CW01658805

THREE SCORE YEARS AND TEN

Best Wishes
To Gloria
From Ron [signature]
31/7/04

THREE SCORE YEARS AND TEN

by

Ron Priestley

CENTRAL PUBLISHING SERVICES.
West Yorkshire

© Copyright 2004

Ron Priestley

The right of Marjorie Hands to be identified as author of this work has been asserted by him in accordance with copyright, Designs and Patents Act 1988

All rights reserved. No reproduction,
copy or transmission of this publication may be made
without written permission.
No paragraph of this publication may be reproduced,
copied or transmitted
save with the written permission or in accordance
with the provisions of the Copyright Act 1956 (as amended).
Any person who does any unauthorised act
in relation to this publication may be liable
to criminal prosecution and civil
claims for damage.

All characters in this publication are fictitious and any resemblance to real persons, living, or dead, is purely coincidental.

Paperback ISBN 1 903970 52 0

Produced
by

Central Publishing Services.
Royd Street Offices
Milnsbridge
Huddersfield
West Yorkshire
HD3 4QY

www.centralpublishing.co.uk

Contents:

THREE SCORE YEARS AND TEN.

THE FIRST TEN YEARS.

I was born at an early age on the 25th October 1921 in a terraced house of two up and two down at 87 Brompton Road, Attercliffe, Sheffield in the County of Yorkshire, England. On November the 9th I was baptised George Ronald at the local Parish Church by Canon Smith. My parents were of humble but proud families with my father originating from the Derwent Valley in Derbyshire - actually being born in the village of Birchinlee just below Howden. He had just finished service with the Royal Artillery during the Great War of 1914 - 1918 seeing action on the Western Front in France and partly in Egypt. He lost his younger brother Jason during that conflict in the Battle at Pashendale on the Somme.

Esther Evelyn, my Mum, was the youngest daughter of a large family called Willis who hailed from the St. Thomas' area of Oxford. She had worked on 'munitions' during the War where she had met George Fell and later married him at the Attercliffe Parish Church on the 29th September 1917. He was 23 and my Mum was 20 years of age. Unfortunately, George Fell contracted pneumonia and died in May 1920. I learned later from one of my Mum's sisters, Auntie Amy Howard, that he was a good footballer and won a gold medal whilst playing for St. Alban's Church on Coleridge Road.

It was as a young widow that Mum met my father George Priestley when he was in lodgings at a Mrs. Smith's in Don Place, Brightside just opposite where two of his sisters lived. They were Auntie May Battersby and Auntie Polly Parr.

From the day I was born I was pampered and mollycoddled with the slightest of any upset the Doctor being called. He was a Scot, Dr. Michael Pettigrew who was short and plump with a small well waxed moustache. He used to do his rounds on a pushbike and charge sixpence a call. Later he moved up to a motorbike. The locals affectionately knew him as 'Mick' and he had a brother nearby called Archie Pettigrew, he too was a doctor.

My Mum was a frail person and seemed to have difficulty, as many young mums in those days had, in breast feeding me and had to revert to a breast pump which was shaped like a small glass motor horn, placed on the breast firmly, the bulb was squeezed and then released to draw milk from the breast.

Dad was a tolerant and patient man and worked shifts on the railway for the London Midland and Scottish Railway (L.M.S.). He was a steam raiser in the sheds of the depot in Brightside Lane and was what one might call a 'grounded fireman' because he never went on the footplate on the 'roads'. He was able to drive a locomotive, which was essential when moving engines about the yard getting them ready for their respective destinations.

As a baby, one doesn't remember much but as I started to take notice, one memory I do recall, perhaps because of a snapshot that was taken of me, was the time my Mum took me to see some friends in Edinburgh. We travelled by train via Carlisle on a free pass because of my Dad being employed on the railway and passes and privilege tickets were available to employees. The main recollection was a day on the sands at Portobello. My shoe had come off and I showed a puckered lip and wanted to cry because I couldn't put it back on.

The following year, 1924, I was so ill with my chest that my cot was taken down stairs and put under the front window in the living room for two weeks. To get some relief, Mum decided to go out to the 'pictures', (a local cinema) and with Dad being on the afternoon shift, she asked two of Aunty Edie's daughters to baby sit for me.

They were Amy and Mary Furness and lived nearby on Swan Street in a back-to-back house. Because I was feeling much better the girls let me out of my cot to play. They were busy painting and drawing on the table and I was playing under the table with my toy motor car. Whilst under the table I could see a pair of legs, I didn't know to whom they belonged but being curios, I couldn't resist putting my hand up between them where I could feel a wet crevice which my little fingers played with. There was no objection from the owner and I think we were both enjoying it when there was a knock at the door and in walked Dr. Downey our other doctor who had called earlier in the evening but had left his gloves. Amy and Mary were about 11 and 13 and that was my first experience of the female anatomy.

The following week their mother, Auntie Edie, came down and made me a brown paper vest, which she covered with cotton wool and goose grease to see if that would ease my chest and asthma. That's how I was mollycoddled

My Grandmother, Margaret Rachael Willis, lived at number 10 Winsbury Road near the top of Leigh Street which was about 500 yards away from where we lived and there she ran a small greengrocery and home made ice cream business from the front room of the house. My cousin Sidney Furness, Mary's brother, who in his teens would help my grandma by taking her pony and dray full of vegetables and fruit around the Wincobank area. The pony's name was Bob and I liked him very much, he was so lovable. On several occasions I was allowed to go with Sid on the dray just for the ride and it was good to go to the Sheffield Market and Cold Store for fresh vegetables and blocks of ice for the ice cream. Sometimes on return I would be allowed to turn the handle of the tub in which the block of ice was broken down and the ground up fine in the crusher. In the yard at the back of the house Grandma also had some hens and ducks, from which she sold the eggs. Bob, however, was not stabled there, he was taken to a stable near the local library up Beverley Street just off Leeds Road.

Grandad, Henry Francis Willis, was a traction steam engine driver and was a very well read man. I loved Grandad Willis but through drink and nattering with Grandma he left home and returned to Oxford. He had read the Bible twice from start to finish and often quoted from it, so deep down he wasn't a bad man.

In his younger days he went to school with a lad called Italian Joe and his other pal was William Morris who later on became Lord Nuffield - the founder of the Morris Motor Co. As they grew up, Grandad and Joe were often asked to pay a visit to the Morris household.

One outstanding feature of my Grandad was when William Cody (Buffalo Bill) brought his Rodeo Show to London. He and several others grew a little tuft of hair in the middle of their chin just below the bottom lip, just like Bill Cody. Right up to him dying in later life, Grandad wore his little tuft.

In the early years when I went to stay with Granny Priestley at Derwent, I was not allowed to go out to play by myself because there was a Golden Eagle which had its nest in the vicinity of Howden Dam. It had been known to attack sheep and lambs and carry them off up into the hills nearby. At the age of three, I weighed about the same as a sheep and could quite easily have been carried away by the huge bird of prey, therefore I was never left to play alone outside Jubilee Cottage.

In 1924 or thereabouts, the eagle was caught and it eventually finished being stuffed and put on display in the Weston Park Museum in Sheffield, where it is today.

In 1926 - November to be precise - I started my education at Maltby Street Infant School. I shall always remember my first day at school because my teacher was dressed in her Girl

Guides Uniform and her name was Miss Rackham and we were in the first classroom on the ground floor. It was a large building built in the shape of a Letter 'E' There was a lower floor but this was allocated to multiple showers where children from other schools and us of course, were able to wash and shower because terraced type houses didn't have bathrooms in those days

It was during this period that a smallpox epidemic broke out and many children and adults caught it, including me. Children were sent to an old wartime army camp at Redmires on the outskirts of Sheffield and put into isolation whilst adults were sent to a hospital at Dart Square near the centre of town.

There was one night during the stay in isolation at Redmires that the men in the ward set up a rat-a-tat on the window. That is, a length of cotton was attached by a safety pin to the window frame with a button hanging loose near the glass. Every time the nurse came into the ward the cotton would be pulled, concealed under covers and the button would rattle against the window. The nurse would try to locate the sound, thinking it was someone prowling outside.

After three attempts she called in the Matron who also had difficulty in finding it - that is, until the cotton caught her on the nose whilst she was looking out of the window. The Matron made no comment, went out and half an hour later returned with two porters. She pointed to three beds opposite to myself and George Bosworth, who was also from my school, 'Now.' she called and the porters immediately turned the three beds upside down.

"That will teach you!" Matron said. How George and I laughed.

During the epidemic when the houses were empty, fumigation teams were sent in to clean everything - in some instances white sheets were put into bins along with black lead cloths, which were used for cleaning the traditional fireplaces and stoves. Before fumigation was organised, everyone with the illness or suspected of it was confined to their own homes and not allowed to go out, even to go shopping. However, neighbours who were thought to be clear of the illness, did the shopping for us but everything had to be passed to us through the downstairs window. Thank goodness it was only for about ten days.

On one of the instances when I was off school because of chest trouble and asthma, Mum as usual sent for Dr. Pettigrew. To try to help my asthma I had been using a steam kettle and beside that I had been using an old-fashioned remedy. This was to soak blotting paper in a solution of saltpetre, dry it on the top of the hob against the fire, take a small square of it, about three inches across, place it on a shovel and put a match to it. The action was similar to lighting a firework because it didn't burst into flame but smouldered and the smell of the smoke was supposed to relief my breathing.

This had just taken place when the Doctor walked up the stairs.

" Good God, Esther!" he cried, "Get those bloody windows open - no wonder he can't breathe."

I might just add that nowhere in No. 87 was fresh air allowed to enter - no wonder I was so chesty; plus the fact the coal fire was always well lit and gave off too much heat in such a small living room.

Because Mum kept me off school so much when I was little, I had several opportunities to go to Derwent where Granny Priestley lived - she was widowed - I never knew Grandad David Priestley. Granny was good to me, she was a frail white haired lady and said the change would do me good playing in the fields with the local children, like Joe Shirt and Sidney Wilson who lived nearby. I loved going out there and sometimes watched Uncle David - Dad's youngest brother - playing cricket for the village in the grounds of Derwent Hall which belonged to the Duke of Norfolk and was situated by the side of the River Derwent.

There was one occasion when I was staying with Uncle Ernest and Aunty Elsie who lived lower down the village near the church in an Army type hut for their home. It used to belong to a family called Hasland who was the local grocer and served the community from his mobile shop. If you heard his motor horn then you knew it was Haslands.

I was playing outside when a tall gentleman came by - he was walking with a stick and limping because he had only one leg. He asked me if I would like to walk with him up the valley for a short while. It was good and at one point he showed me what was once an open air swimming pool. It wasn't large but it had been tiled with white tiles when it was in use sometime ago. He kept on asking me questions about my family and various other things until we arrived back at the hut. Having reached there he bid me good day and he called me Ronald and I thanked him for the pleasure. Uncle Ernest came out and said, "Thank you very much, Sir." Then turned to me and asked if I knew who the gentleman was. When I said that I didn't know, Uncle said that it was Captain Howard - the Duke of Norfolk's brother - and that he had lost his leg during the Great War.

Uncle Ernest had also lost a leg but that was due to an accident when he was helping to build the King Edward VII Hospital at Rivelin Valley, on the outskirts of Sheffield. However Uncle Ernest was the local postman, which didn't prevent him from riding his modified bike up hill and down dale. The local Post Office was just across the road in the small village and was managed by a Mr. George Bingham and his sister Hattie - who incidentally was fancied by my Dad in his younger days before he met Mum. In summer, the post office was a picture postcard sight with various coloured roses spread all around the door and windows. The Binghams were residential there.

Several weekends were spent at Derwent and at one of them there was quite a gathering and because the Priestley family was quite big, sleeping arrangements were a bit hectic and even though there were four large bedrooms, it was a bit cramped. On this occasion I was put into the large front bedroom and told to sleep with Irene Emerson who was a blonde six year old and the same age as myself and she was the younger sister of uncle David's wife, Betty. It seemed alright but as we settled down for the night I couldn't help feeling !!! Well, what do you think, those female parts seemed to attract me - but it was only a touch. It was on one of those family weekends that Aunty May, Dad's eldest sister, and Aunty Winnie decided to try their hand at riding Uncle Ernest's motor bike, which he had now acquired. This was an O.K. Supreme with a square tank for petrol, was belt driven, had no kick start and the gear system was a gate change on the side of the petrol tank.

Ladies in trousers were unheard of in the 20's but my aunties borrowed some of Uncle David's and Uncle Ernest's slacks, put them on and pushed the bike up onto the main road out of the top gate. They then wheeled it down to a private road on the right, which led to the topside of the Derwent Dam wall and the Doss house.

Having reached the road they switched on the petrol, set the gear stick and whilst Aunty May held the clutch in, they started to run. At a reasonable speed the clutch was let out, Aunty May jumped on the seat with her big bum, got a successful roar from the exhaust, held on until Auntie Winnie could get on the pillion seat and set off up the road. Unfortunately they had trouble slowing down and the five-barred gate across the road was locked and into it they went.

Aunty Amy, Dad's youngest sister and I were running behind them and when we caught up with them both Aunties couldn't get up for laughing. The bike had no serious damage to it but I think my Aunties had to urgently change their trousers when we arrived back at Jubilee Cottage. The Doss house, by the way, was a wooden rest centre for people who had worked on the building of the Dam when it was being constructed way back in 1914. Mr and Mrs. Smith lived there and she ran a small shop to which Aunty Amy used to walk me for sweets. Mr. Smith was the watchman\caretaker of the Dam wall and though only having one arm he used to walk across the top of the wall, which was 20 feet wide, to clear any debris which might have become lodged.

Aunty Amy was still at school when I used to go to Granny's before starting school myself. She was a pretty looking girl and attended the local school in Derwent Village. We used to play at shop in the plantation next to Jubilee Cottages and used bits of broken pottery and bottles, which had aimlessly been left there by hikers. One thing I enjoyed there was helping to feed the hens and chickens, which Granny had.

Although I called her Granny Priestley, by law she was Granny Harvey because as a widow she remarried in 1921 just before I was born. As a young child one didn't understand those things and so it was a shock to me that in August 1928 Elizabeth Harvey (Granny Priestley) died of cancer. My Dad, being the eldest child had the job as executor of the estate to divide any assets amongst the family. The house was left to Uncle David who had just married Betty Emerson, the piano went to Aunty Amy who had married William Kelsey from Tinsley in Sheffield and the rest was shared equally between Uncle Ernest, Aunty May Battersby, Aunty Polly Parr, Aunty Dolly Winter and the spinster sisters Alice and Winifred. Money didn't come into it.

As the next few years went by I used to go with my parents on the train to Bamford to visit Aunty Edie Furness' family, this was apart from going to Derwent. This reminds me that when I was small, about five years of age, we went to Derwent and my Uncle Ernest picked me up, put me on the carrier of his pushbike and then peddled with his one leg the seven miles to Derwent via Ashopton, whilst Mum and Dad walked it. On odd occasions we were able to cadge a lift on the 'Leyland' lorry, which belonged to the Derwent Valley Water Board and was travelling up the valley to the Derwent and Howden dams. Jubilee Cottages, where Granny lived, were situated at the top of a small hill just before you came to Derwent Dam Wall.

On other odd visits, Mr. Dimberline, one of our local shopkeepers, used to take Mum and me on his motorbike and sidecar. I once burnt my leg on the exhaust pipe. Occasionally there would be an open aired chara-banc running out that way and we would take the opportunity to go by it to Ashopton and then walk the last two miles down the leafy lanes to Derwent. In summer it was a beautiful sight walking along side the River Derwent, watching the rabbits hopping about and then the lambs gambolling in the fields and as we walked under the over hanging trees, in the distance we could see the clock tower of the Derwent Church, it was glorious.

To return to Bamford from Derwent one day, Uncle Ernest decided to take Dad and me on the back of his motorcycle. Uncle David also wanted a lift into Bamford so I sat at the back of Uncle Ernest, Dad sat behind me and Uncle David sat just on the edge of the pillion seat behind Dad. We did very well until we reached the top of Bamford village near the Institute when we hit a bump in the road. Off came Uncle David into the middle of the road and we hadn't noticed until we heard him shouting. He wasn't hurt but we all had a good laugh.

Going back to infant school days, our head mistress was Miss Bellamy, a short dumpy person but very kind. She used to walk in and out of the classrooms with both fists clenched with one on each of her large bosoms and pupils mimicked her. The only fault I had with her was that another pupil, Ken Goodyear, was mistaken for me and I for him because we were so much alike with the result that either of us would be chastised for something the other one had done wrong.

With the small pox epidemic abating and children returning to school, everything got back to normal with our lessons and I progressed as best I could because of all the absenteeism. Bobby Western, the School Inspector, came around quite often to our house but my absence was legitimate and no report was made to the authorities. When I was in the infants, Mum used to bring me a hot cup of cocoa to the school gates during the winter months as did several of the other mothers to their children.

On my fifth birthday I had a lovely surprise because my Mum's elder brother, Uncle Sid Willis, called in to see us. He gave me a present which was a story book called "Comrades True' and all about bravery and friendship. The surprise was that uncle Sid never bought any child in the family a present. Not because he was mean but because he just couldn't afford it whilst trying to bring up a family of four boys and two girls.

He was a jovial person, liked a drink and a laugh but the Christmas following my birthday he called again to ask Dad if he wanted to go to the local for a pint. Dad agreed and went to change his shoes whilst uncle Sid stayed in the living room. For years we had a wire mesh fireguard to keep me away from the fire but because it was Christmas, Mum had taken it away to make the hearth look tidier. It was an open range hob with a coal fire and a steel oven and Mum had put a large iron saucepan on the fire to boil the Christmas pudding in a basin. Unfortunately, Uncle Sid hadn't noticed that the fireguard had been removed, went to rest his backside on the edge of it but sat straight on top of the pan of boiling water. What a shout he gave.

The air was a little blue but Mum and Dad rushed in and attended to him. Dad found him a clean pair of trousers, went to get his coat and as he did so, Uncle Sid did the same trick again. They didn't go for that drink and Uncle was off work for two weeks, he could hardly walk and daren't sit down for days.

I tried to keep up with the other children in learning but with the pampering and being kept away from school as in one instance, to have my Adenoids and Tonsils removed, I found it difficult. Because I suffered with my breathing so much, it was decided to have the offending organs removed and at the age of five years I was taken to the Royal Infirmary in Sheffield. I remember someone putting a piece of gauze over my mouth and nose and then remembered nothing else until I regained consciousness a short while later. The floor of the Ward was covered with children, lying on mattresses, who had also gone through the same treatment. The air smelt terrible due to the ether, which had been put onto the gauze over our faces to anaesthetise us.

After I came back to reality, I was allowed to go home. Dad was with me and asked for an ambulance to take me but he was told that it would have to be paid for. Dad refused and explained to the authorities that he paid into the 'Penny in the Pound Scheme' and this covered any such necessities. The 'Penny in the Pound Scheme' was a method by which work people were stopped a penny from every pound, which they earned, and this paid for any medical assistance, which was required by the worker or his family. I did eventually go home by ambulance.

At the age of five and a half years I was taken to a chest clinic to see a Dr. Lytle in Queen's Road, Sheffield. It became a ritual going for check ups etc., and eventually I was admitted to Nether Edge Hospital being suspected of TB (Tuberculosis). It was so prevalent in those days but I was found to be clear after staying there for one or two weeks

During my first stay at the hospital I was fortunate to be entered into a race for small children. We had plenty of exercise and fresh air and during one of these sessions I won my race, which was about fifty yards, and I was so pleased when I was presented with a wooden elephant on wheels - it was my first trophy.

Later on I was admitted again - twice in three years to be exact - and one of my cousins was also admitted. He was Aunty Amy's youngest son, Sydney Howard, but pleased to say we were both discharged from the hospital and it was good to stop taking cod liver oil and Parish's chemical food, it was horrible

Aunty Amy was one of Mum's older sisters and the life and soul of any party. If anyone locally became pregnant Aunty Amy was the first to be sent for.

Dr. Pettigrew always sent for her for assistance in midwifery. She had married a soldier, Jack Howard, from World War I and they had twins - a boy and a girl. The girl died as a baby but George survived, then they had their second son Sydney.

Although very young I can just recall uncle Jack passing away. He was a tall man with a big bushy moustache and a true soldier. It was said that as a bugler he called 'Taps' in front of King Edward VII, who turned and said "Well done, Lad." His funeral was a military one and that's why I recall it because he was taken to Tinsley Park Cemetery on a gun carriage that was pulled by Royal Navy personnel - something you don't see in the present day. The mourners followed in a Black van type carriage pulled by two black horses bedecked with black plumes on their foreheads.

Even though being baptised in the Church of England, as I grew up, I was given a choice of my religion because my Dad was a converted Roman Catholic. He was R.C., because in those days if your family was connected to working for the Duke of Norfolk, as was my Grandad and Grandma Priestley then it was essential that all employees should be brought up in that faith.

Whenever possible, because of shift work, Dad would go on a Sunday morning to St. Charles R.C. Church in Attercliffe off Charles Street and Heppenstall Lane. He took me with him several times but mainly I would go to Attercliffe Parish Church.

However, as I became older, I was allowed to choose - I chose neither - I decided to go to the Wesleyan Chapel because most of my friends went there. Also at seven years of age I joined the Life Boys, which was the junior branch of the 14th Company of the Boys Brigade and functioned from the Methodist Church in Bodmin Street. I was really proud of my uniform, which was a Navy Blue jersey with a Lifebelt Badge sewn on the left breast, and also a small peaked skullcap with the crest on the front. With those we wore grey shorts and stockings A Sergeant Fred Webster was in charge of us and took great pride in training us. Charlie Foster, one of our neighbour's sons was also in our Company and over the years we became very good friends. There was never any question or comment as to why I chose that religion but it stood me in good stead, hence our motto "SURE AND STEAD FAST."

Readers may ask why there is no mention of the 1926 General Strike but as they must recall I was only five years old and wouldn't understand politics at that age. I know it was hard for most people with very little money and I recall my father being on piquet duty. Don't forget, the small pox epidemic was with us at that time and everyone's mind was full of other things but one item does come to mind.

A family across from where we lived, the Jackson's, sent two of their sons down to the gas works on Upwell Street to get some coke in a small barrow. I went with them and not knowing any better, I said I was their brother. The man in charge at the gate said that it was a pity because if I had not been part of their family we could have had an extra hundredweight.

Prior to the smallpox, like many other children, I had measles and Mum always said it was because of that, that I had to wear spectacles. It took quite a while to get used to them and many were the times when I would accidentally bend them whilst playing. In any case they had very thin arms and the rims were covered in a type of tortoise celluloid.

In the late 20's the 'Talkies' came and with this, people started to go to the cinema. Locally we had four; the Pavilion and the Globe on Attercliffe Common; the Adelphi on Vicarage Road just below Attercliffe Church and the Theatre Royal at the bottom of Staniforth Road, which was later, named the Regal. It was at the Adelphi that I first saw and heard my first 'Talkie'. It was Al Jolson in the Jazz Singer in 1927. There was also a third rate Music Hall on Attercliffe

Road, which was owned, and run by two brothers, Dick and Speed Walker.

Many artists appeared there and in later years became famous due to the appearance of such stars as Frank Randle, Florence Desmond, Arthur Haynes and many more. At the cinemas there was always an orchestra in the 'silent' days but as the 'Talkies' became` more popular, so the musicians disappeared.

Down Attercliffe, as in other districts, streets were cobbled with granite sets and when the council periodically sent workers in to fill up the cracks and crevices between them, Mum would send me out to watch them and inhale the fumes given off by the hot tar. She said it would benefit my chest and help me to breathe more easily. In fact, in that era, Tar Band was worn around the neck to ward off colds and sore throats.

Opposite where I lived in Brompton Road was a cul-de-sac (we didn't call them that in the 20's). It was Gerald Street with four houses on the left-hand side and five on the right-hand side. At the top, over the wall which was made of clinker and stone, was a green field which was a welcome sight to us in the East end of the city. In the field was a beautiful white horse owned by a Mr. Coney - hence the name we all knew - Coney's Field. It was great to see the horse running around and up and down the small hill it was on. There was a natural spring near the bottom and the horse used to go to it for a drink after chasing about. The field was privately owned and out of bounds to all locals, in fact the small hill gave its name to that particular place - The Hill Top

In Gerald Street in the top house on the left-hand side lived a large family named Jackson, whom I mentioned earlier, and who were more than troublesome at times. A few years earlier, one of their sons, Billy, left home and joined the Royal Navy and once when he came home on leave, he was just passing their front window when a rice pudding in the dish came flying through the window and hit Billy on the head. He had to go to the hospital for treatment. It was shortly after this that all the neighbours gathered and drummed them out of the district by banging bin lids, saucepans and anything that made a noise. We never saw them again except for Billy, who, when he came home on leave stayed at his auntie's house down Holman Street, which was another cul-de-sac opposite Sanderson Bros and Newbould, a steel works, in Newhall Road.

During my early school days it was difficult for people to make ends meet, especially Mum and Dad because his wage was very low at 35/- shillings a week but at the least he had a regular job. He did make a few 'bob' commission by helping to run a 'Templegates Double' for the funds of the local NUR, (National Union of Railwaymen) of which he was a member. He was also the treasurer of the local branch and district. Templegate was a tipster in the national paper the Daily Herald and each day Templegate would tip two horses, which were numbered. If those two numbers appeared on the purchased ticket then a money prize would be won. It was sixpence a go.

To supplement this small income, Mum occasionally took in lodgers. Actually it was mainly family and this also helped their accommodation problems. Our first lodger was cousin Margaret Bunn who worked as a waitress at Davy's restaurant in Fargate in the city centre. She couldn't stay with her mother, Auntie Lily Blagden who was one of Mum's sisters, because the house in Don Place wasn't large enough when her stepbrother was growing up.

Mag, as we called her, was in her late teens and didn't stay more then a few months before going to live at her boyfriend's mother's house in Dunlop Street. She eventually married young Fred Newshum not long after she left our house. Fred worked in the Engineering Dept., as a welder at Edgar Allen and Co., Ltd., in Vulcan Road

Every time we had someone stay with us they shared the back bedroom with me. It was just possible to get two single beds and a small dressing table into it.

It was a great relief when I was on my own but Mum and Dad were willing to help anyone in need. One odd lodger was a Mr. Joe Partridge who worked at Wm. Cooks at Tinsley as a die maker in the wireworks and he used to bring me small cogs and gear wheels to supplement my Meccano set. Somehow he didn't fit in with the family and Dad had to ask him to leave.

In the late twenties families and neighbours seemed to cling together more and help each other out. On one summer holiday a group of us spent a week at Cleethorpes in Lincolnshire, which in those days was like going to the Riviera. In the party we had Mum and me, Auntie Amy Howard with Syd and George, Mrs. Ryder our next door neighbour at No.89. Her sister from across the road Mrs. Millington with her niece Irene and nephew Tommy Mann and Florence Sheldon from No.85. It was at this holiday that I showed myself up. Aunty Amy was having some oysters at a sea front stall and I asked if I could have one, not knowing what they were. Mum said "No." But I insisted. Aunty said to Mum, "Oh! Let him try." I did. The oyster was stuck half way down my throat and I was choking. Mum shouted at me, Aunty Amy hit me on the back and - the oyster left my mouth and shot straight across the counter onto the floor. Aunty couldn't stop laughing but Mum was very cross.

When I was 10 years old, although my health was improving, I had to return to Nether Edge Sanatorium to have another check up about TB but after another six weeks I was discharged for good and in the clear. However, I did keep having small bouts of asthma but managed to keep at school

Overall, the neighbourhood was quite respectable and there were few upsets amongst them but there was the occasional row between families, mainly about kids but they soon blew over. On many a Sunday morning several families sent one of their older members to the local pub with a pot jug to get a pint of the local brew from the 'Off Sales' and one of the highlights of this was a family named Fletcher. More often than not the old man would return to the local inn called the Tram Car at the end of Clay Street. Around 2.PM after closing time he would stagger back and within ten minutes of returning home he would be rowing with his good lady and throwing some punches as well. No one interfered and eventually all was quiet.

We hadn't really any place to play in, so the street became our play area but that didn't suit some of the neighbours because of the noise and possibility of breaking windows. I was playing outside once with a ball and as I went to retrieve it just across the road I was chased by Mrs. Wood's dog from the corner shop in Walkland Road. The dog was a bloodhound and as it went for me it made a grab at my backside with its teeth and took the patch out of my trousers which my Mum had only put in a few days before.

A few years after Mum's eldest brother Uncle Albert died, his widow, Aunty Edie Willis on Staniforth Road, decided to take in a lodger to help her with the finances needed to rear three girls. It was whilst the lodger, Mr Jermy, was staying there that there was an accident.

Fortunately, it wasn't serious but in a way, it was very amusing. Aunty had smelt gas in the front room and when Mr Jermy came in from work, she asked him to help her look for the leak. Aunty climbed up a pair of steps to investigate and said that she could hardly see in the corner of the room and asked for some light. Mr Jermy held the steps and passed her a box of matches and she struck one! **BANG!** She found the leak - the bay window blew out and she landed on top of poor Mr Jermy. The really funny thing was that he was small, slim and weighed about eight stones. Aunty was tallish, very buxom and weighed around twelve stones. Luckily no one was hurt.

It was in the 1930's that Auntie Edie Furness and all her family decided to leave Attercliffe and the back-to-back houses in Swan Street and aim for a better life in Derbyshire. Bamford village was their destination where they all grew up and became part of the community. The eldest son, Alfred, had joined the Coldstream Guards two years earlier and saw service in Shanghai, China. Lily, the eldest daughter married a local lad George Hicks who was from Bamford, Mary and Amy worked at the cotton mill having settled out there in 1928, living in lodgings at Hathersage. George Furness worked for the local greengrocers, Hancocks, Jim married a girl called Zena and lived in Hathersage whilst young Edith was still at school.

One might ask where Sydney was, well unfortunately, he died at the age of 24 when the wheel of his pushbike caught in the points of the tramlines in Attercliffe and threw him onto his head, killing him instantly.

Grandma Willis had a brother and a sister who lived in semidetached cottages in a woodland just outside the village of North Leach in Oxfordshire. Because her sister, my great-Aunt Leah, wasn't in good health, Grandma decided to shut up shop in Winsbury Road and go down to take care of her. My Mum agreed to help her to move and thought it a good idea to take me and cousin George Howard along with her to help. This help was needed because Grandma had made up her mind to open a shop at Aunt Leah's cottage and therefore needed to stock up. She obtained tins and boxes of sweets, blocks of salt and other small essentials from the Sheffield Market and anything else which she might be able to sell to the villagers.

It was a struggle to get everything onto the train but we managed to and with some help at the other end of the journey we made it in one piece to Nor' Lea', as the locals called it. Mum and I stayed a couple of weeks, it was holiday time, and I would take Uncle Dick's dog for a walk in the woods at the rear of the cottages.

George Howard was 14 years of age and needed some work so he said he would stay with Grandma and he eventually obtained employment at the blanket factory in Whitney. One of the neighbours, who lived just up the lane, was very helpful to grandma and Aunt Leah. She was Mrs Brakespere and she had four daughters, one of whom became attracted to our George and this encouraged him to stay for a few years. The romance didn't work out and he returned home to Sheffield.

Shortly after that, Aunt Leah died and because she was so huge and weighed around some twenty-two stones, it was necessary to remove the bedroom window to get her coffin out of the house. It would have been too difficult to try to get it round the bend in the staircase. The loss of Aunt Leah and the upset must have been the cause of Grandma returning to Sheffield where she was able to live in a house on Don Road where my Auntie May Battersby had once lived.

The house was vacant because Auntie had married a widower named Gregory and had gone to live with him in Grimesthorpe on Botham Street. It was just below a public house called the 'Who Can Tell' which was the smallest in Sheffield.

During the past few years, when Mum wasn't feeling too well, I would help by running errands to the shops and by doing little things in the house such as black-leading the hob and the fireplace. The oven plate shelf, which was just below the door, must have been the shiniest in Sheffield because that is how Mum liked it and the brass work on the fender was always highly polished too. My Dad had made me a small wooden box barrow which sat on the axle of two wheels from an old pram and this I used, mainly to go to the local Co-op which was on Attercliffe Common and at the top of Berkeley Street. It was ten minutes walk but was very handy when I had to bring bags of flour, sugar and vegetables, which could be quite heavy to carry in a basket.. Sometimes when I was doing the 'Stores' (Co-op) errand, I would take a peep into the back yard of Kirkup's Ironmongery shop where there was a slaughter house. I didn't actually see any animals being butchered but I would see cows being led into the yard. This was at the top of Leigh Street on the corner with Attercliffe Common. Hygiene of food wasn't as strict as it is in the present day.

THE EARLY THIRTIES

The time had come for me to progress from infant school to the junior school which fortunately involved me in moving upstairs along with the rest of the class. Mr Fred Tilbrook was the Headmaster who was aged about 60, with silvery, grey hair and a moustache to match. He was strict but had a good sense of humour and was very sociable. Other teachers there were Mr Wood (assistant head), Miss Ayres, Miss Chapman, Miss Harvey, Miss Barton and Mr Hall. I started in Std III with Miss Ayres, a very nice lady who had her hair plaited and coiled over her ears like headphones

We were all in mixed classes with twin desks which had twin ink wells at the top. Each morning we had a milk break and ½ pint bottles were distributed at the cost of a halfpenny each. The tops were cardboard with a small centre which could be pressed in to make a hole for a straw to go through or to pull off the top for pouring. These tops were utilised to thread wool through and make various objects such as table mats when they were sewn together.

In the early days of junior school we started to learn our arithmetic and time tables in parrot fashion and at the time I hated sums but I liked English because of the stories that were sometimes narrated to us. As we learned various subjects such as History, Geography etc., we moved at the end of each session to another class room of which there were six. We were with Miss Ayres in classroom one, in classroom two was Miss Chapman, then there was Miss Harvey's class in No.3, Mr Hall was in No.4, in which there were folding doors to enlarge the Assembly Hall. No.5 was occupied by Miss Barton with Std VII and last of all there was Mr Wood in No.6. He had served in France during the War of 1914 - 1918 and at times we could see the effect of the tear and mustard gas used by the Germans and which he had encountered.

When one of the summer holidays came along, my Mum arranged for us to have a break at Aunty Margaret's in Kent at a village called Boro Green. Mum and Dad and I went by train - using one of Dad's free passes - and after changing at St. Pancras Station we hailed a taxi to take us to Victoria Station to catch a train for Wrotham. When Dad asked for 'Rotham' the guard looked 'gone out' at him. The name was pronounced 'Rootam'.

We eventually arrived and Uncle Alec Masson met us at the station where, after a short walk, we came to a building which turned out to be the local telephone exchange. This was where they lived with their two daughters, Ann and Ella who were 19 and 9 years of age respectively. Above the exchange was a three-bed roomed flat where they lived as caretakers but also helped out on the switchboard at night. Aunty Mag, Mum's eldest sister was the black sheep of the Willis family but Mum had kept in touch with her over the years, although the rest of the family hadn't. Apparently this was because at some time in the past, Grandma Willis had misbehaved and had conceived Margaret illegitimately and Grandad Willis wouldn't accept Margaret, who had eventually moved south and married Uncle Alec. There they had Ann and Ella. Also a son called Howard - he joined the Army after the War in the late twenties and served in India.

During this stay, Ella and I became good friends and once, when we were playing together in the lounge and being left on our own, we finished up on the settee. Once again my hands found parts of her I shouldn't have but we both enjoyed our playtime although it didn't happen again. It was a good holiday during which Uncle Alec tried to teach me to fish. He set up a line on a cane with a safety pin on the end, dug up some worms from the garden, put them in a tin box and off we went to the local pond. My Dad also went but after half an hour I lost patience and threw the tin of worms into the water. Dad and Uncle couldn't stop laughing.

The week passed quickly and on the Saturday we had to return home so that Dad could recommence work on the Sunday

When I started my new term after the holidays, my work at school must have improved because I moved up to Std V in the next classroom and was seated at the same desk as a girl named Louie Whittaker - not to be confused with Edna Whittaker, a local greengrocer's daughter, - Louie was a shy girl, especially when she was called out to the front of the class - not for misbehaving but to recite poetry or read something out loud from a book. However, she wasn't shy with me and as time progressed I became more familiar with her in more ways than one. As I was writing with my right hand, my left hand was up her knicker- leg for a quick touch. The moisture on my fingers from between her legs, helped me to turn the pages of my exercise book. There was never any complaint and on odd occasions when her friend Vera Sykes sat with me, the same thing happened but not as often. After school I used to go looking for Louie on Norman Street where she lived but she wasn't always around.

At this time, Charlie Foster, one of my school mates who lived in Gerald Street and was two years older than I, asked my Mum if I could join the Boys Brigade at the Attercliffe Wesleyan Hall. She agreed and so I joined the 19th Company of the BB after having progressed through the Life Boys at the 14th Company of the BB in Bodmin Street Baptist Church. Mr. Bill Woffenden was our Captain and we had a very strong Company. In fact, in those days, it was either the Boy Scouts, B.B. or the Church Lads Brigade for youngsters like us to be associated with.

I enjoyed every minute of being taught PT., First Aid, Firefighting in the work's yard of Brown Bayley's Steel Works, also singing camp fire songs on Parade Night. Every Friday night was something to look forward to. I made many new friends and even started going to Sunday School and evening services. Beside Charlie being in the BB, there was also Fred Tyler, whose father was a Steward at the Chapel. I had met Fred at the Queen's Road Chest Clinic and another family I came to know was the Machins' who lived next door to my Aunty Edith Willis on Staniforth Road. She was the widow of Mum's eldest brother Albert who had passed away a few years earlier. I only saw him a few times and he had left three daughters behind, namely Edna, Edith and Ethel.

I had many happy hours in the Boys Brigade, also some humorous ones such as the night that Fred Tyler had an accident. To raise funds for the Company, we were allowed to buy boxes of matches in quantity from the Captain who bought them wholesale. On this particular evening, Fred collected a gross packet of Capt. Webb boxes which were to be sold at one penny per box. As Fred left the Parade, he ran out of the room towards a small flight of steps which led to the exit. Unfortunately, Fred, who was very tall, jumped down the steps, his forehead hitting the landing of the flight of stairs just above. Blood poured down his face and off he ran home but as he ran he dropped the packet of matches and they burst into flame. Luckily no one was burned and there was no profit from his near sales. He did have a couple of stitches put into his wound.

Over the next few years I was taught to play the side drum and soon became a member of the drum and bugle band. I rose through the ranks and by the time I was ready to leave school I was a corporal. Extra to that I was put into the relay swimming team for our Company with Rod German and Bob Shields who both swam for the Yorkshire Schools' Team in County championships. The one race that I swam in was at the District Gala and I managed to keep my end up by swimming a twenty-five- yard length, Bob swam two lengths and Rod did the last three. We were sitting on the edge of the pool waiting for the others to finish. We received a shell shaped jam dish made from frosted glass which was inset in a silver base.

I attended and played in the band every Whitsuntide Sunday and enjoyed seeing the decorated horse-drawn floats (drays) as we made our way to High Hazels Park at Darnall for the annual hymn singing.

However, I spoiled my attendance record when I was sixteen because I decided to go for a cycle ride with Fred Tyler and another lad named Wally who lived on Stevenson Road.

We set off towards Derbyshire and decided to go to Baslow via the Peacock Inn at Owler Bar. As we were riding along the Baslow Road, where there were many dips and bends in the road, a car started to overtake us. It was a Morris saloon with a running board on either side, just below the doors and as it passed us, Fred's peddle caught one of these running boards.

We were riding alongside of each other and Fred had his left hand on my right shoulder - we often rode like that - Wally was riding just behind with his front wheel positioned between our back wheels. On impact, Fred pushed me into the grass verge and I went over a low stone wall and disappeared from view. The next thing I remember was Fred looking over the wall and as white as a sheet. One of my cycling shoes had come off and wedged between the spokes of my front wheel - he thought that my foot had come off. Apart from a few bruises and a grazed face, I wasn't too bad.

The motorist did pull up and turned his car round, came over to see what had happened and then decided to run me back home. Mum was shocked but pleased to see that I was in one piece but was very annoyed after he had left when I told her that the man who had brought me home had partly caused the accident because he had been driving too close to us.

Back to reality and as I progressed through school I had reached Std.VI and like many others I was given the chance to learn to swim at Attercliffe Baths. This I did and in my second term I had obtained my Life Saving Certificate.

On odd occasions we were taken to one of the local cinemas - not just our school but others in the same locality such as Huntsman's Garden School where Fred went to, Newhall School where several of my cousins were taught, Carbrook and Coleridge Road Schools. The purpose of this was to see some educational films and then take part in a mass fire evacuation exercise in which we may be needed to take part in a real situation.

Another instance of these gatherings was for the Armistice Service in which we all took part each year at the Attercliffe Parish Church on the 11th November at 11 o'clock in the morning, in memory of those who had fallen during the Great War of 1914 - 1918. On the actual day of the 11th November, children would take part in a remembrance service with whichever organisation one belonged to, i.e. Boys Brigade, Scouts, Church Lads Brigade, Girl Guides or Girls Life Brigade.

As I was nearing the age of puberty, I had the misfortune to get dermatitis. Mum had bought me some new underpants, the ones that were held up inside the trousers by loops at the tops which were attached over the braces. For once Mum hadn't washed them as she did with everything else that was new in the line of underwear. In those days, material of that nature was processed through a lime solution, hence the fact that, not having been washed, the lime affected my skin, actually my foreskin.

As it became worse through itching, chafing and scratching, I ended up by being taken to see Dr Pettigrew who referred me to the Royal Infirmary Skin Specialist. The answer - the only way of clearing it was to circumcise me and so it was. However, prior to being done, Mum's youngest brother Jim, thought that he knew best when he was shown it and suggested bathing my penis with a solution of diluted Lysol, a disinfectant. Take my word, whatever you do, never use Lysol on tender parts. After the operation and when it had all cleared, I was having a strip wash in the kitchen because we had no bathroom, when Dad walked in and saw it.

"I don't know about cutting some off. I think they've sewn you a piece on." He said. The operation was a success but it affected me in another way because as I grew up, so did THAT!

The following twelve months saw me befriend another girl in my class, she was Elsie Coulson, who lived in Maltby Street. She was a bonny lass and though not tall, she was very pleasant and like me, an only child. Her father was a counter assistant at the local Co-op on Kirkbridge Road. At least twice a week I would go round to her house to keep her company whilst her Mum and Dad went to the 'pictures'

At twelve years of age most lads were still wearing short trousers and the girls wore gym slips which came just above their knees and this made it difficult at times to control oneself. Instead of playing table games such as Ludo or Tiddlywinks, we finished up PLAYING? Whilst there was no thought of what we today, openly call 'intercourse', we enjoyed it with me lying on top of her on the settee and gently putting my finger on HER problem, we rubbed against each other until we were both fulfilled. We remained good friends until the time came for the 'Merit Matriculation', as it was called.

Quite a few of my friends passed through the exams and went to Secondary or Grammar Schools. So it was that I eventually lost contact with Elsie because she moved to the High Storrs Secondary School at Bents Green and had to do home work every night. Obviously I failed my exams because of being kept off school so much, thus having to stay on to finish in the top class which was Std VIII.

In the earlier standards there was an instance when we had student teachers and one in particular caught me misbehaving with some trivial offence and told me to got to see Mr Wood, the Assistant Head. I knew I was in for a caning but when I arrived in his classroom he wasn't there. I had a quick thought, rubbed some red chalk onto my hands, put them under my armpits and went back to the teacher. I showed her my hands and she said. "That'll teach you a lesson." Little did she know what I had done.

A further instance when I WAS punished for something I didn't do was when someone had dropped a dart onto the floor. It was made from a split pen nib and a paper flight inserted down the split. They were very effective but this time I was caught with it in my hand. I had just picked it up off the floor when Miss Chapman came by. She instructed me to go to Mr Tilbrook, which I did but he refused to accept my explanation and proceeded to give me four strokes of the cane. I didn't need any red chalk on this occasion because it was real.

All lads get up to mischief and in the Bonfire week in the November before I left School, I bought a couple of 'bangers' and had an idea to frighten the girl assistants who worked in the pawnbroker's shop in our own back yard. The shop was owned by the Senior brothers, Percy and Harold who were also our landlords.

At the bottom of each window frame were two bolt holes through which were passed 6" long bolts penetrating wooden shutters which were put up every night for security reasons at closing time, which was 7.00 p.m. I thought that if I lit a firework and pushed it through one of the boltholes, the bang would scare the girls. Unfortunately, I didn't know that there was a rack of clothes inside and up against the window, so that when I put the cracker, lighted end first, through the hole, the sparks from it would set fire to some of them. Mr Harrop, the manager, had an idea who the culprit was and called me out of school. However, because the damage was minimal, he gave me a ticking off, let me go and then told my Mum and Dad. Thinking about it now, it was a stupid trick because a big fire might have resulted in our house being burned down due to the fact that it was in the same terraced block

It had taken Mum and Dad quite a while to let me have a bike and I was about twelve years old before I was finally allowed to ride on the open roads.

This was because my favourite cousin, Sid Furness, had suffered an accident at the bottom of Staniforth Road at the junction with Attercliffe Road. He was cycling home from his work with the Initial Towel Company in town when his front wheel jammed in the points of the tramlines thus throwing him onto his head. He died instantly. He was 24 years of age and I greatly missed him.

It was about this time that Dad bought me a new bike - a £3.19.6d Wigfall's (Wiggy's) Royal. This was to replace a Raleigh 'sit up and beg' which he had obtained for me from a neighbour for £2.0.0. One Sunday morning, when he wasn't working, Dad suggested that we have a run out before dinner on the bikes, he on the old one and me on the 'gas pipe'. So we set off towards Brightside and then on to Wincobank to head for the Blackburn district and up again along Droppingwell Road towards Scholes Coppice and Keppel's Column, which was a familiar local landmark.

We went past the tower and then turned right, down Scholes Lane heading for Wentworth, but this road was a very steep one and Dad kept calling for me to take it steady and use my brakes. I sailed down the hill with Dad behind me and I navigated the 90-degree corner quite comfortably but then I heard a crash. As Dad turned the corner, the back wheel of his bike caught the gravel and he shot across the road with the bike wrapped around his neck. His shoulder was very badly grazed, so we walked back up the hill to the main road again and slowly made our way home for dinner. Mum didn't half grumble but we had to laugh about it.

Now that I was allowed to use the main roads on my own, I finally received permission to cycle to Derwent and stay at Uncle David's for the weekend. On the Sunday, I asked Aunty Betty if I could take her sister Joan, who was living with them, for a walk up the hills nearby. Joan was only seven but even at that age, she was very attractive and a healthily built little blonde. We walked for about an hour but on the way back, Joan said that she felt tired so, I suggested that we take a rest inside a section of a new concrete water pipe which was about three feet in diameter and waiting to be installed into the new water supply. It was cool inside of the pipe and out of the sunlight with plenty of room to sit down and this we did, facing each other. [content omitted] After wiping her hands and tidying myself up, we made our way back to Jubilee Cottages.

There was another occasion when I went to Derwent with some of my cousins, namely Sid Howard, Jack Blagden, George Parr and two of their pals. We had taken refreshments with us so that we had no need to trouble Aunty Betty, who was also Georges' aunty by marriage but not the others. We had a ride around the Derwent and Howden Dams and then had a game of football on the grassed area immediately below Derwent Dam wall, which towered above us. About 3.00 p.m. we decided to make our way back home.

As we climbed towards Sheffield through Ashopton and Ladybower villages and then past Cutthroat Bridge, we somehow managed to split up and with me being the youngest, I slowly finished behind them all, that is except George Parr, who stayed with me until we reached the top of Moscar and Hollow Meadows Church. It had been a real climb to the top but as we arrived on the flat part we were able to freewheel downhill towards Sheffield. Somehow, I managed to get about half a mile in front of George and as we sped down past the entrance to Wyming Brook on the right, my brakes failed to hold.

Round the first bend to the right I went, round the second bend to the left and as I approached the Norfolk Arms Hotel I noticed a private driveway on my left. It was very steep and led up to a mansion type house in its own grounds. I swung the bike sideways, rode straight up the drive and slowly came to a halt. It must have been at this point that George went sailing past, not knowing what had happened. I adjusted my brakes and carefully made my way down the Rivelin Valley Road and up through Crosspool via the town centre to home.

When I arrived, George was there and in a right state because he thought that I had gone straight home and when I wasn't there he became worried. Looking back at the incident, we all thought it rather amusing.

When I was at school, the other pupils and I looked forward to Saturday mornings because a few cinemas allowed matinees for children which was called the 'tuppenny rush'. It was very noisy, especially when we saw cowboy films with such stars as Tom Mix and his horse Tony, Ken Maynard and Hoot Gibson in them.

One Saturday in particular was very disruptive because just before the end someone threw a turnip from the balcony and we saw it whizz through the beam of light from the projector and cast a shadow across the screen. As we left the Adelphi cinema where we had been, I bumped into Sid Howard and mentioned the turnip. He laughed and said that he had bought it for a half penny to eat in the pictures but couldn't finish it, so he threw it over the balcony. I think someone had a sore head.

During this era, gang warfare was very rife and the two main gangs were the Alfred Road mob with the Mooney family and the other lot was the Hyde Park gang with Sam Garvin as their leader. They were always fighting amongst themselves but never harmed any individual person outside of the gangs. I said earlier that Sid Howard attended Newhall School which also had children of the Alfred Road mob there. One night, just after tea, as it was going dark, a group of local kids were playing Delevo, a kind of hide and seek game.

I had just been chosen to put my head on my arm against the wall and count up to fifty before going to find my playmates, when, there was an almighty yelling and shouting and about twenty youngsters came tearing round the corner from Swallow Street, armed with knives, razors, hammers and cellar grates. Obviously I was scared because it was the younger side of the Alfred Road gang. I was pinned against the wall and just as one lad was about to plant me one, a hand reached over the back of the group, grabbed the arm of the offender and yelled, "Hit him and I'll bloody well slaughter you!" I looked up and it was Sid Howard, my cousin. He was the leader of the young gang. They all moved off then to their own streets and left us alone.

I mentioned earlier on that Mr Tilbrook had a sense of humour and one afternoon he took over from Mr Wood to give him a break. This was in Std.VIII and we were reading poetry but after a while he asked us to pay attention and listen to a little ditty he had heard.

"The elephant is a pretty bird, it flits from bough to bough, it builds its nest in a rhubarb tree and whistles like a cow."

"I thought that it would amuse you." He said. "It's something I've always remembered and later passed on to my children."

Having reached the highest standard in my school, Std VIII, I now became the senior boy, partly because of my age. Along with my cousin Sid Willis, who was in my class, we were sports facility monitors and one task was to prepare footballs by cleaning them and setting correct pressure for them for the weekly Friday recreation period. This took place on the playing fields of the Firth Park Grammar School on Barnsley Road. The whole class would go by special tramcar from the top of Newhall Road with Mr Wood being in charge.

One Friday morning, Sidney and I were in the room above Mr Tilbrook's office and having finished our task with the sports equipment, we were kicking the footballs to each other. Mr

Tilbrook rushed in and asked us why we were making so much noise? I told him that we bouncing the balls to test the hardness and pressure. He walked towards me, put his right palm against my cheek and said he didn't like lies and then proceeded to give me one smack on the side of my face with his finger tips. By gum - it didn't half smart but I learned my lesson.

As it drew closer to the time when I was to leave school, I was made School Captain and it befell upon me, the week before I was to leave, to make a speech on behalf of the pupils. The occasion was the retirement of Mr Tilbrook at the age of 65 years. I wrote out the speech, which was brief, and showed it to Mr Wood. He could find no fault with it and told me to go ahead with it. The whole school was assembled in the Hall and I made the short address which became very emotional for the Head as he accepted the small gift for which we had all clubbed together for him. He was a wonderful old man besides being a very good Headmaster. He appreciated every word I said as tears ran down his cheeks but it wasn't the last time Sid and I were to see him as you will read later on.

The following week, on the 24th October 1935, my birthday was next day, I left school and like everyone else I received my Leaving Certificate and Testimonial. Mr Tilbrook had done me proudly but I had trouble finding out what an artisan was because this word was used in describing my abilities. The first week after leaving, I started to search for employment but because the first month was difficult, I returned to school to give assistance to the teachers.

Dad had asked Mr Senior at the pawnbrokers if he had any vacancies and by the end of the week Percy Senior had offered me a place at his shop on Staniforth Road. I had to fasten pawnbrokers' tickets to bundles of clothing etc., which had been pledged for certain amounts of money. This was done by using larges pins which looked like nails. The bundles or articles were then placed upstairs on shelves until redeemed.

I had only been there a fortnight when cousin George Howard found me another place of employment at a cutlery firm where he worked. It was at the bottom of Prince of Wales Road and the working hours were from 7.30. a.m. to 5.00 p.m. and worth 10/- shillings a week as compared to the wage of 7/6d a week which I received from Senior's for working from 9.00 a.m. to 7.00.p.m. Dad advised me to take the new position but said that I must hand in my 'Notice' to Mr Senior but the latter wouldn't accept it. Dad was adamant and on the following Monday - rent day - the rent girl came to our house to collect the rent but Dad was waiting.

"Here's tuppence." He said, "7/6d my lad's wages from 7/8d rent leaves us straight at 2d pence." Mr Senior accepted it and I started work with George at the cutlery firm a week later.

I had only been there for three days when a letter arrived from Edgar Allen & Co. Ltd., offering work to me in the Time Office at 10/- shillings a week. What a difference in attitudes when our George's boss was told, he said for me to take it as there were better prospects and said no 'Notice' was needed and wished me good luck.

So, in November 1935 I started my new job at Edgar's in the Foundry Time Office. My Boss was Mr Vic Sheldon who was the brother of our next door neighbour and he also knew my Mum.

The person who was actually responsible for me starting there was Bernard Harrison who lived in Liverpool Street just down the road from us. He had married the daughter of a friend of ours. The daughter was Amy Holloway who lived with her Mum opposite Aunty Amy Howard in Ordnance Place off Don Road.

Going back to Edgar's, I had to start at 7.00 a.m. so that I, along with two other juniors, could arrange for and collect breakfasts from a little canteen in the middle of the Foundry. This was run by a Mrs Longmuir who was a lovely little lady, very pleasant and kind to us lads. There weren't any full meals supplied at lunchtime but, as some of us did, if you took a pie in a basin to her, she would heat it up for us.

There was one morning when George Blakemore, one of the other juniors I worked with, went for Mr Freddie Lincoln's breakfast which was a full one, consisting of eggs, bacon and tomatoes with a pot of tea. George arrived back at the time office with the full tray and was just about to go through the connecting door when another member of staff came from the opposite direction. Crash! Bang! Wallop!

The tray and the breakfast shot into the air and then finished upside down on the floor. It was an accident and there were no repercussions.

Most of our work was running errands and mashing tea but the highlight of the day was to press the button which set the work's 'Hooter' going, both at midday and at 5.00 p.m. to end the day's work. Lunchtime, which was a one hour break, was absorbed mainly by taking part at the game of pushpenny. This was a football game with two pins either end of the table in the centre, about 1½ pence apart and the ball was a half penny. The players used pennies as footballers and tried to score goals by pushing their penny with a comb onto the halfpenny and forcing it between the pins to score. Mr Sheldon was the past Master at the game and very seldom lost.

I stayed in the time office for six months then Mr Sheldon told me to go up to the Progress Department, which was upstairs.

There I was interviewed by a Mr Arthur Willis (no relation) who was the manager of the department. He enquired about my education but mainly about my eyesight and asked me if I would be able to see steel castings on the floor of the foundry such as the ones on his office floor. I had worn spectacles since I was five years old and with them my eyesight was very good. Having assured him that I was able to detect objects on the floor, he agreed to accepting me onto his staff.

My main duty there was to answer the telephone but I also ran errands and sealed envelopes for the post, not forgetting to get tea and beef dripping sandwiches for the staff from Mrs Longmuir at midmorning break. A classic mistake I made one day, was to answer the 'phone, which was in a little booth at the end of the office. The switchboard, which was in the head office across on Sheffield Road and we were on Vulcan Road, wanted to give some details of a telegram over the 'phone - it was part of my duties to take these messages. The telegram was from G.E.C in Birmingham and was taken down as: - "When can we expect delivery of baby, very urgent?"

Unfortunately I missed out a word from the text and was the laughing stock of the office for ages. It should have read: - "When can we expect delivery of baby 'O' castings - very urgent?"

I worked there in the Progress Dept., for quite a while and made many friends in the Order Dept., and the Drawing Office along the corridor.

We had two Directors in the Foundry. They were brothers and their father used to be the Foundry Director but before he retired, he insisted that they do their apprenticeships as mould and core makers before coming onto the staff. The brothers were Mr Jack and Mr Ernest Wells and that is how we addressed them - Mr Jack and Mr Ernest. It was an unusual sight when in the foundry sometimes, one could see either Mr Jack or Mr Ernest in their shirt sleeves, helping a workman who was having a little difficulty making his mould or core with sand. They soon put the problem to rights and the workmen appreciated their help.

After about six months in the Progress Dept., Mr Willis asked me if I would like to work for Mr Jack Robinson in the Inspection Department at the other end of the office block. Jack was a wonderful guy in my estimation and I fitted in straight away except that when he asked me my Christian name I said Ronald. He thought that I said Donald and he re-Christened me "Donald Duck." That name stuck with me for many years to come but I didn't mind. Jack was auburn haired and about 27 years of age and knew his job.

There was another man in the office called Charlie, who unfortunately died a few years later with what we call today, Multiple Sclerosis. Between them they taught me to use implements and machinery in the Test House down below, to obtain tensile, bends and Izod breaking strengths of various types of steel.

One of the main things which Jack taught me was when, on the first day in the department, he took from his drawer some script cards, like the ones we used to use at school. Every spare moment he would get me to use them to improve my writing. The joined up writing improved with thin up strokes and thick down strokes and after six months he had succeeded, but I still wasn't as good as him. He was a beautiful writer. His was almost copper plate writing

There was a day when we had a visitor. A gentleman called Mr Vincent and he was an inspector from the Government Dept., of the Aeronautical Inspection Dept., in short, the A.I D.

Jack asked me to take Mr Vincent down into the Machine shop to inspect various steel castings which were being turned on the lathes in preparation for the Air Ministry. Amongst these castings were some bomb casings for 250 lb bombs for the Royal Air Force, also some small items called Skid Shoes which were fitted to the tail of certain aircraft instead of the small wheel. After they had been inspected and passed, a labourer punched a government stamp mark on all the castings with a steel stamp which Mr Vincent had brought with him.

As we left the machine shop, Mr Vincent asked the labourer for a piece of chalk and then proceeded to mark sergeant's stripes and epaulets upon my navy blue blazer. "Well done, young man." He said. When we arrived back at the office, Jack and Charlie had a good laugh and Jack also said I'd done well. When I arrived home at night, Mum was a little cross because the chalk took some removing but could see the joke and soon forgot the incident.

Once again, just as I was settling down, another manager, Mr Sam Leach, the Foundry Manager, asked for me to be transferred and work for him in the Foundry Office. Mr Willis objected but after some strong argument, Mr Leach had his way and I was moved into the Foundry Office under the Chief Clerk, Wilf Storr. It was there that I was trained to be a piecework clerk by checking the price and times incurred by the workers on the shop floor.

It was on one of these occasions when I was standing alongside the core making foreman, Mr Billy Major, making notes of the cast numbers, the type of steel being poured from a 20-ton ladle into a mould for a bedding frame, that as I was writing down the details in my notebook, I suddenly found myself lying in 4" of foundry dust and sand.

At first, I thought that some of the workmen were having a game by pushing me over and as I started to pick myself up I saw Mr Major lying beside me. Through his vast experience, he had noticed that the 20 feet by 10 feet bed frame they were casting, had a defect in one of its seams opposite to where we were standing. Sensing danger, he had pushed me out of the way and dived after me. He saved my life because just as he pushed me, hot molten metal came shooting out from the side of the mould and would most certainly have hit us if we had remained there.

A further incident to this, but not as serious, was the time when Mr Harry Jow, the small machine moulding foreman, asked his labourer Archie, to clear an urgent order which was in the form of a small magnet box and had just been cast. He told him to take it into the open yard and cool it off. Archie, being a bit non-compos-mentis, moved the mould with the hot casting inside, along the roller conveyer belt into the open air.

Because it was needed urgently to be fettled, the labourer tried to cool it by throwing a bucket of cold water onto it. What happened!? The mould exploded and the small red hot casting blew back up the bay and hit Archie on the back of the neck as he was turning away. Luckily it wasn't a serious injury - more of a shock - the fool

Prior to starting work at Edgars', Mum had made enquiries about what knowledge I would need for my work in an office and having heeded the advice, she took me to see Mr Hemmings, who was the Headmaster of the Huntsmans' Garden Evening School in Bodmin Street. We had a long talk and Mr Hemmings said that the normal courses to take for clerical duties were those such as English, Arithmetic and Commerce, Shorthand and Book keeping. It sounded a tall order but I agreed to try all four courses. The English class I had no problem with and achieved first class passes for three years. Shorthand I struggled with and even asked my tutor, Mr George Johnson, to coach me at home, which he did for a few periods in the evenings for a short while. I did manage to get to a point of being able to take dictation at a speed of 50 words per minute.

Book keeping wasn't so good but I was able to do that for twelve months and obtained a second class pass. My strong subject was Arithmetic and Commerce where we had a teacher called Mr Chadwick. He was a livewire and had his own way of getting people to learn, sometimes by asking them to express a point in front of the class which occasionally made them look foolish but they learned their lesson, including me. He had a good sense of humour and by his unique ability to get the message across, I learned quickly. Finally, once again, achieving a first class pass mark over the three years I was with him.

I wasn't too happy with Book keeping so, in the second year I transferred to the Technical Engineering Drawing course because that would stand me more in good stead due to the work I was doing at Edgars'. I really enjoyed this subject and advanced so well that on the third year I achieved another first class pass which entitled me to go to the Central Technical College in Sheffield.

However, this was not to be because other things were taking place in the world which prevented me from taking this higher course , as you will read later.

Whenever anyone passed a course at night school, Edgar Allen's rewarded its juniors by awarding them 10/- shillings for each pass achieved, so it was worth making the effort. For five years I attended evening classes, which were between the hours of 7.00 p.m. and 9.00 p.m. during the months of September to March. I did eventually drop the shorthand and book keeping courses because it became obvious that I would not be using them in the work I was doing. This gave me a couple of free nights to find some other interests.

In 1937, I had course to leave Edgar Allen's whilst looking for a better position, so I moved to Davy United Engineering Co., Ltd., on Foley Street just by Norfolk Bridge. I started there in the Cost Office under Mr Smith, who was very strict and a Scotsman. It was a reputable firm who made steel presses, rolling mills and kilns for the cement manufacturing industry. Their products were sold world wide.

Having started at Davy's, I soon made new friends and two of them were in the 16th Company of the BB which was on Zion Lane. One was Marlon Jackson and the other, his cousin Albert. They both lived in Cottingham Street just off Staniforth Road and along with another cousin Bill and a pal Stan Measures from the BB we formed a close friendship, enjoying each others company for the next few years. Marlon and I also joined the small cycling club at Davy's, which was organised by Jimmy Thornton. On some summer evenings we would take a change of clothing with us to work and then go for a cycle ride into Derbyshire. The following morning, we would ride into work, change clothes again and then commence our duties.

LATE THIRTIES.

The cycling club at Davy's wasn't very big but we did have one or two long outings and on one of these we cycled out to Dunham Bridge which is on the River Trent in Nottinghamshire. It was a Sunday and because the weather was so warm we decided to go for a swim in the Trent and most of us had taken our swimming trunks. We made our way up the east side of the river until we found a suitable place to enter the water. We had worked out the current of the river which was very strong and entered the water to aim for a place on the other side which would be about two hundred yards further downstream.

We left our bikes with those who weren't going with us and into the water we went and headed for the opposite bank. The going was tougher than any of us had realised and after about fifteen minutes we eventually arrived at the other side. We were all out of breath and I for one said I wasn't going to swim back, the current was too strong. So, we decided to commandeer a small boat that was lying near to us and climbed into it to row back across the water.

Because the War was getting nearer, the government had decided to set up guards on all river crossings in case of enemy parachutists but we hadn't seen any such activity and as we were half way across the river an Army patrol with fixed bayonets ran across the bridge and were waiting for us as we stepped ashore. Having identified ourselves we were given a good bollocking, not for particularly using the boat but for the dangerous escapade on which we had embarked. We found out later that the place near Dunham bridge was noted for undercurrents and was indeed very notorious for the number of people drowned there. Looking back over the years, we must have been mental to have tried it. That was in 1939 and our last run out, I think we all had learned a lesson.

Whilst at Davy's I also befriended a Peggy Ashcroft who was a comptometer operator and one of the welders there used to give her the glad eye as he passed the office window and this led, eventually, to me passing notes and messages between them. The welder was Bill Cooper who was also a qualified piano teacher. He obtained his Cap and Gown at the tender age of fifteen. As you will have guessed, Bill and Peggy married each other a few years later.

It was at Davy's that I was first introduced to the forerunner of computers The Hollerith System of tabulators and punched cards which all served me in a good stead in later years. However, after eighteen months I decided to return to Edgar Allen's who were good enough to restart me.

One reason for going back was the fact that the immanence of war was very close and John Ward, who was in charge of the Hollerith Dept., was called up as a reservist in the Army. Mr Smith, my manager, asked me if I would take over some of John's work. I thought that this was an opening for promotion but when I was told that it meant me being on twelve hour nights for six months solid, I had to refuse. Let's face it. I was only just 18 years of age. - hence my return to Edgar's.

In 1937 and because I was very interested in popular music Dad asked me if I would like to learn the piano. I never missed the chance to go with Fred Tyler to see the big bands such as Lew Stone, Lou Praeger, Roy Fox and Harry Roy when they were at the Empire Theatre in Sheffield, so when Dad put this proposition to me I was delighted. He managed to buy me a second hand piano for £20 from a chapel on Ranskill Road near Tinsley Park Colliery. The caretakers there were chapel friends of Mum's and that is how the sale was made, through them.

The next step was to find a good piano teacher and fortunately a young lad called Dennis Snaith, who was living with his Aunty across the road from us, was also learning to play. Dennis and his Aunty put us in touch with a Miss Emily Brewster who lived on Staniforth Road.

It was just before the Seniors' Shop at which I had worked. Miss Brewster was a very attractive lady, aged around the late twenties and living with her mother. The fee was 1/6d per hour's lesson plus the cost of any music and tutorial books I needed.

I would go for lessons on the night that I wasn't at night school and it was for an hour between 7.00 p.m. and 8.00 p.m. My progress was rather slow at first but I managed to get in my practice and within six months I was able to play some small compositions. I was rehearsing one night when Bill Cooper called. He was off work with a whitlow on his thumb but that didn't stop him from playing on my piano and explaining one or two things to me about playing.

I stayed with Miss Brewster for three years and became quite proficient but not up to examination standard. This was my first incite to what was to become a great part of my life.

On returning to E.A's, Mr Garrison the Cost Office manager, put me into the Fettling Shop office under the supervision of Bernard Harrison. He was pleased to see me, having been the instigator of getting me started at Edgar's.

The compliment of clerks in the office was nine with Dave Askham then Freddie Bennett, Stan Wild, Mark Smallwood, Eric Lee, Donald Rabjohn, Joe Reardon and a Mr Bool. Our work was to fill in the time and piecework sheets in the office of all work passed to us by the shop floor clerks such as Cyril Markham, Gordon Reece and Irvine Morton. It was in this position that I learned the ability to multiply and add figures in my head when totalling piecework earnings which were put onto wages sheets. We did have a Boss senior to Bernard and we lads and he was responsible for all the fettling and finishing shops which included oxyacetylene welders and burner operators. His name was Billy Hemphill who was a very fair and understandable man.

One afternoon when we had finished our work - around 4.30 p.m. - several of us were playing push-penny in the foreman's room next door to our office when Cyril Markham came in and asked us if we hadn't anything better to do. The next thing was that we were called to Mr Hemphill's office where we found Cyril who had complained. Mr Hemphill asked each one of us if our work was complete for the day and we all answered in the affirmative.

"All right, Cyril." He said. " You've made your point." With that he turned to us and said, "Whilst I don't fully agree with what you have been doing, I will ask you to remember this little motto." 'ONE DAYS' WORK IN TWO AND TWO DAYS' WORK IN ONE!'

Since that day I have always remembered it and abided by it. -Think it out carefully.

Lunch break was between 12.00 p.m. and 1.00 p.m. and if weather permitted we would kick a tennis ball about and this helped to pass the time away. However, during one particular lunchtime, the ball was kicked right over the office roof into Vulcan Road. Eric Lee went for the keys to open the large gates alongside and having opened them, he went for the ball. After a few minutes we heard him shout, " Coming over!"

We all looked up and saw a ball appear in the air and coming towards us. Dave Askham made a short run and jumped to head the ball. OUCH!! Down he went and when we brought him round he commented, "What the bloody hell was that?" When we looked at the ball, we found it to be a steel one of the types we manufactured for use in rotary kilns in cement works. It was the size of a tennis ball and weighed about ½ a pound - no wonder Dave went down. The verbals he gave Eric Lee were well-chosen ones.

There were many sports facilities at Edgar's which included a large sports field on Bawtry Road. I played tennis there, also cricket and football. The league I played in was the Haigh

League for juniors between 16 and 18 years of age

One game of football we had to play was against Stocksbridge, on their ground which was about 12 miles the other side of town.

I wasn't down to play but I was the bag carrier with all the shirts in it and I balanced that on the crossbar of my bike to carry them to the game.

The first half of the game was very even and we were drawing nil - nil at half time. However, it had started raining quite heavily just before then and by the time the second half was due to commence, the heavens opened.

Our lads refused to go out and after some argument, the referee demanded that the game should proceed or else our team would be reported to the League Authorities. A decision was reached, to which the referee agreed, and we sent on the goalkeeper Joe Piper and Dave Askham, the centre forward. It was hilarious because the home team couldn't get accustomed to the situation and with the weather getting worse, everyone was sliding about.

Joe played a blinder, always managing to clear the ball away. Then the crunch came when he booted the ball up-field - Dave ran after it, went straight through the middle and scored. That was it because our two players held on to the end. After the game I had to pack all the wet shirts into the bag and cycle home. By gees, that bag was heavy but with a struggle I managed it.

They were a good crowd of lads at Edgar's and Stan Wild and Freddie Bennett and I would find time to go to local dance halls, many of which were church halls, but we enjoyed every minute. St. John's Hall on Siemens Road, Tinsley, had some very good dances there, also the church hall on Jenkin Road at Brightside. The admission fee was around the one and sixpence mark. It wasn't regular companionship because I also went about with Fred Tyler quite a bit.

In the summer of 1938, Fred and I decided to go on holiday with their next door neighbours, the Drabbles. They had one little son and were going by car but we were going by cycle to Ingoldmells in Lincolnshire, near Skegness.

The Drabbles had agreed to take our luggage in the car with them and we would meet them there later on.

So Fred and I started off at six o'clock on the Saturday morning along the A.57 route which would take us all the way to our destination. We had to have one or two rests on the way because the journey was about 93 miles. We had made very good progress on the way and by 11.45 a.m. we were within five miles of Skeggy. Once again misfortune struck and suddenly Fred had three spokes puncture his back tyre which also buckled his wheel. He borrowed my bike and cycled into Skeggy to get his wheel repaired. This cost us another hour but he eventually returned with the repaired wheel and we set off again.

When we finally arrived, the Drabbles had been wondering what had happened to us but were pleased to see us. We stayed in a converted railway carriage in which there were just three in this huge field. There was no tap water. It all came out of a rain butt just outside the hut. We had a good holiday and every morning Fred and I would run down to the beach, over the sand dunes and into the water. When we arrived back from swimming, we would drink half a pint of fresh milk and then have breakfast.

The holiday ended and the journey home was uneventful but rather tyring and we arrived home safely. That ride today would be very precarious with all the cars and lorries on the highways.

As you will see, I kept company with many friends and at times it was difficult to appease all of them, but I did. There was also the Chapel crowd with whom I mixed, especially after Sunday night service at the Attercliffe Wesleyan Hall.

I did try my hand at being a Sunday School teacher where in the afternoon, a few of us teenagers would take classes of five and six-year-old pupils. I really enjoyed teaching them about Jesus and the lady in charge of us teachers was a Miss Armitage who was always eager to encourage us.

However, I arrived one Sunday to teach my class when Miss Armitage approached with some bad news. One of my pupils, a lovely little five-year-old boy called Jackie, had been killed in a road accident. It so upset me that I discontinued being a teacher

We had a very good Minister there, the Reverend William Cookson. He used to be a professional comedian and he brought that humour with him when he was preaching. He had everyone's attention all the time and it was a pleasure to hear his interpretation of the sermons he gave.

There were special Sunday evening services when, after the service, there would be entertainment from such as the Police band, conducted by Inspector Hespe; The Transport Band and the Salvation Army Band and each year Handel's Messiah would be performed with Harry Jackson playing the large organ which stretched right across the back of the platform and stage. The main auditorium, which held one thousand people, was often packed to capacity.

If the weather was suitable, a group of us teenagers would go for a stroll after Sunday evening service. There was Alan Franks, who was dating Clarice Wild - a policeman's daughter, I and a girl named Florence Rudkin, who hailed from Brunswick Road and was a pupil at High Storrs School.

Florence was my first real date but I only saw her at weekends when she came to stay with her grandmother who lived on Francis Street and that was the only time because of her doing homework. She was a lovely looking girl, very slim, with dark hair and very intelligent. I must have had some feeling towards her because we went about together for quite some six months or more.

It doesn't seem possible today that I only received 2/6d a week pocket money but I managed to take her to the cinema which cost me one shilling, sixpence for each of us, - and I bought her a 2d bar of Cadbury's chocolate. I must have admired her tremendously because not once did I offer to do things I had done in other circumstances.

One of my virtues was that I seemed to be able to make conversation with most people and I befriended many. As you will have read already, many names have been mentioned, both male and female; some old, some young and in due course, you will see the significance of it all.

For two years I mixed with various groups of young people - sometimes keeping the company of one person only. Whoever it was, the front door of 87 Brompton Road was never closed to these friends.

Apart from my close friends, I also knocked about with my cousin Sid Wills and one evening we arranged to go to see our old headmaster, Mr Tilbrook, having obtained his address from Mr Dunkley, his successor. Mr Tilbrook lived in a flat in the Abbeydale area of Sheffield and when we arrived he was more than pleased to see us. We stayed and chatted about old times for quite a while and he commented on how nice it was to know that his old pupils hadn't forgotten him.

It was a few months after visiting him that we learned that he had fallen across an electric fire in his bedroom and had subsequently died of his injuries. We were very shocked and saddened by his death.

I didn't see much of Fred Tyler in the late thirties because he started courting a girl called Norma Bagshaw, another only child, and he was devoted to her. However, I did go to Fred's house one Christmas when all his family and relations were having a party. My Mum knew I would be staying overnight so she didn't worry.

The house was on Stonecliffe Road on the Manor Estate to where they had moved from an old house on Eadon Road in Attercliffe. This house had three bedrooms and on this party night Mrs Tyler, shouted to us to get off to bed. She explained that whoever arrived at the top of the stairs first, then they would get the double bed.

Fred made one dash - arrived at the top of the stairs first followed by Donald Dover, Wilf's pal. CLONK! BANG! WALLOP! . Fred had acquired an enamel potty 'guzzunder' and hurled it down the stairs (empty of course) to stop Donald getting up. It did. It hit Donald on the head and stopped him in his tracks. Mrs Tyler's house was like ours was, it always had open doors and always referred to me as 'PRIESTLEY's bit.

The thirties were nearing their end and war clouds were rumbling over Europe. Back in 1936 there had been the Spanish Civil War which to many, was the rehearsal for thing to come. As you will recall, Poland was invaded in 1939 which resulted in our country being thrown into war against Nazi Germany.

I wasn't old enough to be called to the colours at the start but I did volunteer to become an A.R.P. (Air Raid Precaution) messenger on my bike. This was a reasonably new bike which I had bought with my own money from my wages. It was a sports model in mottled blue colours and was bought from the Co-op at the bottom of Staniforth Road for £6/10/0.

On the 3rd September, 1939, war was declared and unfortunately on that day, Mum had arranged to have all her teeth extracted at home. The Dentist and Dr. Downey attended - finished their task and left our house. Mum stayed in bed to recover and Dad was on an afternoon shift, so I remained in the house to take care of her.

Guess what? 2.00 p.m. and the air raid sirens set off wailing. What a panic! Mum is pestering me to get her under the bed and put pillows around her. She was in a right state and I wasn't too clever either. Fortunately after thirty minutes, the "All clear" sounded. What a relief, it was a false alarm.

Everyone carried on as normal for quite awhile but as air raids were taking place in other parts of the country, it was difficult getting used to the blackout conditions when each night we had to remember to cover our sash windows. Dad had made some roller-blind type of cover which he had fitted onto the outside of the window frames. They were made of tarpaulin material and were very strong and effective, as we found out later.

I was always on standby as a messenger and my local A.R.P. headquarters was at Maltby Street school where I had to report if a warning sounded. In charge overall in Sheffield for the Warden service was Mr Hemmings, the night school headmaster at Huntsman's Garden School

One of our wardens was a young lady called Ann Keeton and aged about twenty-two years. I always tried to be on duty when she was. Sometimes on patrol we would go inside underground air raid shelters to inspect them and make sure there were no people needing help when there was a raid on. Ann lived at a sweet shop at the end of Whitworth Lane, near the Cop shop, and on some occasions we would go there for a break from duty - and a snog.

It was no fun when the sirens sounded, to have to get out of bed in the middle of the night, grab my overalls, helmet and gas mask and then dash off to report on duty. When I did arrive back home after the All Clear, I always had a mug of black Camp Coffee to keep me going. I had to go on fire fighting courses with other A.R.P. Wardens and at times it was very realistic, crawling through huts that were alight and trying to put out the fires within them with a stirrup pump.

After teatime on Thursday, 12th December, 1940, I washed and changed, ready to go to the B.B. because this night I was in charge. Bill Woffenden, our Captain, was on a night shift in the Edgar Allen fettling shop where I worked during the day.

I had now reached the rank of Lieutenant and was next in command to Bill. The Parade started on time at 7.00 p.m. and along with my pal Dennis Simpson, who was the Staff

Sergeant, I began proceedings with all the boys forming into three ranks for inspection and prayers. There were approximately 40 boys present that night and I had planned a Physical Training session along with classes in First Aid and Signalling.

Roll call had just finished when someone cried, "Sir, the sirens!" I told everyone to remain in their places and then methodically put them into groups relating to which area the lived in. One senior lad, Corporal Newton, was detailed to take all those who lived in the Woodburn Road area and proceed carefully with the junior ranks to their homes or thereabouts. Dennis Simpson took the party who lived in his area around Newhall Road and Don Road. For myself I took those who lived around the Chapel area and roads along Attercliffe Common. As it was to prove later, the operation was a success and every boy was returned home safely. Having done one duty, I went home to change into my overalls and then report to the A.R.P. Headquarters

On that Thursday night, Sheffield received its first Blitz. In an attempt to decoy the German bombers, searchlights were set up on the moors around Sheffield in the Peak District and to a point it worked because the town centre and the North West if the city had a right 'pasting'.

Dad was on an afternoon shift at the Brightside Lane Depot of the L.M.S. Railway and when he didn't arrive home by 10.15 p.m., Mum was very worried. He eventually came home in the early hours of the morning looking the worse for wear. He had been sent to the Heeley railway sidings to help them there because rows and rows of railway carriages were set alight with the incendiary bombs. He had made his way home by foot through the centre of town and was horrified at what he had seen. Marples, a well-known pub in the town, had received a direct hit from a land mine and hundreds of people who were sheltering there had been killed.

Whilst the raid was taking place and having returned from the B.B. I went on duty at the A.R.P. centre, taking messages to various people and sections of the organisation in the community. It was very precarious because of the shrapnel flying about from the shells of the Ack-Ack guns. Mum had been on her own in the reinforced cellar under our house. All houses had been converted in readiness of such events.

Everyone had just about settled down again on Friday and Saturday and I had been invited to tea on the Sunday at one of my girl friends' house. She was Margaret Williamson, who worked in the offices at Edgars' and lived in Highgate in Tinsley. Her father was the manager at Dewhursts, the butchers on Sheffield Road at Tinsley.

We were just sitting down for tea at 6.00 p.m. when the sirens went again. This was a night when we didn't fool the Gerry with searchlights on the moors. He had found the East End and the factories. Incendiaries bombs were raining down but Margaret's brother John and I, ran towards St. Lawrence Church just across the road, because the roof had several incendiaries on it. We found a ladder and whilst John held it, I climbed up and managed to throw some of the bombs to the ground. They were about six pounds in weight. We saved the church from serious damage and returned to John's house. It didn't help the area much when a haystack in Harry Justices' farm was set alight. It lit up the whole area, thus offering a bigger target.

I had to excuse myself because I was supposed to be on duty, so I set off to run home and report to the A.R.P. H.Q. On the way I called in to see if my Aunty Amy Kelsey, Dad's youngest sister, was safe, along with their baby son David. They lived on Greasboro Road. Seeing that they were O.K., I ran all the way up Sheffield Road and Attercliffe Common, dodging the electric cables which had fallen from the overhead tram wires and were arcing across the road.

When I arrived home, Mum said that Marlon Jackson, Albert and Bill had called to see if I was going out with them for the evening. She said I was out and then she became very upset because they had only been gone about ten minutes when the air raid warning sounded. That night, the east end of the city received an horrendous pounding and while on duty I had to go towards Staniforth Road Junction.

As I approached it in the light of burning fires from the incendiaries, I saw two land mines floating down by parachute. One was over the Stevenson Road area and the other was over Cottingham Street, I ran for shelter and then the mines went off. The damage was terrible, whole streets of houses had disappeared. A few days later I managed to contact the lads. Health wise, they were all right but all of them had lost their homes and everything. They were devastated

The following morning, after the blitz, I returned to work and fortunately Edgar's had managed to escape any serious damage and we carried on as best we could.

As the war progressed, more people were required to build up the armed forces and many of my family and friends had already been called to the colours. One of the first to be called was Sid Willis, because at the age of sixteen he had joined the Territorial Army in the Royal Artillery branch. The next one was George Parr who also was in the R.A.O.C. branch of the 'Terriers' and slowly and surely 17 of my relations were called into the Forces.

Dad had always been keen on insurance and for years we had a Mr Parker call for the premiums for the Royal London Ins. Co., and also a Mr Elwood for the Prudential. With war breaking out, Mr Parker had retired and Mr Elwood was called up as a reservist.

In Mr Elwood's place we had a young man collecting the premiums called Frank Woodruff. He was good looking and always ready for a chat. He was around twenty-two years of age. We had just become used to him when he too was called into the R.A.F.. In his place, a young lady came and introduced herself as his wife, May. She too was about twenty-two, full of life and very soon became a friend of the family.

Whilst Frank was away, she lived with her mother, Mrs Reading, who lived on Vicarage Road, opposite the Adelphi Cinema. For many months May would call in and tell us how Frank was getting on and in certain instances, she would help Mum decorate and put stippling onto the walls in time to the music of Victor Sylvester and His Orchestra on the radio. Stippling was in place of wall paper which was unobtainable during the war and was a type of paste in various colours which had to be dabbed onto the walls with a small pad.

Everything seemed to be going well, even though the war news wasn't good but one day May walked into our house, she never knocked, she was part of the family. Her face was drawn, unhappiness was to be seen in her eyes which were full.

"What's wrong, Love? " Asked Mum.

" It's Frank." She replied. " He's been killed in a bombing raid over Germany."

Frank was a Rear Gunner in the Heavy Bombers. Tears were plentiful as Mum and I tried to comfort her.

EARLY FORTIES

As the age of call-up came closer to my own, I told Mum and Dad that I really ought to go and because the majority of my relations had joined the Royal Artillery, I also wanted to be part of it - just like Dad had been in 1914. I went to the recruiting office in the Cutler's Hall in Sheffield and applied to join the Royal Artillery. The interviewing officer, Major Griffiths, queried my eyesight because of me wearing spectacles. He turned me down on these grounds and I was so disappointed that I marched down the stairs, straight into the Royal Air Force recruiting office.

This was at the end of February 1941 and I signed on there and then in the R.A.F.V.R., as a Radio Telephone Operator (R.T.O.) I was asked to report on the 19th March following, to go to Padgate, near Warrington in Cheshire, to have a full medical and get documented. On arrival at the Cutler's Hall, who should turn up but none other than Eddie Barrett, one of my school mates from Clay Street. He had signed on as an armourer.

We both spent 48 hours at Padgate after which I was sent home to await further orders but poor Eddie was kept behind for immediate training. Emotionally I was very upset because the onus fell upon me to inform his parents that he wasn't coming home for quite some time. His father was in poor health and his mother was nearly blind and like me Eddie was an only child.

The following June, Eddie's father died and he never saw him again - he did get compassionate leave for 48 hours but due to 'Red Tape', the poor lad missed his Dad's funeral. Because of this upset, my Mum befriended his Mum Lena and over the war years they became good friends - also, by some miracle, Mrs Barrett's eyesight improved.

The war in Europe was getting worse, Hitler was getting the upper hand with the result that on the 4th June, 1941, the B.E.F. had to evacuate at Dunkirk. George Parr was involved in this episode and it was a great relief when he came home on leave, having managed to get back to England across the Channel with his Unit.

It took three months for me to be called up officially and on the 26th June I returned to Padgate where, after a few days of receiving inoculations, drawing uniform and equipment from the Equipment Section etc., I, along with scores of other personnel, was sent by train to Bridlington on the East coast of Yorkshire. This posting was for training and square bashing and the elementary duties applying to all 'erks;'. One number you never forgot when joining the forces and that was your service number. Mine was 1044159.

I was there for eight weeks and during that time I saw a heavy air raid on the port of Hull, just down the coast. The flames could be seen for miles but one night we had a couple of bombs dropped on Bridlington. This was put down to the fact that a warship was anchored in the bay and 'Gerry' had spotted it. The ship wasn't hit but one bomb overshot the bay and landed on top of a garage at the end of York Street where we were billeted.

Our flight instructor was a Corporal Jock Stevenson, a Scot, who knew the drill book inside out. He was a good NCO, and one day whilst out taking drill with us, he stood us at ease for a short rest. As we did this a, beautiful young woman passed us by on the pavement and obviously there were comments and wolf whistles.

"When you've stopped admiring m' wife," He said, in his Scottish accent, "We'll get on with the drill."

The Armoury was in the centre of town and on the day we were to do arms drill we marched down to the building to obtain our .303 Le Enfield rifles. To achieve this they were passed from hand to hand at arms length until everyone had received one.

There were two squads of some 30 men each with Jock Stevenson in charge of our squad and Corporal Jones in charge of the second one. We were in the process of passing them along the file when, unseen, Corporal Jones walked round a blind corner just as a rifle was being passed at arms length. SMACK!! The rifle hit him full in the face.

The air was 'blue' but our Corporal was doubled up with laughing. Jonesey wasn't as popular as our Jock and we all had difficulty trying not to laugh.

We worked hard and played hard - beaches were protected with coils of barbed wire but there was just enough room for us to do PT. and games on them. On Pass out Parade there was a full flight of about 180 men all marching up and down the Promenade with the CO. of the Station taking the salute.

At the end of training we all received our postings to various units for further education in the trade courses which we had chosen to do. I went along with another ten 'bods' to the South East Technical College in Barking, Essex, to be trained as a Wireless Mechanic. Whilst in Brid, I had palled up with a lad from Matlock in Derbyshire - he was Ron Wood who actually lived in Cromford. On the way there we stayed over night at RAF Chigwell which was a Balloon Barrage Training School and the following day we were taken to private billets in Barking. Ron and I were settled on a Mr. and Mrs. Phillips who lived at the back of the College in a three bed-roomed house on Beacontree Avenue

The Phillip's were a good family and had four grown up children. John, the eldest was in the forces but in peacetime was a professional tap dancer with a girl partner. There was also a daughter, Eve, who was in the WAAF, she was married whilst we were there and Ron and I went to the reception at Romford. Then there was Ted, a very nice chap who took Ron and I down to look around Petticote Lane one Sunday on a tourist ticket of 1/- shilling. The youngest son, Wally, was 17 ½ years of age and worked locally. In actual fact Ron would say he was a right 'wally'. He couldn't understand why one testicle hung lower than the other.

At the Tech., we were trained to repair radios and all other ancillary equipment besides doing our normal drills. There was one day when the Flight Sergeant asked if anyone had been in the B.B. and one or two of us put up our hands.

What happened? He chose me to take the squad in foot drill for half an hour. Never volunteer for anything.

It was a six-month course, which in ordinary circumstances would have taken three years. During the course we had the opportunity to visit Bulgin's electrical factory in Barking to see how components were made for the wireless industry. We also had plenty of leisure time and often went out into Barking Town with Wally who had borrowed his father's small car. He couldn't drive but Ron Wood could.

There were many weekends when I was able to get a 48-hour pass and go home - it was 24/- shillings' return by train from London to Sheffield and connections to London from Barking by Tube train were very good.

Sometimes I would write to cousin Ella in Kent and ask if I could go there for the weekend. Her Mum, Aunty Mag, always made me very welcome and once, my Mum and Dad came down to see me and then went on to my Aunty's for a few days' break.

When I was down in Kent I would sit with Ella at night whilst she was doing her shift on the switchboard. On a spare set of headphones I would listen to some of the conversations that were taking place. Some were very humorous but the main interests were the messages that were being passed between RAF Stations such as Biggin Hill, Manston and West Malling, the latter being the local H.Q. One weekend, Aunty's radio broke down and being on a radio course I thought that I could fix it. I took the chassis out of the casing, disconnected the Bakelite knobs just as we had done in class.

I switched the power on and held the bare chassis whilst I tried to tune into a radio station. Unfortunately, as I grabbed the chassis, one of my fingers connected with a live wire underneath.

What a shock !! The whole unit was alive between my two hands and I couldn't let go. Luckily, Ella came into the room and switched off the power. The chassis fell to the floor and I never found the fault. But I did have a scar on the finger involved for several years because the live wire had dug a lump clean out of it, but it didn't bleed.

The course was led by a Professor Holnan who lived on the same road as the one we were billeted on. He was rather a shy person but very amiable. His teaching methods were good and we were expected to do some homework. I did but Ron Wood couldn't be bothered and at the end of the term - guess what? Ron passed and I didn't.

During the latter part of the course we were put to work on Cathode Ray Oscillographs which were the forerunners of today's television, the only difference being that there were no pictures, just a screen with graph lines on it.

In January 1942, our course having been finished the posting came through for us and Ron was posted to another training school but I was posted to Penrhos on the North Wales Peninsular, near to Pwllheli where there was a gunnery and observation school for aircrew.

It was a long and tedious journey from King's Cross Station to North Wales and we travelled by the Great Western Railway to a place which we called 'Rayborn' - it was spelled RUABON and pronounced the same. There were six of us and we changed trains here and embarked on to a place called Afon Wen where we changed trains once more. This train was like a mountain train with a small engine, two or three carriages and - a single line track which took us to the town named Pwllheli. We then boarded a truck which took us another five miles to the camp of Penhros

The group of us were detailed to a hut and issued with blankets etc., where we settled for the night before being shown round the camp the following morning and detailed to our various posts. I was just another GD (General Duties) Bod attached to the planning section of the bomber school.

There were several of us in the section whose work was to plot the readings sent to us from quadrants on the coast. We would mark these geographical readings onto a map with a target marked on it.

The actual target was a 30ft timber and metal pyramid which was anchored out at sea. We would get some readings taken at angles and passed back to us from north and south of the camp. Where the lines drawn on the map crossed each other then that was where the bomb had fallen It was our job to measure the distances between the target on the map and the position given us by the quadrant readers

We had several Army officers with us who were training to be glider navigators and they would go on these bombing trips, learning to read the terrain below and also try some bomb aiming. One day a Captain objected to our plotting and claimed that he had made a direct hit, not knowing, that to us a direct hit was the 12-inch diameter ball at the pinnacle of the pyramid on the target.

When our Officer-in-charge, Flt. Lt. Edwards, DFC, was told about this complaint he said whilst climbing onto the top of my desk, "If the Captain comes in again, get like this." He stood above the plotting graph, "Tell him to look at your readings and then (pause), kick his bloody head in!" He was laughing as he said it and so did I and the other lads

There were several nationalities amongst the aircrews, some French, some Canadians and quite a few Polish ones. There was one Polish Sgt. Pilot, named Paderewski, who was curious as to what made a Varey Light distress signal work.

He opened a spare cartridge and emptied the contents onto the grass outside the dispersal hut. He then took a box of matches, leaned over the contents, struck a match and put it to the powder. WHOOSH1 He was rushed to sick bay with his hands and face badly burned and his eyebrows had completely disappeared.

Apart from our daily routines we still had to do guard duties or early morning calls and on one of the latter I had to go to the WAAF dormitories to call a duty cook at 6.00 a.m. Whilst there I bumped into a young WAAF who came from Doncaster and this led to several dates off the camp and over a period of a few weeks we would go into Pwllehli to the cinema etc.

It wasn't long before I was losing my virginity and more than once we would finish up behind the Camp Gym which was near the WAAF quarters. Then all of a sudden I lost touch with her but later found out that she had been off sick with pleurisy. It must have been caused by lying on the wet grass. My Dad always told me to be careful that's why I kept to the three "Ws'. **W**hip it in, **W**hip it out and **W**ipe it.

I felt sorry for the lass because one night she asked me to take more care due to the fact that as I was withdrawing, my sperm wet the inside of her knickers and it made her uncomfortable as she walked back to her billet. During my friendship with her, my hut corporal confined me to camp for a whole week because I looked so knackered, and I felt it.

Whilst the 'Donny' lass was off sick, I palled up with another WAAF whose father was the Chief Constable of Conway. We went for walks and talked and discussed many things but one night, on our way back to camp, we finished up inside a Dutch Barn on the remains of a hay rick. We had a very hard session but it was really embarrassing when, just as we were on the verge of fulfilment, the movement of our bodies caused us to slip slowly down the rick. We couldn't stop laughing all the way back to camp.

In the Forces, there were many funny incidents and one of these was in our hut. We had a young lad in there who was a member of the Salvation Army. Some of the lads would take the Mickey out of him, especially when they found that he had brought his own enamel potty with him. He was so innocent, but one night the lads nailed his potty to the wooden floor thinking that he would have difficulty pulling it out from under his bed. He wasn't that stupid, because in the middle of the night he climbed out of bed - moved the bed - used the potty and then moved the bed back again to it original position. The laugh was on them!

All pilots had instructions not to bring any bombs back to the camp after a flying practise. They were smoke bombs and weighed about 10 lbs but sometimes the odd one would 'hang up'.

To release them, the pilot would roll the plane to try to shake them off over the sea. By a strange coincidence, on one mission, a bomb would not shake off but the pilot thought that it had. As he approached the airfield, the bomb suddenly broke loose just as he came over the coast, it dropped and landed on the lawn and then bounced straight through the C.O's bungalow window. The smoke filled every room and the Group Captain wasn't very pleased.

A Sgt. Instructor drew a cartoon of a bungalow with the Groupie's head protruding on a thin neck through the window and shaking a clenched fist at the aircraft. This cartoon was put on the wall of the crew room to remind all pilots of the seriousness of the incident.

One type of aircraft on our unit was the Blenheim fighter bomber in which navigators were trained to use bomb aimers. I asked if I could go on one of the exercises and having received permission I collected a parachute from the section and arrived ready to board. This I did and was told to go to the mid-turret position We took off and headed for the practise zone flying over the pyramid targets I mentioned earlier. There were ten bombs aboard and that meant that we had to do at least ten runs over the target. This we did and had no hangups before returning to camp.

Upon landing, the ground instructor gave me a right dressing down because as we took off originally, I sat with my back to the pilot and in the mid-turret seat one must never do that because at some sudden jerk of the aircraft a person's neck could be broken. I did explain, however, that no one had mentioned this to me but I got the message. This was my maiden flight and I thoroughly enjoyed it and I never felt airsick once.

The GD Section was under the supervision of a Flt./Sgt. Gale who hailed from the Isle of Man and one day he took us on Gunnery practice on the Range above the Camp. There he instructed us on how to lie prone and fire a rifle.

"Lay still. Pull the butt of the rifle into your shoulder." He said. He himself did this and pushed his cheek onto the rifle.

"Sight your target." He continued. "Slowly squeeze the trigger. Don't pull it," He fired and when he arose, his right cheek was all puffed up. I think he had put too much effort into it.

When the Squad prepared to fire, one of the boys became nervous - took aim - fired too soon and shot the rope of the red danger flag which was behind the firing butts. The flag slowly fell to earth and the Flt/Sgt was not amused. But we were.

There wasn't much public transport around the camp area so we would go for walks down to Abersoch Harbour or to Llanbedrog onto the beach at the Glen-y-Wydw where there was a small hall which could be used for dancing and there weren't many of those to get excited about.

It was only a short stay at Penrhos because a notice appeared on the D.R.O's, Daily Routine Orders, asking for volunteers for 'B' Release. This was a government scheme to get skilled people back into industry in civvy street to help with the wartime effort. I applied because of my wireless training and very fortunately for me I was selected and believe it or not, I was sent to Sheffield to work for J.G.Graves at their wireless factory in Crookes. Lucky me! I was billeted at home and this was at the end of March 1942.

I wasn't allowed to wear uniform whilst on 'B' release and it was great to move about as a civilian. At the factory there were about 30 girls and young women aged between sixteen and thirty. One of them I knew as Joan Simms, whose father owned a private bus company in Attercliffe. It greatly helped when she introduced me to some of the other girls. There were of course several men employed there to help with designing radio chassis and doing work which might be too heavy for the female staff. A Mr. Hinchcliff was the overseer and the manager was Mr. Bagshaw who was also a Flt/Lt. in the Air Training Corps for teenagers. At times he tried to treat me like one.

I was seconded for six months to this firm to help wire up circuits to radios and help the girls where necessary. This 'necessary' became full time when quite a few of them said that they loved to go dancing at the City Hall Ballroom. Did I dance? Of course I danced and with these lasses I never had a minute off the dance floor. The strange thing was that I never became serious with any of them and we had some great fun. There were times when Dennis Simpson would help me out because he too was a good dancer.

Dennis and I would also go dancing at the Darnall Public Hall which was the main venue for many youngsters. There was a night when I was looking for a partner to dance with when I spotted this lovely looking, dark haired girl with a friend.

I approached the girl and from behind and whispered, "Would you care to dance?" She turned sharply - paused - and then, smilingly she accepted. It was Florence Rudkin whom I hadn't seen since just before I joined the RAF. We had a good chat about old times and she told me that she was an accountant at one of Sheffield's largest stores - Cockaynes'. I dated

Florence a few times and we often went to the Hall to dance again

In the post, one morning, I received a letter from Ron Wood and in it he said that Win, his fiancé, and he was to be married because he had been posted abroad. In actual fact he was to go to Gibraltar where the lucky blighter was to remain for the duration of the war. The day arrived in June 1942 and to look the part of Best Man I took my uniform with me to wear at the wedding because he too was getting married in his. Because of clothing restrictions it was not a white wedding but even so Win looked beautiful in her two-piece suit.

I had gone over to Cromford, where they both lived, on the night before by train and stayed at Ron's mothers. Coincidentally, his father, like mine worked on the railway. There was a little embarrassment in the church because as they walked down the aisle after the ceremony I had to call Ron back because I had inadvertently left all my money in my civvy suit, and therefore couldn't pay the verger. We still laugh about it today.

As I said earlier, I went around quite a bit with Dennis Simpson and on this particular evening he called in to see if I would care to go to a party on an RAF Balloon site on Carbrook Recreation ground near to where we lived. He had met a couple of WAAFs from the site and they had asked him if he could bring a friend along to make up the party.

When we arrived, we were invited into an army type hut where there must have been a dozen Waafs. Food and drink was laid on, also some music from a record player. There was a young WAAF sergeant in charge who was just turned nineteen and she made us very welcome. As the night progressed I was attracted to her. She was smart, shortish but rather attractive, even if she did look a little chubby.

We became more friendly and as per usual I had to make a pass at her with my favourite saying. "Come on, give us a kiss." and gently approached to hold her. The next thing I knew was when I landed on my back in a corner to where she had thrown me. She certainly had been trained in self defence. Apart from that and having had a good laugh, I made a date with her and slowly but surely we became very attached to each other.

Her name was Doreen Daisy Dunne and this caused some comment. She came from the Kensington part of London, feelings became very strong and Mum and Dad said that I ought to bring her home and introduce her. She was an immediate success with Dad who liked her cheeky face and sense of humour - and her Cockney accent.

Before much longer, all her off duty hours were spent with us at No.87. Doreen became my really first heartthrob and when one day she asked me to go for the weekend to meet her parents I thought that this was it. However, not long after meeting her she said she was to be posted to another unit.

I took this to mean that she was leaving Sheffield but she was having me on. The posting was to another site which was in Norfolk Park near to Queen's Road. I would go and see her as much as I could and one evening when I was there, a storm warning was issued and Doreen was busy organising her girls to 'Storm Bed' the large Barrage Balloon which meant fastening thick guy ropes to a concrete base.

Things were getting a little rough with the high winds so I shouted to her to ask if I could be of any help "Yes" She cried. "Grab that rope near the tail fin and pull it down!"

Pull it down! A gust of wind came under the balloon, lifted it into the air and - being only 8½ stones in weight, wet through - I went with it. I rose about twenty feet into the air with the crew shouting for me to let go of the rope. This I did but in reaching the ground I broke my specs with the jolt. Otherwise, I was uninjured.

There was a small lake near the site and very often Dennis and I would go for a swim and then chat to the girls afterwards. There was once when their officer-in-charge walked in but she didn't object to us being there when Doreen explained who I was.

It was here that I made the only sexy pass to Doreen and it almost caused our breaking up. After apologising and a few cuddles and kisses she forgave me. It would have been completely out of nature for me not to have made a pass but I controlled myself, especially when she came down to Brompton Road and we were involved In petting and snogging. DOWN RONALD! DOWN BOY! .

Whilst at J.G.Graves, we had to do fireguard duties on various nights just like all civilians but one of my stints ended my freedom. During the shift I tried to drive the firm's car which was parked outside. The idea being that if it was in danger during a raid I could move it to safety but unfortunately I ran it into a pile of coal which was heaped outside.

The following morning Mr Bagshaw refused to accept my explanation and having moved the car from the heap, he told me to shovel all the coal into the cellar. There was about 20 tons of it and I was so incensed that when I arrived home, I wrote to RAF Records at Innsworth in Gloucestershire and complained.

I told them I had been released to do radio work not to be used as a labourer shovelling coal. My complaint was accepted and on the 5th of September 1942 I received my orders to report to the RAF Camp at South Cerney near Cirencester.

When my posting came through I hadn't a clue as to where South Cerney was but by looking up some maps it was found to be in Gloucestershire, near to the town of Cirencester. I travelled by train on the Bristol Express and followed my instructions telling me where to change at Andoversford and then catch a connection to Cirencester. It was there that transport was waiting for me to take me to the Camp at South Cerney, which was about four miles away.

After reporting to the Orderly Room, I was taken to a huge peacetime barrack block and given a bed in the upstairs flight. There were about thirty beds in the room because a two-bed space was increased to three and things were a little cramped but I did acquire a separate locker for myself.

I was assigned to the Gas Section in which a Flt/Sgt. Jack Waterfield was the NCO in charge, along with two corporals. The Section was next to the Armoury and was a sort of storage unit for clothing which might be needed for personnel to renew their clothing in case of a gas attack. The Chief was a peacetime airman and had been on this camp for quite a while, having risen through the ranks. He hailed from the town of Worcester and was a smashing and friendly NCO.

A posting in the RAF was often a singular one and when arriving on a new camp one had to search for friends. It wasn't long before I met one in the NAAFI and he was playing the piano to entertain the lads. I broke into conversation with him and another airman, Eric Linton, who sang with the Doyle Carte Opera Company. Their accommodation was in a hut which was lower down the camp.

The pianist was Tony Hill who came from Bradford and within days we had cemented a very firm friendship. Tony was a professional musician and had played for Jack White and His Collegians at the Astoria Hotel in London. He now played the piano with the Voluntary Musicians in the dance band on camp. The difference between the full time and voluntary musician was seen by the harp they wore on their sleeves. The regular ones had a crown on the top of their harp whilst the voluntary ones only had the harp.

Musicians and entertainers in the Forces were numerous and many had graced the professional stage. In our voluntary dance band in which Tony played, the drummer Frank Moss, had played for Joe Loss and His Orchestra, Harry Jones, the alto sax player had done many big band jobs and Arthur Mosely, an admin. Sergeant and the bass player, was self taught but quite accomplished.

The rest of the band included Eddie, the trumpet player and then there was Dave on tenor sax. On odd occasions when there was a big dance taking place, we had a vocalist, Jackie Aldrich, who was the sister of Ronnie Aldrich who led the fabulous Squadronaires Dance Band.

After a while I became attached to the Station Dance Band and eventually I became the 'Dots' carrier. That is, taking charge of the music library and keeping it in order.

Over the next few months, Tony, Eric and I kept together as pals whenever we went out of camp but Eric never went with us if we were going out on a band engagement. The CO. had an agreement with the Voluntary Band and that was, if the band played for an all ranks dance every Wednesday night in one of the hangars, then all other engagements outside of camp were not the C.O's worry and no money earned was taken from their earnings for the PSI (Public Services Institute.) This arrangement wasn't too popular with the official camp band but there was nothing they could do about it.

It was approaching my birthday on the 25th October and I had applied for leave so that I could have a party at home. Everything seemed fine until a few days before I was to travel, Flt/Sgt Waterfield called me in and told me my leave had been cancelled because our two corporals in the section had to go on courses.

My face, literally, hit the deck. "You only get one 21st birthday." I told the Chief. "It really hurts."

He said it was the Adjutant's idea because there were no replacements available. I told Tony because he had managed to arrange some leave to go home with me, for days I walked about in a trance.

I was sitting on my bed on the Thursday night when the Chief walked in from his room across the landing. "What are you doing here?" He asked. I couldn't reply. He carried on.

"I don't want to see you on camp tomorrow morning. Your leave starts then, doesn't it?" I was amazed - the Chief was smiling as he said it. "I've fixed it with the Adjutant. I'll do your duty."

What an NCO. He was wonderful and I could never thank him enough.

So it was that Tony and I travelled up to Sheffield and on arriving at home I found that Eddie Barrett had also obtained some leave, it was wonderful.

For a whole week we had great fun and Tony went down a 'bomb' with Mum and Dad. Tony would never sit down to a meal until Mum had done so and he always offered her a chair before seating himself. He was a gentleman.

I introduced him to Doreen who had been keen to meet him and also to some of my friends who were still in civvy street. On the night of the party there was a good crowd consisting of Fred and Norma, Dennis and Joyce, Nora Russon, and old school friend, Florence Rudkin and May Woodruff. Dennis had met a Canadian soldier at the local pub and asked us if he could join in. It was open house at No.87 so we invited him. He was so pleased, with him being so many miles from home. Also, of course there was Eddie.

Although it was war time, Mum had managed to put on a marvellous spread of food, ably assisted by May and we were just sitting down for tea when there was a knock at the back door and who should walk in but George Parr. He too had managed some leave. Unfortunately this made thirteen people so Dad, being a bit superstitious, said he would stand up. So it was and everyone had a good tuck in.

After tea all the lasses mucked in to clear away the pots and do the washing up whilst the lads made the room comfortable to sit in.

It was at this stage that I opened the many presents which my friends had brought me and whilst appreciating them all, there were one or two which to me were very precious. Nora had brought me a beautiful silk RAF scarf, which I wore quite often. Auntie Edie Willis (Uncle Bert's widow), gave me a golden half sovereign in mint condition, along with a gold dress chain key ring which hung from the braces into the trouser pocket. But the one I cherished the most was the gold dress ring which my Mum and Dad had bought me and it had my initials 'GRP' inscribed upon it. It never left my finger and always reminded my of my loving parents.

We had several party games like the old-fashioned postman's knock and others that caused some fun. Tony played the piano - particularly the 'Warsaw Concerto' which was so popular at the time. Eventually the party broke up and Eddie took Nora home because they both lived on Clay Street. I didn't know which of my three girl friends to take but that was sorted out by the Canadian taking Doreen back to her site; Tony took May and I finished up taking Florence home. It could have been embarrassing for me having three to choose from but I got away with it. George Parr had no girl to take because he had left a little earlier in the night.

During the week a crowd of us went to the Hill Top Hotel, a local pub, where the landlord, Frank Sellars, was friendly with Mum and Dad. In the lounge there was a grand piano where before long, Tony and I entertained. If he wasn't playing the piano I was, whilst he was singing. His favourite song was Cole Porter's 'Begin the Beguine.'

Whilst Tony was staying with us, I showed him a piece of music which I had written. It was called "Sahara" and he was so taken with it that he said we should take it back to camp and let the band lads peruse it. This we did and later on I was to receive a great surprise.

The week's leave soon passed but it had been a marvellous occasion and everyone involved had enjoyed it, especially Tony. The time came however, for both of us to return to South Cerney and prepare for the Camp Concert.

South Cerney was a Flying Training School and aircraft had still to be serviced and the maintenance personnel came under Wing WO Thomas. He was a strict disciplinarian but a fair one and when an instance arose where an airman was told by a barrack room sergeant to get his hair cut, WO Thomas showed his authority.

The airman again had his hair cut and reported back to the Sergeant, Sgt. Searle, who told the airman to go back and get it finished. This occurred three times and in the end the erk went to the WO "Sir, is my haircut alright?" He asked.

"Very smart, Lad. Why do you ask?" The erk explained and said that Sgt Searle had told him to go back again to the barber for the fourth time.

The WO told him to leave the matter with him and then he sent for Sgt Searle. Within 24 hours the Sergeant was posted. We understood that WO Thomas had said. "I'm responsible for such discipline around here, not you."

If you were new to the WO's section, he would interview you and his favourite question was. "Can you fight?" The correct answer was. "Yes, sir. Enough to defend myself." Any other answer meant that you had to go down to the gym and have a couple of rounds in the rink with the Warrant Officer. He was once the heavyweight boxing champion of the RAF and I was lucky because I belonged to another section and this came under Mr Slater. He was the Station Warrant Officer. (SWO for short.)

There was another instance when a full military funeral was taking place and just as the cortege was leaving the camp for the local cemetery an ordinary airman decided to walk from one hangar to another. WO Thomas spotted him and as the gun carriage was going through the gates, Thomas let out a roar.

"Airman!" He bellowed. "Get over here." That airman received 28 days detention for discourtesy to the dead. That was discipline.

We had a good entertainment's officer on camp, a Flt/Lt Ronnie Waters, who was the brother of Elsie and Doris Waters of Music Hall fame. Ronnie had put a notice on to D.R.O's asking for volunteers to form a concert party and being interested, I put my name forward and reported a week later to the large hangar where we held dances and other entertainment.

There were about thirty people who came forward, offering their services such as, Singers, dancers, solo musicians etc. These were interviewed by Ronnie Waters who slowly but surely came up with a plan to do a variety concert.

At some of the rehearsals I played the piano, especially for the girls who were to take part in the Mannequin Parade. The tunes chosen for the show were ' A Pretty Girl Is Like a Melody' and 'You Stepped Out of a Dream'.

The effort put into making the show a success was due to the hard work by everyone but most of all by Ronnie Waters. Through his connections with the West End in London, he had managed to acquire two huge baskets full of stage props such as curtains, dresses for the mannequins plus professional wigs for the six of us who were taking part in a mock ballet. We also wore garlands in our hair for the dance.

The official Station Band was used as the theatre orchestra. Ronnie had worked out some blackout sketches which took around three to five minutes to enable changes to be made in costumes and acts. One of these was Peter Sherry of the Sherry Brothers. He was an acrobatic violinist whom I had seen on the stage of a theatre back home. Another act was a harmonica player called Tommy Hazeldene, then there was of course the Mannequins routine. There were three sergeants who dressed up in wigs and gowns and did their version of the Andrew Sisters singing "Sisters'.

It took weeks and weeks of rehearsal before everything dropped into place but eventually the opening night came and the show took place in the Camp Cinema.

On the first night, the leading mannequin, a look-alike of today's Shirley Bassie, had only her pants on underneath her beautiful gown and when the strong, floor level lights in the stage wings were on, they showed all her figure. After the whistles and cat calls from the audience, the producer had the lights subdued. All the girls chosen, such as Paddy, Barbara and Susan were beautiful and looked gorgeous and elegant in their full length dresses.

Another girl, 'Denny', sang 'Daddy Wouldn't Buy Me a Bow Wow'. She was a small blonde with a doll-like figure and wore a short, blue and white small checked dress with her frilly knickers showing. More whistles.

I and five other airmen wore three-quarter length ballet dresses and our wigs had been specially arranged by Gwen the camp hairdresser. We then danced to the tune of the "Rustle of Spring.'

Each pair of dancers did a little dance of their own but when myself and a sergeant did our turn, right in the middle of it, where he had to swing me off my feet, he accidentally let go of my wrists. I went backwards across the stage on my chest and knees. The audience was in uproar and thought it part of the act. Ronnie thought it funny and told us to keep it in the act each time. It was alright for him but my chest and legs were sore for days. He, himself, finished off the dance by coming on dressed in a tutu and brandishing an electric fan in a fan-dance. He was six feet two inches tall and had very sandy hair, so you can imagine what he looked like.

My night was made because the Voluntary Band opened the second half of the show as an actual act and played a few popular tunes including the 'Song of India' with Tommy Hazeldene playing the harmonica. It was great. Then the compere surprised me. I was in the wings at the time, by announcing. "Ladies and gentlemen. We now have a treat for you. The next tune is one composed by AC Priestley and arranged by Harry Jones. It is called "Sahara". I was asked onto the stage and presented to the audience. The band then played my tune. Harry had done me proud and even the regular musicians in the orchestra applauded. I was so proud. More so when, after its first airing, the band played it regularly at all the dances they performed at.

The show was taken on the road and we visited many other camps at Tetbury, Kemble, Lechlade etc., it was a great success. Then one night Tony came and told me that I was entitled to wear the Voluntary Musicians Badge. I felt over the moon.

I did manage to get another 48-hour pass before Christmas and in a way I wish I hadn't. Whilst at home, Mum asked me to go and see Aunty Jessie Willis because she had something to show me. I walked into Aunty's house on Swan Street and I could tell there was something wrong.

"Hello, Love." She said. "Read this"

It was a signal from the War Office.

"Sorry to say your Son, Sidney Willis, is missing, presumed killed."

I just broke down with emotion. He was the first to be called up and the first and last not to return. That was in November 1942. A few months earlier he had volunteered to go as a gunner on the merchant ships and this is where he had been lost. It was on a large convoy which was trying to get to Murmansk in Russia, with supplies. I returned to the camp a very sorry figure, having lost one of my best pals

Tragedy seemed to be accompanying me because a few weeks later I went to meet Tony and could tell by his face that things weren't well. I commented on it and he then told me that he had just received a letter from his Mum saying that his girlfriend, whilst coming out of the factory where she worked, had been knocked down and killed by an American Army truck.

.For weeks, Eric and I had difficulty trying to calm him because every time we went into Cirencester, we had to keep him away from the Yanks We often frequented the Queen's Head pub in Cirencester and each time, after the bad news of his girl, Eric and I had to stand either side if him at the bar to avoid any trouble. Once we were unsuccessful and he gave this G.I. a right beating.

Tony was so distraught that on one evening in town he had his forage cap tucked into his belt. An MP (Snowdrop) pulled him up and cautioned him That was it. Tony hit this copper and shouted for us to run. All three of us did. Three miles back to camp. He was never caught or charged.

Just prior to Christmas 1942, the band was asked to play for the Cirencester Police Ball at the Town Hall. On arrival, as I was taking in the music, a Police sergeant asked me to help him carry in a crate of whisky. "That's for the band." He said. How generous and appreciated it was. Most of it had gone before the night was out.

Jackie Aldrich caused a stir when she gave her rendition of the song, "The Touch of Your Lips."

She deliberately missed out vital words by pretending to cough. For instance, the chorus sounded like this.

"The touch of your lips upon my (cough)
Your (cough) that is cool and sweet
Such tenderness, lies in their (cough) caress
My (cough) forgets to beat.
The touch of your (cough) upon my (cough)
The love in your eyes, a-shine
And now at last, the moment divine,
The touch of your (cough) on mine."

Even the band lads didn't know she was going to sing it that way and could hardly play for laughing. The dancers enjoyed it too.

At one dance where they played, the fog was so thick when we left the dance hall, that Tony sat on the bonnet of the vehicle used for transporting us about so that he could call out instructions to the driver as to where we were going. An arrangement we had, was that no matter what time we arrived back at camp after a dance engagement, we could always go to the Mess and get a meal. On this occasion we arrived back at 2.00 a.m. and the duty Sergeant Chef came and asked us what we would like to eat.

He then saw Tony. "You , Hill." He said, "No yakking, no jokes. I know you so get your food and out you go." That was at 2.00 a.m. At 5.00.a.m. we were still sitting there, along with the sergeant, listening to Tony telling his tales.

In between, I had gone to wash my hands and a WAAF cook came by. We began talking because I knew her by sight but not by name. Within fifteen minutes I was petting her and knowing there was very little clothing under her smock it wasn't long before we were having sex against the swing doors of the Mess entrance. It was good - and novel. As I walked back into the main mess hall, Tony took one look at me and guessed what I had been UP TO! when the WAAF shortly followed me.

Towards the end of January 1943, I was detached to a satellite camp at Bibury, which was some twelve miles away, just beyond a village called Barnsley, which seemed appropriate. All accommodation huts were a mile down the road and away from the main camp which housed the Waafs. In our hut were chaps with whom I became very friendly because of later circumstances.

There was Jack Martindale, he had worked on the railway at Darlington and had a little baby daughter. Then came Taffy (Roy) Morgan, he was only eighteen and came from Port Talbot in South Wales. Jock Inglis was a well built Scot from Glasgow. In the corner of the hut was Reggie, from Bodmin in Cornwall. To us he was old at forty odd years but each morning he would get up at six a.m., go to the top of the camp and yell, "Wakey! Wakey! Rise and shine." Who needed a Tannoy system? Everyone on the camp heard his powerful voice.

There were only fifty personnel on this site which was used mainly as an aircraft stacking place. Our senior NCO was Sgt, Dooley, and he was. He gave me the task of cleaning out all toilets and ablutions on the sites of which there were three. The officers' quarters, the WAAF'S quarters and the airmen's section.

I was cleaning the toilets on the main site one morning when Sgt. Dooley came and asked me if I had finished. I told him I had and he then went into one of the cubicles where there were Elson Toilets without running water.

A few minutes later, there was a bang and a yell and the Sgt came staggering out. I hadn't noticed that during the morning I had been to the Stores to get some disinfectant but by mistake the person on duty had gone to the wrong storage drum and given me kerosene instead. Thus I had put some into each Elson receptacle and unfortunately Sgt. Dooley had dropped his cigarette end into it just as he sat down. That's what the bang was. He couldn't sit down for days.

It was reputed that there was a ghost at Bibury because the airfield was built on top of an ancient cemetery. For instance, there was a night when our corporal Tommy had been to see his girl friend in the village which was about two miles away.

He arrived back at the camp on his bike and came straight into the mess for a drink. His face was as white as a sheet so we asked him what was wrong and he replied.

"That bloody ghost has just accompanied me all the way up from the bottom site!"

He was cycling along when this florescent light, in the shape of a twelve inch diameter sphere, had kept alongside of him for the last ten minutes. Tommy was really shaken. I had seen it once when it went past a window in the Officer's Mess where I had been doing a duty in the kitchen.

A few weeks later I was on guard duty when looking across the road towards the airfield and I could see a light bobbing about in between the aircraft. I went into the Guardroom and reported what I had seen, thinking it could be the ghost. The Duty Sergeant called out the guard and supplied us all with Sten guns.

We proceeded towards the airfield and very slowly made our way towards the light. When within 150 yards of it, the sergeant shouted. "Halt. Who goes there?" There was no reply.

We advanced another fifty yards and again the sergeant shouted, more firmly this time.

"Halt. Who goes there?"

Still no reply and the light kept moving about in between the aircraft. We advanced a further fifty yards, all ten of us, spreading out as we went along. The sergeant told us to cock our weapons. "If there's no answer this time, open fire but mind the aircraft," He said. We all shone our torches and still the light moved about.

"Halt. Who goes there? Advance and be recognised."

This was the third time he had shouted and just as we were about to fire, a voice with the light, answered. "It's me, Cookie!"

It was one of the airmen who was supposed to be on guard with us but had gone out on his own without telling anyone.

He was a dilatory chap in any case, rather fat and stupid looking also. The fool could have been shot. The verbals from the sergeant were undescribable but when things had settled down again, we couldn't stop laughing.

I didn't lose contact with Tony because he was a MT driver and several times a week he would bring the camp supplies from the H.Q. Also there was a duty 'garry' from Cerney between the two camps for personnel to move about in the evenings and this we both used to keep our social activities going.

There was a social evening in the Bibury Village Hall one Saturday and Tony and Eric came up with a crowd from Cerney. Someone asked if they could have some dancing and it finished up with Tony playing the piano. However, he wanted to have a dance himself, so, he persuaded me to go on the stage and play as few waltzes whilst he danced and chatted up some of the Waafs.

It wasn't long after arriving at Bibury Camp that I became acquainted with the Village Belle, Betty. She was gorgeous, having the right figure and a good sense of humour; what a buxom wench. She was nineteen and before long she was my steady date but I couldn't understand why she had attached herself to me when there were better looking chaps on camp.

But that is by the way and we met each other quite frequently. She walked half way towards camp on one night and as I was taking her back towards Bibury, we climbed over a low stone wall and into a field. It wasn't long before her knickers were down and passion took over. As we arose from the grass she commented how lucky we had been because where we had been laying there were lots of cow pats about and we had picked a spot in between them. It *was* lucky. We could have been in the shit.

It wasn't too bad at Bibury because I saw Tony and Eric quite often. Then there was Betty to comfort me. This in itself was beginning to take a toll on me because once again, having taken her towards her home, we finished up against the village Post Office window.

This was about 10.30 p.m. and once more our petting resulted in her skirt going up and her pants coming down. It's a good job we did it quietly. I also remembered the three 'W's, and walked the two miles back to camp.

That particular night must have persuaded me to ground myself by staying in camp for a while. But there again, Betty must have been satisfied with me because she came right up to the camp a few nights later and asked for me. The lads had to tell her that I was on duty. Besides, I found a huge pimple on my 'old man'. I thought I had caught something but realised that it was due to where a brass button on my flies, had chafed against the skin. Thank God for that.

Apart from my duties on the Elson bucket job, there were other tasks such as guard and beacon duties, the latter involved going out to certain points within a five-mile radius of the camp to maintain flashing beacons which guided the military aircraft passing over.

Due to the sanitary facilities being Elson buckets and not WC's, arrangement had been made for the local farmer, Mr Thompson, to come and collect the contents, three times per week. This was excellent because after the visits I would go around and clean and disinfect all latrine buildings. However, Mr Thompson came and said that his labourer and driver, Arthur, had been called up making it difficult to handle the work by himself. He asked if I would be willing to help him carry on and load his lorry, for which he would pay me 10/- shillings per week. This was marvellous because he also said that if I was to go on leave at anytime, he would provide me with eggs or a rabbit.

It was a wonderful arrangement. I also helped him, along with other airmen, to harvest the hay from the local fields, in summer.

There was an incident when we went to clear the WAAF site toilets and couldn't get near because of overflowing Elson containers. Mr Thompson said he didn't like clearing the mess and I didn't. I immediately went to the Adjutant, who herself was a WAAF Flt/Officer, and complained about the situation. When she came and saw the filth, she asked Mr Thompson and I to do the best we could. This we did but following that the officer confined all WAAF to camp for two weeks. It didn't happen again.

Tommy, our corporal, detailed four of us to assist in moving some beds etc., from one WAAF hut to another. We had cleared all but the Corporal I/C's bed and as we took off the 'biscuits' (three square shaped mattresses) we found a long sausage, which was green. The WAAF NCO was a corporal Greenhough, a big ex-bus conductress from Mexborough in Yorkshire.

"What will they get up to next?" Queried Tommy, with a smile.

Entertainment wasn't lacking at Bibury and occasionally we were able to hold a dance in our small NAAFI. At one of them I was dancing with a WAAF and during conversation and small talk, I asked her where her home town was and she answered Sheffield. When I told her I also came from that city the subjects unfolded and it finally came out that she was called Betty Bullock and had worked at Edgar Allens' at the same time as I had but we hadn't met because we worked in entirely different departments.

During the interval we went outside for a breath of fresh air and finished up snogging behind the NAAFI and for once that's as far as it went.

Betty was an MT driver on 3 ton Bedford trucks and worked with another WAAF driver named Flo'. Flo was a true cockney - every other driver on camp gave her the right of way when using the narrow country lanes, of which there were many.

In the NAAFI, one evening, I was having a quiet drink with my mates when there was a disturbance. "You're only in the Services for one purpose." A voice said loudly.

We turned around and an airman was facing a very angry Flo'. "You bastard!" She screamed, "Take this." With that remark she threw the pint of beer she had in her hand, straight at the culprit. The offender ducked and the glass, unfortunately, hit one of my pals in the face. He wasn't really hurt and things carried on as normal. I'm sure that the guilty airman realised that he hadn't to cross swords with Flo'.

I managed to get on one or two 48 hour passes and to get away from camp early, it meant doing a night shift in the cookhouse. This way I was able to get on the road by 7.00 a.m. and hitch a ride as far as I could to catch my train at Andoversford. Sometimes I was able to get a lift by car up to the A40 Oxford road and once I had a lift on an RAF Airframe carrier. This was a vehicle about 50 feet in length and it was very draughty sat on the back of the truck but it was all worthwhile.

I had a 48-hour pass once and decided to go to see my Grandad Willis who lived in Oxford in the St. Thomas' area. He was so pleased to see me and took me to meet the other side of the Willis family whom I had never met. He also took me for a steady walk along the banks of the River Isis where the boat crews used to practise. There wasn't room for me at his place of residence so I stayed at the local YMCA in the city. Being a pensioner, grandad would make a bob or two by acting as a guide around the various colleges.

As I've said earlier, I thought a great deal of Henry Francis and it seemed ironical that this would be the last time I would see him. He died a few years later in Sheffield, whilst I was overseas with the RAF.

I was on crash wagon duty one week and on a particular afternoon of that week, the NCO I/c wagon, told me to go and sit in the canteen and write some letters because there wasn't enough room for me in the cab of the tender.

It was whilst I was writing that the Sgt. Chef came in, went over to the window overlooking the airfield and suddenly shouted. "Oh! My God! A crash." I jumped up and joined him at the window, then realised that I should be on the crash wagon.

I rushed out and just managed to climb onto the platform at the back of the Weeton Fire Tender and off we sped across the field. To make matters worse, with the rough ride we had, I knocked both my knee caps on a bar at the back and that didn't make me laugh.

On arrival at the scene, we all became involved in using extinguishers etc. There were no flames but a huge pall of smoke hung over the aircraft. As we were going about our tasks, we heard a yell.

'Tich', our corporal I/c Tender, had gone into the smoke with a hosepipe and had walked straight into a revolving propeller. Fortunately it was only ticking over but it was enough to fracture his skull. He was in hospital for three months but eventually recovered.

The pilot of the plane had been able to get out of the cockpit but the fool hadn't switched off the engines, hence the accident. There was a Court of Enquiry but we never heard the outcome.

During one of his duty runs from Cerney, Tony found me and said there was to be a dance on the Saturday night at the Village Hall at Cricklade, which was some three miles the other side of Cerney. Would I be interested? But of course, so I caught the duty garry from Bibury and met Tony and Eric at their camp.

We were able to get a lift up to Cricklade around the 7.00 p.m. mark and being a little early for the dance we decided to go into the local pub for a drink. '*Drink'* being the operative word, because Eric suggested that we played Admiral Pope. A silly game really because in the game Admiral Pope says - and each time we did some daft thing like 'Stand up. Sit down, roll about.' After each movement we would take a drink. We were young and daft then and we finished up drinking two pints of cider, two pints of beer and two double whiskies in, believe it or not, one hour.

"It's time for a dance." Said Tony. So we set off for the Village Hall, which was just across the road. I felt marvellous, we paid for our tickets, entered the hall and looked around for a partner to dance with. Apart from the WAAFs, there were quite a few Land Army girls from the Cirencester Horticultural College and I soon made a beeline for a girl.

On to the floor I went, danced one quickstep, going round the hall three times and then the hall went around me. I made a dash for the toilets where I was as sick as a dog and eventually Tony found me on my hands and knees on the toilet floor. He and Eric managed to get me outside but I was hopeless. Tony borrowed a bike from outside the hall, sat me on the saddle and told me to hang on. He pedalled the three miles back to camp and dumped me into the hedge bottom.

"Don't move," he said. As if I could. "I'll be back in a while." He rode the bike back to Cricklade and then ran all the way back to camp. He helped me from the ditch and told me to follow him but be careful of the barbed wire on the perimeter.

Trying to balance myself and regain my equilibrium, I slowly followed him over the wire. He made it easily but when I was half way over, I slipped right into the middle of the coil of wire and in trying to get up, I tore my trousers. Eventually we made it to his billet where luckily, there was a spare bed. I went out like a light but next morning I wondered what had hit me. Whatever Tony did for me that night, it was what I call friendship.

As the light nights came and don't forget, we were in double summer time during the war, time seemed to fly. It was daylight up to 11.33 p.m. on some nights and occasionally we were able to borrow RAF bikes and have an evenings' run to some of the other villages such as Lechlade and Fairford.

It was towards the end of July 1943 that we were called onto parade and the Flt/Sgt in charge at Bibury, called various names out and told us that those people called, would be going overseas. I was one of them and we went for our jabs but tough guy Jock Inglis, passed out when he saw the needle. We all received 14 days embarkation leave and off we went home, not knowing to where we had been posted.

Whilst at home I went round to all the family, including those who lived in Derbyshire, to tell them the news but Jim Williams, Amy Furness's husband, couldn't hold back his tears. He was on leave from West Africa and thought that I was too young to go abroad. Mum and Dad weren't too happy either but they had to accept that in the forces, you went where you were told to go.

During this leave, Doreen and I decided to get engaged and Mum and Dad were over the moon and it lifted the bit of the gloom there was about.

Dennis and Joyce had called and Joyce asked me if I would like another pen friend. I didn't mind and so I was introduced by correspondence to a Sottish lassie named Jessie Rowan. So in all I had plenty of friends to write to because apart from Doreen, there was Jessie, Nora Russon, cousin Betty Willis, May Woodruff and the family.

As I left Brompton Road in the first week of August, tears were in my eyes and a lump in my throat as I walked down the street. Mum and Dad had wanted to go to the Railway Station with me but I thought it best that they weren't there to say goodbye.

I returned to Cerney with the rest of the lads who were going abroad with me and they included Jack Martindale, Taffy Morgan and Jock Inglis. But before leaving Bibury and Cerney I was able to have a farewell night with Tony and Eric, who I was sure to greatly miss.

Those of us who were posted were sent to Blackpool for kitting out and further inoculations. After a week we were transferred to Liverpool to embark to who knows where. This was on the 14th August, 1943.

The next three years covers my war service overseas and this is the final section of the book.

LATE FORTIES

On the 30th June 1946, I left the RAF Camp at Kirkham in my brown suit and herringbone overcoat plus a new trilby hat. This was the standard civilian demob kit issued to all ex-servicemen upon their discharge from the Armed Forces. I travelled by train to my home town of Sheffield and arrived home to find that there was no one in. I had been unable to let them know that I was coming.

Luckily, I had my latchkey and entered No 87 for a permanent stay, or so I hoped. After travelling for several hours I needed a wash and brush up and carried on as though I had never been away. I had just finished when Mum walked in through the front door. She was so pleased to see me but typical Mum, her first words were, " You haven't washed your neck!" She thought it was dirty because the sun tan had become very dark because of being in the Far East for 3½ years.

After having some tea, I made my way down to the Railway sidings on Brightside Lane to find my Dad who was on the afternoon shift. He wasn't hard to find and when I did he threw his arms around me as tears ran down his cheeks. He was so pleased to know that I had returned from the War in one piece, having been through World War I himself.

Whilst I had been abroad, I had received a "Dear John" letter from Doreen and Mum had been so upset that she had written to one of my officers, Sqdn. Leader Pritchard in Kandy, to see if it had affected me emotionally. Actually it hadn't, even if it had been a shock to receive the letter.

However, I had many female pen pals, one of them being a Jessie Rowan. After settling down at home again, the month's leave I had been granted enabled me to visit the family and many old friends. Following this, I made arrangements to go to Scotland to see Jessie. She met me at Lanark Railway Station and then took me on the bus to Forth where she introduced me to some of her relations. They were her Aunt Cath and Uncle Bob and it was with them that I was to stay for accommodation because there wasn't the room at the Rowan's house. Her Aunt and Uncle had no children and at the end of the first week they wanted to adopt me.

Jessie lived a few miles away in a village called Braehead where she resided with her father and family of two sisters and two brothers. Her mother had died a few years ago whilst giving birth to Rosemary, the youngest sister. Mr Rowan was rather a strict person and it was only natural to have doubts about me with not having seen me before. Somehow, he and I were able to communicate and on odd occasions, when I was in their house in the evening, Jessie would persuade her Dad to take me back to Aunt Cath's on his motorbike. He was a hard working man and had his own contract team working down the coal mine at Shotts. He arranged for Jessie and me to go down the pit one Sunday morning when it was quiet and where we walked for two miles to get to the coal face and watch some of his team hewing coal. It is something I will always remember.

The road from Forth up to Braehead was a steady climb for about a mile and a half and was classed as an electric brae because one could freewheel up it in a car or on a bike. Hence the name of the village was Braehead.

Aunt Cath encouraged Jessie and me to make a go of it and one afternoon she suggested that both of us ought go into my bedroom so that we could be away from her and Uncle Bob. This we did and it wasn't long before I was being encouraged to over indulge and as I was caressing her breasts Jessie slid to the end of the bed and as her feet touched she put my hand between her opened legs. This took me a little by surprise but I kept her happy with more foreplay but not once did we arrive in the ultimate sex position.

Because Jessie, who was twenty two years of age, was more or less the 'mother' and housekeeper of the family, it made it a little difficult to be in her company all the time but her Dad really made the effort to help by getting the eldest of the sisters to give Jessie a hand so that she could spend more time with me.

Uncle Bob was a pleasant person and managed to arrange for him and me to go out one night on the local bus which went around the villages calling at various pubs. He soon had me into their ways of drinking - a whisky, then a chaser of beer - but I didn't over do it. Aunt Cath would have grumbled if we had rolled home in an unfit state but we didn't.

I enjoyed my stay with Jessie and we became very close - no, not that close and there were one or two nights when I would walk up to the village to their house and play the piano for her and the kids which they thought was rather amusing for their big sister to have a boy friend. If we did sit together on the settee and possibly hold each others - hands - the children would peep through the window and give little giggles that is until Jessie shooed them off.

However, things didn't last forever and after two weeks I returned home and continued to write to Jessie. In one letter I asked her to come down to meet Mum and Dad but it was Aunt Cath who persuaded Mr Rowan to let her come. A few weeks later she arrived in Sheffield and was able to meet Joyce and Miriam who had introduced me to her. We had to arrange her visit to coincide with my Dad being on nights so that she could sleep with Mum in the front bedroom because we only had the two and I slept in the back one.

On the first Sunday she was with us Dad was teaching her to make Yorkshire Puddings and insisted that she must keep the batter in the middle of the tin. The more she tried, the more we laughed until she saw the funny side of it all but she appreciated the humour and tormenting of Dad. He was like that.

When Saturday came around, I said I would take her to see a first class football match because she had never been to one so I took her to see Sheffield Wednesday at Hillsborough and we stood on the Spion Kop where she really enjoyed it, but not knowing the first thing about the game, she asked me what the object was. When I explained that the players had to get the football between the white posts and into the net to score, she asked, "If that is so, then why does the man in the woolen jersey keep stopping them?"

Jessie was a lovely looking girl with a slim figure which seemed to have been made for the Kashmir dirndl skirt I had brought her from India along with some silk stockings and a beautiful, hand embroidered, white silk blouse. She had an angelic face and a good sense of humour which was enriched by her Scottish accent. We became so acceptable to each other that I thought that this was my destiny. This was the girl for me. We agreed to get engaged and I duly bought her an engagement ring of which she seemed to be so enthralled. Mum and Dad were delighted and very happy for us.

The day after this, Dad was at work and Mum was at the local Chapel so being left alone we became engrossed in a strong snogging session which eventually led to Jessie losing her virginity but how we enjoyed it and our love seemed deeper then ever before.

For a fortnight we had a wonderful time until she returned home but we continued to write to each other for several weeks until one letter I received said that she thought that she was pregnant and was very worried. Obviously I wrote back trying to console her and said I would do the honourable thing. There was a week's lapse before I heard anything and then I had a letter saying that she was all right again but having thought things out, she realised it would be better if we broke off the engagement. I tried to contact here again but to no avail. I really loved Jessie and missed her very deeply. Later thoughts did suggest that her father didn't want her to leave home, especially with such a large family to look after.

It took quite a while to get over another disappointing episode in my love life but the burden was eased somewhat because I recommenced work at Edgar Allen's again. This was a condition laid down by the Government, that all personnel who had been called to the colours during war time, were to be compulsorily re-employed by the employer with whom they had previously worked for and irrespective of what rank you were demobilised with when you came out of the forces, the statutory wage for all males was £4/10/0 per week.

I was detailed to an office which was in a prefabricated hut in the middle of the work's yard. Also there was Stan Wild, who had also been demobbed along with Mark Smallwood, an elderly gentleman Mr Simpkin, who had been called into heavy industry during the war and a Mr Bool. We were responsible to a chap named Gordon Reece, who was our supervisor and one of the people, whom ex-servicemen, called a dodger - he was in his late thirties and had obviously avoided call up for one reason or another.

We all had a separate section in the works for which we kept records for such processes as annealing, oil or water quenching and heat treatment details from Les Mills, another dodger. There were instances when Mr Bool, poor old soul, became the victim of a prank or two. The main one being when Stan put some mercury into Mr Bool's inkwell and every time the old chap dipped his pen into the pot, his pen just pushed the mercury down and no ink went onto his pen nib. Every time he tried to write, nothing happened and the more he kept doing it the more we doubled up with laughter.

Mr Simpkin joined in the fun, he was around fifty-six years of age, but he did ask us to ease off a bit. After the war, pranks were numerous in many places and it seemed to relieve the tension that had been there during the war period. In the treatment shop the Foreman was a Mr Parnell and he was very strict with his workforce but not a tyrant. However, he was standing on the edge of the water quenching tank one day when one of the labourers, who didn't really take to his attitude, thought that he would repay the foreman's belligerent demands and as he walked passed Mr Parnell he pretended to trip and accidentally on purpose he nudged the Boss and into the tank the foreman went. There were titters all around the shop floor and I'm sure that the boss received the message.

I stayed in that office for about twelve months during which time we had that terrible winter of 1947. The thickness of the ice due to heavy snowfalls and frosts, was about four inches thick and solid. Some days, to try to keep warm, we would commandeer shovels and picks from the Stores Dept., to remove the ice in the work's yard to make it easier to move between the workshops.

As Spring approached, quite a few of us began using the sports ground and facilities on Bawtry Road and later on I played cricket for the second team under the Captaincy of Jack Kelk, he was about fifty-two years of age. I would also go and play tennis if there wasn't a cricket match on. Even so, sometimes when a match had finished a group of lads and lasses would stay behind to have a game of rounders on the cricket ground. It was all good clean fun enjoyed by all who took part.

In the summer of 1947 Dad and Mum and her two sisters, Amy and Lily, had booked a holiday through the Co-op, to go to Northern Ireland. They asked me to go with them and also some friends of theirs called Mr and Mrs Pitchford. When we met the train to take us to Liverpool to catch the boat, there were two other couples who had also booked. The two chaps were Ted Hutchinson and Jack Parkin who both worked with me at Edgar's.

We enjoyed the weeks holiday, especially the day trip to Dublin in the Irish Republic. Jack had brought his girl friend Doreen with him and also his sister Joan who accompanied Ted. There was plenty of fun and dancing and Jack did entertain us with a ballad because he had a beautiful bass voice. Whilst dancing I pulled a muscle in my leg whilst 'bobbing up and down' to the tune , Sons of the Sea, so took no further part.

On the way home, the sea was very rough and Dad became very ill. It wasn't sea sickness but food poisoning from some fish which he had eaten prior to leaving Belfast.

Whilst trying to keep my eye on him as he lay on the deck of the ship, I became acquainted with a young lady who was getting some fresh air. To get out of the wind, she suggested that we squeeze behind some containers on the deck. This we did and to keep warm we snuggled up and this resulted in me dating her when we arrived home in Sheffield.

After our first meeting, she invited me to have tea with her on the Sunday and meet her parents. They had a large house in the Ecclesall part of town, the posh area.

Her father was the Petroleum Officer for Sheffield during the War and was responsible for rationing of petrol. Following tea, we went into the drawing room where there was a piano. I played one or two tunes and then her Mum asked her to get on the piano and entertain us by singing.

As she started to sing, I tried to hide the startled look on my face. Muriel had a contralto voice and was trying to sing some classical aria. She had obviously had lessons, but not enough. I was polite and applauded her, then I took my leave after thanking her parents for their welcome.

The Saturday morning following this, there was a knock on our front door and when I answered it, this same young lady was standing there. I invited her in and introduced her to my Mum who, diplomatically, said she had some shopping to do and would leave us to talk. TALK! We had hardly been alone for ten minutes when Muriel made a 'request'. I was a little surprised but went to make a pass at her. I slid my hand between her legs, as requested, and then stopped. There was some padding at the top.

"I can't do that." I told her, but she pleaded with me. I said. "You must be joking!" She reached for her purse and withdrew a £5 note. "Please?" She begged

I know I'm a bit of a lad but no way could I partake in something like that while 'United' was at home. "I'm sorry, Muriel, but you must leave. My Mum will be back any minute now." With that, the young lady left in a bit of a huff but I'm sure that I did the right thing. - at a price - not for a fiver.

When I told my Dad and his mates up at the pub that night, they jokingly asked why I hadn't sent for one of them. A fiver in those days was worth having, like two weeks' wages.

Ecclesall, by the way is where the knobs hang out, but not mine.

Every year, most large firms in the steel industry, would hold their annual dinner dance at large venues such as the Cutler's Hall or the City Hall and Edgar's usually chose the latter.

It was where Fred Bennett, Stan and I would team up with the girls from the Cost Office and Hollerith Dept., and in the Hollerith there were two sisters, Barbara and Flo' Hatton and when they came to a dance they brought their next door neighbours' daughter with them. I finished up dancing with her - she was about as tall as I was and had very fair hair. She was most attractive and a very good dancer. After the dance I tried to date her but she was very coy. I didn't push it but a few weeks into the new year, Stan asked me if I would like to go to another dance at the City Hall. I was a little hesitant until he told me that the fair-haired girl was going again with Babs and Flo.

I agreed to go and once again I finished up dancing with this young lady. I managed to extract from her that she was twenty-four and her name was Audrey Snowball and that she worked at Boot's, the chemist, just up Attercliffe Road near to where I lived.

"How about me meeting you on Saturday after you have finished work?" I asked. She hesitated. "No." She replied - paused, then said, "You can meet me in Rotherham a little later on if you want to." So this I did and from taking her to the pictures that once, things developed rapidly

It wasn't long before Audrey started to come down to No. 87 on Saturday lunchtimes for a break and I in return, started to go to her home in the district of Holmes in Rotherham. The relationship became so serious that I would ring her most lunchtimes at Boot's from a call box on Norborough Road at Tinsley.

We enjoyed swimming together at Rotherham Baths - plus dancing there during the winter months to the music of Brookes' Band, when the pool was closed. Sometimes we would go cycling, not a long way but short runs out into the countryside. Audrey had served in the Women's Land Army during the War and was therefore quite fit and agile.

As usual, affection became very strong and though I really wanted the ultimate with her, I controlled myself out of respect for her but there were times many when foreplay nearly took command again. For twelve months I escorted Audrey and there was once when I went with her family, by car, to a camp site for the weekend at Flamboro Head in North Yorkshire where they had a caravan. Whilst travelling by car, Audrey and I were on the back seat and she pulled a travelling rug over her legs to keep warm and this enabled me to slide my hand inside the zip of her skirt and down to the buttons of her camiknickers. Having undone them, we were in the middle of enjoying a digital exercise when the nearside back tyre punctured and so we all had to get out whilst her father changed the wheel. The car was a large saloon type Standard.

Audrey had two sisters, Barbara the younger one and Marjorie, the eldest, who was married to a chap called Fred. Mr Snowball worked at Steel, Peech and Tozers, a large steel firm in Templeboro.

In July 1947, I was the best man at Fred Tyler's wedding to Norma Bagshaw. They had waited for me to be demobbed so that I could officiate because I had been Fred's best pal for so many years. Because I had arranged to collect Audrey when she finished work, I made two tram journeys to meet her and return to the reception but I was too late to read out the cards and telegrams of congratulations which is the Best Man's duty. Norma and Fred understood and laughed it off.

Fred would call in quite frequently at No 87, even though he was married and sometimes it was because he had been shopping up the 'Cliffe'. The romance with Audrey was progressing very well until one Saturday morning when Fred paid us a visit. He was his usual happy self, laughing and joking, when he asked me if I had enjoyed the dance at the City Hall the night before.

I looked at him inquiringly and said, "I didn't go out last night." His retort was, " I'm sure it was you dancing with Audrey." And then continued, "Well, the chap she was dancing with was about your build and had specs on. You ask Norma. She'll confirm it."

I couldn't believe what I was hearing but then it dawned on me. The chap with Audrey must have been the young assistant chemist with whom she worked with at Boot's. I had seen him several times when I had called at the shop to see her. Fred left to go home around 11.30 a.m. and at 12.30 p.m. there was a knock at the door and in walked Audrey with a look of innocence.

"Did you enjoy the dance last night?" I asked. She kept quiet but began to blush. Her cheeks really glowed. There was no reply, no excuse. I waited and then said, "I'm sorry, Audrey, but you said that you were staying in last night and you didn't. That's lying and two-timing. I don't like people who do that. I think you had better go." Audrey left the house and walked up the street in tears. There was no explanation from her, no excuse, so I took it that the event the night before was true. I never saw Audrey again.

Being so unlucky in love, I was beginning to have doubts about my own attitudes and personality.

Following this upset, I carried on with my work and met one or two friends. On some Sunday evenings I would go with Mum and Dad to meet Dad's sister, Aunty Amy and her husband Bill Kelsey. We would meet at the Beauchief Hotel at Millhouses because it wasn't far for them to come from Totley which was just up the road. We would partake of a few beverages and have a good natter and tell a few jokes and I introduced Dad and Bill to a drink which I had been initiated to whilst serving in India. It was Rum and gingerette. The latter being a cordial, not ginger ale.

With it being a cold night, we finished drinking about seven of these before catching the tram back to Attercliffe, the journey taking about half-an-hour. There was no after effect, such as getting drunk but Dad really became attached to it on other cold nights.

Some Saturday evenings were spent by going to see Mum's brother, uncle Harry Willis who lived on North Hill Road on the Southey Green Estate. We were able to catch a No 5 bus from the top of Brompton Road which took us to the bottom of Southey Hill and then we would walk up the road to uncles' house in around five minutes.

Uncle Harry and his wife, Aunt Edith, had two daughters. The eldest was Betty and the younger one was Una. If the night was warm in the summer months, we would all go for a steady walk through the farm and the fields at the back of their house and this would take us right down into Ecclesfield which was a small village on the outskirts of Sheffield.

Betty was about my age and very attractive. She was always smartly dressed and carried her clothes very well indeed. Una was a little live wire some three years younger with flaming red hair, just like her dad. I started popping up to Southey quite regularly and began taking our Betty out to dances and the pictures or she would come down to our house to stay awhile.

Whilst working in the Fettling Shop at Edgar's in early '48, one of the young fettlers called John Lofthouse, asked me if I knew any girls I could get a date with, for him. I thought of Una and arranged for Betty and I to meet him and introduce him to Una. This we did and the romance blossomed.

The four of us were up at North Hill Road one night and Uncle Harry and Aunty had gone out and left us on our own. We had a few laughs and a chat on various subjects until Una said that she and John were going up the stairs for a while. That left me and Betty by ourselves and being cousins it was a bit embarrassing. However, I suggested that she came over and sat on my knee for a cuddle. At first she hesitated and then she agreed and soon we were kissing and petting and things became a little hot.

As I was kissing her, my hand slowly crept up under her dress and I could feel the soft skin just above her stocking top. I hesitated and she seemed to relax until I went a little further and inside her knickers. She grabbed my hand and struggled a little but when I whispered "Take it easy, enjoy it." She completely gave in, well - not completely.

Una and John eventually became engaged, married and raised a family, having left Sheffield to go and live in Whitehaven in Westmorland, John's home town.

Betty and I knocked around together for quite a few months but her Mum, Aunt Edith, began to get ideas about us and being rather conventional, irrespective of other things I had done, I couldn't accept it that marrying a blood cousin was the right thing to do. A short while after, we cooled off from each other but still remained good friends. John had a workmate called Eric Capille with whom he had arranged to make a foursome with himself, Una and Betty. This too developed into a true romance and Betty and Eric were also married and they too raised a family in Sheffield. I was happy for her and still had feelings for her.

It was in 1948 that I was transferred into the Fettling Shop Office alongside Bernard Harrison again which was much better than working under Gordon Reece. During the War, older people and females had been engaged by Edgar's, to fill gaps made by such as us being called up. However, the time had come for our jobs to be given back to us and this is why I, Stan and Mark were put back into the Fettling Shop area.

There were two young women who were employed to clean office windows around the works' offices and one of them was a very attractive blonde, a suicide blonde. Her hair was 'dyed' by her own hands. As usual I chattered her up and made a date and when I met her one night, she was honest and told me she was married but parted from her husband.

The first night I went out with her we had a short walk and found a deserted place where we had a quiet snog and cuddle before taking her to her home which was in the Railway Cottages just off Broughton Lane Bridge. The time had seemed to fly because when I arrived at my own home at midnight, my Mum was waiting for me. Now, bear in mind that I am twenty five years of age and some mothers don't give in.

"What time do you call this? Where have you been?" My Mum still thought that I was a child.

"I've been out with a dirty blonde." I said.

"Don't be so damn cheeky. Get off to bed." Was her reply. I was always taught to tell the truth and this time it paid off.

I did take the blonde out on a few occasions and her interest in music was excellent because I went with her one Saturday to buy a record at Cann's Music Shop in Chapel Walk in town. It was a surprise to me when she bought a record of Puccini's 'Madam Butterfly', not for the famous aria but for the "B" side which was equally enjoyable. On another night we enjoyed together was at the Empire Theatre on Charles Street. This time we saw the stage show of Ivor Novello's "Perchance to Dream". It was a marvellous show with some fine singing from Nicolette Roige the soloist.

This flirtation came to an abrupt end one day when she said she thought that she was pregnant. "No way!" I said, because she had told me that she had been seeing her husband on odd occasions whilst going about with me and one swallow doesn't make a summer. I wasn't wearing that one and so we finished the association.

As mentioned earlier when in the Foundry, how dangerous it could be if one didn't keep their wits about them, I was proceeding down the No. 1 Fettling Shop to obtain some piecework information from 'Punch' Roebuck, he was a fettler. To reach him, I thought that I would take a short cut in between two shot-blasting bays. I entered the small passage, with the intention of coming out of the other side and into a small area where 'Punch' worked.

I walked out of the passage into this area but hadn't seen the overhead crane coming down the shop. As I turned the corner, I stopped it. <u>BANG!</u> The hook hanging from the 14 tons' crane hit me in the face. Luckily I was wearing a cloth cap with a rubber peak neb and this took most of the weight. I received a cut over my right eye and was taken to hospital for observation and there I had a couple of stitches inserted into the cut.

Upon return to work I challenged the Yard Foreman and told him that if another crane driver traversed down the shop whilst lowering its hook as he travelled, then there would be severe repercussions.

An equally dangerous and serious problem could be to go near to the welding bay and approach the welder himself without shouting for clearance. If you didn't, it was possible to be getting near to him just as he was striking his arc. If the flash from the welding rod hit your eyes, then it could be hours before you were able to get rid of a nasty headache.

You may recall that many pranks were played upon each other and one hilarious incident was the time that Charlie Hunt, a shotblaster, promised a female crane driver that he would bring her a budgerigar because he bred them, or so she believed. This particular day, she asked

Hunty to let her have a peep at the bird which was supposed to be in his lunch basket.

"No." He said. "It's too noisy in the shop and it will frighten it."

But, the woman kept pestering him so he said, "Alright. Come at lunch time, it will be quiet then."

This she did and when she arrived, he picked up his basket onto the bench and slid the retaining rod from the lid. "Now be careful." He said. "Just a peep and that's all." As she came forward, he slowly lifted the lid and then suddenly shouted. "Oh! My God, it's got away." He stared up into the roof of the building.

She ducked. We all ducked. "It must be on your crane." Hunty said to her. So the poor lass chased up and down the shop looking for it and we pretended to look as well and then she climbed into her control box on the crane. It wasn't until she looked down below and saw us all laughing that she realised it was all a joke. From a 'lady', the verbals were not the King's English.

There was an afternoon when it had been arranged for some students from Sheffield University to make a tour of the workshops and as they were walking up the shop floor towards the shotblasting area, Hunty had seen them and asked who they were.

Having explained, he went back into his cubicle, which was some twenty feet square, put on his mask, prepared his blasting gun and then eased his door slightly open for about four inches. Just as the students were level with the door of the chamber, Hunty swung the nozzle of his gun so that the metal shot passed through the gap and sprayed the student's legs. It was like the highland fling watching them dance about but it was only a short blast and no one was hurt. It did look like an accident, although some of the girl-students were not amused.

Money was very scarce after the war and if a shop floor worker in heavy industry earned £7.00 a week he had drawn a good wage. On Friday mornings, I and other clerks like Stan and Mark, would go to the workmen to collect details of the piecework items which they had worked on and then we would go back to the office to record them in ledgers.

This particular Friday, 'Punch' Roebuck said he hadn't much to show so I said that I would check the order books to see if any items had been overlooked and had been missed in the booking in system. I found quite a few items and told 'Punch' to book them onto his piecework card and I would add them to his total earnings. This he did and overall it added some thirty shillings to his wages. As I left him, I passed an old Yorkshire remark and jokingly said,

"I'll be round for the natty money next pay day."

The following Friday I went to record 'Punchs' work and when I was leaving he said, "Here you are, Ron." And offered me a half crown (2/6d). "Don't be daft." I replied. "It was a joke." But, he insisted, saying that it was worth it to him. Other workmen involved were Harry Banner (Grinder) and Bill Scarrett (Burner). Unfortunately, or possibly fortunately, another fettler had overheard the previous conversations and asked me to do the same for him. It was legitimate and for months I received about 15/- shillings a week from natty money.

Bernard Harrison became aware of the dealing and commented.

"You spawny buggar. I've worked here all these years and I have never had a penny from the shopfloor workers, good luck."

After the War, there were many ex-servicemen who were on the belligerent side of life when it came to work and the wages paid for it. Trade Unionism was never so rife and employers were reluctant to increase wages, especially having just finished with the costs of wartime and all that was involved.

My Dad was a strong union official with the NUR (National Union of Railwaymen) and associated with other union officials from other unions. One of these was a Mr. Smeaton, who was the secretary of the Sheffield Branch of the Clerical and Administrative Workers Union. Dad introduced me to Mr Smeaton who persuaded me to join his union and being young and gullible, I was eventually talked into introducing the Union to members of the staff at Edgar's.

It wasn't easy and backing from those who had 'stayed at home' during the war was very poor. However, I did eventually recruit enough of the staff to enable the Union to be accepted by the management. The target for this was one third of the workforce of the staff who mingled with the shop floor workers and therefore received some backing from those respective manual unions. Once recognised, the C & AWU members put in for time and a third to be paid for on Saturday mornings workings. The Union gave us much assistance and we finally went to arbitration.

Edgar Allen's were represented by the CBI (Confederation of British Industries) with Sir John Green, from Hadfield's Ltd, in the chair. The meeting was at the Royal Victoria Hotel in Sheffield and I, along with Ted Hutchinson and a chap from the Machinery Dept., plus the Union representative from Leeds, Mr Smart. We entered the room to be met by some twenty people and these were from various firms and industries in the City and my first thoughts were. Why all these people? The meeting opened and Sir John Green commented, " We have decided...."

I intervened and said. "Excuse me, sir. There's been no discussion yet." Our union rep, Mr Smart, didn't uphold his name. He sat like a dummy so I said to him quietly, "Ask for an adjournment."

This he did and we left the room for fifteen minutes during which time I and the other two delegates had a right go at him. After we returned, he started to explain our case but because of his meandering, Sir John commented. "I think it would be better if Mr Priestley explained the situation. At least he is directly involved and knows more of the actual subjects than you do."

Our official was dumbstruck but after I had explained the case in detail, we adjourned again and upon recall, Mr Goddard-Mander, the spokesman for the CBI, told us that our request had been granted. What a triumph. One month later, we had not received any extra payment and so I went to see George Longden, the Labour Relations Officer with Edgar's and queried the situation. The comment was that the Board of Directors were not going to comply.

My heckles were up so I wrote direct to Mr Goddard-Mander and explained. He in turn contacted Mr Longden and told him that an agreement was an agreement and no matter which way the verdict had gone, the arrangement must be honoured. From then on everyone received their time and a third for every Saturday morning which was worked. We usually worked from 9.00 a.m. until 12.00 p.m. midday so for three hours work we were paid for four.

In September 1948, the annual Isle of Man Grand Prix was taking place. This was a motorcycle race which encouraged riders from all over the world to take part in a gruelling race of 37½ miles course around the roads and through villages and towns of this lovely little island. I decided to take a holiday there and booked my accommodation with a Mrs Gilbert, whose guest house was on the Queen's Promenade in the seaside town of Douglas the Capitol.

On my way over on board the Isle of Man Packet Steamer King Orry, which sailed from Liverpool, I was taking a stroll around the deck when I 'bumped' into one of the ship's stewards who was carrying a tray of drinks. I thought I knew him and when he saw me he became very embarrassed. The steward was my old Chief from Penrhos in North Wales, Flt/Sgt Gale, who had told us that he worked on the big ships, thus giving us the impression that he meant the ocean going ones, not the type on which I had found him. Another 'line shooter' was shot down.

A friend of mine, Bernard, was supposed to accompany me on the holiday but he couldn't get until the following week. I had booked for a fortnight's holiday so the first week I had to find my way around, not having been to the Isle of Man before.

The first day there, Mrs Gilbert arranged for me to sit at a table in the dining room with a Scottish lady in her forties and also the lady's daughter who was about twenty years of age. At the end of the meal, the lady suddenly said, "Come on, you two. Get off and enjoy yourselves." I couldn't believe it because I had only just met them so I thought it was a gift from heaven

However, the girl and I did go for a stroll and the following day we had a game of tennis which was followed by me taking the young lassie for a longer stroll, up towards Onchan Head.

The scenery was very good and overlooked the bay below and as usual, thinking I was onto a good thing, I made a pass at her but after a short snogging session I knew there was no chance of going further, so I didn't pursue the issue.

Mrs Gilbert introduced me to her own sister Wynn who was helping at the guest house and Wynn asked me if I would care to go to a party which was being held locally by some of the bikers. We had a good night out but unfortunately my stomach started acting up again, possibly because of what I had drunk. Upon returning to the residence, Mrs Gilbert was very good, and invited me into their living quarters where she made me some 'pobs'.

These were pieces of dry bread put into some hot milk with mustard and were supposed to be good for biliousness. At least I got some relief and also enjoyed the company of Mr Gilbert who was also ex- RAF. For the rest of the week I went about with Wynn and we enjoyed dancing together but that's as far as it went, although I did write to her after I arrived back home.

Bernard, my friend, did arrive on the Saturday and this helped me to indulge in other activities such as swimming and tennis. There were several ballrooms in Douglas and many big bands played the summer season there in places like the Villa Marina and the Palace. We went one night to see and listen to Roy Fox and his Orchestra and as we were having a drink in the lounge at the interval, a young man approached. It was Bobby Joy, a youthful lad who had made his way to the top as a vocalist. He came from Coleridge Road, near to where I lived in Sheffield. He recognised me and we had a long chat about schooldays etc., and Bernard enjoyed the conversation too, especially when Bobby filled us in about being the resident vocalist for Roy Fox. Other bands playing there, included the Joe Loss Orchestra and Harry Roy and His Tigeraggamuffins.

There were plenty of coach trips going around the Island and we went on one which had a driver named Tommy. He was a right character, full of wit and able to describe our tour around the Island with all the essential details of interest pointed out to us. As we rode up a small hill, past a glade on the side of the road, Tommy slowed the coach down and explained that to go any further, we had to pay respect to the fairies in the glen by saying, "Good morning little fairies and how are you today?" I know it sounds daft but we all said it and then had to stand up and bow to the glade. It was all part of the holiday.

The day of the big race came and Bernard and I managed to get in a good position to see the competitors coming into the nasty bend known as Governors Bridge. This was a very short, sharp 'S' bend which dipped and turned onto a rise before going onto a straight mile past the main Grandstand and Finishing line.

The motorcycles had to do several laps of the Island and the roar of the exhausts was thunderous as they eased up to go round the bridge and then 'rev' up again to gather speed. Some of the speeds achieved in places on the course exceeded 100 mph. The race we saw was won by the peoples favourite and champion, Geoff Dukes.

We had a very good holiday and returned home on the following Saturday. Bernard, by the way, used to work in Senior's Pawnshop on Brompton Road. You know, the one I nearly set fire to some years ago. He also belonged to the Boys Brigade but not the same Company that I had been in.

After the holiday I returned to work and as I was walking through the factory I met Charlie Foster who had been at Edgar's for ten years. Charlie had worked his apprenticeship in the machine shop which was next to the Fettling shop and he was now a qualified engineer. Having greeted each other, he asked me if I was interested in joining the firm's concert party. He knew I might because we had both been taking part in such things when we were attending Sunday School at the Attercliffe Wesleyan Hall. I said I was interested so he asked me to attend a get-together of various people who were willing to take part.

The person responsible for organising it all was a lady named Flo' Hawley and she worked in the Magnet Department which was on the other side of Sheffield Road and away from the Foundry.

When I attended the meeting most of the people there were from the Magnet Dept., and mainly girls or young ladies in their twenties. There were also a few men from various other departments and overall there must have been some twenty individuals.

It was decided to do a type of review by creating cowboy scenes with a saloon bar in the background also there was a South Sea Island setting along with a couple of five minute sketches. One of the favourite sets was the gypsy encampment scene where we were all dressed as gypsies and the girls did a gypsy dance around a camp fire. One tune we chorused to, was, "Oh Play to me Gypsy." Nearly all the props were made up from oddments and all the earrings were made from small brass curtain rings. They were very effective The girls' skirts were made by themselves and this saved a lot on production costs. Many weeks were spent at the end of 1948 in rehearsing, preparing scenery and getting all the props and make-up material ready.

Charlie had always been a good singer and he took on the lead in that capacity. Flo was the producer and managed to get us all organised in various stage sets and coached us in singing the choruses of the popular songs which we were to use in the show. I and a chap called Jerry, were put together as a comic duo for parts in comedy sketches which would bring humour into the shows. Several girls in the South Sea Island scene, wore grass skirts and had to have their legs darkened with some special stain to give the effect of them being dusky maidens. They then danced and swayed to Hawaiian music and guitars played by a couple of the lads.

They also dressed for Western scenes in cowboy outfits of skirts, boots and Stetson hats and all the men wore checked shirts with their western clothes. There were one or two musicians on the firm and Horace Dunwell, a pattern maker by trade who was also a brass band trumpeter, arranged all the music scores. I was so interested that I wrote an opening chorus for the show and Flo' liked it so much that she persuaded Horace to orchestrate it and all the cast learned the words. It was called, "This is the show of the year." And it was used as the opening number every time we put on a show

After months of rehearsal, it was arranged for our first show in the work's canteen. Enough tickets were sold to bring in a reasonable crowd and because it was such a success, it was decided to take it 'on the road'. We had some help from Jerry's sister Jane who was a professional tap dancer and she helped tremendously with the choreographics.

We had a good backing, spiritually, from the Rev. Ted Wickham who was the Industrial Padre for the East End of Sheffield and he often attended rehearsals. He later became the Bishop of Chester. Ted helped us tremendously by getting bookings for us at several Church Halls and we also managed to get several at Working Men's Clubs in the area. Most of the proceeds from the shows went to the local charities attached to the churches etc., at where we played.

We gave one performance at St. Clement's Church on Alfred Road in the Brightside area and at first we were a little apprehensive about performing there because of the past history of that area. It used to be the vicinity in which the famous 'Mooney Gang' of the twenties used to operate and memories still lingered on from those days.

However, we did the show and we had a very good audience where everyone seemed to enjoy themselves. In the Western scene I was leaning on the end of the stage and was dressed up as "Gabby' Hayes, a well known' old timer' cowboy in the Roy Roger's films. My make up included a couple of blacked out teeth, a false grey beard which was stuck on with spirit gum and a holster hung between my legs with a toy six-shooter protruding. This I kept swing to and fro to get some laughs, which I did.

Charlie was singing solo and in the middle of a western ballad called 'South of the Border', I started to look around the stage as though looking for a spittoon. In my imagination I found one and pretended to spit towards it, making a rasping sound with my lips as I did so.

The audience erupted and everyone was in stitches, even Charlie. After things had settled down, he managed to finish 'South of the Border'. But after the show Flo' showed her temper and gave me a right telling off for stopping the show. When I arrived home about 11.00 p.m., my Dad was sitting there having just finished his afternoon shift.

His place of work was near to Alfred Road and just across Brightside Lane where the railway sidings were. Dad was chuckling to himself as I walked into the house and when I asked him what that was for, he explained. One of his workmates, Harry Searle, who lived nearby, had been to see the show and having enjoyed it, he went across to start the night shift after my Dad had finished and told him, "There's an old bloke in that show whose really funny, you ought to go and see him." My Dad replied. "I have seen him. He's my son."

"Don't be daft. He's an old man." It took some time for Dad to convince Harry and we often laugh about the incident.

When I first started going to rehearsals, I noticed a cheery faced girl in the party and I think it was her shoes which drew my attention to her. They were more a type of sandal but the laces were long and these she had wound around her calves and fastened them in a bow just below her knees. It was unusual but very fetching on her chubby legs. It wasn't really just her legs that attracted me because as my eyes moved upwards I could see a fresh, cheeky face surrounded by a mass of shoulder length auburn hair and this had a natural wave running right through it. Nothing was rushed but over the weeks that followed, by accident or not, I always seemed to be her partner in the stage settings. Eventually I became more than attracted and before much longer I was asking her out for a date.

It's amazing how things turn out because George Howard, who worked in the same place as her on Sheffield Road, told me not to go out with her for reasons he wouldn't say. For once I took no notice and continued to see her. I'm glad I did. Her name was Aline Todd and she was twenty-two years of age and came from Thurcroft which was a mining village about ten miles away. It wasn't long before affections became strong on either side and soon we began to visit each others home.

Aline came from a large-ish family. Her father, Joe Todd, was the blacksmith at the local colliery and her Mum, Violet, had two brothers and a sister living in the village. Aline also had three sisters and a brother. Eva, the eldest, was married to Ted Thresh with a family in Wakefield, Freda, the second sister, had one son Ian and lived with her husband Joe Hilton, a miner at Harworth Colliery, in north Nottinghamshire. Then came Joan, who lived in Thurcroft and was married to Bill Hutchinson who also worked as a collier. Aline's only brother, Eric, lived at home and worked in the offices at the pit.

In between doing shows I would cycle over to Thurcroft and sometimes go for a ride with Aline because she had belonged to the Dinnington Wheelers Cycling Club and had her own bike. In fact Joan and she used to ride the ten miles to work where Joan also was employed at Edgar's. There were sometimes when they would use a tandem cycle to do the journey, with Joan steering and Aline using her power at the back.

If we had to arrange a visit to Eva's at Wakefield or Freda's at Harworth, we always had to go by public transport and this sometimes took a full day. It was whilst at Freda's one Sunday, when Joe, her husband, referred to Aline as 'Nip' and when I asked why, Freda said it was short for Nipper because Aline was the baby of the family. From then on, to me, it was always affectionately 'Nip'.

Freda and Joe always referred to her as 'Nip' but the rest of the family still called her Aline but my mind was made up. Aline seemed too formal but 'Nip' was more affectionate and lovable. .

We were fortunate in the fact that there was a private bus service which was run by a company named Wigmore and their buses serviced the route between Dinnington and Sheffield. It was convenient for the both of us because there was a bus stop at the end of School Road, Thurcroft and this was just around the corner from Arbour Drive where Aline lived. My bus stop was at the top of Newhall Road which was at the top end of Brompton Road and this made it ideally convenient for both of us in both directions.

The Todd family originated from Glentham in Lincolnshire but Mr Todd had moved North to find work and had finished with employment at Thurcroft Colliery. They had lived in a small cottage in a tiny village which was two miles away and this was Brookhouse, a very small and picturesque little place with no more than some twenty houses in it and running through it was a brook which gave its name to the place. All the Todd children had been born at the little cottage except Eva but because the family was getting bigger and also growing up, the local council decided to move them into a three bed roomed house which was number seventeen on Arbour Drive in Thurcroft. This took place just as the War broke out.

Mr Todd's brother, Tom, had married Ethel Hope who was none other than Aline's Mother's sister. Also there was Mrs Todd's brother, Ted Hope and he was the manager of the local Co-op Stores. In the early days before raising a family, Violet had worked in service for the Gentry at Thurcroft Hall

During 1949, I still played cricket for Edgar Allen's but managed to see Aline many times during the week. Sometimes she would come straight from work to have her tea at our house and this enabled us to go to the pictures. There was also, of course, the odd night when we would be in the show.

As you will have read earlier, I had several girl friends but now that I was courting Aline, there seemed to be something special, something that wasn't there before. She was so understanding and thoughtful because around this time I started to suffer with my stomach. Most of it was gastritis and there were times when I didn't like to go out and had to be careful with anything I ate. If a spasm came on, I was in agony but still this grand lass took it in her stride and so a strong bond of love developed between us.

During some of these spasms, cheerful Uncle Jim had to butt in and give his advice. "Why don't you eat some orange peel?"He said. "That ought to relieve it." As per usual his knowledge of illness was worthless and having tried what he said I was in more pain. I eventually learned to ignore him.

It was whilst I was over at Thurcroft one evening and feeling good for once and after her Mum and Dad had gone up the village to Aunty Ethel's house, we settled down on the settee in front of one of her Dad's roaring fires. He was able to do this because of the coal allowance he received from the pit.

Before long, the heat must have affected us because having started petting each other and kissing and cuddling, our temperatures rose and so did my ardour.

Things did get a little steamy but for once I was in control and whilst the opportunity arose for me to go further, my respect for her became the better of me and at the vital point I said, "NO" to myself. Nip understood and I think that, that was the time when she finally saw I was seriously in love with her. "Tell you what!" I said. "How about getting married?" She looked at me, gave me a big kiss and said, "YES."

When her Mum and Dad came in, they could tell by our faces that there was something afoot. I did the correct thing and asked her Dad and Mum if we could get married and they in return said that they had no objections.

Imagine my parents faces when I broke the news to them. There was a slight reluctance on their part but both agreed that if I would be happy, then by all means, go ahead.

When it came to the subject of buying an engagement ring, I explained to Nip that because I had lost two other girl friends just after getting engaged, I didn't want to risk losing her. I then suggested that I would buy a small, gold signet ring which she could wear on the little finger of her left hand. Nip thought it was a good idea so we went and chose one and then had our initials engraved on the face of it.

It had been in October 1948 that I had first met Aline Todd and to say that the following eleven months would finish on this note, was more than a surprise. It was heaven. Those eleven months had seen the traditional tour of each others family and both of us were introduced and accepted by each others relations. On my side, being the only child, many of my aunts and uncles were more then delighted, especially Aunty Amy Howard, who was always a favourite of mine. Even Nip's parents and my parents visited each other to become more acquainted.

Things seemed to move very rapidly in making arrangements for the wedding. Eva, Nip's sister, made all the dresses for the bridesmaids and of course, a beautiful white satin wedding dress with a very long train which was twenty feet in length. Freda and her Mum made little white suits for Ian and Terrance, Aline's nephews.

When it became knowledge that I was to be married, several tongues wagged in my own locality. This was because of my past reputation in my youth but I had nothing to hide even though one close neighbour commented, "I knew it would come to that. I've always said he would have to get married." Wrong again, Mrs. Wharton, your daughter's quite safe. As I said a little while ago, I have restraint when it is needed.

All our workmates were delighted with the news and as always happens in large factories, a collection was started for a wedding present for both of us. Because we were employed by the same company, it was decided to pool the money and buy one good present. This turned out to be a large canteen of cutlery. Jack Green, who worked in our department, was able to get a good quality one in a walnut case from Joseph Rogers Ltd, one of the best cutlery manufacturers in Sheffield because his father was the production foreman there.

As I was the Best Man for Fred Tyler, so it was that in return he would do the honours at my wedding. Because I too had many relations, several of whom came from Derbyshire, Dad arranged for them to come to Sheffield and then travel by coach, which he had laid on to take them to the wedding and reception at Thurcroft.. The car taking me and Fred was supplied by Sid Howard who recently had some good luck on the football pools. He had won £10,000.00 pounds and had set up a taxi business. By the way, Dad had also arranged for plenty of 'booze' to be put into the boot of the coach.

So it was that on the Saturday the 10th September, 1949, (Aline's 23rd birthday) she walked down the aisle of Laughton Church in the parish of Thurcroft. She looked so radiant in her white satin dress with her Maid of Honour, Bridesmaids and attendants. At 3.00 p.m., we were married and made our vows and became betrothed to each other - *'til death us do part.'* The church was packed with relations, friends and neighbours. There was just one irony to the service. We could have been married at Thurcroft Church but Nip didn't care for the vicar there, so she had the service transferred to Laughton, which was appropriate because she went to school there. However, on the actual day of the wedding, the vicar of Laughton was taken ill, so we finally finished with the original parson she had tried to avoid. We were pleased with the service and the Thurcroft vicar. He did very well.

We came out of the church with the two of us feeling full of happiness and then the photo call began. The main one of Nip and me by ourselves didn't materialise because of some oversight and it wasn't noticed until the proofs came through.

When it was realised that there wasn't a photograph of us together, the photographer at a later date, managed a marvellous job of super-imposing two single photos of us into one shot and unless one didn't know the true story, no one would tell the difference.

The group photograph included ourselves, Nan, the Matron of Honour who was Eric's fiancé; Brenda, my cousin's daughter from Hope; Kathleen, Eva's step daughter from Wakefield; Wendy, Eva's real daughter; Ian and Terence were the two page boys and they were the young sons of Freda and Joan respectively. Let me not forget Fred of course, who was my Best Man. Further photos were taken which included both our parents and shots of presentations made to Aline by her nephews.

Mrs Todd had booked the Thurcroft Miner's Welfare Hall for the reception and most of her side of the family had helped with the catering, even to the making of the three tier wedding cake which was excellent. Approximately 120 guests sat down to a knife and fork tea and I can't name them all but some of them were workmates from both departments of Edgar Allen's, also friends as opposed to family.

Having enjoyed a good meal and with the normal formalities of the Best Man reading out cards and telegrams of congratulations over and done with, everyone helped to clear away the crockery and the tables so that there was plenty of room on the floor for dancing. Oh! Yes. I had managed to persuade my band leader to come and do the honours. He was Albert Turvey whom I had played for many times and he had brought a further five musicians with him to provided the music.

A small room had been set aside to be used as the Bar but when it came to setting it out it was found that Aline's Dad had only provided a couple of crates of Guinness and two or three gallons of home made Mangle Wurzel Wine.

My Dad was a little 'cut up' about this, considering that the booze in the coach included wines and spirits, Baby Chams and crates of beer. So he asked Bernard Harrison who was my Boss and a guest, if he would organise the Bar but told him not to serve the Todd family with any shorts. I know it sounded mean but Dad believed in principles but I didn't learn of this until sometime later.

Apart from that, the reception was marvellous and everyone enjoyed the dancing and novelty games and I kept the Band supplied with 'refreshments'. There were more than enough wedding presents on display and we had to leave it to Aline's Mum to get them down to their house on Arbour Drive for safe keeping.-

I did learn weeks later on that a taxi driver managed to get Albert Turvey back to his home in Sheffield and Albert didn't get up for three days. He never forgot it and I always remembered the nine Rums and Pep lined up on the top of his piano. Poor old Albert, for months after, whenever I played for him, he told the other players what had happened.

After such a wonderful day, Nip and I popped down to her home so that she could change into her going away outfit. We then left the reception and our Sidney took us back to Brompton Road to collect our cases.

We had arranged to spend our honeymoon in Cliftonville near Margate in Kent and our train left Sheffield for London at midnight. Unfortunately, as Aline was carrying her suitcase down the narrow staircase, she slipped and tumbled to the bottom. At first, we thought that her knee was just bruised but as we settled down on the train it began to swell but she managed to bear it. To complete a memorable day and after an hour travelling in a compartment which we had to ourselves, I pulled the blinds down and we finally consummated our marriage.

We arrived in London at St. Pancras Station in the early hours of Sunday morning and had quite a while to wait for our connection to Margate. This was the nearest railway station to Cliftonville and because of the time delay in London we put our cases into the Left Luggage Office and then found our way down onto the Embankment on the side of the River Thames. Aline had never been to London before so she did enjoy the sightseeing along the river. Whilst we were in the vicinity, I took a snapshot of her sitting on the base of the monument of Cleopatra's Needle which was a well-known landmark and in the background was the Tower Bridge.

After finally making our way back to the station, we boarded the train to our destination. On arrival at Margate and not knowing where we were to go, we hailed a taxi and this took us to the boarding house at which we were to stay. It had been recommended by Mrs. Todd because she had stayed there on holiday once with Mr. Todd, Uncle Tom and Aunt Ethel.

Upon arrival, the landlady had prepared some breakfast for us and after we had 'tucked in' to it, the good lady suggested that because we had been travelling all night, it might be as well if we spent the day in bed. She said that she would call us later. Very thoughtful, very thoughtful indeed.

The weather was kind to us and we had a marvellous honeymoon which included a couple of day trips within the area. The beach at Margate was always full of Londoners who used the place as we would use Cleethorpes in Lincolnshire. Most evenings we would go for a stroll along the sea front and eventually finish up by playing prize bingo on one of the stalls in the amusement arcade. We became the attraction there due to "Lady Luck' being with us most of the time. We had some laughs with the stall holders because every time we won anything, we would ask for cooking utensils such as saucepans, a frying pan, a steamer and anything else which we might need in a kitchen.

It was obvious that we were newly weds and that is what caused the laughter on the stall.

At the end of the week we wondered how on earth we were going to get all the utensils back home and I think we finished up by buying a new suitcase. It was all good fun and we really enjoyed ourselves even though Aline's knee didn't get any better.

The following Monday, the 19th September, we both returned to our respective places of work. I don't know how Nip went on with her workmates but I was tormented and ribbed, particularly by Bernard Harrison. He commented, "It is said that in the first year of marriage, if you put a mark on the back of the bedroom door, for every time you make love to your wife, then for the rest of your life you will be unable to cross the marks off the door whenever you have further sex." I had to take it in my stride but as the years followed, I wondered if he was right.

It took a while for Nip and me to settle down at Mum's house and it seemed rather cramped in a small two bed roomed house with an outside toilet which Nip wasn't used to. We would arrive home from work and Mum would generously have prepared a cooked meal for us. With both of us working all day it was awkward for Nip to help with the housekeeping because she was so tired. However, it wasn't long before Mum mentioned it to Dad and he in turn had a word with me. As I explained, the lass helped as much as she could and shouldn't be expected to do another day's work when she arrived home. Nip was upstairs and over heard the heated discussion and was in tears when I joined her. I apologised to her for the upset and hoped that this wasn't going to be the start of unpleasantness. I didn't know what Mum was getting at because Nip always did our washing and ironing and we both helped with the housekeeping financially.

Somehow Dad seemed to appreciate my concern and realised what I was getting at but it took weeks for the argument to finally settle. Apart from that, things ran very smoothly and to ease Nip's mind we would pop over to see her Mum and Dad.

As Christmas approached, we discussed what we were to do so we agreed to have Christmas dinner with my Mum and Dad and then go over to Thurcroft for Boxing Day and night.

The rest of Nip's family was gathering there and I wondered how we were going to manage for sleeping arrangements but Ma Todd organised it all and Nip and me had the back bed room whilst Freda, Joe and Ian, slept in the small room. The following day, Eva, Ted and their family came over from Wakefield for the day. In the evening we started partying and played a few games but later on I asked Eva to put a special record on the gramophone and play it when I gave the signal. Nip and I went upstairs and she helped me to change into her gypsy costume which she had worn on the shows.

Being ready, Nip tipped off Eva to start playing the record which was "The Sabre Dance' by Ravel. In I went and for five minutes I danced the gypsy dance which was in the show. There was so much laughter when they saw me with the skirt on and those curtain rings hanging from my ears. That brought to an end, a wonderful year and the end of another marvellous decade.

HAPPY NEW YEAR, NIP.

With the excitement of preparation for marriage and all the arrangements to be made, I had forgotten to mention a very important item. Way back in June 1949, my Dad had to go into hospital at the Royal Infirmary for some tests on his heart.

For quite a while he had been having problems because his heart was enlarged and he had been to see a Specialist in a private capacity. I had been with my Dad at the examination and whilst Dad was getting changed after it, the Specialist had informed me that provided he took things easily, he could outlive me.

One of Dad's worries was that he wouldn't live as long as his mother, Granny Priestley, had done. She had died in 1928 at the age of 57 and he was 56 years of age. My Mum and I had a long talk with him about his problem and assured him that he wasn't going anywhere in the near future. It must have had some effect because shortly afterwards, he was discharged from hospital and his tests had found no deterioration in his heart. It wasn't long before he was back at work again and became as active as he had always been.

THE FIFTIES.

Nineteen Fifty started as a new life for me and Aline and we consolidated our marriage by taking things as they came. We enjoyed doing two or more other shows and became more acquainted with each other's families.

We went out a few times with Fred and Norma in the hope of teaching Aline how to play tennis. We booked a game at the Manor Recreation Courts but the idea didn't last long because shortly after starting the game, Fred returned a half volley and the ball hit Aline, SMACK in the eye. That was the end of that and she never attempted the game again.

There were no more problems with my Mum and Dad and he seemed to enjoy the idea of having a daughter-in-law in the house and both took to each others ways which included turns of phrase and banter between them.

Towards the end of January, Aline said that she was going to see the Doctor and naturally I thought that she was a little bit under the weather. When I enquired of such, she had a wry smile upon her face. The next day she saw Dr. Wainwright, who was 'Mick' Pettigrew's nephew. Upon her return the wry smile was accompanied with a beam of light in her eyes.

"You're going to be a Dad." She said. I was so happy for both of us and when we told the families, everyone wished us the best of luck.

From then on everyone became involved in knitting the usual garments for babies and we made a special effort to save enough money for essentials such as a pram. Freda recommended buying a Silver Cross, low slung one, so Nip and I went over to Doncaster to order one because we couldn't get one in Sheffield. It was well sprung and in Navy Blue colours with the price being in the region of £5.00.

To help relax during her pregnancy, we decided to take a holiday in the Isle of Man. We had a pleasant crossing but I didn't see anything of Flt/Sgt Gale this time. Having been there a couple of years before, I was able to arrange for us to stay at Mrs Gilberts' where I had stayed previously. Mr and Mrs Roy Gilbert were pleased to see me again and made Aline very welcome. It seemed ironical that Mrs Gilbert was also expecting their first child.

The week we chose to go happened to be T.T.Week, which was always in June and whilst at Gilberts' we met a Mr and Mrs Harry Hinton from Australia. Harry was over to take part in the races but it puzzled us when he told us that he only had one eye.

However, they insisted that we joined in the fun with the many other riders who were over on their motorcycles, of whom most had entered for the Annual event. This time I was able to book seats in the main stand for the races. It was better for Aline, rather than her having to be in a cramped place near Governor's Bridge. Anyhow, it was more exciting watching the cyclists whizz past the Leader board which was opposite to where we were sitting.

During the day, Mrs Hinton accompanied us on coach tours and visits to such places as Laxey where the famous water wheel was installed. At night we would manage to have a few dances at the Villa Marina and Nip was able to do a few slow dances. On one trip, we managed to book on Tommy's coach again and once more, he introduced us to the fairies. The break worked wonders for Aline and she was sorry to have to return home at the weekend.

Upon return from holiday, Nip carried on working and that helped us to build our finances and strangely enough, her wage worked out at 10/- shillings a week more then mine but we did manage to live on one wage. We did of course put our 'two pennyworth' into the housekeeping to help Mum and Dad with the food etc.

Eddie Kirby, who was Aline 's foreman and Mr Len Parkin, her manager, arranged for her to change to a supervisor's job where she wasn't overworked but earned more money by inspecting materials and components such as electro magnets. By doing this, she was able to stay at work up to within six weeks of the birth and thus obtain a maternity allowance of 36/- shillings per week from the Government.

The big day came and with it being a Sunday, I wasn't at work. When Aline 's labour pains started, I went for Aunty Amy Howard and we had already notified the Doctor who was on his way. I was asked by Aunty to go up stairs to help Nip with her pains by holding her hand or should I say, let her hold my hand very tightly to ease the pain.

Doctor Wainwright arrived and I went back down the stairs whilst Aunty went up to help. At approximately two o'clock in the afternoon the voice of our first born could be heard yelling, very loudly. I was called up and there in Nip's arms lay a beautiful 'Little' 8½ pound baby boy. Prior to the birth we had discussed names and decided that both grandfathers' names would be used along with our chosen one. Thus it was that George Joseph Anthony Priestley arrived on this earth. The added bonus to all this was that it was the 10th September, our wedding anniversary **AND** Aline's birthday, her 24th one.

During the War, Dad had dismantled my bike and greased all the frame to protect it. He had also put Vaseline on my chrome wheels and covered them with a one inch bandage wrapped in between the spokes and around the rim of the wheels, it was then put into the cellar. After demob, it was reassembled and I used it mainly for going to and from work but kept it in the kitchen for convenience. I also used to go over to Thurcroft to see Aline before we were married. So, after our son was born, the space in the kitchen at No. 87 was rather tight when the pram was delivered. To alleviate the problem, I decided to take the bike back down the cellar but not in bits and pieces. It was a struggle getting it up and down if I needed it but that wasn't very often.

So the months progressed, during which time Tony, our son, became chesty just like I was when little. Nip and I agreed that it must be the heat from the coal fire and one day when I was at home the baby had a very bad coughing spasm.

As we tried to help him, a large piece of phlegm seemed to be sticking in his throat. I finally had to get hold of it with my finger and pull it out. After that, as often as possible, Nip would take him out in the pram to get some fresh air. She also took him out of my Mum's way because Mum was beginning to pamper him like she used to pamper me.

We had been married about a year when I had an argument with the management at work and because I couldn't see any progression in my work status, I decided to apply for another position elsewhere.

I was very fortunate because within a fortnight I received a letter to go for an interview at Firth Vicker's Stainless Steels Foundry. The gentleman who saw me was a Mr. Lionel Casson who was the Sales Manager and also an ex-RAF Squadron Leader and I think he was persuaded to offer me the position when I told him I also had been in the RAF. A few days later I received a letter confirming that I had been offered the job at £6/10/- per week which was above what I had been getting at Edgars'. The FV Foundry was on Garter Street in the Pitsmoor district of Sheffield and was involved in making aircraft engine parts for jet aircraft. It was also a much shorter distance from home and I could reach it in a fifteen-minute walk.

So it was that I finally left Edgar Allen's at the end of September 1950, but I did manage to arrange a few days' holiday at Filey in North Yorkshire. We travelled by train and found some 'digs' which were reasonable in price. We stayed from the Monday until the Thursday and the bill cost us £4/10/- for the three of us, the weather was good and we made the most of it.

Being short of space in such a small house, it was starting to tell on Aline but fortune smiled upon us.

Whilst I was in Ceylon and at the time in a hospital with bronchitis, a soldier in the same ward, called to me. "Have you seen this article in the SEAC Newspaper?" He asked. He was from Sheffield and was reading the forces newspaper. He had spotted an article which stated that Sheffield City Council was to build 20,000 houses and anyone in the forces who was from Sheffield, was entitled to put their names down for one on the housing list.

At that particular time I had been engaged to Doreen Daisy Dunne, so I thought it would be a good idea to apply. As you may recall, that lass sent me a 'John Doe' letter and in the upset I forgot to cancel my request for a house.

This is the point which I am trying to make about good fortune smiling upon us. On the 24th May 1951, a letter arrived from the Housing Dept., of Sheffield City Council, offering us a dwelling on a new housing estate at Handsworth on the outskirts of Sheffield.

The key for the house had to be collected at 10.00 am on the day that the letter arrived so I had to have the day off work. We left Tony with my Mum and we dashed off to the Housing Dept., on Cadman Lane which was in town. We took with us our identity cards which had been requested for the three of us. We also had to sign a document stating that we weren't tenants of a house or beneficial occupiers of a house.

Putting my name on the housing list whilst in Ceylon in 1945, had paid dividends and we were over the moon when receiving the keys to No. 8 Ballifield Crescent. We had the option of refusing or accepting and you can guess what we did. We accepted, of course we did. Quite a few of the local neighbours in Brompton Road showed their disapproval at what they thought had been favouritism but it wasn't, it was foresight.

In the afternoon we caught a tramcar from Staniforth Road to Handsworth Church, the tram terminus and wandered down the main road to try to find our new home. It was quite a way down and the Estate was being built on land behind Handsworth Church which used to be the nursery gardens of Fisher, Son & Sibury. We eventually found the house which had just been finished and it was opposite an old building called Ballifield Hall and this was boarded up and stood in semi-private grounds. Apparently it had once been the home of a Mormon family but they had all left the district years ago.

This was on the 23rd May 1951 and the letter we had received informed us that the tenancy commenced on Monday the 28th May and that the inclusive rent would be 22/5d per week. Prior to receiving the notification, we had a health visitor from the Town Hall to inspect the accommodation we had with Mum and Dad to check for cleanliness etc., and to assess us to see if we were suitable enough to be given council property. On top of that, we were partly means-tested to check that we would be able to pay the rent each week from the salary I earned, which was around £5/15/0 per week.

The new house had three bedrooms, a bathroom and toilet up stairs and a second toilet in the back porch. The lounge was large and long at 22 feet by 11 feet. The kitchen was big too, with fitted cupboards and a deep pot sink with wooden draining boards on either side of it. On the right-hand side one there was a two- ringed gas cooker and under the left-hand board there was a zinc, gas fired, boiler for washing clothes. At the far end of the kitchen by the back door was a small pantry which had folding doors and plenty of shelving.

The hallway led from the front door to the lounge door and the staircase was half open with a plaster covered bannister on the open side and another one on the landing. There was also a good handrail on the wall of the staircase. The front bedroom had a built-in wardrobe and was the largest. The back bedroom was also large with a built- in wardrobe and also an airing cupboard, whilst the small bedroom was more like a boxroom but capable of taking a single bed in it.

Out of the back door was the second toilet on the right and immediately in front of you was the coal house capable of holding a half ton of coal. On the left was a ten-feet square outhouse which held a small cupboard with the gas and electric metres in it. Also on the right, just past the toilet, was the entrance to the porch which had three steps going down into the back yard and the garden.

Returning to the kitchen, there was a very handy back- to- back oven which was heated by the fire in the lounge and had a hot plate below it, to put pans on it for cooking purposes. The oven had a drop down door which was very useful when preparing meals.

Having accepted the tenancy, we couldn't move in immediately because we had no furniture of our own and during the building of the houses close by, the workmen had used No.8 as a canteen and break place. This had done us a service because the fire they had kept lit, had heated the water in the fireback boiler and had also warmed the house in general.

Due to the workmen using the house, it took a couple of weeks to scrub the wooden floors and clean the windows. Nan, Eric's girlfriend, came over and helped quite a lot with the cleaning, as did others in the family. We weren't allowed to decorate the walls for six months because of the recently plastered wall surfaces.

It was all go and we had to chase about in order to get furniture, curtains and floor coverings. All the family helped us to get started and each one in turn, did their bit or provided us with some article or other. Quite a few items we needed were given to us as wedding presents such as towels, various types of cutlery, including the cutlery cabinet we had given us by our workmates, a 21-piece tea service, basins, an 18-piece tea service, bedding, mirrors, a clock, an electric iron and many Pyrex dishes.

Whenever Nip and I came to the house on our own, we would put some items in the pram and walked the three and a half miles up to the house via Darnall. On some occasions, we would put Tony into a large holdall type of bag and carry him between us. His little head would bob up and down and people would look and laugh at him but he enjoyed it.

Eventually we managed to get things into shape and when we received the furniture we had ordered, we were able to set a date for moving in. Many people in this era, did their trading with the local Co-op and ours was the Brightside and Carbrook (Sheffield) Co-op Society which had many Branches. We had decided to purchase the bulk of our needs from the Co-op and this we had ordered on the 26th May to be delivered the following week.

We were always looking for ways to save a little money and here was a chance to get some return for what we had laid out for the furniture because by spending our money at the Co-op we would eventually get some back in a dividend at the end of the year.

All that we ordered was from the City Branch on Exchange Street at the corner with Angel Street. We had saved enough money to buy with cash what we wanted and although it doesn't seem much in the present times, it did then. For instance, below is a copy of the cost involved:-

Bedroom Suite	£46/4/9	
Gate-Legged Table	£12/10/0	
Bed Stead 4' 6" long		£5/3/6
30 Sq. Yds Lino (Room)	£11/2/6	
Mattress 4' 6" long		£3/2/0
16 Sq. Yds Lino (bedroom)	£5/18/8	
Side Board 4' 6" long	£21/6/0	
8 Yds. Stair Carpet	£5/15/4	
4 Dining Chairs	£11/0/0	

1 Washing Wringer.	£5/17/8	
Share Number 97153.		
Total		**£128/0/5**

It was only at the weekends and at nights that I was able to give any real assistance but it did help with the light nights of summer time. However, on the 1st June 1951, Aline and I, along with Tony, moved into our new home. It seemed strange at first but eventually we became used to it and having so much work to do by getting things into place, the time seemed to fly. If we were both engaged in doing some odd job, we would take the loose bottom from one of the chairs which Mum had given us, and put Tony inside the frame of it and use it as a temporary baby walker. We still had to keep an eye on him because he would push the chair frame around the floor and laugh at the noise.

The few months prior to this I was trying to settle down at Firth Vickers' and the longer journey to work didn't help. Fortunately I could catch the through tram from Handsworth, near the top end of Orgreave Lane, to Brightside and this dropped me off at the far end of Newhall Road which meant that I had a ten minute walk to get to Garter Street. One good thing was that I had to start work at 9.00 am instead of 8.00 am as I did when I was at Edgars'.

The sales office in which I worked was in a brick building on the corner of Garter Street and Carlisle Street, opposite Firth Brown's Rolling Mills. I was on the second floor and shared the office with several other sales clerks, namely, Fred Whitfield, Bill Scoley, Jimmy Unwin, Roly Grice, Alan Hickman, Alvin Tipple, a Mr Bell and the errand girl Joan Scott. Mr Casson's office was attached to the end of ours. Most of us were ex-servicemen and Bill Scoley, Jimmy Unwin and Alvin Tipple, were all ex-RAF. Jimmy had been in the TDS section of the camp I was on at Kandy, in Ceylon and he remembered me. Tipple was an ex-Squadron Leader (I called him a squabbling bleeder) and had served most of his time in the Seychelles in the Indian Ocean.

Being new to the staff, Alvin tried to come the 'old soldier' with me. The external phone happened to be on my desk and every time he needed to use it, he pushed all my work out of the way and spread himself across the desk. He was a big cumbersome person but it wasn't long before I tumbled him and cured him.

He had left an important quotation on my desk by accident, so I scooped up all the documents and put them into my drawer under some other paper work. For days he was searching for them but I kept my mouth shut until he was in such a state that I slid them in between some of his other papers whilst he was out of the office. I think he received the message because he didn't bother me anymore. All the other lads enjoyed what I had done and said that it served him right.

After some six months had passed, Mr Casson asked me to transfer into another office above the Machine Shop to help with the analysis of costing. This office was under the leadership of a Ken Keys, a bit of a 'know all' and full of himself. There was also a compliment of estimators which included Peter Beeson, the senior one, Jackie Marriott, who played football on the right wing for Sheffield Wednesday, Cliff Bramall, Alan Ball and another junior.

There was one morning when the junior walked into the office and asked us if we knew where 'Buncher' was because Mr Casson wanted to see him. We all turned our heads and Peter enquired. "Buncher? Never heard of him." Then the junior said, "You know him. Buncher Keys." We all doubled up with laughter. A play on words. 'A bunch of keys'.

I remained in that office for nearly a year and then things began to move. All of us who were in that office and the rest of the staff in the old building were transferred into a new complex of prefabricated offices just across the road. I rejoined the sales staff in the largest office but still carried on doing costing. The estimating staff took the office next to ours but in actual fact it was all an open plan office divided by a partition of cupboards.

Apart from establishing myself in my new employment and trying to settle down in a new house, I had managed to squeeze in some driving lessons with the British School of Motoring (BSM) and though I failed my first test and had the second one postponed because of snow, I finally passed my examination on the 17th November 1951 in the School's Austin Devon saloon car.

All through the summer of 1951 I didn't play cricket because I had left Edgars' and therefore I wasn't allowed to turn out for them whilst working for another firm. This had enabled me to concentrate on getting the garden into some sort of tidiness and plan for the future. Both the front and back were on a slope which tapered from three feet on the north east side to one foot on the south west side. This area was also used as farm land and barley must have been the last crop grown here because it was in abundance with little clumps spread around the garden. Aline's brother Eric had managed to come over from Thurcroft one weekend to help me level the front garden and I appreciated it.

It was hard work trying to get it level but because of my tummy troubles I was limited as to what I could do. As I have said earlier, Nip was a good lass and many are the times when she has 'mucked in' to help me, even to the point of using a pick and shovel to move the earth.

Slowly but surely, we started to get on top of it and on the bottom end we were able to grow a lawn on which we would put Tony on a rug to play whilst we carried on with other jobs. My Dad had helped me to erect a rustic fence across the middle of the garden to separate it from the vegetables. We also put some rustic along the boundary which came between us and our neighbours, Ron and Elsie Cox on the lower side and Bill and Emily Hargreaves on the top end. They each had one daughter, Margaret and Jacqueline respectively.

It was on the Whit Monday of 1951 that Eva and Ted paid us a visit from Wakefield in their Morris Ten car. They had travelled down to see us but mainly to see how Tony was progressing. They arrived before lunch as had Freda and Joe who had come over from Harworth with Ian and Graham the baby who was born eight days after Tony.

The reason for the visit was that Handsworth was still a village and a garden fete and agricultural show had been arranged for the holiday. The main event of the fete was a young man who was an up and coming comedian and entertainer in show business and was to appear in the afternoon.. He was Max Bygraves and they all wanted to see him.

We all went up to the show and after a couple of hours we had to leave because of the babies. On our way out of the ground, Joe and I said we would pop up the Handsworth Hill to get some fish and chips, so we took Tony with us in his pram whilst the rest of the family made their way back to our house. It was a lovely warm day and Tony sat up in a quite happy frame of mind. We reached the 'chippy' and placed our order for some eight of us. Having put the brake on the wheels of the Pram, we waited for our order which took about twenty minutes. When we were finally served, Joe and I walked quickly down the hill to stop the fish and chips from getting cold.

We had all managed to get seated around the kitchen table and anywhere else that was convenient, when Eva asked, "Is Tony in the pram, outside in the yard?" Nip looked at me, I looked at Joe who then said, "What the bloody hell! We've left him outside the chip shop!"

Panic stations! We went back up the hill as fast as we could. Arrived back at the 'chippy' and there in the pram was Tony, looking as unconcerned as anything as he watched the traffic go by. When we arrived back home, Nip picked him up and she was in tears, she thought that she had lost him. Afterwards, however, we all saw the funny side of the incident and was glad it had ended happily.

Freda and Joe stayed the weekend with us because Joe was giving me a hand to build a small stone wall on the front path from stones taken from an outhouse which was being demolished across the road at Ballifield Hall. Also, I had acquired some sand, cement and aggregate to use in laying a main path up the centre of the back garden.

I think it was on the Tuesday that we decide to go out for the day to Matlock in Derbyshire. Eva and Ted brought her Mum and Dad over here to get the babies and take them by car to Matlock whilst the remainder of us went by train from Woodhouse Station. We all met in the afternoon in the Park at Matlock and had a good day by going on the boating lake and miniature railway and having a picnic on the grass.

Just after tea time, we decided to call it a day and caught the train back to Chesterfield from where we hoped to get a connection to Woodhouse Station. We alighted at one station in Chesterfield and hurried over to the one where we were to catch our train home. As we made our way down the steps to the platform, we saw the Guard flagging the driver of the train to proceed.

The train had just started to move as we reached the platform. Joe rushed forward, opened a carriage door (they were single compartments then) and we all scrambled in with Ian. Then Joe threw the pushchair in after us and dived in himself. We just made it but the funniest thing was that as Joe ran and jumped into the compartment, his trousers were slowly coming down.

What a day! We finally arrived back at Ballifield, where Eva, Ted and Mum and Dad Todd were waiting for us.

The rest of the year went quietly, by comparison, and Christmas 1951 was shared between both of our parents and it was rather a subdued holiday for us, except that Tony had started toddling and gave us some entertainment with his antics. The New Year was let in by the old tradition of bringing bread, coal and wooden sticks into the house to ensure that we had food and warmth for the following twelve months.

During the Spring of '52, we were looking more ship shape at home because we had been able to do some decorating and my Dad had arranged for a joiner, Harry, who worked with him, to come and put us a storm door on the back porch. This helped to keep the cold out of the kitchen and Dad paid Harry for the work to help us out financially. Dad was like that.

It was around this time that Nip informed me that she thought she was pregnant again and went to see our new Doctor to whom we had transferred after leaving Attercliffe. On her return, I could see she was upset and then she told me that the Doctor, Dr. Nelson, had said that it was about time she had another. OH! She was mad and decided to start looking for another Doctor, but this took time. There weren't many people who liked Dr. Nelson because he was so abrupt even to the point of rudeness.

Because of the news, we decided to have a holiday as soon as possible. So, at Whitsuntide we went to Mablethorpe in Lincolnshire for a week. The weather was glorious and one day we went to a small fete at which there was a baby contest. It was just about to be judged when we arrived so Nip hurriedly took Tony out of his pram, took him in her arms and joined the line of contestants.

With the weather being warm, Tony had only a pair of gathered crepe trunks on and his hair was blonde with a 'crew cut' style which was popular just then. His chubby body had a slight tan and as the judges moved along the line, they kept glancing at him as they approached, each one passing a favourable comment. After a short discussion, it was unanimously decided to award Tony - and Nip the first prize.

Whilst there, we bought him a peaked cap to keep the sun off his head and as he toddled up the 'Pullover' towards the beach, people were saying how much he looked like a miniature

Bruce Woodcock, the heavyweight boxer

After the holiday towards the end of May, I had been offered a small car by a friend, Tommy Hardy, who was our local barber. He was a short, chubby chap and full of life. A pal of his, who owned a garage at Beighton, (Tomlinson's), had a little 1927 Austin Coupe for sale. The registration number was VW3229. It was in reasonable condition with a drop-down hood, spoked wheels and the asking price was a mere £12.0.0 pounds and it included a new battery. I discussed it with Nip and we agreed to buy it. This was our first vehicle and whilst people would give us a second glance, we were happy because it saved us fares on public transport

It was a bonus for going to work and popping over to Thurcroft to see Aline 's Mum and Dad. It also enabled me to call and see my parents on my way to and from work. The car was like a box on wheels with headlamps which looked similar to two huge eyes on either side of a small face which was the radiator with the chrome Austin badge on it.

Shortly after returning from Mablethorpe, we had a terrifying accident at home. Because Nip was pregnant again, I would help her as much as I could and on this particular night, just after tea, I said that I would bath Tony and then put him to bed.

Rather than take him upstairs and put him in the big bath, I decided to wash him in the large, white, pot sink in the kitchen. He just fitted in and was enjoying himself splashing the water when I reached over to get the soap and accidentally caught the hot tap with my sleeve.

Scalding hot water poured onto his left leg and he screamed and screamed. I turned the tap off, Aline rushed in, saw what had happened and grabbed a towel to cover the leg. We put some soothing stuff on it but I cannot remember what, and it calmed him down so we rushed him up to Dr. Nelson in our little car. The doctor wasn't able to help and told us to take him to the Children's Hospital in Sheffield which was five miles away.

After wasting a half hour we eventually arrived at the hospital and there he was admitted for treatment and kept in for that purpose. We both arrived home in tears and I felt so guilty that it was my fault for not being more careful.

For two weeks we visited him but only one parent was allowed at one time into his isolated ward where he had a cage over his little leg. Slowly but surely it started to heal and one day, when I was visiting him he was sitting up and laughing and playing. As I looked at him I could see his leg was uncovered and very pink. It was his new skin growing but the large scab, which had covered the scald, was under his cot. He had pulled it off himself. A few days later he was allowed home but he had a scar for a very long time.

I was getting more involved at work and analysing cost sheets from Headquarters in Weedon Street at Tinsley, resulted in my producing statistics for Mr Ron Wainwright, the engineering manager. There were several production meetings and the results of these were passed on to Mr Alf Thornton, our Foundry Director.

Mr Thornton was generally referred to as AET (his initials). He was a well-built man with a supercilious grin permanently on his face. Every time he spoke, everyone had to jump. He was a metallurgist and was well conversed in foundry work, often giving lectures up and down the country. He was also pompous and very much disliked by all the staff and the management.

Because production was in the ascendency, it was found necessary to increase the staff levels. A gentleman, in his early fifties, was brought in to do the ledger entries and his name was Colin Gill. He was a nice person, very amiable and appeared to be interested in the work but soon we became aware of his slowness in his abilities.

He smoked like a trooper and in one instance he fell asleep, which resulted in the cigarette he was smoking, falling on to the ledger and burning a hole through several pages.

My little Austin, with the registration number VW3229, was proving very useful when driving to work because I was able to offer a lift to Bill Scoley who lived near to me. I was driving along Carlisle Street one morning when a gust of wind blew under the roof cover and lifted it off its seatings. Was I glad that Bill was with me because he was able to hold it down until we arrived at work. We couldn't stop laughing all morning.

Having settled to having Tony back at home and nursing him, Nip was busy knitting again in readiness for the arrival of our new baby. Some things, which Tony had grown out of, were saved in preparation for the new event. The pram was in a good state and that would save us some expense.

During the summer, there were many times when Aunty Amy Howard would come up and take Tony, in his pram, for a walk down Orgreave Lane or on some occasions down Beaver Hill Road. In either place she enjoyed it because in the small disused quarries which were on both roads, there were plenty of wild blackberries to pick. It was one of Aunty's hobbies making wines and jams.

As the time approached for the next happy day, Nip and I once more asked Aunty Amy to be at the birth and this, she agreed to do. We liked having her with us because she was so jolly and full of fun. There was never a dull moment.

The signs were that the arrival may be close to Aline's birthday again but time passed the 10th September and on the 8th October 1952, son number two arrived on the scene. The names we had chosen for him were Geoffrey Alan and his weight was about 7½ pounds. Both Nip and the baby were doing very well and Aunty came up each day until Aline was on her feet again. I brought Mum and Dad up in the car and later on in the week I went over to Thurcroft to get her Mum to come over to see them.

That little car came in very handy when fetching my Mum and Dad and the other grandparents over for the Christening a few weeks later. This was at the Handsworth Church of St. Mary's and performed by the Canon Ferriby, whereas Tony's baptism had been at Laughton, in the church where we had been married.

There were the usual restless nights and we had put Tony into a single bed in the little bedroom. Being still new to parenthood and still suffering with my stomach, my patience wore a little thin at times. One night I had been in and out of bed to Tony so much that I lost my temper with him. I picked him up, shouted at him to stop crying and then threw him onto his bed. He quietened down but I felt awful afterwards. I had forgotten that some of his teeth were still coming through and that was the cause of him crying.

Christmas Day '52, we had Mum and Dad up for dinner and Dad, more than Mum, helped with the cooking. After the meal, it was good to see Dad playing with Tony, and Geoff was just starting to sit up. Dad was so chuffed to have two grandsons and he really spoiled them and kept saying to them, "Come to your Gandipop Gud!" For years it was never Grandad, always Gandipop Gud. Boxing Day we had a run over to Thurcroft to see the other grandparents and let the rest of the family over there take a look at the new arrival. It had been another good year and we thanked God for it.

Early in the New Year I was moved once more into another office. This time it was just around the corner into the area where the estimators were working. There was a new member to the staff and I was now partnered with a young man, Arnold Precious, who was to work with me on the cost analysis side of things. He was studying to be a cost accountant and attended evening classes in his spare time. There was also a young lady by the name of Doreen Schemeld who was doing general clerical work. She was very cheerful and a friendly lass about twenty-four years of age and I found out later on that she lived near to my Mum and Dad at the top end of Brompton Road. She had also attended the same school as I had attended in Maltby Street.

Arnold was involved with the ATC (Air Training Corps) which was for young people who were interested in the Royal Air Force. He held the rank of Warrant Officer and like I said earlier, he was studying Cost Accountancy and had been transferred from Weedon Street Head

Office to gain some experience.

A few weeks prior to Princess Elizabeth marrying Prince Philip, our family had an upset because in the National News it was reported that an air crash had taken place near to Finningley in Yorkshire.

An RAF Meteor fighter had crashed in thick fog and the pilot injured was Tony Whittaker, the son of our Mary Whittaker (Furness). The following morning, I went into Mr Casson, because he was the C.O. at the RAF Camp at Finningley where Tony was stationed and asked him if he could tell me any more about the crash.

Apparently, Tony was bringing the aircraft in to land but couldn't find his bearings because of the thick fog. He told his navigator to bail out due to the fuel getting low whilst trying to find the airfield.

As the navigator ejected, his intercom came away from his head and therefore Tony didn't receive confirmation that his pal had jumped clear. This caused Tony to circle and circle until it was imperative that he must leave the aircraft. Unfortunately, as he jumped, the lower part of his leg, just above the ankle, caught the leading edge of the wing. His ankle was partly severed which was bad enough and then his parachute caught up in a tree and he couldn't release himself. It was hours before he was found and though losing a lot of blood, he was rushed to a hospital and survived. However, it was necessary to amputate the damaged part of his leg.

Mr Casson did a marvellous job in keeping me informed of Tony's health and at times, my news was more up to date than what his Mum received.

The reason I mentioned the Royal Marriage earlier on was because Tony and other patients in his hospital, were given a grandstand view of the wedding but one wouldn't call it consolation. Tony tried to carry on with his career but his artificial limb persuaded him to leave the RAF and his wife wasn't too keen on him staying in, either.

As Spring approached, my Dad had a chat with me and suggested that it would be better to get another car because of the kids. He knew I couldn't afford one but he went with me to Woodseats Motors where he had seen that there was a Saloon car for sale. It was a black Ford Popular Ten model and having looked it over, Dad asked me if wanted it. I said I would like it but hadn't the money. "Don't worry." He said. "It's a gift."

I was so grateful to him. In a deal for my old car as part exchange, it cost him £100 pounds and I had a vehicle which was far more comfortable and reliable. On the following Monday when I arrived at work, I received a terrible Mickey taking because the registration number was AET 145 and the lads pointed out the coincidence of Mr Thorntons' initials, AET . "What are you trying to do?" They asked. "Get some favours from him?" Even Mr Casson had a smile on his face and I must be honest, the initials didn't ring a bell when the car was bought.

Nip and I made sure that we had a holiday of one sort or another and this year, with having a better car, we decided to go to Barmouth in central Wales. It was along drive but we made it, even though at one stage, as we were driving down we had a little problem. Because the weather was so warm, I had opened the windows and as we were driving down this main road I saw something flash in the driving mirror. I slowed down and then saw a car behind us flashing his lights. As I stopped, the driver of the other car came up and asked us if this was one of the children's shoes. It was. Tony had taken one shoe off and thrown it through the window. It's a good job that the other motorist and his wife saw it but we thanked them and enjoyed the laugh. The boarding house in which we stayed, was only a few minutes walk from the beach. We had one or two trips in the area and it wasn't far up the main road to Harlech Castle and then on to Porthmadog and Criccieth, two lovely Welsh towns. With the sands being so handy, it was marvellous to play with the kids and watch Geoff trying to dig with his little spade and bucket. He was just toddling then. We returned home after having enjoyed a very pleasant holiday.

One Sunday, we took Nip's Mum and Dad in the car to see his brother Dick and sister Fanny on their farm in Glentham in Lincolnshire. The lads loved the animals and we took a photo of Tony sitting on a harvester tractor. We enjoyed the day out but my Dad was a little cross when we told him. "I didn't buy the car for the Todd's pleasure, you know."

It was unlike Dad but I could see his point of view. After that I only took them out once more in the car and that was to see Eva and Ted at Wakefield.

I was speaking to Mr Gill at work one day and the subject turned to cricket. He was telling me that he had played with Sheffield United Cricket Team and had been coached by the famous Yorkshire and England player, Wilf Rhodes. He asked me if I played and when I explained about having turned out for Edgar Allens' and had not had a game since joining Firth Vickers, he invited me to go for a trial with the team of which he was the President. It was a private club and was registered in the Norton and District Cricket League under the name of Leadmill Old Boys. Their ground was in Graves Park and after going up for net practise at the beginning of the new season, I was picked to play for the second team. I had earlier explained to Mr Gill that I was a slow off spin bowler but hadn't been given much encouragement in the Sheffield Works League.

The first game in which I played for LOB, Mr Gill, who wasn't playing, had a word with Arthur Ludlam, the Captain. After some ten overs, Arthur threw the ball to me and told me to go on the top end. Having set the field placings, I trundled up because I only took six paces to the crease and in my first over I bowled the batsman around his legs. The pitch was slightly sloping to the left from my end and this had helped to bring the ball in from off the seam.

I had a natural fault when bowling because I would turn my wrist as though I was sending an off break but the ball would go straight and this had helped in my first over. I finished my stint by bowling two other batsmen in the same way without conceding many runs. After the match I was accepted as a regular player in the second team.

The whole of that season was great for me and at the end of it the Club held their Annual Dance in December at the Abbeydale Ballroom where presentations were made for the best performances throughout the season. I"m pleased to say that I headed the 2nd Team bowling averages, the breakdown of which is below.

LEADMILL OLD BOYS CRICKET CLUB

Newsletter 5th December 1953.

Bowling	**O**	**M**	**Runs**	**Wkts**	**Avge**
Priestley	44	5	129	21	6.3
Ludlam	126	43	249	34	7.9
Dungworth	106	22	235	27	8.7
Peel	108	27	244	26	9.4

Priestley Bowling Analysis

TEAM				
Hackenthorpe	1	0	8	0
Handsworth	2.3	0	4	3
Richards Sports (A)	5	1	11	3
Mosboro Trinity	5	0	19	0
Richards Sports (H)	2.3	1	3	5
Prince Of Wales	5	1	10	1

Handsworth (A)	5	1	14	2
Crookes YMCA	5	0	25	1
Mosboro Trinity (H)	3	0	7	1
Hollinsend	9	0	28	5
TOTAL	**44**	**5**	**129**	**21**

Although I bowled so well, it wasn't until the following season that I was awarded my Club Cap, of which I was very proud. It had navy blue and red quarters with the logo LOB on the front red quarter. Later on, when I played for other teams the players would shout "Watch out, Lobbies about.."

Having the car enabled me to take Nip and the kids to several matches and it was treated as a picnic, just as many other player's wives did. At one home game in Grave's Park, Tony was sitting just outside the boundary line near to the pavilion when a batsman hit the ball hard. It sped along the ground towards Tony but a fielder wasn't quick enough to prevent the ball from hitting him in the back. Luckily he wasn't injured but his little back bore a bruise for days.

The summer of '53 had been a warm and sunny one so we were able to set up the play pen which we had bought for Tony and put it on the lawn for Geoff to play in. We had also acquired a rocking type gadget which was shaped and painted like a bull. Tony was just about able to sit on it without assistance and rock to and fro. He called it Barney the Bull.

Around this time we had befriended a young school girl who lived across on Retford Road. Her name was Maureen Matthews and she was about twelve years of age and attending a private school. Maureen had seen Aline out with the pram when she was shopping and had said that if we needed a baby sitter at any time she would be willing to do it for us. From then on Maureen was a Godsend to us and though we didn't go out too often she was always ready to help. It eventually became a friendship and Maureen would call in just for the pleasure of our company.

In Whit Week that year we managed to have another holiday and this time we went to North Wales and stayed in a little cottage in the village of Mynytho near to Llanbedrog which was a short way down the coast from Pwllheli. The cottage was small and had a picture postcard appearance with the bedroom window so small that one had to get down on hands and knees to open it but on the whole it was very comfortable and we were made to feel at home by the landlady. I was annoyed when we took the kids to the beach at Llanbedrog because there was now a charge to go on to the sands. It was all free during the war when I was stationed at Penrhos, even if there was barbed wire all around. Before returning home, I took Aline and the lads up to the camp where I had been and was surprised to see that it was now a Polish Community. I spoke to a few people there and explained my visit, where upon they made us very welcome and showed us around the place. It was good to see the old site again.

It was during this holiday that I put some 'L' plates on the car and try to teach Aline to drive. She did quite well until the day she tried to do a three-point turn in a narrow lane. Nip managed to get it into a position across the road with about eighteen inches to spare at either end and blocking the road completely. Luckily, there wasn't much traffic about in those days but it took me quite a while to get it back on track and facing in the right direction.

After returning home from a good holiday and later on in 1954, Aline carried on with driving lessons with the BSM and had just become accustomed to the car when I decided to change it. This time I financed it alone and so pleased myself as to whom I took in it. No discredit to Dad but it made me feel more independent.

The new car was another Ford, a Prefect, but a more modern shape and it had a two-tone red and white paint work. Nip took to it right away and she looked more comfortable in it and with a cushion she could see easily over the steering wheel which she couldn't do in the old one. After several months learning and failing twice, she eventually passed her driving test.

It was whilst we had this car that Nip had to visit the hospital for a check up and I went with her to give her some courage because she was so nervous. As she drove up Glossop Road she made to change gear and as she moved it, the gear stick came out of its socket and into her hand. At first she panicked but I calmed her down by saying, "Oh. Throw it out of the window. You don't need it."

This eased the tension and she laughed, calling me a silly fool. I took over and managed to turn into a side street, where I was able to screw the gear stick back into place and complete the journey to the hospital.

It was shortly after this that everything went wrong with the car, which I had purchased from Brocklehurst's in Chesterfield. Handsworth Motor Co., managed to get it back on to the road but at some expense. We decided to get rid of it as soon as possible, vowing never to buy another Ford car as long as I was able to drive.

Having managed to scrape some more money together, my Dad and I went to look at an Austin Ascot saloon and this time we took along Mr. Ward, with us from the Handsworth Motor Co., for advice for which Dad reimbursed him. It was at a garage on Middlewood Road just past the tram terminus and upon the 'Dukes' advice I bought it for £250. The registration was ERR45.

There was so much room in this new car that it was a pleasure to go out for picnics and journey to the coast for the day. As I have said before, Dad was so generous and very often bought four gallons of petrol which was only 25d per gallon so for two pounds we could make it there and back to Scarborough or Bridlington quite easily.

Many times we went to these two places and the journey up there, entailed going to Thorne, up the A614 and then through the centre of the little towns of Market Weighton and Driffield. This obviously slowed down the journey and after stopping at a little restaurant for lunch at Howden, it took about 3½ hours to reach our destination. In some instances, Tony would guess where we were bound for and said he felt sick and Dad would panic and ask me to stop the car. After it happened a few times, I said I would cure him (Tony) and threatened to turn around and go home. My ruse worked and it didn't happen again. It was all worth it in the end and the lads enjoyed themselves playing in the sand and playing ball games etc., on the sandy beach. Dad also enjoyed it when playing with the lads as Mum sat with Aline.

This car had a sliding roof and Aline's Mum loved going out on a sunny day with the roof wide open. We caught a shower one day but her Mum told us to leave the roof open because the rain was so refreshing. On some occasions we took Maureen with us as a reward for helping us with the children.

Back at F.V's, because I had been accustomed to experience on a foundry shop floor and had studied engineering drawing, I was asked if I would help the estimators because they were so busy. I enjoyed reading drawings again and getting involved with the pattern makers and the pattern stores.

I have previously mentioned 'Buncher' Keys and what a clever clogs he was but there was one occasion when he queried an estimated cast weight which I had done on a quotation. Having actually worked in the foundry at Edgar's, I was well aware as to what certain castings could weigh and this particular one I had estimated at 114 lbs. It was a flywheel, of which I had seen many, but my 'friend' Buncher had done his calculations and had arrived at an answer of 112 lbs.

He insisted that he was right but it was his attitude which niggled me. "Come on." I said. "You're not going to argue for two pounds? You could lose that in the 'Head' when it's cast." He hadn't a clue as to what I meant with the 'Head' but Pete Beeson, the senior estimator did and he sided with me. Ken Keys wasn't very pleased with me.

In a further incident, all the estimating staff were having a chat at coffee break and things became a little frivolous over something but I had my head down, engrossed in some costing figures.'Buncher' came storming in, told me to shut up and get on with some work. Pete Beeson said that I wasn't involved but Keys wouldn't accept it.

I sat there, never said a word but my knuckles went white as I gripped my chair arms. Another minute and I would have panned him one. Mr. Gill was sitting just behind me and saw my face. He jumped up, put his hand upon my shoulder and told me to go for a walk up to the Pattern Stores. This I did but it took me half an hour to calm down. I thanked Mr. Gill afterwards.

I wrote earlier about an accident in the Foundry at Edgar Allen's and once again, in 1953 I encountered a similar incident. This time it was in the Centrifugal Casting area in the MAP (Ministry of Aircraft Production) of Firth Vickers.

As I was walking up the office corridor, the door at the far end burst open and AET came through it in a terrible state. At first I had to smile because he had on his Anthony Eden hat also his suit jacket but his trousers looked like shorts. It was then that I realised something was wrong and called Ron Wainwright, who was a senior officer in the St. John's Ambulance Brigade.

It seemed that there had been an incident in the Foundry and it turned out to be tragic. As AET had been explaining to the MD of Rolls Royce, Derby, how the centrifugal system of casting steel was processed, the accident occurred. Apparently, as they were watching the casting of a component, the centrifugal machine broke down and flying segments killed outright the gentleman from Rolls Royce. Even though AET had lost the bottom half of his trousers, he wasn't hurt but very shocked. Although the incident was so serious, I still couldn't refrain from chuckling at the appearance of AET standing in the doorway, without his trousers.

In early 1955, Bill Scoley returned my favour of giving him a lift to work, by helping me to erect a garage on the Communal Site just behind the shops on Ballifield Drive. It was a corrugated iron garage and measured 14 feet by 8 feet by 7 feet and had been approved by the Council. Of the 23 on the site, mine was number 21.

I had ordered the sand, gravel and cement to make a concrete base for it and Bill and I mixed it all by hand. The awkward part was carrying the water from our house to mix it all. It took us two weekends to complete it all and then over the following weeks I was able to paint it an olive green which also had to comply with the Council's wishes.

Working at F.V.'s wasn't always easy with AET and 'Buncher' breathing down one's neck. However, whilst doing standard costing analyses, I had to keep in contact with the Cost Office on Weedon Street at Tinsley. In some instances it was necessary to go down there to co-operate with the Cost Accountant, Mr. Eddie Drabble and other members of his staff. His office manager Billy Osborne, was a fussy and strict chap and he, believe it or not, still used an abacus to do his calculations. The senior clerk there was Cyril Points and he and I worked closely together and we both had the same temperament and liked the same type of humour which, at odd times, was difficult to find.

There was some light relief because occasionally a group of us would pop out at lunch time from Garter Street and go for a swim at Sutherland Road baths. It was only five-minutes walk away and Mr Lol Bower, the General Manager, would organise it so that we had a break for lunch when we returned. It was during one of these sessions that whilst I was swimming under the water, one of the female staff thought I was going for her legs. She lashed out with them and broke my nose with her foot. I had no such notion in my head when she kicked but my nose was sore for weeks.

It was in this year that Tony started to go to school at Handsworth Infants which was under the Headmistress, Miss Meredith, along with Mrs Bartlam, her assistant. She ran a very efficient outfit and was always willing to discuss any problems which parents might have. The school was on the corner of St. Joseph's Road and Fitzalan Road which was just across the way from the Handsworth Recreation Ground. It was a steady climb from home and took about fifteen minutes to walk there but Nip always walked it and took the pram with Geoff in it. Rain, snow or blow, she always wrapped up well along with the kids and enjoyed the exercise.

Prior to Tony starting at school, Nip had her hands full trying to watch him playing in the yard and trying to attend to Geoff at the same time. Once or twice Tony disappeared from view and caused Nip to start worrying as to what might have happened to him and would have a quick look round for him.

Across the road from us, Ballifield Hall had been converted into an old peoples' home with a Matron and staff to care for some fifteen old gentlemen who had no homes but needed care.

The Hall, was under the supervision of the local Social Services Department and was being slowly completed with its own flower gardens and garden seats for the old men to sit on but as yet there was no fence or hedge to make it completely private.

I described this because it happened that if Tony was out of sight, then nine times out of ten we could be found across the road at the Hall, talking to his 'Grandads', as he called them. It was from there that Aline was less worried and one or other of the staff, or even the old folk, would let her know that Tony was over there. To try to stop him wondering off, Dad and I decided to put a gate on the corner of the outhouse to the dividing wall of the garden. We drilled the wall and fixed some 4 x 2 inch battens to the walls with coach bolts which were cemented into the brickwork. We then made a divided gate which had a slip bolt at the bottom to fasten it to the ground. To keep them closed, we put a drop-over metal square hoop at the top of the gate halves. This served its purpose for quite a while and thus brought some respite to Nip.

For quite a few years it was very pleasant to sit and listen to the Police Band, the Transport Band and the Salvation Army Bands which would come and entertain the old folks on summer afternoons at weekends. There was also Whitsuntide when the Sunday Schools children would parade in the grounds and sing hymns to them.

It was about this time that we eventually found a new doctor at the top of the hill on the Handsworth Road area. We transferred from Dr. Nelson and we now had a Dr. Shrivastava who was of Indian origin. **NO!** Not a Medicine Doctor Indian but one from India in the Far East. He was a little fat man and his manner was charming. He would also listen to what patients had to say and in my case, when I said I had been to India during the War, he was exceptionally nice. In later years it proved to be a good change.

In 1956 I decided to change my car again and this time I bought a black Morris Oxford which looked like the then modern day police car. The Austin I had was sold to Eric, Nip's brother at Thurcroft, for £100 but he only had it for some six months when due to an electrical fault, it burnt out in his garage. Nip and I were so sorry for him and I felt guilty that I had sold him a duff car but he said not to worry as this was one of those unavoidable incidents.

The new car was needed because Aline was expecting again and we had been so careful but not careful enough. On the 30th May 1956, she had another son and we named him David Michael, after Eva's two sons. It suited me because my Grandad Priestley was called David. Here we had another buster, whose weight at birth was just under 8 lbs.

For this birth, Aline said she would like her Mum to come over and take care of her and the baby, so that is what we did. It so happened that Aunty Amy wasn't available, so no ones' feelings were hurt.

Having a family could be expensive when it came to clothing the children but I had a wonderful wife who managed to reduce these costs by making most of the blouses, shirts, shorts etc., by herself. She was also a marvellous knitter and all the boys' jerseys were made by her own fair hands. At one stage she ended up by knitting special garments for the wool firm EMU.

It was in 1957 that we had a setback. The weather had been shocking in the early few months of the year and prior to the light nights coming in, I was driving home from work and it had been snowing heavily since mid afternoon. As I approached Handsworth church, I could see that the road was treacherous and changed down to a lower gear, ready to go down the hill. As I started to go down, I had made my mind up to keep to the crown of the road and not touch my brakes. I was passing Phillip's garage when I noticed that a lorry had skidded on the snow and had finished up being rammed tightly against a telegraph pole. My first thought was, keep to the middle of the road and even if I skid, I would slide past it.

No chance! I could feel the back wheels sliding towards the causeway edge but couldn't do anything about it. The back wheels hit the kerb first and then the front wheels slewed round into the same position. That was bad enough but the car then started to slip along the icy road and the next thing I saw was the car bonnet coming up towards the windscreen. Luckily, the movement was slow as the car went under the tailgate of the lorry jammed against the pole and although I wasn't hurt I was very shocked.

After sitting there for a few minutes to collect my thoughts, I left the car and decided to walk down home and tell Nip what had happened. She was very upset but pleased to see that I was alright. I had a hurricane lamp in the outhouse and decided to take it up to the crash and put it there to warn other motorists because the daylight had gone and it could be dangerous.

The accident happened just below the junction of Handsworth Road and Handsworth Grange Road but as I reached the corner, I had another shock. A second lorry had done the same as I had done and slid into the kerb and then carried on into the back end of my car and made a sandwich of crumpled metal. What a mess. The following day, Phillip's Garage towed me free and took me up to the Handsworth Motor Company for repairs. It took weeks to repair and cost the insurance company some £240 pounds.

We gradually overcame our misfortune and later on, around Whitsuntide, we arranged to take a holiday in Scarborough, it was David's first birthday and we found a good boarding house in Trafalgar Square on the north side of the town. Whilst we were there, we met a smashing young couple who hadn't been married for very long. They were from Bramley in Leeds and introduced themselves as Margaret and Dennis Eastall. We all palled on together and they took to the lads immediately. Denis was a motorcycle fanatic and had taken part in several road races. We all went one day up to Oliver's Mount race track to watch some races taking place and the lads were more than thrilled to watch the bikes whizzing past.

It's amazing how a little thing can cause so much distress. I was playing with the baby on the floor of the lounge at where we were staying and as he was lying on his back on the carpet, I playfully tried to pick him up by getting his clothing in between my teeth.

Unfortunately, I also grabbed some of his flesh under the clothing and he let out a terrible yell. Oh! He did cry. I was so upset at hurting him and Aline didn't mince words with me either. Margaret and Dennis were there at the time and they didn't look too pleased. One good thing was that I didn't break the skin on David's chest but it did leave a bruise and he soon calmed down.

We were down on the North Bay beach playing with the lads and watching Tony and Geoff build sand castles etc., when Nip told Tony to do something and she had to ask him twice. Because he was defiant, she scolded him and, in his temper, he threw his metal spade which hit David just below his eye and left a one inch cut. Another inch higher and the spade would have possibly blinded him.

That was it. I grabbed him and spanked his backside. Some people passing by said that I shouldn't hit a child like that. My comment was. "Keep that out." Pointing to my nose. "You didn't see why I did it." We enjoyed the rest of the holiday and one day took the lads to see the Warship Battle on the lake at Peasholme Park. At the end of the week we agreed to keep in touch with Margaret and Dennis when we arrived home.

It was around this time that the AEU (Amalgamated Engineering Union) called a strike which meant that most firms in Sheffield were forced to almost close down and this included F.V.'s. To keep part of the works operational, members of the staff took on responsibilities as did Ron Wainwright, the Works Manager. He climbed up and operated the overhead crane in the Foundry and charge hands and foremen did their bit whilst other people were asked to help. I was asked to drive the inter-departmental minibus which was responsible for carrying mail between Weedon Street and Firth Brown Laboratories and Workshops on Saville Street.

I was glad it was all over after two weeks because I never associated myself with being a blackleg.

After the holiday, we kept in touch with Margaret and Dennis and paid them a few visits to their house in Bramley in Leeds and though we didn't see them on a regular basis, we did keep contacting each other.

It was at the period when I wanted, once again, to change the car and this time I bought an Austin A55 which was a two-tone green, Registration JGK 804 and trying this time to make it last longer than any previous cars had done.

In October, Geoff started going to the same school as Tony and was made just as welcome by Miss Meredith. Prior to Geoff going to school we had noticed a slight cast in one eye and took him to see Dr. Shrivastava who recommended that we went to the Children's Hospital for advice. At the Hospital, they carried out various tests and part of the suggested treatment, was to set him up with a pair of spectacles and blank out the lens over the bad eye. This had the effect of pulling the affected eye back into a natural position. It was a success over a period but we hadn't realised that it would mean that Geoff would need to wear glasses for the rest of his life but we accepted the fact.

We had to watch him because, for a child so young, such things took some getting used to and he would often come into the house with them twisted or bent. In one instance, he had managed to get a piece of dirt on to one of the lens and tried to rub it off by holding his face near to a concrete gate post and trying to rub the dirt off by moving his head up and down. Obviously, this scratched the glass and we had to take him up to see Mr. Livesey who was the local chemist and also an optician. He was able to get the lens re-polished and adjust the frames to suit. Mr Livesey was so helpful that I decided to go to him when I needed an eye test or new spectacles.

In the back yard, at the bottom end of the garden, I had managed to make a small pond. It wasn't very big but large enough and deep enough to sail small yachts in and thus keep the lads entertained during sunny days. The pond was only about four inches deep and if the weather was suitable and warm, they would put on their trunks and go splashing about to keep cool.

As the boys grew up, Aline always insisted on a routine, whereby they all went to bed early but obviously this became more difficult as they became older. However, to save any arguments David was put to bed just after teatime at 6.00 p.m. and Geoff followed at 7.00 p.m.

Tony was allowed to stay up until eight o'clock to watch a little of the television program which suited him. T.V. had become a household must in 1953 when commercial television was introduced to the nation. David had a cot in the small bedroom and Tony, along with Geoff, had a single bed each in the large back bedroom. There were never any grumbles as they were told to go to bed and on a long term basis, this idea paid off..

Our summer holidays in 1958 were spent at Weston-super-Mare and having booked in advance we travelled down and found our accommodation to be a small boarding house. We had a large bedroom with a large double bed, a three-quarter bed, in which the two older lads slept and a cot for David. It wasn't luxurious but we made do and the dining room was more like a sitting room. At meal times, the bread was put onto the table in its wrapping paper, not on a plate as one would expect. Fancy cakes were rationed to one each.

The weather was kind to us and we were fortunate that the week we had chosen was the one for the National Milk Race in which scores of pedal cyclists took part from all over the world. Weston was one of the stages in the race and we all enjoyed watching the activities on the Promenade.

We had a good laugh one day, when down at the paddling and boat pool. David was playing in the water and we thought that there was something strange about him. When we looked closer, we could see that he was wearing his toy sunglasses upside down. All week he had them like that and no way could we persuade him to put them on correctly.

There was an upset one day when a load of hooligans came down from Bristol and created havoc in the streets. There were policemen everywhere and it was very frightening, especially for the children. However, we were fortunate not to get caught up in any of the disturbances.

By the end of the week we were glad to be leaving but, once again we had a laugh and in the first instance it wasn't humourus. As we were about to leave the boarding house, Nip asked the boys to make sure that we hadn't left anything behind, even under the beds. So, Geoff went under one of them and when he came out he was covered in fluff. It looked worse because he, along with Tony, was dressed in grey shorts and a navy blue blazer. The owner hadn't bothered to dust or sweep whilst we were out each day and Aline was fuming at the time. But like I said, on our way home, we saw the funny side of things and we had enjoyed the break.

At the end of summer term in 1958, Tony was transferred to Athelstan Junior School just off Richmond Park Road. The Headmaster there was a Mr. Thomas, who was a good, understanding but strict teacher. It made it awkward for Nip to take Tony to one school and Geoff to another so I agreed to take Tony in the car, on my way to work. This served two purposes because I could pick up Bill Scoley at the top end of Richmond Park Road and drop off Tony at the school at the same time. It was ideal, due to the fact that school commenced at 8.45 a.m, and I started work at 9.00 a.m. It just gave me time enough to do the journey to Garter Street.

At Christmas, 1958, my Dad had bought the obvious present for the lads now that they were a little older. It was a clockwork train set and on the Sunday after Christmas Day, Dad brought a railway friend, Len, and his wife to our house. His friend was a train driver with the LMS Company, so, guess what? He and Dad played with the train set on the big dining table. The kids didn't get a look in. I think that they were the 'Kids' and my Mum and Len's wife said that they ought to have had more sense.

The New Year,1959, saw Tony and Geoff settling down at school and the first indications were that they would do well. They both enjoyed going to school and when they came home we tried to help them in any way we could with regards to their education.

We carried on taking them out on picnics and day trips, sometimes by ourselves and sometimes with my Mum and Dad. We always had to have a watchful eye on them because some years ago when Tony was about three years old, we had gone out to Bradwell to see Aunty Edith and on the way back, Dad insisted that we called in at the Brough Inn at the junction of the road to Bradwell and the Castleton Road. We went and sat outside, after parking the car and Dad went to get the drinks. We had been sitting there for some twenty minutes when Dad reached to get his pint of beer. It wasn't where he had put it on the grass verge but looking round he saw Tony with the empty pint pot in his hand. The little devil had drunk the lot.. We couldn't stop laughing but on any future picnics we ALL kept our eyes open.

It was at a later date that we went out to picnic and Dad pointed out that if we pulled up on the A57 road near to Cutthroat Bridge, the lads would be able to paddle in the brook. This we did but my Dad, wanting to join in, took off his shoes and socks to join the lads. He kept telling them not to fall off the boulders and to be careful. ***Careful!*** Practise what you preach, Dad.

One minute he was O.K. The next minute he was sat in a pool of water. His trousers were soaked through but all we, or him, could do was laugh. The kids thought it was hilarious and it finished by putting a car blanket around him whilst his trousers dried in the wind after being tied to a road barrier railing.

In the Spring, I decided to change the car once more and this time I bought another Morris Oxford but this one was more spacious and was of the new design. It had a large boot and it was an evergreen colour with the registration YRC 980. This time we both agreed that it **HAD** to last quite a while before we thought of changing again because now that we had three children, money was a little tight.

Many firms in the Sheffield area would have inter-departmental football and cricket knockout matches and once at F.V's, when we had a staff team playing against the Foundry team, we had a real laugh. During the game, Jack Marriott was batting and scoring a few runs but at one point he hit the ball hard to mid-wicket and as he hit out, the bat flew from his hand and followed the ball. Not knowing the laws of cricket, Jack ran after the bat and was subsequently run out. Incidentally we lost the game which was played on the Atlas and Norfolk ground on Roe Lane.

Each year we tried to go to a different place for holidays to attempt to educate the lads about local geography etc., and this time we decided to take them into a rented caravan at Primrose Valley camp site, near to Filey.

Aline had been busy knitting again and this time she had made three identical jerseys for all three boys to wear on this holiday. The pattern was of stags and pine trees in fawn on a light green background and when the lads stood together they looked really smart and people would comment as they went past. I always said that my lass was clever. I used to say that she was the biggest 'knit' on the estate.

There were plenty of places to see on the East coast of Yorkshire and we took them to places like Filey Brigg, Sowerby Park, Bridlington and the best place was Flamboro' Head and a visit to the lighthouse. I think it was on this holiday that whilst at Sowerby Park we agreed to take them on the pitch and putt greens. There the lads could have a swipe at the balls and release some energy. However, I was so engrossed in the game that I hadn't noticed Nip doubled up behind me. At first I thought that she had hurt herself or was in pain but it turned out that nearly every time she tried to hit the ball, she missed. This caused her to start laughing and the more she missed, the more she laughed and the more she laughed she wet herself. We were all doubled up with laughing but felt very sorry for her. We eventually finished the game and made our way back to the caravan and after Nip had changed herself, we had half an hour in the amusement arcade..

This decade had been an eventful one in raising a family. We had both experienced various incidents with the children, with the different cars and being able to take part in my favourite sport, cricket and enjoy the ups and downs of the three boys. As the next ten years approached, little did I know of what was to be in the near future.

THE SIXTIES

So we entered the sixties with the usual carry on of a happy family, sometimes laughter and sometimes tears. It was on the way back from Thurcroft one Sunday that as we passed through the village of Whiston where I saw a small bicycle for sale. I stopped the car and Aline and I took a look at the bike and asked the shopkeeper how much the price was and he said it would be fifty shillings. Not having that amount on me, I left a deposit and said I would be back to collect it the following day.

I did collect the bike on the following evening and managed to get it into the car by taking the front wheel off the cycle. It was a good buy and Tony and Geoff would take it in turns to use it. It was a twenty-inch frame, Raleigh sit-up-and-beg model and after checking that everything on it was working efficiently and cleaning it up, the lads had many happy hours on it. Tony had settled at Athelstan School and Geoff had become a favourite of Miss Meredith at Handsworth School. David kept Aline busy at home because he was such a chubby bundle of action.

As Whitsuntide approached, we prepared for our holiday which we had booked in advance. I always took Whit Week as a holiday because by doing so I was able to 'steal' an extra three days holiday in lieu a little later on in the year. This year we had decided to go to Rhyl, which was in North Wales, and had booked at a rather large guest house. It was whilst we were there that we befriended one of the living in staff whose name was Margorie Fisher. She was really helpful to us and on her day off, she would spend it with us and the children on the beach. It was during this holiday that an incident occurred which was embarrassing but also funny.

At one of the meal times, we had all seated ourselves in the dining room at our designated table near to the wall. Nip, with David next to her and then Tony sitting on one side of the table, whilst Geoff and I sat at the other side.

The meal was put onto the table before us and as we prepared to eat, Geoff decided that he wanted some tomato ketchup on his food.

He reached over and took hold of the bottle and as we had taught him, he shook it to loosen the contents. Unfortunately, someone hadn't fastened the screw top on securely and as Geoff moved the bottle up and down, the top came off. There was ketchup all over. We and other guests were caught in it but the worst thing was that the main force had formed a huge crescent right across the wall. The dining room had recently been redecorated for the current season.

The other holiday makers were tittering whilst wiping themselves down and Aline and I didn't know where to put out faces, we were so embarrassed. The owners were furious at the mess and in apologising profusely, I offered to pay for any damage caused, but the offer was refused. The knives were out for us for the rest of the week, especially with the landlady. One crumb of comfort was that Margorie would come up to our room to console us but also have a laugh. Margorie was a lovely girl and for ages she kept in contact with by us writing regularly.

A short while after returning from holiday, I was collecting my morning paper from the local newsagents' when a chap approached me and asked if I worked on Garter Street. Having satisfied his curiosity, he informed me that he was the Rolling Mill Manager at Firth Brown's on Carlisle Street and his name was Ben Wilkinson and he lived at the end of Ballifield Drive which was quite close to me. He had seen me in the Carlisle Street area and then in the conversation he asked if I would be good enough to pick him up each morning and evening, for which he would willingly contribute towards the petrol. This we agreed upon and after a little while we became friends but not bosom pals. His office hours were the same as mine and the arrangement suited him down to the ground.

Things became very unpleasant at work - that is, with regards to AET bossing everyone about and thinking that he was the only one right each time something occurred. He was a pain in the arse and just after 'shut down' holidays in August, he called me into his office, along with Ron Wainwright. NOW! AET had a nasty habit of speaking to someone and looking at another person at the same time. This occasion was one of them. He rambled on about some cost figures and looked at Ron Wainwright and said, "Now, Ron, I would like those figures on my desk by 10.00 am tomorrow morning. Right? Then off you go."

So myself and Ron left his office and went about our normal duties. The following morning I was sitting at my desk when AET came barging in and bellowed right down the office.

"Ron, where are those figures I asked for yesterday?" I looked up "Figures?" I queried. "You didn't ask me for any figures."

AET. "Oh! yes I bloody well did." Me. "Oh! no you bloody well didn't."

There was a deadly hush in the office and AET stormed out. I realised what had happened the previous day. He had addressed me but looked straight at Ron Wainwright. Off I went to Ron's office and explained. He started laughing and said,"No. Not again. He's always doing that."

I felt relieved and he continued, "Leave it to me. I'll go and explain it to AET. By the way, how long will it take to produce the figures?"

I told him half an hour and we agreed to take them in together to AET as soon as they were ready. This we did but AET was in one of those moods and having partly apologised for the misunderstanding previously, he suddenly turned to me and said, "I could get a girl of fifteen to do your job."

That did it. "Well bloody well get one because I'm leaving." I stormed out and Ron Wainwright followed me and begged and prayed of me to calm down. "No chance, Ron" I told him. I was so infuriated.

Because things seemed to be coming to a head I had taken precautions of insuring myself by looking for another position elsewhere by looking in the local press and this had paid off because during the two weeks' notice I was serving. I had the good fortune to get an interview at Tinsley Wire Industries Ltd., on Sheffield Road at Tinsley.

I had received one interview with a Mr Leslie Potts, who was the assistant Sales Manager, on the 13th September and he had written on the 19th, a few days later asking me to go for a further interview on a short list of three other applicants. This time a Mr D.A.Bonaker, the Sales Manager interviewed me and he asked me how I was able to get people to work for me and my answer was.

"I ask them to do something."

"What if they don't do it?" asked Mr Bonaker."Then I tell them to do it." was my reply

"And if they still don't want to do what you ask?" he carried on.

"Then you will tell them." Was my final comment.

That must have persuaded him to employ me because the following day, the 23/9/1960 I was offered the post of Senior Pricing clerk at the salary of £14/10/0 per week

Mr Casson at Firth Vickers, accepted my notice with reluctance but I had worked it out that I wouldn't be paying 30/- shillings a week towards my pension and although the TWIL offer was only 2/6d a week more, overall, I would be £1/12/6 per week to the good because the TWIL pension scheme was non-contributory.

So it was that I left F.V's on the 7th October, 1960 with a leaving present from my workmates in the shape of some bathroom scales. I was sorry to leave some good friends behind but I couldn't stay any longer under that man AET. Looking at things in perspective, it had been a pleasant and enlightening decade but during that time I had taken a terrific dislike to two people and Mr Alfred Thornton was both of them.

October the 8th was one of those historical days to the point that each year, when the children were little, we tried to celebrate it with a birthday party for them. On this particular one, not only was it Geoff's 8th birthday but also the day when the last tramcar was to run in Sheffield. The route chosen was the one which ran from Millhouses, through the town, down past the East End and then to the Tinsley tram sheds from where it would eventually be sold to T.W. Ward's for scrap.

To mark the occasion and as a special treat for Geoff's birthday, I bundled our three lads and Geoff's pals, who had come to the party, into my car and along with Aline, I took them down onto Attercliffe Common. From opposite the Globe Cinema, we saw the tram, No.510, coming from town with its blue and cream livery, and the driver clanging his warning bell near to his foot, to let everyone know that the tram was coming. There was quite a number of people lining the route as it went past and many older people took this to be the end of an era when persons could move about easily from one part of the town to another for the full fare of three pence. We were supposed to be moving with the times - or were we? As a note of interest, the last service tram was No. 222 and ran from Millhouses to the Queen's Road Depot.

On the 11th October, I made my appearance at Tinsley Wire Industries Ltd. The office block was part of the factory and was situated on Sheffield Road just past the Tinsley tram depot at Weedon Street.

I was shown into an office upstairs in which there were several other clerks. Most of the desks were against the outside walls and under the windows for natural light. I had the second desk, with a young man from Grindleford in Derbyshire, namely Roger Mount sitting behind me. The next desk up the office had Arnold Marshall at it and he was responsible for the agricultural sales. Next came Peter Miall who was a pricing clerk and also a lay preacher. He was in his early thirties.

We also had two junior clerks who were both called Michael. One of their names was Dickinson but the other one's name slips my memory at this point. Across the corridor there was a Miss Lilian Weightman who checked all outgoing invoices for any typing errors. She was a bit sharp with people which was possibly because she was a spinster in her late forties. To complete the set-up, also across the corridor, there was the typing pool of some six girls and a supervisor, all of which I was responsible for.

Next door to the pricing department, my department, there was a smaller office in which two gentlemen worked in conjunction with my office. One was Alan Pears, who was to teach me how to use the firm's pricing book and the other person was Roger Farris. He was the Chairman's son and he too, took me under his wing.

In the lower part of the building, underneath the works' canteen, there was a staff dining room in which we received some good meals and drinks facilities. All this was controlled by a Miss Montague, another frustrated spinster who thought highly of herself. It was laughable at times to watch her bringing Mr Bonaker some refreshments or other and bowing and scraping to him as though she was going to be **pleased** at the first opportunity. To finish the office compliment there were two offices further along the corridor and on either side of same. In these were the Export staff under the guidance of Mr Louis Jaques with his second in command, Ray Towers.

Just beyond them was Mr Bonaker's office and across was Mr Potts office with an adjoining room for their secretaries, one of whom was Mrs Barbara Winskill. She was a lovely person and in her late twenties and the other was a small, red headed teenager, Pauline Wood.

That was the compliment of the whole of the Sales staff and there I leave it to settle down and try to learn all about my new position.

It was interesting work and during my education of the job, I was shown around the factory to see how wire was drawn from steel rods. Also how wire products such as wire netting was woven, barbed wire was produced and other wire products used in the agriculture and electrical industries. It was around this time that TWIL had invented a product called Welded Mesh which was composed of many designs of rectangular patterns from a small mesh of half an inch to sizes of four inches and was sold in rolls or panels. Russia had just placed an order with TWIL for the same product in hundreds of tonnes.

The weekend before I commenced at TWIL, Dad had been out for a social evening with Aunty Amy, his sister, and Bill Kelsey, her husband. When Dad told them that I was starting at TWIL.

Bill said it was marvellous and he had worked there for over twenty years and was now a charge hand in the Die Shop. He mentioned that TWIL was a 'nobbing shop'. In other words, what you received, you earned.

I realised that as I was learning to price orders, I wondered at one stage if I had made the right move because it seemed so difficult. However, Alan Pears and Roger Farris assured me that one day everything would suddenly fall into place. It did, but it took a few months for it to happen. I didn't drop any 'clangers' because every price was doubled checked on all invoices.

As the first Christmas at TWIL approached, I was informed that if I had any children, they would be able to attend a free party in the Works' canteen. Tony and Geoff were of the required age so I took them down on the named evening and like many other parents who took their children, I left them in the capable hands of Sport Club officials who were under the supervision of George French, the Transport Foreman.. The lads had a wonderful time with refreshments, ice cream, a concert and to finish off, Father Christmas gave each child a present of very good value. Around nine o'clock, we parents went back to collect the kids. It was such a wonderful night for them all.

As the New Year began, I became more settled in my new position but it was a while before I reconciled myself to returning to Saturday morning working, even though everyone had the third Saturday free. It was as convenient as when I was at F.V's because I was able to call and see Mum and Dad to keep them in touch with things.

Once I had settled in, Roger Mount asked me if I cared to go for a drink during the lunch break which was of fifty minutes and this I did by going to the Tinsley Hotel where we had a small drink and a game of darts. The Hotel was rather small but convenient, because it was at the bottom of Lock House Lane on which stood part of the factory.

It was through Roger that I learned of the Sports Club facilities. The sports ground was through the factory and on the other side of the South Yorkshire Navigation Canal. There was a sports hut which wasn't up to high standards and here some people practised archery. There was also a football field and a cricket pitch which had once belonged to Wm. Cook and Co Ltd who had been bought out by TWIL.

It was during the summer that I played for the staff in the works K.O. competition and for the first time in my cricketing career I took a hat-trick in which all the batsmen were clean bowled. I felt over the moon until one of the unofficial umpires said he had never seen such rubbish bowling. There is a saying in cricket. It is, "A bad ball never took a wicket." I leave you to work that one out.

When I first started at TWIL, I was able to park my car at the top end of the works' yard but as more people acquired cars it was decided that all ordinary work people and staff must park their cars on the waste ground, across the canal just behind the Sports Hut. It made it inconvenient with regards to taking a good five minutes to park in a morning and collect it at night. However, we did have the privilege of being able to leave and enter the firm by an entrance on Shepcote Lane.

December 1960 saw a new interest for Tony because he joined the Boys Brigade at the Handsworth Methodist Chapel on Handsworth Road under the Captaincy of Mr. Bowers. The Company was very strong with some thirty boys in it and at that particular time the Company had the best bugle band in the Sheffield Battalion. I was more than pleased that he had joined because the number of the Company the 14th, was the same as the one which I used to be in many years ago at the Bodmin Street Baptist Chapel as a Life Boy. Tony and Geoff had been attending Sunday School at the chapel for quite a while and had been informed that they were eligible to join the B.B. when they were eleven years of age.

To compensate for Geoff being two years younger than Tony, he joined the Life Boys organisation which was the junior section of the B.B. and he could join at the age of nine and prepare for the time when he could join the senior section. The Life Boys were under the supervision of Mr. Slack and one good thing about this organisation was that the Parade night finished at 9.00 pm and took place every Friday night.

In the Spring of 1961, I played my first game of cricket for the TWIL team in the Sheffield Works' League on a ground on Limb Lane at Dore. All the players were new to me and the Captain was Ken Taylor who worked in the factory. When it was our turn to field, we had a reasonable start and we contained the opposition quite well. However, after half an hour, Ken threw the ball to me and told me to bowl from the bottom end of the wicket. Ten overs later I had taken five wickets for thirty one runs. The first wicket was a caught and bowled by me and my hands were stinging because the ball was struck very hard by the batsman and I caught it at ankle height. It was a screamer.

A few weeks later, some of the players asked me if I would like to go to the 'nets' at Bramall Lane where Sheffield United played both football and cricket. I took this as an honour to go to the 'nets' but I soon regretted it.

No one had warned me that because the 'nets' were indoors, the ball would swing in the enclosed atmosphere. I took my stance at the wicket and one of our bowlers, Charlie Burke, ran up and bowled a fast delivery. I thought that it was going down the leg side and moved across the wicket to let it go by. **NEVER!** It swung in and hit me on the left ankle just behind the pad and it really hurt. I naturally rubbed it and tried to carry on but I couldn't because of the pain.

Unfortunately, I had to drive back home and how I made it I don't know because every time I touched the clutch to change gear, a pain ran up my leg. On getting home, Aline helped me to bathe it but it still hurt. The following morning I had it X-rayed but there was no fracture but severe bruising, which made it impossible to go to work, in fact, I couldn't go for a further two weeks.

As Bill Kelsey had said earlier, TWIL was a 'knobbing shop' and you earned what you received. When I rang in to tell them what had happened, Mr. Potts asked if I would be able to do some work at home and I agreed. For those two weeks, I had delivered to my home, two car boot loads full of box files and I went through hundreds of invoices to analyse prices. Eventually the ankle healed and I was able to return to normal duties but I must stress that Mr. Potts was grateful for what I had done whilst off work.

The Works Manager here was a Peter Morecroft of whom I disliked at first because he was so blustering and always speaking bluntly and loudly but as time went by I became accustomed to him and took any comments with a pinch of salt. He was a few years younger than me but efficient in his job.

Being rather new to people it wasn't long before I had a run-in with the typing pool staff where Sandra, one of the girls, objected to my criticising her work and being a little fiery she retorted, "If you can do any better then get on with it?"

I had to chuckle. I sat down at her desk and fed an invoice into her typewriter and typed in the details, luckily with no errors.. "There you are, Sandra, OK?" She looked at me bewildered. From then on all the girls accepted my judgements and everything ran smoothly.

For a holiday this year we decided to go to Primrose Valley Holiday Camp once more for a week and as I said before, I always tried to give the lads a break, plus of course, their Mum, who worked so hard at home to look after us all.

The rest of the year passed quickly and as we entered 1962, little did I realise what was in store. I did, however, become proficient and confident in my new work and everything seemed to be running smoothly until Aline said that she was pregnant again.

We hadn't really wanted this but things do happen and Nip let it pray on her mind which didn't help when complications set in. She kept visiting Dr. Shrivastava and he helped as much as he could but eventually she was admitted into the Northern General Hospital. For a couple of weeks it was chaos with me trying to get the kids to school, going to work and paying her visits.

It was during this period that I was forced to try and do some baking and when I took her a blackberry and apple pie, which I had made from fruit in the garden, up to the hospital she couldn't believe it and other patients in the Ward asked me to make another because they had all had a piece and enjoyed it. At the end of the second week the doctors discharged her but asked her to attend the clinic each week for a checkup. Nip resigned herself to the fact that there was to be another addition to the family and really tried to settle down.

Whilst she was in that ward there was another patient called Mrs. Childs who was in the next bed to Aline and she was from the top end of our estate so they had plenty to talk about. Also, there was another young woman in there who was the wife of Derek Ibbotson, the under-four minute miler and Olympic runner.

For a few months, things got back to normal until one Friday night when I had to go out to a social engagement (which I will explain at a later stage) and this meant that I would be away all night.

I arrived home at six o'clock the following morning and quietly let my self in so that I wouldn't wake anyone. I crept upstairs and entered the bedroom. **My God! What a shock.**

There was Aline lying in a blood covered bed with everything soaked in it. She was in pain and sobbing loudly. "Come on, Luv" I said and putting my arms around her , I continued. "Whatever has happened?" Nip replied. "I don't know. You had better call the Doctor."

This I did and in a short space of time Dr. Shriv arrived and after examining her, he arranged for her to go back to hospital. The lads had awakened and keeping them out of sight of their Mum I told them that she was ill and would have to go back into hospital. I told Nip that I would be up at the hospital as soon as I'd sorted something out for the lads. After the ambulance left, I got changed and gave the boys some breakfast and took them in the car, down to Mum and Dad.

Having explained to them , my parents, what had happened, I went back home by myself to clear away the mess and then made my way to the Northern General in the afternoon wondering what I was going to find.

This time they had put Aline into Ward 10 and she looked a little brighter when I arrived. I tried to cheer her up by asking her if she thought that she was on the Tele because one of the popular programs was called 'Emergency Ward 10' and was all about hospital life. She smiled a little but she wasn't well.

"Where are the lads?" She asked. I replied. "Now don't you worry about them. I've made plans to cope with them." I stayed with her until teatime and then returned to Mum's to collect the boys.

It so happened that the summer holidays were approaching and during the past few months Tony had been sitting his exams for the Eleven plus. I had contacted all of Aline's side of the family and Eva, at Wakefield, said she would have Tony during the school holidays. Joan at Thurcroft, had agreed to have Geoff, and David was to stay, during the daytime, with my Mum and Dad and I would collect him in the evenings after visiting Aline.

Recently, at work, one of our Reps had been taken off the Road to come in and be General Admin Manager for the offices. He was John Roberts, who was a very pleasant person and my immediate supervisor. When I had explained to him what the situation was at home, he immediately said. "I don't want to see you before ten o'clock in the morning or after four o'clock in the afternoon." How kind and thoughtful. It was wonderful because I was able to carry on taking David to Mums' in the morning and pick him up later on.

After a few weeks I received permission to take David into the Ward to see his Mum and this cheered her up immensely, especially when on one visit, as I was talking to her, I could see the bottom of her bed slowly rising. When I looked to see what was happening, there was little David slowly turning the handle at the foot of the bed and this caused the bed to rise. We had to laugh as he began winding the bed back to its normal position.

Everything seemed to be happening at the same time because whilst all this was going on with Aline in hospital, the Sheffield City Council had decided to remove all the back boilers and kitchen ovens which were heated from the fire in the living room grate. It meant that the kitchen had to be cleared of furniture etc., and the food in the pantry covered up from the dust because of the dismantling of the oven and half of the kitchen wall having to be knocked out.

I was wondering where I was going to find the time to clear up after the workmen had finished but there is always a helping hand somewhere. This one belonged to Mrs Bette Jackson who was one of our neighbours who lived over the back garden. I had left a key with her and when I finally arrived home from work, Bette was on her hands and knees scrubbing the kitchen floor which was the last cleaning job she needed to do to complete her task. Oh! I was grateful for everything she had done. It pleased Aline too, when I told her.

I had other help from Maureen Matthews, our baby sitter. She had now grown up and was herself, married to a David Donnison and lived quite close by. Maureen would often pop in to see how Aline was and if needs be she would do little jobs like making the beds for me or dusting around the house. She was a little treasure.

Aline stayed in hospital for some two months or more and at one stage the doctors seemed confident that Nip and the baby would be alright and in herself she seemed to be more cheerful. We even thought that the baby would be born on Aline's birthday, just like Tony was.

As each day grew nearer, I would ring the Ward to check that everything was OK but on the 6th September, 1962, I received bad news. The hospital staff asked me to get up there as soon as possible and this I did but upon entering the Ward, I knew that something was wrong, terribly wrong as I approached the bedside.

Nip was in a sorry state and crying heavily. As I arrived at the bedside, she looked up and greeted me with, "I've lost the baby." I tried to comfort her but I too was in tears. At least I hadn't lost her. The awful thing was, apart from it being just before her birthday, the baby had been a little girl and this didn't help matters.

After a further week in hospital, I was able to have Nip home again but I had to bring a bed downstairs into the living room until she overcame the trauma and pain. As she slowly recovered, she unfolded to me that the doctor had done all that he could and the main trouble had been that somehow the baby was twisted inside her womb as it was born. The doctor had decided that it wouldn't be worth while to let it survive because he was sure it would be deformed for the rest of its life.

This is what had made Aline feel so ill, especially when at last we had a girl, but not to keep. We had agreed to call the baby, if a girl, Alison Margaret and this is what we announced in the obituaries when she was buried on the 8th September, privately by the B&C Co-op straight from the hospital. I never saw Alison but Aline did get a glimpse of her and the memory stayed with Nip for a long time.

If there was any relief from all this upset, then it was on the 11th September when Tony was to start at his new school, the Firth Park Grammar School. It had been way back in June when we had been informed that he had passed the Eleven Plus examinations and had qualified to go to this Grammar School which was known as the 'Blood Nut School' because of the crimson blazers and caps the pupils wore.

When we first learned of his success, both Aline and I had taken him into town to get him rigged out with the necessary uniform and sports clothing he needed, such as white shirts, shorts and plimsolls. I remember the day very well when we received the news because I called in, on my way to work, to tell Mum and Dad the good news. Dad was resting in bed but Mum said to go up and tell him. When I did, we were both full of the tears of joy and very proud of what Tony had achieved.

Slowly but surely, Aline began to come to terms with what had happened and as Christmas approached, she was well enough for me to take the bed back up the stairs by the end of October. We had the lads back home and each one of them did their best to be good for her and help us both.

Patience was needed by me to help Nip fully recover from the loss and it did take quite a time before she started to relax and settle down to normal routines. We talked things over and decided that when we did fully get back to marital relations, steps must be taken along with precautions, to avoid another incident like the one just passed.

Nip attended a post natal clinic in Orchard Lane in town and they suggested that when she was able to carry on as normal, she should use a 'Dutch Cap' to prevent further pregnancies. However, at times, she found it cumbersome and many times, inconvenient, so to give her peace of mind, I commenced to regularly use rubber sheaths, (known today as Condoms), but even this didn't fully suit her and there were occasions when Nip would outwardly reject me. I must admit, that it did unsettle me and sometimes I became frustrated but my love for this grand lass, helped me to co-operate with her as much as I could.

1963 arrived and as time went by, Aline returned to 90% fitness and before long we were planning for another holiday. This time we decided to rent a caravan at Mablethorpe and the lads looked forward to going to somewhere where they hadn't been before - except for Tony, but he wouldn't remember when he was there as a toddler.

We settled in at the caravan and one night, in the middle of the week, we had all retired to bed after spending a day on the beach, and had just made ourselves comfortable for the night when there was a loud bang. I jumped out of bed, grabbed a torch and cautiously went outside of the caravan to see what was amiss but I couldn't see anyone or anything.

We finally settled down again and managed to go to sleep. It was when we came to get up the following morning, that we found the cause of the bang. In this caravan, the double bed, in which Aline and I slept, was a drop-down bed and when it had to be used, it was lowered from an alcove in the wall and fastened down to the floor by an attached hook and spring.

What had happened the night before was that for some unknown reason, as we moved about in the bed, the fastening ring in the floor, was stupidly screwed into a knot in the wooden floor. Through constant use, the knot had worked loose from the knot hole and banged against the bottom of the bed. We laughed afterwards because we had visions of the bed folding up with Nip and myself inside it and upside down. It really amused the lads

During the holiday, we went onto the beach one day and decided to see how far it stretched because the sands here were wide open and went as far as the eye could see. So we started walking at a leisurely pace, splashing in the sea, barefooted and playing about generally with the boys. We must have walked about two miles before we saw a large, wooden tower on the edge of the shore and shaped like a pyramid on stilts.

Up to it we went and became interested in some spent bomb casings that were lying about in the sand. The lads were fascinated as much as I was and just as we were starting to examine one we heard a loud hailer. "Come away from that area immediately." We heard the cry. Looking up and towards the place from where the message was coming, we saw a Royal Air Force lorry, with armed guards in it and they were coming towards us.

An NCO jumped down and approached us and told us that we were in a prohibited danger area and having been in the RAF, I asked him where the warning signs were.

"Over there." He said and pointed towards the sand dunes from where the lorry had come. "They aren't much use over there if people approach from the beach which is five hundred yards away, are they?" I asked.

He saw the point and offered to give all of us a lift back to the safety of the sand dunes. The area was a target zone for practise bombing runs and the place was called Donna Nook. Later on you will see the significance of it all.

We finished our holiday and returned home at the end of the week after a rather eventful time.

All through the year I helped Aline to take things easy in order for her to recuperate from her ordeal and apart from the holiday we stayed at home relaxing and I spent some time doing various jobs in the garden.

Just after Geoff's eleventh birthday, the 16th October, to be exact, he was transferred from the Life Boys into the senior section of the organisation which was the Boys Brigade. He soon settled down and being alongside Tony, it helped him to take an interest in such things as First Aid, Art and Craft, Signalling and Discipline

Towards the end of the summer, a new office block had been completed, over on Shepcote Lane on the other side of the canal and factory. Not all staff were moved over immediately but the Sales staff did, along with the accounts and cost offices. The building was a two storey one and very spacious. I was situated up stairs with the Pricing section which was put at the end of an open planned office over-looking a new canteen and we also had a good view of Wincobank Hill and the East End Steel works. My section included Roger Mount, Peter Miall, Michael Dickinson and Miss Weightman.

Arnold Marshall moved into the main section as agricultural wire organiser and Alan Pears and Roger Farris were at the other end of the office to me, in charge of industrial wire products.

Through the door at that other end was Mr Potts, Mr. Bonaker and the two secretaries, Mrs. Winskill and Pauline and beyond them were the Directors offices. The office block was square shaped with a vacant area and garden seats under a few trees in the middle of it all. The accounts staff under the direction of Mr. Harry Kershaw and Mr. Len Brown, the Chief Cashier, were on the ground floor near to the back entrance. In the front of the building was the main reception, switchboard and post rooms with a side room for interviewing visitors.

The move across from Sheffield Road made it more convenient for me to get to and from work because I could approach it from the Darnall area and turn right, down Shepcote Lane, instead of having to travel along Greenland Road and Broughton Lane to get to the entrance on Sheffield Road.

Christmas approached and the lads were invited to another works' party and this time David was able to go whilst Tony went to a pantomime at the Playhouse Theatre which was in town.

The older children like him were treated as too old for a kids party but old enough to appreciate a more adult entertainment.

I asked Aline what she would like for Christmas and she said a new washer would be nice because of the amount of shirts she had to wash and iron for the lads and myself. On Christmas morning, Nip took hold of a woollen sock I had filled for her. It was the old fashioned way of doing things at this festive season and I had put an apple, orange and nuts in it, a small box of chocolates and some silver coins for luck. As she reached the bottom of the sock she felt a piece of stiff paper.

"What's this?" She queried and pulled it out. It was a luggage label and on it I had written. "Merry Christmas, Luv." Attached to it was a new steel, metal washer. "You Buggar!" She said and took it in the spirit it was meant. Shortly after Christmas, Nip received her new clothes washer. It was because of pranks like this and such like that we were a very happy family.

1964 was to herald a new era in my life because a few months after moving over to the new office block, Roger Farris approached me and asked if would like to help him set up a new Data Processing Department on the ground floor. Having been given time to think about it I talked it over with Aline and she gave her support and told me to accept the offer. When I told Roger I would be willing to take part in the venture he asked me to carry on with what I was doing until arrangements had been finally settled.

I had been asked to take on this task because on my CV when I applied for the position at TWIL, I had mentioned that I had some knowledge of punched cards and the Hollerith System when I was working at Davy United's in the thirties.

In the meantime, Mr. Roberts had agreed to employ another clerk to help with the pricing of invoices. When the new chap arrived, everyone in the office had a grin on their face. The young man was about eighteen years of age and when he arrived he came smartly dressed in a navy blue suit, which was a good start. However, his other dress sense, as he entered the office, was a trilby hat, which sat upright upon his head; thick rimmed specs, which were necessary but the final touch was that he was carrying an umbrella and raincoat over his arm.

My immediate thought was - Harry Worth - a popular TV comedian. His training tried my patience because he seemed to work kek handed. That is, he reached over to turn pages on his right hand side with his left hand and wrote any details with his right hand, on paper which was on his left hand side. You work it out.

I told him one afternoon to go and see Mr. Ken Tupling, in the accounts department and ask for a long rest so that I could open the window above my desk. Off he went and I rang Ken to put him in the picture. Once this John, as he was called, arrived at Ken's desk, he was told to sit on a spare chair and Ken carried on working. This went on for an hour before I rang Ken and asked him to send John back to us. When John arrived, he had the long rest with him and this was a pole with a hook on the end with which to open windows.

"Go on, John, open the window." I said. He put the hook through the loop at the top of the window and pulled and pulled and pulled. Nothing happened. "Give it here!" I said As I put the hook into the loop, I knocked off the window catch which held the window tight. Incidentally the loop at the top of the window was attached to the frame and not the window, so it would never work. I pulled the pole, nudged the window open with my elbow and we had fresh air.

"Now, John, try again." But as I handed him the pole, I quietly fastened the window catch without him seeing it. The more he tried, the more he failed and it finished up with all the staff in hysterics. John Roberts had popped in and seen what was happening. He called me over, "Come on Ron, you've had your fun." He left the office with a huge smile on his face.

Around Spring time I was transferred downstairs into a large office which was occupied with the Cost Office staff but in the small outer offices was Roger Farris, in the corner one was Mike Sara, a management trainee and a programmer called Bill Wass. A new Data Processing Manager had been appointed to oversee the department and he was a Scotsman named Mr. Adamson. He was quite a nice guy and he seemed well organised. Unfortunately his wife couldn't settle in Sheffield so as suddenly as he had joined us, so he left us.

Included in the setup were two young women who worked in the Accounts Department and were the first punched card operators to be used by our department. They punched details into the cards and these were sent to United Steels Ltd., on Glossop Road to be processed through the Tabulator Systems of ICL, which is the International Tabulating Co.

As the year wore on, two more programmers were employed and they were Bob Little, who commenced in October and Geoff Wright, who started a few months later. It wasn't long before some 'wag' worked out a compilation of the programmer's surnames. "Little, Sara, Wass, Wright."

Having settled into my new position in the Data Processing Dept., I was just beginning to enjoy it when tragedy hit the family once more. Aline's Dad had been feeling unwell for quite awhile and it appeared that his many years of working at the 'pit', was beginning to get to him. He hadn't had much retirement when he became worse and Nanny Todd called in the Doctor but he slowly became worse. I would run Aline over to see him as much as I could because there weren't many personal phones about in those days and any communication was by writing or travelling.

It was on the 5th March, 1964 that Joe Todd passed away. He had been a strict father but a good one and if any of his kids misbehaved, he would threaten them with a metal two foot ruler. Even grandchildren, as they came along, would be threatened with the 'two-foot', which was always kept on the mantle piece in the kitchen. I can't recall him ever using it, only to pretend to reach for it and the threat always worked.

It was in June that a further family problem arose. My Dad had suffered with his Angina for a number of years and a Specialist had told me at one of Dad's examinations, that if he, my Dad, took it easy, there was a possibility that he could outlive me. This had gone on for some time and in one instance when I called at no. 87, he was so ill that Mum had called the local Priest to give him the last rights. But he survived and was still reluctant to slow down, with the result that he had to go to hospital for further checkups. He was admitted to the Princess Elizabeth Ward at the Royal Infirmary for ten days and it didn't help when he said that he was afraid of not living as long as his mother, Granny Priestley, who had died of Cancer of the Liver when she was fifty seven and Dad was just approaching that age.

It took us a while to talk him round to thinking on the positive side and even though the hospital staff had said that he had an enlarged heart, there was no reason to think other than he would carry on for some time yet. He was discharged from hospital and did carry on as normal but was kept under strict medication by Dr. Wainwright, his local GP.

Things seemed to be looking up socially until later on in the summer. I was playing cricket on a ground near to Dropping Well Lane, which is part of Wincobank, and Mum and Dad had agreed to have David for the afternoon and then bring him up to the match after tea. Aline and the other two lads, Tony and Geoff, went with me in the car to the ground.

The game had almost finished when Mum, Dad and David arrived, having steadily walked from the Wincobank bus stop which was about a mile away. The last couple of hundred yards to the ground was uphill all the way which made Dad a little short of breath by the time they arrived. However, by the time I had changed, they had rested and so we filled the car with all of us and as we set off for home, Dad, as usual, suggested that we call in for a drink at the Blackburn Hotel, which was just down the road. It had been a lovely sunny day and quite warm, so I parked the car and we all sat outside whilst Dad and I went for some refreshments.

It must have been about 8.00 pm when we decided to leave for home and as usual, Esther, my Mum, must 'pay a call' at the loo.

She must have been gone for some ten minutes when Aline and I thought that we had better go and look for her. When we went back into the pub we found the manager of the pub with my Mum who was sitting on a chair. He said that she had fallen down the small step leading from the toilets and he had helped her onto the chair. Unknown to us, he had rung for an ambulance which, because the Hotel was just inside the Rotherham boundary, had to come from the Rotherham District.

When the ambulance arrived, the attendant examined Mum and said he thought that she might have fractured her hip. We followed the ambulance to the hospital in Doncaster Gate and after waiting, for what seemed an eternity, we were told that Mum had, in fact, broken her hip and they would keep her in and operate tomorrow.

We took Dad home to No. 87 and said we would pick him up the following afternoon when we knew the operation had taken place and we finally arrived at our house about ten o'clock at night. The following day I rang the hospital from a call box but it wasn't until the evening that I was able to pick Dad up and go to the hospital to see how Mum was.

Nip had stayed at home with the lads but when Dad and I arrived at the hospital we found her in bed with her leg in traction because this was necessary after such an operation. Before we left we had to see the police because the accident had happened in a public place. It was suggested that we put in a claim to the brewery because of insufficient lighting in the pub and the step, down which she had tumbled, wasn't painted white to indicate that it was there. Later, Dad put it into the hands of a solicitor, Mr. Keeble-Hawson.

A few weeks later, Mum was moved to an annexe of the hospital to recuperate and this was at Rosehill which was just beyond Rawmarsh. She was there for a long time but I managed to keep taking Dad to visit her and sometimes we would take the kids to see her, hoping it would cheer her up.

Unfortunately, from the day it happened, Mum complained because the operation hadn't taken place in Sheffield. Eventually she was discharged and came home but from then on, it was unbearable, with insinuations that the Rotherham staff were useless. I know one thing and that is, the constant travelling to and from Rosehill amounted to some five hundred miles but having said that, it was the least I could do, especially for Dad's sake.

Whilst all this had been going on, we had some relief in the fact that our Geoff had sat his eleven plus exams and had been successful. His marks weren't as high as Tony's had been, so therefore he had been recommended to go to Rowlinson's Technical School which was on the South side of the city. We kitted him out with a navy blue blazer, cap and grey socks, which was the standard uniform but with regards to travelling, it meant him catching a special service bus at 7.45 am so that he could get to school for 9.00 am.

The Headmaster there was a Peter Dixon with whom I had several meetings when attending the Parent Teachers Association. It upset Geoff to think that his pass standard wasn't as high as Tony's had been but we explained to him there wasn't any criteria with regards to standards and Aline and I were just as pleased with him as we had been with Tony. It was to be proved in later years, that academically, Geoff was more intelligent then his two brothers.

Back at Tinsley Wire, a works magazine was produced bi-monthly and any employee could contribute to it and in this particular issue, an article, or should I say cartoon, was accepted and printed. It had been submitted by Jack Parkin, you know, the chap who had been on holiday with me in Northern Ireland in the forties. He now worked for TWIL in the Sales office. It so happened that very shortly after we moved into the new office block, several of the female staff, some married, some not, became pregnant. Why, we know not, even though I recieved a few bland looks. However, the cartoon depicted the office block with the Stork in full flight over it, carrying a baby.

As the holiday period arrived, we decided to go to Scotland and try a holiday at Castle Douglas in Dumfrieshire. I had written earlier, to a boarding house for accommodation but at the last moment, the lady had to refuse us because of ill health but rather than let us down, she had arranged for us to stay at a farm about two miles away. The farm was called 'Ballyfield' and was owned by Mr and Mrs Hannah.

The journey from Sheffield took some six hours because we did have one or two breaks on the way to stretch our legs and to change over for Aline to drive and give me a rest.

Although I had planned the route, the place had to be found and after arriving in Castle Douglas, we still had to ask directions. We were told to take a 'B' road for another mile and a half before we finally found the entrance to the farm. As we turned into the gateway, we wondered what we had let ourselves in for because it was a typical cart track up to the farmhouse with rucks in it where tractors etc., had travelled up and down. We parked outside the front door and I then went up the few steps and knocked on the front door.

A lady came and answered it and the welcome was a true Scottish one. As we entered, Aline looked at me and smiled in approval. The hallway was highly polished and in the old saying, "One could have eaten off the floor" Mrs Hannah, the hostess, showed us to our bed room, which was down stairs and that too was immaculate. When she took us upstairs into the boys' bedroom, she showed them a cupboard which was full of books and table games.

She said to the lads, "You can use them if you want to and bring them into the lounge if you wish." They accepted her offer and made good use of them.

One of the first things we did after settling in, was to run down to Dalbeattie in the hope that I would see my old RAF pal, Tony Hill. I had his address and I had no trouble locating it but when I knocked on the door and asked if he was in, the lady answering the knock said he didn't live there anymore. Then she followed up by saying, " It could be that young man who removed yesterday, but he didn't leave a forwarding address." I was so disappointed and I haven't heard of him since, even though I've made enquiries in many places.

It was a relaxing holiday and contrary to England, one could walk across fields without being challenged by farmers. Some days we took advantage of this and on one of them Mrs. Hannah's mother, Mrs. Finlay, who stayed with them at the farm, took us for a walk to the old ruins of a large country house where she had worked as a kitchen maid many years ago. Tony picked up a small carved stone from the ruins as a souvnenir and he still has it today.

We took the opportunity to go and visit Threave Castle which was only a short journey from where we were staying. It was quite small and was of a square shape but to get into it we had to park the car about half a mile away and walk along a public pathway where we had to ring a small bell to summon a small rowing boat, which was operated by a guide to take us across the moat to the castle. It was a novel idea and the lads were thrilled.

A few days after arriving at the farm we had a run around to explore various places of interest and found a small bay called Brighouse Bay. It was ideal for us because the water in the bay stretched out some hundred yards and was still only three feet deep. It was great for swimming and playing about in. We spent many hours there during our stay and the only other people in the vicinity were two families in caravans on one side and up on the other side of the bay was a working farmhouse. The cows from the farm would graze just a few yards from where we had settled on the bank but there was no unpleasantness from them.

On one of our daily run-arounds we had a good laugh, or the lads did because I was inclined, on occasions, to mis-pronounce names and I had said that we would have a run down to Fleethouse of Gate. In fact I should have said Gatehouse of Fleet. It is often brought up in conversations today. So what!. At least I pronounced it right when we went down to Kirkcudbright - it is known as Kir-koo-bry.

On the Thursday, we had noticed a poster which was advertising a motor cycle scramble at a little place called Cross Michael and when we mentioned it to Mrs. Hannah, her Mum, Mrs. Finlay who was in her sixties, said that she loved scrambling and never missed it on TV. So, we took her with us.

Having parked the car, we had to climb up one or two small hillocks to get an advantage point and Mrs. Finlay trudged along with a little help from all of us. For an hour we really enjoyed the spills and thrills of the scrambling. We finally set off back to the farm but when we arrived, Mr and Mrs Hannah were in a right state. Apparently, unknown to us, Mrs. Finlayson suffered with her heart and had forgotten to take her pills with her. That's why there was a panic when we arrived back.

Mrs. Finlayson wasn't worried. "I'm alright." She told them. "I've enjoyed every minute." Then she thanked us for taking her out for a change.

The rest of the week was enjoyed by touring around and when we were finally ready to leave for home, Mrs. Hannah thrust a small packet into the car and it was addressed to the lads. On the way home they opened it and a note inside said,"Thank you for being good lads." I think that this was due to the fact that Tony had sorted and tidied the cupboard with all the books and games in, plus of course, everything else that had been used during the week had been put back into the cupboard. It was one of the best holidays we had indulged in and we all fell in love with SCOTLAND. The people are so friendly and helpful and everyone is made so welcome. We intend to return at a later date

Upon return, the lads became more involved with the Boys Brigade, which, funnily enough, was founded in Glasgow in Scotland by a William Smith. Tony and Geoff passed tests in First Aid, Signalling and Wayfaring.

The Company had an open night and Aline and I went along with other parents and witnessed an excellent display of drill by the boys, also First Aid on pretend accident scenes. A Colonel (Ret) Bradley, who lived nearby, presented awards to a number of boys but the highlight of the night was a presentation of marching music by the Company Bugle Band.

It was well organise by Roger Dunwell, a junior officer, and to finish it off, all the drums were lit up with small fairy lights. The main hall lights were put out and the effect was wonderful.

This just about wrapped up another interesting and eventful year. What was to come next?

Early in the New Year, I was sent to the Head Office of the United Steel Co., which was situated in a building called 'The Mount' which was owned by the Gentry in days gone by. It was at the top end of Glossop Road on the South West side of the city. I went there to be trained in the use of Data Processing equipment such as card sorters, collators and tabulating machines which were the forerunner of the present day computer and were used in the ICL Computer system.

The Supervisor there was Miss Kath Taylor who was about my age and very efficient. Also in the department she had an assistant named Barbara and working under them were eight young female staff who operated the various machines. There were also two semi-permanent ICL engineers there for maintaining the machines. One was Albert Livesley and the other one was Jack Brewster and he was the jovial one with a ready turn of wit.

Having to travel through the town centre meant that I had to be up earlier and I also returned home later in the evenings. It was very interesting work learning how to operate the various machines, plus the fact that I had to learn how to programme the various plug boards that were put into the machines to make them work.

In March I was sent to a place in Cookham in Berkshire, for a two- week course on how to officially programme the 902 Tabulator. The place was a type of school which was run by ICL and was just outside the village where the surroundings were very pleasant with being in the open countryside. The accommodation was excellent and leading from the main buildings, which were all on the ground floor, there were four extending corridors, like fingers from a hand. Each trainee had their own room and the dining room was in the main section behind the classrooms.

To get down to the school, I had arranged for Aline, to run me up in the car to Meadowhead, in Sheffield, for 7.30 am, from where I would be picked up by one of the ICL staff named Bernard. He too was going down to Cookham but on a different course. We went down in his Austin Mini and he would bring me back home for the weekend before returning to finish the course. Whilst down there if I had any queries about my course, Bernard would give my advice.

On my course I learned how to insert one pin plugs of various lengths of covered wire connections into certain holes in the insulated metal boards to make the tabulator read and produce details onto continuous stationery. The boards were quite heavy and on a large programme, as many as one hundred plugs could be in use. When a programme had been fully wired, the board was inserted into an open frame which had slides on either side, for the programme board to be slid into and then spring loaded into a locking position in the front of the Tabulator. Where plugs had been inserted on the outside, the metal contacts of the same, penetrated brass contacts on the other side and these were called teeth, which came into contact with similar ones connected to the tabulator, thus, when the power was switched on, so the machine read the punched cards which had to be fed into a hopper, face down, and thus produce the necessary documents.

Punch cards were plain pieces of thin card which measured 7½" x 3¼" on which was printed various columns with subsequent headings needed to assist the punch card operators when entering the necessary details for which the columns were designated. These columns were read and fed into the Tabulator by many electrical impulses and thus interpreted into specific values and text needed to let the print unit of the Tabulator print on such documentation as may be required. These documents could vary from Sales Analyses, Wage Envelopes, Share certificates or any other information normally required when running a business. On each card, small elongated holes were punched and these holes represented numerals, if a single hole, but for alpha details, a combination of two or three holes was needed. It took me some time to become used to it but eventually I was able to read a punch card, just by looking at it.

There were odd occasions when a particular card had to be found in a pack and this could be located by passing a thin five inch long flat piece of steel down the holes until it stopped. Then the cards were split where the needle, as it was called, came to a halt. This was carried out down a field of holes until the required card was found. This method was quicker than passing the whole pack through the sorting machine.

At the school in Cookham there was a young man called Tony who was sent by his employers in the Midlands to train on the same course as me. He had come in a little van and quite a few times we would go out at night after lessons, in the van, to view the local habitats such as Windsor Castle, Boulter's Lock (of Three Men In A Boat fame) and some evenings we would go to the nearest cinema where we saw two magnificent films, Sergeants Three with Frank Sinatra, Sammy Davis Junior and Dean Martin in it and also that great film Becket (The life of Thomas-a-Becket)

We were the only two on the course and the instructor commended us for the effort which we had put into it and on the reports to our employers he remarked that we had completed it in a record time.

After returning home I remained at the Mount for well into the New Year but I still managed to fit in a holiday. For quite a while, Eric, Aline's brother, had been encouraging us to try camping because it was so economical and very relaxing. To help us decide, he let us borrow the whole of his own equipment and frame tent, to try it out.

Having been to Castle Douglas, we decided to return there because we had seen a good camp site on the municipal park by the lake when up there last year. Freda, Nip's sister, agreed to go with us and take her daughter Pam, in their car, and bring along a large ridge tent for them both to use.

Freda had never driven as far since passing her test so to make things easier, we had decided to break the journey by staying a couple of nights at a camp site on the side of Lake Windermere in the Lake District. We enjoyed the short stay and we were able to take in some of the beautiful scenery in the area. Eventually we arrived at Castle Douglas, booked in at the main gate and then set up our tents. The following day we showed Freda around the town to familiarise her with the shops and she couldn't believe how friendly the local people were.

Aline and I were able to take Freda and Pam to places of interest which we had visited previously but one disappointment was when we took them to Brighouse Bay because the Camping Club of Great Britain had purchased some land there to make a camp site. The effect was that the area had become commercialised and was over run by new campers.

At least we made the most of it and the weather was good. Freda hadn't taken a swimming costume but to get the most of the sun, she had partly undressed down to her corselet. Fortunately, where we were parked, it was rather secluded.

One night, on our camp site, we were just preparing to retire to bed for the night and it was nearing 'lights out' time about 10.00 pm, when someone quite close to us outside, was flashing a torch and this was making silhouettes of people against the canvas of the tent wall. As the light flashed onto our tent, I jumped up, pulled the tent zip up and dashed out to have words with the culprit. It was a young lad messing about and as I dashed out to chastise him, I had forgotten that the tents had guyropes attached.

I caught my foot on one of them and over I went. I was only wearing my pyjamas and flat I fell, face down into a puddle of water. It had been raining heavily earlier on and I was soaked from head to foot. As I walked back into the tent, the family were in uproar. I must have looked a real sight and I wasn't allowed to forget it for many a long day. Because I hadn't brought a spare pair of pyjamas with me I had to sleep in my underpants.

Prior to our coming on holiday, David had fallen out of a tree near to home and had fractured his forearm. It was only a greenstick fracture but he had to have it in plaster. However, it didn't deter him from going into the sea and even though his Mum had an idea to cover it with a plastic bag, he still enjoyed himself by trying to float on an empty oil drum which had been left lying around on the beach. Tony and Geoff tried having a go but with the drum being round, the more fun they had. When we eventually arrived home, the hospital staff said the wet 'pot' hadn't delayed his arm in healing.

Overall we enjoyed ourselves and Freda and Pam were more than pleased with their first visit to Scotland, more so, when Nip and I decided to call up at Ballyfield Farm to see how the Hannah's were getting on.

When we arrived, Mrs. Hannah was more than delighted to see us and invited us into the kitchen. It wasn't long before the table was set and the good lady prepared a meal for all seven of us. For an hour, we talked of our previous visit and other things in general and Freda couldn't get over the hospitality we had been shown.

At the end of the week we set off for home and this time we didn't take an overnight stop although we had one or two breaks to give Freda a rest from driving. Like I said earlier, she hadn't driven as far before and really, she did very well.

David's arm had mended quite well and he had the 'pot' removed but it still didn't keep him out of mischief because during the summer, we were in the house one day and we could hear the Fire Engines which seemed to be quite close and somewhere on the estate.

Into the house came David and when we asked him if he knew where the Fire Brigade was, he said, "Up in the cow fields. I was playing with some matches and accidentally set the grass alight." It had been a hot few weeks and grass was tinder dry. "Did anyone know it was you?" Nip asked. "No." He replied. "I just ran." He received a 'clip' around the earhole for taking the matches but afterwards, when we were on our own, Nip and I had to chuckle at the little devil.

Whilst I had been working at The Mount, a new DPM had been brought in to replace Mr Adamson. This new manager was Stewart Bannatyne, a debonair looking Scotsman with a good personality and a willingness to please everyone.

On one of my visits back down to TWIL, I was introduced to him and we had a natter about various things such as work progress but above all, about my salary. When I told him that I had three sons and what my salary was, he commented that he thought that it was too low for the work I was doing.

"What do you think your salary should be?" He asked.

Well, not having given it much thought I replied. "At least £1.000.00 pounds per annum." I wish I had told him more because within weeks of our conversation, he had arranged for my money to be increased to that figure.

Stewart was a dapper little man and very pleasant to get on with. When I told him that I was a semi-pro musician to supplement my wages, he asked me if I would be interested in teaching his two young sons. I declined because I wasn't qualified to teach and he took it in good faith. He was also a generous person because as Christmas approached, he asked me if we usually had an office party and when I informed that we did, he put his 'hand in his pocket' and gave me £20 to get some drinks for the staff. Who said that Scots were 'tight'?

During the year, due to my Mum having difficulty in climbing the stairs at home with her broken hip, (which was now on the mend), my Dad had asked Dr. Wainwright if he would give his support to try to get them moved into a council flat. The houses in the East End of the city had already been earmarked to be demolished under a slum clearance operation in the near future.

Although it took a while, arrangements were finally made and they were moved into a new flat, No. 72 Spinkhill Road at Richmond and this was convenient to the point that it was only a mile and a half away from where we lived. It was a ground floor flat with a bathroom and inside toilet which they hadn't had before, one double bedroom and a medium sized lounge. The gardens outside were tended by the local council so they didn't have any problems there. It seemed to be the ideal place except that before long my Mum started complaining that the place wasn't warm and it was drafty. Of course there was bound to be a difference after living in a small terraced house for the past forty years.

I found it helpful when I could find time to call on them more often and on Saturday mornings, Nip and I would take in any necessary shopping which they needed. The nearest shops to them were at a shopping area called the Fishponds because of the small pond nearby.

This was some three quarters of a mile from the flat and it was a pull for Dad to go there and back. Sometimes however, he would make an excuse to go up there to the shops to get out of the flat and out of Mum's way - and sneak a crafty pint in the Richmond Hotel.

In moving, they had to say goodbye to Dr. Wainwright and Dr. Gethin, his assistant but they soon found a good doctor on Richmond Road who had a practise just around the corner from the flat. He was Dr. Crowther and he had a partner named Dr. Porteous.

As was the norm of things, I went in the car and picked up Mum and Dad and brought them to our house for Christmas Dinner just as I had always done over the past few years. With Mum not being able to get around much, due to her hip, most of the housework fell upon Dad and in some ways, it always had done. Mum was a born Hypochondriac and moaned at the tiniest illness so that when they came to our house, Aline and I made sure that Dad had a rest. I know at the time when Mum was in hospital, he loved to come to us and enjoy the boys' company and the good food that Nip prepared for all of us. It was a pleasure having him but I can't say that about Mum, I'm sorry to say.

Even in our own home, when Mum was with us, it was "Close the door, shut the window, it's drafty." Then we had to stoke the fire up until it was unbearable. It did make Aline mad because she liked her fresh air having come from a village in the countryside. As soon as I had taken them both home, Aline opened the windows for some air.

Into the New Year I was still working at the United Steels and slowly but surely becoming more knowledgable about computers. Preparations were being made structurally to set up space in the offices at Twil for the installation of the equipment we were to use. It had been decided that TWIL would take such hardware from the United Steels and that is one reason as to why I had been seconded to the Mount to learn how to operate it. Some of the analyses which were produced were connected to work done by one of TWIL's subsidiaries. This was a firm called Barnards Limited, who were based in Norwich and produced chain link fencing for industry and agriculture

New programmes had to be created to cater for their production lines so it was decided to send me down to Norwich to arrange things. It was also decided to send Miss Taylor with me because she had done so much to organise the data in the past. For convenience, it was arranged that she would pick me up in her car, a small and new Austin 1000, and take us both to previously booked accommodation at the old Coach Station Inn in Norwich which was the King's Head. We did have separate rooms with an adjoining door, which, incidentally, was locked.

Whilst sorting out the problems down there, we were shown around the factory on Mousehold Road but I was surprised to see that the main office was only an old army Nissen type hut. The accountant there, with whom we dealt, was a Mr. Cecil Jenkins who was a fussy little man but eagre to please. Kath and I sorted out their difficulties but it meant staying over for another night.

On the first night, we were invited to dinner at our own hotel by Cecil but when we went down to join him in the bar, there was another gentleman there who he introduced as Mr. Gillan. He was a tall Scottish chap and I took to him straight away. Over dinner, we discussed what work we had been doing and when it came to the point of withdrawal, Mr. Gillan and Mr. Jenkins became a little heated as to who would foot the bill. Mr. Gillan won and overall, the evening had been very pleasant.

The second evening there, Cecil Jenkins took us out to some secluded restaurant which was on the side of the River Wensum. Kath and I really enjoyed the hospitality and the view overlooking the river, as we ate our meal, was idyllic.

To fit in with the United Steels setup, it was necessary for me to work flexible hours and there was a time when I had to do a night shift. I started work about 8.00 p.m. and arrangements had been made for me to get some refreshments, later on in the night, from the staff canteen. There I was engrossed in operating the machines by myself and making sure that everything was in the current order when there was an almighty banging on one of the windows.

I had been so cut off from anything but my work, that I must have jumped a foot into the air with fright. All I could see at the frosted window was a head and shoulders of someone wearing a crash helmet. I made my way, tentatively, to the main door of the building and saw a security guard there.

"What are you doing?" He demanded. "I'm working a night shift in the machine room. Haven't you been informed?" "No, I haven't." He replied. I told him to do some checking and after half an hour he returned to say that everything was alright. What a shock it was. I told Kath Taylor the following afternoon and she apologised for the lack of cooperation with the caretaker and Securicor. Apart from that upset, I had been having problems handling the punched cards when 'knocking ' them up because my right hand was in a plaster cast. This was due to one of those occasions when my stomach had been acting up and so had my son No.2, our Geoff.

At home, we had been sitting having a meal in the kitchen and Geoff was reluctant to get on with it. "Come on, Geoff." I said "Eat your dinner." He just sat there, said nothing and did nothing. "Geoff." I said more firmly, "Get your dinner!" Still no comment. Still no movement. "I won't tell you again. Get it eaten!" Nothing. My temper was on the verge of erupting and my stomach was very agitated too.. "You either eat it or get upstairs." Still nothing. Just dumb insolence. "MOVE!" I yelled and he went to the bottom of the stairs.

I followed him and he just stood there looking at me as if to say, 'Get stuffed' That did it. "Move now or I'll crack you one." He still didn't move but I did. I took one swing at him and cried, "Shift. Now!" As I swung, he ducked and I hit the handrail leading up the stairs, with my right hand.

It was painful. Bloody painful and I knew that I had broken something. Aline took me up to the Northern General Hospital where they x-rayed it and a fractured little finger was confirmed. They set it there and then and that's why I was slightly incapacitated. When I went back a week later for a checkup, I had to explain to the orthopaedic surgeon how it had happened. He couldn't stop laughing and his nursing staff said it was the first time that they had ever seen any smile from him. Apparently he was a tartar with them. The staff at TWIL and the ICL engineers thought it was hilarious. I didn't.

My hand was usable again after six weeks and we were able to take our annual holiday. This time we travelled down to Tenby, in South Wales, where we found a good camp site not far from town. This time we had our own tent which was a large ridge tent with a big door flap on either side which made it easy to get in and out of. The locality was good and we had the chance to visit various castles in the area and this suited the boys. The only draw back was that the local people reverted back to their native tongue whenever visitors were about. We made friends with a young couple in the next tent to us. They had a baby and we found out that he was a psychiatric nurse and worked for a private patient.

In May, Sheffield was full of excitement because one of its local football teams, Sheffield Wednesday, had managed to reach the final of the FA Cup again. The last time was in 1935 when they won it by beating West Bromwich Albion but on this occasion they weren't so lucky. Their opponents were Everton and although they gained a two goal lead by half time, the second half went against them and through a defensive error by Vic Mobley, they lost by three goals to two.

There was much elation in the early summer and once again football was the topic because England were the hosts of the World Cup and having surpassed themselves under the managership of Alf Ramsay, (later to be knighted). They had reached the Final and eventually won by beating West Germany by four goals to two. Geoff Hurst, of West Ham United, scored the first ever hat-trick in a World Cup Final.

All this excitement was just about dying out when tragedy struck the Country. I was on afternoon shift at the Mount on the 21st October when one of the staff brought in the local newspaper, The Star. There was a banner headline, "**THE SCHOOL THAT DIED.**" In the Welsh mining village of Aberfan, near Merhyr Tydfil, a 500 ft mountain of slag from the local colliery had poured down in an avalanche upon a primary school, killing 116 children and most of the teachers.

It was a terrible disaster and the sadness lingered on right into Christmas and beyond. I think that everyone felt for the families of Aberfan in their bereavement. At work, it was the main topic of conversation for a very long time but life had to go on and many people contributed to a relief fund which was set up for the relatives of the victims.

It wasn't long after returning from Norwich that I found that Mr. Gillan had been transferred to Sheffield as the Company Secretary to replace the previous one who had recently died. He was Mr. Brierley. It was early in the New Year that final arrangements were made to transfer all the hardware from the Mount to Shepcote Lane and at the same time I returned there to operate it all.

I was doing this exact work one day when Mr. Gillan was familiarising himself with the office block layout and into the machine room he walked. He said it was good to see a face which he knew and we had a nice chat about various things. He then asked me if I knew of a good golf club and I asked him where he was residing. When he said that he had moved house from Norwich to Derbyshire, just outside the Sheffield Boundary, I told him I would ask my brother-in-law, Eric, about Sickleholme Golf Club, at where he was the Steward.

A week later. Eric had arranged for Mr. Gillan to see the Captain and Secretary of the club and he was accepted as a member there and then. It was only a ten minutes ride by car from his home at Curbar to the club. Mr. Gillan was very grateful.

Having returned to TWIL for good, I became involved with Mr. Bannatyne as my manager and his ideas of a department being environmentally friendly, included him asking me to ask the punch room girls what ideas they may have for murals to be put onto the walls and climbing plants to be set against the supporting pillars in the punch room. I think he inherited these ideas from the time when he worked for IBM in Canada.

He was very flamboyant and gave the impression of being a 'wide boy'. I think he really tried to make a go of it but his IBM training seemed to clash with the ICL set up.

The 'Old Man', Mr. Marcel Veys, who was the Chairman of TWIL, was a reasonable man to a point but he could be demanding when it came to getting promises from people with regards to output. Whether it be from the factory or the admin side, one had to make the effort. Unfortunately, Stewart Bannatyne had made several predictions as to when some cost and accounts figures would be forthcoming from the Data Processing Dept.

Harry Kershaw, the Accountant, had requested some of these figures and had told Stewart what a tartar the 'Old Man' could be. Once again, Stewart made a promise too many and when the promise was broken again, so was he. There was no alternative but for him to be on his way. I was sorry to see him go because we seemed to gel together but there you are, just into the New Year, Stewart Bannatyne left TWIL.

Just after Stewart left, because some reports were urgently needed, I agreed to work over one night to try to catch up with the output of same. I had some light refreshments brought in from the canteen and after everyone else had left, I carried on processing cards through the tabulator and producing printouts

Around about 8.50 p.m. I decided to call it a day, I switched off the machine and whilst the motor was running down, I closed the office window, tidied round and went to open the office door. As I opened it, there, in front of me, was a Securicor Guard with an Alsatian guard dog.

"What are you doing here?" He asked. "Just packing up. I've been working over." I replied

"Can you prove it?" Was the next question. "Yes." I said. "I'll go and ring my Boss, who's at home." It was obvious that the guard didn't believe me and as I made to go to a phone, the dog growled, then barked. That was it. I daren't move. The guard told me to stay where I was, and I did. He then made a phone call to his Superior. At 9.50 p.m., Roger Farris walked into the office to identify me. He was furious at having been called out from the other end of the town and he made his feelings felt with the Security people. In fact, they should have been informed that I was staying late and they weren't. Hence the frustration.

For many years after, it was a standing joke amongst the staff but it wasn't funny at the time. Aline had been worried sick because she had expected me home by 9.15 p.m. I daren't move to ring her and let her know what was going on. I must be allergic to security guards for this was the second instance where I had been involved with them.

It didn't take long for a replacement manager to arrive and towards the end of February, 1967, a new DPM was installed. He was Mike Jessop and of Irish descent but without the brogue. In fact his speech was rather 'Cut Glarss' as we say in Yorkshire. He was a good looking young man, a bit of a whizz kid with two University degrees and many fancy ideas. I'm always sceptical of new managers and it wasn't long before I knew there wasn't going to be the same repartee there which I had with Mr. Bannatyne and I think he realised there was a gap, not only in attitudes but also dialects.

I don't know whether it was the pressure of extra responsibilities or not but my stomach seemed to be having a birthday and sometimes the biliousness caused me to lose the odd day at work. On top of that I was worried about my Dad because one Saturday morning when Aline and I had called with the groceries, I asked him if he would like to go in the car on our way home and have a drink at the New Crown Inn at the top of Handsworth.

We did this and Aline took the car home, then I went into the pub with my Dad for the drink. I could see that he was worried.

Suddenly he said, "I'm f........ing well fed up. I've had enough." That wasn't my Dad. Tears ran down his cheeks as he said that Mum was getting him down. It was little things like her asking him to put a programme on the Tele and a few minutes later, asking him to get up and alter it. Then having altered it, she would ask him to change it back again.

I did feel sorry for him because I knew how awkward my Mum could be. All her married life, if she could get other people to do little jobs and errands for her, then she would. She didn't give Dad a chance and once, when I was talking to Aunty Amy Howard, Aunty said that Mum's first husband, George Fell, would have been alive today if she hadn't insisted upon him doing some shopping in very bad weather at the time he was suffering from a heavy cold. George Fell died of pneumonia shortly after.

In the meantime, I had been attending the Hallamshire Hospital for X-rays and Barium meal tests on my stomach and after exhausting examinations, it was found that I had a Duodenal Ulcer which had been there for twenty years and was hard to detect due to being deep-seated.

So it was, that in March, I was admitted to the Royal Infirmary under the orders of Professor Duthie and was told that I was to be operated on. I had heard stories of ulcers being cured by the removal of the whole stomach and I wasn't really looking forward to it.

However, Dr.Geoff Smith, the professor's houseman, said that they were going to try a new technique and this was to open me up and seal off the nerve ends, thus eliminating the removal of my stomach.

Prior to this, I had to have an endoscope put into my stomach and this was a device in which a small tube was pushed up my nose and guided down the back of my throat and then into my stomach. From there it was possible to make a visual examination of where the actual ulcer was lying. Oh! It was horrible and it made my nose and throat very sore, too. After two days I was taken down to the operating theatre and must have been there for two hours or more before being returned to Ward 10 (another coincidence.)

Aline kept coming to see me but wouldn't drive the car through the town, so she came by bus. This really made it a very long day for her but the lads were old enough to take care of themselves now.

Having come round from the anaesthetic, I didn't feel too bad except for the soreness but I was given pain killer tablets for ease. On the second night after the operation, clever clogs me, thought that the Saline drip which was attached to me, wasn't working properly, so I leaned over and adjusted it.

That daft action very nearly cost me my life because shortly afterwards I slipped into unconsciousness and but for the swift action of the nurses, I would have been a goner. With the duty Doctor they fought most of the night to help me and thank God, they were successful. Because I was so ill, they sent for Aline and when she saw how poorly I was she too, nearly passed out. She was so worried and once again her love for me showed through.

It so happened that one of my pals, Ron Schofield, had called in to see how I was getting on and he seemed as worried as Aline did. They stayed quite a while and when it was time to go, Ron said not to worry and he would run Aline home in his car, so that was a relief to me. Sometime later, when I was on my feet again, Ron told me how upset Aline had been and he himself, had cause for doubt about my welfare because I looked so ill.

A few days later I was well enough to be moved outside of the Ward onto a veranda with three other patients. Dr. Geoff Smith was doing his rounds and as he came up the ward, I could see him go to one patient and ask, "Can you cough for me ?" The patient gave a little piffling puff and stopped. "Try again." Smithy said. Once more the same stifled attempt from the patient. Dr. Smith lifted up the back of the man's pyjama jacket and struck him with the flat of his hand, right under the lung area. The patient coughed then. "That's better." Dr. Smith cried. "You must keep those lungs clear."

Having seen and heard this, I was ready for the Doctor as he approached my bed. "How are you today?" He asked me.

"Fine." I replied. "Then try to cough for me." I tried and thought that I had made a good effort but he walked over and asked me to lean forward. As I did so, the palm of his hand went into my back. I coughed alright and he seemed pleased with my progress.

On the Sunday after the operation, the staff were bringing our meals to us and the ward Sister said, "Here you are , George." and offered me some cold belly pork.(Why do hospitals always use the first name on your record and not the one by which you are always called?) "I can't eat that, Sister, it's all fat." I said. "Come along, get it eaten. I promise you it won't upset you." She was right you know because the operation was a tremendous success and to this day I can eat anything without suffering any adverse effects.

A few days later, I was taken down stairs to a small laboratory type room and there one of the junior doctors, named Keith, started doing some tests on my stomach, which had an outlet tube protruding from it just above my waist

Because the drainage didn't seem to be working properly, he suddenly said, "I'm afraid I'm going to have to put a tube down your throat to draw the fluid off."

I looked at him and replied, " You bring another tube near my throat and you can pick your window." He looked at me and I carried on, "Let me try myself by turning onto my side where the outlet tube is and see if it works with me flexing and reflexing my stomach muscles in and out." "OK." He said. This I tried and within a few minutes, the excess fluid was coming away from the outlet into a receptacle.

That was that and after a few more days I was allowed to go home. Aline did an excellent job in helping me to recuperate and within weeks I was almost back to normal, except that where the stitches had been, it was a little sore. They can really hurt sometimes, especially as on the day the Sister came to take them out. Everything seemed fine until she came to one particular suture and tried to pull it out against the knot. I soon got over it and as I said, I was on the mend.

After some six weeks, I was feeling about 75% fit and checked with Dr. Shriv and the Hospital to see if I would be able to return to work. I was given permission but with the strict instructions that I had to take things easy and do no lifting of heavy objects such as boxes of cards which were needed for punching.

I had been back at work a couple of days when Mr. Gillan walked into my office. "What the hell are you doing here?" He exclaimed in his strong Scottish accent. He continued, "You shouldn't be at work yet, Ron, it usually takes three months to get over an operation like that." When I explained that my stomach hadn't been removed and only the nerve ends sealed off, he relaxed a little but insisted that I take things easy.

Everything seemed to be settling down to old routines again, both domestically and at TWIL where the new DPM, Mike Jessop, was trying to re-organise various projects. After a short while, he was given the position of Group Management Services Manager and this entailed installing programming procedures which covered some of our subsidiaries and in turn, this meant employing more programmers and systems analysts.

Jeff Wright had left us and in his place they took on Stan Spencer, who was in his early thirties and very good at maths. Also they had a Paul Mahon join the staff and two trainees who were females. Beth Pearson had applied for a transfer from the Sales Dept., and Sue Thompson had come straight from Woodhouse Grammar School. The latter I found, lived at the top end of our estate and therefore I was able to give her a lift, to and from work.

The Cost Office staff, who had originally taken up space in our open plan office, were now moved into the other side of the office block but again on the ground floor and the space that they had vacated was now turned into a punch room with Sheila Clark as the Supervisor. The small peripheral offices were all now occupied with Mike Jessop, programmers, trainees and myself in the machine room.

I had just about attained 100% efficiency with my work when I received a 'phone call from the Royal Hospital on West Street.

It was the Ward Sister to say that my Dad had collapsed in town and had been admitted for observation. This was in the first week in May and I was given permission to leave my work and rush to the Hospital.

Later on, I found out that Mum had insisted that he go to the Sheffield & Ecclesall Co-op

Pharmacy at the bottom of Ecclesall Road in town to get her prescription. Mum's idea was that the pharmacy there was better than the local chemist. Unfortunately, Dad had rushed too much and collapsed in the entrance of the shop.That story sounds familiar. It meant visiting him every day and he didn't look too bad except that some tests they had been making, had upset him a little. We took Mum up to see him two or three times but mostly I went by myself.

At first he was in the main part of the ward but on one occasion, when I went, there was a horrible, unnatural smell coming from him but I made no comment. I know that I never want to experience that smell again. It wasn't until I arrived back home that I expressed my worry to Aline. "I think there's something seriously wrong with him, Nip."

On the 8th May, I took Mum to see him and he had been moved into a corner of the ward, next to the Sister's office. He now had a monitor attached to him and this confirmed my worst fears. I went to work the following morning but I couldn't concentrate on my tasks and in the middle of the morning, I received another call from the hospital. Dad had peacefully passed away on the 11th May and the death certificate said that he had died from heart failure and cancer of the bladder. He would have been 74 years of age on the first of July next, so he did get his wish and outlive the age of his mother. I was going to miss him - I loved him so much.

After the cremation at Hutcliffe Wood Crematorium, we returned to Spinkhill Road, the only mourners there being Nip, myself and cousin Margaret Newshum (Bunn). I slipped into the bedroom and sobbed my heart out. Then I heard my Mum ask our Margaret, "What's our Ron crying for?" That was my Mum. **SHE** always needed attention. It was interesting to note, that not one of Dad's relations came to the funeral and I never forgave them for it.

We didn't have the lads at the funeral and although Tony was sixteen and Geoff at fourteen might have understood the solemnity of the proceedings, it wouldn't have been fair to not include David, who we thought was too young to attend in any case. At a later date, we did take them, with their Grandma, to see a bronze plaque which she and I had arranged to have put on the Memorial Wall at the crematorium.

There was a little respite for us after the previous few months, when, in June, we received a letter from the Sheffield Education Committee, informing us that David had been successful in passing the eleven plus examinations. The letter informed us that he was eligible to go to the same school as Tony, which was the Firth Park Grammar School. This upset Geoff again because he didn't think that he was as clever as them because he had only passed for Technical College. It took some time before we finally convinced him that this wasn't so.

Once again we had managed to save enough money to rig out David with the maroon blazer etc., just like we had done for Tony when he started at the Grammar School. It became a little expensive because Tony was in a higher Form and was now required to wear a navy blue blazer. It's a pity that Tony's old clobber wasn't suitable for David to wear, but there you are, what does one expect after four years wear and tear.

So, on Tuesday, the 5th September 1967, David started at the 'Brushes', as the school was known and it helped Nip and I tremendously to know that he could go to school with Tony and we wouldn't have to worry about him travelling.

It seemed strange at Christmas, not having Dad with us but we tried to make it as comfortable as we could for Mum, by carrying on as usual and having her with us for the Festive dinner. It did make it awkward, however, when she wanted to go back home just after tea because it meant that I had to be careful at lunchtime when having a seasonal drink and having to drive her back home to her flat. In one way it was a relief because it meant that upon my return, I was able to put the car in the garage and get my feet up, so to speak, and enjoy the remainder of the Christmas Day night with Aline and the kids.

It was always a pleasure to go through the Xmas presents again and take part with the lads in any games which ‘Father Christmas’ might have brought them. Since Dad died, it had been a bit of a struggle trying to make sure that Mum was alright and once a fortnight we would fetch her over, sometimes for dinner and tea on a Sunday, but mostly it was just for her tea.

Mum had a friendly neighbour and her husband, Mr. and Mrs. Savage, who lived across the hall and would keep their eyes on her, even though they themselves were getting on in years. Sometimes when I called, Mum would be in their flat which was also on the ground floor.

As we moved into 1968, it had been necessary to call in the Social Service people to see if they could give Mum any help. This they did by arranging for a home help to call in twice a week to keep the flat clean and possibly do a few errands. Actually, the latter wasn’t supposed to be done by these Home Helps but like I have said before - if Mum could get anyone to do something for her, then she would do.

To help Mum keep her mind occupied, the Social Services had organised it for her to be picked up by mini bus once a week and taken to a Care Centre at the top of the Manor Estate on City Road.

It was here that she was taught how to knit dishcloths and do other handicrafts which were put up for sale and from the earnings, it was possible to take these old folk on day trips etc.

Aline was more than pulling her weight in appeasing my Mum by doing the washing and ironing for her and for which Mum received an allowance, but Nip never saw any of it. I would call in twice a week to see what shopping was required and then we would deliver it on the following Saturday morning and at the same time would tidy up for her and collect the weeks dirty washing.

The flats were a block of four with two upstairs and two down and when Mum and Dad moved in they were lucky to get a ground floor one. As with our house, the windows were metal framed and this created the thought of them being cold buildings.

In actual fact, they weren’t that warm because there was no central heating and the only way of keeping warm was by using an electric fire and by closing all the doors.

After moving from a very warm terraced house, the comparison to this flat was immense and Mum, having always been fanatical about draughts, soon started covering every nook and cranny. That wasn’t too bad until one Saturday, when we called, that she said that the Home Help had flooded the bathroom. I went into detail and then found that Mum had stuffed toilet paper into the sink overflow to stop the draught, so that when the Home Help had run the tap, the water had overflowed onto the floor. On top of that, I once went into the bathroom to use the toilet and found the slop pail wedged in it. When I asked Mum about it, she said it was to keep out the draught again. **PATIENCE!** Mine was running out.

Half term arrived for the lads and their school reports had been issued with reasonable results but it wasn’t very pleasing when we read David’s report because Dr. Wilson, his headmaster at Firth Park, had severely compared his progress with Tony’s and Nip and I took great exception to it. We followed it up when we were called to a parents meeting and we had words with his form master and put in a complaint. This seemed to have some effect but we still had our doubts as to what would happen in the future.

I can’t fully remember, but during the early part of the year, Mum had to have the doctor in and he confined her to bed and somehow, with Mrs. Savage being nearby and the Home Help popping in to see her, we managed to cope. At one stage Mum was very poorly, or so we thought, and I called in every morning before going to work. On the Saturday morning we went round to see her and entered the flat very quietly in case she was asleep in the bed. Aline slowly opened the bedroom door and guess what? Mum was out of bed, dusting the walls with a feather duster.

That did it. Aline, for once, lost her cool. "What the bloody hell!" She cried. " Here's Ron and me worried sick about you and here you are trying to Spring clean. You silly old buggar!"

Mum couldn't believe it and neither could I. "You've never spoken to me like that before." Mum said to Aline. The reply came. "No, and it won't be the last if you carry on like that." As usual. Mum set the 'water works' going but it made no difference to either of us. From then on things altered tremendously. To sooth her, we said that we would try to get her moved into a bedsit flat but it might take quite a while because we would have to go through the usual channels and consult the Social Services people.

By going to the Centre at the Manor Top, Mum had managed to make a few friends and on odd occasions some of them would call in to see her. This also helped her to relieve the monotony of being on her own but Mum still continued to moan and groan.

Back at TWIL, I was trying to concentrate on my work and managed at times to push my family problems into the background. Because I had been having one or two mechanical difficulties with the Tabulator, it was decided to call in some ICL engineers from London to give it an overhaul. Two chaps came up and for nearly a week there was no output from the machine because it was all in bits and spread around the floor.

It was interesting to find out how everything worked and eventually all the new parts were put into place and we were in business again.

Whilst all this had been going on, Mike Jessop was busy organising and preparing for the installation of the new ICL 1300 Computer which was to have four large tape decks and an Input machine which was the card reader. The lead up to receiving it was to get all the wiring into place and spacing out the floor so that it would be in the correct position when installed. Also during this period, Bob Little had been promoted to the position of Data Processing Manager and I became more responsible to him which suited me fine because I still couldn't take to Jessop with his 'cut glass' accent and overbearing snobbishness.

Holiday time had arrived again and we had decided to get rid of the ridge tent and go all modern by buying a frame tent which was suitable to sleep four people. Having bought it we agreed to go to Scotland and do a tour by firstly going to a club site at Barns Ness near Dunbar. The lads were able to go up the lighthouse there and we also enjoyed visiting North Berwick but the highlight of the first week was to go into Edinburgh and have the opportunity of seeing a full rehearsal of the famous tattoo which was due to be given the following week. It was a wonderful sight and very fortunately we didn't have to pay to go onto the Esplanade. Apart from seeing Edinburgh Castle, we were able to visit Stirling Castle and view the fantastic Regimental silverware.

Before leaving Dunbar, we took the chance to see George Furness, my cousin, and his wife Hazel. They lived locally because he was the General Manager of the local cement works. They were both pleased to see us because I hadn't seen George for many a year. At the end of the week we struck camp and moved across to the West coast and headed for a Camping Club site at Culzean (Culane) Castle which was about an hours run from Ayr. We only had Geoff and David with us because Tony didn't fancy having a holiday with his Mum and Dad now that he was turned eighteen.

The Castle itself was rather modern by historical standards but was very interesting to visit with its walls decorated with various types of armoury. The Head Gardener befriended us whilst we were there and the camp site was just outside the main entrance to the grounds of the castle and quite often we would stroll down to see him. He was very generous and provided us with many a few vegetables and eggs from the chicken run. These all came in handy when camping. There was one day, when after his duties, he took us in his car for a short run around the area and pointed out places of interest to us, including the famous golf club at Turnberry.

The price there, per night, was in the region of £114 and that was just for bed and breakfast, quite reasonable, we thought.

Whilst on the camp site, a Feast of Lanterns was organised for the members, who decorated their tents and caravans with whatever bunting they could dream up. During the day, there were various festivities during which David persuaded Nip and I to take part in a mixed game of football. It was all great fun. There were also various stalls selling trinkets etc., and some of them were set up for several games and on one of them David won a prize for the best total scored with three darts. That really pleased him. It was from one of the stalls that Nip and I decided to buy my Mum a tall bronze coloured glass decanter. It wasn't expensive but the thought was there. Mind you, we had to be careful when we packed it.

At night, there was a dance in the camp community hall and later on, towards midnight, a large bonfire was lit in a clearing in the woods and a lone piper played some traditional airs and reels. It was marvellous. We were sorry to leave because we had visited Ayr and Girvan, also the birth place of Robbie Burns, the Scottish poet. This really interested Geoff.

On the day we decided to go home. A nine force gale blew up and being on the top of a cliff just past the Castle, there was no shelter. It was bad enough trying to dismantle our tent because Nip rushed about pulling up tent pegs whilst myself, Geoff and David hung on to the frame. What a struggle. However, just a few yards away, a young family had arrived and it was obvious that they hadn't been camping before by the way they tried to handle their tent.

We couldn't really help them because of our plight and then, unfortunately, a huge gust of wind blew under their canvas and whisked it into the air, over the barbed wire fence and onto the beach below which was about a hundred feet drop. It was sorrowing to watch it all but we had to get off and, sorry to say, leave them to it. They did manage to tell us that they had hired the tent. Poor devils. But there you are, that's life.

I wasn't too pleased when we arrived home because whilst we had been away, Tony, with the run of the house to himself, had foraged around and found some registered envelopes addressed to me personally. This was because I had written some songs with lyrics and one way of making them copyright, was by posting them in a dated envelope, to myself, so my music teacher had informed me. What had Tony done? Opened everyone, thus destroying the copyright. Fortunately, none of them were ever published but I was livid at the time and gave him a strong dressing down.

It was early in 1969 that the new computer arrived at work and there seemed to be bodies everywhere as the task of installing it began. From day one there was a mishap because it had been decided to bring it in by the back entrance to the office block.

Fine. There was enough room for manoeuvrability but no one had informed the engineers that there was a cellar below. As it was eased through the doorway, everything looked great but in the next ten feet - crack!. The floor gave way and the computer began to sink under its own weight. Luckily, it came to rest and after the panic had died down, our works foreman, Keith Cooper and his assistant Frank Sheen, rounded up some labourers and by wedging and levering, the computer moved over the danger area and finally into the computer room.

After its initial introduction, the machine was finally set up but it took a couple of weeks before it was fully operational.

Bob Little had been writing a program to set up product codes, whereby each item produced and sold, could be coded for costing and sales analyses. Another program nearing completion was a name and address file of all customers who had purchased goods from us. This turned out to be a mammoth file because each one had a group of at least five punched cards and there were some fifteen thousand customers to record.

Going back to domesticity, at school, exam time was upon us again and Tony had been persuaded to stay on for a further year at school to try to get some better results.

Prior to his eighteenth birthday he had been busy preparing for his 'A' levels. He hadn't taken life seriously and thought that school was a holiday camp. Wherever possible, he would dodge academic lessons to play in the school orchestra as a percussionist. His final results were very disappointing. Nip and I told him that he would regret it in later life for not taking the opportunity to better his education.

When my Dad was living, he always emphasised that parents should give their children a better education than the one they had been able to have. To a point, I had achieved this because he had made sure that my knowledge alone, was better than his and now all our three lads had or were having a better schooling from the one I had received.

Geoff had worked hard at Rowlinson School and his results, though not excellent, showed improvement all round and comments from Mr. Dixon, his headmaster, were very favourable. Aline and I wondered if his extra effort was to show that he was equal to Tony and David passing to go to the Grammar School.

When David's report came through, his Mum and I hit the roof. Once again his efforts had been compared with Tony's with a comment that it was hoped he would be more conscientious than his older brother. I immediately wrote to the Education Officer in Sheffield and expounded on the thoughts of David's Mum and myself. It was obvious there was to be no reprieve from the stigma of Tony, so I asked if it would be possible at the end of this term to have David transferred to Rowlinson Tech. There he would be under the watchful eye of his other brother Geoffrey who was now in the Sixth Form.

Aline and I knew that a decision couldn't be taken immediately and enquiries would have to be made as to the circumstances involved. We did get a reply to my letter saying that the matter would be looked into and we would be informed at a later date. So we sat back and waited.

For our annual holiday we ventured further afield and having joined the Camping Club of Great Britain we were able to choose a campsite from their camping guide.

We decided to pick one at The Warren which was just outside Folkestone, in Kent. It was high up on the cliff top but also convenient for visiting places like Dover Castle and the cathedral at Canterbury.

One of our neighbours up the road, Mrs. Driver, was a foster parent to a young lad of our Dave's age. He was Martin Williams and a cheerful lad who spent many hours with our David. We asked Mrs. Driver if it was possible for Martin to come with us on holiday and for company for David. It was agreed and we told her he would only need some spending money.

I can't recall our Geoff being with us this time because it's possible that, having joined the YHA (Youth Hostel Association) as a life member when he was just fifteen, he had taken a holiday with friends he had met in the YHA.

In fact having settled in at the camp, the following day we popped into Folkestone to have a look around and not long after arriving, the heavens opened. Rain, thunder and lightning. We were worried stiff as to what state the tent would be in when we arrived back at the campsite. The centre of the town was about a foot under water and the local Fire Brigade were busy pumping water out of cellars under shops and pubs.

When we arrived back at the site, people were dashing about, ankle deep in water and the Warden was giving as much help as he could. He had a large, two inch diameter bar in his hand as he went in and out of the tents. When he came to our tent he went in and came out smiling. "You lucky people." He said. When we investigated, the inside of our tent was bone dry.

We had been fortunate because we had pitched up on a small mound. Apparently these occurrences happened quite often and the only way to release the water was by ramming the iron bar into the chalk ground on which all tents were pitched. As the bar was pulled out again, it had left a hole which seemed to act as a sink drainage hole and thus the water drained away quite rapidly and with the same noise as a sink. Where we had pitched, a hole was already there.

The vacation was made more enjoyable because Aline's sister Joan and her husband, Bill, had booked at the same time for a holiday in Folkestone but were staying in a boarding house in the town. We arranged to meet them one day and go to Romney Marshes via the Hythe and Dymchurch Railway, which ran along the coast.

Martin had not experienced anything like this before and in fact, neither had we. The line was a narrow gauge one and the engine and coaches were rather small. It was laughable trying to squeeze into the small carriages and once in, everyone had to sit with their knees hunched up. It was very awkward for Bill because he was rather tall and Martin couldn't stop chuckling at him trying to get comfortable. We only rode one way and decided to walk back to Folkestone along the beach road and although the weather was dull we enjoyed every minute. I had parked the car in Folkestone so we didn't have to walk all the way back to the Warren.

Joan and Bill had rented a small chalet on the beach at Folkestone and once or twice we would join them for the day down there. The lads seemed to take extra interest in a couple of topless lasses who were sunbathing and who were over here for the day from France. Although the beach was all pebbles, it was quite comfortable to lay on.

Martin also enjoyed it because he liked to go on to a jetty just below the camp site and take a line with him to do some fishing. It was convenient too to go into the sea and play around. Apparently, Martin hadn't had much of a family life, that was why he was fostered out but I'm sure he enjoyed his holiday with us. We only stayed for a week because of other commitments at home.

One of these commitments was to finalise arrangements for moving my Mum into a new flat. The Social Worker from Darnall School, which was the local DSS office, was a Mrs Ann Midgley and she worked really hard to get Mum moved. Eventually, in the summer, Mum was given a brand new bedsit in a complex on Richmond Park Drive and this complex had some twenty such places in it and there was also a caretaker cum warden, who along with his wife, was responsible for the managing of the building. Mum had been allocated an upstairs flat which had a reasonably long room where at one end a bed could be placed. There was a small compact kitchen with a fridge and an electric cooker and plenty of cupboard space.

The toilet was on the left as you entered the flat and there was also a small box room. At the other end of the long living room there was a bay window which overlooked some gardens attached to the flats. There was no bathroom in the flat but there was a communal one on the ground floor but that wouldn't bother Mum because she hadn't sat in a bath for years and preferred a strip wash. She had always been afraid of slipping again.

At first Mum didn't like being upstairs but she was told that there was a lift just along the corridor. When we found out that one of her new neighbours was Mr. Bartrop and his wife, she accepted the situation. Mr and Mrs Bartrop used to live near to Mum when they were in Attercliffe and they had lived at the top of Leigh Street in the last house on the left. Mr. Bartrop had also worked on the Railway at Sheffield Station and knew my Dad very well because of the local Union Committee.

It wasn't long before Mum made new friends and another good neighbour was found in Mrs Brough who lived on the same landing but just around the corner at the top of the stairs. She was an ex-policewoman who had served in the Attercliffe Division.

Ann Midgley called in occasionally to see how Mum was settling in and she also arranged for Mum to go once a week to Housteads Home. This was just across the road from the flats and was a residential home for old folk

The new flat was about one mile nearer to us and was more convenient because there was also a small shopping area, including the local Co-op at the end of the road. Mum now had a new Home Help and also a District Warden called Mrs. Lewis. The latter would call each day to see if everything was alright and go to Handsworth Post Office for Mum's pension when it was due.

When Mike Jessop had settled at TWIL and Bob Little had been made the DPM - a job I thought I might have obtained- Roger Farris handed over the reigns to them and he moved into a new position of creating a Corporate Planning Dept. This was established to work out the costs and involvement with the D.P Dept., for the purposes of reorganising the firm in general.

I was engrossed in running the input/output section of the department and teaching some of the female staff how to use the card sorter, reproducer, decollator, collator and interpreting machines. Having done a wireless mechanics course in the RAF, I was familiar with wiring circuits etc., of the hardware and it came in handy sometimes, if a fault was found.

There were odd times when it was necessary to go to other firms in the vicinity to use their equipment if ours broke down and this was a mutual understanding with all those who used ICL machines. I've had to go to such businesses as T.W.Wards, Firth Browns, English Steels and Davy United's to process some of our cards. It helped me because it was like joining an elite club and very soon I knew many other operators in the same position as me.

In preparation for the 1300 coming into operation, a position had been advertised for an experienced computer operator and on the 2nd June, 1969 a young lady was engaged. She was Sheila Holdsworth who had been an operator at Hy. Wigfalls', a local mail order firm. Sheila was very attractive with fair, almost blonde hair and her figure was really something to be desired. With her using high heeled shoes and knee length shirts it made it a little difficult at time to concentrate on one's work. One advantage of employing her was that she could also operate all the machines we had on line and this helped me quite a lot when I was pushed for time.

I still played cricket for TWIL and our sports ground was shared with the steel firm of Arthur Lee's and was half way up Handsworth Hill, near to where I lived. We were playing at home one Saturday and I took David with me to watch the game. During the tea interval, the captain, Fred, asked me to have a word with our Dave. He was up to his devilish tricks again and was squirting a water pistol.

It wasn't that it caught people but he had used it in the dressing room and wet some of the players change of clothes. We had some laughs whilst playing because there was one instance when at home when the weather wasn't too good and we had been blessed with a couple of light showers. The umpires had called us off and as things brightened up we were asked to take the field again. Whilst off, a card game had been started and the recall to play was in the middle of a hand of cards. Wanting to finish it, one of the cricketers not playing cards, climbed up onto the roof of the pavilion with a watering can and showered water down past the window.

"We can't go out just yet Umps, it's still raining." Was the call. For a further quarter of an hour the umpires fell for the joke and then realised what was going on. We were soon ordered out onto the field but the officials did see the funny side if things. One of the players that day, Hugh Facey, rose through the ranks and after making management levels in sales, he eventually left TWIL and founded his own company and became the managing director.

It was on the 20th July that the world was full of excitement because America had launched a manned space rocket which had three astronauts aboard. It reached the moon and one remained with the rocket whilst in orbit but the other two landed on the surface of the moon by a small module. The first man ever to set foot upon the moon was Colonel Neil Armstrong accompanied by Buzz Aldrin.

I know that some years ago when unmanned rockets were being sent up to explore the possibilities of landing man on the moon, my Dad would say. "They'll go too far one of these days and knock the moon out of the sky." You know, I think he meant it.

It was just before the summer school holidays that Aline had received a phone call from the Northern General Hospital to say that David had been involved in a car accident on his way to school.

The bottom of Staniforth Road at its junction with Attercliffe Road, was always busy in a morning and David had left the bus from Handsworth and run to the corner to cross the road to catch the No.17 bus to Firth Park.

As he was crossing the road, he hadn't seen a car which was approaching from the town and finished up across the bonnet. He was taken by ambulance to the hospital.

Aline had rung me at work and Bob Little gave me permission to dash up home to collect her and then go to the hospital. **WORRY!** There was no need to because after we found him in the casualty department, we could only laugh. He was on the chubby side and he had more or less bounced off the car and there he was with no broken bones and he was just in for observation. We laughed because he was lapping it up by propelling himself about in a wheel chair and beaming all over his face.

We were advised to keep him off school for a week or two and this ran into the holiday period. Just after that we received notification that our request had been granted for David to be transferred to Rowlinson Technical College and that he was to start there at the beginning of the next term in September. The decision Nip and I made, to have him transferred was one of the finest made, as was to prove in later years. One of his teachers there was a Mr. Startup and this man had a big influence on David's future.

This worked out fine because Tony had also finished his education at Firth Park and through the careers office he had managed to get a post at the steel firm of Samuel Osborns' in the Wicker In Sheffield.

So the sixties came to a close and many happenings had taken place, some were sad but overall, we had to thank God for small mercies and I, or should I say we, had to take care of my Mum and still help to guide our family to a better outlook.

THE SEVENTIES

As I started another decade, I became more involved with my work and apart from keeping records of input and output documents in ledgers, I also had to share the sorting and processing of punched cards within the department. As work progressed, it came to the stage where it was necessary to clear out obsolete cards at the end of certain periods. I asked Roger Farris as to what he wanted doing with them and he said to burn them.

Turning it over in my mind, I thought what a waste, so I made enquiries with certain waste disposal merchants and found that there was a reasonable price to be paid for good quality scrap cards. Roger said I could please myself because he wasn't interested, so I started to accumulate cartons of old punched cards, of which 20 boxes, each containing 10,000 cards, were equivalent to one ton in weight. The merchant with whom I had made contact was offering me £25.00 per ton so I made it a quarterly collection and to me it was cash in hand, no qualms, no illegality - Roger had given me permission, albeit verbally.

This arrangement went on for a long time and another perk was that at Christmas times, the merchant brought me a bottle of whisky as a complimentary gesture. In the purchasing Dept., there was a chap called Gordon Hinchcliffe who, after a couple of years, had tumbled to what I was doing and so arranged with his boss to take the collection of cards from me and accumulate the cards in the General Stores across in the works. Being clever, he amassed several tons over a long period but by the time he came to selling them, the price had dropped tremendously with the result that overall, the amount the firm received was negligible

It was a few months into the new year that I decided to get a better car and this time I bought an Austin Cambridge saloon which was a two-tone green and the registration number was JGK 804. There was more room in it and the front seat was a bench seat which enabled three people to sit in the front if the necessity arose.

It was just prior to this, to be precise, the 7th of February at Cedric Crescent, that Aline's Mum died after a long illness in which she had to have her leg amputated because Gangrene had set in. For the past two years Nanny Todd had been suffering and Joan, Aline's sister, moved into the flat with Mum to take care of her. Bill, Joan's husband, who sometimes could be very awkward, turned up trumps and mainly took care of himself although Joan did keep popping back to give him a hand. They only lived a few streets away across the village.

To give Joan some relief, Nip and I agreed that I would take her, Aline, over at the weekends to give Joan a break and a rest. It was on one Sunday when I went to collect Nip, that, although the situation was serious, there was still time to have a laugh. Aline had popped across the road to see Joan and had left me to keep an eye on her Mum, along with Freda's daughter, Pam, who was just a school girl. After about half an hour, Mum said she wanted to go to the toilet. Bear in mind, she still had two legs but still had difficulty in walking.

I eased her up out of the chair and with my arms around her, as if in a dancing position, I managed to waltz her into the bathroom. Now, Nanny Todd was a big woman but my physique was something to be desired and as I eased her towards the toilet, the weight of her body pinned me to the wall. We both started laughing and as we laughed she said that she was wetting herself.

I managed to turn her round and tried to pull down her knickers and put her on the toilet. The more I tried, the more we laughed and - the more she wet herself. It finished up with me calling to Pam to run over and get some help. When Joan and Aline arrived, they too were in hysterics when told the story. Up to Nanny Todd's death it was always a topic of laughter and one which I hope brought some light relief to a sad ending. It was a great loss to the Todd family and Aline took a long time to come to terms with it.

Nineteen Seventy was the year when the Government decided to reduce the voting age from twenty one to eighteen years of age. It was difficult to see the reasoning of this because to the older people, some teenagers didn't know what life was all about as this was to prove a few years later.

David had now settled at Rowlinson School along with Geoff and one of David's subjects was metal work. His tutor was Mr. Startup who seemed to have taken a liking to him and on one project he was sent to a large country home called Bagshawe House which was near the school and on its own estate. The object of the project was to go into the large kitchen, the visit had been arranged previously, and measure up the old fashioned spit which was over the large open fireplace. The idea was that David and two other boys would go back and make one similar so that it could be used at a school barbecue.

Mr Startup was a down to earth man who had served his time in the Royal Air Force as an armourer instructor. I think this had some bearing on David's future within the next few years.

Geoff was finishing his final studies in the Fifth Form, having obtained passes in the GSE 'O' level examinations for English, Geography, Chemistry and Music in 1969. Later on in this current year he achieved further passes in Maths (Adv), English Literature, French, Ord. Maths and Physics. Of the three sons we had, Geoff was the more academic.

Tony had left Firth Park in 1969 with reasonable results and four GSE 'O' levels and had managed to obtain work at Samuel Osborne and Sons' in their offices in the Wicker in Sheffield. Unfortunately his stay was short because of his outspoken thoughts which had offended one of the female staff. Therefore he was asked to leave. On the upside he was helped by an agency through his old school, to obtain another position at Hy. Wigfalls' in the computer department on Walker Street which was just off the Wicker. Apart from shops all over the country, Wigfall's was a mail order firm. It is possible that because I was involved in Computers, Tony decided to take an interest in his work and settle down to do some hard graft.

Having become used to not having Nanny Todd around and having acquired a different car, we decided to take another holiday in Scotland and this time find some places where we hadn't been before but eventually we finished staying in the Girvan area. It was a break and we had always liked Scotland, if only for its scenery.

Upon return from holiday, we found Geoff's name in the local press, the article read :- *'Geoffrey Priestley, an 18 year old student, of Ballifield Crescent, Handsworth, will carry a heavy responsibility on his shoulders in a 25-mile sponsored walk this weekend, organised by Sheffield Christian Aid Committee for one of Geoffrey's sponsors is the Master Cutler, Mr, Tom Burleigh, and it's the first time Mr.Burleigh has ever sponsored a walker. For every mile Geoffrey covers, the Master Cutler will give 40p and there will be an added bonus of a penknife if he finishes.'* Later Geoffrey was presented with the knife. Well done, son

It is often said that there is a lull in one's life and this seemed to be that period between Autumn 1970 and Spring 1971. Life was going on as usual and the lads were starting to go their own way as they grew older. Aline busied herself with knitting garments and sample patterns for EMU, the knitting wool manufacturers. The remuneration wasn't large but it provided her with a little spending money supplemented by a few bob she made by knitting for other people. She fitted this in whenever she could and treated it as relaxation because being a mother to three growing lads and an outstanding wife to me, was no easy task.

There was one incident when she saw something swinging past the living room window and upon investigation she found that David had tied some bedding together and was preparing to slide down it from the bedroom window. That was David who needed watching closely.

As usual, we had my Mum over for Christmas Day dinner but like I've said before, we couldn't settle down because shortly after tea, around six o'clock, she wanted to be taken home. Boxing Day was always a visit to Thurcroft to see Aline's parents but now that they had both passed on we stayed in the comfort of our own home.

So into the New Year where Tony had settled down at Wigfall's, Geoff was preparing for his 'A' Levels and David - well?

Earlier on in 1971, the 15th February, to be precise, the Government had put into operation the plan to decimalise our currency etc. To the youngsters it wasn't too bad but sympathy had to be shown to the older generation who had grown up all their lives with £.s.d. The half a crown went out of circulation as did the old halfpenny and penny and to the ordinary person the value seemed to be halved because the number of the coins was followed by a 'p' and not a 'd'. The sixpence (6d) became 2½p, the florin or two shilling piece became 10p and one shilling (1/.-s) became 5p. However, time must move on and we must accept the future and its committments.

During the Easter Holidays we decided to take David and Geoff up on to Emley Moor where the ITV Television transmitter was situated. It wasn't just to see the mast, which could be seen for miles around, but to witness an exhibition of an old Yorshire game called Knurr and Spell. This was a game where a 'potty' (a small round white marble) which was about 1½ inches in diameter, was suspended on a small type of gallows by a piece of string. As it hung motionless in middair, a player would take a special club which looked like a cudgel, place it by the potty and carefully swing it back and then strike the potty with the intention of knocking it out of its sling and sending it as far as he could. The winner was the striker who sent it the furthest.

At the game which was being televised, there was the presenter Austin Mitchell (later to become M.P for Grimsby) and the Yorkshire and England cricketer, Fred Truman, who was the adjudicator. The cameras were on the celebrities as they interviewed the winner and David managed to push his way near to the front.

We arrived home in time for the Calender News at 6.00 pm and David had to make a dash for the toilet. I switched the TV on and just as I did, there was the recording of the Knurr and Spell. We all shouted to David to come and watch and he ran into the room just as the shot disappeared of him standing between Fred Truman and Austin Mitchell. Hard luck son, but we enjoyed seeing his cheerful chubby face.

I went up to the garage at Handsworth one Saturday morning and as I was being served, the manager, Ron, said he had just had my son in. When I enquired which one, he said, "It was the youngest one. He's just popped in with the tractor from the cricket ground to get some petrol."

It was unbelievable. For weeks, Aline and I knew that he had been helping a Mr. Greenwood up at the Civil Service Sports ground which was just behind the Chemists shop on Handsworth Road. Little did we realise that he had been taught to drive the tractor and was cutting the grass regularly for Mr. Greenwood. I had to go and have a word with the man because David was only 14 years of age. It was explained that it was a 'one off' because the groundsman hadn't had time to go for some petrol himself. We didn't stop David going up there because it was some pocket money for him and he enjoyed it.

Geoff was still at Rowlinson and all his work seemed to take ages to do. Even his home work would be going on late at night and it worried Aline and myself. He was very keen but slow and at times I had to make him go to bed, even at that age. Little did we know that there was a problem there but that will be revealed at a much later date.

The 10th September, each year was the special day of our wedding anniversary, Aline's birthday and of course Tony's who in this year of grace, reached the milestone of his 21st birthday. Aline and I had planned for months to give him the traditional send off by throwing a party at home for him where he could invite family and friends.

Everything was in place and Aline worked really hard to prepare a buffet and a cake for Saturday the 12th because the 10th fell on a Thursday. Although it was his official birthday date on that day, he spruced himself up and went out to meet some friends - or so we thought. About 11 pm we heard the key in the door and in he stumbled. Nip arose from her chair, looked into the hall and called me. "Look at this!" She cried. There was Tony, legless and stoned out of his mind.

We pushed him towards the sink in the kitchen, Aline turned on the cold water tap and held his head under it. "I feel sick." He said. "You will be bloody sick when I've done with you." I yelled. "Birthday or no birthday, you must have gone out of the house with the sole purpose of getting pissed up and trying to prove you were a man."

He wretched and was sick on the floor. I more or less threw him into the downstairs toilet where he became wedged between the toilet basin and the wall, on his hands and knees. If it hadn't been for Aline I would have knocked hell out of him. After some black coffee, we slowly sobered him up and he did apologise.

"For two pins." I said, "I'll cancel the party." It was an idle threat because there was all that food and I had bought a certain amount of soft drinks and one or two other stronger types of refreshment. Saturday came and many of his friends attended, including John Thorley and his girl, Des Woolhouse and Susan Fisher, Keith Toyne and Tony, himself, had invited one of the girls from his place of work. She was Elaine Ramsden. Geoff, I think had managed to find a partner for the night and my Mum had been brought over for tea but didn't stay for the party. David joined in the entertainment.

We had a few party games and a record player which churned out a few pop tunes of the day. The young 'uns did a bit of snogging whilst the grown ups sat in the kitchen for awhile but everything went off fine and no one had too much to drink. By 11.30 pm everyone had gone home and Aline and I decided to leave the room to be tidied up the following morning. At least Nip and I had kept to tradition and headed Tony towards the future, I think.

Geoff's studying did pay off because during the summer he passed his 'O' levels for Economics and Additional Maths. Some of this reward could be attributed to his faith because on the 4th October, just prior to his 19th birthday, he accepted the Lord and was confirmed at the Handsworth Methodist Chapel, to which he had been attached whilst in the Boys Brigade. Geoff was a believer and thoroughly deserved his rewards.

In November, he obtained another 'O' level pass in Art and thus ended a productive educational era for him.

As we moved into 1972, Geoff and David were still at Rowlinson and David was preparing for his 'O' levels prior to coming to the official leaving age of sixteen years. As this approached, the Careers Master had a talk with him and enquired as to what profession he had in mind. "I'm going to join the Royal Air Force, Sir." David said. "No." said the teacher. "I'm talking of a long term career." "Yes, Sir. I've made up my mind. I'm joining the forces."

Following the interview, David had followed this up by calling at the RAF recruiting Office in Sheffield and getting an application form to join. On the tenth of February, we received a letter from the Recruiting Officer, Flt/Lt J M Wheeley, asking us to help David fill in the three forms enclosed and bring them, along with his birth certificate, to an interview on the 25th February at 11 am. If Boy applicants were successful in the aptitude and medical examinations, they would be invited for further test and interviews at the Youth Selection

Centre, at RAF Stafford.

David carried on until the end of term and managed to pass in four subjects at 'O' level and they were Maths, Physics, Technical Drawing and Metal Work, plus a pass at GCE level for Technical Drawing.

It was during April that Nip and I had a shock. Tony had been out in the evening and when he arrived home - which wasn't late - he informed us that the girl, Elaine Ramsden, was pregnant by him. "Are you sure it's you?" we asked. "Yes." Was his reply. "Positively." I turned and bellowed at him. "You bloody fool. Well, you'll have to do the right thing." And Aline agreed but I personally regretted ever having made that statement.

Elaine's parents, Ken and Thelma, had five children, three girls and two boys but they had no money so the onus fell upon Nip and I to arrange for the wedding. In the meantime, they had to look for a house and very fortunately Ken managed to find one on Woodbourn Hill which was quite near to where Ken and Thelma lived in Attercliffe. The house was a two up and two down terraced house and Ken said he would decorate it for them. Where was the money coming from? Not from us, but Ken was the artful dodger in acquiring items that were needed. He hadn't worked for years because he had an official 'Green Card' which stated that he was unable to work because of a bad back. This didn't stop him from being an official referee in local football. His brother, Bernard, used to play at left back for Liverpool Football Club. Whilst Ken and his son Kevin were doing things at the house they asked me if they could borrow some of my tools. Upon return, some were badly damaged, such as drill bits and some I never saw again. I learned my lesson.

Aline and I managed to find items of furniture to give them a start and a good item was an oak bedroom suite which my Mum had started us off with. It was in excellent condition with a tall wardrobe with a full length mirror and also a wash hand stand with a black marble top.

As Elaine became bigger, she finally had to leave Wigfalls' where she worked on the staff and the wedding day was finally set for the 5th May 1972 - Cup Final Day. The reception was held at our house and Aline worked her fingers to the bone whilst making the refreshments and cake. The whole Ramsden family thought that they were on another planet when they arrived and saw the house and spread of food.

The ceremony took place at the Registrars Office on Surrey Street and Geoff was the Best Man. Photos were taken on the front lawn and Elaine was very prominent as were Tony and Geoff with their mops of hair, which was the trend at that time.

I mentioned earlier that it was Cup Final Day and Tony was mad about football - and still is today - so it was agreed that all the men would go up to Susan and Bob Shirts' house at Aston, to watch the game on Telly. We hadn't a TV then. Bob and Sue were Eric's daughter and son -in-law who had been in the same boat as Tony and Elaine the previous year. What a funny way to spend time at a wedding reception by watching a football match. However, everything seemed to go off alright and afterwards, when people left, I took Tony and Elaine in my car back to their new abode on Woodbourn Hill.

Now that Tony hade moved out, we were able to change around a bit in our house and the main thing was that David moved into the small bedroom, which used to be Tony's, and Geoff spread out in the back bedroom. This arrangement helped both the lads when they were doing more homework. Aline said we ought to take the opportunity to do some decorating and David offered to do his own room by himself. He did, and though we disapproved after it was finished, we agreed that he had done a good job. He had painted the ceiling in a deep purple and the walls and furniture, which included an old set of drawers and dressing table, he had painted in camouflage colours. It was so good that when the window cleaner came, he thought that the room was empty because everything blended in.

After his first interview and medical, the main objection to him being accepted was that he was obese and needed to lose some weight. He achieved this by more or less living on Ryvita biscuits for several weeks until he tried again to join. This time he was accepted but had to wait for a vacancy in the trade he had chosen.

On the 16th June, we received a further letter from the RAF Recruiting Officer saying that as a result of his tests and interviews, David would be entered into the November, 1972 competition for Craft List 1 Apprentices which was to be compared with other applicants provided that he obtained the necessary GSE and GCE qualifications.. Would we also forward to him the official results of these examinations by the 30th September, 1972. David's apprenticeship was due to final medical examination on his arrival at the Apprentice Training School.

Whilst all this had been going on, we had decided to give David his last holiday with us so we went back to Folkestone at the Warren Camp Site. This time we pitched on a better plot and like before, we took one of his pals with us for company for him.

The friend was Nick Garewska, whose father was Polish but a good neighbour, married to Irene. Aline's sister Joan and her husband Bill went along again but made their own way there and stayed in a different boarding house to the last time that they were in Folkestone.

There were no thunderstorms this time and we had a good ten days apart from one day when the suspension broke on the car. I was fortunate to find a back street garage which was recommended to us by the Camp Warden. It took a day to fix and this cost me £9.00 pounds, the car being a Vauxhall Cavalier.

We also had a good day in Canterbury and spent a long time looking around the Cathedral and then went to a large open air market where I bought a large battery operated portable radio.

A few weeks after arriving home, David, somehow found himself a part time job in the Sheffield Wholesale Market on the Parkway. We didn't know how he did it but he had to be there in the early hours of the morning and arrived back home around about ten o'clock. He earned enough to stop him nattering us for pocket money.

Whilst we had been on holiday, Geoff had stayed at home, mainly to swot for his final exams, prior to leaving school. His efforts weren't in vain and although the grade wasn't as high as he had expected, he did achieve an 'A' Level 'E' pass in Geography. He was disappointed that he didn't obtain two passes at 'A' level because it would have assured him of a certain chance to go to University. However, it didn't deter him from trying to obtain a place at one of a number of other Universities with the qualifications he had obtained. He almost made it to Cardiff but the standards they set were just out of his reach. He was almost twenty years of age when he left Rowlinson. Although downhearted, he made up his mind to try to find a position where there was a future for him To him there was no rush and he decided to wait until the New Year to really make an effort.

On the 29th August, there was jubilation in the family because this was the day that Tony rang up to tell us that we had our first grandson. Elaine had given birth to a baby boy weighing about 8½ pounds and both were doing well. They had agreed to name him Mathew Gary but at a later christening his name had only been given one 'T' instead of two but they decided to let it stand and it looked unique.

Returning to the saga of David joining the RAF, and having acknowledged receipt of his GSE results, Flt/Lt Mills, the Recruiting Officer, informed us that David had qualified academically to be entered in the Craft List 1 competition. This was on the 22nd of September 1972.

At the end of October, we received a request from the Royal Air Force Recruiting Office in Sheffield, asking us to take David and witness the Attestation Ceremony prior to him being fully accepted into the service. On the first of November we witnessed him taking the Oath of Allegiance to the Queen., along with four other young lads who were joining. They had decided to go as apprentice armourers and on the 2nd November we took David to Sheffield Midland Station to catch his train to Halton via London and Wendover to the No. 1 School of Technical Training at Halton.

There were other parents there to see their sons joining the Armed Forces and obviously there was a lump in all our throats as we waved goodbye for awhile. Mr and Mrs Sutton, who were the parents of a young lad call Trevor, said that they came from Ulley, which was a tiny village between us and Thurcroft. We had a short conversation about the lads and then Aline suggested that we take them home in our car to Ulley. I didn't mind and it eased the tension and during the journey home we became very friendly and told them that we passed their house frequently whenever we went to Thurcroft. It was only four miles further to take them home and the journey is always pleasant when going out there.

When Aline and I were on our own we shed a tear or two because the 'Baby' of the family had left home and we wondered how he would cope with the new life. On the 4th November, we received a letter from David and that eased our minds.

It had his address on it, Room 5, Anson Flight, RAF, Halton, Bucks. Typical David, even to this present day he puts no date on the top of is correspondence.

Dear Mum and Dad,

Arrived alright. Five hour journey. A farce on the Underground, London, Don't worry about badly fitting suits. Have been measured from head to toe & for the length of the rifles. Lost sideburns. Kept tash and cigs. Please send me a couple of quid and a pack of cards. Had to pay for a haircut and new locks. Need to buy other necessities before the week's out.

Love,

Dave.

This was his first letter and several more informed us of his progress. Aline said that once he stopped writing to us, then he would have settled and this eventually happened and we settled down too. He was only 16 years of age.

It would appear that all parents were kept informed as to what was happening to their sons when they reached Halton and on the 8th November we received a pro forma type letter from Group Captain W E Dainty which was signed by him, explaining what was to happen.

First of all we were informed that David had been fully accepted as an apprentice and who his Flight Commander was to be. It was a Flt/Lt Yates and also the actual flight he was to be in and that was the Anson Flight. There were three pages of notes for parents to read and most of it was very informant. David had been selected for a two year course to train as an Aircraft Fitter (Weapons) and if successful he would pass out as a Junior Technician. Also we were informed that over the year he would be entitled to nine weeks leave which would be split over certain periods. The notice of interest was as to how much pay he would receive upon joining. This was shown as follows:-

Craft Apprentice	Weekly Pay	Amount Saved (Spending Money)
Ist Year under 17 yrs	£3.50	£2.08 (At 18
2nd Year at age 17 yrs		Apprentices
(Terms 1&2)	£6.00	£2.31 Go on full pay)

2nd Year, 3rd Term (And at age 18 yrs)	£9.00	As required

We were also informed that we would be invited to visit the school and see where our son lived and worked.

On the 16th December, we had another letter, this time from his Flight Commander, Flt/Lt Yates., saying that David was being moved into new accommodation and as from the 3rd January, 1973, we were to address his mail to 'Invader Flight', Apprentice Wing, RAF Halton (Building 13). We were also invited to a 'Parent's Day' on Friday the 2nd February, where we would have lunch in the Apprentice Mess with David. We looked forward to the day.

Christmas was a bit special because David was granted leave for the holiday and when he walked in we were so proud of him in his uniform. On his sleeve was the shiny Apprentice Wheel with the four propeller blades and also his peaked cap which had a red coloured hatband denoting he was an apprentice. He was proud too and no one was allowed to pick up his hat by the peak because the finger marks would show.

It was good to have all the family with us for Christmas dinner and especially Baby Mathew, who was now beginning to take notice. My Mum was also here and as usual and she enjoyed the day with us. David eventually returned to Halton and said he would see us in February when we went to the parent's day.

As we moved into 1973, I still couldn't take to Mike Jessop at work and I began to notice a relationship developing between him and Sheila Clarke, the punch room Supervisor. I mentioned it to Bob Little but he said that there was nothing in it but it seemed strange that on more than one occasion when I went to see Mike, his office door was locked and Madam was missing. It was obvious that she was keeping him informed of everything which was said in the department and this was beginning to wind me up. I proved my point by deliberately making some false remark about work and within a short while Jessop came to my office to see what was going on. The Chuff!

This man had two degrees and what in, I didn't know but one afternoon he came and asked me to go and fit a new petrol cap onto his car for him. I ask you? Then on another occasion, I had been working on the Interpreter machine for hours and just as I had finished, he came into my office. "What's wrong with the Interpreter, Ron? I can't get my cards through."

"That's funny." I said. "I've been on it for a couple of hours and I've had no problems but I'll have a look."

Now, to operate the machine properly, there is a metal weight which is placed on top of the pile of cards in the hopper and this helps them to lay flat and thus pass through the feeder. I picked up the metal plate and found the fault. The daft buggar had left a rubber band around the cards he was trying to get through. No wonder the machine wouldn't work. DEGREES? He must have been two under.

Bob had persuaded Jessop to let me have an assistant and early in the New Year they engaged a reasonably attractive lady called Jean Wright. She was willing to learn and eventually took quite a bit of work off my hands and she also picked up the way to operate the various machines. Jean was very fair, wore specs and hadn't too bad a figure and at this particular period, mini skirts were becoming very popular but that didn't distract me from my work because most of the female staff were wearing them.

Finding out more about her as each day went by, I learned that she was married to an ex-RAF pilot and that they were both in their mid forties. I eventually met him and Colin, as he was called, was quite a nice chap. Jean became a great ally because it wasn't long before she tumbled as to what was going on between Jessop and Clarkie. Jean also became a good pal of

Sheila Holdsworth, the other good looking blonde in the Computer Room.

As promised, on the 1st February, Nip and I made our way down to Halton for Parent's Day to find out how David was getting on and it was interesting to see the classrooms and work shops. I managed to have a word with his Instructor, as to what progress was being made. The sergeant told us that David must abide by what he was told to do because one day the class had been instructed on how to dismantle a sub-machine gun.

This had been done by all the class but when he, the sergeant, returned to David's bench, the gun had been re-assembled - correctly. But as the instructor said, one error could mean life or death in real life. David learned his lesson.

With regards to his barrack room, his Flt. Officer, who was now Flt/Lt Hood, said he was doing fine but one could hear David's voice on 'Bull night' when he was giving 'verbals' when telling other apprentices to get off his 'bumpered' floor before the inspection of same. A 'bumper' is a traditional weighted polishing tool which one pushes up and down to make the surface of the floor look like a mirror. Even I used to do it when I was in the RAF.

We returned home feeling satisfied with what we had seen and it help us to clear up any apprehension as to how David was coping with his new life.

It was during May, that I was trying to clear the reproducing machine at work which had jammed and to try to find the fault, I went and borrowed the engineer's ammeter. As I was bent down looking for a connection, Jessop came in. "You shouldn't be doing that. You should call the engineer." He said.

Now Ray Bamforth, the engineer, and I had an understanding that if I could diagnose the fault, then I would give him a ring and tell him if a new component was needed. Unfortunately, Jessop didn't know that I had been trained to use an ammeter in the RAF.

I turned to Jessop and told him that I knew what I was doing and in any case it saved the firm money if I could solve the problem and stopped the engineer from making a call out journey. He wasn't too impressed but he didn't bother me again. I can't repeat what Ray Bamforth said about him when I told him what had happened.

As to my being promoted up the ladder, I had no chance with Jessop and this was proved when on the 11th June, they started a young man called Sandy Glossop, as the assistant DPM to Bob Little. Agreed, Sandy was a programmer/analyst and I wasn't and that was because Jessop refused to send me on a programming course. At first I was reluctant to cooperate with Sandy but I soon overcame my inhibitions and managed to work alongside of him.

Whilst all this had been going on, our Geoff had managed to find work in February and had obtained a position in the GPO Headquarters in Fitzalan Square in the centre of Sheffield. His educational qualifications had helped him and from what he explained to us, there was every chance of him being promoted within the organisation but like every other job he had to start at the bottom.

This meant him getting up really in the morning to get to the main sorting office at the back of the headquarters. It was strange to him with it being his first position but he soon became used to it and he found some new friends. It also helped, now that he had some money of his own and didn't have to rely on his Mum and me.

Towards the middle of the year, around May time, David had told us that he had joined the Pipe Band at Halton. I didn't know that the RAF had bagpipe bands but I soon found that out when David told us that there was to be a massed bands display in Yorkshire at the RAF Camp Church Fenton. It wasn't far for us to go, so we made arrangements to meet him there and when we arrived, there were seven Pipe Bands from many units of the RAF, including one from Akritiri in Cyprus and many others from RAF bases around the country.

As we walked into the hangar, where they were all gathering, we were met by Pipe Major

Macleod, with whom we had caught a glimpse of when we were at Halton. He was an NCO who was proud of his lads and he was the only Pipe Major in the Royal Air Force.

There was a competition between the bands and there was also a competition for the best solo instrumentalist. The display of set marching patterns to fit in with the music was fantastic to watch and at the end of the day it was out of this world to see the mass bands marching and playing together.

We were very proud of David as he marched in his cadet uniform and wearing a large bear skin because he was the bass drummer. I took some photographs of him but at a later date we were able to obtain some professional photos of him and a side drummer and a piper. It stated underneath the photo that David was from Sheffield and the other two lads were from Leeds It was a good writeup in the Yorkshire Post newspaper.

Now that Aline and I were more or less on our own, even though Geoff was still living at home, we again decided to take our holiday with Bill and Joan. With there being just us four, we all went in our car and this time we went to Ilfracombe in Devon, for which Joan had done all the booking of apartments.

None of us had been there before but it was very pleasant and the weather was kind to us. The only fault with Ilfracombe was that it was in a sort of basin and to get out anywhere, one had to walk up a hill, no matter which direction one took. However, having the car did enable us to get to various places such as Saunton Sands, Bideford and Lynmouth, where those terrible floods had wreaked havoc a short time ago. We also went to Clovelly with its steep cobbled road to the beach. We had a shower whilst we were there and had to hurriedly buy some lightweight pakamacs.

Later on in the week we went to Westward Ho to have a look around the place and once again we had a short but heavy shower and this time we doubled up with laughter as Aline did a 'Gene Kelly'. She was obviously dressed for summer with a light frock on and just sandals on her feet. There she was singing "I'm dancing in the rain." and splashing up and down the kerb in and out of the puddles. She was so full of fun

I don't know why but the journey back home seemed to take ages and admittedly we had a couple of breaks but having left Ilfracombe about 10.30 am, it shouldn't have really taken us ten hours to get home. But it did. It's possible that I might have taken one or two wrong roads because all normal routes such as the A5 and A6, seemed to have disappeared. I also had to take Bill and Joan back to Thurcroft and this added a little time to the journey.

All this year had seemed to be about David but he was the youngest and we were pleased to see him adapt to his new life. In early November we received his first years' report and it was signed by Sqdn/Ldr W R Collins. The report was excellent in all areas with a 76% 1st Year General Service Knowledge result being classed as above average for an entree.

The only slight blip in the report was a reference to his Flt/Commander's comment regarding conduct and discipline. "Exemplary conduct. A cheerful lad. Doesn't know the meaning of the word 'Volunteer'".

In the middle of November, his name appeared in the local press again, saying that two local boys, who were at No.1 Technical Training School at Halton, had been two of 100 Apprentices selected to line the route between Buckingham Palace and Westminster Abbey for the wedding of Princess Anne to Captain Mark Phillips. The two 17yrs old boys were David Priestley from Handsworth and Trevor Sutton from Ulley Nr Rotherham. Once again we were very proud of our son and it seemed a good note on which to end 1973.

Going in to 1974 we had noticed that Geoff wasn't enjoying his work and when we asked why, he told us that one or two of the shift supervisors were pushing him too much and we understood that it was because Geoff had only one pace. We asked him to try to put more effort into it and we know that he tried. However, in the meantime he looked round for other employment and in March he was successful in finding a position at Samuel Osbornes' which was at Ecclesfield.

It was quite some distance for him to travel but if the weather was alright, he would go on his pushbike. The position seemed more to his liking because he was taken on as a telephone salesman, selling stainless steel forgings, bar ends and billets. The money was a little better and he didn't have to get up in the mornings as early has he had been doing whilst working at the GPO.

In May, on one of the Sundays that Tony and Elaine came to us for dinner, they were delighted to tell us that another baby was on the way. This pleased Aline and me and we were overjoyed to think that we were going to have another grandchild.

Within the correspondence we received when David was accepted as an apprentice, rules were laid down that parents were to discourage the boys from riding motorcycles, scooters etc., whilst in training. However, now that he was 17 years old and in his second year, David somehow managed to get around the situation and on one of his official leave periods, he arrived home on a CZ 250 cc machine. We couldn't believe it and when we asked him where the money had come from, he said that he had saved it out of his pay.

The bike wasn't a new one and hadn't cost a great deal but I think the leather cycling outfit he wore, including the leather boots, must have cost more than the bike. It had taken him four hours to get to us and he said it would have taken longer if he hadn't come up the motorway.

Nip and I both shouted, "Motorway?" "Yes." he replied, carrying on with, "I tucked my 'L' plates under the luggage rack." We couldn't help but laugh at his audacity and cheek, but we were glad to see him. It's a good job he wasn't pulled up by the police because it was illegal to ride on the M1 motorway whilst being a learner. He returned to Halton after a week but shortly after that he wrote to tell us that he had been involved in an accident but was O.K.

Apparently a French tourist was travelling along the Wendover road and had suddenly braked. David was a fair distance behind but hadn't time to fully pull up and had hit the back bumper of the Frenchman's car. The bike stopped but David shot headfirst over the length of the car and finished up in front of it on his back. There were some bruising but no serious injuries and the Frenchman accepted full responsibility.

This year Nip and I had agreed to go on a holiday by ourselves and we decided to try a Camping Club site at West Runton in Norfolk. So on the 9th June we travelled down and eventually found the site which was approached by turning off the main road to Cromer, down a side road and then turning right and slowly going down a cutting between the trees.

As we arrived at the end of the lane we came into a clearing at the beginning of which was the Warden's Hut which was the reception point. Having booked in advance, a pitch was saved for us and we set about putting up the tent. We were both tired with travelling and more so after knocking in the tent pegs and fixing the guy ropes.

We stayed fourteen days and enjoyed every minute by visiting Cromer, West Runton, East Runton and Sheringham. All were within either a fifteen minute run in the car or fifteen minutes walk across the fields into Runton Village. It was there that we would go into the parish hall to play bingo. The prize money wasn't big but our attendance, like that of other holiday people, helped to boost the funds. The locals too were very friendly and made us very welcome.

The walk to West Runton was very pleasant in the evenings and as we came out of the fields onto one of the small roads, there was the village green with its duck pond and as many as thirty different birds in it or waddling about. Typical country life, it was great. Being members, we always pick a Camping Club site because most sites were secluded, no non-members were allowed to stay on them and a noise curfew was imposed on all sites at 11.00 pm.

Whilst in this area we took the opportunity to visit Norwich for the day and this time on my visit I was able to see more because I wasn't working, as was the case when coming down to Barnards. We both enjoyed the visit round the Cathedral and wished we could have stayed longer but we had to get back to the campsite. It was a very pleasant holiday and we had enjoyed it so much that we said that we would return in the not too distant future.

Shortly after returning from holiday, I decided to look out for another car and a smaller one now that there was only the two of us to use it. So, in August, I managed to find one which was advertised in the local press and quite conveniently, the vendor's address was about two miles down the road from where we lived and on the Boden Wood Estate, just off Handsworth Avenue..

Aline and I went to have a look at it and found it to be a Vauxhall Viva which had low mileage, one owner and the colour was a fawn metallic one. The registration of the car was VWJ 197L and we said we would have it straight away. Within the week I had sold my other car, the blue Cavalier, which had given us some very good service and mileage.

Our Silver Wedding Anniversary was approaching and many of the family and friends had been invited to the function. I had also written to David's CO, to ask if David could be granted leave to attend the celebration which was to be held on Friday the 6th September.

On the 5th September, we received a reply from Halton saying that unfortunately, the Halton Pipe Band, on both Friday the 6th and also Friday the 13th September was engaged on important duties. "As the Bass drummer, your son is one of the key members of the band and it is virtually impossible to do without him on these occasions. Had he notified us immediately after his August leave, we might have been able to find a replacement." It was suggested that we alter our date of celebration to Friday the 20th Sept., because David had been granted a 48 hour pass for that weekend. Aline and I were very disappointed but it was too late to alter our arrangements.

We had managed to book a room with a bar at the Handsworth Working Men's Club which was just up the main road from where we lived. I had also managed to get Ron Chapman, a pianist I knew, to come and give us some light entertainment. Apart from the family, Fred and Norma Tyler came and also George and Marion Cottam.

There was a small problem when Eva, Aline's eldest sister and her husband Ted arrived because a few years earlier Eva had been unfortunate to have a brain haemorrhage and this had left her paralysed down one side. This meant that she had to have a wheel chair and whilst we were pondering on how to get her up the stairs to the function room, several of the young men there made nothing of it and bodily carried Eva and the chair up the steps. Ted couldn't have helped because many years before that, he himself had fallen off some scaffolding whilst working for a builder and badly injured himself. Ted was a Master joiner but could still do some light work.

My Mum also attended the celebrations and she too was still hobbling about with her bad hip and trying her best to manage with a walking stick, so, Tony, Geoff and two others did the same thing and carried her up the stairs. She wondered what was happening but she enjoyed it. She always did when anyone made a fuss of her. It was nice to have all the family together, except of course for our David.

All the previous week, Nip had been extremely busy preparing her own buffet and she managed to cater for all of the forty guests who were to attend. She was a wonderful cook and I suppose that we could have had outside caterers but she was very proud and took delight in what she did. In the same afternoon, prior to the do, I was busy running up and down with the car to the club to prepare the tables and set out the display of food. I later had to find another spare table so that we could show off some of the many presents of silverware etc., that people had bought us for the occasion.

Everything had gone marvellously for a few hours and everyone joined in with a dance or two but one thing was missing. DAVID. It must have been around 9.30 pm when there seemed to be a commotion on the stairs and I thought that we had acquired some gate crashers. It was. Into the room walked David and one of his pals. The Parade, on which he was supposed to be on duty, had finished early and he had obtained permission to come home for the weekend. His arrival finished off the day for Nip and me and it had all worked out well.

Whilst he was home, David had mentioned that one of the dates he had been refused leave for, was the 13th September because the RAF Massed Pipe Bands were to appear at the RAF Camp at Leuchars which was in Scotland and not far from St Andrews on the coast.

After the celebrations of the past week had died down, I suggested to Aline that the car needed a good run so how about going to see our David at Leuchars. She readily agreed, so on the following Friday, the 13th, we set off about 10.00 am for Scotland and the long journey North. We eventually arrived just before teatime and located David on the Camp. The surprise was on him this time and he helped us to find accommodation in a small boarding house near to the camp for the weekend.

On the Saturday, we went onto the camp to see the display and it was as good as before, perhaps a little better but we enjoyed seeing and hearing it all again. As Nip and I walked into the large reception hangar, Jock MacCleod, the Pipe Major, came over and said in his Scottish brogue, "Where the heck have you'se come from, Mr and Mrs Priestley?"

"We came to give the Halton Band our support." I replied

The Pipe Major said he could do with some support after the journey up from London. He told us that he had instructed the boys not to take any drink on to the train and he was sure that he had gotten the message home until he spotted our David struggling to carry the Bass drum It shouldn't be heavy, the bass drum, it's like an empty vessel. However, upon inspection, it was found that our lad had taken one of the skins off the drum and packed the inside with cans of beer. He got away with it because of his cheek and the Pipe Major commented that in a way, he had admired David's initiative. In the evening after the show, Aline and I joined in the fun in the local pub and mixed with the rest of the bandsmen

On the way home we stayed overnight at Dunbar so as to break up the journey a little and spent a few hours looking around the lovely small town of Dunbar itself. We set off early the following morning and when we arrived back home, everything was buzzing with activity as to Elaine's health with the new baby nearing its appearance and sure enough, on the 11th October she presented Tony with a baby girl, weighing about 6½ pounds. It was also our second grandchild and we were happy for both of them. Elaine had chosen the names of Lisa Ann, the latter being her grandmother's name. It had been hoped that the baby would be born on the same date as Geoff's which was the eighth but it wasn't to be.

October was turning out to be a busy month, because during the first week I received a phone call at work. It was Geoff, saying that he was supposed to take his driving test but the instructor hadn't turned up with the car for the examination. I told him not to panic, go and get some 'L' plates and I would meet him with my car at the Test Centre.

I arrived within twenty minutes, stuck the 'L' plates on my car and went with Geoff to explain to the examiner. He accepted our story and also that Geoff had never driven my car. Off they went whilst I waited in the small waiting room. Half an hour later they returned and I could tell by Geoff's face that he had been successful. I ran him down home and then returned to work again. Nip and I were both pleased for him.

In September, we had received an invitation card for the graduation ceremony of the apprentices at Halton, in which David would be taking part. That day, the 23rd of October, was almost upon us and David had managed to get us some accommodation in Wendover, so we met him at the entrance to the camp and he showed us where we were to stay.

We were both looking forward to seeing him in the Passing Out Parade but unfortunately the weather was dull and damp, which spoilt it for all those present. At first we looked all over the Parade Ground but couldn't see him and all those on parade were wearing white gloves and white webbing belts but we still couldn't spot him. Suddenly, Aline said, "He's there!", I looked and she pointed to the Pipe Band. He was there, not in the actual ranks of the Parade but in the capacity of the bass drummer.

It wasn't long after passing out that he was granted leave and was then to go direct to RAF Binbrook in Lincolnshire, This was his first posting. Having passed out as Junior Technicians, both David and Trevor Sutton (Sooty) were posted to Binbrook which was handy for them getting home at weekends. As JT's they were qualified to wear the badge of rank on their sleeves and this was a four bladed propeller embroidered on a dark background.

Getting back to reality, it made my day and year when, during December, just prior to Christmas, it was announced that Mike Jessop was to leave TWIL and also Sheila Clarke.

"I was right Bob, wasn't I?" There was a collection for a leaving present for them but Jean Wright and I agreed that they had no chance of getting anything from us. Very shortly after they left, Dorothy Pilley was made the supervisor of the punch room and were we glad?

Early in the New Year, Bob Little took over Mike Jessop's office and became the Group Management Services Manager, Sandy Glossop became the DPM and I was shunted into Bob's old office. I was doing less operating now but was still in a supervisory capacity with the machine room. Because of my position, I was able to take leave in urgent circumstances and one of them arose in April. Geoff had arranged for an interview for a new position which was to be held at a shipping firm in Grimsby. I took the day off to take him there and whilst the interview was in progress, Aline and I popped into Cleethorpes for an hour to pass the time away.

Geoff had always wanted to do something in the traffic industry and constantly wrote for vacancies which appeared in the local press. This was one of those occasions when he had been successful and when he rejoined us, he was beaming all over his face. The position was his but - he had to move to an office which was situated in the port of Felixstowe in Suffolk. He handed in his notice to leave Osbornes' on the 1st June 1975 and on the 7th July I took him by car to this east coast port to start his new employment. The firm had helped him to find a terraced accommodation which was not far from where he was to work.

He appeared to be settling down but it wasn't long before he felt homesick. Fortunately, Aline and I had decided to go once more to West Runton for our holidays, so we told Geoff to come up and join us for the weekend, because the tent was big enough for three people and still have some room in it. The journey wasn't a long one for him and he was pleased to see us, even though it had only been a few weeks from leaving home. We decided to take him back to Felixstowe in the car and it would be a run for us. This we did and hoped that the weekend together would have cheered him up somewhat. As we left to return to West Runton both of us had our doubts as to him staying down there so far from his home and friends.

Shortly after returning from holiday, it was on one particular Sunday when Tony brought his family for dinner, that we noticed that Mathew had a cast in one of his eyes and Nip and I suggested that they take him to a Doctor to get it seen to. It would appear that during one morning at their house in Woodburn Hill, the electric meter reader had just barged in at the back door where Mathew happened to be standing. The kitchen door hit him on the side of the head and we had always wondered if that was the cause of the cast in his eye.

Tony and Elaine did get Mathew examined and it finished up with him having to go to Lodge Moor Hospital where the Doctors successfully turned his eye but he couldn't see out of it. It was a pity because he was a lovely looking boy and although the operation made him look normal, the loss of sight in that eye was to be detrimental.

Everything seemed to be running smoothly until Geoff came home one weekend in the middle of August and told us that he was in trouble with the police. Apparently he had been feeling so lonely that he had been out for a drink and had taken a little too much. Because he felt drowsy, he had entered an empty car on the forecourt of a garage and fallen asleep.

The following morning, the proprietor had called the police and Geoff was charged with 'loitering with intent'. It upset Aline and I very much but we told him we would get a solicitor to fight the case and this we did. It was one from a firm which had just opened up at the top of Orgreave Lane and was quite near to where we lived.

Geoff gave all the details in explaining what had happened and the solicitor said to let him know when Geoff was to appear in court.

He went back to Felixstowe and he eventually received a letter from the authorities telling him he had to appear on the 8th September next. Geoff booked us some accommodation and Aline and I went down on the 7th Sept., and stayed overnight in a boarding house, close to where he himself was stopping. We both gave him encouragement and told him not to worry too much as things were sure to work out alright.

We arrived at the Court House at 11.00 am and a solicitor, not the one we had seen back home, but one who had been contacted by ours, had been given the brief. When Geoff was called into the court room there were also about twenty elderly ladies from the Women's Institute in the public gallery and they were there to see how proceedings took place.

The charge was read out and Geoff's solicitor rose to his feet. He put the case so eloquently, explaining about this lonely young man, with a good education, trying to make his way in life and sacrificing the home comforts of a loving mother and father, to better himself. He was so good that the old dears were in tears and so were we when the magistrate only stipulated a fine of £20 and dismissed Geoff. We expressed our deep felt thanks to that wonderful solicitor. He was great.

Under the circumstances, Geoff didn't serve any notice with the shipping firm and after the court case we had a look around Felixstow and even had time to take a short trip in a boat across to Harwich where we had a meal and then made our way back to the car, picked up his belongings from his digs and made our way home with Geoff in the back. The relief on Geoff's face was a picture to watch and we were happy and relieved too. Upon returning home, it wasn't long before he found another job as a stock controller at a small firm on Rutland Road and this was a firm called Crusteel Ltd.

It was during one of many visits to the Accounts Dept., at TWIL whilst reconciling accounts records with our computer record, that I came into conversation with Gilbert Catton, who was one of the senior clerks. Gil had a small diamond shaped badge in his lapel with a small 's' showing on a blue background. I asked him what it was and he said it was the official badge of an ex-servicemens association called 'The Fellowship of the Services'. It was an organisation of men who had served in His Majesties' Forces in all services, irrespective of rank.

Gil asked me if I was interested in joining and if I was he would sponsor me if I could get a seconder who was also in the organisation. Now fortunately, I had worked with several members wearing the badge whilst I had been at Firth Vickers. I contacted one of them, namely

Fred Morris and he turned out to be the Secretary of one of the Messes which was part of the setup. Having decided to join, Gil gave me an application form to fill in and he signed the proposal form for me to take to Fred to second it. It took quite a while to go through the necessary proceedings but eventually I was called

On the 27th September, two days after my fifty fourth birthday, I received a letter from Fred Morris saying that I had been accepted for membership to the Fellowship. I let Gil Catton see it and he arranged to go with me to No. 163, King Edward Mess which was situated at the King Edward Hotel on Poole Road in Darnall. The invitation was for my initiation on Thursday the 11th December 1975 at 8.00 pm. I had to wait outside the room until called but Gil had gone in because he was a Passed Chairman. So at 8.15 pm that evening I took the necessary oath and became No.60015 Companion G.R.Priestley in the Register.

I soon learned of the benefits in the Fellowship and a meeting, or concert, as it was called after the Ritual, was held every month at the same venue. On initiation, I was given a voucher with my membership number on it and this would always prove that I belonged to the FOS, also I received my small lapel badge by which I would be recognised. The two hours after ritual were taken up by being paired off with another Companion for the night by which you bought refreshments for each other and no one else. One or two Companions would render a song and some would entertain by telling jokes which were the Armed services type.

Women were not allowed to join but at varying intervals during the year, a Mess could hold a Ladies Night and on these occasions, wives and girl friends were allowed in after the Ritual or at other places of entertainment where the Ritual wasn't carried out. There were some four hundred and thirty messes in Fellowship and they were spread, not only all over the country, but also as far a field as Australia and New Zealand.

There were some forty men in our Mess and each year a new Chairman was elected and this depended upon his seniority and service in the Fellowship. Also each year, there would be a Chairman's Dinner and this was one of the occasions when ladies could attend and usually a dinner was booked at some special rendezvous. I was invited to the Chairman's do on my first year and we went out to a large hotel, The Royal Oak, at Taddington in Derbyshire. I was able to take Aline with me and we both enjoyed the dancing which took place after the marvellous meal we ate. We also enjoyed meeting many new friends.

It was early in '76 that I stepped out of the bath to dry myself when I noticed that my Scrotum was inflated like a huge bag. There was no pain but I called to Aline to come and have a look and when she saw it she said that I ought to go and see the Doctor. I went to see Dr. Shaikh and he referred me to the Hallamshire Hospital for examination where I came into contact again with Professor Duthie's Department. I was diagnosed as having a Hydrocele, which was excessive fluid in the Scrotum and I was given an appointment to go and have it attended to. A couple of weeks later, I went to the Hallamshire and was directed to a cubicle and told to strip off my lower garments. Having done that, a young doctor came in to look at my predicament, went out and returned, accompanied by Prof. Duthie. The young doctor picked up an instrument which looked like a huge knitting needle but with a plunger attached. He performed with the needle and it was obvious that he hadn't used it before.

He hesitated, looked at the Professor, who very sharply said, "Get on with it, young man!" The junior doctor still hesitated so the Professor took the instrument from him, came towards me and said, "It won't take a minute and shouldn't hurt." Oh No! He pushed the point of the tool into my Scrotum and slowly pulled up the plunger and drained off the fluid. There was no anaesthetic.

"There you are Mr. Priestley. See how you go on but if it refills, you will have to come back. In any case I'll see you in two month's time." That time soon passed and sadly to say, the fluid accumulated again. When the Doctor saw it he told me I would have to undergo a minor operation to correct the trouble. So it was that shortly after, I was admitted to the Royal Infirmary because the Hallamshire, as a surgical hospital, hadn't been built. I had to chuckle to myself when I reported to the hospital because I was put into Ward 10 again, the Ward where I had been for my ulcer operation.

I felt a little embarrassed because the 'houseman' was a lady doctor and she came and examined me, telling me that I would be in for a couple of days. The operation was a success and no further discomfort occurred. However, there was a humorous ending to it all because after I was on my feet again, I paid one of the weekly calls to see my Mum. She was glad to see me again and when I explained what had happened, she replied in her hypochondriac way, "I've had one of those, a Hydrocele." It so happened that Tony was with us on this visit, he disappeared into the hall, Aline went into the kitchen and I went into the boxroom. We were helpless with laughter. Poor old Esther.

Mum had kept up her regular visits to the centre at the Manor Top and as the holiday period was approaching, we had made arrangements, or should I say Dr. Crowther had made them for Mum to go into Housteads Nursing Home whilst we were away. It was just across the road from where Mum lived and we knew that she would be fed and cared for whilst we were on holiday. She was a little reluctant at first but the Doctor insisted that this would be for the best and in any case, he told her that Aline and I both needed a break.

Still taking a great interest in camping, Nip and I thought it a good idea to find 'fresh fields', so we chose another camping club site which was at Norman's Bay on the Sussex Coast.

In the last week of June we set off for the long journey down to the south coast and the route took us down the A1Trunk road and through the centre of London. Not having passed directly through the big city before, it was a bit of a nightmare and with the heat of the day affecting traffic light systems, it wasn't easy. I finally found my way through the Hyde Park area and down the Edgeware Road which seemed to be the most direct route.

When I mentioned the heat, the temperatures were up in the 80 degree mark and we had all the windows open and Aline was sat with her feet up on the dashboard trying to keep cool. I know that one or two lorry drivers who passed us, must have had a real eyeful of her lying there with her dress up around her knees.

We eventually made it to the campsite and after making a drink, we set about pitching the tent. The site was very flat with only a short distance from the beach which had large pebbles and was supposedly the same one that William the Corn Curer landed on in 1066. The next few days were spent exploring various places of interest, such as the small town of Battle and the Abbey which was a historical place during the Battle of Hastings.

Having the car, we were able to go down to such places as Pevensey Bay and Beachy Head with its famous lighthouse. Bexhill was just up the road from the camp and we made a few visits to there and Hastings. It was during a visit to Bexhill that I had an idea. Maidstone wasn't too far away so I said to Aline that I would look in the 'phone book in the nearest 'phone box to see if I could trace Howard Masson's address and telephone number. Howard was Aunt Mag's son whom I had mentioned very early on and lived in Maidstone.

It was a thousand to one gamble when I saw the name, H.Masson. Now Howard is an unusual Christian name but I rang the number. A female answered and I said, "Is that you Queen?" Which was Howard's wife's name. "Yes." Was the reply. "Who's that?"

When I explained, she couldn't believe it because it was some forty years since I had seen them. I told her what we were doing down there and she asked us to call in and visit them.

At the end of the first week, on the 1st July we left Norman's Bay and headed for

Maidstone. With Aline navigating, I eventually found the address and both Queen and Howard greeted us. We had lunch with them and talked over old times also discussing the fact that Howard had just retired from the local paper manufacturers having worked there for many years after leaving the Army. He had contacted Ella who lived on the other side of town and had arranged for us to pop over and see her whilst we were in the vicinity. We left Howard and Queen in the afternoon and made our way over to Sussex Road where Ella lived with her husband Rob Robinson and following the instruction given by Howard, we found them. It took us about thirty minutes and Ella was looking out for us when we arrived.

She was so pleased to see us because I hadn't seen her since 1942, when I was stationed at Dagenham. She introduced us to Rob, her husband and two of her daughters were still living at home. There was Lorna and Gwenda, the youngest one, they were both nurses in the local hospital. It was good to reminisce about old times and when I used to go down for the weekend to her Mum's at Boro Green.

We left after tea and made our way back to Norman's Bay and enjoyed the rest of the holiday. That is as best we could because all the time we had been down there, the heat of the sun was unbearable. Every day it was up in the eighties and the weather reports said that we had been experiencing the second highest temperatures this century. Because of the heat, we decided to set off for home early so we left at a quarter to eight in the morning and it paid off because we missed the heat of the day and arrived back in Sheffield at 12.45 pm in the afternoon. Mind you, we had to have one or two breaks on the way and with the heat we needed them.

Upon return to work, I asked Bob Little if I could do an exercise to reduce the work load of the computer operators. The position was that each month, they had to feed in 75,000 punched cards into the computer to obtain a list of sales customers for sales analysis and this meant emptying and refilling 38 trays, each one containing 2000 cards. My theory was that if we took out all customers from the file, who hadn't made a purchase over the past five years or more, then the file would be reduced tremendously.

Bob consulted other managers and they reluctantly agreed to try it. A program had to be written to decide which customers would be involved and that task fell to Sandy. For each customer there was at least five punched cards, so one can imagine the impact it would have if my idea was successful. It took many hours of hard work going through the necessary lists and extracting manually the relevant cards of each customer with whom we had not done business with over the past five years. The effort was worth while because the outcome was a list of 15,000 customers was reduced to some 5,000 and the time saved was very valuable.

Because of this exercise, it meant that I had to go down to one of our subsidiaries to check the records and this was a firm called Goodwin's who were based at Watford in Hertfordshire and they made wire staples for the stationery business. Because our accounts department was involved, it was necessary to take someone from that department with me. They chose the office manager, namely, John Hunter who was some fifteen years my junior but was compatible with me in thinking and working.

The work involved resulted in John and I searching through many files of invoices which at times was very monotonous so, instead of trying to do it all in one day, we had arranged to stay overnight at one of the Hotels in Watford where the accommodation had been booked in advance by Head office at Sheffield. This gave Clive Skinner, the office manager at Goodwin's, the chance to invite John and me out for the evening to a meal and a drink at the firms' expense.

The night out was to one of Clive's favourite restaurants which was Italian. John and I returned to our Hotel for a couple of hours so that we could freshen up before meeting Clive, who by the way, very conveniently resided just about a hundred yards up the road from the factory.

From 7.30 pm until 11.00 pm, we sat and talked, sat and joked, discussed the work we were doing, had a few drinks and more than one cup of coffee which we think was the cause of our following illness. John and I returned to our hotel but to different rooms and as soon as I laid down, I started. I was sick all over the room, I couldn't get to the bathroom in time and I felt so ill and embarrassed at the mess I had caused.

I eventually managed to get some sleep and when John came knocking at my door at 8.00 am I thought it was thunder. I let him in and he helped me pack my belongings so that we could get out as soon as possible. He said he would hand in my room key because I didn't look capable and I wasn't. Oh! I did feel ill and when I reported in at Goodwin's I couldn't do anything but slump helplessly in a chair in the foyer of the offices.

Apparently I wasn't alone because John felt ill too and then Clive Skinner turned in at 10.00 am and he looked terrible, just like me and it didn't help when one of the reps from Sheffield, Tony Ball, came in the front entrance. "My God. You look rough." He said.

The rest of the day was a struggle but John and I eventually completed our task. We arrived back home just after teatime and the next day, word was put around that we had been on a binge. NO WAY! It was food poisoning and did we know it. Obviously the story had come from Tony Ball.

Our David was still at Binbrook and on several occasions, in the capacity as an armourer, he had to go with a detail down to the beach at Donna Nook to accompany a civilian bomb disposal expert. Donna Nook was the place where a few years earlier, the RAF Security had taken us off in a lorry.

It was on one of those visits that the civilian's job was to dispose of some highly dangerous explosive waste and Donna Nook was an ideal place because it was isolated and partly desolate. Apparently this civvy had prepared the waste for disposal on the sand when, the detonation went wrong and he was critically injured. He was carried back, or what was left of him, to the service vehicle and everyone was in shock but somehow, David calmed down the other personnel and made them a drink to steady their nerves. The civvy lost his life and several months later, David received a written commendation from the Group Captain for showing his initiative in such a terrifying incident.

This year was another milestone for the family because my Mum, on the 22nd November 1976, reached the ripe old age of 80 years. To celebrate the occasion we had arranged a party for all the family to come to. Aline had excelled herself with the catering and she had also made a birthday cake with an "80" in icing on the top.

How Mum managed to reach this age I do not know because since Dad had died, Aline and I had many a problem looking after her. We were always up and down to the flat but that was by the way. It was Mum's special day and we tried to make it a happy one for her and along with all her grandchildren and great grandchild, I'm sure that she enjoyed herself.

To celebrate a little independence of her own, Aline kept looking in the adverts of the local press for part time workers and in January 1977 she went for an interview at a small bakery named Hardy's in the Heeley area of Sheffield. She came home full of smiles because she had been offered a position as a shop assistant in their bread shop in Union Street in the centre of town. It meant getting up early in the morning to be at the shop by 8.30 am because besides selling bread they also made sandwiches etc., which was a thriving business in the centre of a busy city. She soon took to the job and it made it better when she found out that one of the other assistants, Mrs Renee Foster, lived a few streets away from us but higher up the estate on Ballifield Avenue. The money wasn't good and she finished at 3.00 pm but it was sufficient for Aline to buy necessary things which normally we couldn't afford. It also helped her to build up some savings for a rainy day.

Early in March, on the 8th, I went down to Watford again but this time I was booked into a different hotel which wasn't too sparkling but suitable for one night. I did a decent day's work considering that I arrived at 11.00 am from Sheffield but as we closed down for the night another member of the staff, Dan Bridges, asked it I would care to go out for the night, down to his club. I thought, well, it couldn't be as bad as the last night out down there.

I accepted his invitation and he also invited Clive Skinner so that he could take me in his car. It was necessary because Dan's club was down in Slough, which was a thirty minute run away. Clive picked me up at 7.00 pm and off we went. He hadn't been before so it took a little time to locate the club but he did and Dan was on the lookout for us.

It was a pleasant evening and I enjoyed the company of the chaps but I made sure that I didn't have too much to drink this time. It must have been 11.00 pm when Clive and I left for Watford, the night was clear and dry and the traffic was rather quiet. It was a good job because Clive had drunk enough and didn't I know it as we 'sped' homewards towards Watford. The traffic lights in Slough were numerous but if you timed them properly, you could go through all the sets without stopping.

We did. The speedo was showing 80 mph and my knuckles were white as I hung on to my seat. I was dropped off at my hotel and was I glad to get into bed. There were no ill effects this time and I finished my task at Goodwin's the following day before driving back to Sheffield, in one piece. With the information I had obtained at Goodwin's, I was able to process many items connected with my special project but even so, I still had to make a further visit down there.

My next journey was on the 10th May and once again I was booked into a different hotel. Not for any misdemeanour but because of the convenience. I only stayed the one night but Clive invited me to a meal and then onto his club. This was the Bushey Conservative Club and it possessed a three table snooker room.

Clive asked me to make up a foursome with his friends and we had an enjoyable evening. Incidentally, Ray Reardon, the World Snooker Champion was also a member of this club. This turned out to be my last visit to Watford but I made the most of it.

Before leaving Sheffield, I had asked Bob if I could have a couple of days off whilst I was down there, to which he agreed. This enabled me to drive down through London and pay a visit to see Ella and Rob at Maidstone. They were both glad to see me and made me very welcome. We were able to carry on where we had left off last year except for the fact that as I arrived, I could tell by Ella's face that something wasn't right. No it wasn't, because the first thing that greeted me was that Howard, her brother, had passed away after a massive heart attack. What a shock and a tragedy to think that he had lived a good life and was just looking forward to enjoying retirement. I stayed overnight and the dismay didn't make my visit a very pleasant one.

Once again, Geoff didn't seem to fit in at work and in June he left Crusteel but once more he had luck with him because by July he had found another position at a similar small steel firm named Rowland Tucker which was down on Tyler Street in the Brightside area. Here he was employed as an estimator and storeman and this hepled me to a point because my garage on the communal site was getting the worse for wear and Geoff was able to get me a supply of galvanised metal sheeting to repair the doors of the garage which had worn at the bottom due to the bad weather in the winter months.

On the 25th June, Aline and I went camping again and this time we chose to go to Lyme Regis and this too was a camping club site but the actual site was at Charmouth which was a little way inland.

It was whilst on this site that another camper showed us their trailer tent and we were very impressed by the layout and of everything being compactly stored.

We made this a leisurely holiday and the weather was good again, so we just took our time and visited one or two places of interest such as Bridport, Honiton and Chard. A different venue each year seemed to keep us interested in life in general.

In November, 1977, there was a National strike of the Fire Brigade and this resulted in the Armed Forces being called upon to give any assistance that might be needed. During the War, small vehicles called 'Green Goddesses' were used by the services to suppliment the Fire Brigade and these were now called into service again to help in the strike.

David was still at Binbrook and he was one of those detailed to give assistance which meant him being put on detachment at Church Fenton in Yorkshire. He was based at the RAF Camp and had to be called upon several times but on one occasion he was overcome by smoke and for weeks he had a bad chest.

He did manage to get a weekend leave and turned up with a 'pot' on his leg. We thought that he had done it whilst fire fighting but he told me on the quiet, that he had been enjoying himself in the WAAF's quarters and the WAAF in the next room had called the RAF police because of the noise our David and his enjoyment were causing. Upon hearing the police coming up the stairs, David had jumped out of the bedroom window and broken his leg. So he had two 'jumps' in one night. Boys will be boys.

At the end of the Firemen's strike, David returned to Binbrook but his pal Trevor decided to leave the RAF. It appeared that he was afraid of the dangers of being an armourer.

Being in the Forces, one had to be prepared to be sent anywhere as was the case in April 1976 when David, along with the rest of the Camp, moved to RAF Leconfield whilst the runway at Binbrook was repaired. It was whilst there on this camp that he met a young nurse called Heather Phillips and in the six months he was stationed there, he surprised us by bringing her down to meet us. She was a quiet lass but very pleasant and her family hailed from a small village called Eckington which was near to Pershore in Worcestershire. Her Mum and Dad worked for the RAF but in a civilian capacity. She also had a brother, Malcolm, who was in the Air Force and her sister Cynthia kept up the tradition by marrying an airman.

It wasn't long after returning to Binbrook that David's application came through for aircrew training. This meant him going to RAF Finningley, where he was to train as a winch man on the Air Sea Rescue helicopters. He appeared to be doing quite well for several weeks until it came to passing out.

Upon passing out, all cadets took part in a ritual from within the Mess and this ritual entailed each person to be thrown into a pond which was situated just outside the main entrance to the Mess. David had been suffering a long time from the smoke inhalation which he had sustained whilst firefighting and when it came to his turn to be ducked, he objected. No one was supposed to refuse and if they did then they were physically manhandled and dumped into the pond.

Several other Cadets approached David to take him outside but because of his chest infection, he flatly refused. As they approached him, he picked up a bottle from the Bar, smashed it and then threatened the advancing party. "The first one to touch me, gets this!." He cried. They all fell back but he was later charged with the offence. The CO refused to accept his explanation and he was taken off the course. I think he returned to Binbrook for a short time before being posted to Honington to carry on in the trade he had been trained for, an Armament Technician.

Geoff had done well to stay at Rowland Tucker's for nearly eight months but his ambition was to get into transport had encouraged him to do some research and he had managed to come upon a Government Scheme whereby he could gain more knowledge in this subject.

On the 6th February, 1978, he set off for Thurrock Technical College where he was to train for freight forwarding with the possibility of getting a good position in that field. Thurrock wasn't far from Tilbury in Essex and also very near to the Dartford Tunnel. This came in handy on a couple of occasions when Geoff wrote home to say he was at a loose end at the weekends.

I suggested that he went down to Maidstone and stayed with Ella and her family for a change so I contacted her and she was more than delighted to have him. That eased his mind somewhat and he completed the course by the 30th June. This was classed as higher education and by receiving his Diploma, he had added another feather to his cap to go with his other achievements.

I mentioned last year that we had been shown around a trailer tent, when we were at Lyme Regis and we were so delighted with it that this year we decided to buy one. We had seen an advert in the Camping Magazine for a Concraft Ranger Trailer Tent which was on offer. This was possible because we had to get it direct from a small factory which was situated in Tusmore, which was a little village near to Bicester. On the 9th June, 1978, Aline and I set off down south to collect our new tent. It took a little while to find the place, which, when we did, turned out to be a converted farm house and building. The people were very kind and checked everything out, including the towing bar and trailer lights and they made sure that everything was in perfect order before accepting any money.

The invoice for the whole unit came to: -

Trailer and Tent	£291.80	
Extension and spare wheel	£83.41	
Extras	£9.26	
Bogie	£14.30	
VAT	£31.89	
Total		£430.66

The base of the trailer was galvanized metal and we bought the bogie extra because the width of the base was too wide to go past our outhouse into the yard. The idea of the bogie was that it slotted into two supports near to the wheels and then was tipped onto its side and wheeled to where it was to be stored. It took us a couple of hours to get back to Sheffield and following instructions, we finally put it into the back yard for the night. Because the galvanized base was so heavy, it took both of us to tip it up and move it and then took both of us once more to lower it back onto its wheels. Over the years, it proved to be a very good investment with the interior being a colourful and comfortably upholstered. The actual tent and extension, by the way, were made by John Hawley & Co., one of the top manufacturers of tents in the country with their factory being in Walsall.

Having bought the new tent, we looked through the Camping Book again for a different and suitable site on which to try it out and we chose Slapton, in Devon. It was on the 24th June that we set off and after a long journey we eventually reached a small place called Strete and as we passed through it and came to the top of a small rise, we had a marvellous view of the beach down below. We thought it would be ideal for swimming but we couldn't understand why it was so empty with no one about. It was later on that we found out that it was a beach of tragedy and that hundreds of American soldiers had lost their lives on that beach whilst training for 'D' Day in World War II.

Whilst on the camp we befriended two young London lads who were in the next tent to ours and one of them asked one day if we liked fish. When we asked why, he said that he and his pal were going down to the beach to catch some. Aline and I were a bit 'iffy' about it but they came back later on and not only prepared the fish, it was Mackerel, but they also cooked it for us. It was surprising how tasty the meal was.

.During our holiday we had a good tour of 'mouths' in the area and these included PlyMOUTH, to which we paid a visit to and saw naval ships in the bay. There was also SidMOUTH, ExMOUTH, Kingsbridge and Salcombe but the most interesting place was DartMOUTH where the Royal Naval College was situated.

There was a carnival taking place whilst we were there and after having a trip across the River Dart on a small ferry, we went to see this carnival. Also anchored in the bay was a Royal Naval Minelayer which was open to the public.

After seeing the carnival,we went on board the minelayer and had a good look around it and found it to be very interesting. As we were leaving we made our way down a steep gangway onto a small picket boat but as we were descending, someone shouted from above, "Look out." and as I looked up, some idiot had dislodged a lifebelt from its hook and it was just about to hit Aline. I pushed her out of the way and took the weight of it upon my shoulder. Naval personnel rushed to help and took me back up the gangway onto the ship and into the Sick Bay to see if I had sustained any injury. Aline was OK but I felt a little bruised. Afterwards we both left and went down the gangway again but very carefully. As we reached the shore, Nip asked, "Do you want to go for a drink of coffee?" "Yes." I replied. "What time is it?" I looked at my watch. It wasn't there. Then we realised that in the melee, the lifebelt must have knocked it from my wrist and into the water.

Later on we returned to the quayside where a naval officer was standing. "Excuse me, sir. Are you from the ship?" I asked. "Yes. I'm the Commanding Officer." He answered.

I explained what had happened and asked him to let us know if anyone came across my watch and I gave him my address but I never heard any more about it. I suppose the watch was two or three fathoms down below in the water. Aline in a jocular manner said, "I won't buy you another one." One consolation from the day was for me to acquire a pair of very strong binoculars which I purchased from Boot's the Chemist but taking all things into account, Aline and I had a marvellous day.

Having enjoyed a full ten days' holiday, we started for home but on the way, as we were cruising up the M5 Motorway, I looked in the rear mirror and saw a motorist flashing me and pointing to the trailer. Wondering what it was I waited a short while until I could pull over onto the hard shoulder and put on my hazard lights.

As I opened the door to get out I could see smoke coming from the off side wheel of the trailer and the tyre was almost flat. Taking the necessary precautions, Aline helped me to get the spare wheel out of the trailer and between us we managed to replace the defective one.

We set off again and I said to Nip that rather than make an unnecessary journey to replace the wheel, we might as well cut across country and head for the place from where we bought the trailer at Tusmore, near Bicester. I know it was making the journey longer but it was worth it.

This is what we did and after leaving the Motorway we headed along the A40 road towards Cirencester and just on a whim I said to Aline that it would be interesting to pass through Bibury and take a look at the camp where I once served during the war. At first it seemed a good idea because we were headed in the right direction for North Leigh, where my Grandma once lived, and then on through Whitney towards our destination. Bibury had altered tremendously over the past thirty six years since I was there but unfortunately, as we arrived in Bibury, Aline said that she didn't feel too well and I think it was due to the long journey and the heat so we didn't stay more than ten minutes to stretch our legs and we then set off again for Tusmore, which, though not on the map was just besides a village called Fritwell.

On the way I did manage to point out to her the camp where I stayed and also Mr Thompson's farm from where I used to get perks for helping him.

I eventually found the farm buildings at Tusmore, from where we had bought the tent but there was no one about except for a couple from Sheffield who were camping there. After explaining what had happened, they very kindly told us to leave the damaged wheel, which was under guarantee and they would bring us a replacement one when they returned to Sheffield. It was a generous offer and a week later after getting home, we had a phone call from the couple to tell us that they had obtained the replacement wheel for us. A few days later we travelled over to thank them and collect the new wheel.

When we arrived home, Tony came up to see and tell us that he had been taken off the computer staff at Wigfall's and transferred to the Auditing Department. This entailed him visiting various shops up and down the country and it suited him because he met many types of people working in the shops of which some were amiable in giving the Auditors assistance and others were awkward, to say the least. He was able to make a little extra money too, because they were allowed travelling expenses for their cars etc. He travelled to such places as Southampton on the south coast and then up to Newcastle on the Tyne.

Geoff moved into a council flat, number 457 Oxford Street, which was on the opposite side of Sheffield to where we lived but we helped him to settle in by providing furniture and bedding, plus cooking utensils and crockery, some of the latter was provided by Esme Crick, one of Aline's associates at Hardy's Bread shop. It was whilst at the flat that Geoff had one of his pen pals up to see him. She was a lovely girl with very fair hair, called Christine and she hailed from Southampton. He brought her to see us and a few weeks later he went down to meet her parents. Unfortunately, nothing came of it as a romance.

July 1978 and Geoff was able to put his new qualifications to good use by obtaining a position at Andrew's Ballantynes', a freight forwarding company which was situated on Shepcote Lane and just a few hundred yards up the road from where I worked at Tinsley Wire Industries. He was employed as an import clerk with his own department and was responsible for pricing and auditing. Although it was quite a way to travel to and from Oxford Street, he wasn't too bothered because he now had his own car, a Triumph Herald. There were odd times when he had to call me for help at TWIL and I was able to get one of my workmates to pop up and help him out.

There was one lunchtime when I was approaching the small passenger lift in the foyer of our offices, to go to the top floor, that Mr Gillan was returning from lunch with a guest. I stepped back, out of courtesy, to let them enter the lift. Mr. Gillan looked at me and said, "Come on Ron. There's room for another one." On the way up I asked him how his health was and he said, "Fine, thank you. I'm hoping to play a round of golf this weekend."

Sad to say, Mitch Gillan did go for his round of golf and it was his last. He suffered a massive heart attack and died on the golf course. It was a terrible loss and he was only in his early sixties. Many members of staff, including me, went by coach to his funeral which was to be held in the small village of Curbar in North Derbyshire.

When I look back to couple of years ago I can hear him now asking Miss Leone Hargreaves, his secretary, "Where did that come from?" He was referring to a small flowered arrangement on the wall of her office.

To fill in some spare moments at home, I had made some designs from half inch welded mesh which I had bought from the factory floor. In one of these designs I had put some Oasis flower preservative and inserted some roses from my garden and presented it to Leone as a gift. The whole unit was only twelve inches high and this is what Mr. Gillan had seen. She told me that he thought it was a lovely idea.

A few weeks after borrowing a nibbler from the welded mesh foreman (a nibbler was a small hand machine made by Black and Decker for the use of cutting welded mesh into various shapes), I had made a number of designs and one in particular was shaped like a sled. I had put on a small Yule log, which I had cut from one of my trees, along with a miniature Santa Claus, a piece of holly and some tinsel. When I took one to work to show the girls in the office, some wanted one and others asked for another design which had artificial flowers and a coloured candle in the middle to use as a table centre decoration.

Unbeknown to me, Mr Gillan had mentioned the designs to Mr Jim Fouldes, our Managing Director, and he had arranged for me to go to the studio of our industrial photographer on the other side of town. Mr Platts did a really good job of taking various shots of all the made up pieces and some included me as the designer. The photo's were published in the works magazine and the Sales staff were asked to investigate the possibility of getting one of our customers who bought welded mesh from us, to manufacture the designs as products, with us being the supplier of the raw material. Sorry to say, due to lack of interest and the dilatoriness of certain people, the idea never left the ground. Not to worry because as Christmas 1978 approached, I was inundated with orders and the Table Centres £1.00. each and the Sleds for £1.50 pence at a time, so I proved that the articles were sellable.

At the end of last September, I had a few days holiday to come, so Aline and I decided to take the trailer tent to a small camp site at Sewerby, just a few miles to the north of Bridlington. The site was so small that there was only room for twelve caravans and a half dozen tents. Being a club site, all the facilities were available and it was also convenient for visiting Scarborough, Filey, Flamboro Lighthouse and Bridlington. We always had a liking for this area.

In May 1979 we were invited to go to visit Heather's parents, Dennis and Edna Phillips, at their home in Pershore, so on the 20th May, Aline and I travelled down to see them with our David showing us the way. It was a two and a half hour journey and we were made very welcome upon arrival. We didn't know that Dave and Heather had decided to get married and this visit was to arrange for the wedding day. A date had been set for the wedding on the 9th June and we returned home to make arrangements and notify the rest of the family as to when the event was take place.

Heather had managed to get some leave and David had arranged to get some time off as well, so that things could be settled. Heather's home was set in a corner of two main roads near to the village of Eckington and within that area, Dennis and Edna ran a smallholding of garden produce which supplied the local markets.

On the 9th June we set off with Geoff, Tony and Elaine in the car and Elaine's Mum had the kids for them. David couldn't make up his mind as to who was to be the Best Man and to avoid any jealousy between Tony and Geoff, one of whom would be the natural choice, he chose to ask me. I know it sounded strange, being his father, but I was very proud and honoured to do it for him. To save expense, Heather had made her own wedding dress and instead of having a veil, David had designed a lovely Juliet Cap, the mould of which was made from a half football case. She looked beautiful in it with her long flowing hair handing down her back to just above the waist.

Our family were the only guests there because Heather's brother Malcolm couldn't get leave and her sister, Cynthia, was abroad with her husband who was also in the RAF. Edna had booked the reception at a local hotel and to help out, I paid the bill for the meal etc. The wedding took place at the little village church which was very close to where Heather lived and after service it was only a short ride to the hotel reception.

They weren't able to take an immediate honeymoon except for a few days up in Cumbria because Heather had to return to Wegberg in Germany and David to Honnington. In July, David was posted to Belize in Central America. The RAF had a base our there because of some unrest in British Honduras. It wasn't anything serious but the base was there just in case of anything happening.

The middle of June saw us going off camping again and as always, to a different site. This time we chose a place at Embleton which was just outside Morecambe in Lancashire. We again used it as a base so that we could visit such places as Carnforth, Grange-over-Sands and Lancaster. If we went out for a drink at night, we called into a small pub not far from the campsite, where Jim Bowen started his TV program called 'Bullseye' It became very popular over the years.

On the 7th August, I had to go to Warrington to one of our subsidiaries, Rylands-Whitecross. We had dispensed with our card sorter at work and unfortunately the occasion had arisen when we needed to sort some old files. Bob Little contacted John Cowling at Rylands, who at one time had worked as an analyst at Sheffield and made arrangements for me to go over to use their machine.

Whilst there I was able to meet my old boss, Les Potts, who was now the Operational Director over there.

It was only a few days after being over there that the terrible news broke that the IRA in Ireland had murdered Lord Louis Mountbatten by blowing up the boat in which he was sailing. Having served on his staff in Ceylon during World War II, this was a terrible shock for me and on the day of the funeral I was sitting in my office when Bob Little came in. He could see how upset I was as tears welled in my eyes. "I think that you had better go home, Ron." said Bob.

I was grateful because I was able to watch the funeral service being televised from London. I know it sounds uncalled for, but to me, Mountbatten was the finest leader of men in the second world war and as the cortege moved down Whitehall, I just sat and cried. What a sad ending to such a great man.

Geoff had always taken to wearing a uniform and in November he went and joined the Territorial Army Volunteer Reserve. The branch he joined was the Royal Signal Regiment and was based at the Manor Top on Mansfield Road. He quickly settled in to learn his trade as a signalman and having joined, he soon palled up with another young man, Andrew Steel, who was to become a very firm friend of Geoff's. It wasn't long before they were taking part in the activities of the Sheffield branch of the Youth Hostel Association. Andy was not in the Terriers as a signaller but as a Medic and this came in very useful as the years went by. I think that Geoff had joined the TAVR because he wanted something to do due to the fact that once again he couldn't hold down a job but as things were to prove over a long time, we found the answer.

I have just remembered that back in 1970 there was plenty of land available for building on the bottom side of Rotherham Road across the old farmland down to Orgreave Pit. The owners had given up farming in the area and had decided to make a bob or two by selling it to industrial builders. The area became an Industrial Estate and many little businesses were built and new roads laid for access.

The largest sites were occupied by Ackroyd and Abbott, well known in Sheffield as builders of houses and the other one became a Superstore which sold anything from food to timber, even petrol. It was a Leeds based firm created by Associated Dairies and became known as ASDA. This was a godsend for local people and it made it possible for them to shop there at much lower prices than the local shops. We were able to walk there in ten minutes from home.

So another decade came to a close and many things had happened, including accidents, births, marriages and deaths but we took it all in our stride in the hope that there would be better days ahead.

BACK TO BASS-ICS

In the narration of the past thirty years it must have been obvious to the reader that there were gaps of unaccountability but that was intentional because my interest in music had increased since being in the Forces and meeting and playing with many musicians.

After being demobbed in 1946, my Dad had bought me a brand new upright grand piano from Crane's Music Shop on Lady's Bridge, just up from the Wicker. It was a Russell piano and was made of a beautiful Rosewood material and cost £100 pounds. He had bought it so that I could carry on learning to play as I had done before the War. In the offices where I worked at Edgar Allen's, there was a chap who was called Irvin Morton and during a conversation with him about music, he suggested that I contact his old music teacher.

Harry Izett worked in a music shop, Milner's, in Pinstone Street in Sheffield and after going to see him I was taken on as an improvement pupil. That is, I had learned the basics of piano playing but wanted some tuition to improve my technique and also learn the theoretical rudiments of the music language.

Mr.Iizett was a fine musician and taught the piano, organ, piano accordion and the violin. He himself was deformed by having a pigeon chest, a hunched back and a club foot but most of all he had a marvellous personality and his fee was reasonable too at 7/6d per hour.

I attended Harry's studio on Crookesmoor Road until 1949 and improved my playing ability besides being able to compose music, some of which Harry approved of and advised me to send it to such people as Ann Shelton, one of the wartime forces sweethearts. I did get one favourable reply from her agent but at that time she wasn't able to fit it into her program.

The mention of being with Harry until 1949 and no further was the fact that the main reason was my getting married and not finding the time to do much practise but I still played for my own amusement. Also, upon returning to civilian life again, after the War, I went back to Edgar Allen's as this was a compulsory statute laid down by the government, that all employers must re-employ the personnel who had left them to join His Majesty's Forces. The only thing wrong was that everyone returning was given the same wage of £4/10/0 per week, irrespective of position.

That is why I took the chance to earn some extra money when offered it. This was in the way that I renewed my acquaintance with Ronnie Hulme, the sergeant I had met in India and who had persuaded me to take to playing the Double Bass. In conversation with him, one day, he said that there was a young draughtsman, Arnold Johnson, who worked in the drawing office, who was interested in forming a small band and would I be interested?

I told Ron that I was interested but hadn't an instrument on which to play. I talked it over with Mum and Dad and they said that if I was so keen then why not take the chance. I met Arnold Johnson, an eighteen year old blonde lad and he said he was in the Musicians' Union and might know someone I might contact as to how I could get a bass.

He put me in touch with a musician named Harry Edge, whose father was a pawnbroker. Harry asked me to go up to their shop on City Road at the Top of the Manor Estate because that is where he had the bass for sale. I went up there and Harry brought in the tatty old instrument from the store room. Not being an expert, I thought that it seemed OK and it sounded reasonable so we came to an arrangement and I bought it for £5.

Now, Harry Edge, I found out later, was noted for smoking on the stage whilst playing for Bernard Taylor at the City Hall and if Harry flipped or put out a cigarette whilst playing, he would put the tab end into the shell of the bass. This I found out after I arrived home with it.

I wondered what the rattling noise was when I was moving it. So, the first thing was to get my Dad to hold the neck of the bass whilst I held the bottom end and then we lifted it upside down and shook it to and fro to get the filth out of the '*f*' holes.

God knows how long Harry had been doing this habit because when we had finished, there must have been two shovels full of tab ends, tram tickets and match sticks. Many people asked me why I had chosen a double bass and my answer was, "I'm single and it has the nearest shape to a woman, a long slender neck , plus the fact that it also has two '*f*' holes"

Having obtained the instrument, I told Arnold and Ron and we agreed to have some practise in the works' canteen on Vulcan Road. It was a little awkward for me because I didn't have any transport then and the only way I could get about was to put it in the front bay of a tramcar, just behind the driver. They were all very good and understanding about the situation and I had to be careful because I couldn't afford to buy a cover for it at that time so I used to strap the neck under the front staircase of the tramcar.

After some weeks of practise, an arrangement was made with the works sports club secretary, Arthur Greenwood, for us to play for a dance at the Tinsley Working Mens' Club for the sports section. Arnold Johnson managed to get a sax player and a trumpet player to make up the band. This was the first public appearance in this country for me and the first time that I had some 'dots' in front of me to play from. This started my career as a semi-pro musician. One minor hiccup was that one of the sports committee objected to us being paid when he wasn't paid for playing football and cricket for the firm. It was through Arnold that we played at one or two more venues but Ronnie Hulme soon gave up because Arnold asked us to join the Musicians Union and Ronnie didn't agree with unions.

I contacted a George Hallam who was the secretary of the local branch of the MU and he played trumpet in the orchestra at the Empire Theatre in Sheffield. It was from there that I joined the MU in September 1948. The first thing I learned, that to became known in the business I had to get some business cards printed with my name address and telephone number on them. Unfortunately, I didn't have a telephone but in our row of houses, the pawnbrokers shop was now used as a printing shop and Mr. Rowley, the owner, not only printed the cards but also put his telephone number on them so that people could call me. I really appreciated the offer and it came in very useful.

It was necessary, as a musician, to have a dress suit and once again I was lucky because Bob Green, who worked in our Cost Office at Edgars', told me that he had one for sale. I bought it from him, it was single breasted and fitted me quite well, he also threw in a couple of hard butterfly winged collars for good measure. The lot cost me £5 again. How lucky can one get?

Joining the Musicians Union paid off because I started to get calls and although they were few at first, once I managed to get into the circle of musicians, the bookings increased. The Sheffield Branch of the MU had some four hundred members just after the War and the Dance Hall craze was in full swing because of the promotion of dance and big band music by such people as Glen Miller, Ted Heath and Joe Loss.

My first full break came in 1950 when a drummer, Maurice Moore, asked me to play for his band at the Limes Club on Barnsley Road. This was a six piece band and they played every Thursday and Saturday night for a free and easy dance night. It was just for three hours each time for which we were paid 7/6d a session and this was given to us in a little brown envelope by the treasurer. Each night I would put the envelope into the cupboard at home because with Aline working as well, we really didn't need the money and it was like a savings bank.

However, there was a time when I needed some change so I went to an envelope because I knew that there were three half crowns in it.

That is what I thought because when I opened the envelope there were only two coins in it. When I mentioned it to the Club treasurer he told me that I should have checked before leaving at the end of the session. That was another lesson I had learned.

I did much of my playing as a free lance and turned out for many outfits such as Jack Knight and his Band. It was at a sixth form dance at the Rowlinson Technical School that we had a good laugh. Jack Smith, the drummer, was a 'right' card and when the MC asked Jack to announce the next dance, he slowly walked down to the microphone on the front of the stage and said, "Ladies and gentlemen, please take your partners -(pause) - for a blood transfusion." The guests and the band lads couldn't stop laughing. The MC wasn't amused

Later on he did it again by announcing that one of the band members would play, by special request, a solo, whilst he accompanied him on the Hobbing Foot, (a last). I wonder if he had already heard of the German big band leader. James Last?

I played at Newton Hall in Chapeltown, one night and Jack Smith, who lived on Barnsley Road just below the Limes Club, said that if I could carry my bass down to his house, he would take me with him in his Morris Minor shooting brake. Jack was a self employed painter and decorator and had always parked his car on the main road just outside his house. On the night I joined him and as we were driving to the Newton Hall, he told me that a new policeman on his patch had stuck a notice under the windscreen wiper of his car saying that he wasn't allowed to park there. "I soon cured him." said Jack."I took the wipers off my car." That's how amusing Jack was and I couldn't stop giggling all the way to the dance.

It didn't stop there because as we came out of the car park at the end of the dance at one o'clock the following morning, Jack drove across the road. He pulled away from the junction to head for Sheffield but as he went under the railway bridge, a police car pulled up in front of him and stopped him. A police officer left his vehicle, came over and accused Jack of ignoring a 'HALT' sign

I supported Jack by saying that there wasn't a light on the sign so I didn't see it either. "What's your registration number?" asked the cop. This is where the fun started. "Just a minute officer."Jack slowly got out of the car, made his way to the front of his vehicle and with deliberation, looked at his number plate and then read it out loudly and very slowly.

The policeman was so frustrated that he turned to Jack and said, "Piss off." With that, Jack returned to the driving seat of his car and we drove off.

In 1948 there was an up and coming young musician, another drummer, Alan Furness (no relation to our family) and he had assembled a small band which did dances here and there. I played for him a few times and on odd occasions he would drop in at No. 87 to give me some bookings. Mum used to laugh about his laid back attitude as he sat in a chair, talking as though he had known us for years. Alan eventually became a probation officer.

In one or two circumstances I had found it necessary to ask cousin Sid Howard to help me out by taking me in his taxi to dance venues such as Nether Edge Hall because access by tramcar was difficult. I didn't ask any favours with regard to fare and even though he was so generous, I insisted upon paying him.

Prior to getting married, I had played for Albert Turvey's Band on several occasion when his resident bass player, Arthur Platts, was unavailable. Albert had the residency of Glossop Road Baths and was very popular. At one of my piano lessons, Harry Izett had asked me if I could get a small group together to play at a wedding of his friend and I finished up by having Albert on piano, Harry on accordion, myself on bass and another band leader, Jack Start on the drums. It's not everyone who can call on well known local band leaders to sit in on a booking but I managed it and it went very well.

At Glossop Road Baths, a floor was laid over the empty swimming pool and most dances were under the guidance of a dance teacher named William Collinson. He was a bit of a tartar because if any musician turned up a little late, he would deduct a 'bob' or two of their fee. Classed as a grade 'A' ballroom in Sheffield, that fee was 25/- shillings which was the top fee for three hours playing.

In Albert's band I became acquainted with a very good drummer by the name of George Cottam. George wasn't any old drummer, he was a very good reader of music and also an amateur comedian in his own sphere. One night, Albert asked George to put up the next dance which was shown on a unit made from a tramcar indicator box.

George altered the box by winding on the names until it came to show a quickstep and then very calmly he took hold of the microphone and announced. "Please take your partners for a quickstep via Attercliffe." The rest of the band were in tucks. Many routes on which tramcars were headed for the Eastend of the city, indicated that the destination was shown as being 'via Attercliffe' because the tram depot was at Tinsley and to get there, one had to travel through the suburb of Attercliffe.

Albert Turvey wasn't a young man and he was a batchelor who mainly taught the piano for a living. He was a pleasant and honest man, that's why I had asked him to bring his band to play at my wedding.

Another venue at which I played for Albert was at the top of Burton's shop at the junction of Staniforth Road and Attercliffe Road. It was called the Astoria and I became the regular bass player there. It was at that time when my ulcer was acting up and on one or two occasions I had to leave the stage because of the bile and flatulence which was forming in my mouth. As I said, Albert was a good man and never grumbled about my breaks.

It was on one of the nights at the Astoria that Albert asked the lads in the band if they would be interested in helping him to play as the resident Saturday night band at a new dance hall called the Azena. This was a place which had been purposely built by a local farmer on White Lane at Gleadless, who had sold his land for building purposes. The farmers wife was called Zena, hence the name of the dance hall, Azena. It was a large hall with a big stage, two dressing rooms and a restaurant up the stairs at the opposite end to the stage.

So it was that Albert obtained the contract to play, not only on Saturdays but also on Tuesday nights for Old Time dancing and Thursday nights for modern ballroom dancing. The band was comprised of piano, bass, drums, violins and alto sax for Old Time dancing and the rhythm section plus alto, second alto and tenor sax in the reed section with trumpet and second trumpet in the brass section for modern dancing..

Albert played the piano as leader, George Cottam was on drums and I was on bass. Jack Richardson was lead alto and Harry Sisman played the tenor sax. The brass section was Derek Ashmore, who was later joined by his brother Jack. The Old Time strings were provided by Terry Lally and Jack Undy.

For twelve months everything was marvellous but the farmer's wife Zena seemed to rule the roost. Towards the end of the first year, Albert seemed to be getting past it so the lads had a discussion and suggested that he get another pianist and he could then 'front' the band. This he agreed to and he managed to get a very good replacement in one Arthur Frost.

Even then the years seemed to be catching up with Albert because he would get a chair and sit down in between dances, the conducting seemed to be taking it out of him. Unfortunately, he sat down one night and we wondered why the dancers were looking at him and tittering. One of the bandsmen suddenly noticed that Albert was laid back on the chair with his flies all undone. No wonder that the customers were laughing.

It wasn't long before Albert realised that he was past his best and had seen a good life, so he decided to retire and it was agreed that George Cottam would take over the running of the band. Everything worked well until Jack Richardson decided to leave and without notice, so we were short of a lead alto up to within half an hour of starting. Fortunately, someone remembered that a Ron Innocent lived almost next door to the ballroom therefore George popped round and found him in. Ron came and helped us out and finished playing with us for quite a while. There was only one problem, he always seemed to blow 'sharp'. We managed with this setup for quite a while but the sound of Ron Innocent's tone was beginning to put the other musicians out of their stride and eventually George had to find another alto player.

The Azena was getting well known as a venue for entertainment and in our second year there, Arnie Fidler had managed to book a young man who was taking the jazz scene by storm. It was Johnny Dankworth and his Band and he brought with him his new wife, Cleo Lane. They played for most of the evening and we were there just as a backup filling outfit.

I now had a reasonable car to get about in, moreso when I look back to the first one I had, which was a 1927 Austin Seven Coupe. In the early fifties I was playing a little with a group from the Beighton area and although it wasn't much we did go to one of the players homes in Renishaw occasionally to practise. The sax player, Ray Tomlinson, would pick me up in his Ford Pilot car along with Tommy Hardy from my hairdressers, he lived at Hackenthorpe. One night, Ray said that he had a car for sale and it was an Austin Seven with a detachable fold back roof.

I bought it from him for £12 and that included a new battery. Ray ran a garage with his father at Beighton and so was able to do me a good deal. It caused many a laugh because to get the bass in the car I had to fold down the roof and wedge it on top of the back seat with the neck protruding between me and the passenger seat.

It was funnier still when I gave Tommy Hardy a lift because he was short and dumpy and I was a little taller and very slim. The other lads in the band said we looked like Laurel and Hardy as we drove about. When I was with that band, we played at a dance at Eckington Hall and one of the dances was Latin American so the leader of the band asked me to put down my bass and take up the maracas for sound effect. They were home made and were filled with granite road chippings. They were effective until the dust from the chippings came out and went all over the players dress suits.

Having joined the MU, at one of their monthly meetings, George Hallam asked members if any were interested in going to the Melody Maker Band Contest which was to be held at Belle Vue, Manchester. This was a place where there was a circus, a zoo, a speedway track and a large hall for the purpose of various contests such as wrestling. The reason for asking us if we were interested was mainly to give support to a jazz quintet from Sheffield, who had entered the contest. George also announced that wives and girl friends could go along also, and therefore I persuaded Aline to go. She really enjoyed the outing and met many of the musicians with whom I had played with. The coach was filled to capacity.

The compliment of the individual bands varied from large outfits of eight or more, down to trios and quartets. As each entry mounted the stage to play their chosen piece, a panel of adjudicators went into a hut type box which had no windows but was able to allow the judges to hear every note of each group. As they listened, they awarded points for individual solos and also the section work of each band. The small groups were the last to appear and play and the five from Sheffield were led by Stan Dawes on Alto sax, Dave Howett on piano, Jimmy Clayton on bass, Ted Needham on acoustic guitar and Lenny Briggs on drums. As they entered the arena we gave them all the encouragement we could by clapping and cheering. They started their program with confidence and after playing some wonderful music for some ten minutes, they left the stage to await the final results.

We had all sat patiently as each band had played their program and eventually, about 4.30 pm the judges came onto the podium to announce their decisions. As I had said, there were many categories and almost at the end, it was announced that the best Combo outfit was Stan Dawes and his Band from Sheffield. As Stan received the Silver Cup we all stood up and applauded them. Upon return to the city the Cup was displayed in the window of Milners' Music Shop on Pinstone Street for all to see.

I played with Albert Turvey's band at the Azena for two years and then the beginning of the guitar pop groups started coming onto the scene. As usual, if a band size had to be reduced, it was always the double bass player who had to go or the trombone player. Seeing that we didn't have the latter it was me who had to be sacrificed but I had gained a lot of experience and through this I made my way in free lancing with other bands.

For quite a while I was sort after by bands such as Hal Baker, Stan Hardcastle, Lily Wrigglesworth's old time orchestra and Maurice North, who, along with his brother, ran a six piece band. It was on an engagement with him when we played at Doncaster baths that we witnessed an amusing incident.

The stage had been set in three tiers and Tommy, the drummer and I were on the top flight which made us level on eyesight with the surrounding balcony. As we were playing, Tommy called across and shouted, "Look at that." He pointed with his drumstick to the balcony on the right. We couldn't stop laughing because we could see a bare bottom going up and down and we guessed that some lucky chap was knocking hell out of some poor lass.

I also did a gig at the Cutler's Hall for Walt Chapell, the resident band there. I was asked to play because his bass player was his sister Margaret and she had left to join the all girls band of Ivy Benson.

In the meantime, in the early fifties, I had been approached by a trumpet player called Bert Barlow, to join his band which played residentially at the Southey Green Working Men's Club, I was glad I did because I gained more experience of musical arrangements when they played military music and semi-classics besides popular tunes.

We only played at Sunday lunchtimes from 12 pm until 2 pm and like many other clubs, artistes were booked for entertaining the sometimes, large audiences. There was one Sunday when the committee had booked Sandy Daw, a Scottish comedian and Jack Doyle, an Irish singer who at one time had been the heavyweight boxing champion of the world. The latter had recently married a movie star called Movita, a South American beauty and they were all appearing at the Attercliffe Palace Theatre.

Sandy Daw came on to do his act and it was obvious that he had drunk too much as was clear in his gyrations about the stage. He went off and we played the intro for the entrance of Jack Doyle.

His signature tune was 'When Irish Eyes are Smiling' and he came on from the wings of the stage, sang the first line of the refrain and then beckoned to everyone in the audience to join in.

That was it, that was Jack Doyle's act but it didn't work here. Members of the committee of the Southey Green Club were mainly from the Alfred Road district of Brightside from where a ruck of gangs had been re- habilitated in Southey during the slum clearance days. They booed and whistled and told Doyle to get off. As big as Jack Doyle was, it made no difference and he and Sandy Daw were turfed out and they didn't get paid.

I played at the club for a long time and in the band was Les, an orchestral drummer with all the percussion equipment, including the xylophone and tympani; Stan, who played alto and was an excellent clarinetist; Bert played trumpet and there was myself on bass but I always had to chuckle when I looked at the pianist because he was the double of Arthur Askey, the comedian.

There was a story going around that a few years ago, Bert Barlow had taken over the leadership of a circus band. He wasn't too keen on the music being played so he decided to put in his own program. Little did he realise that the animals were trained to follow set pieces of music so obviously, when his choice of music was played, the circus came to a standstill. Bert was a good musician but he didn't hold the circus job for very long.

On odd occasions there can be embarrassing moments and the one for me was when I had been booked to play for Edgar Godber's Orchestra for a dinner dance at the Royal Victoria Hotel in Sheffield. Obviously a lot of functions like this were in the winter months and on this particular night it was rather cold so I popped on a flat cap to keep my head warm.

Without thinking, I walked into the foyer of this top class hotel wearing my 'penguin' suit and a good top coat with a white scarf around my neck - and my flat cap and as I entered, the drummer, Jim Oxley, who was waiting in the foyer, came over to me.

"Ron." He said. "Take a tip, don't wear a flat cap in places like this." I blushed but didn't mind because I had played alongside Jim on several occasions and he was always immaculately dressed. He had helped me tremendously in my short period as a semi-pro musician and had given some good advice to me on protocol in that capacity.

In 1954 I was asked to deputise for Bill Spencer, the bass player in the orchestra at the Attercliffe Palace Theatre. He was going on holiday and I had been recommended by George Cottam. Here was a chance to gain some more experience and learn another side to the music business.

With it being a temporary position, just for two weeks, I still had to ask for a couple of hours off work each Monday morning in order to attend rehearsals with the new acts that were arriving. Most of the entertainment was by revue companies who travelled the country with lead singers, comedians and chorus girls.

The first rehearsal was an eye-opener because we had just started to play the first orchestration when the safety curtain went up and the cleaners were sweeping the dust from the stage, straight into the orchestra pit. Frank Payne, the leader, put down his violin and shouted, "That's it. Everybody out." He told us to leave our instruments and leave the pit. By the way, I wasn't using my own bass because Bill had told me to use his. In any case his instrument was far superior to mine.

We wasted about twenty minutes rehearsal time before we were able to play again. The other musicians were Barry Goode (pianist). He used to be Bernard Taylor's dance band leader at the City Hall; Jim Cole was on trombone, Arthur Jones on trumpet- come-flugel horn, Bill, (a policeman), was on alto sax, I was on bass and George Cottam was on percussion. We eventually managed to finish rehearsals and prepared for the evening show.

When I returned to work after the rehearsals, Ken Keys, the office manager, passed some snide remark about me having time off but I had prepared for that by asking Mr Lionel Casson, the sales manager, for permission. He had agreed because he used to go to the Palace Theatre to see some of the revues.

It was commonly known that the Palace had, what was known as 'leg and tit' shows and quite a number of male audiences frequented the place, especially if there were nudes on it. Phyllis Dixie was a great favourite but artistes like her were not allowed to move whilst on the stage in poses but could do so if they were 'fan dancers'.

I never had the privilege of playing in the orchestra whilst such a turn was on but I had been to shows as a member of the audience. I would get ribbed at work as to what I saw on the stage whilst playing there but believe me, I hadn't time to look up at the artists until at least Wednesday night because I was so busy keeping one eye on my music score and the other on the Musical Director.

That brings me to another interesting point and that is, most shows brought in their own MD which we called the Travelling Musical Director. Now, the MU had a ruling, nationally, that all TMDs should be members of the Musicians' Union. On the following Monday at rehearsals, Frank Payne, our leader, asked the TMD for his credentials who said that he would bring them with him for the opening of the show. We all arrived and set up for six o'clock which was the starting time and the TMD climbed into the orchestra pit, the audience waited in anticipation for the overture.

We could see Frank having a quiet word with the TMD and then Frank turned to us and said, "Out. Everybody out." and we all left the orchestra pit. Wrangling went on for an hour and it ended with George Hallam, our union branch secretary, being called into the dispute to try to settle things. There was further discussion and after an hour's delay we were called from the bar of the Queen's Head hotel which was nearby, and told the matter had been resolved. The TMD did join the Musicians' Union and the show went on.

I deputised for Bill again the following year and the experience I enjoyed but the money wasn't too good for the hours we played. For twelve hours of rehearsing and playing we were only paid £7.10.0 each. Incidentally, if there was need for natural relief in between the acts, then we went below the stage and slacked down the dust on a pile of coke which was used for heating the boilers of the building.

It wasn't long after, that the Palace was closed as a Theatre so Bill Spencer decided to retire. He was in his sixties and asked me if I wanted to buy his bass. It was a Tarby bass and of well known manufacture, so having agreed, I went to his home, which was in the Hillsbro district, and bought it for the sum of £20, along with two bows and a solid brass bass mute.

Around this time I received a letter from a Harry Richmond, asking me if I would like to play for him at the 'Green Room' in the Gaumont Cinema in Barker's Pool in Sheffield. My immediate thought was, 'Harry Richmond, the BBC Theatre organist' but when I went for an interview, I found that it was a pianist who played by 'ear' and was looking for a bass player to make up a trio at the Gaumont. He explained that it would be a twelve month's contract with the Rank Organisation and the salary would be £1,000 per annum.

In that era, the sum was lucrative but having talked it over with Aline, I decided not to accept because there was no garauntee of future contracts and it meant me giving up my day job. It later transpired that I had made the right decision because Harry Richmond left the 'Green Room' to run away with the manageress there and take up residence in the south. It proves without saying that some names can be deceiving. Harry Richmond, indeed.

I don't wonder, that through this encounter, I was approached by a Hoover sales rep, Johnny Gregory. He called at our house and said that he wanted a bass player to make up a trio at an Inn called the Angler's Rest in Bamford in Derbyshire. The Inn was owned by Mr Benny Goodfellow who happened to be the General Manager at the SUT which was the Sheffield United Transport Company on Charlotte Road and it was a coach operating business. Johnny took us out one night to meet Mr. Goodfellow and show us the layout of the so called stage from which we were to play.

Johnny explained that it involved playing Thursday and Saturday nights for dinner dances and the money was thirty shillings a night.If I drove to his house on Richmond Road and left my car there, in his driveway, he would take me in his car and pick up the pianist on the way. I hadn't any engagements on at the time so I accepted his offer and commenced playing on the following Thursday. We picked up Ken Watkinson, the pianist, as we headed for Bamford.

I don't know how Johnny Gregory managed to get his connections but he asked me if it was possble to get an afternoon off work to play for him at the Cutler's Hall. The occasion was a fashion display which was organised by Norman Hartnell, the well known fashion designer and we were to play incidental back ground music for the models as they paraded down the cat walk.

To do the engagement I rang up the office and said that I wasn't feeling too well and that I wouldn't be at work. I played at the Cutler's that afternoon but just as I was leaving, who should I 'bump' into but none other than Ken Keys. "I thought that you was ill?" He enquired. "I am."I replied. " but this was an emergency and I couldn't let them down." He wasn't too pleased but I went to work the following day and no further comment was made.

To get back to the Anglers Rest Inn. On our first night there, we found that the set up was that the piano was set on top of a small stage above the bar in the dining room. There was just room for Johnny to set up his drum kit, which wasn't that elaborate and I was to play on a three feet square platform which was attached to the top of the bar and at the side. For all of us to get into position, we had to climb a small ladder. It took some getting used to and I was the last one to climb up.

Ken Watkinson was a self taught pianist and was very good. He also had been the resident singer with Bernard Taylor's band at the City Hall. Johnny couldn't read a note of music and couldn't even do a roll on the drums when we played the National Anthem but he was a nice, debonair, smooth talking guy with a sharp wit and some very good 'stories'.

Over a period of time we did very well out of the gig and many business people ran functions there, including a top class tailor. Benny Goodfellow was so impressed with our playing that he arranged for the three of us to be measured for 'bum freezers' to be made by this tailor in a powder blue material at a cost of £5 each. The fittings were perfect and on our first night to wear them, we really looked a top class trio.

The three of us played there for three years and quite often on our way out to Bamford we would call in at the Millstone Inn which was on the Surprise Hill just above the village of Hathersage. There, another trio, under the leadership of 'Freddy 'Chick' Needham was in residence and occasionally we would give them a break and play a couple of numbers for them. In 1957, we lost, what I thought, was a good opportunity to go big time. Benny Goodfellow would annually put on a dinner dance for SUT customers at the City Hall Ballroom in Sheffield and called it Blackpool Night. This particular night he had asked us to play incidental music in the dining area where each table had a centre piece of a replica of the famous Blackpool Tower.

Johnny had arranged for Brian Cooper, a wonderful pianist and accordionist to supplement the trio and the four of us looked great in our blue tunics. Brian had managed to find a blue coat to match our 'bum freezers' and we all looked the part for the night.

In the main ballroom, Benny had booked Billy Ternent with his BBC Dance Orchestra and on the other side of the revolving stage there was Reggie Dixon, the world famous organist who played at the Tower Ballroom in Blackpool. By the way, Reggie originated from Sheffield.

What a night. As we had played, we saw a gentleman in the dining area and he was more or less sitting opposite to where we were playing. We didn't take any notice because he looked as though he had drunk one or two too many and couldn't care less.

However, at the end of the night he came over, quite sober and told us that he had been very interested with our performance and that he was a talent scout for Granada Television in Manchester. If we cared to go over for an audition, he was sure that we would be successful.

He gave Johnny his card and we talked it over but Johnny didn't think that we were good enough, so we didn't take up the offer. Ken and I were interested but that's as far as it went to.

I mentioned a while ago as to how the three of us would call in at the Millstone Inn and it was on one these calls that we ran into some tragic news. It was February 1958 and we were just having a drink in the bar when the landlord asked us and Chic's lads to pop upstairs and watch the television. We wondered what was happening but as we entered the landlord's lounge, we were greeted with the news that Manchester United's aircraft had crashed.

The Manchester United football team had been playing in Munich in Germany and after the match the plane had started to take off from the runway but ice had formed on the wings and the weight at lift off had made the aircraft crash just after take off, killing eight of the team and attendants. The team was known as the 'Busby Babes' because the manager of the team was Matt Busby who once played for them in his younger days. He too was terribly injured but after a long illness from injuries, he did survive, as did Bobby Charlton, Harry Gregg and one or two others. It was a sad blow to English soccer also, for it took a very long time for recovery from the shock.

Being out at the Angler's interested my Dad because of him being born a few miles away from Bamford in the village of Birchinlee to the west of Derwent. It so happened that 1956 was the 60th birthday of my Mum so Dad asked me to book a table for them to celebrate the occasion at the Angler's. He also asked for some grouse for dinner and at the interval of our playing, he arranged for me and the lads to join him and Mum. Benny Goodfellow was very obliging in arranging everything. I enjoyed my meal but the taste of grouse didn't appeal to me because it had an acquired taste. However, Mum and Dad enjoyed their night out.

Another reason for mentioning my Dad's interest in Bamford, was the fact that back in 1945, preparation had commenced to build the Ladybower Reservoir and when this entailed flooding the Derwent Valley and the village of Derwent, it was decided to uplift all the remains of villagers buried in the local graveyard and re-inter them in the cemetery at Bamford Church. Dad's parents, David and Elizabeth, my grandparents, were amongst those who were moved, hence the interest.

Benny Goodfellow had been very good to us and sometimes he gave us a steak and chip supper on the house to show his appreciation. In the winter months, if the roads were treacherous, he would ask us to drive up to Dore Moor Inn, which was on the outskirts of Sheffield and was about half way to Bamford and just climbing into the Peak District. When we arrived there, he had laid on a coach from his company's garage for the purpose of, not only getting us out there to the Angler's to play but also to pick up some of his customers. He was a very thoughtful man.

Playing at the Angler's Rest had been very lucrative, especially when it came to the festive season and New Year's Eve dinner dances. There were also many private functions there and one of these was organised by a young man called Ralph Weston. Shortly after this period he became head of Weston's Chemists with a chain of shops all around the South Yorkshire Area. He also owned a large warehouse which was just down the road from where I lived and it was here that in later years, our Geoff was to work for a short while. Ralph Weston was Jewish and as many in that faith, he was a self made man.

There were one or two instances when we were given extra tips on top of our fees in acknowledgement of the good entertainment we had provided. However, the good times don't last for ever and after three years there, other opportunities arose and the trio split up and we moved into other venues of the music game.

I went freelancing again and one of the bands I played for, or should I say, was offered the chance to play for, was Jack Fretson's band at the Roxy Ballroom at Page Hall near to Firth Park. Jack Fretson's name was a pseudonym for Fred Jackson and he was an alto sax player and leader of the five piece group.

Also in the band was a pianist, Peter Baker and he was one of the sons of Hal Baker, a big band leader in Sheffield. Peter was an accomplished player and was an under graduate in law but played in the band to supplement his income. He also had a filling -in job as a lorry driver at Wm Jessop's the steel firm. It was later on in life that he not only graduated as a lawyer but eventually became a Circuit Judge.

The Ballroom was owned by Harry Sylvester, who was also of Jewish descent and he ran dances along with his wife Connie Grant, who was an international dancing teacher. They also had a small private ball room on West Street called the Cavendish Ballroom and their daughter Judy helped in running it. Harry, being a business man, did everything by the book and when I received my first pay packet, it should have been for twenty five shillings for the three hour session but it was only twenty two shillings. He had stopped the tax.

The following week I received a letter from the Inland Revenue saying that I owed them £110 in back tax. I took a couple of hours off work to go to the tax office where I was interviewed by an under manager. He said that Fretson's band played three nights per week at 25/- shillings per night and over the past year had earned ex-number of pounds, so therefore I owed the Inland Revenue £110.

"Hang on a minute." I said to him, "I have only played the one Saturday night and that was last week. In any case, I have a wife and three children to keep." We sorted the problem out and he said that if ever I played in 'Sheffield', I must declare my earning as a musician. 'Sheffield' was the operative word because from then on I only played in Rotherham, Barnsley, Chesterfield and Stocksbridge, anywhere bar Sheffield. I only played another twice at the Roxy, it wasn't worth it. Besides, I was glad to leave because on the second Saturday night I was there, a fight broke out on the dance floor between some youths and it only finished because as they fought their way towards the stage, Jack Fretson leaned over and clobbered one of them on the head with his clarinet. Incidents like that were very rare but not welcome.

I was now working at TWIL and one of the sports club committee, Ken Tupling, who worked in the accounts section, approached me and asked if I knew a band who could play for a dance in the work's canteen. Through being in the MU, it was always possible to make contacts and this is what I did. I contacted Ron Schofield who, I later discovered, had worked at Edgar Allen's. He booked the job and included me in the band.

It was from this that I became a regular member of the Ron Schofield Orchestra and this blossomed into many engagements over the years from trio work to big band engagements. The main stay of the band was Glynn Roden on piano, Gerry Nugent on tenor sax, Norman Moorhouse on trumpet, myself on bass and Ron Schofield on drums.

Ron had built up a good clientele of people in various walks of life in the steel industry, in sports organisation and one or two small businesses who held annual functions and needed entertainment. A regular venue for us was at the Rotherham Co-op where the restaurant above was often used for firm's sports club dances. I enjoyed playing there because at the intervals we would go into the kitchen for refreshments and I loved there small crusty rolls.

In the early days with Ron Schofield's Band, there was only himself, me and Glynn, who had cars. Glynn's was a firm's car but between us we would arrange to pick up Gerry and Norman, depending on the destination of the booking. On one of these bookings, I had arranged for Gerry to come up to my house on the bus because he lived with his parents on the Triangle Estate down Handsworth Road and our journey was going in the opposite direction to where he lived.

The dance was a private one at the Three Horseshoes Hotel at Wickersley and it was more convenient for Gerry to meet me. Now, to load my bass into the car, I had to rest it upright on the grass verge with one hand whilst I opened the car door with the other. I would then lift the bass up with the back of it facing downwards and gently slide it across the back of the passenger seat with the bottom of the bass resting on the back window ledge.

This I had already done when Gerry arrived, so the only thing he had to do was get into the back seat. He slid his sax case along the floor and then climbed into the seat and off we went. We had been playing about half an hour when Ron said that there was a smell somewhere. We had a good look round and at first we couldn't find anything.

A short while later, Ron commented, "What a stink. It smells like shit" We laughed at first and then Glynn remarked, "What's that on Gerry's coat?" We all looked and there on the back end of his dress suit coat was some dog dirt. "Oh! Bloody hell." I cried. "It's my fault." As I had loaded my bass back at home, when resting it on the grass verge, the spike of the bass had penetrated a dog turd and as I had lifted it into the car, the turd had come with it and dropped off onto the back seat of the car. Gerry had sat on it and that was the reason for the mess on his suit and the smell it had caused. We managed to clean some of it at the interval and after the dance I obviously told Gerry that I would pay the cost of cleaning it. After that incident, I always checked before loading my instrument into the car whether going to or from a dance.

We all had a night out together on a 'busman's holiday' to listen to a new big band which had come over from Manchester. They were to give a concert at the Royal Victoria Hotel and Ron had managed to get tickets for all the band lads. The band was the Syd Lawrence Orchestra who specialised in the musical arrangements of the Glenn Miller Orchestra which was popular during World War II. At that time non of us realised how famous and world renowned the Syd Lawrence Orchestra would become. It was a fabulous night out and greatly appreciated by the large audience.

Engagements and venues varied immensely from church halls to the large hotels in town. We were booked to play at the Grosvenor Hotel one night and unbeknown to us, the hosts who had engaged us, had also arranged for a top class singer to come. She was Kim Cordell who broadcast regularly with the BBC. Kim was very popular and was very attractive both in looks and as a singer.

Ron had a quick word with her as to how she wanted her music playing and she produced some very specially arranged 'dots' which were encased in fine plastic covers. This is where musicianship came in because none of us had time to rehearse and it was a case of immediate sight reading. Kim gave us the tempo and we accompanied her for a couple of numbers. After the dance, she came over and commended us by saying we were one of the best small bands who had played for her.

Another place at which we played often and enjoyed, was at the Chantry Hotel at Dronfield. They were always dinner dances and the Hotel was owned and run by two professional entertainers who also lived together as 'friends'. They were good to us and provided a full meal for us each time we played there but the interesting part was that one of them played the marimba and later on in the night, he would come and join us in our performance. He had a lovely ' touch'.

Of the number of engagements at which we played, it was only the odd one where there was any trouble with unruly elements who were usually the worse the wear for drink. It was when we were doing a favour for one of my workmates, Roger Mount, that such an incident occurred.

Roger, who lived at Grindleford, had engaged us to play at a Young Farmer's Ball at Edensor at the entrance to Chatsworth Park. Up to the interval, everything had gone smoothly but shortly after, a couple of young teenage hooligans managed to find their way back stage and crept up behind the band. We were actually playing at the time and one of them knocked over a pint of beer which one of us had left on the floor to the rear of the stage.

As we heard the glass break, Ron left his drum kit, grabbed hold of the youngster and hit him with a beauty. The lad's feet didn't touch the floor and he crumpled into a heap at the bottom of a small flight of stairs. Ron was a tall and very athletic person and he also had a short fuse. His concern was for his musicians and their instruments and that is why he hit first and asked afterwards.

Roger Mount had called in the police and the troublemakers were taken away but Roger kept apologising to us but it wasn't his fault and the rest of the night passed peacefully. As I have said, incidents like this are far and few between.

To try to recall details in datal order would be a bit of a task so please bear with me as I slowly try to remember. Such places as Lomas Hall at Stannington, Rawmarsh Baths and the Blind Institute on Mappin Street were all good places to play at and it was at the latter that I had a nasty mishap.

I had recently bought a brand new bass and a strong cover to protect it. After the dance had finished at 11.00 pm I went to the car park to put my bass into the car. Unfortunately, someone had blocked me in so I rested my instrument on its side, on top of a covering of snow and against a light coloured car. I thought it's sure to be seen if anyone comes along. I started my car and eased it out into the open so that I had room to get my bass in. Guess what? As I walked over for the bass, some idiot, in reversing from the row of parked cars, had backed into my new bass. The belly was broken, the bridge was off and there were marks all over the cover. I could have cried and what didn't help was the fact the culprit didn't even stop to check any damage. It took a fortnight for Milner's, the music shop, to repair it but they did an excellent job of it.

Two special places we really liked to play at were the Maynard Arms Hotel at Grindleford and the Kenwood Hall in Sheffield because we were always treated to a full evening meal as part of the fee. Then, of course there was always the Rising Sun Inn at Bamford which was on the main road to Castleton. It was on such dates as these which made being a musician worthwhile. At the Kenwood, Ron, Glynn and myself would play light music for dinner before we had our meal along with the rest of the band who didn't arrive until later after the official dinner speeches.

Festive seasons were always very busy for us and one we always looked forward to was the Caledonian Dance at the Cutler's Hall.

It was all hell let loose after the dinner but one reason for looking forward to it was really mercenary. We would play from 8 pm until 2 am the following morning and the fee was time and a half so that at the end of the night we would come away with £14 each, which was excellent money at that time.

This was an era when large businesses, especially in the steel industry, would hire such places as The Cutler's Hall, the City Hall and the Grosvenor Hotel plus the Royal Victoria Hotel for their Annual Dinner dances. It was also an era when Rock Groups, who, by the way, were supposed to be in the MU as we were. It was at the City Hall that as we were setting up on the stage, a young man was sitting at the grand piano, with the lid down, fiddling about with his guitar. Bill Tindall, our trombonist, had just arrived and as he climbed onto the stage to pass the young man, Bill asked, "Shall I give you an 'A' on the piano." Now this was the standard procedure for all musicians, whether dance or orchestral.

The lad looked up inquiringly, "What for?" he asked Bill, who replied, "To tune it in." The lad's reply was, "You don't have to tune in guitars, they're electric." We all fell about laughing and it makes one wonder today if the majority of these so called guitarists ever do tune in there instruments..

Another annual dance we played at was for the Faculty at the Sheffield University in the Refectory. This was another big occasion but one highlight was when the organiser came to speak to Ron. This gentleman was Dr. Roger Bullivant and he was Head of Music at the University. The first time we played at the Refectory we had a surprise because after the interval, Professor Bullivant came and asked Ron if he could sit in with us for a number or two.

He could tell by our faces that we were amazed and told us not to worry, he wouldn't let us down. Glynn left the stage and Roger Bullivant took over the piano. He was terrific and proved to a point that in some respect, all music is of an equal. At the end of the dance, we all applauded him and he rewarded us by buying us all a drink.

The dancers enjoyed the music so much that the professor booked us there and then for another special occasion for a Faculty Dance at the Cutler's Hall. There were fourteen musicians in the band and the sound was marvellous and it was a pleasure to be able to play some big band arrangements for a change from the normal 'pop' music. After the interval, the evening warmed up and requests were made for us to also play some speciality dances such as the Gay Gordons, the Lancers and Eightsome Reels, not forgetting the Dashing White Sergeant. As we played these tunes the dancers really became involved and on top of the booze it was all hands to the pump, or should I say all hands on deck. Before long, all the males were down to their braces and the ladies weren't far behind in swirling their skirts and dresses. It was worth playing when you saw the customers enjoying themselves

When we were in full swing with some of the big band arrangements, some tunes were given another title by one or the other of the lads. I know that one favourite tune of mine was 'String of Pearls' as played by Glenn Miller but some one referred to it as a 'String of B....cks'. Another title, ' I Cover the Waterfront' was referred to as 'The Tampax Blues' and the tune we all said was difficult to do was, 'Come, Dancing'. Yet seeing some of the holds that many partners had on the dance floor, it made us wonder if it was.

'What Is This Thing Called, Love?' was another twist of a title and during one well known song I couldn't resist because as the second chorus started, I sang out quite loudly, 'I've Got You Under My Skin' and automatically followed it up with the beat and sang, 'One, Two, Three, Four-skin' Ron doubled up on the drums and the other lads could hardly play for tittering.

Towards the end of the evening, when most dancers were tiring, we would play some lovely lilting foxtrots and watch as the couples embraced each other and appeared to be in a different world. This type of music we would refer to as 'Knicker Wetters or Womb Tremblers'.

These were some of the memories I cherished.

Word went around and this time we were booked for the Medical Ball at the Cutler's again and whilst talking to some of the young student doctors, I managed to make arrangements to sell my old bass, my Tarby bass, to one of the students because he belonged to the University Jazz Band.

Steel, Peech and Tozer, was one of the largest steel works in our area and they had a large office block at Templeboro which was quite near to Rotherham and within the building were catering facilities for the staff there. These rooms were different in size and were regularly hired out at night for various functions such as weddings, conferences and dances.

For small parties there was the 150 Room, then came the a larger one called the 250 Room and the largest held some 500 people. All these were under the management of Wilf Peacock who used to be the comi-chef in the canteen at Edgar Allens' but over the years he had risen to the position he was now in at Steelo's.

The building was well known as the Phoenix Rooms and Wilf had performed a marvellous task in promoting the place and getting it on the map as a viable place for entertainment. Knowing him helped because whenever we were there he always made sure that the musicians were taken care of with regards to refreshments. Wilf did surprise me to the fact that when he worked at Edgar's, he was a stripling of a lad and now the good living he had become used to, had broadened him out very well and he fitted the part well, both as catering and entertainments manager.

With Ron Schofield working on the staff, it enabled him to make contacts with people who were going to use the facilities at the Phoenix Rooms and thus he was able to get some plumb booking for us.

Each year, Victor Sylvester and his Broadcasting Orchestra would appear there for some top party which had been organised for a large firm in the area and Ron had managed to get the booking for us as the support band. It was marvellous to perform opposite such a man as Victor Sylvester because he had a world wide reputation in the dance business. One of Sylvester's fads was that he insisted in continuous dancing and this was proved when arranging with Ron that as each session was ending, his pianist, Oscar Grasso, would carry on playing whilst myself and Ron slipped onto the stage to accompany him (Oscar). As the first tune was coming to an end, Glynn would replace Oscar and the rest of the band would change places. This happened each half hour so I can say that I actually played with the Victor Sylvester Orchestra.

We only played opposite Sylvester the once, even though it was an annual event. This was because Ron also had a fad and that was that he insisted, at any dance, that although on the drums, he would sit at the front of the stage. Sylvester requested him to move but at times Ron could be very obstinate and wouldn't co-operate. The outcome was that Sylvester told him, "You'll never play opposite me again." And we didn't.

Another engagement which we had there was when Ivy Benson and her All Girls Band appeared. Ivy was great and had a word with all of us. They were a fabulous outfit and at one break her lasses were leaving the stage, that is, all except the drummer, a young woman of eighteen. We prepared to go on stage but Ivy said not to and told us to carry on with our rest period. The girl on the drums then proceeded to entertain the audience with the best drum solo I had ever witnessed in my life. For twenty minutes she played various phrases which included flams, drags and crescendos and at one point she appeared to fade away, the audience started to applaud, thinking that she had finished but she hadn't. From the rim of the 14 inch cymbal she rolled up into another crescendo and played a further three minutes. The dancers clapped, shouted and whistled etc., and so did we as we stood in the wings.

During this long break, Ron had been talking to Ivy's lead alto player, Maisie and apparently she was leaving the band shortly to return to her native home in the Barnsley area.

It didn't happen immediately but not long after, Maisie did leave Ivy and married a tenor player named Eddie Webb. They both eventually joined our band and what an asset was Maisie.

One night when playing at the City Hall, she asked Ron to pick a Latin American number and she would do the rest. She did. Maisie was a beautiful looking dark haired young lady and as we started the intro, she arose and went to the microphone. Firstly she played the melody on the piccolo, then she played the flute and to crown it all she sang the words of the chorus and swayed her body rhythmically to the tempo. The crowd went wild and the band lads couldn't hide their feelings either. She was terrific.

A few months after that, I mentioned to her that my son, Tony, was looking for a saxophone to learn on. "I have one at home and it's an alto. I'll bring it for you to see." The following week Maisie arrived with Eddie at our house with the sax. It was a silver plated one and she demonstrated it to show that it was in a sound condition. Tony seemed pleased so I asked her what she wanted for it, money-wise. "Oh! Give me £12." It was a very good buy.

Before Eddie and Maisie left, I noticed that she had brought her clarinet with her. "Please, Maisie?" I asked. She knew what I meant and as Aline, Tony, Geoff and myself settled, Maisie sat on the edge of the settee and played Acker Bilk's signature tune, "Stranger on the Shore." Oh! She was a beautiful player.

At a later date we had the opportunity to play opposite another top band and this was at the

Phoenix Rooms. Not far away from Sheffield was the Batley Variety Club and many famous entertainers performed there and on this occasion the act was Eric Delaney and his band.

Eric had agreed to do a show at the Phoenix Rooms for a private engagement and we were booked as the backing band. He too was a drummer, or should I say, percussionist and in his line up he only needed four other musicians because the biggest part of his act was played on the six tympanies, marimba and tubular bells.

His masterpiece was the tune, 'Baubles, Bangles and Beads' which was based on a theme by the composer, A.Borodin and this was closely followed by 'In a Persian Market'. What a sound, what an act. It was some years later that I had the pleasure of meeting Eric again but that was when I wasn't playing, it was purely social. It was over a number of years that I had the opportunity to meet some wonderful musicians and each time it was an honour to be associated with them.

Tony had practised very well on his sax and had become so proficient that I persuaded him to join the MU and get the chance to learn the profession. Not long after joining, I asked Ron Schofield to give him a run as second alto to Maisie in a big band night at the Pitsmoor Club where Ron's brother, Harold, was the steward. Tony didn't let me or the band down and he soon did several other gigs. Maisie commented that he should keep at it and had played very well on the night at Pitsmoor Club. One big band number we played was 'Canadian Sunset' and this required an effort because none of us had seen the score before the night.

Certain instances remain in one's memory and one of these was when Ron had been given a booking to play in an ante room of the University refectory one afternoon. The University was holding some convention or other and all the senior faculty was there and others too from across the country. The booking had obviously come from Roger Bullivant but he only wanted incidental music played, to give a back ground atmosphere and there was to be no drummer, just piano and strings. The music was only required when guests were having a long interval during the convention and when they were partaking of refreshments.

When we too were taking a break to get out some more scores of music, Glynn, very quietly, started to tinkle on the top octaves of the piano and gave it a soft rhythm. Haydn Godfrey was the leader and he looked at Glynn, smiled, picked up his violin and joined in with the melody. The next thing was that Terry Lally, the other violinist, also picked himself in and then I lifted my bass and added a rhythm.

Bill Levitt, on cello, couldn't resist the temptation and joined in with the rest of us. I think the tune was George Gershwin's 'Lady Be Good' and we kept the volume down but suddenly one or two of the guests started jiving to the tempo and before long, there must have been a dozen or so couples joining in. At the end of the tune we were asked to do some more, it must have sounded like an augmented Stephan Grapelli outfit. The slight diversion had come to the ears of Roger Bullivant and at the end of the afternoon he came over and commended us for using our initiative.

When I was writing about the early 60's, I mentioned that I had been out on a social engagement one night and upon returning home I had found Aline in bed in a serious condition whilst expecting a baby. That particular night I had been playing with Ron Schofield's band at the Hall of Residence at the University. It was to have been an all night session and I had left home at 6.00 pm to commence playing at 7.00 pm and then we were to play until 5.00 am the following morning with appropriate intervals during the night. One must imagine how I felt when I came home at 6.00 am, having played through the night and found that lass in the state that she was in. As I explained, I did what was necessary and it was about four o'clock on the Saturday afternoon before I could get to bed for some rest, having been on my feet for some thirty two hours. I vowed there and then, never to do an all night session again - and I didn't.

By March, 1967, I had recovered from my operation and was able to carry on playing and this led to my being asked by the TWIL Sports Club secretary if I could put a band in at the Phoenix Rooms for a buffet dance. This was the first time that I had the pleasure of having a billing as Ron Priestley and His Orchestra.. To be honest, I had to borrow a spare music library from another band leader.

It was at this dance where I thought that it was going to be a flop because on starting time, my drummer, Haydn Cook, hadn't arrived and this was unusual because most musicians were loath to be late.

However, I decided to get the dance going and started up with a quick number to liven up proceedings. There was Jackie Walker on the piano, Harry Bush on the trumpet with Bill Tindall on the trombone and they were the truly professional back up I needed.

Half way through the second number, Haydn arrived, prepared his drum kit and then apologised. Apparently, he had been almost ready to leave home and was just putting on his dress suit trousers when his foot went through the backside of them. We had all wondered why he had a dress jacket on with grey flannel trousers. Fortunately, with being behind the drums they were hardly noticeable. By the way, I had taken our Geoff with me to get some experience of dance music and he sat just behind the piano.

The dance was a success and because of this, Mr. Sadler, our cost accountant, asked me to get him a band to play at Kenwood Hall. This was for the annual party which was held for the personnel who had worked at TWIL for 25 years or more and was called the 'Twenty Five Year Club.' Mr. Walter Sadler was responsible for anything connected with the club and as we had done for other functions there, we played firstly for dinner and then dancing later on.

For some people at work it was hard to understand that I had been to the '25 Club' dinner when I had only worked there for about eight years. I was given that booking for several years to come and at one of them there was Bill Kelsey, who qualified to attend, and his wife, my aunty Amy. Whilst she was dancing with a friend, she was so interested in trying to speak to me that as she went around the floor, she went arse over tit and finished on her backside. Luckily she wasn't hurt.

I was able to get several engagements with my own band, especially with the TWIL Sports Club and I did one or two at the Cutler's Hall for them. I still played with Ron Schofield but as Rock and Roll was becoming more popular, he shocked us one night at the Cutler's by saying that it was the end of his band and he wasn't playing any more.

We were all left high and dry and from then on we all had to look for other individual engagements.

It's amazing how the word spread because it wasn't long before I was approached by such as Stan (Rocky) Ward. He had his own little outfit and he played accordion and marimba, along with a drummer and a pianist/keyboard player called Millie. Stan's bookings were for small and intimate occasions but sometimes he would get one out at the Marquis of Granby Hotel or the Rising Sun Inn at Bamford.

It was on one of these engagements at the Rising Sun that Stan had a nasty accident. To get our kit onto the stage we had to pass it through one of the downstairs windows just off the dining room. It was as he was going through the window himself that he caught the crown of his head on the upper part of the window frame. Now Stan was a very bald headed man without any hair to protect him from such an incident as this and it put a right tuck in his crown. There was blood all over his head but eventually the bleeding stopped and he carried on playing but all night he had a terrible headache.

I don't know why it was but quite a number of bands were run by drummers such as Jack Start, Ron Schofield, Morris Moore and now another one had broken away from Walt Chapell's band to form his own. This was Colin Whitehead and he asked me to go and play for him on a permanent basis depending on what bookings he received and I would be his regular bassist. It was great because Colin had some good contacts and George Merrill, who had played lead alto with Ron Schofield had also joined him and even Glynn Roden and Gerry Nugent played on odd occasions. Eventually Jack Walker became Colin's regular pianist and a trumpet player named Rod Johnson came to join us.

We were playing at the Grand Hotel in Sheffield one evening when one of the dancers caught my eye. At the interval, I went onto the dance floor and sought him out. It was Marlon Jackson from my Boys Brigade days, way back in the thirties. "What are you doing here?" I asked him."It's my firm's annual dance." He replied.

"I'm the managing director." I couldn't believe it but there again he had done his apprenticeship as an engineer at Davy United's. He now was at Neepsend Steel and Tool Company and as he had said, he was the MD. A short while after that, I read in the local press of a scandal at Neepsend and Marlon was involved. He had been found guilty of embezzlement and was sacked and given twelve months 'down the line'. Why do people have to be their own worst enemy.

Colin had booked an engagement one Saturday night at Elsecar Village Hall near to Barnsley and it was the time when Rock and Roll was really getting established. It was a young crowd and as we played the usual music, it became obvious that they only wanted 'Shake Rattle and Roll'.

At the interval as we were having a drink of tea at a table, a group of youths came up and asked us if they could have a go on our instruments. I looked at Colin and to be honest I felt scared in case we gave the wrong answer. It ended with Colin and myself saying yes but if there was any damage they would have to pay and the cost of some of the instruments was around £300 pounds each. This seemed to deter them and we had no trouble but we must have played 'Shake, Rattle and Roll' about thirty times because there were very few orchestrations of that type on the market.

I played for quite a while with Colin but in between, I also did the odd gig when available. It was due to a double booking fault that I turned up at the Ecclesall Co-op Restaurant one Friday night thinking that I was playing for Stan Ward and having lugged my bass all the way up the stairs to the dance hall, Rocky told me I wasn't booked there for that night. I looked in my diary and found that I should have been playing with Colin at the Stocksbridge Victory Club. I returned to my car and set off as quickly as I could but arrived at Stocksbridge half an hour late. I apologised to Colin and told him I had been working over on the Computer at work but unfortunately, a few days later, Colin rang me at work and said he had bumped into Rocky Ward who had told him about my turning up at the wrong place.

That was it, because Colin said he didn't like lies, not even little white ones and in any case he objected to me playing with any other outfit. That suited me because technically, I was a free lance musician and could choose who I wanted to play for. I never played for Colin Whitehead again but it worked out OK because shortly afterwards I saw an advert in the 'Star' - the local rag - and it asked for a trio to play at a local country club.

Within a few days of applying for the contract, I was offered an interview by a Miss Mildred Arthurs, who was the secretary of the Norton Country Club which was on the western outskirts of town. We talked it over and a fee was agreed for three musicians to play on Saturday evenings from 8.00 pm until 11.30 pm.

I had some cards printed for advertising purposes and called my trio, ' The Five Over Forty' which in technical terms was a musical *f* for forte, inserted under the figure 5. It also meant that I could produce a group of five people and they were all over forty - years of age

It so happened at a Musician's Union meeting, I came across George Cottam again and he had been away in Jersey for a few years as a pro in a hotel in St. Helier. George was looking for work, both daytime and as a musician. I managed to get him a place in the accounts department at TWIL and then offered him a place in the trio. He agreed and suggested contacting an Alan Price to play the piano.

Alan was the postmaster at Dyche Lane Post Office and jumped at the chance to play on the doorstep, so to speak. He also ran a taxi type service for the local barmaids who worked in the area so that he could get them home after their duties at the various pubs which closed at half past eleven. It all fitted in with his plans and we played at the club for a few years. Sometimes we did extra nights for the fishing section, bowls section of the club and also two annual dinner events which were put on for the Lord Mayor of Sheffield whoever he may be in the current term of office.

The first night we played there, we were introduced to the President of the Club who was Percy Hollis and he was a self made man in the rag trade. He had two factories in Cyprus and many connections in Lancashire although he was a Yorkshireman. It was during a conversation with him that I learned that he used to live on Newark Street in his younger days, just near to where I lived in Attercliffe. With Percy, formalities were dispensed with when he was around and at the end of the each evening, it was he who went into his wallet to pay our fee.

There was of course, the seasonal social evenings such as Easter, with it's bonnet parade, and the normal Christmas and New Years Eve dances. It was one wintry night when it was so cold, I think it was the winter of 1974 and because I felt so cold, I partook of a Barley Wine to get warm.

I enjoyed it so much that I had another three but by the end of the playing time I knew I wouldn't be able to drive home safely so I rang Aline at home. Now, David was on leave from Binbrook at that time and he had a small Mini Van in which he was learning to drive and had only just come in at home from being out with Geoff.

Geoff hadn't passed his test either so Aline came up for me in the van after giving both David and Geoff plenty of black coffee and bringing them with her. It finished up with me sitting in the van with David as a qualified driver and Geoff sat alongside Nip for company whilst she drove the car back home. One good thing was that I nearly always left my bass at the club and this was one of those nights so it didn't interfere with her driving. It's the first time ever that I've been in that state as a musician but I had the presence of mind to use some common sense and not risk an accident. I think George Cottam was more worried about Aline driving home than my state of health.

As we were playing one night, I noticed a young man standing at the bar and as he turned, I recognised him as Charlie Barnes, who had worked with me in the thirties in the Foundry at Edgar Allen's. At the interval we had a good natter and he introduced me to his wife and mother-in-law. I also found out that he was the good friend of Percy Hollis.

During the conversation, his mother-in-law asked me if I would care to borrow some music which had been left to her by another musician, Dave Egerton, who used to stay with her when he ran his big band at the Lacarno Ballroom in Sheffield at the bottom of London Road. Apparently he had run up some debts and repaid some of them by giving the lady his music library because she so loved music.

I borrowed the books which had over a thousand tunes in them from 1913 up to the present day and most of them were the 'evergreens' in every type of tempo. She said that there was no rush, so over the next few weeks I guiltily photocopied them on our Rank Xerox machine at work. They were to be invaluable in the years that followed. One of the members there was a

Mrs. Shaw and she was having a retirement party at the Hallam Towers Hotel and asked us if we would play for the party there and this we gladly did.

We became very popular at the club and it helped also that George was a fairly good vocalist which he could do whilst playing. There were times when I had to take my holidays and more then once I was able to call on my son Tony to deputise for me and it also helped him out financially with his little family.

There were other odd times when Alan couldn't get so I managed to obtain the services of Ken Watkinson who deputised for him. This was an added bonus because Ken too, was a good vocalist and as I've said before, he used to the resident singer with Bernard Taylor's Band before becoming a musician. Some of the tunes we played encouraged George and Ken to sing in harmony and this really suited the club members.

I had my trio right up to 1978 when one evening, the committee asked us to play until 12 o'clock midnight instead of 11.30 pm. George and I didn't mind but Alan said that it was inconvenient because of the ferrying service he gave to the local barmaids. Alan gave us time to get a replacement and George managed to contact a lovely young lady Jean, who could play and sing but not busk. For a couple of weeks we carried on until one Saturday when I walked in, George and Jean - who's married name I can't recall - were having a conversation at the bar, prior to starting. I sensed that something was amiss and just before we started playing, George said that Jean had commented that the fee for the trio should be split exactly into three. Now, the total fee was £21 for the night and I gave George and the pianist £6.10.0 each which left me with £6.10.0 for my fee plus the balance of £1.10.0 which I kept for buying music and any necessary expenses which may occur.

Bear in mind that I had found George employment at TWIL and given him the chance to play at the club with me, I couldn't believe it when he said that he backed Jean's request. You can understand why I don't want to remember the girls full name. I waited until the end of the night and then told George he could run the trio and that I wasn't interested any more. I then told Percy and Miss Arthurs what had happened, thanked them for their support in the past few years and walked out there and then.

Over the years, there had been happenings of all kinds and although on the whole there were happy ones, there were some which were rather sad, as when told at one MU meeting that a pianist, Curly Mason, had committed suicide by putting his head in the gas oven due to domestic circumstances. Then there was the case where Jackie Bates, Taylor's original drummer, was driving up the High Street, felt ill and pulled over to the curb. Jackie collapsed and died on the spot. Jack Smith, the drummer, also died of a heart attack whilst in his early forties. You may recall the name of Jimmy Clayton who was in the award winning quintet at Manchester, he too collapsed and died whilst in his late thirties. So, it wasn't all a bundle of laughs being a musician. A few years later on I paid my respects to Colin Whitehead when I attended his cremation and there he set he new trend because he had asked a pianist friend to record the song, 'I Wish You Love.' and this was played in the Chapel of the Crematorium,

I never played my bass again and one can tell how incensed I was because after thirty years I resigned officially from the MU. It's rather ironic, that two months after I left the club, Jean became ill and had to stop playing and this dropped George right in it.

Three months later, I advertised my bass for sale in the local press. A lady rang me to see if she could bring her son to see it. This they did and as soon as he picked it up I knew he could play it. I sold it for £70 and was more than pleased when I found out that the young man played in the Sheffield Youth Orchestras. As they left, I must admit that there was a tear in my eye.

THE EIGHTIES

In January 1980, we welcomed the return of David from Belize and his posting was to Waddington in Lincolnshire. This was the base for the famous 232 Squadron which was now equipped with the also famous Vulcan Bomber. Shortly after his return, Heather had managed to get a posting from Wegberg in Germany, back to England, so that she could be near to him

It worked out fine because she was sent to the RAF Hospital at Nocton, which was more or less a stone's throw from Waddington and by doing this she was able to arrange married quarters for them both on the Nocton Camp. Aline and I were glad for them and it also meant that we were able to visit them on two or three occasions because it was about an hour's run in the car from Sheffield. They also popped up to see us whenever duties permitted them to.

Back in 1979, the Tory Government had introduced a scheme whereby 'sitting' council tenants were given the 'Right to Buy' their council homes and although it didn't go down well with a lot of Labour Councils, especially Sheffield City Council, the Government pressed ahead and early in 1980, the Bill was passed in the House of Commons for this to take place.

We had been tenants in No.8 Ballifield Crescent since it was first built in May 1951 so, we were eligible to apply but we didn't know what was entailed or what the deposit was going to be. Also, the local council were issuing threats to people who were interested and it became necessary for me to contact a Mrs. Christine Smith. She was a Conservative Councillor who lived on Poole Road at Darnall but was actually a councillor in a different Ward to ours. Over the next few months, she gave us tremendous assistance and advice as to all procedures.

Having finished playing as a musician in 1978, I was at a loss as to what to do with my time on Saturdays. It was whilst out shopping that I bumped into a Dick Brewerton who once worked in the Cost Office at Edgars. He was a cricket umpire in the Sheffield and District Cricket League and asked me if I still played cricket and when I told him I was too old, he suggested that I might try umpiring.

I hadn't even thought of it but he asked me to go to a meeting in Sheffield and he would try to get me registered. Dick was successful and the first match at which I umpired, happened to be with Dick at a match up at Loxley. From then on I began to learn the business and enjoyed every minute. The fee at that time was £5 per game and Dick encouraged me by advising me what literature to buy so that I became familiar with the Laws of cricket. In the winter period I went to organised lectures and prepared to sit the Association of Cricket Umpires examinations. I failed the first time and no wonder because the pass mark was 75% which was extremely high but it didn't stop me from carrying on umpiring.

At the end of June, Aline and I set off on a camping holiday once more with the trailer tent. This time we intended doing it in stages and our first stop was Barns Ness again and just against the Light House there. We stayed there a couple of days and visited North Berwick and had a look around the small town of Dunbar before pushing on over the Forth Bridge, up through Stirling and then along the north east coast of Scotland until we came to a place called Newburgh.

Once again we stayed a couple of days and camped on a lane just outside a pub, from where we were able to get water and use their toilets. We walked up the lane the next day and after some fifteen minutes we came to a small estuary, Newburg Bar. As we walked over the small dunes, we came to a beautiful long beach which stretched right down to Aberdeen. We could have camped at Aberdeen the previous day but the site was on a municipal car park and we didn't fancy it so we had moved up the coast to our present position.

We walked along the beach for a good mile and then decided to find our way back over the nearby sand dunes. I hadn't seen so much sand since I passed through the Middle East during the War.

We were on holiday and it was fun. The dunes were huge and at one point I took a photograph of Nip sitting on the top of a telegraph pole. That was possible because the drifting sands had piled up against the pole, almost to the top. I couldn't have imagined Nip climbing one of these poles just to have her picture taken. It was whilst we were having a drink in the pub at night that the landlord explained that the dunes had been used for Army exercises in the past, hence the debris we had seen lying about.

Having enjoyed our short stay, we headed across Aberdeenshire in the direction of Macduff on a part of Scotland I always called the flat bit. We had a couple of refreshment breaks on the way and eventually ended up on a large camp site at Lossiemouth. Having pitched the tent and had a good night's sleep, the following day we had a look around the various small towns which lie along that part of the coast and they were so close together. On one visit, we had a look around the famous Baxter's canned food factory. The point of being at Lossiemourth would be significant in later years and one noticeable feature was that after 5.00 o'clock at night, there was no flying from the local RAF camp, so we didn't get disturbed whilst camping after dark.

On the 6th July we headed for home via Morayshire, up and down the glens until we came to Kinlochleven where we stayed for another couple of nights on the loch side. After two days we left the site and drove up the well-known Glencoe Valley. What a beautiful sight to see, with the lone piper standing there and playing some Scottish airs on his bagpipes. All the holiday we had been fortunate with the weather until we arrived at the top of Glencoe. What a difference. Gale force winds, heavy rain and we couldn't see a thing as we travelled along the A82 route down to Crianlarich. It did ease a little but as we drove down the side of Loch Lomond, the cover on the trailer tent became saturated.

As we passed through Paisley, I pulled up to get some fish and chips because we were so hungry and after eating them in the car, we finally set off again and headed for the lovely little town of Moffat in Dumfrieshire. Here we had a slight mishap because we found that one of the support bolts on the trailer had snapped. We only found it when we came to erect the main canvas rods but the camp warden came to our rescue by telling us to go to the local blacksmith who was just down the lane of the camp site. This I did and I left Aline to do what she could in setting up the rest of the tent. The blacksmith was very obliging and found four identical bolts for which he only charged me ten shillings. It was worth it.

Moffat was a friendly little town and we camped there for a couple of more nights, one of which we used by calling in one of the pubs named the Station. This was all set out like a railway with a track line at the bar to put one's foot on. The lounge was the guard's van, the snug was the signal box and the main saloon had all sorts of memorabilia in it.

We had experienced a wonderful holiday and after a long drive from Moffat, we eventually arrived back home at three thirty pm on the 11th July.

During the following week, our Geoff had told us that he had arranged for us to go to the TA Royal Signals unit on Saturday the 19th July. The purpose being that HRH The Princess Anne, was to do an inspection because she was the Colonel-in - Chief of the Regiment.

Aline and I arrived at the centre by 10.15 am because we had to be seated in a specially erected small stand which would accommodate about one hundred people. Our seats were in the third row and after the Royal Salute, which was played by the Band of the 34th (Northern) Signal Regiment (V), Her Royal Highness was invited to meet some of the guests, both distinguished and otherwise.

As she came level with our area of seats, Princess Anne looked up directly at Aline and me and asked, "What do you think about units of this kind?"

"They are very good, Ma'am, for training young people. I have a son in the Royal Air Force."

"Oh! Really?" She replied, enquiringly.

"Yes Ma'am, but of the two, I lean towards the RAF."

She lifted one eyebrow as in astonishment and walked on. My comment made her laugh.

Aline couldn't believe that we had been addressed by one of the Royal Family but I wondered what HRH would have said had she known that David had been on the parade in London at her wedding to Capt. Mark Phillips when David was stationed at Halton. At just after 2.00 pm, Princess Anne left in the Royal car to proceed to Sandbeck Hall, the residence of Lord Scarborough.

After her departure, Nip and I were given a guided tour around the unit by our Geoff, who really looked smart in his uniform. He was so proud of it and we were proud of him too. He told us that whilst all the preparations for the visit had been going on, he has caused a little upset but also a laugh.

He had helped to erect a twelve-foot square tent for the display purposes of signalling equipment and just as the main guy rope was being pegged down, he had stepped back, caught the tent peg and the whole tent had collapsed. It wasn't long after that when we found out the cause of his clumsiness. We enjoyed the day out and were both pleased to give our support to him because during his service with the TA, he became a proficient signaller and had passed his examinations in signalling courses.

Apart from our holidays, I umpired many cricket matches and had enjoyed taking part during the summer in a game I loved and I was sorry when the season came to an end. However, as winter approached, I carried on attending the lectures which took place at the Sheffield Transport Sports Ground at Meadowhead.

Unbeknown to Aline and me, Geoff, who had been working at the GPO since March, had handed in his notice on the 3rd October because he had applied to join the RAF and had been accepted. His CO at the TA unit was disappointed because Geoff had progressed so well. He was to report to RAF Swinderby, in Lincolnshire, for training on the day before his birthday which was on the 8th October.

Geoff had been accepted as a Supplies Clerk and was to commence training immediately. We didn't see him during his six weeks initial training, at the end of which, he managed to get a weekend leave. We thought that he looked well in his TA uniform but when he came home in his RAF uniform there was a lump in our throats. With being tall, he carried it very well.

During the year, Christine Smith, the councillor, had been busy supporting would be buyers of council houses and eventually Aline and I decided to apply and it was in October that our final application was sent to the Town Hall. This was because we had to apply within eight weeks of Royal Assent to the Bill in Parliament which was the 3rd October. So we sat back and awaited an answer, not knowing what was involved or what finances were required.

An acknowledgement was received from the Town Hall on the 27th October and a whole load of objections to the scheme were given as to why we shouldn't buy our home but we took the chance again, not knowing what the outcome would be and so we waited for the final result.

In the first week of December, Geoff had let us know that he had hurt his arm in the Gym and had been sent to the RAF Hospital at Nocton Hall for treatment It wasn't too serious but whilst there he was able to call in and see Heather who was a nurse in the Maternity Wing.

Following this accident, Geoff had been put back into a holding unit which usually finished up with the personnel being dismissed the service if their attainment wasn't achieved. I took it upon myself to write to my MP Pat Duffy, whom I knew personally. I explained the circumstances to the effect that why did the Ministry of Defence go to the expense of kitting out and partly training people before they had passed the basic medical and physical requirements.

Back at work I had been busy for many months travelling up and down the M1 motorway between Birnam's and Lace Web, setting up information on VDU's and teaching the staff in those establishments how to feed in information and operate the hardware.

I worked alongside Clive Morris, the DP Manager at Birnams, also Mick Morris who was the TWIL Handling manager at Eastwood.

On my way up from Sandiacre, I would call in at Birnam Products and collate information about car seat springs and mattress details. I looked forward to lunchtime at the 'Moon and Stars' pub at Eastwood and don't forget I was on expenses when travelling for TWIL so the cost didn't matter within reason.

It was upon return from one of these visits to Birnam's that Bob Little called me into his office and I thought, what on earth for? "Sit down, Ron." Bob said. I could tell by the tone in his voice that all was not well and I began to think of what I may have done wrong. Bob carried on, "I'm sorry, Ron, but I've some bad news for you. David Young, the Chief Executive, wants you to leave at the end of January next."

Obviously I was taken aback and for a minute I couldn't comment. "What's all this about, Bob? Have I done something wrong?"

"No." Said Bob. "It's just that right now cut backs have to be made and you're one of the people to be made redundant."

" Well. Is it possible for me to stay until I reach the age of sixty?" I asked. That was until October. "I'm afraid not." Said Bob. "David has made his mind up and I can't persuade him."

So it was that I received my Christmas Box a little early and when I arrived home and told Aline, she was very upset. She asked about compensation and I told her it would be settled in the New Year but I didn't know any details. The year had ended on a sour note but somehow I wasn't too shocked and decided to take it in my stride. I was sure that things would turn out for the best in the long run.

It seemed ironical that during December, Aline and I had been and purchased a whole new Schreiber bedroom suite and units. We paid cash of around £200 for it and we were happily of the knowledge that we hadn't any outstanding debts. That's the way of the world and we accepted it because Aline and I were that sort of people who could take things in our stride and smile at adversity.

Geoff was able to get some leave at Christmas and this helped to break the disappointment of my being made redundant, also Dave and Heather were able to come up to us as well

After the Christmas Holiday and upon return to work, I had several meetings with Terry Murphy the Personnel Advisor and Reg Hill, who was the Pensions Manager. Terry had explained to me my entitlements with regard to Statutory Redundancy payments and what was involved. He told me that I would no longer be required by TWIL after the 30th January.

With regard to Geoff's problem, Pat Duffy replied eventually and said that he had taken it up with the MOD and would contact me when he received an answer. It was the 19th December when he finally received that reply from Geoffrey Pattie, the Minister of Defence which explained the details of the medical report about our Geoff from Swinderby. Because of the Christmas break, Pat hadn't sent it on to me until the New Year and it was now the third week of January. But, having the letter, which was dated the 20th January, in my possession, along with Aline, I read the explanation and details about Geoff's abilities and disabilities and they were very disturbing. It was a case of sitting back and waiting for any outcome.

For two weeks I carried on helping people who were to be involved with any tasks which I had been doing and Bob arranged for a bit of a leaving party for me in the Manager's Dining room before I left. It was a case of visiting various departments and saying cheerio to work colleagues with whom I had been associated. It also enabled me to pick up a few little perks such as a 50-metre roll of 'damaged' wire netting which would be useful when gardening and also on my last trip to Birnam's I was able to scrounge a car foot pump with a gauge which was a by-product of that factory.

In the last week of my employment, Reg Hill had me in his office to finalise my redundancy pay and my pension, to which, fortunately, I was to receive from the 1st of May and not when I was 65 years of age. Because I had been there for just more than 20 years, it entitled me to receive 29 week's pay in lump sum and in lieu of notice. It was £2,910.15 and very welcome.

Along with this, I was told that I could have a pension (which had been non-contributory) of approximately £40 pounds per week from May the first. However, to avoid any tax problems, Reg Hill said there would be no guarantee that any increase would be forthcoming in the future and suggested that I take a reduced pension of £28 pounds per week, along with a cash lump sum including an ex-gratia payment which amounted to £6000 pounds.

I talked it over with Aline and we agreed to accept the lump sum and invest it and take the reduced pension of £28 per week which, incidently, didn't come into force until the end of April. Aline and I always worked as a team when discussing our future and I think this is what enabled us to have such a successful marriage.

On the 30th January, I had my leaving party with certain invited guests because the number was limited but such people as Bob, Roger Farris and one or two other bosses, were automatically chosen to be there. I was presented with a Black & Decker Jig Saw, some bathroom scales and a made-up farewell message in punched cards to remind me of my workdays. The only regret was that the works' photographer forgot to load his camera with film and at a later date this was rectified by my calling in at the office and having some photo's taken with members of the staff to make amends.

As we entered February, I was trying to settle in to being out of work and trying not to get under Aline's feet. We were just getting over some of the problems with Geoff when Tony called in to say that he had been made redundant at Wigfall's. However, he managed almost immediately, to get a job as an auditor with a clothing firm named 'Jean-Jeannie'.

This entailed him travelling about the country visiting the many shops which the firm owned and taking stock of supplies and auditing the books. Sometimes he would be up in Newcastle-upon-Tyne on the North East coast and another time he would be down south in the Southampton area. He appeared to be enjoying the challenge plus the fact that he could claim expenses on the top of his salary.

Having recently left TWIL and having a fair amount in our account in the bank, I talked it over with Aline about having a new car - and I meant a 'new' car. We had always wanted one, so she said, "Why not?" And off we went and chose a Vauxhall Cavalier with a 1300 cc engine and agreed upon the colour of dark blue. We bought it for around the £4,000 pound mark from Kirkby Central Motors in Rotherham on Wellgate and we paid cash for it. I was pleased with the customer service there because the number plate I was given reminded me of the year we bought the car - it was KHE81W. My old car, the Vauxhall Viva, went to Tony and this was VWJ176L, which I had driven for six years.

Aline and I were just having a coffee break one afternoon when the 'phone rang and Aline answered it. "You're wanted on the telephone, Ron. It's the Royal Air Force."

My first thought was that David had been involved in an accident. Many years ago, whilst he was in training he had told us that the life expectancy of an armourer was seven years and this was at the back of my mind when I picked up the phone.

Apprehensively, I said, "Hello! Mr Priestley speaking. Can I help you?" A voice replied, "This is Sqdn/Ldr Cowper at RAF Swinderby and I'm the medical officer." That gave slight relief, knowing that it wasn't about David. "Yes, Sir." I replied, still showing respect for the rank. "Is there a problem?"

"Yes and no." He answered and then carried on by saying, "Is it possible for you and Mrs. Priestley to come down to Swinderby to discuss the physical implication we are having with your son Geoffrey?"

My voice must have indicated that I was worried but he assured me that whilst a problem was there, we ought to know the full story. I made an appointment for us to see him and he did say that the Senior MO, a Wing Commander, would also be present.

He rang off and Aline and I had a good talk as to what we were going to find and a few days later we visited Swinderby and we were introduced to the two officers. Sqdn/Ldr Cowper said, "We would like you to see a video of Geoffrey in the gymnasium and watch the difficulties he has been having." He then called in a sergeant and asked him to bring in the video tape. After five minutes, the NCO returned, minus the film.

"Sorry, Sir, for some unknown reason the tape has been over written."

The look on the officer's face said it all. "I'll speak to you later, sergeant." He said, and the NCO left the room. The two officers couldn't apologise enough and regretted a partly wasted journey but they asked Nip and me to accept their findings at face value. We couldn't do anything else, could we. Apparently, as Geoff was exercising on an upturned bench by jumping on and off and straddling the bench, he couldn't keep his balance and kept falling off. Also in the field events he couldn't keep up with the rest of the group, even though he tried so hard.

The Wing Commander had made some serious enquiries into the cause of this and had come up with the answer that it was Cerebellum Ataxia which meant lack of coordination of the brain with the limbs. Due to this finding he said that there was no alternative but to discharge Geoff from the services. So **this** was the cause over the years of Geoff's clumsiness, how I wished we had known earlier.

I asked, "Is that really necessary, seeing that Geoff's trade is mainly doing clerical work?"

"I'm sorry." Was the reply. "But all servicemen have to be of a physical standard which may need the requirement to kill if in a military conflict." Aline and I were taken aback but realised that we must accept the verdict. Geoff was devastated when told of the outcome because he had set his heart on following in a career in the RAF just like his brother David. It was a blow to the whole family and more so to our Dave.

The officers had been kept in touch with what had taken place between myself and my MP and I think this is what had prompted them to talk to myself and Aline. It was a few weeks before everything was finalised and on the 18th March, 1981, I went down in the car again to collect Geoff and his belongings. As he signed for his release, I had a word with the Admin Warrant Officer, Mr Arbuthnot, who said he was sorry to see Geoff go because people of Geoff's mental qualifications and intellect were needed by the RAF and had it not been for his physical inabilities, he's sure he would have been officer material.

Geoff was put on medical release and though he left Swinderby on the 18th March, his actual release date was the 23rd April and this was the date up to which he had been paid. The following week we did what we could to make up for his disappointment and one of the immediate priorities was to re-register him with Dr. Hasan with whom he had been a patient prior to his enlistment. I went with him to see the Doctor and he was very sympathetic when we told him the findings and he said he would do all he could to help him under the circumstances.

We were just getting accustomed to having Geoff at home again when further bad news was brought in by Tony. Once again he had been made redundant, this time from Jean-Jeannie. Obviously we were upset but it's strange how fate takes a hand. However, in April, we eventually had some good news. David, who was at Waddington, had been promoted to Corporal and the pay increase came in handy.

For the past few years I had been a member of a three-man billiards team for Handsworth Social Club but recently I had been playing for the Darnall Conservative Club. In our team were Jack Kirkby, Cyril Hartley, Cliff Sutton and myself. I was the youngest of the team and just a moderately rated player but I helped to take an interesting part in the fortunes of the team.

It was whilst playing against the Burngreave Conservative Club at their venue in Pitsmoor that I was drawn to play against Ted Vickers. He was in their team along with Eric Ball, with whom I used to work at Firth Vickers and another chap called Alf Todd.

Whilst I was waiting to play my game, I mentioned to Ted Vickers that I had just been made redundant.

"I'm sorry about that." Ted said. "If you had been a little younger, you could have come and worked with me as my assistant." I thought, what a pity, but he carried on. "I'm looking for someone to help me and eventually take over when I retire." He was also an ex-police inspector.

" I'll tell you what, Ted. I've a son who has also been made redundant and he's looking for a job. He's thirty years old."

"Where was he educated?" asked Ted, and I replied."Firth Park Grammar School."

"That's good enough for me, " said Ted. "Send him down for an interview in a few days' time."

I did this and immediately after the interview, Tony rang to say that he was to start right away. What luck!

Trying to get used to not having to go to work was a little difficult because I couldn't sit around doing nothing so one day I said to Aline, "I'll think I'll go into security."

"But you don't know the first thing about it'" Was her reply.

"Then I'll go and find out." So I went up to the Manor Top, where I knew there was a local police office and asked for any officer who was conversant with Crime Prevention. I was lucky because I was introduced to a Detective Constable Graham Highfield. I explained what I wanted to do and he advised me as to the necessary procedure for being registered with the South Yorkshire police. He took down all my details and said I should submit a photograph of myself for their records. This is what I did and when I returned a few days later with the photo, he put it in their files and told me I had already been checked out with their records in case I had one.

He introduced me to his superior who was a Sergeant Ward who told me to abide by their rules and had a laugh about me not being on the records. Graham advised me to have some leaflets printed, giving details of the sort of security I was offering and my home telephone number but not my address so that I could be contacted. Graham advised me to go to the Manor Press which was just down City Road below their office and tell them that he had sent me.

Graham and Sgt. Ward were attached to the Hackenthorpe Police which was a Division of the South Yorkshire Police and they both asked me to keep in touch with any work I did. Graham also told me where I could buy security fittings and claim the trade discount. This was a large security business in Sheffield and was a family business named Harrolds and they were situated on Shalesmoor not far away from the S.Y Police Headquarters.

I went down to town to make myself known and told them that Graham Highfield had sent me and one of the sons commented that he, Graham, would do that because he had been at the same school as they when they were young. He also said that Graham was the longest serving Detective Constable on Crime Prevention in the whole of the country.

Graham persuaded me to have some leaflets printed and I agreed with the Manor Press to the following format.

SAFETYCARE

Be Secure With SAFETYCARE
Assist In Crime Prevention

HELP US TO HELP YOU BE SECURE
BY ASKING US TO INSTAL ONE
OR MORE SECURITY FITTINGS
AT REASONABLE PRICES

Door Chains   Door Viewers
Door and Window Bolts
Personal Hand Alarm

CHECK YOUR PRESENT SECURITY
REPLACE OLD FITTINGS
INSTAL NEW SAFETY DEVICES
MAKE CONTACT WITH **SAFETYCARE**
ENSURE YOUR POSSESSIONS ARE SAFE

WHY NOT RING Sheffield 695992

SAFETYCARE

So on the 3rd June, I collected my 1000 leaflets which cost £16 and for the next few weeks I went around the Handsworth and Woodhouse areas distributing them and hoping that I would soon get some business. It wasn't long before I was doing small items like door viewers and chains but as the orders increased I thought that to be legitimate I had better register as an official business. So I did and on the 27th July I registered with the Government Department as 'SAFETYCARE'

One of the first big jobs I did was to put some large mortice locks on the doors of the flats just across the road from where I lived. There again Graham had been helpful when I told him that I hadn't fitted one before so he told me to get an old piece of wood and practise on it in the outhouse. This is what I did and eventually I became very proficient and more ambitious and did sash locks as well. I didn't make a lot of profit but I enjoyed having something to do and talking to old people.

On the 10th of June we received notification that a surveyor was being sent from the Town Hall on the 16th to measure the house and land of No 8 to fix a valuation of the property following our application to buy. It didn't take him long and the gentleman said he would notify us in due course. In anticipation of the result we had arranged another holiday and this time we headed for the West of Scotland to another Club Site which was on the Mull of Kintyre.

The actual site was located on the West Coast of the Mull and to get there we knew it was going to be a long journey from Sheffield. There were no short cuts across country to get there, so having two weeks in which to enjoy our holiday, there was no urgency in our travelling time and once again we had a break at Moffat and stayed there for two nights. We then set off for our next stop which was to be Oban in Argyllshire so we headed for the Loch Lomond area by which route we were to take. Everything was going well, the new car was pulling the trailer beautifully and the weather was fine.

As we approached Luss on the South West side of the Loch, traffic began to accumulate and we were just entering Luss when a vehicle, some several hundred yards in front, was late in indicating his signal to turn left. The result was that the six vehicles behind had a chain reaction in taking evasive action. Unfortunately, our car with the attached trailer, was the last one and although the speed was below 30mph and having changed into a lower gear in anticipation, I wasn't quick enough to stop hitting a Morris Mini in front of me. I had swung towards the kerb trying to avoid an accident but I couldn't help my front offside wing bumping into the back of the mini in front. The wing received a huge dent and bent inwards onto the tyre.

No one was hurt but as we pulled up, the driver of the mini climbed out and said he had a baby in the back. Luckily, it wasn't hurt and I was sorry for him and his wife but he insisted on calling the police who eventually arrived and asked me to pull over to the other side of the road into a small layby.

Why is it that the law always blames the chap at the back?

Even though I had tried very hard to avoid any trouble, the weight of the trailer had helped in pushing me into the car in front. The police wouldn't accept my explanation and I couldn't help commenting upon them ganging up on a Sassenach

I was more annoyed and upset and my pride was hurt because I had finally managed to acquire a brand new car and the first long run I had been able to do, I had become involved in an accident.

After being held up for about an hour we were able to carry on after easing out the wing from the tyre and headed for Oban on the A85, having left the A82 route.

Once again we had a two-day break at Oban on a small campsite before proceeding down the A816 and A83 to Loch Gilphead and then Tarbert, where we had a meal break. Carrying on down the A83 we travelled down the coast road and eventually came to Campbeltown, the largest place on the Mull. We had driven some 500 miles since leaving home and this last stretch had made us feel hungry as we came into the town. But, we hadn't finished yet because we had to turn off the main road and go another six miles before reaching our final destination which was Machrihanish and it was right on the coast. It was desolate but in years to come it was to be significant to David.

We booked in and found that there were only three other units on the camp so we could pick our own spot. This we did and set up just at the bottom of a ridge so that we had a little shelter from the wind. The facilities were good with the Warden's residence being in a brick building which also had a bar and a small play area for children. We stayed there from the Thursday until the following Wednesday and visited many places of interest.

One of these places was the lighthouse at Bein na Lice but because the road down to it was so steep, we parked the car in a small parking place. We then walked to the edge of the road just above the lighthouse so that we could take some photographs. Back in Campbeltown which was a small quiet fishing town, we enjoyed looking around and then we had a meal in one of the cafes.

Another day we spent entirely by strolling along the harbour bay and along the shingle beach up to the Castle. We had always taken an interest in looking at castles, especially in Scotland, possibly because the boys always enjoyed it when we were on holiday with them. On our way back, we noticed several fish boxes scattered along the bay and I commented to Nip that they would be useful in the garden at home mainly for putting bedding plants in .

They were strong plastic ones and about three feet by eighteen inches and four inches deep, so very nonchalantly, I put two into the car boot. The funny part of the holiday was that when I needed a daily paper, I had to go by car into Campbeltown to get one and this was a twelve miles round trip each time. Across the bay near to the camp site was an airfield and we had a run round one day to have a look at it. The bay itself was very sandy and we wondered why there weren't many people using it but when we had a walk along it, we soon found out because it was littered with flotsam and jetsam and the Atlantic winds made it very cold.

On our way home from the holiday we travelled up the B842 road, which was on the East coast of the Mull, just for a change of scenery and once again because of the long journey home we made for Ayrshire and this time we stayed at Kilkerran for the night, which was another Club site. We eventually arrived back in Sheffield at 5.pm on the 2nd July, having travelled some 1200 miles which, apart from the accident, had been very enjoyable.

The 24th July was when I had a letter from the Procurator Fiscal's office in Glasgow telling me that he had received a report from the police about my accident and although it warranted criminal proceedings, he had decided not to take me to court but warned me that any other offences would be taken into account. I think the decision was mainly decided because at that time the legal establishment was on strike and a tremendous backlog of court cases had piled up. Lucky me.

Just prior to this letter arriving, we had another letter from the housing department at the Sheffield Town Hall, asking us to go and see a Mr Bownes to discuss the price of our house and the means by which we would be paying. The valuer, who had called earlier, had assessed the house and grounds to be worth £14,750 but because we had been tenants for over 25 years, the price to us would be £7,375 and Freehold. This complied with the Tory Government's decision to reduce by 50%, any house sale where the tenancy was over 25 years. Here was a good chance to own our own home and we intended to do just that.

Mr Bownes still tried to talk us out of buying it, as was the request of the Labour Council but we had made our decision and when it came to the method of payment and a mortgage, Aline and I had already agreed to use my redundancy money and buy it outright in a lump sum. Mr Bownes looked surprised that we were able to do that and on the 31st July, we received another letter confirming the figures agreed to. All we had to do now was to wait for finalisation of the documents and to make sure that everything was done by the board. We commissioned the solicitors of Slater, Elliot, Todd, Cooper and Co., whose office was in Paradise Square, to deal with the legal proceedings. Mr Elliot was our personal representative.

Also in July I had decided to buy a small wooden hut so that I could keep all my gardening equipment and seed boxes etc., in it and also to make some room in the outhouse. It meant clearing the water from the small paddling pool which I had made for the kids years ago when they were little. The hut was 7ft x 5ft and I went down to Shalesmoor to a small business called Metro Buildings. That was on the 17th July and three days later they delivered it and erected it for the price of £107. It just fit in onto the concrete base where the pond had been and looked very tidy and accessible. The next job was preserving it by giving it a good coating of Creosote.

Since coming out of the RAF, Geoff had really tried to get employment and his first try was to apply to go back as a postman. However, the Superintendent there told him that having left the GPO service twice before, he couldn't take that chance again. Once more Geoff felt down in the dumps having had no success. To try to help him to adjust, I asked Geoff if he would be interested in joining the Fellowship of the Services, the ex-servicemans association I was in.

He was a little reluctant at first but I arranged for him to have an interview with the Mess Committee and make up his own mind because I wasn't going to press him. On the 12th October, Fred Morris, the Mess Secretary, sent him a letter inviting him to a Mess concert so that he could assess the situation.

Geoff enjoyed the company of companions there and agreed to join. It was the 19th October at Mess Committee that he was officially interviewed and produced his documents confirming that he had been in Her Majesty's Forces.

During the interview, when asked about his opinion on joining, he commented, "I think I'll get along with all you old foddy-doddies." This caused a laugh, especially from John Cobb who was the senior member there. The Companions weren't that old but to our Geoff, some of them, who were ten to fifteen years older than he, seemed a lot older.

Because of what was called 'Remembrance Mess' in November, new initiants weren't accepted, so it was on the 14th December 1981 that our Geoff was enrolled as a Companion of the Fellowship into 163 King Edward Mess. I think another reason for him deciding to join was that David, being a member of the Forces was allowed to attend the Mess as a Serving Friend and his comments about the odd visits he had paid may have persuaded Geoff to enrol.

For the early part of my retirement-cum-redundancy, I seemed to have had little time to spare and though it was rather hectic, 1981 had been a full year with some things regrettable and others memorable.

Having had a good Christmas again with family and being able to have my Mum for her Xmas dinner, we settled down and looked forward to a more possible productive year. This started off well with Nip and me deciding in January to replace the old pot sink unit in the kitchen with a completely new stainless steel unit. We purchased it from MFI at a cost of £44.95 and Tony arranged for his father-in-law, Ken Ramsden, to come and fit it in for us.

Ken was of the scrounger type and would do anything for a bob or two but no way would he take on full time employment. He held a 'Green card' to confirm that he was suffering from back trouble to exclude him from any manual obligations but, it didn't stop him from refereeing football matches for which he was a qualified official.

On the 26th January we had a request from our solicitor, Mr. Elliott, to go and sign for the Deeds of Conveyance which indicated that we were on the last lap of buying our house and having both given our signatures, we were told another couple of weeks should see it through.

Mr. Elliott wrote to us again on the 15th February asking us to visit him to sign the final documents for the sale of the house and then everything should fall into place. There was also the final invoice from him which included his fees and this along with the cost of the house came to the grand total of £7,494.51. I made out a cheque for that amount to be drawn on the Yorkshire Bank account because either signature of a joint account was acceptable.

By the way, over the past few years, Aline and I had a joint account with the Nationwide Building Society and through saving and depositing my redundancy pay into that account, we had amassed a total of some £16,000 plus. However, because the interest was so heavily taxed, we agreed to transfer all our assets into a Premium account at the Yorkshire Bank. Besides, it was more convenient and accessible at the Darnall Branch of the Bank.

In February, Geoff had the good fortune to get employment at 'Mr. Minit', which was a Midlands based shoe and travelling bag supplier and they had moved into Sheffield. They had taken over the building which was once occupied by Weston's the chemist. This was where Geoff had once worked in the past. Incidentally, just prior to this, in January, Geoff had registered as a blood Group 'A' donor. He was taken on as a warehouseman and although the wages weren't exceptional, he was glad to be employed, plus the fact that he could walk to work from our house in ten minutes. As he settled down to it, his outlook changed, and he seemed much happier than he had been for a very long time. His whole being seemed on the ascendance.

Trying to find employment for myself, I had answered an advertisement in the press whereby a hypnotist based in Cambridge, was asking people to offer their residency to be used as a clinic.

Having received a reply, asking me to go for an interview, I went down to Cambridge and took Geoff with me for the ride and the company. The interview went very well but the implication of me using my home as a therapeutic hypnosis clinic seemed a little too much and with me having had no dealings in the treatment, the whole scheme was dropped. The interviewer did give me expenses for travelling and Geoff and I enjoyed being able to take a look around Cambridge and the King's College Chapel.

On the 23rd March, Mr. Elliott notified us that the sale was now complete and the Title Deeds would be forwarded to Mr.Fletcher, the manager at the Yorkshire Bank, for safe keeping. We were now the proud owners of No. 8 Ballifield Crescent.

With everything being settled and still having a little money in our account, we thought it was time to invest in some modernisation so we had the bathroom and bedroom windows replaced. The new ones were all pivot windows and made of white wood which meant that we could clean and paint them without having to use a ladder. We also had the kitchen window replaced and this included a transom and a casement window. These were all purchased and fitted by the son of a near neighbour and companion Geoff Wilson. The total cost was £455 plus VAT of £68.25 and that was all completed and paid for on the 29th March.

In May I was able to prove to Geoff the advantages of being in Fellowship because being on the District Council of the organisation, I had to go to a monthly meeting. On this occasion I decided to travel by bus but after the meeting, I was offered a lift home by a Companion, Derek Burgess, who lived at Woodhouse and he would be going past where I lived.

On the way home, he commented about people who refused to accept work and when I asked him to explain, he told me there was a short term vacancy going at the business where he was the Personnel Officer and this was at British Tissues at Oughtibridge where they made toilet rolls and tissues. He explained that an industrial painter was required, just for two weeks, to help smarten up the place for a VIP visit.

"Would I be able to do it? Derek?" I asked. "I don't see why not. It's only painting railings, barriers and road marking." He replied. "Come down for an interview and see George Alcock. He's the foreman and he's also a Companion in 284 Mess at Woodhouse with me."

So the following week I saw George and told him I could hold a paintbrush the right way up. He set me on to start on the 11th May. Having been on the staff most of my life I found it a bit much having to get up at 6.45 am so that I could travel out to Oughtibridge for an 8.00 am start. It was some 15 miles away. We worked until 4.30 pm but one consolation was that the rate of pay was in the top grade. It was £2.2462 per hour but taxed.

It should have be for just two weeks but the Manager told George to keep me on for a further two weeks to do some extra work. Having done a whole month, I was entitled to a perk of three dozen toilet rolls, like everyone else.

During March, Aline spotted an advert in the local press advertising the sale of two mopeds. When I rang the necessary telephone number, it was answered by a lady who said that she and her sister no longer required the vehicles. I arranged an interview and we went to their house, which was just below Millhouses Park, to see the ladies who we found to be in their late fifties. The mopeds were 50 cc pedal types and in very good condition with the number plates being consecutively numbered as AWE 29M and AWE 30M. We struck a deal and bought them both for £120 and having already bought helmets, we were able to ride them home. We didn't need 'L' plate because we were both qualified drivers of cars and with the mopeds being 50 cc it wasn't necessary to take another driving test.

The main reason for the above detail is that whilst at British Tissues, if the weather was good, I would use my moped to do the fifteen mile journey to Oughtibridge. One other bonus for me was that whilst at British Tissues, I came across another relation I had not seen for a very long time. It was Eric Furness who was one of Alf Furness' sons of the large Furness family which I mentioned way back when.

In June we took the opportunity of having the roof insulated because the Government were allowing grants towards the cost of having such work carried out. We were given permission by the South Yorkshire County Council to have the work carried out and the total cost was negligible because we were allowed £69 towards it.

On the first Sunday in July, which was the 4th, I was working in the garden in the morning when Aline called to me to go to her in the house. When I enquired what for, she said she couldn't call out the reason but would I go into the house to her. I know I seemed a little impatient at having to break off from what I was doing but eventually she persuaded me.

"Will you check me my bingo card numbers in the Sunday People?" She asked. She seemed all tensed up when asking so I granted her request and checked the card. She had marked off all her 15 numbers for Game No.7, eleven of them on the previous Sunday which she had kept quiet about. The last four numbers had come up on this particular Sunday, so she asked me to ring up the newspaper to confirm that they were correct. This I did and it was confirmed that she was a winner.

The following week it was also confirmed that she was the outright winner and would be sent a cheque for £10,000 pounds. During that week a photographer was sent to take a picture of her receiving the cheque, which was on the 14th July, but I wasn't in at the time. However, our Geoff was and the following Sunday their photograph appeared in the paper showing them both full of smiles with the cheque held between them. No wonder, for it was to be the last time a winner would be receiving the large amount of £10,000. Shortly after Aline winning, the total was reduced to £5,000. Who was a lucky girl, then?

If in conversation I referred to 'her' winnings I was always rebuked by Nip who said that it was 'our' winnings and I was to accept is as such. Being of a very generous nature she gave Tony, Geoff and Dave £500 each and her two widowed sisters, Freda and Joan, £50 each. The rest was invested so that we would have some benefit in later years. And don't forget, neither of us was yet officially retired and was not receiving an official state pension.

After the first month at British Tissues I was asked again to stay on another fortnight and though the hours seemed long I was beginning to get used to it and enjoyed the company of the chaps I worked with. There were only five of us in the team and that included the charge hand, Fred Rutter, who helped me along the way, he was the professional painter.

There were various jobs to be cleaned or repainted in the many departments of the firm and at times we had to climb scaffolding to get to the ceilings of the departments.

I didn't think that I would be able to climb to such dizzy heights at the time but I did. It was coming up to the annual 'shutdown' for the holidays and I was asked to stay on and help with the cleaning down and painting of some of the machinery and at times this was dangerous because it meant climbing into small receptacles to fettle and refurbish but we always went in twos because the rule was that we could only go in one at a time for two minutes only, because of the fumes.

One very good thing about the firm was that it had a marvellous canteen and the food was good and was needed when working long hours. It was really hard work doing 'shutdown' and I worked for a whole fortnight, including Sundays, with out a break but the money I drew with overtime was really worth it in the end. Just after 'shut' the manager told me that I would have to go but I explained that if I could stay a further fortnight I would have been working for thirteen weeks continuously and this would entitle me to go back on the 'dole' and draw security benefit. He said he would look into it and a few days later he returned and said the firm had granted my request, so on the 7th August I finished my stint and was some £2,500 better off, minus tax of course.

We allowed ourselves the odd luxury and one of these was on August the 24th because Aline had always wanted a new bathroom suite and this we ordered on this date from Morlite Bathrooms in Commercial Street, in Sheffield. We both agreed on the colour of champagne for the wash basin, pedestal, bath and WC. The bathroom was large enough for the full suite.

Whilst in the mood we decided to have an Aquatron shower installed with a 7KW heater with a riser rail and we paid a deposit of £50 towards a total cost of £340.40 which included the cost of the plumber. The contract was signed on the 24th August, the suite was put on order and on the 1st October we were informed that it would be delivered in the second week of October. On the 14th October the suite arrived and also the plumber, a nice young man, who didn't waste any time in dismantling the old units and he had to break the cast iron bath into pieces with a clump hammer so that he could get it down the stairs. The bathroom looked in a right state by the time he had dismantled everything.

As soon as the bath was taken out, he firstly installed the shower system because it was easier for him to work on an open floor and he had to do some pipe work after putting in a water tank in the loft above the bathroom. Having done that he set about fixing the WC so that we would be able to use it during the first night because he said that it would take at least a couple of days to finish. He was a methodical person and by teatime on the 15th he had finished fitting all that we had ordered and he had cleared up as much of the mess as he could. The balance of the invoice was due so I wrote out a cheque for £290.40. If there was any trouble, he told us, don't delay in calling us because it's all guaranteed for twelve months.

Since finishing work at TWIL, I was able to help more about the house with the decorating but Aline always did the papering and painting because of my asthma but I did the preparation and cleaning up afterwards. So it was with the bathroom when we purchased some tiles from the ASDA Superstore which was about five minutes walk away from home. However, because of the weight of the tiles we used the car to get them back home and Aline had chosen donkey coloured ceramic tiles which were six inches square.

We needed enough to cover the whole wall above and beyond the bath, plus all above the wash basin and toilet, right up to the ceiling. In all we required thirty dozen and with 24 in a box we needed the car to fetch them. Of these, there were sixteen with a flower motif on and we interspersed them to break up the monotony and make a contrast. We didn't do it all in one day and we took it in turns to put the tiles on to the wall.

Whilst we were working on the bathroom I decided to alter the surface of a huge box area which covered part of the staircase and protruded into the bathroom. It was about thirty inches by forty two inches and had a depth of three feet. I allowed for a top shelf of fifteen inches wide and then cut down to a depth of eighteen inches.

I then measured up and bought a heavy duty work surface in a cream colour to contrast the tiles and this I fitted onto the lower piece to make a seat top and I also bought some cream coloured Melamine for the top shelf and a back rest to the seating area. When it was finished we had a bench type seat on which we could sit and dry ourselves (separately) after having a bath or shower. It also came in useful to stand on when we were decorating the ceiling or changing the light bulb.

We had some fun cutting and shaping the tiles and sometimes patience became a virtue but eventually we finished it off and Aline put the finishing touches to it by putting a washable wall paper on the other walls and I completed it by laying cork tiles onto the floor.

It was just after finishing the bathroom that Dave and Heather came up from Waddington to tell us that he had been posted to RAF Bruggen in Germany. Whilst at Waddington, Dave had shown initiative by having a jersey embossed with the outline of the Vulcan Bomber and on each wing he had put RIP because the squadron was shortly to be disbanded. One of his flight commanders spotted it and asked him whose idea it was and when David said it was his own idea, the officer told him to borrow some money from the PSI funds and order enough for the whole squadron. The jerseys were vee necked, blue in colour and the logo was on the left breast.

Not long after this, in September, Aline and I and the rest of the family were sitting in the kitchen having our Sunday tea when the back door opened and in staggered Geoff with his arm in a sling. He had been out for the weekend in the Buxton area with his best pal Andy Steel, whom he had met a couple of years ago at a meeting of the local YHA. Through the Youth Hostel Association, Andy and Geoff had become very firm friends and although Andy was a little younger, he tended to keep an eye on Geoff.

Apparently, whilst crossing some fields, they had to climb over a small stile and Andy had negotiated it without any trouble but Geoff, through his awkwardness, wasn't so lucky and as he had try to get over the stile, the weight of his back pack had caused him to lose his balance.

Andy had gone on in front but when Geoff had failed to catch up with him after fifteen minutes, Andy had turned back to look for him and found him in the ditch below the stile. He went and raised the alarm and it ended with Geoff being taken to a hospital in Cheshire where he was detained for the night for shock. Due to Geoff having to stay overnight, it also meant that Andy had to find accommodation for the night in order to bring him home the following day. That's Friendship. He had dislocated his collarbone and had to have some time off work but was able to resume after a couple of weeks.

Geoff had joined the YHA way back in 1979 but since leaving the RAF he had taken more interest in the organisation and had become a fully paid up Life Member. He made many new friends who included 'JB' John Brightmore, Tom Curtin and many female members who happened to be in the nursing profession at some of the hospitals in Sheffield. Caroline worked at the Royal Hallamshire Hospital and Jo and Rosemary were Sisters in the Childrens' Hospital. This was a good thing because incase of accidents, there was always someone handy to give assistance.

In Geoff's case, there were to be many incidents because of his disability and awkwardness when out on their walking expeditions. Caroline was married to Martin Boler and Rosemary was married to Andy Fletcher, the whole crowd being good friends and willing to help each other out whenever needs be.

We still had Geoff at home and this kept Aline busy having to do his laundry besides doing ours. Also keeping an eye on my Mum helped to occupy some of our time because apart from doing her shopping each week, Nip also did her laundry and ironing for her. Although there wasn't much involved, it was another chore for the lass.

Having decided to manage on the income that was immediately to hand, we found it a bit of a struggle at times but the money from British Tissues had helped and I was again signing on for my dole money each week in Woodhouse village. I was also discretely doing one or two jobs on security which brought in a little remuneration..

An acquaintance of Alines' who lived at the top of the estate, had mentioned a part time position she was engaged in and suggested to Nip that she ought to try to get on to it. This was an escort scheme which was run by the Sheffield Education Committee whereby responsible ladies had to use taxis to collect disabled and other types of children and make sure that they were taken to their respective special schools.

Aline applied and after a couple of interviews she was accepted on to the scheme. It meant that she had to leave home at 8.00 am and go into town to a rendezvous where all the other escorts were detailed to their special passengers. She soon settled down and really enjoyed it, even though occasionally she became emotionally involved. Nip would be home for 10.30 am but had to set off again by 2.00 pm to pick up her charges and return the children back to their homes. Sometimes there would be one and sometimes three children to care for.

With my DHSS money and the few pounds which Aline received for her escort duties, we were able to manage without touching our bank account. That is, unless we needed to buy anything out of the ordinary.

It was one of these special instances when on the 7th December, Aline bought me a special Christmas present. We had noticed that there was an electric organ sale on at the B&C Co-op in Woodhouse village so we went to have a look. After browsing round, I became interested in a lovely looking instrument, not just for the key board setup but as a piece of furniture.

The model was a Cavendish Loretto 902V and it had a built in rhythm section with various instrumental innovations, a double key board manual which was covered with a roller shutter and the other outstanding thing was that it had Wurlitzer speakers. The salesman played it and the sound convinced me that I ought to have it.

My only hesitance was the price which was £1,095. "Do you want it?" Asked Aline. "Yes please, Luv." I answered. She was generous to a fault and bought it for me.

When I told the salesman that I already had a small EKO Elite One keyboard organ, he said he would take it in part exchange. We agreed on a deal and I was allowed £495 on my EKO which I thought was a very good bargain. The exchange was made a few days later and what a difference between the two. Being a considerate person, it was very rarely that I used the bass pedals because the Wurlitzer would have made it too powerful in volume with respect to the neighbours.

Having said that, a few weeks later I saw Jackie Walker sitting in his car on our road whilst waiting for his lady friend, Muriel Smith, who was widowed and lived up the estate. Muriel used to be the singer at the City Hall when Jack played there.

I popped over and asked him to come and have a look at the new organ. In he came, sat down and started to play. I think he thought that he was still playing in the City Hall Ballroom because everything was moving.

Aline, who had just been up to the shops, walked in and cried. "What the bloody hell are you doing?" And then she saw Jack sitting and playing the organ.

. "Oh! I'm sorry, Jack." She said. "That's alright." He replied, with a smile on his face "I got carried away. It's a lovely instrument and I hope that you enjoy playing it." And off he went

. There was an official letter arrived one morning and it was addressed to Aline who was as surprised as I was when she opened it. It was from the local authorities telling her that she had been called to do jury service This is something which one cannot be excused from unless in exceptional circumstances and she wasn't looking forward to it at all. However, she did go and the case she was put on lasted a fortnight and each night when she came home from the Courts, whilst not being allowed to discuss it with anyone, including me, she said she was getting into the swing of it. At the end of the trial she did admit that there was a delay in the juries verdict because she and another person couldn't come to a decision but eventually they were persuaded.

She was more then pleased when it was all over.

Now that Dave and Heather were in Germany, it was going to be different and somewhat quiet this Xmas but we were still going to have Geoff here and Tony was bringing his family - plus, of course, I would be fetching my Mum for her dinner.

Not long after Christmas, Aline said she wanted a new cooker, so we went into town to shop around and after visiting one or two places, including the British Gas showroom, we eventually finished up in Cole Bros., in Barkers Pool. Nip decided on a New World Nova cooker which was neat and compact in design with four gas burners, a grill and a large oven. Even with the splash screen on the back, the height was no more the four feet and it fit comfortably into the space where the old one had stood. Invariably we paid cash for it and we thought it was a bargain at £190.

In February I started to dig up part of the front lawn so that I could put in a hard standing to put the car on. Having excavated to the depth I wanted, I decided to let it settle down before putting in an aggregate base. The next step was to apply to the South Yorkshire County Council for permission to make a vehicle crossing over the pavement and into the road.

Whilst waiting for a reply, I had busied myself by cutting out part of the front privet hedge so as to make access available. On the 28th February I received a letter from the engineering department of the Council, along with some diagrams of the area to be worked upon. On the diagram I had to indicate the measurements and materials needed to affect the driveway and I then returned them to the Council for approval and also give 28 day's notice of the proposals.

In the meantime, with the help of Tony and Geoff, I had levelled the front garden area and ordered some aggregate, sand and paving flags from a nearby builder. I couldn't do much else until I had my plans approved by the Council and I knew that wouldn't be yesterday.

To get away for a while, Dave and Heather had invited us over to Germany to stay with them at Bruggen. He suggested that we took our car over so I made a booking by the ferry from Dover to Zeebrugge and he and Heather would meet us there in their car. We travelled to within ten miles of Dover and stayed overnight at a local inn before catching the ferry to Zeebrugge. It took about three hours for the crossing but when we arrived and drove off the boat, Dave was there to show us where to go for customs etc. Heather had brought some sandwiches and a flask of coffee for us to have during the journey to Bruggen and off we set to follow Dave and Heather. It had cost me a little extra for the car because on the Continent, two wing mirrors were essential by law but I only had one on the drivers side of the car. A new one for the passenger side had cost me £21 but I was glad of it as we left Zeebrugge to follow Dave and start to learn to drive on the right hand side of the road, it all seemed so strange.

We didn't see much of Brussels as we drove through because I was concentrating on my driving but eventually we arrived on the autobahn. I know that the Cavalier had only done 10,000 miles on the clock but I hadn't expected to be driving at 80 - 90 mph up the German motorway. We had been travelling about an hour when I noticed that the petrol gauge was nearing the empty mark so I tried to draw Dave's attention by flashing my headlights.

It must have taken fifteen minutes for him to catch on but he eventually pulled into a layby marked Ausfahrt and asked what was wrong. When I told him he went to the boot of his car and took out a five gallon drum of petrol and put it into my tank. We took the opportunity to have a bite to eat and a drink before setting off again and soon we were doing 80 mph again with Aline keeping an eye out for me when traffic was overtaking on my off side which was the left hand side of the car to me.

After two and a half hours drive we eventually arrived at Bruggen or somewhere near because Dave had driven straight to a garage where he was to collect his new car but he hadn't told us that. He had been racing all the way because he had to pick it up by five o'clock due to the garage closing at that time. We arrived there at exactly 4.55 pm where upon he did the paper work and then set about changing the headlights because they were on a different alignment out there. Another half hour finally brought us to their flat and were we glad to settle in a chair and get a drink. The new car Dave had bought was a Ford Escort and his idea was to use it for the holiday and get some mileage on the clock.

Although the flat was supposed to be at ground level, it was actually three feet above that and outside from the lounge door was a small balcony on which Dave kept his crates of booze and when needed, he also used it for barbecues. The flat was well laid out with two bedrooms, a lounge and kitchen, all of which were reasonably sized. Our bedroom window gave a good view of the RAF camp at Bruggen because the flat was actually in the small town of Erkelenz and about five miles away down the road was Wegberg Hospital where Heather was a nurse.

Dave had planned ahead for our visit and after a day's rest we all piled into his new car and set off for a Cook's Tour, leaving my car on the parking lot near to some lockup garages on the site of the flats. He assured me that it would be safe there whilst we were away. We headed south to Cochem on the Mosel River. We had just avoided the floods there but the height of the water was marked on the side of one of the buildings and showed the level of the water as having been above the height of any of us.

By doing a little searching round, Dave had managed to get us booked into a Zimmer (B&B) at a cost of 12 marks each, which was about 25/- shillings in our money. This enabled us to have a good look around the picturesque town of Cochem and also take the opportunity to go up to the castle there which had a lovely young German girl to guide us and who spoke very good English. For a better view of the surrounding, Dave persuaded us to go up a ski lift to an advantage point overlooking the town but he insisted on sitting next to his Mum on the lift. No wonder. As they rode higher and higher, he deliberately shook the seats for devilment to try to scare her. It didn't work but she enjoyed every minute and at the top we had a coffee in the cafe there. Before we left Cochem, he took us round the back streets looking for a wine seller. He finally found one, knocked on the door and enquired about buying some wine. A lovely old German Frau invited us in and introduced us to her husband. They must have been in their late seventies and were interested in talking to Dave and Heather who could both speak a little German. The old lady took us into the cellars to show us the vats and barrels of wine and the place was larger than it looked from the outside but it was worth seeing.

Back in the living room, the old man asked Dave how much wine he wanted and Dave said, "Two, please." The old man enquired "Two bottles?" "No." Said Dave "Two dozen."

The look on the old man's face, he couldn't believe his ears and, upon which, he asked his wife to get some glasses and immediately opened a bottle of his own wine in gratitude.

We left Cochem and headed south again through Baden-Baden to Freiberg and eventually reached a beautiful place called Tittersea. Here was a lovely little tourist town sitting on the side of a lake which had boats for hire etc., and numerous shops and cafes. Once again Dave found us a good and reasonably priced Zimmer which we booked into for a few nights.

We went down to the lake side one day and hired a paddle boat, for that is what they were mainly and we had a good hour paddling up and down the water and David getting up to some of his daft tricks to make us laugh. When we came off the lake he managed to get us into a private hotel to use their sauna and swimming pool for a nominal fee. He had the cheek of the devil when it came to getting favours done. The weather was glorious but Dave said he would show us a contrast, so he took us in the car the following day, for a short run and within 20 minutes we were on roads with three feet of snow on either side. It was incredible how the climate had changed in such a short distance.

We used Tittersea as a base and had a trip down to Freiberg to have a look around the town and how picturesque that was because the centre was full of flower sellers and everyone seemed to have a different coloured type of flower on display. Also in the town centre was a building which had recesses high in the wall and in each one was a different type of bell which rung on the hour.

Our next stop for the day was Zurich in Switzerland and Nip and I were really looking forward to this. Dave parked the car and we set off towards the central square but just as we were reaching it, sirens started wailing and there were police everywhere. In the centre of the park area was a huge bonfire set up in readiness for some festival announcing the end of the snow season.

However, it had been reported that someone had put a bomb at the base of the fire so the immediate area was cordoned off and the crowds waited whilst the bomb disposal people arrived. It ended being a bit hilarious because this soldier went in with all his gear on and after half an hours inspection he shouted a warning and ran away from the scene. Suddenly there wasn't a bang - but a plop. We couldn't stop laughing and there was our Dave trying to take a photo of the explosion that didn't come.

After the scare, things returned to normal and we manage to have a look around a fair ground whilst looking for some toilets. After that we walked past where the disturbance had been and managed to see some of the coloured and beautifully decorated floats that were being used in the festive procession and they were all led by a parade of musicians in splendidly coloured uniforms. We returned to Tittersea for one more night and then headed for home, Dave's home but he decided to go a different route on the way back because this time we went through part of France and headed for the Mosel River again. This time we travelled down the eastern side of the river before crossing over to a town called Bitburg. Here we found accommodation for the night in a local inn.

Also in the inn were some American soldiers who were on leave. During conversation they were telling us how they enjoyed the bottled beer called Grolsh and said that they had it shipped over from the USA. Dave and I had to laugh because he could pop over the border into Holland from Bruggen and get as much as he needed. Typical Yanks. Ship it from Holland to America and then back again. We left Bitburg and Dave said he would finish off the holiday by taking us to Luxemburg on the way back where upon arrival the first thing to do was find a parking place and toilets.

He parked the car and then found a cafe in which there were toilets but we still felt hungry and Aline said that she could eat a horse. Dave ordered the food and when it was brought to us, Aline couldn't believe what she saw. He had chosen a huge bread roll full of meat and salad. It was about four inches thick and about fifteen inches long and as she lifted it to take a bite I whipped out my camera and took a picture of her trying to put it into her mouth

After that we had a good look around the city and saw the guards on duty outside the Palace doors and after a quiet walk into a park we headed back to the car. Dave loved driving and this time we travelled via the Belgium countryside and through Aachen before eventually finishing at the flat in Bruggen.

I'm just trying to recall if it was on this holiday that he took us to Fantasialand which was a big theme park and it had many features such as Chinese pagodas, a Wild West American town and a fun house where we had some laughs because all the internal fittings seemed to be lopsided. Even a small billiard table was funny because the balls rolled up the sloping table as you pushed them with the cue. We had a couple of rides on one or two things, one of which was a large water shoot, down which all four of us sat in a log shaped boat and as we hit the water at the bottom, we were all covered in spray.

Because Dave and Heather had to return to work, he couldn't personally show us the way back too Zeebrugge but he drew on a paper which route we were to take and once we were on the E5 road it was straight through. At least he did lead us to where we could get onto the autobahn and it was a case of learning as we went along, with Aline doing the navigating. That is until I managed to negotiate the Brussels traffic and head for the port of Zeebrugge.

As we approached it I was convinced that we had to turn left and so I did for several miles until I realised that we were in Ostend. I turned around and headed back to where we saw the sign for the docks. It's a good job we had some time to spare and was able to catch the ferry on time.

Shortly after our holiday, a letter had arrived from the Council approving of the plans to finish the driveway and cross the pavement. Tony came up to help me and we had been working for an hour trying to remove some of the kerb stones when John O'Halloran came past. He was a neighbour from down the road.

"You shouldn't be struggling like that. Here's what to do. Dig a foot behind the old kerb stones and about the same depth and you'll find that you can just push over the kerb stones with your foot."

Paddy, as we called him, used to work for the Highways Dept., and he said that they could lay a hundred yards a day and knew the tricks of the trade. He was right. In the next hour, Tony and I had moved the necessary old kerb stones and replaced them with dropped and bevelled ones and cemented them in. We were just completing the job by putting down paving flags where the grass verge had been when a car pulled up just below us.

A young man emerged and came towards us. "Is Geoff in?" He asked. Tony and I looked at each other and asked who he was. "I'm Lackie, a pal of Geoff's from the YHA." He said. "Oh! Just a minute, I'll get him, he's in the house."

Geoff came out and had a chat with his friend and Lackie then told us that he was the Highway's Inspector and had come to check the driveway. He had a good look at our work and then jumped up and down on the flags before saying. "That looks fine to me. I'll endorse it when I get back to the office."

It's not what you know but who you know on occasions like this. The old kerb stones were used to enhance the entrance to the drive and looked great when painted white and with some of the flag stones being of a tinted red colour, the whole effort had been worth while.

Having enjoyed our holiday we settled down again and in June, Aline and I decided to have the old metal framed windows in the living room, replaced with a patio door. Prior to having it done I had contacted a Companion in the Fellowship and he was also the Chairman of the Darnall Conservative Club at which I was a member.

He was Tommy Hall and along with his son, he ran a small building company. Young Tom came and gave me an estimate for the job and we agreed for him to carry out the work. On 17th June both Toms and another chap came and took out the old windows and put in the patio door. Old Tom did the pointing work and by teatime it was all done. It cost us £450 but we were pleased with it all.

With all the spare bricks, which had been taken out to make room for the door, I used them to make the base for the patio itself. And having ordered some 24" x 24" slabs I put them onto the brick lattice base for support, making sure that they sloped away from the house for drainage. I then built a small brick wall some three feet high and finished it off with some concrete coping stones.

We were so pleased with the patio door that we asked Tom Hall to fit a tilt and turn window into the end wall of the living room to replace the metal framed window which was remaining. Nip chose this type of window because she had noticed the ones which were fitted in our Dave's flat at Bruggen in Germany. It could also be cleaned from the inside thus making the use of steps unnecessary outside. It was fitted at the end of July and cost us a further £230.

It meant having to redecorate the interior walls but we soon did that and Aline re-papered either side of the patio door and the other window when the plastering had dried out. This Tommy had done when inserting the patio and new window.

I had managed to obtain some thin, stained wooden panelling and when the papering had been done I measured the panels and fitted them inside of the window and patio. This now finished it all off and the difference in the living room was unbelievable and it was much warmer.

Our mopeds came in very useful for running small errands to Darnall or Attercliffe and it was on the 22nd September when I did a run down to the east end to get my hair cut at an old established barbers called Hewitts. However, on the way home I went up Attercliffe Road to the junction with Staniforth Road and halted at the traffic lights. When they changed to green I started to move off when a small blue van overtook and cut across me. I followed it round the corner to the left and then, without warning, it started to turn into an entrance to the back of the Burton Building.

No signals! I tried to brake but the van stopped so suddenly to let someone pass that I hit the back of it with the front wheel. My speedo was hardly moving at 5 mph but the force made me knock my right leg onto the steering column. Off I came and someone rushed to help me get up. With difficulty I was able to prop my moped against a wall and then a shop assistant, from Burtons, help me up a flight of stairs above the shop and phoned for the ambulance.

Someone rang home for me and told Aline who set off by bus immediately. The journey was four and a half miles and she arrived just as the Ambulance did and though she wanted to come with me, I persuaded her to push the moped up to the Rainbow Motorcycle shop which was about 200 yards away up Staniforth Road. It was agony having to negotiate getting down the flight of stairs again but the ambulance attendant gave me as much assistance as he could and Aline saw me go with a tear in her eye.

I was taken to the Northern General Hospital Casualty Department where, after an x-ray, I was told that I had broken my right knee cap (Patella). Aline had found her way home after leaving the moped at the Rainbow shop and then made her way to the hospital.

I didn't feel too bad but casualty wards are always noisy and this was no exception plus the fact that I had to stay in for a couple of nights and when Aline came to see me a she brought my football coupon but she said she didn't think that there was anything to come but upon checking it I found that there was something.

The following week I received a cheque for the magnificent sum of £11.60. It broke the monotony and we had a chuckle about it. I was allowed home shortly after and was on elbow crutches for about two weeks. The surgeon had inserted two thin wires into the broken patella to hold it together and it was a success because I am still walking alright.

Shortly after the accident, a young policeman came to our house to confirm a previous statement and, though technically the man at the back of a road accident is to blame, the policeman said he would do what he could to apportion the blame on the van driver. He was very sympathetic.

The few days I was in hospital, Aline obviously came up to see me but the afternoon visiting time cut across her times for the escort service so she had contacted the person in charge of the system, a Mrs. Sims, and explained about my being in hospital and it would it be possible to get a relief for the afternoon run?

It takes some believing but the stupid person refused to accept Aline's explanation about me and unfortunately it resulted in Nip losing the job, even though the lady who had recommended her for the position, had confirmed my accident. Nip was upset but she soon settled to it and accepted it for what it was. At least she didn't have to get up early any more.

On January 6th, 1984, I received a letter from the South Yorkshire Police referring to my accident last September and in it they said that after due consideration, no further action would be taken about my driving without due care and attention. The young policeman who had visited me, had kept his promise about no blame being attached to me.

Having had the patio and side windows installed, Aline suggested that now we ought to be thinking about having central heating put into the house. I wasn't too keen because of my breathing difficulties which, whilst not too serious, were still there. After much discussion, I agreed with her and Tommy Hall suggested a friend.

So at the end of February, this friend, Barry Dawson, came along with his son and measured up and we arranged with him as to what type of radiators we required in each room. He quoted us a price of £1,120 pounds for seven radiators of varying sizes and this included all the pipe fittings, boiler and labour. We accepted the quotation and at the end of March everything was installed and working perfectly. It took us a while to clear the mess which wasn't excessive and because of prompt payment, Barry reduced the bill by £50. It certainly made a difference not having to go into a cold bedroom at night.

Just after this, Geoff decided to leave home again in an effort to become independent and after a few weeks the local council found him an empty flat on the Norfolk Park Estate. This was the same district where I used to court the WAAF Sergeant on the barrage balloon site during the War but was now a built up area containing maisonettes and tower blocks.

Geoff's flat was right at the top again just like the one he had when on Oxford Street a few years ago. His address this time was 201 Tower Drive. We all helped him to move in and managed to obtain small pieces of furniture from family and friends. The view from his window was marvellous because he had a good sight of the city centre and was almost directly overlooking the Sheffield United Football ground. It was also very convenient for getting into town to do his shopping and doing any transactions at his local bank which was on West Street.

Even though he had moved away from us he often called in for a meal on his way home from work or if, as sometimes he did, he required anything he may have left behind when moving from us.

He was easy to please for food and one of his favourite meals was a small tin of tomatoes cooked in a pan with grated cheese and about four slices of bread and butter.

We didn't see too much of Tony because approximately twelve months ago, April '83 to be exact, he and Elaine had serious differences which culminated in them getting divorced.

Aline and I were very upset because of Mathew and Lisa being so young but the arrangements for the divorce had been amicably agreed upon and Elaine went with the children to live with a chap called David Heard.

He was already separated from his wife and eventually he became divorced and married Elaine. I know that Tony wasn't perfect in many ways but I still think the separation from Elaine was due to her association with this David. Why? I don't know because in comparison, David was a fat slob in appearance as compared to Tony who was handsome and athletic. But that's by the way.

It wasn't long after the divorce that the house on Whitehill Road was sold and with the proceeds being equally divided, Tony went and took out a mortgage on a small and old terraced house at 89 Russell Street in the Eastwood district of Rotherham. He did have access to the kids and very strangely, Elaine and he seemed to have a better understanding of each other now that they were divorced. He frequently called at her new home to see Mathew and Lisa

Because Tony couldn't move into his new home for four months but had to move out of the one on Whitehill Road immediately, Nip and I told him he could come and stay with us until final arrangements were made for him to move to Rotherham. It seemed ironical that Geoff should have moved out to Tower Drive earlier in the year because Tony could now have Geoff's room. It was the 24th May when Tony finally managed to move to Russell Street.

At the beginning of May, Nip and I were invited down to Maidstone to have a few days with Ella and her family. We went by car and whilst there we had a run down to Brighton. The few days holiday was a welcome break but I was beginning to soon get tired after driving some 200 miles so I was glad to get back home.

Having said that, the following week we went to join Freda and Joan in a caravan on the Primrose Valley caravan site near to Filey but that was only an eighty mile ride. We stayed overnight but the main reason for the trip was to look at a the caravan with a view to buying it. Garbutt, a friend and neighbour of Joan's wanted to sell it and asked us if we were interested. We were at first but having had a look round it we saw that it needed some repairs and renovation besides the cost of buying it for £700 but apart from that, it also had a ground rent of £500 to be paid each year and we didn't like the idea of that.

I finished off the cricket season in the Sheffield league and then filled in my evenings with playing billiards in the Sheffield and District Billiards league which meant travelling to several clubs and institutes to fulfil the engagements. It was only one night per week and Aline didn't mind because she enjoyed her television and she always had some knitting to do for one person or another. This too made her a little pocket money beside having the pleasure of doing it.

Back to reality, we kept a keen eye on my Mum as best we could but one night, toward the end of January, we received a phone call from the warden at her flat complex.

Would we go over to attend to her because she was ill. Now, bearing in mind that it was 1.00 am in the morning and I had taken my car into a garage the previous day for a full service and check up, the weather was really frosty and there was no public transport service available, Aline and I got dressed, wrapped up well and set off to walk the two miles to Mum's flat. To shorten the journey, we decided to walk across the fields behind Handsworth Church.

We then went along on to Richmond Road and then turned down onto Athelstan Road which brought us into the block of flats.

It took us about thirty minutes and we both felt exhausted with the cold by the time we arrived. We went into the flat, the warden was there waiting for us and when I asked Mum what was wrong, she said, " My nose won't stop bleeding."

My immediate reaction was, "You've fetched us out for a bleeding nose ?" Having calmed down, I sent for the doctor on call. We waited about thirty minutes before the Doctor arrived but on arrival we found it was a lady doctor. It took quite a while but eventually the bleeding stopped and the doctor gave Mum some tablets to calm her down. It must have been around three o'clock in the morning before we were able to leave her but later on during the morning I popped round again to see how she was getting on and luckily she was much better.

Each year as the holiday season came round, we had to be careful how we approached the subject because Mum always seemed to develop another illness as an excuse to try to stop us going away and leaving her alone. It was one Saturday morning when we were there that her GP, Dr Crowther, called in and the subject of holidays arose. When we explained to him the situation, he turned and told my Mum that we needed a break and we were going to have one because he was going to arrange respite care at the Home across the way which was called Housteads Old People's Home. I could feel for Mum's thoughts because she was approaching the good old age of eighty eight and perhaps thought it would be the last time we would see her but over the years I had become accustomed to her. So at the end of June it was organised by Ann Midgley, Mum's social worker, for Mum to go into the Home for two weeks whilst we were away. In there, she would have a room to herself and also constant attention and still be taken each week up to the Centre at the Manor Top.

We went on our holiday and this time we had booked into a small Camping Club site at Middleton which was quite close to Heysham in Lancashire and easily within reach of Morecambe. It was possible to take a run or two up into the Lake District and we had a good time looking around Grange Over Sands. Near to the Club site was a small private club cum inn where we would call in for a drink in the evenings and we found out that it was the venue from where Jim Bowen launched his darts game of Bullseye which had a long run on Television.

Just across the road from there was a holiday camp run by Warners and upon payment of a small fee, we were allowed entrance to the camp buildings and all the facilities there for the full day.

We had a run down the coast to Blackpool for one day but mainly we relaxed on the camp and took advantage of the reasonably good weather before returning on the fifth of July. Apart from the normal cost of the food etc., the camping fee was £3 per night so actually it had been a cheap holiday and the relaxation was good for us.

During his stay at Tower Drive, Geoff, through the YHA, had befriended an Australian girl named Linda Jones and she lived in the St John's Wood district of London where she taught English to foreign students in that area. One of her pupils was a Japanese Neurologist and she made enquiries with him about Geoff's disability and between them they arranged for Geoff to meet the Japanese doctor and receive a free assessment This was good to one point but the outcome wasn't very encouraging when the neurologist diagnosed Geoff's complaint as the dreaded Motor Neurone Disease. It was in it's early stages and there was medication available.

Late in eighty four, Linda's parents came over from Australia and Nip and I said that we could accommodate them whilst they were in Sheffield and we enjoyed their company and they were very grateful for the offer. Linda was very good for Geoff and joined in YHA activities besides going with us on one occasion on a Fellowship trip into Derbyshire and she often popped in with him to see us..

January 1985 turned into a busy month for me because one of my neighbours, Arnold Carr at No 6, had just retired from a part time job at the builders of Ackroyd and Abbott. They had their office site on Rotherham Road which was just across the main road from us and Arnold asked me if I would be interested in taking over from him and if so he would have a word with the transport manager, Jack Gardener. I said that I would be glad of the chance so shortly after, I was interviewed for the position of general dogs body.

I was taken on to work three mornings per week from 8.00 am to 12.30 pm. It also incurred popping over at 9.00 pm each night to check the plant over and twice a day on Saturdays and Sundays. I enjoyed the odd jobbing and running errands and sometimes I was asked to take a van or car and collect equipment and materials from various places in South Yorkshire and I think there was one instance when I had to go down into Lincolnshire for some spare parts. The wage was about thirty pounds per week and it came in very handy when added to my works pension.

In February 1985 we had another setback because whilst across at Housteads Home, Mum had either sat down too suddenly or had been released too quickly into a chair by one of the helpers at the home and the result was, they had to get an ambulance to take Mum to the Hallamshire Hospital where they found that she had broken her femur (thigh).

She was kept in for quite a while but eventually sent her home with a zimmer frame. This meant extra care for her but she still had home helpers and a daily district visitor, Mrs Lewis. Mum wasn't the best of patients and at times tempers wore a bit thin but we did our best. As it became more difficult to attend to her, we finally managed to get her taken into St George's

Hospital which used to be the Isolation Hospital I mentioned in 1926. It was now a special hospital suited to the needs of old people and it had a full compliment of nurses and helpers. The wards were communal and there was a relaxation-cum-rest room for mobile patients.

It meant that we were obliged to visit her at least once a week but we managed to take it in our stride. The Sister in charge and other nurses were very good to the patients and on odd occasions I would assist them if they needed beds moving from one ward to another. Nip and I hadn't envisaged the length of her stay there and the time eventually covered the whole year. There was one instance when the resident social worker at the hospital suggested getting Mum an electric wheel chair.

We didn't know this until on one Sunday when we arrived, there she was sitting in this chair. Now Mum was never mechanically minded and as soon as I saw it I didn't like the idea. She tried to show us how it worked but she kept bumping into furniture and people and I told the Sister it was too dangerous for Mum. The Sister said to give a little more time for Mum to get accustomed to it but the following week we were told she had been relieved of the chair. It wasn't a cheap item to be used by a novice and the cost of it was in the region of £350 so it wasn't a plaything. Nip and I were relieved too at the outcome.

We had a little respite because in March, Dave and Heather had returned to England. He was now a corporal posted to Marham in Norfolk and their accommodation was at 49 The Chase in Ely but this was because Heather had been placed at the RAF Hospital there. Dave had to travel quite a way up to the camp at Marham and shortly after being there they decided to buy a house of their own. This was our break because the small house which they were buying was brand new with a garage attached and the back of the house overlooked some fields. This house was on Croft Hall Road at Littleport and on a private estate which was part of Ely. We had a few days down there and had to chuckle because Dave had turned his garage into a workshop. It paid off due to the fact that whilst down there he made not only a double bed in pinewood but also a settee and two easy chairs. Heather did all the upholstery side of the operation. It was so made that it fit together like a furniture kit and was easily dismantled and folded up which proved very useful whenever they had to move to another posting.

During the summer I had carried on umpiring at cricket in the Sheffield League and more often than not I was paired with Keith Parsonage who lived next to the Handsworth Grange School which was just around the corner from where we lived. Keith was also a football referee and was very well known by the Handsworth footballing fraternity. His day time job was that of a delivery van driver for the Chemist, Smith and Nephew which came in handy if we were umpiring together and we wanted an easy route to the match. He knew most of them.

As the year went by I had been getting more involved with the FOS and over the past year I had slowly progressed through various stages of what was called the 'Top Table' It was now my turn to do a full year of office as Chairman of 163 Mess. It was an honour and I was proud to have attained that status. During my year of office, which I started on the first Monday of 1986, I was obliged to go each month to committee meetings besides going to Mess nights. It also meant that I could groom Geoff for that rank if ever he was in a position to accept a top place in Fellowship. He was doing very well and had taken on the thankless task of Social Secretary and the Editor of the Mess News Letter into which he put his heart and soul. He called his newsletter 'The Natter' because that was what most of us did on Mess night and his research into useful information for companions, was more then gratefully accepted.

Having taken on the job at Ackroyd and Abbotts, I had to do some thinking about how to fit in my own security business of fitting locks etc. Graham Highfield knew that I had been engaged by A & A but still contacted me if there was an emergency due to a break-in, in the vicinity.

It was on one of these recommendations when I was fitting a new door lock for an old lady in a flat at Woodhouse, that a run of good fortune came my way. I was knelt down fitting this mortise lock, which was recommended by Graham, when an old gentleman hesitated as he passed by. "How much would one of those cost?" He asked me. "Including fitting." I replied, "About £10.50." "Good." He remarked. "Will you come and fit me one, please?" The gentleman's flat was just across the way from where I was working and I arranged to go there the following day. The good fortune I mentioned, was that from this one contact, I finished up installing door locks for the most of two blocks of flats and this kept me occupied for several weeks. Not full time because I had to fit it in with the part time work at Ackroyds.

Graham Highfield couldn't believe the price which I charged and said that I was a fool but that was me. I enjoyed doing it and I made about 25% profit on the deal after buying all my equipment at Harrold's Security Shop at trade prices.

Apart from fitting in my security with the work at Ackroyd's, I also had to work out how to get around umpiring when the season started because I was supposed to check the premises at 6.00 pm.

I figured a way around it by taking the gate keys with me and calling in straight from any games of cricket which varied in finishing times from 7.00 pm to 8.30 pm.

Aline and I didn't have our usual holiday break this year because being chairman of the Mess tied me down somewhat with regard to recreational activities. Apart from going to the local Mess and District meetings I was also deeply involved on the Area Council of the FOS. This had come about because way back in October 1984, I had been asked to step up from the Deputy position to the full position of Area Advisory Officer, due to the sudden death of Past Chairman Ken Turner who had been the Area official. The Area covered districts as far as Barnsley, Blackpool, Chesterfield, Penistone and Rotherham besides all the messes in Sheffield. Ken had unfortunately passed away from a sudden heart attack at an age in his mid fifties. He was a very quiet and unassuming but a very good companion in Fellowship and resided in Deepcar.

After buying the house, we slowly but surely carried on with improvements and in June '85, Nip and I had a run out to Dinnington to a manufacturer to look at some doors. We wanted a new one for the front of the house and decided on a design which consisted of fifteen small panels. Seven were of wood with a flower embossment and the other eight were of a semi-smoked glass with a flower motif inlay and this cost us £75.21. We managed to get it into the car and this saved us the delivery charge.

I had made one or two new friends whilst at Ackroyds and one of these was Barry. He was the senior joiner. Nip agreed with me to ask Barry to come and fit the door and its furniture for us because we wanted a good job doing and I hadn't the time or the confidence to do it. He came on a Saturday whilst I was out umpiring and as I arrived home about 7.00 pm he was just tidying up and looked very tired. He was only a little chap and had struggled with the heavy door. But had done a very good job so I gave him £20 for his labour. At first he objected but I insisted and thanked him for his good work.

During the summer, Graham Highfield had contacted me again and asked me to go to a bungalow which was out at Woodsetts, a little village just past Dinnington. There, a family friend of his mother's needed some window locks putting on, which I gladly did. However, shortly after going there, Graham rang me again and this time he asked me to do some security work a the small chapel in the village. I think he arranged this when he visited there as a lay preacher.

In December, I completed my year of office as Chairman of 163 Mess and the social secretary asked me where I would like to hold my Annual Chairman's Dinner. This was an occasion which occurred each year in Fellowship and the retiring chairman had the pleasure of choosing his own venue for the event.

Normally it would have been at some local function room but I felt so proud of having been chairman that I asked for the dinner to be held at the Royal Victoria Hotel which was one of the top places for such events. I had played there several times as a musician so I knew the service would be good. The ante room was booked for forty guests which included the wives of Companions in the Mess and as usual, several of them enquired if dancing would be available.

This was agreed to by the Social Committee and being in the music business I was able to arrange for some of my musician colleagues to entertain us at a reasonable fee. The group of five were led by Stan Dickson on accordion, Lew Tindall on piano and Keith Peters on drums along with two other chaps on alto sax and trumpet All this took place in the second week of January 1986 and to put the finishing touches to the momentous occasion, I asked for all companions on the Top Table to wear formal dress. It really finished the year of my officialdom on a bright note.

At the end of January, I decided to buy a small green house which I bought from the Asda Superstore for £99. It was 6 feet by 6 feet with a galvanised frame and was made by Hall's, a well known manufacturer. We were fortunate with the weather when deciding to erect it and Aline, as usual, rolled up her sleeves to give assistance.

I was still at Ackroyd's and was able to get hold of some breeze blocks which I used as a base to put the green house on and bolt it down securely. I set it just above the recess in the yard which Geoff had helped me to dig out some years earlier to put the trailer tent in. I bought the green house mainly to grow tomatoes in but it also came in handy when raising seedlings.

When David was posted from Bruggen to Marham in Norfolk he was still a corporal but had taken his exams for promotion and just as he was settling in at Ely, where he and Heather were living out, he was posted again. He had just completed 12 months in Cambridgeshire when he was sent down to RAF Manton in Kent. That was on the 17th March. However, the good point of this was that he was promoted again and this time to the rank of sergeant. Aline and I were very pleased for him.

Because we had missed our holiday last year, Nip and I decided to go camping again and once more we went to West Runton in Norfolk. We liked it down there because it was quiet and secluded and the camping fees were reasonable. When we arrived this time we found that the site had new ablutions which were all modern and purpose built in a brick amenity unit. The break did us good again and when we went into the village hall to play bingo, the locals recognised us and made us very welcome. It was fully worth the trip from Sheffield and it was a pleasure visiting Cromer and Sheringham again. This time we went on the 6th July '86 for a full ten days.

I finished off the cricket season in mid September and commenced playing billiards again whilst Aline carried on earning a bob or two with her knitting.

Although Nip and I were now officially retired pensioners and on a full state pension, I carried on for a while at Ackroyds but had asked Jack Gardner to find a replacement for me because I was going to retire from any work and didn't need the small wage which I had been receiving there which incurred tax. With myself and Aline being on the full state pension, including graduated pensions for work done during the War, we were now quite comfortable financially but still watched what we were spending.

We had no mortgage to pay and my TWIL pension helped us along quite nicely if we needed something out of the ordinary. It was during this period that Geoff had been busy making enquiries into buying a house of his own and in he walked one day to announce that he had negotiated a deal to buy a terraced house on Norborough Road at Tinsley.

At first, Nip and I tried to discourage him but we were too late. Everything had been finalised all by himself and on the 1st November 1986, Tony and I helped him to move his furniture and belongings from Tower Drive. The house at 66 Norborough Road was really too big for him but he said that he would do what he could and his Mum and I kept popping down to help him with the decorating. That was a task because it had two large rooms and an off shot kitchen downstairs and two bedrooms, a bathroom and an attic upstairs. It was an old building having been built around the 1908 period but it was sound and solid. It also suited Geoff because it had a small garden at the back and he was keen on growing his own veg etc.

Just before I finished at Ackroyd's, I was able to get a brand new back door for Geoff's house and I obtained it for nothing due to the yard foreman's generosity. The house was on the market at £9,500 and Geoff had worked everything out to the last detail regarding the mortgage. I don't know how, because his wage at Mr Minit was only £75 per week. However, he was a thrifty lad and searched around for bargains in the food line but still fed himself well. He could even afford to have a telephone and later took advantage of his small garden at the back make other saving by growing his own produce.

In the middle of November, Graham Highfield contacted me from the Abel Alarm Co. He had left the Police Force and was now working as a rep for this security firm and wherever possible he passed work onto me for any conventional security. This time he asked me to go to the Esso Welcome Service Station at Shelton Lock near Derby.

I had to go twice, firstly to assess the work and secondly to fit what was necessary. As it happened, I had to get some steel bars made and drilled from an old contact of mine on Prince of Wales Road in Sheffield and return to fit them. I was acting as a sub-contractor to Able Alarms and there was no argument when I submitted my invoice of £54 plus. Graham told me later that I ought to have put more onto it.

Just before Christmas '86, Dave had rung and invited us to spend the holiday with them at Manton. When we arrived, we went to the Sergeants Quarters where Dave and Heather had a RAF bungalow which was capable of holding three extra bods such as us.

He had also told us to take Geoff with us because he had booked us all on to a Sally Line Sea Ferry for a festive meal. Geoff was pleased to be asked and relished the idea of sailing over to Calais from Ramsgate, even if we were not allowed to disembark.

The day before we sailed, Geoff borrowed David's push bike because he loved looking round new places of interest. Unfortunately, because of his disability, he had fallen off but there was only slight damage to himself and the bike. Dave told him not to worry about it and he was glad he wasn't hurt. Whilst Geoff was cycling round, Dave took Nip and I for a look around the Camp at Manston but only where it was legal to go. Because of the fall, Geoff had decided to stay in the bungalow when Dave invited his Mum and I down to the Sergeant's Mess for a few drinks and introduce us to some of his work mates. Dave and I did manage to get in a couple of games of snooker.

On the actual night of the sailing, David ran us down to the docks in his mini bus, parked up and directed us to the large cafeteria on the ferry. We found a table suitable for the five of us, ordered a few drinks and waited to sail because we couldn't eat before then. When the time arrived, there was more than enough food and the carvery as excellent. One could eat as much as one's stomach could take and to a point this suited Geoff because he certainly liked his grub.

After the meal, which must have taken us about an hour and a half to eat, we retired to a lounge on the upper deck and relaxed after such a good meal. All this was our Xmas treat from Dave and Heather. During the short voyage we sat and drank and Aline and I were having whisky and dry ginger with ice. The ice was in a large bucket which our Dave had acquired from the bar and this seemed to compose us as we drank.

The weather was fair but the sea had quite a swell on and earlier Heather and I had said that we wouldn't be affected but as we sailed on, we both had to go out onto the open deck to get some fresh air to stop our heads from spinning.

As we approached Calais, we all had to prepare to disembark but not for real because the procedure on these trips was that such as us on the special meal ticket had to go down the gang plank onto French soil and then turn left at the bottom and come back up the other side back onto the boat. What a farce because we were carrying our 'duty free' gifts, which were mainly bottles of booze from the outward journey. It was a 'bind' lugging them about but on the return journey we sat and chatted again until we arrived back at Ramsgate having obtained some more 'duty free' goods. Then we had a laugh because as we were disembarking, we had to go down some steps and as I reached the bottom, I slipped off the last step with two carrier bags full of booze. Luckily, I didn't smash any of the bottles but Nip and our Dave said I was drunk. Because Dave had drunk a few extra, he asked Heather to drive the van back to Manston but overall, everyone had a good time.

Before returning home, I used my car to have a run down to Broadstairs and look around the small harbour there. This was another place we hadn't seen before. We set off for home on the 29th December and on the way we had a break when calling in to see Ella and Rob in Maidstone. After a couple of hours with them we moved off again and arrived in Sheffield in the early evening. So another year had gone by but was what in the next one?

Whilst it was a duty to visit my Mum in hospital, it was becoming very tedious travelling twice a week to see her and each time we went, there was always something which wasn't right and upset her. Not regularly, but on odd occasions, Tony would go to see his Nannan and more often than not he would take Mathew and Lisa to see her too and this seemed to please her. I mustn't forget to mention that the Sister and staff had arranged a little party for Mum's 90th birthday last November and the family, including Geoff, went up to the hospital to celebrate it with her. A lovely birthday cake had also been made for the occasion.

In March this year, David was once more posted and this time it was back to Germany to a place called Laarbruch where he was engaged with an actual squadron on active duties and this sometimes meant him doing shift work.

It was during March, 1987 that we had some terrific gales which caused wholesale damage and destruction up and down the country. Acres and acres of huge trees were uprooted and some cases, where they fell over, there was thousands and thousands of pounds worth of damage to property. I got away with eight panes of glass being blown out of my greenhouse and my wooden fence on the side of the garden, had three, five feet high panels blown over.

Aline decided in April, that she wanted a new washing machine, so I went with her to choose one. On the 24th, we picked a Hotpoint model with a spin dryer and once again we were able to pay cash down which amounted to £279.99. We bought it from the Sheffield Co-op and this entitled us to treble stamps which was a method used to encourage customers to buy from them again. The stamps could be used as collateral on later purchases.

Now that Geoff was living in Tinsley, he had decided to transfer from 163 Mess to 232 Temple Mess which was in the Rotherham District of Fellowship and just down the street opposite his house and on the corner of Sheffield Road and St. Lawrence Road. The Mess meeting were held in a pub called the Fox and Duck Hotel on the first Monday of every month. After a couple of months he asked me to transfer there as well along with another Companion Ted Hutchinson, a chap I used to work with at Edgar's years ago and recently at Twil.

I think that this was to give Geoff some encouragement in joining a different Mess and meeting new companions. On the 4th May 1987, I did transfer out of 163 Mess to 232 Mess and on my first visit I recognised a couple of chaps who had worked with me at Twil and Ted knew them also, so this broke the ice when being accepted. It was whilst in my new Mess that I befriended Stuart Gorton, whom I had met on odd occasions at the Area Council of Fellowship.

He later became the Chairman of the Northern Area Council and in my capacity as Area Advisory Officer, I travelled with Stuart to many Messes in the Area to explain the functions of Fellowship administration. We visited such places as Chesterfield, Barnsley, Rotherham and many in the Sheffield district as well. It was all very interesting work and I loved every minute.

I still carried on umpiring at cricket in the Sheffield League and one Sunday, I was working in the garden, when Aline called to me to say that someone in Joe Lister's office wanted to speak to me on the telephone. Now, Joe Lister was the Secretary of the Yorkshire County Cricket Club and my reaction was, "Don't be daft. You're joking." Again Nip called to me and said it was true, so I went to the 'phone and said , "Hello!" and a female voice asked,"Mr. Priestley?" I replied, "Yes." and she carried on, "This is Mr. Lister's secretary. Would you like to umpire a Cup Match between the South Riding League and the Bradford League next Sunday?" I thought this is an honour to be asked to umpire such an important match.

"I would love to." I replied. "What are the details?" The secretary explained that the event would take place on the Phoenix Ground on Bawtry Road in the Brinsworth district of Rotherham and would start at 11.00 am and it would be a 60 overs match." I thought, that's going to be a long day, but there!

"By the way." She said, "Your partner for the day will be Mr. Keith Parsonage." That decided it because as I've said before, Keith lived just around the corner from me. I told her how pleased I was that I would be with Mr. Parsonage and accepted the invitation.

So it was that on the following Sunday, Keith and I turned up at what is known to us as Steelo's ground and officiated. It was an exciting game, with the weather being kind and it ran well into the early evening before the game finished in favour of the Bradford League. We just had one set back. When it came to the payment of fee, Keith and I were only offered £5.

We couldn't believe it but when we lodged an official complaint, we were told that the Sheffield League would re-imburse us with the difference and that was another £3 each. I agreed with Keith that we would never do another match even though we had enjoyed taking part and we both thought that the fee was an insult to our abilities. It worked out at less than one pound per hour and there were no expenses. Stingy beggars.

Geoff was really settling in at Norborough Road and he was knocking his little garden into shape. Health wise, however, he was still having problems but we did all that we could to help him. He would call in from work to see us at least once per week and we were pleased to see him.

During the year I had been having discomfort with Haemorrhoids and it became so painful that I went to see Dr. Hasan, who, on taking a look, made arrangements for me to visit the Royal Hallamshire Hospital. I went there and had a thorough examination and a few weeks later I was admitted on the 16th August into Ward I1. The following day I was operated on successfully and on the nineteenth, a young nurse told me to go and have a warm bath. This was to soften the cotton wool plug which had been put up my anus to stop the bleeding after the operation.

The bath had already been prepared and it felt great to lie and soak there. The nurse told me to call her when I had extracted the plug. **Extract the plug?** Oh! It did hurt. Every time I pulled, it brought tears to me eyes and eventually I had to call the nurse and told her I was having difficulty. "Turn round, kneel up and bend over." She said. This I did and she leaned over and gave a sharp tug.

The plug came out and I nearly hit the roof. I felt so embarrassed. On the 20th August, I was discharged, having successfully been through the trauma but it was all worth while and a peace of mind, knowing that there would be no more hairs stuck up my arse. The operation had cleared them all away.

At the end of August, Aline and I once more agreed to spend something on the house and this time we said that we would get rid of the outdated downstairs toilet with its cast iron cistern and flushing chain. We called in a local plumber who ripped out the old system and replaced it with a duo level cistern and a new toilet basin. The duo system meant that a short push on the handle only used half the water in the tank and a long push gave the full use of all the water in the tank.

It looked as different again and not unsightly like the old one had been. Whilst he was at it, I asked the plumber to fit me an outside tap for use in the garden and this he did from the water system on the downstairs loo. All this he did for the sum of £100 and we were highly pleased with his work.

As the year had progressed, Mum had been slowly deteriorating and the Sister at St. George's told us they hadn't the staff to tend for people in that state of health. We appreciated her explanation and agreed to put Mum into a nursing home. The Social Worker at the hospital gave us as much help as possible when trying to find a suitable place and it took a while to decide. After visiting one or two, some of which were in a terrible stinking state, we finally chose a small home called the Sharrow Head Nursing Home which was at the top end of Sharrowvale Road.

Nip and I eventually transferred my Mum from the hospital to this home which was run by an ex-nursing sister and her husband. The cost was worked out at £184 per week but this was paid for by the Social Services. It looked a nice clean place and only had about twelve other patients in it and my Mum had a room to herself to start with. She was later put into another room with another old lady because Mum said that she felt lonely on her own.

You see, unlike the hospital, this place had no communal room where people could sit together for company. Nip and I still visited Mum twice a week but it wasn't long before we could see her deteriorating even further. Her age was beginning to show and in a way I felt guilty and sorry for her now that she was in this position.

It was only a short period after, on the 13th September, that we received a phone call to say that Mum had passed away peacefully in her sleep. "Sorry, Mum - we did our best." We cremated her at Hutcliffe Wood Crematorium and scattered her ashes in the area of the Memorial Wall which had a small bronze plate on for my Dad. His ashes were in a small urn opposite the Wall under the soil and we thought that if we scattered Mum's ashes about there she would be near to Dad and also near to other members of the family and some neighbours who were put to rest there. So she was in good company.

It was just over twenty years since my Dad died and during those years I, along with Aline, had done what we thought best for Mum. At times it had been very trying and tempers had frayed but I must say to those who follow. **LOVE YOUR PARENTS DEARLY, THEY'RE THE ONLY ONES THAT YOU WILL HAVE.**

For the next few weeks, we were busy clearing out Mum's flat, otherwise we would have had to pay the rent for it. Before Dave had moved to Laarbruch, he had asked for some of the items of furniture such as the wardrobe, dressing table and blanket box and Tony had taken the three piece suite and one or two other things so that eventually we were able to dispose of just about everything. Any suitable clothing went to Oxfam and other stuff was just binned.

Inwardly I really loved my Mum but at her passing it was as though a huge burden had been taken of my shoulders.

In the first week of October, Aline and I told the family that we were going to Bridlington for a few days holiday to rest and relax. We only went on spec but we managed to find a self catering flat for the period of our stay and this only cost us £25 all in. We catered for ourselves and enjoyed every minute and because we were both partial to a flutter we went out to the local bingo hall on the main road for a couple of nights. During the day, we would have a run up to Filey or Scarborough or if it was really nice, we would go for a long walk on the beach on the south side of the town.

Upon returning home, Geoff popped in to tell us that he had become a blood donor and this we could understand, knowing how he thought things out. Also on the eleventh October, he rang to tell us that he had successfully completed a 10K run in the Lincoln Classic Race. In his condition he had excelled himself and had managed to complete the course in 64 minutes and 49 seconds. He just refused to give in to his complaint and was proud to display his certificate of achievement and his medallion.

As the years roll by, one's mind does funny tricks with one's memory and as 1988 approached, I was finding difficulty in recalling incidents which may have occurred recently. Forty years ago my mind could remember but forty weeks ago my mind seemed to go blank and to be honest, I'm struggling to keep the story going.

On the 23rd January, we had an urgent call from Tony saying that he was in terrible pain because he had fallen backwards down his stairs at home and crashed into the wall at the bottom.

He had managed to get to the phone to call us and I said I would be down there as quickly as I could. When I arrived, I managed to get him to a chair but his pain was so sharp that I decided to take him to the Rotherham General Hospital. Eventually he was examined and X-rayed but the doctor thought it best to admit him for observation. I left him there and returned home to explain to Aline. Apparently, Tony had been out boozing with his mates and had drunk too much. On trying to climb the stairs to reach the bathroom, he had lost his balance and fallen backwards down the stairs, thus injuring his back.

He was detained for a few days but even so, he couldn't refrain from drinking some beer which his pals had smuggled into the ward when visiting him. It annoyed Nip and I and she told him so when I took her to see him. He eventually recovered and then returned to work.

On March 11th, I said to Aline that the back door would be more secure if I took out the three horizontal panes of frosted glass and replaced them with just one large pane of Pilkington reinforced glass. It was something to do, so I gently eased out the old glass panes and then cut away the cross members which had supported them. Having measured up my requirements, I popped down to Newman and Watson's, the glass suppliers, whose business was next door to where Geoff worked at Mr. Minit. The cost wasn't much, around £6.45 which included the putty. It was easier than I thought in puttying in the new glass. This was in the top half of the door because the bottom half was all solid wood and very strong. Nip agreed that it did look more secure after it was completed.

It was little jobs like these that we agreed to do in order to improve our property and a month later, on the 10th May, a contractor came to the door to see if we required the front path and back yard re asphalting. He was in the area and had some excess material on his lorry and didn't want to take it back to Bradford from whence he came. Having agreed a price of £65, he and his assistant made good their work, the material having a metal base in it for endurance. What a difference it made to the paths and back yard. Just like new shoes.

In the third week of April, Freda, Aline's sister, rang her to say that she had booked a week's holiday at Sandown in the Isle of Wight, with one of her elderly neighbours, a Mrs.

Johnson. Unfortunately, the old lady had been taken ill and wouldn't be able to go, so would it be possible for Nip to take her place?

Nip asked me if I would mind being on my own for a week whilst she went with Freda on the holiday. Of course I didn't mind and it would be a break from tradition by going away without me. So on Wednesday, the 27th April, I took Aline over to Freda's at Harworth, where we stayed the night because it was an early morning start the following day. After I saw them off on the coach, I returned home and for a couple of days it seemed strange not having Nip about the house. It made me fend for myself and I did miss her.

The holiday was from Thursday to Thursday and I thought it would be good for Nip to have a rest from me for a while. When she returned on the following Thursday, the 4th of May, I could tell that it had done her some good. She had enjoyed every minute and said that we ought to try it ourselves sometime because the Isle of Wight was such a beautiful place.

I was beginning to feel like a hypochondriac because last August I had my piles seen to and now at the end of May, I was going back to the Hallamshire to have my top end cleared. This time, on the 25th May, I was admitted to Ward E1 and the following day I had my polyps removed. At a previous meeting with the ENT Specialist, he had told me that I hadn't helped my cause by using a Vic Sinus Spray up my nose because, although it gave instant relief to breathing difficulties, the residue of the spray set like concrete in the nostrils. This made it more difficult to breath. The operation was a success and when people asked me how my asthma was, I told them it was much better because I now had a clear passage from **Top** to **Bottom.**

Our Geoff kept himself active and if he wasn't hiking with the YHA, he would be out on his bike. He often went on his own and on this one occasion he was cycling along in a happy frame of mind, enjoying the country scenery and taking things easily. He reached the crown of this country lane and started to descend the hill in free wheel. He slowly gathered speed and as he approached the junction at the bottom, which joined a main road, the contestants of the June National Milk Race for cyclists was coming into view. It so happened that Geoff's handbrakes weren't efficient enough to stop him in time and into the middle of the main pack he rode.

Luckily, there was no accident but the speed of his bike coincided with the speed of the racers. To make things worse, Geoff was wearing a bright yellow 'T' shirt and a white cap with the peak turned upwards. As they went past, the spectators cheered because they thought that Geoff was the race leader in the yellow jersey. It is a true story because there were witnesses to the occasion.

Keith Parsonage, my umpiring partner, was unfortunate in having an accident whilst on his delivery rounds when doing his work. Somewhere near to Clumber Park he had swerved to avoid another vehicle but finished up crossing a grass verge and hitting a tree in a small copse.

He wasn't injured as such but was very badly shaken and sorry to say, shortly afterwards, the incident took its toll and Keith passed away. He was so popular with the local sports lads in both football and cricket, that the church at Handsworth was packed to capacity with many mourners. He left a wife and two grown up sons and it took quite a while for the sporting fraternity to come to terms with such a sad loss. He was only in his late fifties.

Dave and Heather had invited Nip and me to go over to stay with them again in the first week of August, but this time we were going to go via Harwich where we could leave our car in an insured compound for the time we were to be over there so that we could relax on our travels.

We sailed overnight to the Hook of Holland and enjoyed the use of a small double bunked cabin. Having had a good night's sleep we disembarked and there was Dave, by himself, to greet us. However, the first thing he did as we approached his car, was to ask us to hang back a little whilst he checked all around and under the car for explosives. This was at a time when the IRA (Irish Republican Army) had been active on the continent and operating against British personnel. Quite recently an Army Warrant officer had been killed in Ostend and two other people killed in Roermond in Holland.

Having made sure that everything was OK, we set off for Laarbruch, the RAF Camp at which he was stationed. It was quite a long ride and took us about one and a half hours. It did enable him to run in his new car which he had just acquired. It was a Nissan Micra and a smashing little saloon type which was handy for reasonable distances and very economical. He was eagre to show off the sunroof facility which was a feature of the new model.

This was our second visit to Germany and their flat this time was in a block of same and on the second floor. Dave had planned the holiday again and part of it was a tour of the three German dams which had been bombed by the 617 Dambuster Squadron during World War II.

They were the Mohne, Eder and Sorp Ennepe dams where the bouncing bomb, invented by a chap called Barnes Wallace, had caused so much damage, but not so much on the Sorp because this was built, mainly of concrete inside an earth bank and the bombs had difficulty in penetrating the earth bedding deep enough to cause the necessary damage. It was interesting at this dam because running down the side of the wall was a salmon leap to enable the fish to reach the waters of the dam for spawning.

We were able to walk or ride along the top of the dam walls and the Mohne had fortress like turrets at each end and this enabled us to walk along the road between them. Dave was happy to show us these places because during his service he had been on duty for a while at Scampton from where the famous 617 Dambuster Squadron operated from during the War.

We went sightseeing another day and he took us to see a famous castle. This was the Burg Eltz Castle of which jig saws had been made from photographs of it. It was quite a way up the mountain and couldn't be seen until one was within a few hundred feet from the entrance because of the trees surrounding the area. It was whilst we were struggling up the main path that a pal of our Dave's, from his camp, caught up with us along with his wife and three small daughters. He was a Chief Tech named Pip and for some unknown reason, his youngest daughter of about five years, tagged onto Aline and me and called us Grandma and Grandad.

I said it was a steep climb to the castle and Nip couldn't believe how Heb (Heather) as our Dave called her, took it all in her stride because she was expecting their first child but that didn't worry Heather and she kept on climbing .

It was more unbelievable because the day was so hot. Everyone was relieved when we finally reached the castle yard so that we could have a cool drink and an ice cream.

Later on in the week we went to see "The Rhine in Flames." and this was a firework display which occurred regularly at various places on the River Rhine. Dave had taken his big frame tent and we had just pitched it and settled in when Pip turned up. "What are you doing here?" He asked. "We've commandeered a large area in the middle of the campsite for all our families from Laarbruch."

"I didn't know." Our Dave replied. "It's too late now and we are nearer to the ablutions here." The following day was hilarious to a point because the camp site was packed and guy ropes were overlapping and cars and caravans came from all over the place.

It was just approaching lunch time when word went around that the IRA were about again and this is where the hilarity came in. All British servicemen's cars had a black number plate with a 'B' at the end of the number and as I have said, there were many civvy cars on the site but as soon as the word went out about possible bomb scares, all the civvy drivers couldn't move fast enough from in between the vehicle owned by our lads.

The scare was due to the fact that the British Army WO had been blown up in his car at

Ostend in Belgium the previous week and everyone was on their guard. As for instance, the next morning, Dave had arisen and dressed and had just gone outside the tent when an English chap from a caravan next to us, went to open his car door.

"STOP." Our Dave bellowed.

"I beg your pardon." Was the reply. "I'm an RAF Officer."

"So what.(Pause) Sir?" And carried on, "I'm a sergeant armourer in the RAF and you should know better than to get into your car without checking it." Dave then went on, "You should get rid of that, too." and pointed to the battery operated remote control which would have opened the doors of the officer's car. "You might want your parents killed but I don't want mine to be." finished Dave.

"Point taken, sergeant and thanks for being so alert." came the reply. That evening, we went round to join Pip and his family and all the other RAF people who were set out in their own reserved area. Nip and I were made very welcome and were treated like Royalty with food and drink in abundance. Pip's daughters tagged on to us again and then we saw the firework display commence.

This took place at the junction of the River Rhine and the River Mosel and on the other side of the river was the Koblenz Castle which seemed to burst into flames as the huge number of fireworks were unleashed. Many boats were decorated and lit up with coloured lights as they sailed up and down the rivers singing and partying. It was gone midnight when we eventually went to bed but it had been worth every minute.

In the morning, Dave took us across the river on a small ferry to have a look around the city of Koblenz and during a break for refreshments, he took a photo of Nip with a big and long hamburger in her mouth, it was so funny. Koblenz was very picturesque and Aline enjoyed it immensely. The following day we went back to Laarbruch and after another day's rest, Dave drove us to Zeebrugge to catch our boat home. What a wonderful holiday. Thank you Dave and Heb.

We didn't seem to have been back home for more than five minutes when we were again celebrating the annual trio of events from the past. Namely, Aline's birthday, our wedding anniversary and of course, Tony's birthday. We didn't splash out for a meal or for a drink but just enjoyed each others company. As the lads had grown up, Nip and I had just taken any of our birthdays in their stride and not made too much fuss about them.

We received a phone call on the 23rd September from Dave to say that Heb had presented him with a lovely baby girl and they were both doing well. They decided to name her Dawn Michelle but wanted to wait until she grew up before baptising her. Both Heather and Dave said she could make up her own mind later on in life. It didn't please either of the grandparents and further comment was a waste of time.

During the year, the Government had been having a purge on women who were suffering from Cervical Cancer and though Aline had no worries in that direction, she asked the Doctor if she ought to go for a check up and he said it would be a good idea. So on the 18th October I ran her up in the car to Nether Edge Hospital for a smear test. Just over a week later she received a call to go for the result. She was all smiles when she came out because she had been pronounced to be clear of any signs or symptoms of the dreaded disease.

At Christmas we were able to see what Dawn looked like because Dave was able to get some leave and they all came over for a few days to stay with us. Dawn was beautiful and had a lovely head of dark hair and Aline was in raptures when holding her. After the holiday they travelled down to Evesham to stay with Heather's parents. So another year had passed and we had been blessed with another lovely grandchild.

In the Spring of 1989, Nip and I found it harder to try to get the trailer tent ready for a holiday. The main base was of galvanised metal and even taking the canvas tent off to lighten the load, it still meant there was total of three to four hundredweights to lift it onto its side to load onto the two wheeled buggy.

Because of this, and neither of us getting any younger, we advertised it in the local press and luckily within a week we had a call from a couple, asking if they could see it. We agreed a day and time but even so we had to erect it to let them fully inspect it.

The couple were in their forties and had two young children and it was the latter who finally persuaded their parents to buy it. I think the kids liked sitting on the coloured seats and being able to look out of the clear plastic windows. We packed it all up after explaining how the folding of the tent frame worked when getting it to fit on top of the galvanised trailer. We included many extras such as a camping cooker, curtains and the spare wheel. The couple were happy at the price of £270 and we were satisfied too as they drove away. Everything must have been alright because they never contacted us again.

Having completed the sale of the tent and feeling a little flush with money, Aline suggested that we ought to go modern and buy a video recorder. So, the following week we went to town and had a look in various shops but finally opted for Curry's on the Moor in Sheffield. The lady assistant was very obliging and having chosen the model we liked, she went into the storeroom at the back of the shop and came out with box containing a model for which we paid £120. We had taken the car to town so that we were able to carry the unit to the car park where we had left the car. We paid cash again and we were eager to get home and set it up.

It was a Logik model and when we came to unpack it from the box, we found that it wasn't the one which we had chosen but a far more superior one which had a 21 day 8 program timer on it and should have cost £180. Of course we took it back to the shop. (We should cocoa.) It was just one of those instances of dishonesty- so what? Curry's had more money than we had.

I have mentioned earlier about our Geoff's many friends who included nurses, well, on the 27th May, he was invited to the wedding of Joanna Lodge and Andrew Steel. Jo and Andy, as we knew them, were Geoff's best pals and he seemed to be with them more than his other friends. Jo actually came from Drayton which was a district of Portsmouth and that's where the wedding was to take place. Andy was a Sheffield lad and a little bit younger than Geoff but they always enjoyed each others company and both Jo and Andy kept their eyes on him.

At the end of July, we had a few days break down at Ingoldmells where Tony owned a small caravan. He had bought it a short while ago from a man who used to employ Elaine in his sandwich shop in Sheffield. Tony had started to rent it out to people to obtain a bit more income but some of his bookings turned out to be rather undesirable because one couldn't vet them over the phone. Because of some damage caused by such people in the caravan and the increase in ground rent, he eventually had to let it go.

Now that we had sold the trailer tent, we had no further use for a car with a tow bar, so on the 22nd August 1989, having had a good look round various forecourts, we agreed to go to D.C. Cook's and exchange our Cavalier car for a small Fiat Panda GL which had a registration plate of D401RAK. It was only three years old and had been used by a disabled person in Rotherham, who had obtained it through the Social Services. It was in good condition, coloured grey blue and had just 21,500 miles on the clock. It cost us £2,500.

Sorry to say though, that after a short while Aline took a dislike to it and refused to drive it. It wasn't as comfortable as the Cavalier had been and she said it was like a tin box on wheels. At least the engine was a 998cc and it ran on unleaded petrol which made it very economical.

As usual, Nip and I went to Bridlington again, in the flat which we had been to before on Tennyson Avenue. We always went in the first week of October and always seemed to pick good weather. This time the lady owner asked us to let ourselves in and out of the house because she was a postwoman and would be out doing her rounds during the day. She was also helpful to Nip when it came to odd bits of wool for knitting. It was useful to Nip because she was knitting little coloured squares from which she was making a large bedspread.

In November, I had some trouble with one of my teeth so I went to the Charles Clifford Dental Hospital near to Weston Park in Sheffield. I went there because I had no regular dentist and I knew that the treatment would be free. Little did I know what I was letting myself on for because after treatment I was put under the Dental Conservation department for further treatment, all of which was for my own good. For months I attended clinics which would have cost me a fortune at a private dentist. All the treatment was carried out by trainee students and my first one was a Richard Emms. He was excellent.

Dave and Heather weren't coming over for Christmas this year but Dave had made a video of Dawn as she played and splashed about in her bath. I'm glad that Nip persuaded us to buy that video recorder.

EARLY NINETIES

As I enter the beginning of the last decade of the twentieth century, my mind goes back to the earlier days of my life and the many changes that have occurred over those years. Things like the silent movies to the 'talking pictures', the cats whisker radio sets to the modern portable radios which can be concealed in the hand, from Edison Bell gramophones to the present day stereo units with twin speakers; vinyl records to cassette tapes and compact discs and the invention by Logie Baird of the modern television set. But the biggest communicator of all time must be the modern day telephone system by which conversations can take place between two people from anywhere in the world.

Because of modern technology, we were able to follow the progress of Dawn due to the fact that Dave had made a video recording of her in 1988 and had sent it over from Germany for us to look at. It had been lovely to see her playing with the presents and toys which she had received last Christmas and Dave had asked us to send it down to Heb's Mum and Dad in Evesham, so that they too could watch Dawn's progress.

It was in March this year that we had the good news that Dave had been posted back to the UK and this time he had been sent to RAF Lossiemouth in Scotland. He and Heb had been allocated a small terraced house which was on a street called Hythe Hill and about two miles away from the camp. This suited Dave because being a fitness fanatic, he could jog into work and in the other direction he could get to the nearest golf course in ten minutes. One asset was that 'phone calls were cheaper from Scotland as opposed to Germany.

By attending the monthly meeting of the Retired Persons Club at TWIL, it eventually befell upon me to be elected onto the committee of same at the March AGM. I hadn't been in the position very long before I was asked to become the Social Secretary and this meant organising coach trips during the summer months.

My beginning as social secretary was very busy and my first effort was to organise a coach to take a party down to Newark, in Nottinghamshire, and then go on a boat trip down the River Trent for the fare of £6.60, included a fish and chip lunch which we had served on the boat. It was an hour's journey on the river and upon return, we had enough time to have a look around the ancient castle ruins. The weather was kind all day and everyone enjoyed their day out.

Later in the year I arranged some other outings and the next one was on the 17th August which was a Friday. It was an awkward day for many but I managed to persuade thirty three people to come out that day, which was to Southport in Lancashire, and I think that was due to the fact that the fare was only £3.50.

In between all this social work, things had been happening at home and after returning from Germany, Dave and Heather revealed that another baby was on the way and so on the 29th June, 1990, they had a little brother for Dawn. They decided to name him Craig Phillip (Phillips) being Heb's maiden name but due to some worry about the birth, Heather had to go to hospital to have the delivery and this was in Aberdeen. Everything turned out fine for them and the baby was a strong healthy lad.

At the end of August, Dave and Heather invited Nip and me to go up to stay with them for a week and have a short holiday with them, so we went and booked our seats on the National Express which was a coach company who would take us the whole way to Glasgow and there we would catch a connection to Inverness. That's what we thought and down to Pond Street bus station we went with our luggage and stood at the place from where we thought that the coach would depart. After about twenty minutes, we saw a coach arrive with the indicator showing 'Glasgow' and we set off to go aboard.

As we showed our tickets, the stewardess said that this wasn't our coach but another one which went a different route. After making enquiries, we learned that the one we should have boarded, had left some ten minutes ago.

I had a right go at the Regulator and complained that we hadn't been informed about the different boarding points. Eventually, he told us to get on the one we had first tried to enter and when we arrived at Leeds we were to contact the Regulator there and he would direct us to another coach.

We arrived at Leeds, unloaded our luggage and went to the Regulator. He informed us that there wasn't another vehicle available, so would have to get back onto the coach from whence we had alighted. This we did and this one seemed to go all over the north of the country before arriving at Glasgow. We disembarked, asked the Regulator there about our connection and he said that we had missed it by thirty minutes.

One can imagine our annoyance but the Scottish Regulator was very helpful. Having explained that our son was supposed to pick us up in Inverness, he asked us into his office and made several 'phone calls. He then told me to ring our David and tell him that we would be in Inverness around about ten thirty at night.

The answer was, that because it was the fault of the National Express Co., he was obliged to get us to our destination and therefore he had booked us a taxi, free of charge. It was rather hilarious because when the young taxi driver arrived and asked, "Where to?" he couldn't believe it when the regulator said. "Inverness."

The driver was a grand lad and said he had never had a fare like this one before because it was about 180 miles to Inverness and during the journey he really tried to find us a place to get a drink but without success. We eventually arrived at our destination but even then he told us to sit in the cab until he had located where Dave was parked. We couldn't do anything but give him a good tip for his thoughtfulness. I'm glad we didn't have to pay the fare.

The young man found Dave and having thanked him we finally set off and arrived at Dave's house at 11.15 pm. One good thing was that Dave had brought a thermos flask of coffee with him and were we grateful for that drink?

Because the house on Hythe Hill was only a two bed roomed one, Nip and I had to sleep on the lounge floor in sleeping bags but we didn't mind because it was so good to see them again.

Dave managed to get a few days of work and was able to show us around one or two places and it was nice to go into Elgin which was a short journey down the road from Lossiemouth, past the RAF Camp gates and then past the famous school of Gordonstoun where several of the Royal Family had been educated.

Craig was still in the crawling stage but Dawn was turning into a lovely little girl and full of energy. When we went to Elgin, Heather showed Aline the shop from where she bought most of the kiddies clothes. Heb was always thrifty and this shop, whilst being on the cheap side, also had good things in it. We enjoyed our stay and once again the weather was good. On our return journey home, we had no problem and Dave ran us back down to Inverness to catch our connection. From there it was no trouble and this time we travelled on the through bus which was the one on which we should have started our holiday in the first place What a difference in travelling time. The return journey only seemed to be half as long.

Almost a month later, we had a day out at Bridlington and this included a visit to the Hornsea Potteries. Many old people enjoy a day at the seaside and Brid was very popular. This trip was made better because I had booked it on a Wednesday - the 12th September. A month later on, having contacted the Chocolate Factory of Cadbury's, we had a day out there to look around the factory to see how they made their products and this was more than interesting.

We had one point of dissention which was that the prices in the cafeteria appeared to be rather extortionate, but there, it's part of the Tourist Industry. It was the largest party that we had taken on an outing and this time the cost was £6.00 each. It all depended on the coach proprietors fee for some charged the earth but I always shopped around for the best deal until I obtained the right price to suit our Club's finances and the pockets of the pensioners.

Towards the end of the year and having family contacts in Derbyshire, I had managed to contact a Mr Peter Middleton at Castleton to ask when their Christmas Lights would be on and if the shops would be open.

The lights at Castleton Village were not a huge display but all the main street was lit up with fairy lights and each cottage and shop has its own lighted and decorated Xmas Tree outside the front door. Besides being a shop keeper, Mr Middleton was on the local council and was gracious and understanding when I made arrangements with him. After explaining that our coach trip was a pensioners outing he said he would arrange for most of the shops in the village to be open until seven o'clock so that they could browse around them until our meal was ready at the Peak Hotel. The Peak was one of many pubs in Castleton but I had chosen this one because one of my late cousin's daughters (Jean) worked there and I knew we would be well looked after. Once again I had all this at an inclusive price of £5, which included the coach at £3 and the buffet at a further £2.

Occasionally, we would have a social evening at the Club House on Ferrars' Road and this entailed getting sources of entertainment on the musical side. It was on one of these nights that I booked the small Concert Party of Companions from 308 Mess of the Fellowship. They were a group of fellows who were organised by an ex-police inspector from Maltby and they did a whole show in mime. The inspector was Jim Gunn who was a Past Chairman of their Mess and he put everything into entertaining us and the whole group were fully appreciated. By the way, none of the concert party were under 45 years of age but you wouldn't have thought so when seeing the antics which they got up to.

Each year, Tinsley Wire made arrangements for some three hundred pensioners and friends to go the Grosvenor Hotel for a Christmas Dinner and this year was no exception, it was all free and an excuse for the Managing Director to read out the state of the firm during the past financial year.

This was followed by a reply to the speech, from the Chairman of the Pensioners Club. Sorry to say that out of the three hundred guests, there were only about fifty who ever attended our Monday Club.

It was on one Sunday morning that Tony caught the bus to Catcliffe from Rotherham and walked up from there to have his Sunday lunch with Nip and me. As he walked past the gateway of a small business who hired out Porta Cabins, a chap passed the time of day with him and asked Tony if he was coming from work because of the small pack on his back..

Tony told him that he had been doing some football training and was on his way to see us for his Sunday lunch. The man commented that he was a football referee and also a cricket umpire. "My Dad is an umpire in the Sheffield League." Tony told him. "But he's thinking of trying to get a change."

The man commented that he was in the Bassetlaw League and if I was interested, he would put me in contact with that League's officials. "My name is Norman Angell and I live in Woodhouse. Ask your Dad to call in after you have had lunch. I'll be here at Pasuda, (that was the name of the firm) all afternoon." I duly obliged and went to meet him at about 3.00 pm and after an interesting chat, he gave me the name of the secretary of his association and asked me to ring him.

I was so keen to get a new start that I contacted a Peter Stafford within a few days and shortly afterwards he rang back and asked me to go down to Killamarsh Cricket Club to be assessed on the Laws of Cricket by a Brian Rivington who was a qualified umpiring instructor in the Bassetlaw Cricket League.

After a few questions and a chat, Brian said that he would contact Peter Stafford and give his verdict as to whether I would be acceptable and ask Peter to let me know in time for the coming season.

It was in November, 1990 that I received a letter from TWIL, informing me, like many others who had been on the staff, that as from next May, 1991, my pension would be increased annually by 3% until I 'kicked the bucket.' It didn't seem much at the time but it was guaranteed and I knew that over a long period, God willing, that there would be a benefit from it.

As Christmas approached, Nip and I were looking forward to it because Dave and Heather were travelling down from Scotland to show off their new arrival, Craig, to the family. It was lovely to have them and it was the second time that we had been able to see him and like Dawn, he too had a full head of thick hair. It was later on that they found out that Craig had five crowns to his head. After spending Christmas day with us, they all went down to Heb's Mum's at Evesham to show Craig to Dennis and Edna, the other grandparents.

Early in the New Year I was put on the list of umpires for the Bassetlaw League and I received my fixture list for the first three months of the coming season. The first two matches were arranged so that I would be visually assessed again but this time on the field of play. At the first one, I had Peter Stafford, the Secretary and the second match I had Eric Jackson, the League Umpires chairman. I was eventually accepted as a full member and paid my yearly fee of £2.00.

The association was well organised and the official Bassetlaw League hand book was more than useful and on the last few pages it contained all the names, addresses and telephone numbers of umpires taking part. Each match had 92 overs as opposed to the 80 overs of the Sheffield League and I found that the actual cricket grounds were far superior to the Sheffield ones. Most of them were ex-colliery grounds and had been well maintained. Umpires could more or less choose where they would prefer to go to and I measured out a twenty mile radius on a map, from Handsworth to regions within North Nottinghamshire and North Derbyshire. It was well worth the change. During the close season, Umpires were able to attend meetings on the first Saturday of each month in Worksop. The purpose if this was to keep up-to-date with the league news and also have the privilege of listening to well known and famous members of the cricketing fraternity. Our own League President, Nigel Plews, was a first class and Test Match umpire.

Our Geoff had always had one ambition in life and that was, unbeknown to us until a later date, to walk the Pennine Way which was a public footpath along the top of the range of mountains dividing the West of Northern England from the Eastern side of the country. The beginning of the walk was at a little village called Edale, which was in North Derbyshire and about twenty miles from Sheffield. Geoff referred to the walk as the Benign Way in later years but on the 27th April, 1991 he set off on the first part of his quest. For the next two days he made his way along the path and after an overnight stop, he arrived at Marsden. On the way he was accompanied by several YHA pals and one in particular was Ann-Marie Sandilands.

Her name will arise at a later date but to follow his progress one must read the write-up in another book about Geoff's life. It was the start for Geoff and we thought that he had done well because we thought that his disability might hinder him but it didn't. He was so determined.

Geoff had chosen this particular week for his walk because Aline and I had agreed to hire transport and take all the family for a holiday in Scotland and Dave was in the act because we had asked him to book an eight berth caravan on the site at Lossiemouth where Nip and I had stayed some years earlier. We had to juggle with the dates so that Tony could get time off work and also make sure that Mathew and Lisa would be available. We finally agreed to go in the early part of May so that Geoff could get in his arranged walk and everything worked out fine.

There was one slight hiccup when the first vehicle we had booked, was cancelled so we finally acquired a twelve seater mini bus from Smith's Hire, which I picked up on the Saturday morning.

It was a long drive to Lossiemouth and in the region of 450 miles but Tony was able to take over for a while once we had crossed the Scottish Border. The hire people had taken out a double seat at the back because all our luggage wouldn't fit in, especially with Geoff having brought all his hiking outfit with him. He had arranged to meet Andy Steel, Andy Fletcher, Tom and JB, besides the female friends who were going to be there. He was to join them at Ullapool after spending the week with us at Dave's. We didn't get to Lossiemouth until late afternoon due to one or two breaks which we needed to stretch our legs and answer the calls of nature.

Having collected the key for the caravan from the Warden's office, we soon sorted out the sleeping arrangements and then after a drink and a snack we walked up to where Dave, Heather and the kids were living on Hythe Hill, just to let them know that we had arrived safely. The house was an RAF accommodation and wasn't that big but it was sufficient for their immediate needs. It seemed smaller still when all our gang arrived but at least there was a small garden to which some of us dispersed. Whilst there, Dave pointed out the nearest chippie, just up the road.

He had managed to get some time off duty and had made one or two arrangements to entertain us whilst we were up there. It was good to have all out family together in one place because this doesn't happen very often. One of the trips he organised was to do the 'Whisky Run' which was a must for all tourists in the area. This was a standard thing which meant visiting about seven distilleries from which whisky was produced. We called at one place where they made Glenfiddich whisky and as we arrived, we saw two coach loads of American visitors who had come to look around. The custom on these visits was that all tourists were offered a free tot of whisky and a look around the vats etc. This didn't seem possible for us to get a look at all the processing plant, but Dave said to go in. We did, received our free tot and then came out again to visit the next distillery. Cheeky devils!

We went another day down the Spey Valley but because he wasn't too keen to go with us, I agreed to let Tony borrow the minibus and please himself where he went to. Dave took the rest of us in his own minibus, dropped us off at a particular point and told us where to walk and he would pick us up further along the Spey Valley.

Because he couldn't have all the week off, Dave helped us to enjoy the holiday by telling us the best places to visit. Elgin, the nearest town, was a beautiful little place with a magnificent church, which some said was a Cathedral, to look round and it also had some nice shops too.

In the middle of the week he told us to have a run down to Aviemore, the famous Scottish ski centre, so off we went. The weather was glorious so there was no snow on the slopes but we, that is myself, Geoff and Mathew, decided to go up the ski lift to get a better view. Tony and Lisa agreed to stay with his Nip whilst we proceeded up the mountain on the lift.

There are two stages of the ski lift, one which goes half way up for the novice skiers and the final one to about 1,000 feet below the summit of the Cairngorm Mountain. Having reached the final stage, we had a breather and then set off to climb the rest of the way to the very top. At nearly 70 years of age that was no mean feat for me but I tried to follow Geoff and Mat up the very steep incline but within about 500 feet of the peak I had to give in. Mathew went to the top and came back down again to see if I was alright and then proceeded to go back up again.

Geoff amazed me and Aline couldn't believe it when I told her that irrespective of his disabilities, he had managed to reach the summit through sheer determination, but that's Geoff. He was a very determined lad and after making the journey, one would have thought that he had climbed Mount Everest.

I took my camera with me and whilst up there I was able to get some shots above cloud level and on one shot I could see the Solway Firth in the distance to the West. It was a good day out and although Nip, Tony and Lisa didn't do the climb, they enjoyed it just like the rest of us did

The following day, Dave had arranged to take us into the RAF camp to show us where he worked and whilst most of us went with him, he had organised it so that Lisa could spend some time in the Dog Handling section because she was interested in joining the RAF and fancied herself as a Dog Handler .

We left her with a corporal of the section and then we carried on into the hangar where Dave worked. He introduced us to his Boss, Chief Tech. Fitzpatrick who told Dave to let us have a look round one of the Buccaneer Aircraft which had just returned from active duty in the Gulf War.

The cockpit was high up off the ground so he fixed a standard type metal ladder to the fuselage and told us to go up. Geoff went first and was more than overwhelmed when being able to say afterwards that he had sat in the cockpit of a jet bomber. Mathew was next but he was at a loss to understand all the modern technology but it fascinated Tony when his turn came to sit in the controls. When it came to Nip and myself, we just climbed up to have a look and she said that if she climbed into the cockpit, she wouldn't be able to get out again.

As we were taking a look around the hanger, our Dave's Flight Commander, a Flight Lieutenant, came over and introduced himself and then told us to go to the hangar door and watch the last flight of the Shackleton Bomber Squadron which was just leaving Lossiemouth for its last destination prior to being taken out of service. We were just making for the door when the officer shouted to our Dave and pointed to his own ears. Dave received the message and went and obtained a set of ear muffs for each one of us. It was so noisy as the aircraft taxied to the runway and we were thrilled as each pilot waved to us as he passed the hangar. This aircraft had done some very good work on reconnaissance duties over the Atlantic Ocean etc., but it was now obsolete and was to be replaced by the Nimrod and the AWAC aircraft.

We made our way back to Dave's section for a cup of coffee and as we went down one of the corridors, Chief Fitz said to Dave, "What's that carpet doing there?" Dave replied, "It the one from the Sergeant's Mess. I've commandeered it for my brother's house so that they can take it with them when they return home." "I had my eye on that but obviously I'm too late." The Chief said. Dave commented, "Too right you're too late." We then loaded it onto the mini bus which was just outside, picked up Lisa and then returned to the caravan park.

In the evening, Dave had booked a meal for us all at a local restaurant and had asked for a table for eight people plus a spare place for Dawn. It was a carvery and everyone could help themselves to as much food as they liked and this suited Tony and Geoff down to the ground. As we were eating, Dave pointed to a spare place at the table. "That's for next year, if you come." Nip looked across at me and raised her eyebrows. "Yes." Dave carried on, There should be another addition if all goes well and it should be in the New Year." Having enjoyed a goodnight out we went to leave the restaurant and Dave said he would settle the Bill as a gift to the family and this was appreciated by all of us. He was a generous lad.

The next day we called in to say cheerio to Heather and Dawn and to make arrangements for Dave to run Geoff down to Inverness so that he could make his connection to go to meet his pals at Ullapool. In the evening, we went down into the bar of the Camping Club House and had a drink or two to finish off the holiday and then we went and finished the packing ready for the following morning. This was the Saturday morning and we left for home, once more took in the sights of Scotland. Tony relieved me a couple of times with the driving and we had a couple of breaks to stretch out legs again.

The last break was at Scotch Corner where everyone seemed to stop on their passage to and from Scotland and the Lake District because there were public conveniences there. It was somewhere about five o'clock at teatime when we finally arrived home after dropping Tony, Mathew and Lisa. The following morning I returned the mini bus to the hirers. The holiday was a great success and well worth the effort to arrange it all.

Prior to going on holiday, I had managed to squeeze in another day trip for the TWIL pensioners and this had been to Denby Potteries in Derbyshire. After a short film show, which gave an incite into the pottery industry, we were then shown round the small factory and finished in the art room where hand painted items were being finished. It was wonderful to watch the female operatives doing the delicate designs of decorating the many shapes of pottery on display. Before leaving, all the ladies on the coach were given a small piece of pottery clay and then told to make their own models from the small moulds which were on hand. This pleased them all and each one of them carefully wrapped their efforts in tissue paper to take home with them.

Upon return from our holiday, I took them on another journey and this all came about because Nip and I had been into Sheffield one day to have a look at a holiday exhibition which was taking place at the Cutler's Hall on Church Street. We had a good browse round but we were very interested in a stall which was run by the Newcastle Tourist Information Centre.

The young lady at the stall explained that if we took a party up to Cleveland, she would meet our coach at a special rendezvous and act as a guide whilst showing us round the Catherine Cookson Country. For the un-initiated, Catherine Cookson was a world famous novelist from that area and most of her stories originated from the local countryside.

Having taken details and brochures from the lady promoter, I later on contacted her in Newcastle to make final arrangements and included in the tour, she had managed for us to have a lunch at a chosen pub. The price of £1.50 each for the food was extra to the fare of £3.50. So on the whole I think that everyone had a good deal and a good nosh. This journey was undertaken by a new coach company I had managed to come across and it operated from Thurcroft. It was Carol's Coaches and the service and driver were excellent, nothing was too much trouble.

I continued to hire Carol's Coaches because the service was so good and there was always the facility for us to have a game of bingo on the trips whilst we were travelling. Towards the middle of June, I arranged for a small tour of North Derbyshire. It was more or less a half day trip but near the end we finished calling in at Derwent Dams because there were some toilets in the Fairholmes car park. On the way into the Dams area I went up to the front of the coach and sat just opposite to Ken the driver and borrowing his microphone, I gave a running commentary of the events which had taken place there, over the past years. I was able to do this because I had been connected with the surroundings of the place through my family and I must have done a good job with the descriptions and explanations I gave, that several of the group on the outing, and Ken, the driver, said why didn't I apply for a courier's post. Many of our people hadn't seen the Dams where the making of the film "The Dambusters." had been made and this was an extra thrill for them. That was our last trip for the year, so I was able to relax from all the organising duties in which I had been involved.

Aline said that we ought to turn our thoughts to our home again and this time she said that she would like some new carpet in the living room. So, we contacted Homeworld which was a new furnishing outlet at Catcliffe and had just been opened. It was managed by the Co-operative Wholesale Society (CWS). The carpet was fitted on the 9th August and cost us £179.82 plus a rebate in dividend stamps.

I think that Nip caught the bug because a month later on, she said that we could do with a new carpet for the back bedroom. This time we went to the Pyramid Carpet Co., at Darnall and on the 12th September, the fitters came and obliged. The cost this time was a little less at £157.00, the colour was a darkish blue and with having curtains to match, we called it the blue room

This year was to be my 70th birthday and quite recently my pal, Fred Tyler had persuaded me to join the Steel City Bowling Club of which he and his brother Wilf were members. Having had a try out, I agreed to join the club so, for my birthday, Aline bought me a new set of bowls and I started a new hobby but not until the next Spring when the bowling season started.

Dave didn't write to us very often but he had written to us on the 14th of August to say that he was taking Heather and the kids to Leuchars for the RAF Air Show on the 21st September and hoped that he would be alright because it was the day after his operation at the Aberdeen Hospital.

Because he now had two children and another one on the way, he had decided to have the 'Snip' - Vasectomy. Apart from that, everything regarding Heather and the baby was fine. He had enclosed some snapshots of Dawn and Craig in a portable paddling pool in the garden and they really looked fit and healthy.

Now that I had reached the age of seventy years I was aware that somewhere in the Bible, reference was made to the fact that the life expectancy of man was three score years and ten. This was the basis of my autobiography and due to the help of my family and above all, my God, I was now entering into the period of borrowed time. Aline's Mum often referred to it and I agreed with her that we had been blessed with a gift and we must make the most of a golden opportunity to enjoy any bonus in life which had been put before us.

Outwardly I am not religious and I am not a regular church goer but there are times when a person must turn to God for guidance and I am one of those people. It may be necessary at times to ask for his help, it doesn't go amiss to thank the Good Lord for any small mercies he may bestow.

I hope it isn't too late, Dave, but I would like to know if your children will eventually be baptised in the name of the Lord. You, Tony and Geoff, were all brought up to believe, so I'm sure you will grant me my wish.

Going back to Geoff's Pennine Walk, it was on the 20th September that he went on another stage of his quest and this stage two lasted three days. On October the sixth, off he went again but only for one day and like I said previously, to follow his progress, one must read his 'Pennine Way' encounter.

Just prior to Christmas, on the 10th December to be exact, I once more made arrangements to have a trip to the Hyde Park Inn. This time it was organised to be a little more festive with turkey sandwiches and Christmas pudding portions. Paper hats were supplied and crackers to pull, thus getting into the festive spirit of the season, albeit a little early and Mrs. Tomlinson again excelled in helping us to enjoy it.

It was in the following week that Dave rang up and asked Nip and myself if we would be free to go up to Lossiemouth the week after Christmas to baby sit for them because the new baby was due that week and if he had to take Heather into the hospital again, there was no one to take care of Dawn and Craig. Nip was only too willing and Dave said instead of driving all that way by car, why not go by train. This was the day after Boxing Day and we travelled from Sheffield to Aberdeen without having to change trains but we had to change when we arrived at Aberdeen so that we could catch the local train which would take us to Elgin. The whole journey was a change from driving the car and one could relax and take in the views.

Dave was waiting for us at Elgin station after our five hour journey and told us that things seemed to be going alright with Heather and this time she would be going into the local hospital at Elgin.

For the time of the year, the weather was marvellous and although cool, Aline was able to stand outside to smoke her cigarette. Dave wouldn't allow smoking in the house and Nip was appreciative of the fact.

Since our visit earlier last year, both Dave and Heather had been busy getting their new house in order. They had decided to buy a new one because the price was right and they classed it as an investment. It was a three bed roomed house but there weren't any amenities for Nip and me to sleep in it, so we slept in their tourist caravan which was parked on the driveway. The house was on a new estate and was in a cul-de-sac called Ardivot Place where the view from the kitchen window overlooked a gap between other properties to where the local golf course and coast line were plainly visible. Although Heather was in pregnancy, she had 'mucked' in to help Dave with the house, especially the driveway where she had assisted in moving a load of bricks for the driveway. They had been laid by hand by Dave and he told us that his finger tips were sore through laying them in a herringbone pattern. This once again enhances the cause of married couples working as a team.

Adjacent to the back garden, they had a huge garage but he didn't keep the van in it because it was so full of their belongings, some of which hadn't been unpacked since returning from Germany. In front of the garage was the caravan in which Nip and I were sleeping and there was central heating in it if we needed it. Also there was a small toilet which was handy to use in the night.

Dave was able to take us out to local places of interest but we couldn't go far because of the condition of Heather but she plodded on with us and it helped because Nip and I were able to look after Dawn and Craig.

To break the monotony of sitting around waiting for the event, Dave borrowed a small set of golf clubs for me from the RAF Sports section and then took me to a small course which was a few miles away, to have a round of golf and give him the opportunity to relax a bit. It was only the third time that I had ever played but I managed to get round OK and I only lost three balls.

We were able to go down to Campbell's Canned Vegetable Factory where they made their famous soups and at the back of it they kept some Highland Cattle for the pleasure of the tourists and of course, any children. On the way back we went along the coast road through Cullen, Portknockie, Findochty and ended up at Buckie where Dave said we could get some fish and chips. As we drove back to Lossiemouth, we were able to see dolphins playing around in the gulf stream which goes past that part of the coast. It proved just how mild the weather was for that time of the year.

The new baby was due in the New Year of 1992 but for some reason it wasn't ready and Dave had taken Heather down to the hospital for a quick check up and everything seemed alright. We thought that we would only be up there for about a week or possibly ten days even but the way things were going, it seemed that the visit would be longer, but it didn't matter. We had plenty of time and we were enjoying the stay. To stay anywhere is always pleasurable when the weather is in your favour and so it was for us.

I had a regular chore and that was to take Dawn to play school each morning which was just over a mile away and we would walk across a playing field for a short cut and then along the road where there were some cottages before it dropped down to the school where she attended. It was on one of these mornings that, unfortunately, I needed a toilet very badly. As we were passing these cottages we reached the end one and I said to Dawn, "Come with me a minute and I'll ask at the house if I can use their toilet." An old lady came to the back door and embarrassingly, I explained the situation.

She spoke to Dawn and said,"Come in young lady. What's your name?" Dawn told her and the good lady directed me to the toilet which was upstairs and then turned to Dawn. "Come with me, Dawn and I'll get you a biscuit." The hospitality was more than welcome and the relief to me was greater. Dawn had looked a little bewildered at me going into a complete stranger's house but even at that young age of three and a half years, I think she understood and having thanked the lady we set off again.

Dawn was a good little walker and only once did she ever ask to be carried but I coaxed her to carry on walking because the school was just coming into sight. I enjoyed the chance of taking her to the school and going to pick her up again about three o'clock in the afternoon. The fresh air made me feel good and when needed, we both wrapped up well but on the whole the weather was kind to us.

Going into the second week of January, we had bedded down for the night but about 2.00 am in the morning, Dave knocked us up and told us that Heather had started with birth pains and he was rushing her down to the hospital in Elgin. We left the caravan and moved into their bed in the house so that we would be on hand if Dawn or Craig needed anything. I think Nip and I could only doze as we waited for any news.

It was shortly after breakfast, on the 9th January 1992, that Dave arrived back from the hospital to tell us that Heather had given birth to another boy and both were doing well. He said that we would be able to go to see them in the afternoon when Heb had rested and things had been tidied up.

So after some lunch we all went down to Elgin and explained to Dawn and Craig that they had a new brother. The baby was in its own cot next to Heb's bed and Heb looked reasonably well considering having only recently given birth a few hours earlier. Whilst we were there, the RAF MO came to see how they were both getting on and Dave had warned us about him. In features, that is. He was a Wing Commander and his build was that of a huge rugby player but he was a very nice man to talk to when Dave introduced Nip and me to him.

The next day when we went to see them, Dave and Heather were discussing what names to give the new baby and they went through several possibilities when one of us suggested 'James' but Heather said it might be shortened to 'Jimmy'. Both Nip and I said that if they stuck to calling him 'James', then everyone else would. So it was that 'James' was decided upon and Dave said let us add Alan to that (it was our Geoff's middle name)and this is what they did. Dawn said she liked 'James' and that finally settled the matter.

We 'pulled' Heb's leg a bit because Dawn's hair was brunette, Craig's had a touch of auburn in his and James' hair was blonde. We asked her which one of them was the milkman's.

Aline and I stayed on until Heather had been back home for a few days, then we decided to leave them and return home. Dave ran us down to Elgin Station where the ticket collector suggested to us to go back the other way through Inverness and Glasgow instead of Aberdeen. The suggestion paid off because we were able to see more of the Scottish countryside on what turned out to be a round trip, it was very enjoyable.

There was a slight hiccup, because as the train approaching Sheffield, we were held up by a signal failure just North of Rotherham and the guard had no idea how long we would be. We were able to move slowly and when we arrived at Rotherham Station, Nip and I decided to get off and get a taxi to take us to Handsworth. It paid off because we were in our house within 20 minutes whereas we would still have been stuck between Rotherham and Sheffield for ages.

In March, Geoff had a biopsy done on his right thigh and for weeks he had difficulty in walking and had to have some time off work. The biopsy was another stage in trying to find a cause of his Motor Neurone complaint and we patiently waited for any results which may ensue.

He came up to see us one day and said he had seen a short holiday advertised and would we care to go with him. It was to St. Ives in Cornwall but Aline said that she wasn't really interested but said for me to go with him for a break.

This I did and towards the end of April we caught the coach to St. Ives and stayed for five days in a hotel just out of town at Carbis Bay. The food was excellent and as usual, Geoff couldn't get enough but a middle aged couple from Lancs, who were sitting at our table, passed over to him any food that was in excess to them. The holiday included a couple of day excursions to places of interest such as Newquay and the Cathedral town of Truro. On one of these trips, Geoff tired me out because he went and asked the driver to drop us off at a garden centre to have a look around and then we walk back to the hotel for dinner. We completely mis-judged the distance back and as we came to each bend in the road, Geoff said that this must be the last one. Was I glad to get my shoes off, we must have walked two miles but we both enjoyed it, even though I was a little grumpy.

The whole holiday was a success and whilst we were in St. Ives itself one morning, I came across a gentleman who I knew from Sheffield. He was a Mr. Phillips who used to own a garage in Handsworth and his sons went to school with our boys. When I asked him what he was doing there, he said that now he was retired, he came down quite often to the cottage which he owned.

The break did Geoff the world of good and I was pleased to have helped him mentally by being with him. Aline had also enjoyed not having me under her feet.

As the year progressed, I became busier than ever with organising trips for the pensioners and the first one was to go over the Saddleworth Moors, which straddle the Yorkshire and Lancashire Borders. (These were famous due to the Brady and Hindley child murderers because it was in this vicinity that they had hid the children's bodies.) We then carried on up into North Yorkshire to visit the natural setting of the village of Goathland which was the main background for the TV series, "Heartbeat" with Nick Berry, Bill Maynard and Derek Fouldes and we finished off the day by popping into Whitby before returning home.

A few weeks after that trip, the 1st July, our Geoff walked in full of woe because he had been down to his workplace, 'Mr. Minit', to see his workmates and John Ryan, his manager, had called him into the office to inform him that, mainly due to his absence from work, even though it was due to his illness, it had been decided to dispense with his services.

Nip and I were also upset because with being in our Fellowship Mess, we thought that John Ryan would have been a little more compassionate but, as many people know, there is no sentiment in business. We both consoled Geoff and I said that I would go with him to see Dr. Hasan. This we did and explained to the doctor, who very sympathetically said he would do what he could to help.

It took a few weeks to set up but the doctor eventually had Geoff registered as a disabled person. Geoff wasn't too happy with the title because he had fought so hard to master the early signs of the Motor Neurone disease. However, he did cheer up when his Government Benefit came through and his all-in allowances totalled £180 per week. At first he was at a loss as to what to do with all that money because his finishing salary at Mr. Minit had just reached £105 per week.

It didn't take him long to sort out his weekly finances and instead of him scratting and scraping, he was able to put away a reasonable amount of his money into savings for a rainy day.

Once he became accustomed to not having to worry about work, he took his time in achieving his ambition of walking his 'Benign Way' at a leisurely pace and in stages which suited him.

On the 11th August, I organised another trip to a place in North Yorkshire called Eden Camp, which was near to Malton. This was an attraction which was set out in the style of an Army Camp with rows of Huts as it used to be during the War. There were some twenty of these huts and in each one was a display of stages of the Home Front during the WWII.

The tour started with recordings and films of the Prime Minister Chamberlain returning from Munich in Germany to tell us that we were at war with that country. Each hut displayed some aspect of the war from the Blitz to activities of various branches of the Armed Forces and the Civil Defence Personnel who worked under tremendous difficulties. Good meals were served in a reproduction of a Forces Mess and at reasonable prices. In another hut, it was set out as a NAAFI and we were able to get a drink there and sit and recall the war time films that were showing on the placards which hung on the walls.

We had a good two and a half hours looking around every display in the huts and some had sound effects as part of the tableaus which enhanced the realistic displays. Just as we were leaving and boarding the coach, the heavens opened and it rained very heavily. We all managed to get onto the coach without getting wet and we then set off to finish the day at Scarborough. As we travelled, the weather became worse, also it was accompanied by heavy thunder but the Lord must have looked down upon us because just as we were alighting from the coach on the Promenade at Scarborough, the sun came out, the rain stopped and everyone enjoyed the rest of the day.

The weekend following, Nip said that there were some televisions on offer in the ASDA Superstore and if they were suitable, it might be a good idea to buy one for use in the kitchen. I went over with her and had a look at the model on display. It was a 14 inch coloured TV made by a firm called ALBA and the offer price was £95, so we decided there and then to buy it. It was a good set and came in handy if Aline was busy in the kitchen but still wanted to watch a certain programme.

Towards the end of September, I arranged another outing to the Hyde Park Inn and Mrs. Tomlinson was very pleased to see us again, and once more donated a prize for our raffle.

We left about three o'clock in the afternoon, having enjoyed the meal provided, and then went for a short tour again where this time we went to Creswell Crags in North Derbyshire. There it had a nature museum and lovely walks in the area to some very old caves. Once more the work I had put into the trip, was appreciated and we arrived back home shortly after 7.00 pm in the evening.

The firm's annual dinner for pensioners, at the Grosvenor Hotel, came upon us in no time and towards the end of November, Nip and I made the usual pilgrimage to the event. Roy and Mary made the effort to attend where we did manage to get seated at the same table. All the tables were large round ones and seated eight people and this made it convenient to get to know other retired persons with whom I may have had only an acquaintance at work. Prior to sitting down to the meal, it was a pleasure to have a chat with some of the senior management with whom I had worked with over the years and who themselves were now retired. The one I always looked forward to having a chat with, was Leslie Potts, my first boss, but who now lived in Cheshire.

At this particular dinner, there were several complaints about the meal and the main one was highlighted when Mary tried to stick her fork into a sprout. It was so hard and under cooked that it shot off her plate and went across the floor. We both had a word with David Baker, who was the Works Catering Manager and he said he would register our complaint.

Earlier in the year, Tony had befriended a young lady and the relationship had really grown to more than affection and Tony's attitude to life seemed to change all at once. They were ideally matched, although the young lady, named Mary Davies, was a few years older than Tony, he being forty two and she, around the forty five mark. She lived in a flat in Carlisle Place in Rotherham which was about ten minutes walk from where Tony lived.

Mary was very modest but full of life, so to speak and considering that she had fought an eight year battle against Hodgkin's disease, which she had won because the Doctors had declared her clear of the illness in 1987, she was a real live wire. She was also an intelligent woman because she had studied through the Open University and obtained a degree as a Batchelor of Arts. On one occasion when Tony went to visit her at the flat, he found her fast asleep on the floor of the bathroom with just a quilt over her.

She was a bit of a rebel to a point because she thought that she was stronger than she was and decided to go on a march in London to support the Miners and the TUC demonstration. A few days after returning, Mary became ill with dizzy spells and losing vision. This was on her birthday, the 1st November, and two days later she was rushed into the Rotherham General Hospital where a few hours later she was put onto a ventilator but she drifted into a coma.

Tony rang us to tell us the story, so to give him some support, Aline and I went down to the hospital to see her. A few of her family were there but eventually we went into the small ward to see her. The poor lass was out to the world but both of us held her hand and gave her words of comfort, hoping that the sound of our voices might help to bring her round but to no avail.

Mary had contracted the non-contagious Pneumococcal Meningitis and Tony believed that she had lost her fight for life because her spleen had been removed in her battle against Hodgkin's Disease. Shortly after, the decision was left to him by her family, to ask the Doctors to turn off the Ventilator. It was a terrible decision to make but he faced it like a man and not long after, Mary was pronounced dead. Tony, our son, had told us that Mary had proposed to him three days before her birthday and he had seemed to be 'over the moon' as he told us the good news at the time but I think it hit him hard when Mary was taken ill. It took a long time for him to overcome the tragedy. After Mary's death, he arranged for a headstone to be placed on her grave as this was her request, ages before she passed away. He still feels for her and regularly visits the grave to place some flowers there.

In the following weeks after the funeral I was busy helping Tony clear out her flat because Mary's relations seemed to lack enthusiasm and therefore burdened Tony with the unenviable task. Mary must have felt ill because when I entered her flat to help, there must have been eight dirty dinner plates strewn about the living room floor where she had eaten a meal but felt too listless to clear them away or wash up. It was so upsetting for all of us and we did what we could to help our son with his loss. Why do so many years finish on a sad note?

Christmas was approaching and Dave told us that they would be coming to stay with us over part of the holiday before going onto see Heather's Mum and Dad at Evesham. This meant re-arranging the sleeping accommodation but it was all part of family life.

Dave and Heather slept in the back bedroom and Dave fixed up a large cardboard box for James to sleep in. It was rather amusing but it worked quite well and Dawn and Craig slept in the little bedroom on small camp beds. Tony and Mathew came up from Tony's house in

Rotherham on Christmas Day and Geoff didn't come up until late on Christmas morning - just in time for his dinner.

This was to be a memorable Christmas in many ways and Nip and I were so pleased to have all our family together again on such an occasion. The house was full with Dave, Heather, the three little ones and then Geoff, Tony and Mathew. It was so hectic as everyone was opening their presents. Unfortunately, there was one person missing but we didn't forget Mary.

They had a laugh on me because one gift I received was a roll of 35mm film which I said was no good because my camera was a 125 size. It wasn't until later on that Dave gave me a new camera to fit the film.

Everyone enjoyed the mad scramble as each one showed what 'Father Christmas' had brought them and a novelty one was what Geoff received from Tony. It was about four feet long and very thin but it was still wrapped up in Xmas paper. The look of amazement on Geoff's face when he discovered that it was a hand carved thumb stick for use on his hiking expeditions. Tony had arranged to have it specially made.

All this excitement of unwrapping the presents was highlighted by Dave recording most of it on his Cam Corder. It seemed significant that it recorded Nip with James in her arms and Dawn and Craig sat on the arms of her chair beside her and then Mathew knelt down just behind her with his beaming face showing.

The preparation of accommodating and cooking for the whole family had really been worth while and as the future will prove, this was a significant Christmas.

Early in January '93, Dave had persuaded me to buy a new Panasonic Electric typewriter instead of trying to pound out material on an old fashioned portable one. It cost me over a hundred pounds when I bought it from Boots the Chemist shop in High street. I soon found the difference and my typing did improve considerably.

It was in January that Nip started to have, what we thought at first were dizzy spells when she seemed to pass out. They weren't long spasms and only lasted a few minutes but eventually they became more prevalent and it was decided to consult our Doctor. For a while he seemed at a loss because the spasms weren't on a regular basis like every day, but now and again. This went on for several months but we kept a watchful eye on things.

On Thursday, the 21st January, we had some terrific gales all over the country and thousands and thousands of pounds worth of damage was caused by falling trees and property being damaged etc., and **we** didn't escape because the top side garden fence had three panels ripped out and flattened. The strong winds persisted for days and on the following Saturday there was glass flying everywhere as the gusts reaching eighty to ninety miles per hour, attacked my green house and smashed about eight panes of glass. We had to go to a depot in Rotherham to get replacements because of their special sizes but fortunately the cost wasn't prohibitive..

Through a bit of ingenuity I was able to repair the fence myself and I gave it some extra support by wedging 3" x 2" wooden beams into the soil at angles of forty five degrees.

Over the next few months I kept a very careful check on Aline because the attacks were still occurring and to try to give her a chance to get some rest at night, I decided to go and sleep in the back bedroom. It helped us both because I was a light sleeper and tossed and turned a lot and this didn't help her at all. It worked to a point and I was always there if she wanted any help which really wasn't very often because she was such an independent lass.

On the sixth of April I received some good news and this was in the form of a letter from the Company who operated the TWIL Pension Scheme and in it I was informed that as from that date, I would no longer be obliged to pay Income Tax. This had been assessed because I was not now employed in work, either full time of part time, as at Ackroyd and Abbotts and was just living on my pension income which had to cover for both Aline and myself..

In May, I ran another outing and this was to Harry Ramsden's Fish and Chip Shop at Guiseley and then after the meal we went on to Skipton to have a look around the Castle and market. It was a good trip with the coach being full. It also helped Nip to forget some of her past dizzy spells. Some of these bouts had occurred whilst we out shopping and I was frightened to death that she might fall and injure herself, but on this trip, she had a normal day.

I still carried on umpiring but on one Saturday, the 8th May, the match finished late and I had only travelled a mile up the road from Pilsley when I came to a junction in the road with Hardstoft Road. I looked both ways, eased out and an old couple, who were chatting away in their saloon, approached from the right and hit my near side front wing.

It so happened that a police patrol car was just passing and he stopped to see if anyone was hurt but there wasn't. He asked me from which direction I was coming and when I said the side road, he said, "It's your fault then." I was too tired to argue but the couple and I exchanged details and I set off for home. I drove up the M1 Motorway with my off side light on but without a lens, it must have looked funny to other motorists. I didn't arrive home until turned 10.00 pm and Nip had been wondering what had happened to me.. She emphasised that the main thing was that I was alright. It took a few weeks to get the car repaired and it was all settled by the Insurance Company.

I had been trying for several months to contact Taffy Morgan through various channels because I didn't have his address or phone number but by process of elimination I was successful. On the 18th May the phone rang and on answering it I heard Taffy's voice. "Hy ya Man. How are you?" He asked. "I hit on the right address then, Roy?" was my reply and after a good chat and reminiscences we said that we would keep in contact and this we did. I told him I was writing a book about RAF service in the Far East and would send him a copy as soon as it was finished.

On the 10th June, I posted my book 'Over There' to Taff and I also sent a copy to Mrs. Cohen, Stuart's widow, who lived in London. One of the photo's in the book was of Stuart and another pal of his, Ron Worley from Romford in Essex. As a good will gesture I had the photograph enlarged to 6" x 4" so that she could get a clearer look at it.

It was also on that same day that I was privileged to be asked to umpire at a cricket Festival in Sheffield and this was to be a Round Robin Game between the staffs of various Universities from several parts of the Country such as Leeds, Newcastle, Manchester, Nottingham, Sheffield, Leicester, Loughborough and one or two more.

It was the 12th when I officiated at the match between Sheffield No.1 and Nottingham in a 60 overs match, commencing at 11.00 am and carrying on until nearly 7.00 at night. On the following day I umpired Sheffield No.2 against Newcastle.

Each time I was accompanied by a full ACU umpire, namely Alan Bennett. There were eight local umpires officiating at the matches which were played on the University Ground on Warminster Road, the De La Salle Ground and a further ground situated at the back of Beauchief Abbey. Unfortunately we didn't receive our fees until a month later with a letter of thanks for services rendered.

The 29th June was to be a significant day because Geoff had rung us to say that he was sitting an examination for Law at Richmond College in the afternoon and could he come for his tea afterwards? Aline told him he didn't have to ask but Geoff was always polite and very thoughtful.

He arrived just in time for tea at 5.00 pm and after enjoying it and having had a rest, he asked if he could have a shower. "You know where it is." said Nip, "and there's a towel in the airing cupboard." Off he went and came back downstairs some twenty minutes later.

"Can I have a bowl of hot water to wash me feet in, Mum?" He asked her.

"You've just had a shower. Why didn't you put the plug in the bath and wash them in that?"

"I never thought of that." was his reply and we all had a laugh as he carried a bowl of water into the sitting room.

Having done what he wanted and cleared away his bowl and towel, he asked me if I had a cricket match on that night. As it happened, I had to umpire a midweek match on Bawtry Road which was fifteen minutes walk away from where he lived on Norborough Road.

"I'll go down with you, Dad, and watch for a while." Geoff said. This he did until about ten minutes past eight o'clock because he had arranged to go out for a drink with JB and Tom, his YHA pals. He caught my attention, waved and shouted, "I'll see you tomorrow." But little did I realise what was to come.

The following morning the post arrived and there was an airmail letter from Gambia addressed to Geoff. It was from one of his many pen friends and this one was Anne-Marie Sandilands who was doing Voluntary Service Overseas with the VSO in her capacity as a physiotherapist. Aline said, "We're going to the Aldi to do some shopping so we might as well drop the letter in for him on the way home." The Aldi was a retail discount food store and was situated on a new Retail Park at the end of Lock Lane at Tinsley and therefore wasn't really out of our way.

We did our shopping and went around to Geoff's house about 9.45 am but he wasn't in so the letter was put through his door. We went back home via Brinsworth and as we turned to go onto our driveway, Albert Smith, our neighbour, came round and told us that the police had called but would return shortly.

We both thought that something had happened to our Dave, knowing that his job in the RAF could be dangerous. However, some few minutes later, there was a knock on the front door and I could see the police car outside. There were two officers who asked our name and then asked if they could come in. It was something serious and Nip and I sensed something terrible.

"Have you a son named Geoffrey?" One of the officers asked.

When we said 'Yes.' He asked us to sit down and then told us that there had been a road accident and would we go with them to identify the body who they thought was that of Geoff.

Aline and I threw our arms around each other and just sobbed and sobbed. After ten minutes we left with the policemen in a patrol car to go to the morgue at the Rotherham General Hospital. Apparently, the ambulance had taken him there but he was dead on arrival. Aline wouldn't go in to see him but I plucked up enough courage to confirm that it was our Geoff. The Doctor let me into a small room and there Geoff was lying in a peaceful pose after been cleaned up and I automatically leaned over, kissed his forehead and said, "God Bless you, Geoff." I was asked not to touch the body but I couldn't resist it and the hardest part was confirming that it was him and then having to tell Aline.

We were driven back home by the two young policemen who had been very helpful and sympathetic all the time. Just before leaving the hospital, we were told that the Coroner's Office would contact us because there had to be an inquest. In Geoff's belongings they had found an Organ Donor card but the Doctor in charge said he was sorry but due to the state of the body, it would be impossible to use any of them.

The rest of the day was spent informing the family of the tragedy and Tony and Dave just couldn't take it in that they had lost their brother. Neither Nip or myself could settle to do anything and hardly felt like eating. I think the shock of it all must have put Nip's dizzy spells on hold because she bore up to it magnificently.

The following day, a motor cycle policeman came to see us for certain details that would be required when the inquest came up. He was more than kind and told us that if we required any assistance whatsoever, we were to contact him. The officer's name was PC Warrilow who had been called to the accident and who had asked for the ambulance immediately. He gave us a rough outline as to what he thought had happened and he would be called later at the Coroner's inquest to give a report.

There wasn't a spare moment after contacting the undertakers, A. Keeton and Son, whose business was just across the way on Highfield Lane, near to the ASDA. An announcement was put in the local press besides me passing the word onto Andy Steel, his best pal, who in turn informed all the YHA people. I also informed them at Mess as to what had happened and the secretary told the Head office of Fellowship.

As Nip and I were sitting in the house having a break, we heard someone at the back door and we both went to see who it was. There was Andy Steel and he was in such a really depressed state that we had to help him up the back steps into the house. The poor lad couldn't control himself, he was so emotionally upset and tears rolled down his cheeks. Geoff and he had been such bosom pals.

After a drink, he slowly came round and it eased the pain for him as we talked about Geoff in general. Andy recalled some of the happier times that he and Geoff had spent in each others company.

All week we had been receiving cards and letters of condolence and I had also contacted the local church of St Mary's, to make arrangements for the cremation service, which we had decided upon. We expected the local vicar, The Rev. Bruce Leng, to come and we were greatly surprised when, on answering the bell on the front door, there stood a lady curate from the church. Her name was Hilary Hotchin and she was a large person in build but an angel to us during the time we spent with her. After a short prayer, she took details of Geoff's life in readiness for the service in the Chapel at the Rotherham Crematorium.

Because the Chapel wasn't in this parish, Hilary had to get permission to hold the service in Rotherham and sanction was given by the office of the Bishop of Sheffield. The cremation was scheduled for the 8th July at 10.30 am but the day before, Keeton's had rung to say that they had collected Geoff's body from the mortuary and put him in their own Chapel of Rest. They asked us if anyone cared to go over and see him but none of us felt like going as we wanted to remember how he looked before the accident.

Dave had rung from Germany and said he had been able to get compassionate leave and would be over for a few days. He asked me if I would like him to wear his uniform as a respect to Geoff, who, you will recall, had also served in the RAF. Nip and I greatly appreciated the gesture because I had already made arrangements for the Union Flag to be draped over the coffin when the time came. With Geoff being a Companion of the Fellowship, it befell him to receive that honour as an ex-serviceman.

On the eighth July, the cortege left our house at 10.00 am with Hilary in attendance and myself, Aline, Tony and Dave in the one hired limousine. Geoff would have been proud of seeing Dave in his RAF sergeants uniform. Many relatives followed on behind in their own cars and slowly we headed for the Rotherham Crematorium which was about six miles away.

We entered the grounds of the Cemetery there and as we came to the crown of the hill just before the descent to the Chapel below, I nudged Nip and nodded to the front of the cortege. There, in front and lining both sides of the driveway, were at least one hundred Companions of the Fellowship who had come to pay their last respects to a very popular Companion.

I just filled up with emotion because I knew that Geoff was the most likeable and friendliest of Companions in the Rotherham District of the FOS. That in itself was emotional but as we pulled up on the flat at the entrance, there were another forty friends if his from the YHA. Inside the Chapel, the family pews were full of relations and close friends and the guest side was packed with Companions from many Messes. There was an over flow of mourners and they had to go up into a small gallery which over- looked the service altar.

The coffin which was draped with the Union Flag, had been brought in and placed on trestles in front of the altar and the Curate, Hilary, took her place at a small lecturn where she commenced the service which Aline and I said we would never forget. Hilary went through the history of Geoff's short life and recalled some of his many academic achievements and the generosity and kindness he had shown to others. Geoff would help anyone at anytime. The service was so interesting and touching that even grown men in the Fellowship were in tears. At a signal, just before the commital, a Companion from his own Mess, spoke the short poem associated with such occasions;

"They shall grow not old
As we that are left grow old,
Age shall not weary them
Nor the years condemn.
At the going down of the sun
And in the morning,
We will remember them.

The service ended with all the Companions in the Chapel singing, what we call 'The Last in the Book.' but it is generally known as "Love's Old Sweet Song." It is sung at the close of every Mess in Fellowship but on that day it sounded just like a male voice choir.

As the curtains closed and Geoff was committed to God, there wasn't a dry eye to be seen anywhere and we prepared to leave, I just couldn't face up to having a word with the senior companions who were present. I think that they realised what a great loss we had suffered.

The mourners dispersed and most of the family and friends returned to No 8 where luckily we were able to use the patio and lawn because there were so many of us. Andy Steel came back with us along with his wife, Jo, and his Mum and Dad who had thought a lot of Geoff.

Aline's brother Eric, said he hadn't realised how much Geoff had done in his short life and commented on how Hilary Hotchin had conducted the service. Prior to the funeral, there were some doubts about Hilary officiating because normally, a Companion Padre conducted such services but at a later date, when I saw some Companions, they couldn't believe how good Hilary had been and said that they would make a note of it for further reference.

We couldn't believe it either, that with the family, the many YHA friends and the strength of the Companions of the Fellowship, there was something in the region of 180 mourners in attendance to pay their last respects to such a grand lad.

Dave returned to Germany and to help Aline and me to adjust to Geoff's loss, he and Heather asked us to go over to them at Bruggen, so on the 20th July we sailed from Harwich, having put the car in a security compound. We had booked a two berth cabin to enable us to kip down for the night and when we docked at 8.30 am at Rotterdam, Dave was waiting for us but he still checked under his car for security reasons, before letting us get in. There was still enough activity about with the IRA that precautions were always necessary.

Although officially stationed at Bruggen, Dave's allocated accomodation was at Wildenrath and at the time of being posted there, he had objected to the offered housing and through persistence, had finished up with officer accomodation. Lucky devil.

The house had a large lounge - come dining room with a patio door, a fairly sized entrance hall, a kitchen and three bedrooms. To save moving the kids about, Dave had managed to get hold of some empty beer crates and on top of these he had laid some boards, blankets and camping bedding in one of the rooms in the basement. This basement was also large with a washing room, a drying room, a work place which he had set up for himself and then this large room where we were to sleep and where the kiddies kept reminding us that it was their play room. We had guessed that with all the toys in it and a spare TV for them to watch cartoons on.

It hadn't taken us long to get from Rotterdam, from where Dave had picked us up and we arrived at Wildenrath about 10.45 am in the morning. The children were so pleased to see us and Craig, not knowing any better, looked directly at us and asked, "Is Geoff dead then, like a bird hitting the window? Aline said, "Yes, sweetheart. But he didn't feel it."

Apart from the large house, they also had a reasonable sized garden for the little ones to play in. It suited them because there was so much wildlife in the woods across the road and many species of birds would come onto the patio to be fed.

Just prior to our visit, Dave and Heather had taken all three children to a large garden centre and on display was a children's playing frame which was about 10 feet high and some 12 feet long. It consisted of a climbing ladder at one end and a similar thing across the top for support. The other end was supported by a two feet square climbing box with rungs on two sides but half way down there was a small platform from which a slide had been fixed. In the middle if the frame was suspended two swing seats and a trapeze. It looked ideal for the children to play on but they were reluctant to buy it immediately.

When Dave asked the price, he was quoted in the region of 500/600 Marks, so he asked Heather for some paper and a pencil and then did a rough sketch of it all. A few weeks later he had bought the materials required and built one himself for about 125 Marks which was quite a saving. It showed how strong it was because Aline sat on one of the swings and had Dawn and James on her lap. As young as he was, James was forever climbing up on to the top portion and crawling across to the other end. It was a laugh to see him but he saw no danger. It was at a later date that Dave was asked to make a couple more for his RAF pals.

He had arranged for some time off work so that he could take us out and the first run was to Wegberg Park which wasn't too far away and there the youngsters could play on various types of apparatus and go into a tunnel system which had been built into a small hill. They were all enjoying it until Heather spotted the grass being covered with hundreds of ants. Collecting the children, Heb then headed for a huge duck pond where Dawn, Craig and James enjoyed throwing pieces of bread to the ducks. Shortly afterwards we all left and went into the centre of Wegberg, which is a beautiful little town with cobbled streets. Dave headed for the ice cream palour and there we all tucked in to various types and flavours of the local ice creams and having enjoyed our outing we all returned to base, their house.

One night, Heather had arranged for a baby sitter to come, so that all the grown ups could go to the Sergeants Mess for a social evening. As we entered the Mess there was a Chief Tech., checking everyone in and Dave asked if we remembered him. At first I didn't but when he reminded us that he had been to our house some years ago it all came back. The lad was John from Grimsby in Lincolnshire.

Another day, Dave took us to the big military base at Rheindahlen, to show us the NAAFI shop there. He had to go in any case because he wanted to go and collect something and whilst there we went into the NAAFI for a browse and I called to Nip and pointed out a very neat radio walkman which was complete with headphones and made by Sony, a Japanese firm. She looked at it and said,"If you want it, get it. We're on holiday." I asked the price and they were on offer at 50 Marks which was about £25 in Sterling. Dave said it was a bargain, so I bought it.

After that, we strolled about the shop and looked at other goods. I was at the top end of the display area and turning round I saw that Dawn had tagged on to me. As we were looking, I spotted a piece of paper money on the floor. Picking it up I saw that it was a 50 Mark note and asked Dawn, "Have you dropped this, Dawn?" She looked a bit surprised and said "No, Grandad." On catching up with Dave and the rest of them, I asked him if he had given it to Dawn to buy something with.

"50 Marks, you must be joking." He said. We all looked about and no one seemed to be interested, so I put the note into my pocket. On the way out of the NAAFI I asked Nip if she would like a Walkman for herself and when she replied by asking, "Why?" I said, "Well if you do, I'll get it out of the money I found." This was agreed upon so we finished up with two Sony Walkman for the price of one.

Towards the end of the week, Dave took us all across the border to see the Liege Market on the side of the River Meuse. We passed through Maastricht on the way and I asked Dave to drop me off so that I could sort out one or two problems for the Government. Ha! Ha! He managed to find a convenient parking place on the opposite side of the river to the market and the length of the market must have stretched for three or more miles and there were all kinds of nationalities there.

We had just sat down on some stone steps, which led from the main riverside walk, when a woman tapped me on the shoulder and asked me in French, to let her pass. I don't know how but I moved over and answered her in the only few French words I knew. Aline's eyes went wide with amazement. We had a drink and a snack on those steps before carrying on to look at some more of the market. Whatever anyone wanted, then it was sure to be somewhere about because there were so many stalls to choose from.

It wasn't long after, that the kids were getting tired, so Dave said we ought to make our way back to the van. The weather had been kind and everyone had enjoyed the visit. We had just passed through Maastricht on the way home when Nip started to have one of her turns. "Dave." I cried. "Can you pull up somewhere, Mum's not too good?" I turned towards her to give her some support with my arm and my right elbow hit her right on the forehead. Of course that didn't help but Dave managed to pull into a layby and Heather rushed round to give her a drink of water.

As I've said before, these attacks didn't last long and after about twenty minutes we were on our way again but it had frightened the three little ones at seeing their Grandma like this but Nip was soon back to normal. Apart from that one attack, Aline seemed to be a lot better and the break had also helped. On the 28th July, Dave ran us up to Rotterdam and the Hook of Holland to catch our ferry back to Harwich.

It had been good to see the children again and they had been pleased with us being able to play with them but we had to get home. We travelled overnight and managed to get bunks again, which meant that we could get some rest on the way over. Before turning in, we had a walk on the top deck and Aline loved every minute with the wind blowing in her hair.

Having settled down back home again for a few weeks, it was on the10th August that we went on the Bridgewater Canal in Cheshire, along with the pensioners from TWIL. I had organised the outing many weeks beforehand and although the driver of the coach had a little trouble finding the boarding point, we finally made it and had a good day out on the huge barge.

It was just after this that Nip started to have frequent attacks, firstly on the 13th and then on the 20th, which occurred whilst we were out shopping. Two days later she had attacks on consecutive days but on the 28th, Aline was so ill that I sent for Dr. Shaikh to come and see her. On the 30th August, which was Bank Holiday Monday, I was so worried that I wanted to cancel my umpiring fixture at Ashover.

But knowing how much I liked going, Nip insisted that I go, so to get round it I contacted the secretary of the Ashover cricket team to explain. He said that one of their players had a mobile phone and if needs be, Aline could contact me through that, if she needed me. Fortunately, everything went well and she managed without having to use the facility that was offered and for which I have always been grateful.

Two days later I had been playing bowls at the Nether Edge Bowling Club but upon arriving home, Aline had been through another attack, so I sent for Dr. Shaikh again. He couldn't understand it but gave her some sort of sedative.

The following Monday, at 9.30 am, Nip had another attack so I sent for the Doctor again but this time a young Dr. Qaiyum turned up. He was the new junior doctor in the practise but he didn't hesitate and said he would arrange for Nip to see a specialist. I offered to pay to get an early appointment but the Doctor said that it wasn't necessary.

The following day the Specialist arrived at our house and he was a Dr. Austin from the Nether Edge Hospital who gave her a thorough examination and asked her many questions. She showed him a record she had kept in a little book of all the recent attacks. He was a gentle and kind man and said he would make arrangements for Nip to go to his clinic at Nether Edge.

It was the week prior to this that Andy Steel and his pals at the YHA had asked us if they could take Geoff's ashes up to Cold Fell on the top of the Pennine Way and finish off Geoff's ambition to do the whole walk. We agreed and Tony asked to go with them and when we mentioned it to David, he said he would get some leave and join in with them.

The 10th September was our wedding anniversary, Nip's birthday and also Tony's, so in a way it was very significant that the following day the group set off to a starting point to where Geoff had last been and from there they all finished the last forty miles of the Pennine Way for him.

Upon return at the weekend, Tony and Dave said how eerie it had been on top of the mountain where they dropped a rosary into the pointed cairn which acted as a trig point. J.B then sang 'Jerusalem' and the rest of the party all joined in. It was at this point that the lads said a lone Spitfire circled overhead as if the hand of God was in attendance. Andy confirmed this upon their return and he said it was unbelievable.

Whilst up there at the top, most of the men had worn a different hat which Geoff had accumulated over the years and Andy asked if he could keep the peaked sailor 's hat because he always associated it with a holiday he had with Geoff when they went on a boat and Geoff had worn the hat as though he was the skipper. Along with all this, one or two had gone in fancy dress because Geoff liked things like that. Dave wore a clown's outfit with a red wig and Tony put on some old plus fours and a deer stalker hat which Geoff had once used at a fancy dress party. The walk had been sponsored and at the final reckoning a total of £1,000 was collected and passed on the Motor Neurone Disease Foundation.

Back in March, at the AGM of the TWIL Retired persons Club, I had been unanimously voted in as chairman of the club and this had made extra duties for me besides doing the social secretary's work. It did enable me to contact direct, the hierarchy of TWIL and many were the times I had to go into work to liaise with the MD, Dil Scrivens, who always had time to discuss any problems concerning the pensioners.

I was down there on one occasion when, as I was talking to the girls in reception, the Chief Executive, David Young, came down the main staircase with a guest. He looked across at me and excused himself from the guest for a few minutes. "Hello, Ron. How are you?" He asked, in his Scottish drawl."Fine, thanks, David." I could address him as such because I could remember when he first joined TWIL as an accountant. We discussed a few points about the Club and he then returned to his guest. Although he was the Chief Executive, David always had time for the ordinary person and it was appreciated by all.

The receptionists couldn't understand why I was able to talk to David on level terms because to them he was the Big Boss.

Back to September and on the 26th, Aline had a really bad attack just as she was preparing to get out of bed. I was getting very concerned for her and on the 1st October I took her up to the Royal Hallamshire Hospital for a check up. We returned home and had to wait for the results to be sent to our local GP but on the 21st / 22nd of October, she had two more attacks.

Deep down, I think that Geoff's death was getting to her and in any case it didn't help matters with all her other worries. But going back to the 2nd July, we had been asked to go to the South Yorkshire Police Headquarters in Rotherham and ask for a PC Kettleborough, who, after introducing himself, took us to a little office and there we met the Coroner, Stanley Hooper. He offered his commiserations and by asking us many questions about Geoff he said he would have to postpone the inquest until further enquiries had been made. However, he said he had made out a temporary Death Certificate and issued it for Probate and Insurance purposes. On the 10th November we were asked to go to the Coroner's Court in Rotherham and there Mr. Hooper gave his summary and verdict of the accident.

PC Warrilow gave his account as to what had happened and Mr. Hooper said that cars parked on Norborough Road where they shouldn't have been, had contributed to the accident. The driver of the lorry which was involved in the accident, was also present and he gave his version but following the Coroner's summing up, we laid no blame on him and at the end I even shook his hand and told him we were sorry for him

The actual Coroner's report stated that the death was accidental and the medical cause, after the post mortem was; I (a) Multiple injuries. And II. Motor Neurone Degeneration. Apart from Aline and I, Tony had managed to get time off work and Andy Steel had asked us if he too, could attend. We left the Court Room and shed another tear or two but now it was all over and a very sad day we wouldn't forget.

It was on the 9th November that Dr. Austin had arranged for Nip to be admitted to the Hardwick Ward of the Nether Edge Hospital. Here he was able to do some more tests and keep a closer eye on her. Whilst there, Dr. Austin arranged for her to go down by ambulance to the Hallamshire to have a brain scan and an ECG. I was allowed to go with her for company and there was also a young student nurse to accompany us as well.

We returned to Nether Edge after the scan etc., and I returned home but a few days later Nip was allowed home and I was glad to have her back with me but on the 30th Nov., she was asked to visit Dr. Austin's clinic at Nether Edge. Dr. Austin said he had received some reports from the Hallamshire but said he would like her to go for another brain scan. The Doctor did admit that he thought that there were signs of Epilepsy but wanted to have another check. So the following day I took her in our car back to the Hallamshire and went and sat with her as she was put into the CT (Computed Tomography) scanner and this lasted about twenty minutes whilst the monitors were checked by the nursing staff in the next room. We then returned home.

Each year the Retired Person's Club held their own little Christmas Party at the Club house on Ferrars Road at Tinsley but this was mainly for the group of people who regularly attended the monthly meeting and this year the party was to be on Monday, the 9th December. There was a nucleus of about sixty persons and most of the catering was supplied by a committee member, Marjorie French, for which she was reimbursed out of the club funds. Also, through my cheek, I had persuaded David Baker to let us have enough chicken drumsticks to go round and when I offered to pay, he said to forget it. In my capacity as Social Secretary, I also made the effort to obtain the usual Christmas trimmings such as fancy hats and Christmas crackers. There was no entertainment but we did have our usual raffle and games of bingo. All raffle prizes were generously donated by the members of the Club and it was unbelievable how many prizes were brought to make the evening an enjoyable one.

For a couple of weeks things seemed to settle down and on the 16th December, TWIL were giving their Annual Christmas Dinner at the Grosvenor Hotel in town. Car parking near to the Grosvenor had alway been difficult but due to past experience as a musician, I knew that there was a way into the Hotel's personal park and this is what I achieved and access to the dining room was made much easier. Members could take their spouses or a friend and Aline said she was looking forward to going because Roy and Mary Fisher were also going and the night was important to me because it was to be my maiden speech and response as Chairman, to the MD's Annual Report.

Now being the Chairman of the Pensioners' Club, I was entitled to choose my own table of friends and members, so Roy and Mary sat at my table along with another four close acquaintances. My table was next to the MD's table which was handy for passing any comments. All the tables were large round ones and seated eight people.

We were enjoying the meal and chattering amongst ourselves when I noticed that Aline, who was on my left, started to have one of her turns and she flopped towards me. Harry Foster, a committee member, came over to help and someone handed her a drink of water. Harry was fussing but I told him that it was possibly the heat of the room and the atmosphere with over three hundred people present. No one, not even Mary and Roy, knew about these spasms that Nip kept having.

Five minutes later Nip was alright again and everything returned to normal. One good thing about the Xmas Dinner, even though there were paper hats and Christmas crackers and everything was free, the party was always over by 9.30 pm because of the older people having to make their way home.

There were times when the MD couldn't make it for business reasons and this was one of those occasions, so he deputised a new Director, Stephen Morris, to give the 'State of the Party' speech, as we called it and after the speech I was introduced by David Baker who was the MC and our own Catering Manager.

I rose to me feet and thanked Mr. Morris for the report but I couldn't help but make a quip by saying," We're sorry Mr. Scrivens couldn't be here tonight but with it nearly being Christmas, I see he's sent Stephen, (St. Stephen.) It took a while for the joke to sink in but eventually the 'penny dropped' and people applauded. My response was also well received and I was congratulated afterwards by Terry Murphy, our retired Personnel Manager, who was also a past Chairman of the club.

This had been a very sad and distressing year, where, at the beginning, I thought that it was going to be a happy one, especially for our Geoff. It was in January that, having put his heart and soul into Fellowship and doing an excellent job as Mess Editor, he had been made Chairman of 232 Temple Mess. It was an honour that every Companion looked forward to and he was so pleased to know that he had achieved the same status as me but at an earlier age. He was one of the youngest Chairmen in Fellowship at the age of forty years. It was shortly after his death that the Area Chairman, Stan Batters, visited our Mess at the Fox and Duck Hotel at Templeborough and it was on this night that he announced that Geoff had been posthumously awarded his 'Passed Chairman's Badge'. Stan asked me to accept this accolade on Geoff's behalf but in doing so, I was too full of emotion and so very proud to accept it. At a later date I was going to have the Pin made into a brooch for Aline but circumstances made this a non-starter. Christmas was very quiet, particularly this year because our thoughts kept returning to the sad loss of a wonderful son.

As we entered 1994, I was still busy trying to help with Aline's illness and still taking her to the hospital for tests and besides that, it was a problem having to keep visiting Geoff's house on Norborough Road, just to make sure that the property was alright and vandals had not broken into the house. There were occasions when Aline would go with me, just for the run out.

Geoff had earlier put the house up for sale but had received no enquiries from the estate agent Reeds Rains, so I cancelled the contract with them and put a personal sale sign in his front room window. Around that area there were many Pakistanis but in a minority to the older residents who had lived there for many years. One or two ethnics, including the local shopkeeper across the road and the next door neighbour, Mr. Aziz, had asked the price I wanted. At the time, the market price was in the range of £27,000 but as was the case with these people, they wanted everything for nothing.

In the middle of January, a Mr. Nazir asked me to go and see him about the house, he lived not far away, at the end of St. Lawrence Road, where he had a shop. To act as a witness, I asked Tony to go with me and in the discussion, Mr. Nazir and his son offered £24,000 in cash. I was so pleased, I agreed but said that I would have to consult Mr. Wragg, our solicitor.

On telling Mr. Wragg, he said that although it was a generous offer, it would have to go through the normal legal channels and Mr. Nazir gave him a solicitor's address in Dinnington. It took ages to contact the chap and doubt was thrown into the case as to whether the solicitor was bona fide. Things dragged on for such a long time that the deal fell through. It was a chance well missed.

In the process of clearing out number 66, I found in a drawer, many pieces of paper, envelopes and jotting pads with some ditties and poems which I worked out that Geoff must have scribbled them, mainly about his happenings when out hiking or cycling.

Some were very funny and others on the serious side of life, with the odd ode thrown in. Aline read them and we agreed it would be a good idea to tidy them up, type them and make them into a small book. It took me quite a while to finish them and I had twenty copies made before finally putting the pages into some small binders I had left over from another of my projects. Upon finishing them, I gave copies to his best friends Andy, Tom and JB as well as letting some members of the family have a copy. I finished off by letting Miss Meredith have a copy. She used to be the Headmistress of our lads at Junior School and always said that Geoff was the brainiest of them.

Whilst all this was going on, I was having to go regularly for treatment to the Charles Clifford Dental Hospital. I had been going for about five years on and off and it all started when I went to their casualty department with a broken tooth. That department booked me into the Conservation Department and it was there that I was having a good clean up and general repair of my teeth.

On Monday the 24th, I had to take Aline to the Hallamshire Hospital again for a further check up and they referred her to the Nether Edge Hospital and booked her in on the Tuesday, the first of February. On the following Tuesday I took her back there to get the results of some tests and Mr. Austin confirmed that the bouts she was having, hadn't anything to do with Epilepsy. At the time it was good news but Mr. Austin did refer her back to the Hallamshire Hospital.

The next day, the 9th Feb., I was chasing about a bit because I had a dental appointment at 11.00 am and after returning home for lunch I went down to a printing firm in Attercliffe to collect a book which they had been preparing for me. This book, called 'Over There.' had taken me over two years to write and it was all about my service life in the Far East with the Royal Air Force. The compiler had put many photographs and snapshots into the book and it really looked professional. It ought to have because it cost me £600 for thirty copies. I did try to get it published but the general comment was, 'It's of limited interest.' It should be something for my grandchildren to read in the future.

Dave had rung immediately upon his return to Germany from two weeks in Las Vegas with the RAF, to ask about his Mum. It was the week after this last call, that Nip had to go into hospital with a touch of Jaundice and was kept in overnight but released in the afternoon on the Sunday. By 7.00 pm she was back in again and on the Monday she had a liver scan. They kept her in hospital and unfortunately because of this, she missed the presentation at Thornbury Hall Annexe on the 22 nd, of a cheque for £1,023 which had been donated by the sponsored walkers which included Tony, Dave and the YHA pals of Geoff and had taken place last September. Photo's were taken of the presentation by me to Mr. Bill O'Connell, followed by a press release about Geoff's effort to walk the Pennine Way. Aline was thrilled and overjoyed when I took the photographs for her to see.

The next day we had a blizzard and it made it difficult to get to the hospital but on the Thursday I went by bus to see her. As usual she was cheerful in herself and on the following Monday, the doctors allowed her to come home.

During the weekend, Dave had rung as usual but this time to tell us that he had to go on detachment for three months to Dahran in the United Arab Emirates to do his bit in the Gulf War. Nip was upset about it but as I explained, Dave was operating on Tornado aircraft which was well behind enemy lines. It seemed a coincidence when on Monday 28th Feb., Nip was able to come home and this was the same day that Dave had left for the Middle East.

The car I had been driving since the end of August 1989 was a Fiat Panda and had served me well but Aline wasn't happy with it and always said that it was a box on wheels. It was due to this dislike that she said she would never drive it and she didn't. At the beginning of March 1994, I decided to let Tony have it for £700 and when I handed it over to him it was in really good nick with only just under 40,000 miles on the clock and I had made sure that it was regularly serviced.

I was able to let Tony have the Fiat because I had seen a car advertised in the local press by a chap on the Coalbrook Estate just down the road from us. I asked Brian Gleadle to go with me to check it out because he was always working on cars and knew what to look for. We had a short run in it and Brian said that it was in good condition. The car was a Nissan Micra, Special Edition and a beige colour; the engine was 998 cc and the mileage was 38,500 on the clock. The owner, a young chap, was wanting to get married and needed the money. He asked for £2,700 but when offered £2,500 he accepted. It was a bargain and the registration number was F911GKW which I said I could always remember because I called it '**G**eoff's **K**ilometre **W**alk'.

Aline seemed to be a lot better and was able to go with me down to the Monday Club and on one or two shopping trips. It was at the Monday Club when we broke the news to the members about Geoff, that one of the members, Jack Green said, "I didn't know it was your lad, Ron, who was killed near me." Having confirmed his belief he told me that the morning prior to his death, Geoff had called down at Jack's home to see if his wife wanted any shopping doing. That was Geoff, willing to help anyone and he knew Jack and his wife because Jack's brother Ernest was a companion of 232 Mess to which we both belonged.

Aline had one or two small spasms and unbeknown to me, she had been keeping a record of any bouts she had experienced during the night. She kept all this to herself and I hadn't witnessed anything because, as I said earlier, two years ago I moved into the back bedroom to help both of us get some rest.

During March we learned that her brother, Eric, had gone into hospital in Blackpool with some stomach problems and this uneased her because as children, they had been very close. At

Geoff's funeral, Eric seemed quite fit and was looking forward to going on holiday. It was a set back for Aline when Nan, Eric's wife, had rung to say that he had passed away on the 5th April. Whilst he had been in hospital, it appears that two buttons were available to Eric, one to call the nurse for help and the other for him to press to receive a shot of Morphine to ease his pain. It was assumed that he had pressed the wrong button and accidentally overdosed himself with the Morphine. It certainly didn't help Aline to fight her cause and she was so full of grief.

On the 12th April we went to the funeral and Aline and I were able to get into Terrance's car to save taking mine. What with our Geoff going and now Eric, Aline became as bad as ever. She even stopped knitting and that was a big part of her life.

Things settled down again for a short while and on the 27th April she was able to go with me on one of my organised trips to Skipton and Ilkley.

I had arranged for a boat trip at Skipton and upon return to the moorings, the whole party went into Bizzie Lizzies Chip Restaurant for a meal which I had booked earlier in the year. Just around the corner, to finish the day, we set off for home via Ilkley where we stopped for about half an hour to let people have a look round. We hadn't the time to go on the famous Moors B'aht hat.

The following Monday Aline and I had a run up to Bridlington for a couple of days to stay with Joan and Freda who were staying in a caravan at Primrose Valley. On the Tuesday I said that I would run them down to the market town of Malton and do some shopping, if necessary. It was whilst walking round the big clothing stores of Boyes there, that I was taken short but luckily I had just bought some new underpants which I needed so I went into the nearest pub and whilst they were ordering a meal I went into the toilet to clean myself. I know it wasn't nice but I left my dirty pants in the toilet. I wasn't going to carry them around with me for the rest of the day. The three lasses couldn't stop laughing. Just after returning home Dave gave us a call to say that he had returned from the Gulf and this cheered up Aline tremendously.

On Wednesday, the 1st June, Nip was admitted to Ward L2 in the Hallamshire to have another brain scan where, unfortunately, we were informed that a tumour was slowly getting bigger. I went and saw Dr. Hasan, our GP, to keep him in touch with what was happening and he was so full of sympathy.

Whilst visiting her on the following Monday afternoon, we were introduced to Dr. Raban Krishnan who couldn't help but smile when Aline said that she knew his brother Harry. 'Harry' Krishnan was a world famous Indian Guru. This was Aline all the time, looking on the bright side but Dr. Krishnan couldn't understand why she wasn't in pain. Just before he left us I managed to get him to one side to ask him the truth but I wasn't prepared for the answer he gave. His reply was, "I'm sorry Mr. Priestley, the cancer is terminal and I would say that your wife has three to six months left."

I was deeply upset and under stress, I managed to go back to Aline and put a brave face on the situation and no way was I going to let her know. When I arrived home, I just sobbed and sobbed. But eventually I was willing to accept the outcome but the next hardest thing was to let Tony and Dave know.

Tony was at home and as I told him I could imagine his emotions and he asked if I needed any help, to which I replied, "Not at the moment." I contacted David straight away after speaking to Tony and told him the bad news and he and Heather must have had a discussion about things because he arrived home unexpectedly on the 12th, which was a Sunday, just as Tony was helping me to get Nip up the back steps of the house. I had brought Nip home for the weekend. It cheered up Aline when she saw Dave.

Upon return to the Hallamshire, Aline was transferred up the road to Weston Park Hospital and put into Ward 2 and it was then that my worst fears were known. Dave went with me and

Aline said that she was to have 20 shots of Radiotherapy. This was the decision of Dr. Kishnan who told me earlier that Nip, at the age of 67, was too old to go through any operation.

When Aline was told about the treatment, her comment was, "If Roy Castle can take it, then so can I." Roy Castle was a top class all round entertainer who had developed cancer because of passive smoking which he had encountered during his long career. He had never smoked.

Dave returned back to Germany at 2.30 pm on the Thursday to tell Heather and the kids how ill their grandmother was. He had been a comfort to both of us and had visited his Mum every day since he had been over. It had been a thankless job ringing round the family but Joan helped a lot by passing the message on.

I had a nice surprise on the Friday because I arrived at the hospital to see Nip and the Ward Sister told me that I could take Aline home for the weekend for respite but must return with her on Sunday afternoon. It was lovely to have Nip at home and I enjoyed getting her meals for her and being able to sit in comfort to talk to her. Having her at home also helped the hospital staff to take a break from the wonderful work which they were doing.

A wheel chair had been ordered from the Social Services but for the time being we used one from the hospital. Although Aline looked well in herself, she was too ill to climb the stairs so I made up a bed on the large settee which we had. There was a little hand bell on the whatnot so we agreed that if she needed anything in the night, she would ring it. I could just hear it because the back bedroom, where I slept, was directly above the living room.

Just after tea on Sunday, I managed to get her back into the car to return to the hospital. I stayed with her for a while but she insisted that I go home and get some rest. It's amazing how visiting a hospital daily, sometimes twice a day, can put such a strain on a being but I didn't mind because this was my lass. I had only been home for a little time when Dave rang to see how things were and couldn't believe it when I told him that his Mum had been at home for the weekend.

On the Monday, an appointment had been booked for me to see the hospital social worker, Miss Chris Milnes, who put me into the picture about any help which I may require and it was through her that I was able to temporarily obtain a wheel chair to use when fetching Aline out for the weekend. That wasn't available until Friday the 1st July.

Tony came to see his Mum regularly and once he brought Lisa with him. That's something I regret with Lisa because Aline told her that not finding time to visit us at our home, even occasionally, had cost Lisa an eighteenth birthday present. Nip was going to give Lisa her own moped. Lisa took it the wrong way and the discussion became heated. I had just walked back into the ward and heard the tail end of it all. I can never forgive our Lisa for upsetting Nip, especially under the circumstances. Whilst in Ward 2 and when I was visiting her during the week, it befell upon me to take her to the toilet. This was to ease the work of the nurses and having watched how they lifted patients into wheel chairs, I copied their method by pushing the chair up to the easy chair in which Aline was sitting. I put the brake on and then went to lift her. The method was to put one of my legs in between hers, get her to loop her hands at the back of my neck and then I would put my arms around her waist, take the weight on the leg between hers and slowly lift her into an upright position. As I eased her round to sit in the wheel chair once, I said, "Do you want to waltz or do a quickstep?" The other patients laughed as she called me a silly fool but at least it raised a smile.

Because Aline still liked a smoke and the staff didn't mind, I would take her in the wheel chair, either up to the top floor, where there was an area on the flat roof on which one could relax or I would take her down to the ground floor and through into some quiet gardens. There she enjoyed her cigarette but there was one instant when it had just started to rain and as I was saying that it wasn't fit to go out, a hospital porter said he would lend us an umbrella. People must have thought we were daft as I sat next to her in the pouring rain, holding an umbrella over the both of us. I couldn't care less, that lass was enjoying her smoke.

One afternoon when I was visiting her, a porter came into the ward to take her down for treatment. He was on the small side and seemed to be having difficulty in lifting Aline into the wheel chair. She looked at him and said, "Let Ron lift me. I trust him." The chap didn't know what to say but this I did and commented to him.

"If you put one leg in between hers, it is easier to make the lift."

"I'm sorry, Sir." He said. "But I daren't do that in case there was some misunderstanding." I couldn't believe it at first but apparently it was a rule of the hospital.

From the first day that Aline went into Ward 2, she became friendly with a young woman whose bed was in the far corner opposite and it helped both of them. The young lady was from Hoyland Common which was on the Sheffield side of Barnsley. Aline explained to me on the quiet, that she was called Catherine Jaques and was having Chemotherapy because this was her second time in Weston Park and she was full of Cancer and at the time in terrible pain.

Unfortunately, her husband had difficulty in visiting regularly so if Aline had more than one visitor to see her, I would go over to Catherine to keep her company. She was a wonderful and cheery person considering her condition but I'm sure it helped Aline along and between them they kept the Ward alive.

On July the 1st, I had been able to obtain a new wheel chair from a centre near to Bramall Lane football ground and this was a relief being a new one because it saved me from having to pump up the tyres on the one I had borrowed from the hospital. With a bit of practise, I was able to fold the new one up so that I could get it into the boot of the car.

Next door to us lived a staff nurse from the Children's Hospital and her name was Karen and one weekend she saw me arrive home with Aline. She climbed over the small fence on the front and said she would help me to get Aline from the car into the house. **Help!** She hadn't a clue and we put this down to the fact that she was only used to handling children all day. We were grateful and eventually we succeeded in lifting Nip up the three steps at the front door and into the house.

At an earlier meeting I had with Janet Howard, the Social Worker at the Hospital, it was agreed that she would contact out local GP and get him to arrange for the District Nurse to pop in and keep an eye on Aline when she was at home for the weekend. This was done and one day, when Nip was at home, I answered the front door bell and a young man was standing there. "Mr. Priestley?" he enquired. "I'm the District Nurse and have come to see Mrs. Priestley. My name is John Webber." He was a smashing chap, very efficient and he took some notes about Aline's condition and told us that if ever we needed him urgently, we had to contact him and he would come right away.

Because of her condition and having put on weight, Nip started having sweat rashes under her bust and it was getting sore.

"Don't worry." I said, "There's some Zinc and Castor Oil cream up the stairs." So I went to fetch it. Bringing it down to her I told her to lift up her blouse and I would help her to put some on the sore parts. I'm glad that I thought of it because the soreness went and the nurse at the hospital said that I had done the right thing.

We had some light moments as when one night, whilst trying to settle her down on the settee, she asked to use the commode, which had been supplied by Social Services. As usual, I picked her up and shuffled her round until she was able to sit on the commode. That was alright until I tried to lift her off because, unfortunately, her bottom stuck to the small receptacle and as

I lifted her onto her feet, the pot came up as well and spilled all down her legs and onto the carpet. Nip was upset about it but I told her to forget it and we both finished up having a good laugh. "Remind me in future to put some talcum powder on the rim." I said.

On Wednesday, the 29th June, Dave had made contact with a private individual who was to buy the new Mitsubishi Spacewagon which Dave had brought over earlier and had parked it on my driveway, so whilst Brain Gleadle drove it to a rendezvous in West Yorkshire, I followed in my car, completed the deal for Dave who was still in Germany and then returned home with Brian in my car. Because Brian had helped him out, our Dave gave him £20 for his kindness.

Because he had seen his Mum in the state she was in, Dave had taken extra leave for a week to be with us. I'm glad he had because on Saturday, the 9th of July, Nip took a turn for the worse and not being too happy, I contacted John Webber, the District Nurse. He arrived within the half hour and tried to comfort Aline but the poor chap seemed at a loss as to what to do so he called for the duty locum doctor.

Within the hour the locum, who was a female doctor, checked one or two things with Aline and she was in the middle of her examination when Nip went into a convulsion. The poor lass couldn't hold a limb still and the doctor said that it was an Epileptic fit.

On odd occasions I have seen such fits but not one like this because it got worse and lasted quite a while. We, our Dave, John and myself managed to lift Aline from the easy chair onto her side onto the settee. Here, the locum was able to insert a special type of suppository and eventually Aline quietened down. The fit had lasted an hour and at the end of it the doctor said that Aline ought to go back into hospital so rang for an ambulance and expressed the urgency of it.

It was terrible to see Nip in this state and I felt so sorry for our Dave to witness his Mum in that position. The ambulance came and I told the driver she was under the Weston Park Hospital, so he set off for there and Dave and I followed in my car arriving at the hospital at 5.30.pm. We had thanked John and the doctor for all they had done and John said he would call again to see how things had progressed.

Because Dave had witnessed the state of his Mum, he had rung Heather, told her of the circumstances and had contacted RAF records in Gloucester and applied for extended compassionate leave and this had been granted. All this had been done after we had returned from the hospital, where we had seen Nip put into a special side ward to receive urgent treatment. We couldn't do anything to help but after seeing her settled, we returned home and contacted Tony to put him in the picture and inform the rest of the family.

Just before we left the hospital, Catherine, in Ward 2, caught David's eye as we passed by and she called us in to ask why we had brought Aline back into hospital. We didn't go into every detail but when we told her of the epileptic fit, she was very upset.

From there on I had a very busy week because apart from going up and down to see Aline everyday, I was contacting the Northern General Hospital about a special cushion for her when she came home again. I also had to get in touch with the limb centre about a wheel chair and Dave was very helpful and supporting at all times.

Because of the present situation, Tony managed to come up to the hospital so Aline had all three of us there at one time. It was on one of those visits that we had to chuckle at Aline because a nurse came in to give her some tablets and addressed her by saying, "Come along, Alice, it's medicine time." Aline was propped up on pillows at the time, looked straight at the nurse and replied in a very strong tone. "My name is Aline -. **A - L - I - N - E."** The nurse also had to smile.

It was a traumatic week and I could see the determination in Nip as I visited her each afternoon and as I reached over to kiss her, I told her how much I loved her but it was hard not to show my emotions in front of her. I knew things weren't right.

The weekend she was at home prior to going back in to hospital, she was sitting in her chair when she looked at me and asked, "Will you say the Lord's Prayer with me?" I replied, "Of course, Love. You start it."

"The Lord is my shepherd, I shall not want --." She said. I interrupted her and told her that what she was saying was the 23rd Psalm."Oh! Alright, we'll do that then." So we went right through the Psalm, oh! It was so difficult to hold back my tears but I did so because I didn't want to upset her.

The Lord is my shepherd; I shall not want
He maketh me to lie down in green pastures;
he leadeth me beside the still waters.
He restoreth my soul; he leadeth me in the
paths of righteousness for his name's sake,
Yea, though I walk through the valley
of the shadow of death, I will fear no evil;
for thou art with me; thy rod and thy staff
they comfort me.
Thou preparest a table before me
in the presence of mine enemies;
Thou annointest my head with oil; my cup runneth over.
Surely goodness and mercy shall follow me
all the days of my life:
and I will dwell in the house of the Lord forever.

After Aline went back into hospital, I decided to record the 23rd Psalm on a small tape I had on one of the Sony Walkmans'. I spoke into it very slowly so that it would be clear when I took it up to the hospital for her to listen to.

Late on Monday afternoon I received a phone call from the Staff Nurse at the hospital, saying that it might be a good idea to go up because Aline had taken a turn for the worse.

I told Dave the news and then I rang Tony to tell him, so Dave and I went straight up and Tony followed a little later. As we walked into the small ward, we could see the difference from the day before. How poorly that lass looked and she couldn't recognise us or speak to us. She seemed all bloated up and was laying partly on one side with her head drooped. After a while, Dave went out with Tony, who wanted a smoke and I remained on my own with her.

To try to help her die in peace, because that was what was happening, I had taken the small tape recording and held it to her ear so that she could listen to her favourite psalm. Slowly and surely she was sinking, so I called Tony and Dave back to her bedside. It was such a sad sight to see our loved one gradually leaving us.

A short while after I looked at the poor lass and said to the lads, "That's it. She's gone quietly." We all put our arms around each other as we broke down. We left the ward and called the male nurse, who said that he would call the duty doctor. An Indian lady came and pronounced Aline as dead at 9.15pm on Monday the 18th July, 1994.

The staff took us into an ante room and provided us with a cup of tea whilst the doctor went to make out the death certificate. As the nurses tried to comfort us, it slowly turned into a funny session and the lads had them in stitches. The Sister commented that in all her experiences she had never seen anything like this at the death of a wife and mother. Between us, we explained that Aline would have been the first to join in because that was the kind of person she was. Half an hour later the Doctor brought in the death certificate.

The certificate stated that the cause of death was:-
1a Glioma (Dessimated) and the document was signed by (could be decimated)
A. Anand BA.
The interpretation of Glioma was Brain Tumour.

The Doctor then told us that Aline had been laid out and made presentable and if we wanted to see her, one of the nurses would take us to where they had put her. We went with the nurse but not to the side ward because Aline had been taken downstairs into a Chapel of Rest.

She looked so peaceful as she lay there and for the last time I kissed her forehead and said, "God bless you, Nip." Our sons paid their respects and we returned home having thanked all the staff for all that they had done.

All day Tuesday I was busy making arrangements for the funeral with Keeton's and Sons and also contacting Hilary Hotchin, the Curate. Aline had made only one last request and that was that her wedding ring was to remain on her finger. Having pointed out to Mr. Keeton, I decided to have Aline's body cremated at Rotherham, so that she would be near to her Mum and Dad and also Geoff who were all cremated there. Some officialdom had to be sorted out because Aline had lived outside the Diocese but I think this was overcome when it was pointed out that she was actually born and married in the Diocese of Rotherham. Hilary Hotchin had once again been required to get permission to do the service in the Crematorium Chapel.

Wednesday, I was also busy sorting out financial problems and getting the necessary copies of the death certificates to send to the people involved, such as the National Savings Bank and Insurance Companies. In the afternoon, I had gone upstairs to make my bed when I had a terrific pain in my stomach and for a while I tried to get rid of it by doing some exercises. However, the pain was so acute that I shouted for Dave at the top of my voice, he was downstairs.

He rushed up and could see that I was in agony as I rolled about on the bed. I asked him to call the doctor but because it was out of surgery hours, a Pakistan doctor arrived who was on call. After he had examined me, his diagnosis was that he thought it could be a kidney stone and after injecting me with a painkiller drug, he said he would call an ambulance. He also gave me some tablets to take to help ease the pain and by 7.30 pm I was in 'K' Ward at the Hallamshire under a Mr. Moore. By the way, part of the injection which the doctor had given me, had spilled from the phial onto the set of drawers and stained them. I wasn't too happy about that when I later found out.

Dave followed the ambulance to the hospital to see me settled and then returned home to tell Tony. The following day Mr. Moore examined me and said he would send me for some tests and X-rays. I told him about Aline and said that in no way was I missing the funeral. Even if it meant fastening the bed to the hearse.

They say that God works in mysterious ways and I became more convinced of that when after all the tests etc., late on Friday, I felt tremendous relief. When the doctor came on his early rounds on Saturday morning, I told him that I had no pain and felt fine. "You're not saying that because you want to go home, are you?" He asked . "No." I replied, "I'm dead serious."

"Right." Said the doctor, "If that's how you feel, you may go home at lunch time but I'll see you in a month's time." I rang Dave and he came up to collect me and I told him that the doctor said the kidney stone must have flushed its way out of its own accord. Was I relieved?

On the Monday, Hilary called in to finalise the arrangements for the funeral service and cremation and also to get some background to Aline's life in general. She showed the same sympathy as she had at Geoff's passing and was such a wonderful and understanding person.

The following day, Tuesday, 26th July 1994, most of the relations turned up at No.8 and that included, Heather and the children. After Nip had died, Dave had telephoned Heather and between them they had arranged for her brother-in-law (also in the RAF at the same camp) to bring them over in Dave's vehicle and take them to Worcester to Heb's Mum's house and then Dennis, her Dad, would bring them all up in his car. This he did but didn't stay long and returned to his home that same evening. Heb's brother-in-law was coming over to England in any case so it also did him a favour.

The main funeral service was held at St. Mary's Church at Handsworth at 11.00 am and Hilary, in her address, spoke highly of how Aline had been such a good and jolly wife besides being a much loved mother and grandmother. The hymn I chose for the congregation to sing was obviously Nip's favourite, The 23rd Psalm but I was too choked up to get the words out.

The grandchildren were all there, Mathew, Lisa (Tony's children) and Dawn, Craig and James (Dave's children). Comment was made later on how well behaved Dave and Heather's little ones had been during the service. It must have seemed strange to them with them being so young.

As we were leaving the church to go for the cremation, many friends and workmates from TWIL Pensioners Club were there but the one surprise was when I turned to look out of the back window of our funeral car and saw Dil Scrivens nodding to me. I couldn't believe that the Managing Director would come to the funeral of someone who hadn't worked for him. However, a few days later, I went down to Tinsley Wire to thank him and his reason for being there was, he said, "Because your wife has given you so much assistance whilst you was the Chairman and Social Secretary of the Pensioners' Club." I appreciated that very much. Thank you Dil.

Not many mourners went down to Rotherham for the cremation but there was all the family and one surprise was to see Elaine there. She was Tony's ex-wife and mother of Mathew and Lisa. The committal service was short and as the curtains closed around the coffin, I bid farewell to Aline, perhaps in body but never in spirit.

The following day, just before lunch, Dave and his family left for Worcester in his Mercedes car, which he had over here, to go to see Heather's Mum and Dad and collect their mini bus for Heather to drive back to Germany by following Dave in his car.

I popped over to Joan's for an hour in the afternoon, but upon my return I felt so lonely - but I had to cope with the distress and a prayer helped.

On Saturday the 30th July, I had a cricket match booked to umpire at Sheepbridge, which was near to Chesterfield, but I didn't really feel like going to it. However, Tony said that the outing would be a change from all the worries I had gone through. To give me some support, he said that he would go with me just in case I needed any help and this is what I did.

The following Monday I was busy again chasing round to get various financial items sorted out such as altering any joint accounts that Aline and I had held. On Tuesday I went to town to put an acknowledgement in The Star newspaper for all those who had been at the funeral and had donated gifts to the Ward 2 of the Hospital Fund.

It helped me tremendously to carry on playing bowls on Wednesdays and umpire at cricket on Saturdays. In the middle if August I had found a beautiful photograph of Aline which Roy Fisher had once taken of her on one of my organised TWIL outings. I took it to Boot's, the chemist and had several copies taken off to give to Tony, Dave and the rest of the close family and friends. My copy I put into a frame to put on the mantlepiece at the opposite end to where I had one for Geoff. It was nice to see them both each day as I entered the living room and to wish them, "Good morning." To me they were still there.

Mr, Keeton called one day to say that he had received several donations from certain people and did I wish to pass them on. In total there were cheques to the value of £163 which I took up to the Ward 2 Sister for their fund. Mr.Keeton also brought me a container, in which were Aline's ashes from the crematorium. She had requested that if anything happened to her she wanted them scattering at Brookhouse Village, the place where she was born.

Another regular chore was to keep in touch with Mr. Wragg, the solicitor, about the sale of Geoff's house and the settling of his estate. This was a long and drawn out process but progress was being made.

On the 12th September I had an appointment with Mr. Moore at the Hallamshire again and this was a good visit because he said that my kidney stone, having cleared itself, allowed me to be completely discharged and he didn't want to see me again unless of course I had further trouble with it, in which case I was to contact him straight away.

Tony had been pestering me to take a holiday with him and Mathew for quite a while and eventually he persuaded me that the holiday would do me some good. So, on Saturday the 24th of September, we flew from Manchester Airport to arrive in the early hours of the following morning at Malta. The holiday hadn't been booked through one of the recognised agencies and as we were shown to our rooms I could see the difference. They were clean and en suite but that's about all. Tony had a little room to himself along the corridor whilst Mat and I shared the larger room.

Having been there before, Tony was able to take us to places of interest and to see some beautiful churches. In one place we went to, there were some famous catacombs where one of the Saints had hidden from the Romans. We had a day out in Valletta, the capitol of Malta, which was the target of many German and Italian air raids during World War II. Another day we took a ferry to the small island of Gozo. It was only a short journey but was very pleasant and enjoyable. There wasn't any beach near to the hotel but we were able to go for a swim in the small inlet nearby but it wasn't ideal. I enjoyed one day out when we went in small motorised boats to a place called the Blue Grotto and here we were able to go into some small caves where the water was very clear and had a blue tint, hence the name Blue grotto.

Most nights were spent down in the bar of the hotel but it wasn't my scene or Mathews' and very often he and I would go to our rooms to get away from the noise. There were odd nights when I would take him across the road to a billiard hall which was owned and run by Tony Drago, the international snooker player. Over all it had been a break and Tony had said at the start, "You either love Malta or you hate it." My reaction was, even though Tony had tried his best for me, I wouldn't go there again.

Sunday the 30th October, I went up to St. Mary's Church where Hilary Hotchin was holding a Memorial Service for bereaved people who had lost a loved one during the year. It was amazing to see so many people there with whom I had been in contact over the years but not enough to know of their problems.

Speaking of bereavements, up at Weston Park Hospital, there was a group called 'Footprints' and this was organised by two Social Workers and a retired Sister from the hospital who had recently lost her husband. This was a get together where people could express their feelings. Each month we would meet at the hospital to have refreshments and a natter. There was only a dozen or so of us and it eased the minds of others by talking but some were reluctant to come out of their shells and express their feelings.

At one of the meetings, when I was asked if there was some comfort I could do with, I said that it would be nice to put my arms around someone and get a big hug for comfort. There was a tall chap there from Barnsley who had lost his wife and he was a lecturer at the college there. He looked at me and said. "You're not putting your arms around me." This of course brought some laughter and relief and that's how we tried to help each other.

Having decided to make an effort to sell Geoff's house, I thought that one way of disposing of some of his household goods was to take the small items to a car boot sale. I went several times to one at Kiveton which was held on the library car park and though not a great success, I managed to sell a few things and received around £40 which I put on one side towards his estate. He had a lovely cupboard which I managed to sell by advertising, also an oil filled electric radiator. His settee was collected by Joan's son, Russell, so eventually I cleared most of the house and waited for a buyer to take the building off my hands. I didn't sell everything in the house and I realised that some of it was going to be of use to me.

Not long after our Dave obtained that carpet for Geoff, he had also managed to get hold a set of chairs and an office desk which helped to fill up Geoff's house but after his death I swapped the chairs for some of my old ones and also moved the desk to my house to use as an office accessory in the little bed room.

In between all this I was still playing billiards on most Tuesdays in the Sheffield League and this gave me some extra relaxation - I won some and I lost some but I enjoyed the night out.

I was also still very involved with the Monday Club at TWIL and on Monday the 21st November, I had arranged for a pea and pie supper and the entertainment would be provided by the Eskafeld Brass Band. The booking of the band had been brought about because Companion Alvin Ibbotson, in 232 Mess, was the bass player in the band. I arranged with him that if they played for us, we would donate £50 to the band funds and this was agreed. The night went well and everyone enjoyed the program and the members of the band also enjoyed their pie and peas.

The first week in December, Dave came over from Germany, I think mainly to persuade me to spend Christmas with them because Tony had taken me to Malta for a break and thought that he would do his bit to keep his eye on me. So I agreed and he told me that there was a 'service' bus which left Liverpool and passengers were picked up on the way through to Germany and it passed through Sheffield. He did all the necessary booking for me and I was to catch the Trans-line coach in Brown Street in Sheffield.

Prior to this, I was able to go to the Christmas Dinner again at the Grosvenor Hotel with the Tinsley Pensioners. It seemed strange to be without Aline but I had enough courage to get up to my feet and address the 300 people there in my capacity as Chairman. It was also nice to see some old faces again who weren't able to get down to the Monday club.

I left for Germany on the 22nd Dec., and the journey took some 14 hours of travel but I did get a break when we went on the ferry at Dover and the one good thing was that the coach stop which I needed was outside the NAAFI at Wildenrath where Dave was there to meet me in the early hours of the morning.

With it being early in the day when I arrived, Heather and the kids hadn't got out of bed but when the children finally came down stairs they were all over me. The look on their faces was well worth the trip and from then on I enjoyed being with them. I think it was Craig who asked if Grandma had gone up in the sky. He was so thoughtful.

Being the shut down at the RAF camp, there was plenty to do and one night Dave took me over to another house across the back and introduced me to 'Biggles'. This was a 'nickname' given to corporal who had made some beautiful model aircraft. In his cellar he had done a conversion and turned it into a proper bar where he could entertain his friends and at this time, some of his relations, who were over for Christmas.

Dave took us out on two or three occasions including a run up to Rheindalen, the big forces base with the shopping centre. There was snow lying about but it wasn't too deep to prevent us going out. Heather enjoyed the snow because she made three separate snowmen for Dawn, Craig and James, It was pleasant on their patio because several types of bird would come down to feed. It was lovely to watch the three young ones opening their Christmas presents on Christmas morning.

I think it was just before New Years Eve that we went to the Sergeants Mess for a social evening, but the children weren't allowed there, so a baby sitter was booked. At the Mess, I sat with a group of Dave's fellow NCO's and their families and watched and bet on horse races which were made possible by having cut out horses about three feet high. Three wives, including Heather, took some very large dice and rolled them on the floor and dependant on what number was showing at the top of the dice, then that was the number of moves a horse could be moved forward. It was all good fun and being on holiday I didn't mind spending a bob or two on the horse races.

On New Year's Eve, we were all invited to a Senior NCO's house to celebrate and there he had his parents over from England so I didn't feel out of it and I enjoyed their company tremendously.

It was so strange not having Aline with me and I knew she would have been happy being over there with the kids but I made the most of it and Dave and Heather were positive about me enjoying it all. The time seemed to fly and on 3rd January 1995 I caught the coach back home from where I had alighted outside the NAAFI when I had first arrived. I gratefully thanked Dave and Heather for having me and it had helped me to get over the recent loss of Aline.

LATE NINETIES

In settling down again, I made it a point to take down the Christmas decorations on the twelfth night, which was an old superstition and this was Friday the 6th January.1995. Yes, I had put them up, irrespective of being on my own.

At the end of January, Mr. Wragg had given me a ring to ask if there had been any progress about selling Geoff's house but I had nothing new to report and he hadn't heard from anyone either.

It seemed so different to twelve months ago when Aline and I had received postcards from Dave when he was on detachment with the RAF in Las Vegas in America. He was over there on special exercises but he found time to get in a couple of days of golf and visit Disney Land. I was kept busy with the Monday club but I also carried on playing billiards for St. Mary's Church and going to the 'Footprints' meetings at Weston Park Hospital. I had also received invitations to a Friday meeting at the Aurora Club for retired persons who had once worked at Edgar Allen and Co., and whilst it was nice to meet old workmates from there, it wasn't the same atmosphere as we had at the TWIL Monday Club, besides that, the Edgar's meeting was on a Friday morning at 11.00 am and was rather inconvenient on that day.

Aline and I had always enjoyed a game of Bingo and for years we were members of the Top Rank Club in Sheffield, where we had won a few hundred pounds but it got to the stage where it was too much trouble to get ready and go there each Saturday night and now being on my own I didn't fancy it at first. However, for company, I joined a new club called the Gala, which was built on the Parkway by-pass into the town. It was there that on the 1st March, on a Wednesday evening, that I won £200. I wondered if this was a turning point for good luck.

On the 14th March, Dave arrived from Germany and brought over a new Mini Metro car which he hoped to sell privately. He stayed almost a week and it was lovely to have him around. There was no immediate sale so he left the car on my driveway which I wasn't too happy about because of the risk of vandals interfering with it.

A little while back I referred to good luck and I wondered if it was working again because on the 5th April, whilst at the Gala Club, I thought that I had won the National Game for thousands of pounds but due to a fault at the Sheffield end of communications, the game was played on a local basis. However, the management put in an extra £1,000 but unfortunately I had to share it with three other contestants and we each received £360.

On the eighth of April, Dave took part in a NATO charity run which takes place every year at Bruggen. It was a 10K road race and Dave entered it to obtain more money on sponsorship for the MNDA as he had done with Tony in '93 when going to Cold Fell. He sent me pictures of the race which were published in the Forces Newspaper and there in the middle of shot was Dave's beaming face. Having completed the run, he was sponsored for the sum of £250 for which he sent me a cheque to pass on to the Motor Neurone Society.

To try to help me in my bereavement, various people put forward suggestions and one was from Ella , asking me to go down and stay with her over the Easter weekend. I agreed and went down by National Express coach to Victoria Station in London and then I caught the train to Maidstone. Ella was there to meet me and from there we took a taxi to her address in Allington Park where she had a bungalow. This new address was on Tintern Road and had two bedrooms with a small gardens at the back and front and it also had a small conservatory attached to the back of the building. I liked it and it was so different to the last time I was down there in 1976 when Aline and I visited her in Sussex Road on the other side of Maidstone. I liked this new place of residence which was on a quiet and private estate with a small shopping centre within a few hundred yards walk. Ella made me very welcome and though she wasn't too good in health she enjoyed my company.

I stayed over the Easter weekend period and Lorna, one of her daughters, came and took us out in her car to one or two places including Folkestone. Overall it was a good break for me and the company helped a lot. It also suited Ella because it was her birthday, which is six months after mine.

The last week in April I had mixed fortunes because on the Monday I missed my footing on the stairs and tumbled from top to bottom and fortunately I didn't do myself any injuries but my pride was hurt because I didn't think that I could be so daft as to do a thing like that. Dave rang me at night and when I told him he said that I was a 'silly old fool'.

Tuesday was another visit to see my dentist friend, Tina Rackham for some more treatment. The other side of mixed fortune was the next day went I went to the Gala Bingo and won another £20.

On the 10th May, Wednesday, I sat in for Tina's examination final and before the exam came, she commented, "If I pass --." I interrupted her and said, "When you pass - I'll take you out for a meal." She replied, "Oh! Thank you but what about my boyfriend?" My answer was, "That's OK. Bring him along with you." Twenty minutes later the examiner checked Tina's work which she had carried out on me and commended the lasses good work. She passed and a few weeks later became a qualified dentist.

Dave rang me on the Thursday the 18th to tell me that he was going on detachment to the Gulf again but only for a short visit. He really looked forward to it. The War was nearly over and their base was well behind the front line, so to speak.

Since going on holiday to Malta with Tony, he had pestered me to go again but I wasn't too keen so, as an alternative, I persuade him to go with me to Jersey in the Channel Islands. Having agreed, I booked the holiday through the travel agent 'Travelsphere' to go for eight days at the end of May. We travelled by coach to Weymouth and stayed overnight at a local hotel and put in an early morning call so that we could catch the 8.00 am Condor Hovercraft with the rest of the party.

Unfortunately our early call was overlooked and we arrived at the dock just as the Condor was leaving. We were told that we would have to catch the afternoon sailing and it wasn't pleasing to think that we had lost half a days' holiday. When we finally arrived at St. Helier we reported the incident to the courier but was told that it was the fault of the hotel staff not the courier.

We were accommodated at the far end of the town in a guest house as part of the package deal but every time we wanted to go into town we had a fair walk to do. The guest house was excellent, particularly the young lady serving behind the bar. She was very friendly and advised us on ways to enjoy our stay.

Tony hadn't been before and I enjoyed showing him the sights and there were two coach excursions around the island which helped in pointing out the interesting places. There was the Elizabeth Castle near to St. Aubin's Bay in St. Helier. The castle was approachable by 'motor duck' at low tide but it was also possible to walk across. I took him to the famous German hospital, used during the World War II and the very large Castle and Fort at St. Brelades Bay which we walked to one day.

Having reached it after a half hours walk from the guest house, we had a short rest and then went to the castle. There we had a good look round and eventually finished up right at the top, from where we had a marvellous view of the small harbour and the surrounding district.

But Tony, deciding to see as much as possible, wanted to walk back to the guest house a different way. This we did, got lost, had to ask for directions and a couple of hours later we arrived back jut in time for dinner. I was definitely knackered.

Towards the weekend, the bar lady asked us if we liked music and when we both said yes, she told us that the Jersey Big Band were rehearsing on the Sunday morning at one of the pubs in St. Helier. So, off we went and found the place where the band were playing and that was up the stairs of the pub. It sounded great and at one recession, as the Band Leader walked past, I enquired if they played requests.

"What do you want?" He asked and I replied, "The String of Pearls as played by Glenn Miller." "OK." He said, "are you a musician?"

"Not now but I was a semi-pro for thirty years in Sheffield."

"Sheffield?" He queried. "Just a minute."

He went back to the stage and spoke to the drummer who came over and said his name was Wally Thompson and used to play in Sheffield some years ago. During our conversation, it turned out that he used to play for the Bernard Taylor Band at the City Hall and knew a lot of my friends such as Albert Lobb, Harry Bush, John Ogden and Barry Goude, all of whom were good musicians.

When I told him that I was a double bass player he asked me to take over from their bassist in the band because he thought he was rubbish and had no drive. I had to refuse because, not having played for such a long time, my fingers were too soft, but there, I would have longed to have played. I had my request played and afterwards Wally invited Tony and me to see the Cabaret at another hotel at which he and an organist/pianist from the Northern Dance Orchestra in England, were resident. Before we left Tony and I managed to get a photograph of Wally in between us. He also asked us to go to an outdoor charity event at which there were many entertainer of all kinds and many of them were professional musicians. This seemed to make our holiday and as we arrived at the show, who should be there but the lady from behind the bar at our guest house. Apparently she knew quite a few of the entertainers and although we didn't know many of the people there, we were made to join in as though we had known them for years.

Before the holiday ended, one of the day trips was to the famous Gerald Darrel Zoo and Park. There were so many birds and animals to see and Tony could hardly believe the size of the place. One really needed a full day to take in all the park and areas where the creatures were on show.

The holiday over, we returned to Weymouth after having had a comfortable voyage on the Condor Catamaran which took about three hours. On disembarking, we went straight to a coach to start our journey back to Sheffield but it turned out to be a deplorable one because after travelling for a while, a horrible smell developed at the rear of the coach. Eventually one of the other passengers found out that the receptacle in the loo hadn't been emptied and cleaned. It made quite a few people feel sick and after arriving home, Tony and I reported that incident and the one where we were left in Weymouth at the start of our holiday. Travelsphere refused to accept any responsibility and the latter was blamed on the coach driver who was sub-contracted.

After my holiday I continued to visit the Dental Hospital and now that Tina had qualified and left I was put in the hands of a young man called Banton. He was likeable but not half as good and gentle has Tina had been.

Each Thursday I would go to St. Mary's Church where, for a nominal fee, a lunch was supplied to pensioners in the parish. I sat at a table with five other people who were all sociable.. One was an ex - police inspector with his wife and another man was Polish and had married an English girl during the war. The other chap was Albert Flint who only had one leg and he was in the Fellowship of the Services like I was, so there was always something to discuss.

However, there was one Thursday, when starting our meal, someone came to tell us that several cars had been broken into in the car park. I was one of the unlucky ones and entry to the car had been made by a screwdriver being forced into the door lock. Nothing was taken but the facia had been smashed as the thieves tried to start the engine. It was suggested that some schoolboys were responsible but nothing was followed up when we notified the police.

After the incident I asked Brian Gleadle to fit an alarm in the car and that cost me £45 but I felt that the car would be more secure and it was worth it. Expense seems to come in sets and two days later it cost me another £49.50 for a new motor for the washing machine.

Cousin Ella had rung me on the 12th July to say that she was going into hospital to have a heart by-pass which, over a period, turned out to be a success but it took months to for her to get over it.

I was still popping up and down to Norborough Road to keep an eye on Geoff's house and on one occasion the 'Sale' sign had been stolen, so I had to contact the Agent to get a replacement. This was a few days after the first anniversary of losing my Nip.

On the Channel 4 Teletext, there was a programme which displayed contacts for ex-servicemen and it was called Service Pals. On one of them I saw an advertisement for a trip to Singapore for Changi personnel who had served out there, to celebrate the 50th Anniversary of the end of the War in the Far East. I had made enquiries and details were sent to me from a Mr. James, who lived in Bristol. The journey was to be in February 1996 so I sent the deposit necessary on the 21st August to the gentleman and made sure my seat was booked for that event.

One will recall that I promised to take Tina Rackham for a meal when she passed her exams and this promise I kept on the 30th August. I drove up to Crookes to pick up Tina and her boy friend David and then took them to the Woodroffe Arms Inn, which was situated in the small village of Hope, which was in Derbyshire. Just before we set off I passed a small parcel to Tina and told her that it was for being so good to me in my treatment. When she opened it she was more than pleased and said to David, "Look at these, aren't they beautiful?" I had bought her a pair of ear rings in the shape of crystal clear teardrops and she put them on straight away. They suited her and I had chosen them because during some of my treatment I had noticed that she wore that sort of thing as she leaned over me. We had a very pleasant evening and a good meal and during conversation it was disclosed that David played cricket and at one time he had been captain of the Lancashire Second Eleven. With me being an umpire, we had lots to talk about and Tina was enjoying it too because she always went with David to watch him play. That season he had played as a professional for one of Sheffield's oldest clubs, the Abbeydale Cricket Club. I took them back home about 10.30 pm, having enjoyed their company.

A few weeks ago, Andy Steel had said that several of Geoff's friends wanted to go up to Cold Fell again, in commemoration of the last time they were there. He had already temporarily booked accommodation and wondered if myself, Tony and Dave would be interest. They were all for it when I told them, so on Nip's birthday and Tony's birthday, the 10th September, we started out to climb the 2,930 feet haul.

We had travelled up on the previous day, Saturday and after making a rendezvous with Andy, we followed him in my car which Dave drove. We arrived at the little village of Castle Carrock on the borders of Cumbria and Northumberland where Andy had booked us into a lovely pub called the Weary Sportsman and the large picture sign on the wall outside, reminded me very much of our Geoff. The features on the face of the man in the picture was Geoff, to a tea.

Dave slept on his own in a small bedroom and Tony and I shared another bedroom but due to Tony's snoring, I had to get up and go into a small lounge next door to get some sleep.

The meals were very good and the company was excellent with Andy, Jo, Caroline and Martin and Andy Fletcher with his wife Rosemary, plus JB and Tom. One surprise was having Lackie and his wife Elizabeth with us, so overall there was quite a crowd. There were one or two children but they were very good and caused no upset in a group of grownups.

We set off on about 10.00 am on the Saturday morning and started the first part of the climb which wasn't too bad and I seemed to be coping well, considering that I had never done anything like that before. All the others were rigged out in the proper hiking gear but the only thing extra which I had, was a good pair of shoes. Tony had put our Geoff's plus fours on again but Dave decided to wear some shorts instead of trousers.

After a while we all rested and had some refreshments and relieved ourselves where possible, we then started to attack the hard bit. By the way, we didn't take any children with us and it's a good job because after an hour I was beginning to feel the strain but I was determined to make it. Our kid did. As we climbed each small hill and went higher and higher, our Dave would shout, "Come on Dad, it's only over the next hill."

Over the next hill!!? And the next and the next. After about three hours, the first of the party had reached the trig point at the top and waited for me to make the final push which I eventually did and was I glad for the rest? I had made sure that I had put some of Aline's ashes from the urn into a small container so that I could scatter them amongst Geoff's ashes which the rest of the crowd had brought up two years ago.

Tony, Dave and I stood against the trig and very kindly the others stepped to one side so that we could have a quiet reverent moment. The three of us then took a handful of Nip's ashes and scattered them around. It was a very touching moment and more than we three had tears in their eyes. Whilst up there, Andy Steel checked the trig because on the original visit, they had put a rosary inside to keep Geoff company in thoughts and spirit. From that point both Nip and Geoff had a wonderful view together. No wonder Geoff loved the open air so much.

We stayed up there for nearly an hour and after having some more refreshments we started the journey back down. I thought that the climb up was difficult but I eventually found that it was equally as awkward to descend. It wasn't a straight walk down and because of the moorland tufts of grass and the sloping hillside, one had to walk down sideways and this put a lot of strain on one of my knees. If I could have laid down and rolled, I would have done but that was impossible. Within the last half mile to the flat bit at the bottom, I could go no further and it finished with our Dave giving me a piggy back for a couple of hundred yards. At least it broke the monotony and we couldn't help but laugh at the situation.

It was still a good mile from the pub and I trundled along as best I could but I suddenly missed our Dave. As we arrived at the end of the track where it met the road, I saw a car coming towards us. It was Dave, who had trotted off in front to get the car to take me the last few hundred yards. Oh! Was I grateful and don't forget, I was nearly 74 years of age so I hadn't done too badly.

After freshening up, all the party went down to dinner in the dining room and we all enjoyed an excellent meal. Dave had brought over a couple of bottles of some special German brew but one or two were reluctant to try it because it was so potent but those who did, thoroughly recommended it. I was ready for bed about 10.30 pm but Dave and Tony stayed up and entertained those who remained in the lounge.

The following morning, after a good breakfast, we all assembled outside for some photo calls and then around 10.00 am we all made off in our own direction. Being near to the M6

Motorway, Dave suggested going down to Preston to visit his RAF pal, Marcel. He was a character and we finally found his house at which he made us very welcome. Marcel was stationed at Coningsby in Lincolnshire but commuted each weekend between there and Preston because he had bought a house at Preston and was renovating it.

We had an hour or so with him and his wife before deciding to head for home down through Lancashire and over the Woodhead Pass back to Sheffield. There was one little falter when, after getting some petrol, Tony directed Dave up a road and we had gone about two miles when Dave commented that we were heading for Liverpool. He turned the car round and having found the right route, in a couple of hours we were back in Rotherham where we dropped off Tony and then made our way back to No.8. It had been a memorable weekend and I thoroughly enjoyed it but the next day Dave had to set off back to Bruggen.

Trying to sell our Geoff's house was still an on going thing and after consultation with Mr. Wragg, the solicitor, it was agreed to put it up for auction by Eadon, Lockwood and Riddle the estate agents. Mr. Riddle made all the necessary arrangements and on the 4th October I went along with Mr. Wragg to the Quaker House on the corner of Vicar Lane, off Church Street in the centre of Sheffield. It took quite a while because other properties were being auctioned before No.66 Norborough Road was put up. It started at £18,000 but no one seemed to be interested and the outcome was that, not having reached the reserve price of £14,000, it was withdrawn. There were several ethnic people there who were looking for a cheap buy but I wasn't being succumbed.

It was disappointing and with the housing market being in the doldrums, at a later date I had to let it go to a Mr. David Whitehead who lived in the Brocco Bank Area and was acting for a Pakistani business man, Mohammed Yuosaff. They both came to see the house and whilst I tried to stick it out for a reasonable price I had to let it go for £12,000 and by the time the agents fees etc., had been paid, I finished with a net figure of £11,634.49. It was regrettable to have to let it go for that price but in the long run the hassle of not having to go up and down to No.66 was a great relief and I was then able to relax.

Mr. Wragg tied up all the loose ends and the finalising of Geoff's estate ended in a monetary value of some £52,000. It was a surprise to us all and although he hadn't made a will, Geoff had made sure that the family, including nephews and nieces, received some gain from his estate. We found all the bequests on a piece of paper in one of his drawers. Some of his assets had come to hand shortly after he died and this had been distributed according to his wishes and Aline and I had made sure that his request had been met.

The rest of the estate that arose, after Aline passed had on, was now shared amongst the rest of the family. I'm sure that she would have been surprised at the final figure of Geoff's estate, I was.

I had some good news in November and it was that Dave was being posted back home and this time he would be nearer to home having been assigned to RAF Coningsby in Lincolnshire, so therefore would be able to meet up with his old pal Marcel again. Once he had settled in, he asked me to go down and spend Christmas with him and the family. The house was a terraced one on a small forces'estate and about a mile and a half from the camp. The address was 9 West Drive, Castlefield, Tattershall, Coningsby. The back of the house overlooked some agricultural land which made it very pleasant. I really enjoyed being with the children again and they were pleased to have me with them. It had also been convenient to be able to drive down in my own car, the journey taking around a comfortable two hours. I returned home on the Wednesday, 27th December.

This year had been eventful in parts and I was glad that many anomalies had been overcome and towards the end of the year, prior to going down to Dave's, I had won another

£15 on the bingo one Tuesday and on Friday the 15th December I once more enjoyed my Christmas Dinner at the Grosvenor Hotel with my TWIL pensioner friends. To finish of the old year I had invited Tony and Mathew to come up and have lunch with me on the day of New Year's Eve.

I was looking forward to the New Year, 1996 because a few months ago, having written to a Mr. James in Bristol in answer to his advertisement on the Teletext and I had now been accepted as a traveller to Singapore with the party which he had organised. This meant arranging for the necessary inoculations (which I received free because the nurse at the local surgery told me that if ethnics could get it for nothing, then why not me) It was on the 5th January she gave me the anti-typhoid injection, the following week I returned to receive my jab for Polio and Hepatitis B. To make certain that I arrived at Heathrow Airport on time, I had to travel down to London and make an overnight stay in a nearby hotel which was included in the coach fare from Sheffield by The National Express Company. This I booked on the 18th January to make sure I had a seat reserved on the coach.

I managed to get to another meeting of the 'Footprints' at the Weston Park Hospital on the 29th and enjoyed the company of the other bereaved people there. It's amazing how talking about losing loved ones, does help to ease one's mind.

It was all go getting ready for my long journey and on top of that, Ella had arranged for us both to go on a River Rhine 5 Day Holiday in the second week in April. On the 5th Feb., I sent her the balance for the fare to Germany.

I had recently had a sharp pain in my groin and when I went to see Dr. Hasan, he said it looked like a double Hernia. However, on the 12th February, I kept an appointment at the Royal Hallamshire and after an examination, the doctor there said it was small, single Hernia on the right of my groin and they would contact me at a later date.

The next day I was up early, called a taxi to run me down town to catch the National Express coach to Heathrow. I was dropped off at a designated hotel and after a good meal, I settled down for the night. The following morning a courtesy coach took me to Terminal 4 at Heathrow Airport where I eventually contacted other members of the party I was to travel with. Along with the organiser, Mike James and his wife, there were about fourteen other people in the group. Having made the long trek to our departure point we finally boarded our 'plane and shortly afterwards we took off for the 14 hour flight to Singapore.

It was a different flight from the last time I flew in that direction in 1946 when I travelled most of the way from Bourne in Cambridgeshire, in a Liberator, four piston engined bomber to Karachi, in India.

Fourteen hours of non-stop flying can be very tedious and cramped and I'm one of those people who cannot 'drop off' to sleep, not even on a coach, so by the time we touched down at Kuala Lumpar in Malaysia, I felt shattered.

We stopped here to change to another aircraft on a short service flight to Singapore Airport. It didn't take that long, with the main delay being due to the changing over of the luggage etc. By teatime we had reached our destination by means of a courtesy coach which took us to our hotel, The Allson, where upon arrival, I was asked to share a room with a gentleman called Malcolm Warren.

Prior to arranging my holiday in Singapore, I had mentioned it to one or two friends at TWIL and they had told me to contact Andy Marshall, who used to work in the Sales Department. Andy was now resident in Singapore and was the Rep for the parent company, Bekeart's of Belgium. Upon arrival at the Allson Hotel, I gave Andy a ring and he was more than pleased to hear my voice.

After a few friendly exchanges and after asking at what time I had arrived, he said that if I hadn't planned anything for that evening, he and his wife, Nancy, would pick me up and take me for a meal and have a chat for old times sake. This he did and at 7.00 pm he met me in the Hotel reception, introduced me to Nancy and he then drove over to the famous Raffles Hotel where we booked a table and ordered a meal.

We had a wonderful meal and a good reminisce and I found Nancy to be a lovely charming person. She was Malaysian and had met Andy shortly after he had arrived out there and subsequently married him. Having contacted Andy, it paid dividends later on in the week as one was to find out.

The following Friday, Feb., 16th, Mike James had arranged transport to take our party to see the Kranji Cemetery and War Memorial where so many of the Forces were buried. After alighting from the vehicle, to approach the Cemetery we had to go through an archway at the entrance, where the stepped pathway climbed up to the memorial, in front of which was a curved concrete wall some ten feet high and on this there was an inscription dated 1939 - 1945, saying that the walls of the Memorial contained the names of 24,000 soldiers and airmen who had died out there.

The main line of text in the middle of the wall was:

"THEY DIED FOR ALL FREE MEN."

This wording is also shown below in many Far Eastern languages such as Urdu and Hindi . The huge monument was high and about 150 feet long with two end walls and three dividing walls, each some thirty feet wide which supported the roof. On each wall, on either side, were the names, ranks and regiments of those who had fallen. On the top of the memorial and in the centre, was a high and thick concrete column with a star shaped golden ornament at its pinnacle. Overall it must have been sixty feet high and could be seen for miles around.

There seemed to be peace everywhere, it was so quiet and the only noise was from a few birds above and on the ground below, local Malaysian attendants were sweeping the paths and trimming the surrounds of the many graves. The graves themselves were laid out in plots of countries, sub divided into regiments which enabled visiting families and friends to locate the remains of their loved ones. Some headstones were laid out in arcs but most were in regimental rows. It made one so proud to visit this place of solemnity, thanks to the Singapore Government. Before leaving, we held a two minutes silence in memory of all those who had fallen.

On Saturday the 17th, Malcolm and I used our free day to take a look around the Sentosa Isle which we reached by catching a service bus on Keppel Road. To me it was a strange coincidence seeing the name Keppel, because about ten miles from where I lived, in the Rotherham district of Scholes, there is a tall stone built round tower with a square observation platform at the top. It is one hundred feet high and one has to climb 365 steps, (one for each day of the year) to reach the top. The tower is known as Keppel's Column and was built many, many years ago. Some people called it Keppel's Folly but it was a favourite place for picnics and family outings.

After a fifteen minute ride on the bus, we arrived at a place called Mount Faber, where we were able to pay and board a cable car which carried Malcolm and me well above the Singapore River. From the car we had a marvellous view of Singapore City in the distance and the docks just south of there. It took another fifteen minutes to reach Sentosa Isle but there was no rush because the view was so great.

Sentosa Isle is a kind of leisure place with an ornamental, rising dragon fountain at its centre and then in various directions there was a war museum, an aviary, a restaurant and further afield, at the southern end of the isle, was Silosa Fort.

The first stop we made was at the museum where there was a lifelike setting at two stages of the surrender of the Japanese to Admiral Lord Louis Mountbatten. The wax figures were so real that it was possible to think that you were at the actual meeting and the features of the officers taking part, were easy to distinguish . We spent quite a while there before going to the aquarium.

This was a passage way which was covered with heavy duty reinforced glass and as we made our way along this glass tunnel we had a wonderful view of sea life with hundreds of types of various coloured fish. At the time we were looking, we could see an attendant in Scuba gear, slowly moving in and out of the fish whilst feeding them. It seemed so uncanny to watch as a couple of sharks, some five feet long, slowly approach the attendant for their food. There was even a couple of sting rays swimming around him besides a variety of other exotic fish.

We must have spent an hour in there and even as we left the aquarium, we had the chance to look at some specially designed water tanks in which there were many multi-coloured varieties of these tropical fish. Having decided to give the aviary a miss, we made our way down to Silosa Fort where we had a close look at the barracks and in the forecourt there were several 4" guns which had been pointing out to sea in 1942 to stop the Japanese invading but this had been a failure and helped to bring about the surrender of Singapore.

As you will recall in history, the guns permanently faced one way and when the Japanese attacked from the mainland, the guns couldn't be turned round to defend. Thus we were routed.

Having browsed around the courtyard etc., we then walked up to a lookout post from where we had a marvellous view of the shipping lanes into Singapore and from where the enemy was expected, but didn't come. But that's history and we finished our day out by taking refreshments in the nearby restaurant. We returned via cable car to Mount Faber but this time we went right to the end of the cable run so that we could take in more views from the Mount itself. Eventually we walked down to Keppel Road and caught the bus back into town.

Although we stayed at the Allson Hotel, we didn't have our meals there because they weren't included in the package price. We tried the restaurant on the first morning and cereals and toast with a pot of tea cost about £7.50 so after that, we found an open air cafe which was adjacent to the hotel and for what we required, it was adequate. We did however, buy teabags and milk and also some biscuits at a local shop so that we could have a drink in our hotel room.

The following day, Sunday, Malcolm asked me to go with him to Sembarwang which was a part of Yishin City. He wanted to go and take another look at the area where he lived as a child with his parents. His father worked as an engineer in the shipyards there and he was eager to see if the house where they had lived, was still there.

We went most of the way by Metro Train, the SMRT, which runs from the centre of Singapore and part of the way by under ground. The train travelled north towards the famous Causeway which joins the Island of Singapore to the mainland and after half an hour we alighted at Yishin City where we were able to catch a bus to Sembarwang. After reaching our destination we must have walked around for a couple of hours before we finally found his old home and by the time we had walked back to catch the return bus, I was knackered.

When we arrive back at the bus terminus at Yishin City, Malcolm asked me if I would like a quick look around North Point Shopping Centre. This was a massive place and very modern and our shopping centres at home bore no comparison. There were hundreds of shops and stalls and the local residents packed every lane and aisle in it. Having looked around the place we then crossed over the main road and climbed the steps to the SMRT station to catch the tube train to return to Singapore.

On the Monday, we went into town to look at some of the old haunts such as Clifford Pier and other places of interest like Kavanagh Bridge and Anderson Bridge which spanned over the Singapore River within a hundred yards of each other. I remembered Clifford Quay because when I was there in 1946, our offices were in the Union Building on the top floor of Winchester House and overlooked the area.

One embarrassing moment was when I needed a toilet badly, so I said to Malcolm that I would ask at the reception in the main entrance of the Singapore Cricket Club which was nearby. In I went and asked the Malaysian receptionist if there was a toilet handy and she took me back outside.

As we went down the steps she pointed to a small building just to the left and said that it was the toilet. In I went and it wasn't a modern toilet but what is known in the Far East, as a squat. There is no seat, you just bend and squat and hope for the best because there is no toilet paper but I happened to have a couple of tissues with me and made them do. Flushes are out and to get rid of the necessary, one has to turn on the water, which is connected to a short hosepipe, and swill away all the "s...t" down the drainage hole in the floor. I had to use the system because it was a must.

We returned to the hotel to freshen up and then, after a meal at the cafe just around the corner, we cut across town, up by Raffles and into Chinatown. On the way we went through Raffles City which is another large and modern complex of shops etc. At one of the shops I bought two large tubes of 'Oral B' toothpaste because it is unobtainable in the UK. It's a revelation crossing the roads in the centre of the city because there are at two main lanes in and out of town and each of these lanes has six lanes of traffic full of all types of vehicle. There are no holdups and the pedestrian crossings are synchronised to perfection. It's a wonderful sight at night to see the many signs flashing, not only in English but in Cantonese, Chinese and many other languages because Singapore has a multi national populace. Everything was so colourful and at times it looked just like fairyland.

On the Tuesday we had a half day excursion in a coach and went to see the infamous Changi Jail where so many servicemen had been imprisoned during the war. There were still armed guards at crucial points overlooking the jail and we were only allowed to go into the small museum and further on have a good look at the wooden chapel which had been built by the POW's. It was a touching sight - but the Jail was now the official prison for the Republic of Singapore and used only for civilian offenders. We also went a little further up the road to see the old RAF camp at Changi which was now occupied by the Singapore Air Force. We were guided around one small part of it just near to the entrance but elsewhere was off limits.

As we sneaked a view up the main road of the camp past the barrack blocks we used to occupy, I commented that the old metal air strip had now been dismantled but one clever 'Johnny' in the party, said that there had never been one there and he had been in charge of the party which laid the first air strip which is now Singapore Airport and that was over two miles away. I didn't argue because I had been on the camp before him in 1946.

Upon return to the hotel, the management had arranged for a Chinese Dragon Dance group to perform along with a type of musical band who accompanied the dancers. It was all in conjunction with the Chinese New Year. The dance took place in front of the hotel and part of the ceremony was to offer a platter of fruit to the dragon in thanks for the New Year. That year happened to be the Year of the Rat and after the dance the Dragon went into the hotel and waddled its way up the main staircase and then through the building. This was to bring everyone good luck

After the show, upon returning to our rooms, we found a beautiful red, four inch square folder on the cocktail cabinet and on the front of it was imprinted a Golden Rat with the 'Year of the Rat' embossed upon it and inside were two brand new Singapore Cents about the size of a farthing. Going back to the front cover, under the embossed Rat was a Happy New Year in Chinese. "GONG XI FA CAI."

Malcolm and I agreed to visit the Botanical Gardens the following day and it was well worth going to. As we went through the large ornamental wrought iron gate, the first thing we saw was a small area surrounded by box privet and it that, there must have been twenty different animals shaping from giraffes to cows which had been cut by the topiary method. We had a good look at these shapes before making our way to the other sections of the gardens and it was wonderful to see a full area of various cacti and other exotic and tropical plants.

We then went into the orchid area and it was unbelievable how many varieties there were. Many were outside but there was a small greenhouse type place where young plants were being nurtured and constantly watered with a system of electrically operated sprays which were on a time system. We must have spent a couple of hours touring in and out of the gardens and finally finished our visit by strolling round a large artificial lake which displayed aquatic plants of many kinds.

Andy Marshall had arranged to take Malcolm and me to the huge Singapore Zoo, along with Nancy and their two children, Ben and Kim, and this was on Wednesday 21st.Feb. It was a magnificent place with partly open spaces to create a natural habitat for some animals but which were fenced off for the safety of the public. Right in the centre was a water feature, which was large enough for types of birds such as pelicans, flamingoes, ibis and storks to move around as if they were in their own natural environment. There were also many species such as wild fowl and several types of the everyday duck quacking away to the noise and songs of the other birds.

In another corner we were just in time to see the feeding of the pigmy hippopotami and the kids loved it. On the far side was a widish stream which was fenced off on the main path side but across the water there were two beautiful fully grown Bengal tigers lounging about on the embankment. There were so many animals to see but one animal which is usually associated with a zoo, wasn't there and that was the elephant. However, there was a compound for monkeys and orangutans with warnings not to feed them. The alligator pond was a little lively with their thrashing about in the water enclave.

Andy's children, who had been cared for by their nursemaid most of the day, behaved very well until just before we decided to leave but they had traipsed about for about three hours so there was no wonder that Ben and Kim were tired. Andy took us back to their house which was near to Tanglin where some barracks used to be during the war and as is the custom, we had to take off our shoes before entering the house. Nancy made us very welcome and we stayed and chatted for about an hour and their Malaysian maid, made us a cup of tea and put on some biscuits. Andy then took us back to our hotel and we, Malcolm and I, thanked him and Nancy for a good day out. Before leaving, Andy told us that he had made arrangements for Malcolm and me to visit the famous the famous Bird Park and Aviary at Jurong and the visit would be free.

The next day we made our way by bus to Jurong Park and this was a large area, some two hectares in size which was covered with welded mesh which had been supplied by Tinsley Wire in Sheffield and the sale had all been arranged by Andy Marshall, that's why he had some influence in getting us into the Park. There was a man made waterfall which was a hundred feet high and the water fell onto the foliage below with the TWIL mesh stretched well above the top of that, thus creating the effect of a tropical jungle and keeping the birds in. It wasn't captivity because the birds could fly freely within the area and on a plaque at the entrance it stated that there were 1,200 birds to be seen.

Right at the entrance was a special aquarium type building in which were housed many penguins included the King Penguins which were so colourful. It was strange to be in a tropical country but in this building it was like being in the antarctic.

The park had been upgraded recently at a cost of six million Singapore Dollars and there were now 1800 birds there of which there were many, many varieties. It was possible to really get up close to some exotic birds and take some snap shots of them. One modern innovation was a monorail car to go around the park to get better views but we didn't take advantage of it. We left the aviary and strolled about the park looking at other features in the bird world where in huge welded mesh cages, we saw other species such as Toucans, Vultures, Eagles and Owls.

All the large birds were kept separate from the aviary area. Lower down there were places where birds of the fowl family were kept and in one corner, some had been bred with pink feathers. To finish off the day we went to the huge glass roofed building near to the aviary and this was a refreshment place where we had a drink before catching the bus back to town.

When we first visited the Changi Camp on the half day excursion, Malcolm and I weren't too impressed. Not with the visit but because we had little time to really take a good look. So, on Friday 23rd we caught a bus to the camp to see if we could get a better look at it. On the way I noticed that there were several workers employed and armed with petrol strimmers and black bin bags. There job was to keep the grass edges short and tidy and also pick up any litter which unfortunately had been left lying about. It's a crime in Singapore to drop litter anywhere, particularly cigarette ends and if one is caught, then it's not a fine but a short stay in jail.

When we arrived at the camp we firstly went to the Air Force Museum because I had promised to let the curator have a copy of a book I had written whilst serving in the Far East. It was called 'Over There' and whilst my service in Singapore and Changi was minimal, the Singapore Captain in charge of the museum, accepted my offer to put the book into the library for any future reference. It was whilst taking a longer look inside the museum at the memorabilia there that Malcolm called me over to the wall at the far end.

"Ron." He said. "Take a look at this." I went over and on the wall was a small photograph about 8 x 6 inches and on it was an air strip made in metal. The caption read,

"The original air strip at Changi which was built by British Prisoners of War under the supervision of the Japanese Army."

"Thank's very much, Malcolm." I said with glee. "That's what I was trying to explain earlier on in the week but was rudely contradicted by Mr. Knowall."

Malcolm commented that I should know the truth because I was at Changi long before the other person had arrived out there. Another significant thing was that it was about fifty yards below our barrack block and we used to watch aircraft arriving and departing from it. Not operational aircraft but the mail planes and VIP transport bringing in important people.

Having left the museum with its display of obsolete military aircraft on a concrete display pad behind the building, we made our way to the guard room and asked if we could just stroll up to the barrack blocks in which we had once been quartered.

There was a little heated discussion with the Singapore Air Force guard and he eventually called out his officer to talk to us but as much as we tried to explain about just walking one hundred yards to take some photos of the barracks, the officer flatly refused our request. As we argued with him, I had to chuckle because next to the Guard Room was a reinforced small building which was the armoury and this, funnily enough, was the last place at which I had ever done a twelve hour guard duty with the RAF.

We left the Guard Room and made our was down the main road through the rest of the camp to Changi Village and ironically this took us round the rear side of our old barrack blocks, so after all that hassle we were able to take the photographs - plus some of military equipment in the foreground. **SECURITY?** What security?

As we walked on for some twenty minutes, Malcolm pointed out a building at the back end of the camp and asked me if I recognised the old NAAFI. For a moment I hesitated and then I said. "Yes, but where has the sea gone to?" When I was stationed there, several of us would go down to the NAAFI with our swimming trunks, have one or two soft drinks and then go into the ablutions and change before going for a swim in the man made pool. This was a part of the shore which had been fenced off with railway sleepers to keep out the sharks.

This had all altered since 1946 and since then the Singapore Government had reclaimed many miles of land from the sea and this was one of the areas which had been reclaimed. The shore was now three miles away.

We carried on walking until we reached the village of Changi Creek. How things had changed because now there was a small complex of modern shops, of which there was only a muddy road through the area when I was there during the war. We purchased one or two souvenirs, one of which was a Chinese wind chime for Ella. We then went to a restaurant called Millies' Bar where we had a good lunch and a drink of beer. The whole district was new to me and after enjoying the meal we made our way back to Singapore and the Hotel.

As we were approaching it, I suddenly said to Malcolm, "Oh! There's the remains of one of the Three Worlds." During the war there used to be three worlds, the Happy World, the Great World and the Little World. The first named just had the gateway left and all of them used to be places of leisure and entertainment. Malcolm said that they were all now in ruins.

We arrived back at the Hotel, had a wash and brush up and then rang Andy Marshall to ask him if we could pop into his place of work at Bekeart's office (TWIL) to say cheerio to him and thank him, not forgetting Nancy, for helping us to enjoy our stay in Singapore. He told us how to get there and when we arrived it was on the top floor of a huge office structure which gave a marvellous view of the city sights. We didn't stay very long and he introduced us to his staff, pointing out to them that I used to work at the TWIL Industries in Sheffield, England.

For the last day of our holiday, Saturday, Malcolm and I had a stroll down into Little India and watched the locals making baskets of various shapes and sizes, plus the trinkets they produced for tourists. It's amazing that in Singapore, the population is made up of many Far Eastern races and many have their own little townships within the city, such as Chinatown, Little India and a lovely area called Orchard Square. It was whilst there that I bought some beautiful tea shirts, three to be exact and all were of different colours with the name 'Singapore' embroided across the front and each letter in a different colour.

We popped out at night for our last meal in Singapore before retiring early because we had to be up the next morning at an unearthly hour to get to the airport at 4.30 am and fly to Kuala Lumpar to catch our connection home. Not all the party were going home to England because some had decided to stay on for another week and go up to Penang in Malaysia. After a very tiresome and long journey, we finally arrived at Heathrow at 4.30 pm on Sunday the 25th February and I personally arrived back on my own doorstep at 10.30 pm but it had all been worth it and I wouldn't have missed it for the world, whether it was the Little one, the Great one or the Happy one

It was good to be back home and get back into a normal routine and one of the first things I arranged, was to send for a PEPs Investment Plan. Our David had been briefing me for a little while and had persuaded me to invest some of my savings for future years. On the 1st March, I invested £6,000 in the Schroder Organisation to mature with bonuses in the year 2001. To do this, I withdrew the amount needed from my National Savings Account and hoped that I had done the right thing because it would be all tied up money for the next five years. To obtain the money I needed I had to give a month's notice to my bank but eventually the Banker's draft arrived.

On the 26th March, I lost a good old friend when I attended the funeral at Handsworth Cemetery, of Bill Cooper, the musician I had known since 1937. Having taught Tony and Geoff the fundamentals of the piano, he was always willing to have a chat about old times and even called in to see Aline and me when passing by. He had reached the ripe old age of 82 years but kept teaching the piano right up to his death. Bill had always played in public besides doing his daytime job and his teaching and it was at the young age of fifteen that he had obtained his Cap and Gown for music. He was one of the youngest in the country to achieve this honour of LRCM.

The first week in April I travelled down to Kent because I had arranged to go on a coach holiday to Germany with Ella. The trip was down the Rhine Valley to a small town called Born Hofen and the hotel was owned and run by a young German chap named Werner. It was awkward climbing up two flights of marble steps to get to our bedroom and I was fearful that Ella might slip and not be able to cope but we soon settled in to the twin bedded room.

We went with the Travel Agents, Travelsphere and in our stay there we had three day trips visiting places of interest, the two main ones being Mount Lorelei the place of the so called legendry siren and (Khon) Cologne Cathedral. We did have a full day at Cochem on the Mosel River and I enjoyed seeing it again, especially to see it without the floods we experienced when being there with Nip, Heb and David in the late 80's.

The food at our hotel was excellent and for entertainment, Werner would play the keyboards and sing both German and English songs besides playing music for dancing. To help the guests enjoy their holiday, he also organised some party games. On one half day trip we went up to some huge monument which was historical to the Germans and to get back down we came by cable car which Ella really enjoyed. Having enjoyed the holiday, we returned to Maidstone on the 15th March which happened to be Ella's birthday and unbeknown to her I had bought a cassette of Werner's music for that occasion.

On the 28th April, I had a nice surprise when I received an invitation to have lunch at the Abbeydale Cricket Club. It was from Tina and David in appreciation of my taking them out to dinner at the Woodroffe Hotel in the village of Hope. I enjoyed their company and walked around the boundaries edge with Tina because David was taking part in the game. Before leaving them, David introduced me to his Mum and Dad, who had popped over from Lancashire to see him play.

As Chairman of the Pensioners Club, I still organised trips for members and on the first of May I had arranged for a visit to RAF Conningsby Air Museum. Our Dave had done the booking side of it because he was now stationed there and was able to get all the details I needed. We had hoped to see the last Halifax Bomber but unfortunately it had been sent to Bristol for a complete overhaul. However, the journey wasn't wasted because in the hangar were other famous aircraft such as the Spitfire, Hurricane and an Argos transport plane which had all been operational during the War. Terry Murphy was really interested, having been a bomber pilot during the War and Harry Foster showed some interest because he had been an Air Gunner during the same period. We left there after an hour and then went on to finish the day at Skegness which was only a short run from there but the weather wasn't too good. It was cold and damp and by five o'clock we had all had enough and were we glad to set off for home?

Four months ago at the Bassetlaw monthly cricket meeting, I had been asked by Bernie Jarvis if I would like to take part as an umpire at a cricket gala in Sheffield. After explaining it to me, I accepted and on the 8th May I officiated at several matches. The teams were representative of Universities from such places as Sheffield, Leeds, Leicester, Loughboro, Manchester and Durham and there were eight umpires to be in charge, including Frank Richardson, Albert Burkinshaw (both County Standard umpires) so I was in good company. Bernie Jarvis had become involved due to the fact that he was a senior lecturer at Sheffield University.

There were two umpires designated to each game and the matches would last the full week. The weather was good and I enjoyed all with being in the company of such people. For my part I received a fee of £22. At one of my matches on the lower pitch it was lovely to hear the bells ringing across the valley from the beautiful Ranmoor Church at Fulwood. It was so heavenly.

On the thirteenth of May I had arranged for another day out with the TWIL Pensioners and once again I had organised a buffet lunch at the Hyde Park Inn at Dronfield Woodhouse again. The food and the service was excellent and Mrs.Tomlinson once more donated a bottle of wine for one of the prizes in our raffle. We stayed until about 3.00 pm and then finished off the afternoon by asking the coach driver to take us to Hardstoft Garden Centre. After having a good look round, we had a light refreshments and returned home at 6.00 pm. Including the meal at the Inn, the committee only charged £6 each for the whole day. It had been such an enjoyable one that it was agreed that we do a similar trip in June and on the 11th we returned to the Hyde Park Inn but after the meal we this time went down to Newstead Abbey, which is a historical building with plenty of interest and some wonderful gardens and lakes to explore.

Towards the end of June I was returning from a bowls match with two other players and to take a short cut back to Steel City Sports Club, I made my way onto the M1 motorway intending to leave it at the Chapletown exit. As I was trying to look for the turn off, I inadvertently eased over onto the hard shoulder. I hadn't realised that until the moment I left the motorway and was heading for Ecclesfield. Then a car behind me flashed me and after pulling over I was confronted by a policeman who had been following me in an unmarked car. He asked me to get out and go to the police car where he explained that I had been driving on the hard shoulder with proof of same on the camera his companion was holding and it was an offence. I didn't offer any excuse because it was obvious they wanted a late booking to make up their quota for the day. That daft little error cost me an instant fine of £40 and a three point endorsement on my license. It was the first in forty years of driving and it was enough to make one spit.

Way back in February I attended the Hallamshire Hospital because having seen Dr. Hasan about a pain in my nether regions, he had decided that it was a double Hernia. After being examined at the hospital I was told that it was only a Hernia on the right hand side and not a double one and they would notify me when it was possible to operate. I received notification in the last week of July and the operation was on the 30th. There was no messing about and I only stayed in the hospital overnight and sent home the following day. Tony collected me because I was advised not to go home by taxi or bus. It was very uncomfortable for weeks and I had to cancel many of my bowls and umpiring fixtures but eventually it settled down.

It was now getting nearer to my trip to Barbados and the day following my coming out of hospital, I decided to send a cheque to Mike Hall for the balance of the fare. I had already taken him the deposit of £102 in the first week of June and now I paid him by cheque for the balance of £595. On Saturday the 5th October, Tony kindly agreed to run me over to Retford to Nigel Hall's house so that I could travel in his dad's car, along with Nigel and another player called John Cosgrove, to Gatwick Airport. Mike Hall had arranged for all of us to stay at a guest house overnight before going down to the Airport which was only a twenty minutes run away. We met up with other members of the party which included Ashley Metcalfe, the Yorkshire and Notts batsman and we left England late on Sunday night headed for Barbados. We were late getting in and arrived there one and a half hours overdue on the Monday. With Mike Hall being the principal organiser, he had arranged for a courtesy coach to take us to our places of accommodation. He said that the coach would go a pretty way and allow us to see some of the island. As we went, he pointed out to us in the centre of the capital, Bridgetown, a place called Trafalgar Square of which he insisted was the original Trafalgar Square, not the one in London. He must have thought that we were thick.

Where we were to stay was in the St. Thomas area of the island which was on the Western coast near to Holetown. Our accommodation was in a well built villa and was shared by the four of us who had travelled together. I had to share a room with Mike who kindly offered me the choice of beds whilst the other two, Nigel and John shared the other bedroom.

There was a dining room come sitting room and also a small corridor, off which was a toilet and shower. The kitchen was quite large and had all the facilities needed for our use, including a large fridge. The other members of the party were in different villas and the one next door had Ashley Metcalfe, two young chaps and another man who was a policeman and had brought with him his lady friend who was also a cop. The rest of them were in villas just down the road except for a couple of friends of Ashley's from Leeds and they were staying in one of the large hotels nearby.

The villas all had their own lawned areas and palm trees bounded by shrubs but I was surprised to see that the doors and windows had iron grilles on them and when anyone went out, Mike made sure that the door was double padlocked. The shopping precinct was a ten minute walk away so we were able to get some general groceries in and Mike suggested that we all put $20 into a kitty. After a short meal we all kipped down for the night and because it was so humid I switched on the wall fan. Mike told me to switch it off because of the cost. I thought, 'Aye! Aye! I'm going to enjoy this.' As I undressed I noticed that there was a small seepage on my underpants but it was possibly due to being sat so long on the aircraft in a cramped position after my Hernia operation.

We went to Bridgetown by the service bus the following morning to collect three small jeeps which Mike had arranged to hire for the purpose of getting the team about to the various venues. We needed them that day because it rained continuously and was therefore not possible to play the first match, so we hung about the villa and Nigel and John played Trivial Pursuit.

Mike took one of the jeeps and went into Bridgetown on business which I later found out was for his hobby, horse racing and he went there nearly every day to the bookies.

The second day I was up early along with the people in the next villa and we were swimming in the sea by 7.30 am. It was lovely and warm and I enjoyed it tremendously - in fact most days it was to become a habit. At lunchtime we all piled into Cirio's Restaurant for lunch and that was almost on the beach, it was like a MacDonald's but apparently that firm was banned from the island. In the afternoon most of us had a run up to Holder's Hill to the Bar Marshall which was familiar to the Hall's and was opposite the well known cricket ground. On the way back, Mike pulled up to go into a shop - come - cafe to speak to a Barbadian lady there who was Julie Stephenson, the wife of Franklyn Stephenson the West Indian cricketer who was coaching in South Africa. Julie was running the shop and cafe whilst he was away.

Because we had no match on the Wednesday, most of us went down on to Folkestone Beach. It wasn't too far so we walked there and managed to get a drink and a snack but the place was snided with cats and the birds were like gannets. We didn't go down there again.

On Saturday 12th, Julie Stephenson had told Mike to take all the team up to the cafe because she had laid on a special meal for us and that would be followed by a Karaoke night. The meal was very appetizing and there was plenty of drinking going on. The team were all drinking bottles and bottles of the local brew which was like a lager and made by a firm called

Banks. Everyone seemed to drink it out there and whilst it wasn't too bad, I only had a couple. Because of this I think I was ostracised by the team perhaps because I was unable to keep up with them and in any case I couldn't afford to keep buying a round for the whole team. I was sat on my own when Julie came over and said that I looked out of it. Perhaps so, but she sat and talked with me for some twenty minutes and I felt that I had known her for a very long time . She was very attractive and more so in her shorts but she also had a pleasing personality.

As the Karaoke got underway it was more pleasant and everyone was taking part. Suddenly one of the players asked me to do a turn and at first I declined because non of the tunes seemed to be in my era. So, he passed me an album with all the tunes listed and told me to pick what I liked. Then I told him I would do one of Nat King Cole's, 'The Very Thought Of You.'

The DJ announced me as the first 75 year old to take part and he started up the disc. The pitch was right, the tempo was right and I'd handled a microphone before. As I started to sing, everyone stopped talking and the only sound was the music and my voice, which luckily, held. At the end, the applause was terrific and was led by Julie Stephenson. Mike Hall said, "I didn't realise you could sing like that." Neither did I. It was late on when we finally arrived back at the villas and I can't disagree that I hadn't enjoyed it.

The next day we went down south a few miles to a place on the other side of Bridgetown called Miami Beach and there we had a good afternoon swimming and playing about on the beach. We were able to get a few refreshments. In the evening we all drove from the villas to a special pub like place where for two dollars one could have as much as they wanted. There was also some local entertainment for us. After a couple of hours the young ones took off for a longer night in Bridgetown, so Mike and I returned to the villa. I followed Mike into the villa but didn't lock the grille behind me and he said it must be locked at all times, even if someone was in during the day or night.

"I'm responsible to the owner for this building and in any case I don't want to be sat here and suddenly get mugged". Mike said.

I replied, "Well, you're big enough to take care of yourself, aren't you?" He was about six feet two inches tall and well made.

"I'm not taking that chance." He relied. "I'm scared as to what can happen out here."

I retorted in shop floor language, "You must be ********sick. If I was like you I would go and see a ********doctor. You're bloody pathetic!"

Back came the answer, "No one has ever spoken to me like that before."

"Well it won't be the last you stupid pillock." I then went to the bedroom.

He must have been a bag of nerves because he sat in the lounge until 3.00 am, waiting for Nigel to return to the villa. Now, Nigel was a big thirty three year old so I leave the reader to decide what my thoughts were and it didn't help with the lights reflecting up the corridor and into the bedroom. No way can I sleep with the lights on. However, he didn't speak to me for a couple of days. The mardy arse.

We were unable to get in any cricket because of the heavy rain showers we kept having and to pass the time we took ourselves off up to the hotel where the other couple were staying and there we were able to go in the open air swimming pool. It wasn't that big but we were able to have some fun. On the Monday of the second week, I went with the younger ones to the Bel Air Golf Course on the other side of the island. I didn't play but went round with them for the laugh because it was set amongst a series of small pools and it was an art in itself trying to clear them. Those who played, hired the clubs and eight golf balls each, which was 48 balls in total. At the end of the game only four balls were returned, so to some it up, it was a bit expensive.

On the Tuesday we finally managed to get a game of cricket on the Holders Hill ground but it wasn't ideal because the outfield had been mown and the grass put onto the wicket and rolled in. Apparently, that's how they prepare their wickets out there.

The first over started and our team were batting with Nigel and Ashley opening the innings. The West Indian bowler ran up and delivered the ball and I instantly called a 'No ball' for a foot fault. The second ball was the same so I called again. After the second ball, Ashley slowly walked down the wicket to me and laughingly said, "No eight ball overs, Ron, It's too bloody hot." So from then on I bent the laws to accommodate everyone. Mike Hall was umpiring at the other end and some of his decisions were to be desired and for which Ashley took some skyward looks at me as if to say, "I give up." Both teams made high scores but our team won by three wickets. After the game we all retired to the pavilion for a meal of bread and soup.

On the Wednesday, Mike came round a bit and asked me if I wanted to go to Bridgetown with him because he had some legitimate business to see to. I'm not one to bear a grudge so I went with him to some council offices where he told me to go and have a look round the town and he asked me to see him again in about an hours time. So off I went and had a good look at some of the places of interest in the town and also the so called Trafalgar Square and then I walked back to the council offices. I was stood out there in the hot sun for quite a while when I saw a young Barbadian lady and asked her if Mr. Hall was still in his meeting.

"Come with me." she said and took me through the back entrance to the offices and into the reception area. After another twenty minutes, Mike appeared and gave a look of disapproval at me being in the reception. We collected the jeep and on the way back, he said that if I hadn't seen the Test Match ground, he would take me into it to show me the famous stand named after Walcott and Weekes. This he did and I was pleased to have been able to see the well known ground.

On the Thursday, we played Holder's Hill cricket team again and the wicket was better. We had to start early at 12.pm because the light soon went out there and at half past five it was dark. The boundaries were short and any loose ball was punished, because we lost eight balls in which the home team beat us; scoring 350 for 8 off thirty overs to our 208 for 5. Ashley scored a marvellous eighty.

Friday the eighteenth and I was still a little upset after that argument and because of my age, I seemed to be out of it again so during the day, being on my own in the villa, I managed to ring our Tony at home in Rotherham and told him I was fed up and wouldn't be stopping for the third week but would be coming home with Ashley Metcalfe and one or two others who would be returning on the Sunday. I'm glad I contacted Tony because that night I went for a walk by myself and was nearly killed because as I was walking along the side of the badly lit road, a bus came so near to me that I had to dive into a roadside ditch. It's a good job it was there otherwise, who knows. I dusted myself off and made my way to Cirio's where, on seeing the state I was in, everyone showed their sympathy and asked me to join them at their table.

The next night we all went down into a large - bar - come hotel on the dockside in Bridgetown and listened to some good music played by a decent band and they played my kind of music which included a bit of jazz. We stayed there drinking until about 11.00pm before returning to the villa. Saturday night was a good night because the whole team went down through Bridgetown and found a pub called the Ship Inn where apparently most British holiday makers spent their time. There, we ordered a good meal but after that, they dispersed to the bar and I was on my own again. However, some people from Newcastle called me over to their table and I finished the night in their company so it wasn't too bad.

The last day of my tour, Sunday, we played Holder's Hill again and won by 177 runs to 115. One of their bowlers had played in England with aTest Side and was known as the

'Dentist' because he bowled so fast that it was known for him to knock out peoples' teeth. After the match, I was just having a shower after the rest of the team had finished and was just drying off when Mike Hall came in and asked me to pop outside a minute. When I told him I wasn't dressed yet he told me to just put on a pair of trousers and follow him. As I hobbled outside in my bear feet and just a pair of trousers on, he called for everyone's attention and said, "Because he has stood out here in the hot sun for three matches and done such a marvellous job for us as our Umpire, it gives me great pleasure to present the "Ashley Metcalfe Trophy to Ron on behalf of us all. Thank you, Ron." After the hassle between Mike and I, it was unbelievable and I was just too lost for words but I did thank them all. After the match we all finished up again in Stevo's - Julie Stephenson's bar, so we were able to thank her before we left. Mike Hall said that he was a godparent to one of her children and, funnily enough he had taken me up to Julies house one day to see her children, but that's by the way.

On Monday the 21st, those of us who were returning home, made our way to the airport just after tea and at 7.20pm in the evening we took off for England. I had enjoyed the change of climate etc., but in general I was disappointed with Barbados because as soon as one left the main areas, even like Holder's Hill, it was like a shanty town with rusting corrugated sheets on the roofs of the houses.

We arrived back at Gatwick at 7.40 am the next morning and after saying cheerio to Ash and the others, I was able to catch a National Express coach direct to Sheffield and that cost me £22, but it was worth every penny to be home.

My 75th birthday was very quiet but I did receive eleven birthday cards from friends and family. On the eleventh of November I was discharged from the Hallamshire after a final check up for my Hernia. It took a while to settle in at home again but I was able to carry on with the routine pastimes of playing snooker for the ChurchTeam, going to the TWIL Monday club and once again going to the Grosvener Hotel for the annual Christmas dinner which was always organised by TWIL. That was on the 6th December and on the 10th the MondayClub held its own Christmas Buffet up at the Hyde Park Inn again.

The Fellowship of 163 Mess also held a Xmas Dinner at 6.30 pm in the Angler's Rest pub on Richmond Park Road. The meal was good and afterwards some of the committee ran a quiz which was enjoyable but I didn't win anything. My one regret was that the ceiling was low and when people were smoking it became unbearable for such as me who was a non-smoker, nevertheless, I enjoyed it. Following that, my Christmas was very quiet with Dave being away again although Tony did pop in to see me when he collected his Xmas Box.

It had been a long haul to write up my lifestory and I was now at the point that after three years and having completed 1996, I wasn't going to go into so much detail of anything happening in the years up to the Year 2000, if I managed to reach that milestone. I had told Tony and David of my decision that I would do a synopsis of any main events in that period. Tony didn't seem too happy but I had made up my mind and my memory wasn't as good as it used to be after all the hard work which I had put into it.

Early in January, 1997, I had developed a skin rash on my back and the itching was driving me mad. Also my face was being affected so the Doctor sent me to see a Dermatologist. This was at the NGH and the specialist there, examined me but seemed at a loss as to what was causing it. He gave me some ointment for my back and told me the face rash could be ROSACEA and gave me some leaflets to read about the subject. I was asked to return on the 2nd February to see if the treatment had worked but this time I saw a Lady Doctor and she gave me a type of gell to put in the water whenever I had a bath. Eventually the rash disappeared but not the facial problem. Even the bed clothes caused me to itch around my face and at times I could have gone mad.

On the 11th February I was obliged to close my account at the Yorkshire Bank because since they had been taken over by an Australian Company, the service hadn't been half as good so I transferred to the Royal Bank of Scotland who had a Branch in Attercliffe so there wasn't too much inconvenience.

I received a letter last summer from New Zealand telling me that Aline's cousin Alison and her husband John, were coming over to England for a holiday. At the end of March this year, they arrived in London and I patiently waited to hear further from them so that I could arrange accommodation, but I heard nothing more for ages. In the meantime I had arranged to go to evening classes in town for a ten weeks' course at the Hi-Tech School, to learn about PC's (Personal Computers). This was because Dave had persuaded me to set myself up with a second hand one and this would help me with my book. I finished the course and received a Diploma for my efforts but I had been helped by the fact that I had worked on ICL Computer Equipment at TWIL.

We had seen a PC and printer advertised in the Midlands in a Computer magazine so I sent for that and it was in good nick. Dave brought over from Germany a load of Software which included Windows Word Perfect 6.1 and this enabled to to get off to a good start. The Tutor, Tom at the college had also given me MS Works for Windows 95 which also helped.

In May I received a phone call from Alison saying that whilst staying at John's brother's house prior to coming to me, she had been involved in a road accident with a motor cycle and had been in hospital for several weeks. She had broken her leg, cracked her pelvis and had some head injuries but was now able to get about on crutches.

She told me that John's brother was going to bring them up in his car on the 21st May. This he did and I had to make up a camp bed for Hubert to sleep in. He only stayed the one night before returning home down south. It was lovely to see Alison again after all those years because she was only twenty one the last time she was over with her Mum, Auntie Elsie. I had never met her husband John and it wasn't long before I wished I hadn't. He was good to a point and quite generous but in some things he did, he appeared to be a penny short of a shilling. Also after almost every question or statement he said, 'Ron' and it really got to me.

I did my best to entertain them and fortunately they had brought a wheelchair with them and this helped tremendously. I was able to take them round to see the immediate family but I drew a line at going to Stoke to see Harold and Betty her other cousin and wife. Don't forget, Alison was a cousin to the Todd and Hope families, not mine.

I didn't begrudge having them because being the only one with a car I was able to show them the Derwent Dams, which John hadn't seen but Alison had on her last visit. We had one day out at Chatsworth House and it pleased her when I was able to get her into part of the House without paying. John enjoyed the gardens and fountain area there. He hadn't seen anything like that before and took advantage of being able to get some good photographs to take back to New Zealand.

It was awkward trying to decide on other places of interest but I managed to find one or two, including Cresswell Crags and the Great Oak in Sherwood Forest. Because I still had my umpiring to do, I took them to a match near to Retford and with the weather being good, they enjoyed that day too.

Tony invited us to go to the Yellow Lion pub at Greasboro with his friends Dennis and Doreen and our Mathew also went. We were able to have a short walk across some fields where Dennis pointed out certain landscapes. We had a few drinks at the Lion and then I ran them back home because the night air was turning chilly.

Overall, they stayed for three weeks and there were lighter moments such as watching John help Alison to do a little washing. He hung out each handkerchief with a separate peg but when he went to take in the washing line, instead of winding it around his thumb and elbow joint of one arm, he was trying to wind it on the floor like a lariat. I'm sorry, but things like that always amuse me. I shouldn't grumble really because he did his best when helping Alison in and out of the wheel chair or getting her up or down stairs and steps. I kept forgetting that they were now in the mid-fifties. Early on I said that he was generous and quite often he insisted on paying for the meals if we called at a pub on our days out.

On the third week, they rang Hubert to arrange for him to come and collect them, ready for their journey home to New Zealand. Although it had been tiring, I had enjoyed having them but I was also glad to be back on my own. Hubert came up a couple of days later and I said cheerio to them both and they thanked me for all I had done for them.

On August the eighth I lost a really good old pal, Fred Tyler because we had grown up together as lads and later on in life we were the 'Best Man' for each other at our respective weddings. We really had seen some fun and incidents in our lives. Fred was three days younger than me and died at the age of 75 years. His funeral was on Thursday the 14th and Norma, his widow, asked me back to the wake because of the good friendship we had shared. Fred and I had been pals since the age of twelve when our parents were taking us both to the Queen's Road Chest Clinic in town. In those days many children were taken for check ups with their chests because there was so much Tuberculosis about but neither of us contracted it, thank goodness.

Almost each time I visited the Charles Clifford Dental Hospital, I was able to call on my friend Jessie Catton who lived in a private flat just above the hospital. It was on one of these visits that she asked a favour of me and it was, would I care to go with her as a companion on one of those four day weekend excursions. Having agreed, she did all the necessary booking and having paid her my deposit at the end of August, I let her have the balance on the day we set off. It cost £115.50 each and it helped us both financially by sharing a room and saving the single room supplement. Jessie was two years older than I so there was no other motive in sharing.

We travelled to Moffat in Scotland and stayed at a hotel which was just below the park and luckily our room was on the ground floor. The coach people had arranged a couple of outings for us and once again the weather was good. On the Sunday we bought tickets for a charity duck race on the small river which flowed through the park. I've never seen a duck race and neither had Jessie and wondered how it was possible to get ducks to race, so we had to wait until the actual race. There were various breeds of ducks all around the park and we soon found out that the racing ducks were actually small yellow plastic ones which had a number painted on it which corresponded to the number on our tickets.

The small river was blocked off with a net at one point and higher up the stream the race was started. It caused great enthusiasm at they floated down stream to the net which was about a hundred yards away but our ducks were nowhere at the finish.

I had noticed that I was having to literally push Jessie into doing something and even at the meal times I saw that she seemed to be confused when ordering her food. Thinking no more of it, we finished our short holiday and returned home. We had both enjoyed the break and shortly afterwards, her daughter, Marylin, rang me and thanked me for taking her Mum away and giving their families a break from looking after her.

On one of my afternoons at the Steel City Club where, being in the winter season we met to play indoor games, I was asked by Albert Dyson if I was interested in going to watch the World Indoor Bowls Championships. This was always held at the Preston Guild Hall in Lancashire and I thought it would make a pleasant change. So on the 1st August, having paid my dues, I joined the rest of those who were going, at the Sheffield Sports Stadium in

Attercliffe. It was an exciting day and it was good to watch the game live instead on the TV. Many of the worlds top players were there including Andy Thompson, Ian Schumaker from Australia and David Gourlay from Scotland besides many other well known players. It wasn't a bad day out for the price of £9.50 which included admission and the coach fare.

On Thursday, the 23rd October, I went down to Ella's again for a few days but this time I went by National Express to the Victoria Bus Station and then caught a connection on the Greenline coach service which dropped me off within five minutes walk of where Ella lived. My birthday was on the Saturday and Lorna, Ella's daughter, was off duty so was able to take us out for the day to see Leeds Castle which is in Kent and not in Yorkshire. It was a very interesting place to visit and to help me with the history of the Castle, Lorna bought me a book giving the history of the place and she said it was my birthday present. It was a break for me again but by Tuesday, I had really had enough so returned home. In any case, I had another appointment at the NGH at 9.30 am on the Wednesday and also the following day at the same time.

Saturday, 1st November, was a mixed day because I had been invited to the wedding of Tina and David Jones at Ranmoor Church at 2.30 pm. Also Tony and I had been asked to go up to the YHA Hostel at Brecon, which is near to the Gliding Club at Hucklow, high up in the Derbyshire hills overlooking the Hope Valley area.

I went to the wedding which was really a high brow one and had to be if it was held at the Ranmoor Church because it was **The** church at which to get wed in Sheffield.

I saw the marriage ceremony and took one or two photo's of the happy couple and managed to apologise to Tina and David for not being able to attend the reception later on. They both understood the circumstances and said that they would see me at a later date.

The reason for going to Brecon was because the local area YHA committee wanted to show their appreciation and thank me for the donation which Geoff had made in his financial arrangements following his death. This time the sum of £500 had paid for a new cooking range at the Hostel. Tony and I enjoyed the evening out and by 10.00 pm we were on our way home and I was driving carefully because snow had fallen a few days earlier.

Way back in early September, I had attempted to contact Aunty Betty Priestley at Bamford but her sister Joan had answered the 'phone and was pleased to hear that it was me. It had been several years since I had last contacted them and though it sounded cheeky, I was ringing them to asked if they new what had happened to the Family Bible which had been at the Jubilee Cottages many years ago. I was enquiring because I was the last of the male line in the Derwent Priestley's and I would have liked to have gotten hold of the Bible because of that reason. Joan said that she would have a word with my Aunt and ring me back. This she did a few days later and said that the Bible was with Aunty Betty who was thinking of passing it on to the Bamford Church. When she rang, she told me that if I wanted it I was welcome to go and collect it from my Aunt, so this I did a few days later. It was a good job that I did because when I opened the front cover, inside was an inscription written in ink and it said, "Presented to our dearest brother George from his loving sisters May and Pollie on the 1st July, 1914 on his 21st birthday, with best wishes."

This proved to me that because of the inscription I had done the right thing in asking for the Good Book, it proving that really the book did belong to my father George and in turn to me, being his only son. The Bible was a beautiful piece of work and was some twelve and a half inches long and ten inches wide with a depth of four inches bound in a cover of black with gold clasps and hinges. Aunty said that she was pleased that I had taken charge of it instead of it going to the church. I was so pleased to be able to bring it home for my father's sake and don't forget, I had two sons to whom I hoped it would be handed down and to their sons also. On getting it home the first thing I did was to create a family tree commencing with my Mum and Dad . I then put in it into the front of the Bible for history's sake. Ironically, it was shortly after seeing Auntie Betty and collecting the Bible, that she passed peacefully away aged, 90. What had to be, had to be.

The year faded out quietly, except for a further visit to the NGH on Wednesday 30th November and as I said earlier, there wasn't anything of significance to write home about.

Early in January 1998, I made up my mind to take a holiday and decided to go back to Scotland, so I paid my deposit with the Wallace Arnold Coaches and waited for the 12th April to arrive because that's when I was going. My lads kept telling me to spend my money and that is why I had firstly booked this holiday and also had decided to spend some money on the house by having the small windows replaced. On the 22nd January a surveyor from Cold Seal Windows came and measured up and agreed on the installation being between May and June.

The following Wednesday I went with the bowling club to Preston Guild Hall again to see the World Indoor Bowling Championships and though it was on the Television I don't think any of our group managed to get on the big screen.

During February I was spending again and this time I thought that I would replace the living room carpet. It had been down over ten years and was getting rucks in it which became dangerous, so on the 3rd February, the carpet fitters came and luckily the weather was dry and sunny and enabled the workmen to prepare the room.

Being dry helped tremendously because it was possible to take the heavy furniture on to the patio and this included the organ. This gave the fitters the chance to put down the underlay and carpet grippers prior to laying the new carpet in one piece. The old carpet had been removed before that and put in the hut ready for Tony to collect it and use it in his home. The men told me that the reason the old carpet had rucks in it was because the previous fitters hadn't put any grippers down. The new carpet had a flowered design and it was all in a medium blue colour and cost me £350.

For an early break in the New Year, Dave had invited me to go over to them for a few days and on Friday 13th I went by the North Sea Ferry from Hull and Dave picked me up at Rotterdam. I always enjoyed seeing the children and though it was a quiet weekend we did manage to go to Holland to see the Voolon Museum. It was a type of park with wartime vehicles strewn about the area and in which children could please themselves inside some of the tanks etc. There was also a large building in which there were military displays and other wartime memorabilia. On Tuesday Dave ran me back up to Rotterdam, which was a two hour drive, to catch the return ferry home and after sailing overnight I arrived home in Sheffield at 11 am on the Wednesday morning.

The following morning I was up at the NGH again because following some earlier results Dr. Quiyam had found a ripple on my left nipple and wanted an X-ray to see if it was of any importance. Those results were to be passed back to the Doctor at a later date.

Having been to the cremation of Aunty Betty on the 22nd January, it seemed strange that within two months I would be going to her sister Joan's cremation. It was possible that after all those years of being with her sister Betty, she couldn't cope with the loss of someone who had literally been a mother to her.

On the 12th April I set off on my holiday to Scotland, in fact I had chosen a place called Ullapool on sentimental grounds because this was the place where Geoff had spent his last holiday before his accident in 1993. I wanted to look at the place and visualise what he might have been doing on that holiday. I even went to the local YHA to see if that was the hostel that he had stayed at and the staff were very good in looking up their records to confirm that he had really been there.

The Wallace Arnold Coach tours were well renowned and our hotel was on the top side of the town which was situated on Loch Broom in the Highland district of Scotland. It was used as a base for the holiday and the coach driver took us to many laces of interest during the week and with the snow laying about it made the scenery exquisite. Although the coach was only half full everyone was friendly and sociable and joined in the fun. One of the days out was to go to the famous Glencoe Pass and another day we went down to Fort William near to Ben Nevis. Just before dropping down to that place we were taken to see the Monument of the famous Commandos. I enjoyed the holiday and on our way home we stayed at a hotel in the centre of Glasgow when, as we left the following morning the driver gave us a quick tour of the city which included Sockiall Street and the Gobbels district. I arrived back home on Saturday the 18th April in time for the forthcoming cricket season.

On the 27th April, Cold Seal came to renew all the little windows such as the one at the side of the front door, the pantry window, the outhouse window and the downstairs toilet one which had a locking transom window put in. They were all double glazed and the pattern on the glass matched the small panels in the front door. They made an excellent job of it and the total cost was £569.

At the end of May I measured up for some new blue curtains in the living room so that they would match the carpet and the three piece suite I had recently purchased from a shop in Darnall at a cost of £150.

The curtains I bought in Rotherham from a shop which Aline used to go to when she wanted new materials. Having chosen the material I had to wait for a couple of weeks for them to be made up and they cost me another £65 but in the end, the room took on another appearance and looked completely refreshed. I'm sure that Nip would have approved.

On the 5th June I had arranged to see a Mrs. Helen Botham who was a financial consultant for the Wesleyan Mutual Society. She arrived and rung the door bell and when I opened the door, there was a very attractive 50 year old lady and without thinking I said, "Do you want to go straight through to the living room and do it in comfort or would you rather we did it on the kitchen table?" I realised straight away that I had 'dropped one' but she saw the funny side of the remark.

Half an hour later I had agreed to invest the sum of £5,500 in her Society for a period of five years with possibility of accruing a final bonus of 33% over that period. I had to take the risk because investments can go down as well as up. It was on the 9th July that Helen Botham called again to collect the Banker's Draft which I again, had to get from my NSB Savings Account. I only hoped that I had done the right thing but there was a guarantee that irrespective of what happened, I would get my original investment back.

It's amazing how time flies and as the 18th July came around again, it didn't seem four years since I lost that lass of mine and also that five years had passed since the loss of our Geoff on the 30th June.

At the end of the cricket season I felt like a rest so I decided to go to Bridlington, on my own, for a few days. I hadn't booked anywhere so I headed for a guest house on spec and rang the bell. As soon as I saw the landlady I knew it was the place I wanted because she was the landlady when Nip and I stayed there for our Ruby Wedding anniversary and she had a deformed arm which was shorter than the other because there was no hand there but that was no criteria. I was fortunate because there was a vacancy and I booked in for three nights. The guest house was the 'Springfield' on Trinity Road and once I had settled in I told Mrs Fielding about the last time I had been and she commented that at the back of her mind, she could recall Nip and me being there. She and her husband had made some alterations to the place and there was now a licensed bar.

I enjoyed the company for the few days I was there and in the evenings I would take myself off to the local Gala Bingo Hall. That brought back happy memories because Nip and I always went there.

On the 19th October I made arrangements to change my telephone company from the BT and Cable & Wireless to Yorkshire Cable because by paying monthly by Direct Debit, I found that it was cheaper. Also, if I required it, I could also have Cable TV through them.

In the last week of October, Dave rang to say that they were coming over to buy a dishwasher because they were cheaper over here than in Germany. They all arrived on the 28th, just after my birthday but only stayed the one night before travelling back to Bruggen. Although the stay was short it was good to have them over again.

As I mentioned a way back, I had been having trouble with the rash on my face and Tony had suggested me using a shaving foam instead of the brush and soap stick. So, over the past few months I had been trying it and also I decided to rinse my face in clean fresh water instead of using the water in which I had shaved. I'm pleased to say that I now have no problems at all and Doctors don't know everything. It also helped when I put a bed sheet on the bed just under the duvet. It stopped any irritation.

On the 5th November, Ella rang to ask me to go down for a few days because she had a surprise for me. So down I went and when I arrived she informed me that one of her neighbours had managed to get some tickets for the Royal Albert Hall in London.

The occasion was a concert by the massed Bands of the RAF and also the USAF for some anniversary or other but I really enjoyed the music and the programme was varied and excellent but at times, as usual, the Yank musicians tried to outdo our lads by playing double forte but I wasn't impressed. It was a novelty to me because I had never been inside the historic hall before and I appreciated being there and could well visualise the scene when the annual Remembrance service was held there each November. The break was enjoyable once more.

Way back in the 40's when I mentioned my 21st birthday and the night at the Hill Top Hotel, well it was with sadness that on the 17th December, Frank Sellars, who had been the Landlord there, had been cremated at the ripe old age of 104. It was only last year that I had called in to see him in his flat in Woodhouse.

Nothing had been planned for the coming Christmas so I had an idea to ask Tony to bring Mathew over and I would provide the Xmas Dinner for them this year for a change. It felt like good old times, having someone sat at my table on Christmas Day. They both had a good feed but by six o'clock they decided to go home and I didn't mind because I had enjoyed having them with me.

I knew I wouldn't be seeing Dave and his family because he had arranged to take them on a ski-ing holiday and it was to be their Christmas Present. The video he took of the holiday with them showed how much they appreciated it and proved how good they were on their skis, young James in particular.

The year ended quietly and as usual I had to let in my own New Year, not forgetting to bring back into the house some bread, to keep me fed; some coal to keep me warm and some silver coinage for luck.

What a difference to the previous Christmas when Dave and his family came for a few days. One of the lads had done something of which I disapproved and when I aired my feelings, Heather turned on me and our Dave seemed to lean to her as well. Perhaps it was a storm in a tea cup but it ended with me walking out of my own house on Xmas Eve. I first went to Tony's but he wasn't particularly interested so I drove over to Joan's and received some solace but I hadn't told Tony where I was headed for.

What hurt me more than anything was that I stayed at Joan's until 10 pm and she agreed with me that one would have thought that Tony and Dave would have rung each other just to check where I was. Missing for four hours and no one seemed interested. However, eventually I calmed down and returned home and as I drove up, Dave was on the doorstep and readily apologised.

I never bear grudges and I soon forgot the incident but I don't think Heather had because at later times, when I was in her company, I was lucky if I had more than a few words out of her. She wouldn't enter into any conversation at all.

The first few months of Ninety Nine were very quiet and apart from Tony telling me he had been notified that he had obtained his degree through the Open University and that the presentation ceremony would be at the Harrogate Conference Centre. I went along with Mat and Lisa where we claimed our reserve seats in the hall and then waited for the ceremony. It must have taken an hour before Tony's name was called and as he mounted the stage to receive his diploma I had a tear in my eye because I was so pleased and proud of him and he looked smart in his Open University Gown - They were not permitted to wear a motor board in the OU set up. There he was with a Batchelor of Arts Degree plus a diploma with honours in Music. He had really worked hard for it and it had taken him five years to achieve his aim.

Wanting a break, I had booked a five day holiday at Great Yarmouth in Norfolk and this started on the 12th April. Whilst on this holiday there was another man with his wife and his sister-in-law and they asked me to go and sit with them on their table in the dining room.

During conversation it turned out that he originated from Bradwell in Derbyshire where many of my relations lived. His name was Jim Lloyd and he knew nearly all my relatives so we had something in common, plus the fact that he was also a Companion of the Fellowship.

We had one or two coach trips whilst we were there and one of them was to Norwich, where it snowed and where we had a good look around the Cathedral, the other trip was to Wroxham. On the quiet, Jim told me that his sister-in-law was the widow of a Mr Turner who had owned a business park near to where I lived and that she was a millionairess but that didn't interest me.

We had one laugh at the Hotel because I commented that my room was rather cold and the following night when I went to retire, someone had hung a hot water bottle onto the door handle. No one in our party would admit to it but I did take it home with me.

On May 20th I paid a visit to the Nurse at our surgery for a routine blood pressure check up. She was new to the practise and looking at my notes she asked me how my Diabetes was going. I asked, "What Diabetes?" and she replied that I had been diagnosed two years ago. "Well, no one told me." I said. "Just a minute, Mr. Priestley, I'll get Dr. Shaihk to take a look at you."

A few minutes later he came in, asked me to drop my trousers and lay on the couch with my knees under my chin. He then inserted one of his fingers, in a rubber glove, into my Anus and after a few seconds he said, "That's not Diabetes, it's a prostate problem but I think that it is benign." Turning to the nurse he told her to book me an appointment at the Hallamshire Hospital for a confirmation check up.

It didn't take long for the appointment to come through and on the 5th July I saw a Mr. Smith in the Urology Department of the hospital. Before going into him I had been asked to drink two pints of water and this was to take a flow reading when I was passing water prior to the examination. I eventually was called in to see Mr. Smith, the consultant, who, like Dr. Shaikh, asked me to climb onto the couch. He performed the same inspection but this time he said he was sorry but he must disagree with my doctor because the Prostate wasn't benign but malignant. In other words I had Prostate Cancer and he arranged for me to have further blood tests and a bone scan.

At the end of July, Dave arrived home for the weekend because he was on an environmental course in England for the RAF and it was taking place in Sheffield. He had brought some more computer equipment with him and he eventually set me up on the Internet and also made it possible to use an e-mail system. He was making sure that I lived in the modern times.

Once more I had to go and have some tests at the Hallamshire and this time I saw a Dr. Cato who explained to me that he was going to take some biopsies off my prostate.

Having explained that there would be some discomfort, he asked me to strip off from below the waist, put a gown on and lay on the couch in this type of mini theatre. Two nurses gave me some comforting by talking to me as he inserted a type of camera up my back passage. To me it felt like a Kodak Brownie Box Camera. Through it he could see a picture on his monitor screen and as he moved it around he called another Doctor to see where he was to take the biopsies. He then said that he was going to insert this special instrument which would sound like a staple gun when he used it. Each time he used it I heard a click and the action made me wince and each time a small section was cut from the Prostate gland. There were six shots in all and each one seemed to be going higher and higher up my bum. After this minor operation I put my clothes back on and the auxiliary nurse made me a cup of tea as I sat in the corridor just outside the small theatre in which I had been treated. It is all part of the treatment and helps the patient to settle down.

Whilst Dave had been here the other week, he had arranged to have a digital box installed. He had wanted to get one, which was free from any reputable TV shop, to take back to Germany and install it himself but the contract stated that although the box was free, it had to be installed by a qualified engineer at a standard fee of £40. On the 10th August, the box was installed so I was able to get 'Sky' television on it and many more programmes to watch. I took it that after the twelve months were up, Dave would disconnect it and take it with him to wherever he might be stationed. After all, he signed the paper work so it must be his.

Early in August I had asked our Betty to go with me to a furniture company called Courts because I had been and had a look around the store at an earlier date and in my mind I had chosen a wall unit come cocktail cabinet but I wanted a second opinion. She agreed with my choice when she saw it and it was about eight feet long and six feet high. It had a large glass fronted cupboard at each end and the centre contained two glass shelves at the top and the cocktail cupboard below them. Underneath that was a recessed shelf and it was finished off with three long drawers and a normal small cupboard at either end down below. The top area had mirrors on the back upper cupboard and behind the glass shelves and to really set it all off, there were three partly concealed lights in the top of the unit. I had paid a deposit of £55 but it wasn't until the anniversary of our Geoff's birthday that it was delivered. I paid the balance of £519 and there was an insurance included of £50 which, if I didn't call them out to renovate any accidental damage over five years then I could reclaim the £50 pounds.

My bone scan had been on the 29th July and after that I had to go for a set of x-rays of my chest, right shoulder blade and my head. August the 23rd I was called to the Hallamshire for the results of my tests and Mr. Smith said that the scan had shown that the cancer had gone into my shoulder blade and ribs. He did explain that it was cancer in the bone and **not** bone cancer which is something more serious. When I asked the consultant what his prognosis was he said, " Two to five years." It was a blow but I was assured that with certain treatment it could be controlled. As I went home I had a tear in my eye for I was thinking of Aline. The diagnosis really knocked me back and my lads were really upset when I let them know the bad news

I returned again on the 1st September for treatment, which I was to have each month for the next three months. Staff Nurse Carline was very good to me and when I told her that a friend of mine had suggested castration to cure the cancer, she said, "Why loose your acutriments for nothing because even that won't cure the complaint." She also commented, "I know it's difficult to say but try not to worry because I'm sure you will find that the treatment will ease your mind."

With that she stuck a needle into my stomach and that was my first injection of Zoladex.

The following week I took our Betty out for the day to Newstead Abbey. She had never been before and she really appreciated it as we toured the building and then after some refreshments we had a steady walk around the extensive grounds and gardens.

On the 11th Sept., Dave was over again for another course but popped into to set me up with a new monitor and update my system by installing Windows 95. He also put in a new Modem which we bought at a computer fair in Rawmarsh. Three days later Dave returned to Bruggen. He really knew his stuff about P.C's.

I had to go to see Dr. Shaihk again because I was getting those palpitaions and miss a beat - double beat situations, so he sent me back up to the NGH for further tests and another ECG but it proved negative.

On the 27th September I had my second injection of Zoladex but another nurse did the treatment this time and asked on me which side of my stomach I had received the first one. When I told her the left side then she said that this one was to go in the right side and in future each visit would be alternatively monitored.

I really don't know why but on the 29th I went down to Ellas' again for a few days but apart from going to Lorna's for Sunday lunch, it was all so boring and it didn't help with Ella moaning and groaning most of the time. I was glad to get back home.

Tony had persuaded me to go on holiday, with him and his friends, Dennis and Doreen, also his new lady friend Sandra, was going. She was his senior by about five years. We left Rotherham on the 16th October and the journey took twenty four hours to a place in Spain called Rabat. It was very tiring and I wasn't too happy with the stops we made in France on the way down. The toilet facilities were atrocious for a modern country and it didn't help when looking for one, I tripped over the causeway edge in the dark and grazed my knee.

When we arrived, the hotel was OK and the room which Tony and I shared, was quite cosy. We went on the train to Lloret a couple of times but the weather wasn't too kind. It was really tiring because Dennis would set off at a quick pace when going anywhere but counteracting that we had Sandra. Although she was on medication, her pace at walking was unbelievable and we kept having to wait for her to catch up with us. One day I was so fed up with her slowness and Dennis was 'miles' in front that I shouted for him to wait and I then set off and ran about a hundred yards towards him. It put the wind up both him and Tony. It was a pleasant change and another country to add to my list but I was glad when we arrived home.

My appointments for treatment at the Hallamshire could hardly be overlooked because the third injection was on my birthday the 25th October and the fourth one was on my Mum's birthday, 22nd November. The latter visit also included a further interview with Mr. Smith and this time I was much happier because further investigation showed that the cancer had gone from my shoulder and he was more than pleased to tell me that my PSA (Prostate Specific Antigen) blood count had been reduced from the original reading of 38 to a very welcome 4. Anything below ten was classed as excellent. When he had told me the good news he followed it up by saying that he thought he could find me a few more years to live, so you can tell, I really felt chuffed with life. Mr Smith, therefore, decided to put me on quarterly injections instead of the monthly ones. The nurse in attendance asked me to wait until she had been to the hospital pharmacy to get the equipment and as she was leaving the room, I asked her if it meant getting a bigger needle for the injection because I was going onto the longer three monthly treatment. She gave a little chuckle and commented that she didn't think so. Ten minutes later she was back and although the needle wasn't longer, it certainly was thicker.

In between these two treatments, on the 10th November, Dave had rung me to inform me that he was going into a German Hospital to have his polyps re-done. The first attempt, a few years ago, hadn't really been successful, thus the reason for having it done again. He was kept in for about a week before being discharged and when he contacted me again he said that he felt fine except for the bruising of his eye due to the operation.

Prior to that though, he had been over again because on the 30th October he had finished an environmental course at RAF Halton and had made the journey up home to see how I was coping. I know that neither of my sons commented much but I also know that they really cared about me.

The annual TWIL dinner at the Grosvenor Hotel fell on a Thursday the 2nd December and this year I had remembered that I could take along a guest, like I used to take Aline. So, I asked Tony if he would like to go with me and though at first he seemed reluctant, he finally agreed because I had persuaded him to say the night at No.8 to save him chasing about. He enjoyed the night out and the meal and also to be able to talk to one or two of my workmates such as Bob Little and Janet Perrins, with whom he had once worked alongside on his vocational training whilst he was still at Firth Park Grammar School. During the evening we sat at the table for our meal with Terry Murphy and his family and best of all was the fact that the Chief Executive of Tinsley Wire, Neil Pursehouse, was in our company, or were we in his?

Having arrived back at No.8, and after a little natter, we retired and having taken his shoes off, Tony followed me up the stairs in his stocking feet, not having brought any slippers with him. It took me a couple of days to get rid of the smell of his sweaty feet but it was a complaint he had been lumbered with for many years.

At three in the morning on Saturday 11 December, I was awakened with a terrific pain on the left hand side of my head. It was excruciating, so when I had arisen and had a little breakfast I went to see Dr. Shaihk. Being a Saturday morning there wasn't much he could do but gave me a blue card and told me to go to the NGH to have my head x-rayed on the following Monday morning. This I did and trailed to the hospital, only to be told that they wouldn't do the X-ray and would I go back to my Doctor and they would contact him. I was fuming. There was no explanation and I returned immediately and was just in time to catch Dr. Shaihk again before surgery closed. He was at a loss but the hospital had contacted him with the outcome being to tell the receptionist to make me an appointment to see a consultant at the NGH.

A week later I received the date of the appointment and guess what? It wasn't until the 15th March, 2000 and I was to see a Doctor Liddle, who I was to find out later, was a lady doctor. Efforts were made to get an earlier date but to no avail. The pain did ease a little but it was still there and I had to wait.

Dave was taking his family on a skiing holiday at Xmas to Mayrhofen in Germany but on his last visit, he had brought my present with him on strict instructions not to open it until Christmas Day. He had taken their presents back with him except his. It was a surprise because it was always difficult trying to buy things for him due to the fact that he had most of the things he needed. I ordered a pullover from the RAF Benevolent Fund catalogue and posted it direct to him. That surprised him as it was on 50th Anniversary of the founding of the Fund and on the front was a special crest.

Tony had been up on Christmas Eve for his present of slippers and a £10 note, Mathew's present was a football encyclopaedia plus a £10 note, Anna and Dylon had a musical board each and not knowing what to buy Lisa I gave her a cheque for £15 which unfortunately she lost a few days later.

I found out later that Dave had asked Tony to contribute to my present and when I opened it on Christmas Day, I found it to be a JVC CD/Cassette player with a built in radio. Tony's contribution was a set of four Jazz Classic CD's and Dave and Heather's children had bought me a set of CD's of Great British Bands from the forties era. It was good to listen to some of the old time greats.

So as the Christmas Festivities subsided, everyone was getting excited about the so called New Millennium which was about to descend upon us. One thought I had for it was that our Dave would be successful in finally getting his promotion and also emulating Tony in getting his degree at the Open University.

Who would have thought that way back in 1921 the little weakling who was born in No. 87 Brompton Road, would live long enough to see the year 2000. I did, with lots of love and care from my loving Mum, Dad and family and of course, My God.

OVER THERE

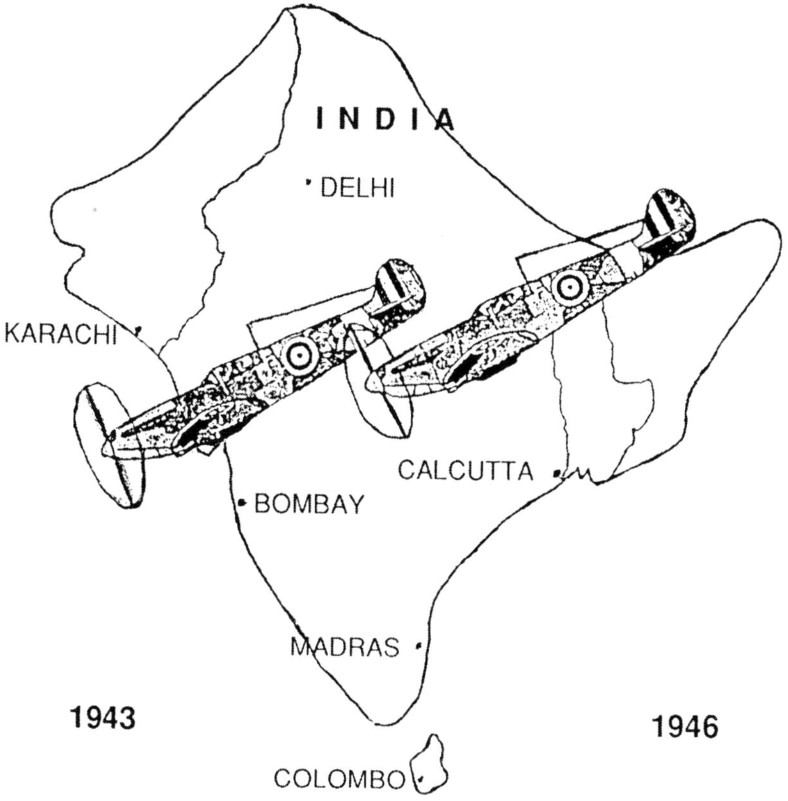
INDIA
DELHI
KARACHI
CALCUTTA
BOMBAY
MADRAS
1943
1946
COLOMBO

Chapter One

OUTWARD BOUND

To those who have the first experience of boarding a large liner, there must be a thought in their minds of fascination and mystery. But on the other hand there is no thought at all but shall I say, discontentment when the embarking is forced.

I had this experience when I walked up the gangplank of the Monarch of Bermuda on the 11th August 1943. The Monarch was a two funnelled liner of a well-known shipping line and was normally used for holiday cruises in peacetime but had been converted into a troopship for wartime purposes. The first thing that came into our minds, as it must have done to others, was a few hours shore leave before we left England for an unknown destination. We were due for a disappointment. Once on board we had to stay until we reached that certain place. The order of the day was definitely, "no shore leave." The party of us who had been sent in advance set about getting to know the ship generally and doing the few odd jobs we had been assigned. Officially we were the BAGGAGE PARTY, and was fortunate to be settled in a small room suitably fitted with twelve bunks, just enough for our party. This was on the left hand side of the ship, which for all innocents like ourselves we learned to call the port side. With the early dawn of August 13th, the first batch of drafts of personnel detailed came aboard. These were quickly dispersed to the sleeping quarters on the lower decks and the loading of the baggage, food etc., helped to pass the day well. By the evening there were only a few odds and ends to come aboard and by sundown we were almost ready to sail. This we did on Saturday the 14th August, from the Mersey through an opening in the minefields and out into the Irish Sea. The Monarch set her bows on a north-westerly course, this bringing the idea into all passengers heads that we were going by way of Northern Ireland.

Sunday morning we found ourselves off Greenock in North West Scotland and I can honestly say that I have never seen a more beautiful sight than the small but picturesque Scottish town across the bay. The sun had just risen and was reflecting on the red roofs of the white cottages on the shore. In the afternoon we moved out of Rothesay in the glorious sunshine, keeping a slow speed until we reached the Clyde. Off Rothesay we joined our convoy and escort but we didn't sail immediately. It was Monday 16th August when we actually sailed on what was to be more of a cruise than a dangerous voyage.

Each night members of the band, who were on board, congregated on the Fo'c'sle of the ship to play music to the LADS AND LASSES. Yes, I forgot to mention earlier that there were members of the A.T.S., V.A.D. AND RAF Nursing Sisters with us. This was certainly helpful because we were able to hold some dances on the deck but one could hardly call it a ballroom. As the sun reclined in the west, dancing would cease and the sound of voices would rise above the calm to swell into a refrain of some popular song. If one could imagine some thousands of people who had never met before, joining in the songs or hymns to make it sound like a professional choir, they would have a look of envy upon their faces. I shall always remember the beautiful scene that met our eyes on the morning of Saturday 21st August. There in the glorious colour of an Eastern sunrise, we saw on the Port bow Gibraltar with its well-known Rock, the gateway to the Mediterranean and the Middle East.

It was here that our escort left us and we waved goodbye to the destroyers, corvettes and aircraft carrier. The Captain of the escort signalled a message to us relating to the pleasure it had been to escort us and hoped it would occur again someday. He concluded by wishing all personnel the best of luck on our future mission.

There was no sign of life on shore as we sailed slowly through the Straits guarded as it were by the mountains of Spain on the one side and Spanish Morocco on the other.

Before continuing the story I would like to put you in the picture as to what was happening on board before we reached the Med.

To celebrate our first day at sea we held a concert on board on the main Mess deck. Personnel from all over the ship and from all branches of the Services participated to give all passengers a really good evening. There were singers of straight and popular songs, a conjuror, well known in England as Salin the Chinese Magician; comedians, pianists of which I was one; impressionists and impersonators. A great laugh of the evening was an impression of a Blitz by 'Taffy' Morgan. It was so effective that he burst the ships' Tannoy system, which was being used by kind permission of the Captain.

'Taffy' – or George Roy Morgan as the records showed, was a bespectacled bonny lad of 19 years old and hailed from Port Talbot in South Wales. We had been together in the same billet on a camp in Bibury in Gloucestershire and had been drafted overseas at the same time. If there was a noise to be copied then Taffy would try to do it. Like I said, his impression of an air raid was the cause of the ship's address system being damaged but it was soon repaired and the concert continued.

The biggest ovation of the night was given to non other than Pilot Officer Oliver Wakefield. He was a very popular broadcasting comedian and could be heard regularly on the BBC variety programmes. His forte was to break up or leave sentences unfinished; the rest was left to one's imagination. I remember how he held the attention of the audience with his witticism and flashing but cheeky smile. What a laugh we had when he referred to the Desert Rats fighting in the hot sands; this was his remark

"Just think for one moment, as you sit there on your on… (laughter), of the wonderful lads of the Eighth Army, out there in the desert smoking camels and riding Egyptians..."

Another roar of laughter could be heard all over the large ship as he corrected himself in his inimitable way. Camels by the way were a type of cigarette. I don't think there was anyone who didn't enjoy him or herself.

For the next four days we saw no land and we carried out the general routines of the ship including boat drill in case of emergency. Don't forget that we were sailing south down the east of the Atlantic Ocean and a zigzag course was maintained at all times to elude any possible 'U-boats' that may be in the vicinity.

We became very interested one day when five Seafires from the escorting aircraft carrier started "shooting up" the convoy for practice. It was marvellous to see them just skimming the waves and suddenly shooting up into the sky. There was a bit of excitement when one tried to land on the flight deck whilst flying out of wind. The pilot made four approaches but each time he came in too high. At the fifth attempt he made a bumpy landing with his wings beating a tattoo on the deck. It was only with sheer luck that he missed the watchtower.

Now to return to where I broke off, when we were entering the Med.

We couldn't actually see the coastline, just the tops of what appeared to be crimson mountains. From then onwards groups of people crowded at the rails to see what they could of one of the greatest battlefields in history, northwest Africa.

The first big place of importance we saw was Oran but only in the distance. Coincidence or not I cannot say but on Sunday night as we passed Algiers we were to be privileged by another concert under the directorship of Oliver Wakefield. I mention coincidence because the concert seemed to be in memory of the great victory we had won after the invasion of Algiers. This second concert was organised as a review and this time we had a chorus of dancing girls from the A.T.S.

Also there were several witty little sketches and these were compared personally by Oliver Wakefield.

The 24th August brought us to within reach or should I say view of Bizerta another base we had fought hard for and won. It was here that we really got sight of eastern beauty.

In one sense it could hardly be described as beauty for as we sailed past this great barren rock, or small island, just off the coast, the setting sun cast a rare colour upon it. Just imagine the slanting maroon shadows given off by the jagged edges of the lone sentinel; as the golden ball of fire sank lower in the heavens, the rock changed. This time it seemed to be a thin huge sheet of jet black cardboard set in a murmurless and ripple-less pool with a background of sky-blue above coming down to a deep purple and black velvet to be lost beyond the horizon. The island was Pantelliria.

The 25th August saw us leaving Cap Bon behind and we started to leave the coast of Tunisia for open sea again. It was during the afternoon, approximately half past two, that Jack Martindale, my buddy, mentioned that there was a column of smoke on the horizon. I immediately spotted it; an argument ensued when we told another of our boys. He said it was a cloudbank and we said it was smoke. The argument was settled however when the evening came and darkness descended. Yes, it was a ship burning at sea and the column of smoke suggested it being a tanker. Torpedoed or bombed we didn't know, nor did we ever find out. At a guess we could say that it was some thirty miles away and it certainly was burning, casting a red reflection along the surface of the sea. Here and now I can truthfully say that this was the only piece of excitement we really saw and had regarding enemy action.

A short while ago I mentioned my buddy Jack Martindale. He was a few years older than myself and he too was stationed at Bibury with Taffy and I. He came from Darlington and before being called up he was working on the L.M.S. Railway. He was married with a little girl whom he idolised and often talked about.

The last few days had passed quietly as we nosed our way eastwards and on Thursday afternoon some of our ships left the convoy and headed for Sicily which we had sighted on the port bow. Friday we saw the North Cape of Cyrenaica and along the coast towards Egypt. All this time we had spent sailing through the Mediterranean and we saw not one enemy aircraft, neither did we have any interference from submarines.

Sunday the 29th August we were nearing the half way mark and there before us lie the historical town of Port Said and the Suez Canal.

What ships remained in the convoy worked into position of line astern and slackening speed we nosed our way into the Canal.

The Monarch of Bermuda was the flagship and being the first ship to enter the Canal we could look back and see all the other ships stretching like a long chain into the distance. It was a fantastic sight.

How great it was to see such signs as 'Johnnie Walker'; 'Dewar's Whisky' and 'Craven 'A'; and there were the Egyptians shouting to us as we sailed very slowly down the Canal. We were lucky that our ship was the first through because of the clear view we had ahead. Also we saw some of the Desert Rats convalescing on the shore. Calls and slang phrases were exchanged such as, "Get some in. Get your knees brown" and "Join up Sprogs". It was all in good clean fun.

So we arrived at the half way with the knowledge that we had made history; we were the first convey through the Mediterranean since 1940 and without loss too.

Chapter Two

HELLSHIP TO INDIA

It was the dawn of the famous Arabia that we sailed into the port of Teufik on Monday 30th August and it was here that we heard the rattle of chains as the anchor slid into the quiet waters of the bay. This was our first stopping place since we left England. Then started the usual panic as we were told to stand by for trans-shipping.

There were troop-deck officers and N.C.O's nancying about getting their respective deck of troops ready; men panicking to get their kit together and all around was a general hullabaloo.

In the afternoon, by walking down the gangplank in single file, we left the Monarch and boarded a tender which then carried us over to a large black painted dirty looking troop-ship. When we arrived there with a full pack on our shoulders and a kitbag under one arm, believe me, never in all my some twenty-odd years; never have I sweated so much as when standing under that broiling Eastern sun. Not being accustomed to a cloudless sky and temperatures of 100° plus, there was little wonder that our K.D. was wet through.

After a wait of some twenty minutes or so we finally boarded the SS ASCANIA as the thing was called. It was here on the 'ALTMARK II" as we later named it, that the worst part of the journey was really had. On Wednesday morning the 1st September, we had just passed our first night's sleep aboard the somewhat unpleasant ship when the sergeant in charge of our Mess deck came around with the following order,

"At 1100 hours today all personnel will stack their kit onto the racks provided. Nothing, repeat nothing, will be left on the floor or hanging from these racks."

When the stated time arrived we commenced to carry out the order; within five minutes the first trouble started. One of the boys was trying to squeeze a kitbag into a space six inches wide under the supervision of the sergeant. The lad exclaimed, "How the hell can I get that into such a small space?" The sergeant immediately turned upon him with the reply, "You're not bloody well trying!"

This of course aroused Jock's temper and he told the sergeant to see if he could do any better.

"Don't you get tough with me because I can get tough with you also you bastard you!" said the sergeant.

Believe me one could have heard a pin drop on the mess deck. I thought Jock was going to kill the sergeant and his Scottish tongue was going fifty to the dozen.

"Report to the Officer immediately," continued the sergeant. As it happened the Officer I/C was just coming and asked what was going on. Jock told him what the N.C.O had said and continued, "… neither you or anyone else is going to call me that."

"Forget it Scotty, forget it," said Flying Officer Roberts. The Officer knew that if Jock Inglis carried the matter further both he and the sergeant would get a severe reprimand, after that everything carried on as normal.

Digressing slightly, Jock Inglis hailed from Glasgow and he too was with us at Bibury and I vividly remember one night what happened when we returned to camp. He had had one or two drinks too many and just for fun and in good humour he walked up to the old iron stove in the billet, very coolly clenched his fist and hit the chimney pipe which protruded up through the roof of the hut. There was a tremendous crash and the whole lot collapsed. There was soot and dust everywhere – I was glad the incident went no further.

We couldn't see much of Teufik from the deck of the ship but we could see the lighted town sparkling in the night, it was a grand sight to see the streetlight again.

Part of the baggage party went ashore with some kit the next day and their description of the town was non-too satisfying. One of the lads told us that whilst on shore a convalescing Eighth Army soldier was found with several knife wounds in his body. To avenge his death some of his unit pals went out and 'polished off' one of the assassins.

At 1900 hours on Thursday 2nd September, we sailed from the port of Teufik out into the sea, the Red Sea, having passed the port of Suez. We were very grateful that portholes could be left open at night because sleeping on the mess decks was worse then sleeping in the Black Hole of Calcutta. Men cramped together in hammocks, on tables, under tables and for the first few nights sleeping was forbidden on the open deck. The air conditioning was insufficient to take away the smell of all those sweaty bodies first thing in the morning.

The meals were the worst I have ever had; mouldy sausage and porridge which tasted like ground stone and bread, well, solidified rubber was too good a description for it. Surely we were right in renaming the ship ALTMARK II.

To the uninitiated, the Altmark was a German prison ship, which held hundreds of our soldiers captive in the early part of the war near Norway.

Sunday, September 5th we had our second spot of trouble. Thirty of us were detailed for fatigues. Yes, the fatigue was carrying lemonade and lime juice to the officers who had cabins, a decent mess, smoke rooms and all the comforts that some of them never deserved.

It was all very well but we had to carry crates on our shoulders from the hold of the ship up flights of stairs that were treacherous even for the ship's cat to walk up. I remember one of the lads telling the Chief Steward he only needed a whip in his hand. The steward immediately challenged the lad and told him to mind his own business.

"Why should I? Do you think it right that we ought to take orders from civvies?"

"You'll do as you are told or else I will report you," cried the steward.

"That's what you think. Twenty of us slogging away while you have four of your men standing over us as if we were slaves."

At this the steward closed his mouth because he knew he couldn't really do anything. It certainly had some effect because after this things were much easier.

Monday the 6th September we passed a group of islands named the Perin Islands, which were a British possession and we knew we were nearing the great port of Aden. The following morning found us steaming into this port, another British protectorate. It was known that here temperatures could rise to 140 degrees. To many people Aden stands out as a place of beauty and romance but we on board the Ascania received a great shock as we sailed in. To us there was no beauty, just a great black jagged and ugly coastline that resembled a broken-down disused quarry.

Jack Martindale who on seeing it commented, "To think we are fighting for such a place as this," gave a good summing up of it. He was right, even if it is one of our great Middle Eastern ports. Why should people praise it up to what it isn't? The only comfort we received from Aden was as we sat on the decks in the cool of the evening and we could see the lights of the traffic moving along the shore road. One thing we will always remember about Aden and that is it was here that we heard the news, "Italy has capitulated!"

As it came over the ship's radio a great cheer could be heard all over the ship. We left Aden on the 8th September and had only been at sea a few hours when trouble broke out again. The meal just served was the worst ever and the lads, after standing the degrading since we left Teufik, let out their wrath. Some of them even went to the Mess for the officer in charge of our deck. I wasn't actually in it at the time but the next thing I knew was when the Officer came down to the mess deck.

"Let me warn you now," he said, "if there is anyone of you in an organised mutiny you will all be put in the Brig to cool off."

This was certainly a surprise to me because this Officer's statement was the first I had heard of a mutiny. It must have reached the ears of the Commanding Officer because the food was much better from then on.

September the 9th was a very hot day and funnily enough there was a very large swell on and the ship was rolling all ways.

This particular morning we had a good laugh; Jack and another boy were sitting waiting for dinner when through the open porthole, WHOOSH! A wave crashed through and drenched the two of them to the skin. However, there is an old saying that he who laughs last, laughs the longest. This was so because the very next day I too received a soaking in the same way.

We were now leaving the Gulf of Aden and heading into the Indian Ocean with the Island of Socotra (BR) to the south of us.

It was Monday the 13th when we sighted land, then a lighthouse. Was this our destination? At lunchtime we knew the answer was 'yes.' Once again we were the first ship to dock and by teatime we had manoeuvred into Alexandria Dock, Bombay, India.

Just after docking we were instructed to parade on stated decks for our money, which was to be exchanged into Indian Rupees. After parade drafts and contingents were given their orders for disembarking.

So with the dawn of Tuesday 16th September, we were ready to start our service in India, for how long? We did not know. At the last minute we received a message from the Royal Air Force Padre on board and like everyone else I shall always remember it.

"We have been together on this ship for a number of weeks and now it is time to say goodbye. All that remains for me to say is, may Christ be with you always, wherever you are, whatever you do. Goodbye, good luck and God Bless you all."

Chapter Three

A FIRST IMPRESSION

As we came down the gangway onto the dockside, a fleet of Chevrolet lorries was drawn up and here we grouped off, twenty men to a lorry. It was a grand feeling to feel terra ferma beneath our feet once more and contrary to what we expected there was no swaying as we moved towards the lorry.

As soon as we set off through the town we found out what an Indian driver was like. There we were speeding along and every time we came to a bend the lorry hung dangerously onto one side. The speed we were travelling at made it impossible for any of us to see much of Bombay. Twenty minutes later we arrived at the camp.

Down we jumped onto the road and formed up three deep with our kit then the first thing we did was hand in our paybooks. A Corporal took our party up to a section of the camp and what a walk. Full kit and a kitbag and the heat was terrific with the distance being between a half and three-quarters of a mile.

When we at last arrived there a sergeant by the name of J. Michael Nash took over from the Corporal and oh boy! what a sergeant. He was more like a gorilla in manner and looks but his physique spoiled the effort. When he commenced to give orders he stalked rather than walked about and his arms almost touched his knees as he bent his back whilst putting emphasis on everything. His favourite saying was, "I'll do the talking," and I'm sure he did.

At last we were detailed to a hut F4 by number and I am certain that no one could have been more glad than we were to get our packs off. Jack and I managed to find two charpoys next to each other in the large brick and plaster building.

A charpoy is a timber frame made from 3" x 3" wood with legs the same thickness and about 24 inches from the ground. This is all bound together with long pieces of dried grass, a sort of heavy-duty raffia. On top of this we had a kind of palliasse, which was simply a large bag of straw and was really quite comfortable to lie on.

As we found out later during our service over here, these charpoys were ideal for insects to nest in, some of which could give you a nasty bite.

The building was divided into three sections and there was accommodation for approximately 200 men. On the end of the top section there was a wash place and showers and adjoining this we found the toilets. On the front of the hut was a large veranda from which we had a marvellous view of the Indian Ocean and the promenade below. So it was that we settled down to a good night's sleep in 'F' Camp, Worli Camp, Bombay.

Wednesday the 15th September was actually our first full day in India and coincidentally our first payday. To start with we handed in our blankets at the stores and in exchange we received a mosquito net and another pair of shorts together with a towel, which was bottle green, possibly for camouflage reasons. Then after having a real good dinner or 'tiffin' as it is called out here, we paraded for pay. What a parade too, all the camp was on it, so just imagine some eight to nine thousand men being paid.

After each man had received his Rupees he was sent to a Rahat Villa to have an inoculation, which was only a small one and no one suffered any after effects.

We were not allowed out of camp for three days but on the first night off we, that is Jack, Taffy and myself had a walk along the promenade and then we went to the Coffee Café, which stands at the end of the prom.

Just picture a large mound of rock some twenty feet high upon which stood the cafe. A yellow stone building with steel barred windows, no glass and projecting from this a medium sized awning under which were situated twenty tables.

The three of us sat down at one of these tables and an Indian waiter dressed in white slacks and navy blue waistcoat came for our order. After studying the menu we decided to have an RAF special as it was called. When it was served we had a great surprise. There were two eggs, onions, steak, fried bread and potatoes, also bread and butter with tea. However, the second surprise came when we received the bill. For all this the cost was a mere one Rupee and two annas, which in English money is worth one shilling and eight pence. To the people back home this would seem a luxury compared to the food they were at present able to get for their rations.

The next few days we spent getting to know the place, there being very little to do with regards to duties. There were one or two lectures including one from the Padre, he reminded us about going with the native women with this little ditty:

"Mere was a man called Starkey,
Who went and married a darkie.
The result of this marriage.
Was a four-wheeler carriage,
With one white, one black and two khaki."

Friday the 17th September, we further explored the camp and found the cinema. This was a long building and had a seating capacity for eleven hundred personnel and the prices were very moderate at nine annas and one Rupee two annas a seat. We found the machine to be quite modern when the three of us went to see Bob Hope in 'Thanks for the Memory'. One laughable thing about the cinema was that the favourite star was none other than 'Popeye' who had a film shown every night. The show was so enjoyable that all three of us went the following night, Saturday, to see Abbott and Costello in 'Hold that Ghost'.

It was Sunday the 19th that Jack and I were unlucky enough to be detailed for fatigues along with thirty other boys. We had six bags of potatoes and two bags of beans also one bag of onions to peel then we were finished. All of us waded in and by half-past two everything was cleared.

On Monday the following day we had our first impression of Bombay. We boarded a B.E.S.T. bus at the camp gate, paid our four annas fare and set off for the city. The ride itself was well worth the money and we had a marvellous view from the front seat of the upper deck of this open topped bus. It was good to feel the cool breeze blowing through our hair as we rode along the sea front.

All but a mile from the camp we came to the famous race course bound by an avenue of palm trees on one side and the arterial road on the other. As we passed we came to the European Swimming Pool at Beach Candy. At this point permit me to say that the lads who were keen on swimming, spent many a happy hour there.

From there we drove through a small village and then back to the sea front where, as we sped along Marine Drive, we had our first glimpse of modern India.

We could see block upon block of up-to-date flats, six stories high with their flat roofs. As we came to the last of these flats we turned left down Church Gate Street into the centre of the city. About 400 yards down this wide street with its new buildings we passed Church Gate Station on our left and then went by the Oval, which is a beautiful green park in miniature. At the corner of the park we saw what is known as the latest cinema in India, the Eros. A few minutes later the bus pulled in at the terminus in front of the offices of the British Tabulating

Company, in future years to be known as International Computers Ltd., (I.C.L.)

We commenced our sightseeing by visiting the Army and Navy Stores, which had a definite English touch about it. There were some really beautiful things in this store; jewellery, leatherwork, toys, sweets, fruit and one thing which I knew was scarce at home, cutlery. From there we walked up the Mahatma Ghandi Road from where we saw the Prince of Wales Museum and the Prince of Wales Memorial. Prince Teddy of course.

It was getting near to teatime so we decided to go to the Services Canteen of which we had heard so much. It was self-service. The canteen itself was marvellously set out and the first thing we did was to get change at the desk. We then followed the queue around until we came to a rack of wooden trays and on these we put our food as we moved along, paying as we went. The tea was excellent and consisted of eggs and potatoes, bread and butter, pot of tea, Swiss roll with custard and the cost was a mere twelve annas.

Praise must be given to the staff in this canteen, the majority of whom by the way, were European. All their work is voluntary; they were efficient and of course very beautiful.

Let me stress, it was impossible to see all of the sights of this historic city in one go, so to acquaint ourselves more we had to make several other visits.

During these visits we saw such places as the Sir Alwyn Ezra Canteen, which is in the Town hall, Elphinstone Circle, Crawford Market Place and Bazaar. At this market one certainly had some amusing moments. There's the excitement that is shown by the shopkeeper or stallholder as you try to knock his price down and then the delight on your face at having beaten him and again the happiness on the vendor's face at having made a bargain.

Taking everything into consideration there was plenty of entertainment in the city, cinemas, dance halls, and rest rooms, writing and reading rooms. I for one definitely enjoyed my visit to Bombay.

The next few nights were spent lazing about with nothing to do but write air-graphs to those at home etc., in the evening we would go for a walk and then sit on the sea wall and watch the sun disappear.

September the 23rd was the only busy day for a week or more. We paraded at 8.30 a.m. and were marched into a small field by the mess. All the camp was mustered for postings and there we stood for five solid hours listening for our names to be called. This was all very well but when one has to stand beneath a blazing hot sun, it was no joke.

During the parade we had a slight distraction, which really could have been serious. As we stood there someone suddenly shouted, "SNAKE, SNAKE!" People hurriedly dispersed, there in the cleared space was a cobra snake. An N.C.O. called an Indian bearer who in turn called for a snake charmer. How good they are! He quickly took out his bulbous flute, charmed the snake and within ten minutes it was in the bag and being carried away.

After this was over we had tiffin and went onto pay parade. Here we had another three hours stand, so one can quite imagine what we felt like at the end of the day.

The next seven days we passed our time away with one or two visits to Bombay and also going to the camp cinema. It was during this time that it was one of India's holy weeks and every night we could hear the wailing of the pipes and people together with the beating of the tom-toms but after a few nights we became accustomed to it.

The only point of interest during this interlude was the sunset on the 28th September. Earlier on in this book I described a sunset in the Mediterranean but the one we saw this particular evening was due to full honours. It would be foolish to try to describe this scene because the only way to appreciate God's beauty such as this is to see it.

The following week was again very quiet and my pals and I passed away most of the time by seeing films as before or sitting on the sea wall talking about old times back home. How we wished for a posting!

However, we did break the monotony of this by going down to the European swimming baths at Beach Candy. This was on Tuesday 5th October and it was about two miles from camp. The baths were of the most modern structure having an indoor pool along with an outside one. Everything inside was spotless and lined with white tiles and at the deepest end of the indoor pool there were splashboards up to a height of twenty feet or more. One excellent feature of the beautiful architecture outside was the landscaping and a closely cut lawn where teas could be taken.

Wednesday and Friday the 6th and 8th respectively, we caught the tail end of the much talked about monsoon. It so rained that Taffy and I received a soaking never before experienced. The wind was blowing at a terrific pace and the rain was working its way under the rafters of the roof. There were pools of water all over the hut. One spectacle of this freak storm was the display of lightning flashes; at one time the whole camp was like daylight for about three minutes. Briefly it resembled one of those never-to-be-forgotten blitzes of 1940, that is to say, in the light and noise effect. Tuesday the 12th October saw such another of these freak storms.

A week after this storm I was posted to New Delhi and my moral was lifted by some 50% on hearing the news; a posting at last to the top of the tree so to speak.

To start with we were taken to a railway station in the same 'Chevs' I mentioned before and then onto an express train. To describe this would be rather difficult and our passage being third class I can only say it was a glorified cattle truck. It was 1930 hours when the train was fully loaded and at 2000 hours we left Bombay.

The sun was just setting when we pulled out of the station and before long we were travelling into the night. This made things rather awkward from a sightseer's point of view but as we travelled along we became accustomed to the nightlife of Central India.

As we journeyed north we passed through a vast desert but before this we came to a stretch of swamp land and in the blackness of the night we could see something like fireflies glowing in the air and hear bull frogs croaking in the swamp. This was also a breeding ground for the dreaded mosquito, the carrier of malaria.

The Thar Desert, through which we passed, was nothing but barren land without much habitation but what small town or village we came to, the train stopped. On the journey we had plenty of food to eat, in fact there was too much so we gave what was spare to Indian peasants as we went through their stations. Sleeping accommodation was terrible and I personally had bruised sides and ribs after sleeping on a shelf that was like a springboard.

During this long journey, if we needed a drink of tea, we soon became addicted to a local custom. Every time the train stopped, people ran to the front of the train to mash their tea in any vessel available by using the hot water from the boiler of the engine.

Wednesday, 20th October, we crossed into the Province of Delhi and before long we could see the buildings and factories etc., telling us that we were nearing our destination. After five weeks of anxious waiting since landing in India we were finally going to do our bit and the joy of it was that our 'workshop' as you might say, was to be the City of New Delhi, the jewel of the British Empire.

Chapter Four

TONIC FOR MORALE

After waiting on New Delhi Station for some twenty minutes our transport finally arrived and when we pulled away from the station our lorry was crammed choc-a-bloc with kit and of course ourselves.

This time it was an open truck and we were able to get a glimpse of this very old city. Perhaps it wasn't so modern as Bombay but there were the usual sights of street vendors etc., and beggars calling "Baksheesh, Sahib."

As we moved to the outskirts, dwellings and buildings thinned out until we were driving along a straight, tree lined road. This road, Lytton Road by name, brought us round to the city of New Delhi and so to our place of residence for a while.

This was Irwin Stadium, which is a large and modern sports ground and has facilities for playing football, hockey, rugby and tennis etc., and is situated two miles outside of town. The building is made of sandstone and has some very fine sculptural designs on its wall faces. At the moment the Stadium is being used for the accommodation of RAF personnel who are nearly all under canvas with four men to a tent.

We all climbed down from the transport and were taken in charge by that nice man the S.W.O., - the Station Warrant Officer. Such a nice man, especially this one, from the stock of the good old English bulldog; some five feet, six inches tall, red in complexion with brown wavy hair; the typical regimental moustache and of course, the bark. "Yes sir! Slater's the name."

FRUITS

There were several bungalow type brick barrack blocks about and it was on the veranda of one of these that we were detailed to sleep. We had Tiffin, which was the best service one since we left Blighty and then we decided to take a good look at the Stadium surrounds.

In it we found first of all the dining hall which was moderately furnished, then the Sergeants Mess and rest room. Further along we came to the Bok's Canteen, which is similar to the NAAFI but more lavishly furnished with easy chairs etc., in fact it was so set out that it looked better than any Sergeants' Mess I had ever seen in England.

It so happened that on the night of the 20th October there was a dance in Bok's Canteen and being very keen on the subject two or three of us tried to get in. A corporal gave us some complimentary tickets and later we found out that he was Paddy Correl who used to keep wicket for Leicester County Cricket Club.

For once luck was with us and we proceeded to enjoy a very entertain-able evening but this was not all for as I was looking around the room my eyes turned to the band and stopped. No! it couldn't be, but it was. There playing the drums was one of my hometown workmates sitting with as much surprise on his face as I had on mine. Naturally, as soon as the dance was over we indulged in telling each other any home news of importance.

In the centre of New Delhi there is a circle of shops, offices, restaurants etc., and in the middle of this was a small park. This circle was named as Connaught Circus and from this ring of buildings, streets and roads led out to various outlying districts of the province.

My first night in Delhi was certainly a tonic for morale. That night I went to bed with the feeling that I was going to enjoy my stay in Irwin Stadium. The following day we were busy going through the usual paraphernalia of new arrivals and then we were split up and sent to our respective sections to commence our new jobs. I was detailed to the Maintenance Statistical

Department and reported to a Flt/Lt. Wheen, an Australian. He was a gentleman and told me that if I had anything to clear up with regards to settling in I could have the afternoon off and report for duty the following morning.

This I did and in the evening I went down town to keep an appointment with Ron Hulme, my workmate, whom I had met the previous night.

Ron was a few years older than I and had been out here about two years and had reached the rank of Sergeant in the supply Headquarters. He thought it a must to put me wise to any pitfalls one might encounter having only just arrived out in India. I was forever grateful.

KING GEORGE V MEMORIAL FROM THE TOP OF INDIA GATE MONUMENT WITH IRWIN STADIUM IN THE BACKGROUND

He took me to a high class restaurant, Wengers, where we had a marvellous dinner and Ron, being the host allowed me to pay not, shall I say, one anna. After the meal he took me to a cinema, so altogether I had a very enjoyable evening.

Friday the 22nd October, I started my detail in my new environment and before the day was through I decided that it was going to be very interesting work. There were three offices, rather on the small side and the floors were of ordinary red brick, which gave reason as to why there was so much dust lying about. The lighting was not too good and suspended from the ceiling was a large fan to cool the air, commonly known as a Punnka.

My first day at work was tedious after having two months of nothing to do but laze around but I enjoyed it and by the end of the day I was ready for my charpoy.

The next three days I spent getting to know everyone in the offices and I took a great liking to Corporal Ken Haywood with whom I was working alongside. Everyone was considerate and willing to show me how things should be done and I also was pleased with the jovial way all of them carried out their duties. It wasn't long before I had that feeling of being an old hand.

THIS IS A CLOSE-UP OF IRWIN STADIUM

A CLOSE-UP OF KING GEORGE V MEMORIAL

Monday the 25th October happened to be my birthday and upon hearing that Ken and his pal

'Boggy' were celebrating a similar event, I asked them if I could join in. "Certainly," said Ken.

So we all went into town in a big way, firstly having a slap up dinner and then going for a drink of good old Scotch. To say that this was my first birthday in India, I enjoyed it immensely.

The day after my birthday I was making my way to have dinner when, who should I meet, none other than Taffy, my pal whom I left in Bombay. What a surprise it was and when I asked him what he was doing here he said that he had been posted to this Unit so I knew that we were both going to have a grand time.

INDIA GATE

The India Gate Monument is a war memorial to the gallant Indian troops who fell in the First World War, 1914-1918.

We used to walk through this Monument every morning on our way to work and it was situated at the south end of Kingsway, which was a wide road flanked on either side by beautiful flower beds, small ponds and huge grass verges.

In the next week or so nothing untoward took place except for a few dances here and there until Sunday, 7th November, when we had a surprise at camp with the personal appearance of Ralph Reader of Gang Show fame and did the boys go for his act. The following night there was a talent spotting competition and several lads took part in it. The first prize went to Ken Speed, a soldier who played "Rustle of Spring" and "The Warsaw Concerto" on the piano. He truly deserved it too. Taffy took second prize with his impressions, which he certainly has a gift for and a violinist came third. I myself took part playing two of my own compositions on the piano but I wasn't even in the running.

The sixteenth of November was a really big day. We were told to parade at the nearby Tiffin Room to be spoken to by none other than that great man Admiral Lord Louis Mountbatten who had just been appointed Supreme Allied Commander for South East Asia Command.

The S.W.O., had us all on parade with everything spic and span and all the 'bull' necessary for such an occasion and as the Supremo arrived we were all called to attention. When he came he just strolled up, one hand in pocket, greeting us with, "Gather round lads, I just wanted to see your faces and I know that you want to see my mug."

The Admiral went on to tell us about his world famous Commando raids of North Africa and Sicily, continuing with, "If I was in England I would not be allowed to say this but I am in India so I can say it. I firmly believe that the European War will be over by March or early summer of 1944 at the latest. When it is, then we can get all our might out here and take it from me, when we do, the Japs are certainly going to get it."

Was this not a different tonic for morale?

The 20th November I had a setback. I was unfortunately admitted to the British Military Hospital with Sandfly Fever (but what happened there will be described later on in the book).

Me on the left and Taffy on the right when we were at one time under canvas in the grounds of Irwin Stadium. Taff's assignment here was to be detailed to work under the supervision of Sgt. Ron Hulme in the supplies section.

The first big night I had when I came out of hospital was an invitation to one of the sections' dinners. Actually it was Taffy's invitation but I went along with him to keep a fatherly eye on him – sort of thing. He had been asked to entertain at this dinner, which was being held at the most flashy hotel in town, 'The Imperial.' Just before Taffy did his turn, once again who should appear but Oliver Wakefield who did an act similar to the one he did on the boat. This gave my pal plenty of encouragement and he went onto the stage and gave an excellent performance.

It came to my mind that whilst we were out here we would get the opportunity of seeing many great theatrical stars and this was confirmed when on Christmas Day we had the chance to see two American film stars.

Of these two stars there was one world famous for his big mouth and the other not so well known but co-starred with Bing Crosby as an instrumentalist. Yes, your first guess is right, Joe. E. Brown and the other was Harry Barris a very fine pianist and composer. Between them they put on a marvellous two man show along with an all-American Swing Band, conducted by another film star, Melvyn Douglas. If you have forgotten what these great entertainers looked like then overleaf is a photograph of them in concert. By the way Joe E. Brown had recently lost his son, killed in action.

Many artists came to entertain the troops including our very own Elsie and Doris Waters. Coincidentally Ronnie Waters their brother became our Entertainments Officer at the Stadium. I recall being in one of his concert parties back in England at South Cerney.

After a swell Christmas everything quietened down until New Years Eve. What a night!

Corporal Ken Haywood above and on the left another L.A.C. named Benchly who worked in our section down at the secretariat at the other end of Kingsway

Joe E. Brown

Especially when my two, Senior N.C.O's joined in getting me drunk. Flight Sgt Pawsey held my head back whilst Sergeant Roberts poured gin down my throat. Then we all had a good singsong and the last thing I remember was just getting into bed.

And so into the mysteries of dreamland. I closed my year for 1943 full of the tonics of morale hoping that the morrow would bring us into a year of peace and victory.

Goodnight Taffy, goodnight Mum and Dad. A very Happy New Year to you all.

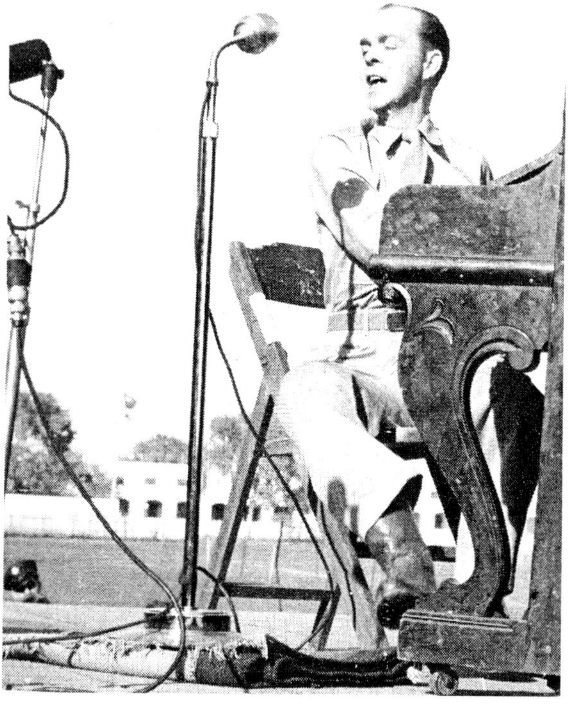

Harry Barris

Chapter Five

BRITISH MILITARY HOSPITAL

Monday, 20th November, I was feeling rather ill so I reported sick. I was examined by the M.O. who ordered me into B.M.H., for observation. It is about twenty minutes by ambulance through lovely avenues of trees and along straight arterial roads, and then we turned into a driveway and up to the Hospital buildings. On entering I handed in my forms and was then shown to a bed, which was in Ward M3. Now for some sleep or so I thought.

I have had some terrible nights' sleep in my time but never one like I had last night. Someone asked for a number, someone asked for a correspondence file; requests started coming fast, faster and faster. Numbers, files, letters, cards: with this I saw faces of people I knew at home. Mother, father and all my pals, as the power increased I thought my head would burst. Still more they came, faster they came, faster and more faster. Obviously I was delirious. I awoke to find myself wringing wet through with sweat and my heart was beating fifty to the dozen.

Tuesday the 21st, I was awakened at about five o'clock in the morning to have my temperature taken by the orderly but he didn't tell me what it was. After this I had a bedside wash and then waited for breakfast but I don't recall eating it. At ten o'clock the doctor came to see each patient and when she came to me she took rather a long time.

The doctor was a loveable young thing of some twenty-four years with Anglo-Indian origin of slight build, a trim figure and about five feet four inches tall. She had a beautiful complexion and eyes of a burnt blue, one of which was covered by a curl of light brown pageboy style hair. Her touch was that of an angel as I found out when she examined my stomach; after giving me a thorough testing both back and front she became hesitant before finally marking up my chart. All day I felt anything but great and I hardly had anything to eat.

Nighttime was drawing near and I was dreading going to sleep. After tossing and turning for a couple of hours I finally went to sleep and dare I say it, I had another dream. This time I dreamed that I was transferred to the Middle East Command within an Intelligence Unit amongst the ordinary ranks to find out certain information.

I was doing quite well until we came to a chasm which the Sergeant said had to be crossed and when he managed to get a line to the other side he asked for volunteers to try it and being enthusiastic I volunteered.

So I started to swing along and it seemed quite safe until I was about half way across when – the line broke. For a minute I was suspended there, then down I went swinging towards the other side of the gap. I tried to swing myself around so that when I hit the rock face my pack would take most if the blow. I was now travelling at a terrific speed and I closed my eyes waiting for the crash but it never came.

I found myself being carried upwards and when I opened my eyes I was in the arms of a burly airman hanging from a rope ladder suspended from a helicopter. All this happened in a matter of seconds and he told me to let go of the rope, which I did in earnest. We climbed up the ladder and into the helicopter where we found some of the crew giving us a helping hand to get us aboard.

"Thanks a lot, lads. Whose idea was that?" "His," said the chap who saved me.

I took a good look at the pilot and saw that he had a Joad beard and I at once recognised him as my bosom pal from South Cerney.

"Tony," I cried. "What are you doing here?"

"Shut up and don't ask questions, I will explain later," he said. Rather mysterious I thought but I did as I was told and put two and two together.

When we landed I found myself on a German airfield and this confirmed my curiosity. When we were alone Tony told me that he was doing a similar job to myself which was very interesting. Again someone woke me up but very soon I was off to sleep again. I continued my dream but in a different way.

This time I had a brainwave to write a book and have Tony as the leading character. It would be all about the hero defeating the crooks by sheer mental ability. These people were out to get something secret in the HQ and by encouraging them and helping them, the hero comes out on top.

The beautiful spy tries to trick the hero but he turns the table and in the end he destroys the gangs' hideout by fire in which he narrowly escapes being trapped himself as he sees the villainess, half naked, being burnt to death. Could I write such a book? I wondered. Then a voice cried, "Come on, temperature time."

Tony Hill was the best friend I ever had in the RAF, and came from Bradford. He was a character within himself. Stockily built, with wavy sandy hair, who was at home with everyone, especially the ladies. He was also a very fine musician and used to play the piano for Jack White's Collegians at the Astoria Restaurant in the London West end.

November 23rd, we had some very nice visitors. They were four ladies from Delhi and came to see if we required any stamps or airgraphs. They also handed around some boiled humbugs. The one speaking to me was an Officer's wife and said that she came from Surrey in England. Luckily I was feeling much better and was able to speak to her.

All was quiet for the next few days with nothing much to do. One night we had some good entertainment from Tommy Handley's 'Half Hour' on the radio. Another night the lads amused themselves by making paper aeroplanes and flying them up and down the ward, just like little boys, but it was a laugh.

Our ward had about thirty-two patients and quite a mixture there was too. They were mainly English but we also had an Aussie, a Scotsman and five Italians. Jock the Scot was a very cheerful chap and gave us many a laugh with his witty remarks. He was slight of build with his hair brushed straight back and his features slightly on the thin side. He was in with Yellow Jaundice.

Of the five Italians, the best English speaking one was Sergio Bacotta. He too was of thin features but rather tall, in the region of six feet, two inches and had a very pleasant disposition. Before the war he had been in the Italian Merchant Navy and had travelled many miles from his hometown of Trieste. He had visited such places as England, Russia, Estonia and then to San Francisco. Also he had been east to India, Singapore and Hong Kong; so on the whole he had seen quite a few things in his time.

The reason for his being in India at the present time was that he had been taken prisoner in the Libyan campaign and had been shipped to India as a Prisoner of War. He did not mind and seemed to be content in his new surroundings, he was very good company amongst his fellow patients. His other four countrymen were quite decent chaps too, very jolly and I can say this not, one of them mentioned the war in any shape or form, until a little later.

We also had two nursing orderlies who would do anything for us. The sister in charge of the Ward was of the fussy type, always rushing about and generally making herself busy. Being rather on the plump side this attitude seemed to suit her admirably but on the whole she was quite harmless but very efficient.

After tea on the 2nd December, I had a very interesting talk with the Italian in the next bed to me. His name was Gabrielle Miglietta and he came from Lecce in Southern Italy. His English wasn't too good and myself not being able to speak his language, we managed to understand each other. He was of medium build and had an immaculate head of hair set in jet-black waves; his age was twenty-two. I learned from him that he was taken prisoner in Bardia and like his friend Sergio was trans-shipped out here to India.

One story he told me about when he was in Libya surprised me greatly. He said that the British Tommy was very good to him and if it had not been for the Tommy he would have been treated badly. He told me of an Aussie who wanted to take his family photograph away from him but the British soldier stopped the Aussie and said it was not right. Before the Tommy came up the Aussie threatened to shoot Miglietta if he didn't hand over. Gabrielle continued by saying that our prisoners in Italy were looked after very well because Italian women said, "If we treat the British Tommies kindly then our boys in England will be looked after also." Miglietta told me that he hated the Germans and Japanese but had great respect for the British. His mother and father lived with his only sister and he was looking forward to getting back to them someday. After all, the Italians were like other people in this war, why had we to fight? No man is better then another.

During the afternoon of the 3rd December, the Scots chap and I had a slow quiet walk for about half a mile up the road to the crest of a small hill from where we had a marvellous view. We had a clear picture of some ten miles around and in the distance we could see the white buildings of Delhi jutting above the horizon and further to the right we could see the Dome of the Viceregal Residence.

Once again I felt sadly disappointed at the scenery before me. Although there was a vision of so many miles there was nothing to see but a vast plain of barren land strewed with rock here and there, this once more showing that India had been over glorified, except for the large cities.

On the 4th December, there was quite a commotion when we had to move into another ward. This was about 10.00 a.m. and we found it was because some smallpox cases were coming into our ward. As a precaution we received another vaccination against this disease but as the lady doctor came to me I remarked, "I had smallpox once, in 1926 in England when an epidemic was on."

The doctor replied, "Well, in that case you are immune, however I'll do it just as a precaution."

The vaccination never took on me.

We moved across the way into Ward M2 a much larger ward but not as comfortable as the one we had left and being the unlucky kite I am, I finished on the veranda which I found out later was rather cold at night.

Also we left our fussy little sister and beloved lady doctor. Before we left, the doctor came to the conclusion that I had had Sandfly Fever and not Malaria, but its still very unpleasant and has all the same signs and symptoms.

The 5th was our first full day in the new ward and it was rather quiet and cold but in the evening I had a very interesting time listening to two of the Italian patients talking to each other. They were conversing in French and it did cause quite a deal of amusement.

It was a great relief that on the 6th December, the M.O. said I would be discharged on the following day because I was just about fit for duty again, so on the 7th December 1944 I left the British Military Hospital.

Chapter Six

HERE AND THERE

For the first six months of 1944 I spent a quiet time except for one or two occasions, which I intend to recall here.

The first of these occurred on the 25th February. One forward WAACI in our office invited several of us to a cabaret and dance, which was being held in the WAACI quarters near Irwin Stadium. So, that evening, a party of us went to the occasion, the first object being the bar, where we had a drink and then began to explore the surroundings.

In two rooms adjoining each other dancing was in progress to the music of the Royal Signals Band. In the quadrangle was a large marquee, which was packed to capacity with the middle of the floor being kept clear for the cabaret to come. There seemed to be plenty of 'snogging' going on, (this is a term originating in Delhi which means petting a partner etc.). There weren't quite enough girls to go round, therefore some of us were without partners but we didn't mind because we had the bar. It was impossible to dance however because the floor was too crowded.

Around ten o'clock the cabaret started with a Hawaiian Dance performed by six dusky coloured WAACI's dressed in grass skirts and flowered brassieres. It was marvellous and the boys didn't want them to leave, eventually they did but gave us another performance half an hour later. The floorshow finished and the last dance came, also the bar closed so everyone decided to make their way back to the billets. All had had a wonderful time but the next morning we learned that some of the lads had been able to have a better night still. Some of them had found their way into the girls' quarters and were thoroughly enjoying themselves but when the WAACI Commandant asked them to leave they refused. The result was that the Military Police were called in and order was restored.

The 27th February I was up early because I was going to Agra on 48 hours leave. I had arranged to go with three other lads and the trip had been arranged by Sgt. Perry a Sheffielder like myself and in the same section as myself.

We had booked for a long weekend and this morning we were rushing around getting everything ready. At 8.00 a.m. the Station Wagon picked us up at the main entrance to take us to the station in Delhi. The train pulled out at 9.15 a.m. and we were on our way. We travelled second class and there were about ten in our compartment. To pass the time away Ken, Ralph and myself had a game of cards Brenchly did not play. The journey took about four and a half hours and on arrival at Agra we hailed a 'tonga' and proceeded to the Salvation Army Hostel where we were to stay. What a good job these wonderful people do for our troops overseas.

The hostel was a medium sized building standing in its own grounds and was managed by a Major Lee and his wife who were very nice people indeed. It was lunchtime when we arrived and after being told where we were going to sleep, we had a light lunch. It was very good food and set out in that certain way which everyone looks forward to. It was plain and simple but we all enjoyed it. The dining room reminded me of the rooms of the hostels we used to visit at home and I am sure that Mrs Lees had tried her best to make it look as English as possible.

After lunch we went to our own rooms and had half an hours' rest then the bearer came and asked us if we were going to see the Taj Mahal and if so there was a guide outside who would take us. We agreed to go in two tongas because two soldiers were joining us and we couldn't get six people into one tonga, which is a horse drawn carriage seating two in front looking forward and two sitting in the back facing backwards.

As soon as we saw our guide we almost burst our sides laughing because he was the exact double of Moore Marriot the film star from the Will Hay films. Height about 5 feet 4 inches, on the tubby side, bald head with a fringe of white hair around the back, one tooth in the centre of his mouth and bandy legs.

We set off for the Taj, three in each tonga and old Moore following behind on his bike. We had not gone far before we in the rear tonga were rolling about laughing again. The first tonga had taken a wrong turning and old Moore shouted to the driver who didn't hear him. So off old Moore went with his bandy legs pushing the cycle.

It was so funny and the sight of him made the thought of the actor more realistic.

Our tonga kept on the right road and we lost sight of the other one for about ten minutes. Suddenly we came to a blind corner where our road joined the main road. We swept along onto the main road and as we did so the other tonga almost collided with us. Old Moore being unable to stop his bike, cut in between us shouting at the top of his voice. It was so funny and everyone just roared with laughter.

We arrived at the Taj Mahal, which is often called the most beautiful building in the world. It is a tomb built by the Emperor Shah Jahan for his wife-who died in 1631. She was called Mumtaz-i-Mahal, 'chosen one of the palace' and from that title the big building took its name, Taj Mahal. The Emperor too was buried there after his death in 1658. It is approached through a red sandstone gateway, which leads into a beautiful walled garden in which a watercourse runs between rows of Cypress trees. At the far end of the watercourse the Taj Mahal stands on a marble terrace. This domed building of white marble and four minarets is decorated with all types of jewels including diamonds, rubies, sapphires etc. Truly a 17th Century wonder.

On 48-hour pass at the Taj Mahal in 1944
I'm in shorts as usual.

The big disappointment for us was that it was under repair at the time and scaffolding, which obscured most of the beauty, surrounded the dome.

We spent a considerable time viewing this wonderful building and to go inside the tomb we had to take our shoes off and leave them outside and I can tell you that it was very hot to ones feet on the sun-baked marble. At one stage we climbed the stairs inside one of the minarets but looking down onto the forecourt below caused one to go dizzy because of the glare caused by the reflection, so we hurriedly returned to ground level. After taking several photographs we went back to the hostel for tea and then rested in our rooms until dinner. We had taken a bottle of gin with us and it certainly kept up the cheerful spirit we all had. After dinner we went to see a film and then called into a cafe on our way back to have a snack and finally reached the hostel again about midnight and snuggled down to sleep and dream of the wonderful sight we had seen.

The following morning we were awakened about 8.30 a.m. by the bearer who brought us a cup of tea and told us that breakfast would be ready by 9.00 a.m. After the meal we arranged to go and see the Red Fort in Agra but Ralph wasn't feeling too well so there were only five of us.

The fort was of the old legendary type and we enjoyed every minute of the tour. We descended into some dungeons under the fort and when the guide struck a match for us to see in the dark, bats started screeching and flying around us so we beat a hasty retreat. All the weekend was very enjoyable and in the afternoon we caught the train back to Delhi not forgetting to thank Major and Mrs Lee.

The next few weeks seemed to fly and all my time was fully occupied. Ron Hulme asked me to help out with their dance band by playing double bass. The first time was at the Annual Delhi Hunt Ball where there were no officers below the rank of Squadron Leader or Major but I must say that the behaviour of these so called 'gentlemen' was deplorable. Whilst the 'erks' were doing their best to entertain them at the interval by putting on a good cabaret, these officers were so drunk that they were sprawled about the floor giving loud ignorant guffaws over senseless little things and not paying the slightest bit of attention.

The second occasion I played was at the Roshanara Club the M.C.C., of India. This time it was entirely opposite, stuffed shirts and all starch. Alas I learned of some aristocratic scandal. Dancing on the floor was the Air Chief Marshal and the Viceroy's wife who, one of the band told me, were always together, ahem.

On May 1st I was elected onto the committee of the Irstad Services Club. This was a club at the Stadium organised solely for the benefit of junior ranks, the 'erks' and no one over the rank of sergeant was allowed to be a member. It provided for every sport and later from the funds, we were able to have our own clubroom furnished with wicker chairs, teak tables and lovely carpets. It was on this committee that I spent most of the following months outside of working hours. Below is a table of one week's duties.

Monday	General Meeting
Tuesday	Tombola or Whist Drive
Wednesday	Committee Meeting
Thursday	Musical Evening
Friday	Tombola
Saturday	On duty in clubroom.

The musical evenings were record sessions given by Flt. Lt. R. Traill and L.A.C. Ron Worley with anything from classics to jazz.

This is only part of the work because so much has to be done in town, i.e., buying furniture, organising games and arranging dinners and dances. However. I enjoyed every minute and became very involved.

On my days off I went swimming at the Post and Telegraph Grounds where there was a pool, which was a godsend and quite a crowd used to gather for relaxation. Many friends were made down there and two in particular were very charming. They were members of the WAACI's and their names were Joan and Jacqueline (Jackie). A Scottish Regiment had brought Joan out of Burma in the retreat and now no one dare say anything against them in her presence. She was well proportioned and her bathing costume showed every contour of her body. I liked her because she was the exact double of my friend's fiancé back home. Jackie was on the slimmer side and had a trim neat little figure. She too was an excellent swimmer and when she stood poised on the diving board ready to dive, one could but admire her shape. When they swam they didn't have bathing caps on and when you saw them under the water it reminded you of the South Sea pictures with their black hair flowing behind them, the skirt of their costumes rippling in the water trying to conceal a little light brown figure. Although they were both Anglo-Indian they spoke perfect English. I remember dancing with Jackie one night, it was a tango and I can honestly say that it was the best tango I had ever danced, she was so smooth and light on her feet.

Whenever I went down to the pool I passed what I thought was a Hindu Monument but it turned out to be a huge sundial commissioned and build by Maharajah Sawai Jat Singh in 1724. The time of the day was calculated by noting the shadows cast by the straight walls in the centre onto graduated markings on the curved inner walls. A photograph of the sundial in shown below.

On one hot, indeed very hot day. Our Chief, Flt/Sgt. Pawsey came into the office and commented how still the air was and passed a remark that things wanted cooling down so, without warning he turned the switch for the ceiling fans to full and guess what – it was like a snow storm with the paper work being blown around the room in a sort of whirlwind. What a comic?

On the 16th July, Taffy and I went on leave, and the adventures of which will be found in the next chapter.

Prior to this leave and since I arrived in Delhi, the chances of sightseeing have been limited but eventually, over a period, I was able to view some of the beauty of this historic city, or should I say 'cities.'

In actual fact there is Old Delhi about five miles away and this lies on the west bank of the River Jumna where on the plains for many miles around there are scattered Tombs, Mosques and various ruins. The name 'Old Delhi' is used for the capital built by the Mogul Emperor Shah Jahan in 1638 and is surrounded by massive battlements. The most famous of the streets is Chandni Chawk or to us Silver Street which is reputed to be the richest street in the world with its gold, silver, ivory and particularly Indian carpets of oriental design. The domed Jumna Masjid of religious fame, or Great Mosque, is crowded every Friday with worshippers.

New Delhi was laid out as a modern city in 1912 and the best way of describing it is to imagine one of those horizontal steel wheels we played on as children in recreation grounds back home. We called them spiders and this is how New Delhi was set out. Connaught Circle was a ring of shops, banks etc., centred by a small green park, then came the Outer Circle with cafes, restaurants and more shops. From these Circles the main roads lead from the City in straight avenues of trees for a distance of some two miles or more into the outlying districts. One of them was the Lytton Road, which we went along when we first arrived. Another road was known as Queensway and lead to the Princes Hall which was the equivalent to our Houses of Parliament and circular in shape.

From the Irwin Stadium end of Lytton Road we used to walk to work through India Gate, along Kingsway, which was about two miles long. This lead to the Viceregal Lodge, which was flanked by two Secretarial Buildings and these were used as the offices of the HQ, South East Asia.

In the winter months we wore blues to go to work but by lunchtime we changed back to K.D. because of the heat.

Chapter Seven

TEN DAYS LEAVE

Taffy and I left Delhi on the 1809 hours train on our way to Mussoorie, which is a Hill Station in the foothills of the Himalayas where we had planned to have ten days leave. We had booked second-class reservations on the train and found the berths to be moderately good, which are by Indian standards.

As we pulled out of the station, last minute arrivals made frantic efforts to board the train. Those who couldn't effectively get into a coach hung perilously onto the running board. This, by the way, was the favourite custom of the third class Indian traveller on the railway.

It wasn't long before we were out of the city boundary after first passing over the River Jumna and five miles further on over the Hindon River. There wasn't any really interesting scenery because all the land around was a rolling plain of scrub. We passed several small villages where the people built their houses of mud, this being collected from the streams and ponds, which were very numerous. Also we saw herds of cows and water buffalo attended by the herdsmen. The cow is the sacred animal of India. I was rather surprised myself to see some of the herds to be of large numbers. In parts the small coppices and streams brought back to me the beauty of our own English countryside but the dark skinned and sometimes filthy looking peasant spoiled the memory.

What was that!? Just then we caught a glimpse of that beautiful bird of paradise, the peacock. This was one of the many instances when amidst all the misery of India there appeared something out of the ordinary life like this it broke the monotony.

A mile or so further on we saw the wife of a farmer ploughing the land in a primitive way with two bullocks pulling the plough. This was the custom out here that the women did their share of the work, like for instance, in the cities, many Indian bricklayers used their wives to do the carrying of bricks and this was done by balancing around a dozen or so upon their heads, even going up and down ladders. For this effort the wage was about two annas a day, two pence to us.

Thus we rumbled along the rails towards our rendezvous and as the shadows lengthened the setting sun moulded patterns of beauty with the silver fleeced clouds. There's a war on! But would you think so as the stars appeared like silver studs set in a sky of black velvet.

So with the night descending upon us we turned our thoughts to sleep, kipping down on our berths and dozing off into the mysteries of slumberland. The next morning we awoke about 6.30 a.m. and dawn spread her light onto the countryside once more.

We arrived at Dehra Dun in the north of India at 8.00 a.m. and the first set back we had was when the R.T.O., told us there were no reservations for us on the return date. However, we skipped that and said we would chance it. The station was a quaint little place with its small booking and ticket office and wooden railings at each end of the platform. It reminded me so much of the average village station in the country at home. The next item on the agenda was some breakfast and although there were only eggs and chips to be had in the little cafe we enjoyed them. This was our first meal since we left Delhi.

After the meal we went to arrange transport and were told that the bus was full but after arguing for five minutes or more with the proprietor we managed to get some seats. We then started our journey up the hills with Taffy and I sat in the back seat facing five local travellers and to be honest I felt out of place but there we were. On the outskirts of the town we stopped to pick up more passengers and two Indians tried to squeeze in beside us. Then I decided it was time to speak and after convincing the driver that there was only room for ten and not twelve, he went back to his cab and once more we started off.

The first half hour was very good and everything felt all right but then it started to drag, 1000ft., 2000ft., 3000ft., all this time we were twisting and turning along the mountain road and being in the back seat made it worse. Every time we took a bend we swung across the road and our backside across the seat; on one side sheer mountains and on the other a drop of thousands of feet.

Twisting and turning, winding, banking, it seemed worse to me than the first plane ride I had and now my stomach was beginning to feel it. I could feel my egg and chips on the move and at any minute I was expecting to have to rush to a window. At five thousand feet we were in the clouds, which were rather low and if anyone had said it was impossible to ride in a bus in the clouds I wouldn't have believed them before we started out but now I know it can be done, and how! As I said, the ride made me feel ill and this turned out to be true. On one side of the bus was seated an Indian family of some standing, the mother and one child on one seat and two other children on the seat in front. After a while one of the children felt sick and his mother put his head out of the window for some fresh air. This he did and was then sick. Unfortunately the wind blew it all back into the bus but fortunately not over us. YAK! It was horrible.

At last we made it. We arrived at Mussoorie, 6000ft., up and it was all blanketed in cloud. As I alighted from the bus my knees trembled and Taffy said I was as white as a sheet, I felt it too. To make things worse the deluge descended upon us. There seemed to be hundreds of coolies and rickshaw wallahs.

"Pukka coolie, Sahib," "Rickshaw, Sahib?" was all we could hear and not feeling too good I could have punched them. "Thyroa!" I said, "give us a chance to arrive." Thyroa (pronounced tiroe) means wait in Urdu.

After checking with the S.S.O.! We booked two coolies and started for Zephyr Hall, then came another shock. We had to climb another 500ft., walking and just like the bus, winding in and out up the hill, but we made it.

We found Zephyr Hall to be a very large bungalow and as we walked into the courtyard Mr Back, the proprietor, met us. He fixed us up in a medium sized room, which had an adjoining bathroom and also a dressing room. He told us that lunch would be at one o'clock and we were ready for it too. On time the dinner bell sounded and Taffy and I made our way to the dining room where we were seated with three ladies and a gentleman of whom I found their dispositions very interesting. This is how I summed them up after finishing a very good lunch.

On the right was a lady somewhere in her forties and she came across as the quiet weekend type because when I asked her if her husband belonged to the RA's, she said something I didn't catch and carried on with. "Were you taking this gentleman to be my husband?"

"Why, of course not," I replied.

"He's in the RA's, and this is his badge I am wearing," she answered.

"The badge was the reason for my question," I said.

Whilst she had been talking her face coloured up with embarrassment. There wasn't much to say about Alec the gentleman because he spoke so very little and I rather liked his manner, he sat at the opposite end to the lady on my right.

On my left was Mrs Searle, an innocent looking, and fair-haired lady in her early twenties and from the conversation across the table I figured her out to be a 'gold digger'. She was just an ordinary person putting on a classy show, but she had no class.

Now my fourth character and opposite me, was Mrs Westcombe, a lady of some fifty odd years. One of the original gossipmongers knew everyone's business and who was going with who in the hostel. However, she was amusing and her English was none too moderate. I think that covers all on our table but on the whole they were very good to us.

Mussoorie was a small but pleasant town and lie in the foothills of the Himalayas where from the main street one could see the snow-capped mountains in the distance with their peaks breaking through the clouds. Mussoorie was also a summer retreat for the Europeans who usually stayed on the plains but as soon as the hot season began they all came up here and to other Hill Stations such as Simla, to cool off.

There were two other boys in another room who were from our billet in camp and they asked us to go roller-skating with them. Taffy and I had never done any before but we took a chance and down to the local rink we went. For two hours we skated or should I say, tried to and I for one got a few bumps but nothing to worry about. At frequent intervals the four of us went over to the bar to have a drink, each time three of us having rum and gingerette and Taffy having whisky. Altogether we had four each and at 7.30 p.m. decided to go back to the Hall for dinner.

I forgot to mention that the other two lads who were on leave with us were named Bill and Syd and after we had enjoyed a marvellous five-course dinner we all decided to go for a walk. I think we had only been walking for ten minutes when we agreed to go to a local cinema. There was a bar open and there it started again, this time we all had rum. For an hour we drank and Taffy was getting worse minute by minute. He even started telling himself off in the mirror which was by the wall. Suddenly Bill had a brainwave to go and see the film, which was showing and after an argument with Taffy we went in. It was an Indian film and none of us understood one word of the language but Bill and I did get interested in the acting and by that we followed the story. After an hour however, Taffy and I fell asleep so Bill thought that we ought to go.

Taffy and I on leave at Mussoorie in August, 1944

Yes, we went. As soon as we left the cinema Taffy disappeared but we soon found him sitting amongst a crowd of rickshaw drivers. They were all doubled up with laughing at Taffy who was rabbitting on in his native language Welsh made worse by the booze so Bill and I lifted him up whilst Syd looked on.

We had only gone ten yards after finding Taffy when he conked out. We carried him to the bottom of Zephyr Drive and after a rest Bill just lugged Taffy over his shoulder and started running up the drive. He did it for fifty yards and then put him on the ground, just by a water pump. Lovely! Down went Taffy's head and down came the water over it. It did the trick so we took him to the bedroom, undressed him and threw him onto the bed, just like a baby.

Myself, Syd and Taffy at the roller skating rink with the proprietor in the background.

So for the first day we had a good time. The next morning we went roller-skating again but enjoyed ourselves without any drink. Once I was going round and trying to turn a circle when I lost my balance, made a grab for the handrail, which gave way and I finished up amongst a pile of chairs, which were stacked at the end of the room. I gave my ribs a crack and I grazed my arm but apart from that I was all right.

After lunch we arranged to go horseback riding to see Mossy Falls, which was a local attraction. My horse was a lovely jet-black animal but was blind in one eye, this causing him to keep veering to the right but with a gentle touch I could correct him. We must have gone down the mountainside along the narrow paths for some thousand feet or more then we dismounted and walked down to the Falls leaving the horses behind. We were expecting something spectacular but there was only a small stream. We didn't stay long and after taking a few photographs we re-mounted and set off back. My horse took the lead and as soon as we came to a little flat ground he broke into a trot. This could have been because leaches had become stuck to his legs whilst we were looking at the Falls. It took us an hour to get back and by the time we did the clouds had descended but we enjoyed every minute of it.

Following dinner we went out and had a few drinks and then went to another cinema, which lie in the other direction and was showing a British film. This time we all walked back to the Hall.

Wednesday was the last day for Bill and Syd and at 2.00 p.m. they started on their return journey to Delhi, Bill leaving his camera with me.

At lunchtime the people on our table were speaking of a dance and I asked, "Is there a dance tonight?"

"There's a Tea dance at Hackman's," replied Mrs Searle.

"Would you mind if I came along with you to show me where it is?"

"No, not at all," was the reply, "I'll see you in the courtyard at a quarter to six."

So, as arranged, I met Blondie and off we went. Hackman's was just up the road, about five minutes walking distance.

It was a two-hour dance and I thoroughly enjoyed it, especially one of the cabaret turns; a smashing looking girl doing a French Can-Can. It was an open dance with cabaret included and was for any B.O.R., or officer on leave in Mussoorie and the place was packed out. We were so interested in the floorshow that we forgot all about the time and had to rush off to get our dinner at the Hall. We were half an hour late.

After dinner Taffy and I went to see another film called "East of the River" and on our way back we were soaked to the skin but didn't mind because we had enjoyed the film immensely.

Thursday the 20th we went to see where the S.S.O., was situated, also to post some airgraphs and buy some new film. Off we went and this time we took our monsoon capes with us in case it rained. We hadn't gone far when it did but we still carried on. All the time we had been climbing up, winding in and out of the bazaar and after half an hour we came to the photographic shop. Outside we asked some soldiers where the S.S.O's office was to be found and they told us to go around the corner and up the hill, follow the arrows and it wasn't far.

No, it wasn't far. We followed the arrows on the signs and climbed for another 30 minutes but still no S.S.O. was to be found. Taffy was 'binding away' like hell but I was determined to post my mail. We kept going and ten minutes later we asked two more soldiers for directions. They asked us why we were going up and I told them.

"There's no need to trail right up there," one said, "you can post them at Hackman's in town."

Taffy and I nearly fainted. All that trail for nothing 'cos one of them said he would take my mail up for me.

We started back and this time we had all on to stop ourselves running, it was so steep. We arrived back at the photo shop and bought some more film and Taffy bought some views of the area. It had been raining all the time that we were out and when we arrived at Zephyr Hall we were soaked all about the legs where the water had dripped down our capes.

We took a few photos after tea and then with it brightening up a little we had a short walk.

We didn't go far and on our way back an MP stopped us because we weren't wearing hats. The rule here is that you can wear mufti up to 8.00 p.m. and then you must wear uniform. We told the MP that we had misunderstood the rule because at the time we were wearing K.D. and that was his reason for stopping us. He advised us to buy civilian shirts and then we would be all right, so the next thing we did was to go straight to the bazaar and get ourselves a shirt each.

The bazaar was a very narrow street and could be described more easily as a small market place. There were a few shops selling many things such as ornaments, silks, and carpets and of course the shop where we bought our shirts.

After dinner we hit another snag. Last night we had been soaked coming from the cinema; this morning we had managed to get our other pair of slacks wet, therefore we couldn't go out. However, Mrs Westcombe told us to get one of the bearers to dry them for us, and this we did. We were able to go out for an hour only, and then we came back and went to bed.

Friday we stayed in all day because it rained heavily but by reading, writing letters and playing games of cards we were able to pass the day quite well. About 7.00 p.m. it had cleared up a little so we made our minds up to go and see another film but after dinner it came on to rain again so we gave up the idea and retired to bed once more.

The next morning we had to stay in again, it was still raining but by 11.00 a.m. it cleared again. Mrs Westcombe at lunchtime noticed some round sores on Taffy's arms and said they looked like Ringworm. I and one or two others were inclined to agree so we finished lunch and went to the M.O's residence. She wasn't in when we arrived and the bearer said she wouldn't be back until 4.00 p m. so we said we would call again at the time stated but I'm afraid it was not to be.

On our way back to the Hall we saw a somewhat small chap, English, arguing with some coolies and he asked us if we could help him to make them understand. In the short time we had been in India we were soon able to understand enough Urdu, which was the main language, to use to success on this occasion. After more arguing everything was fixed up.

We made the coolies realise that the gentleman only wanted one of them to take his horse back to his house. Having done this, Taffy and I made to go our way but the chappy called us back and asked us to have a drink. We accepted and one drink led to another, which absolutely made all three of us drunk. We learned that the man was Chris Hadley an English jockey and during conversation he said he used to live in Sheffield my hometown. This made things perfect and he just wouldn't let us go but in the end we managed to get away and arranged to meet him in Delhi in a week's time.

We both staggered back to the Hall and as soon as we made it Taffy passed out on his bed until dinnertime. I laid on my bed wondering how I was going to be able to go dancing with Mrs Searle but what seemed only five minutes one of the other B.O.R's came to our room to tell me that the lady was waiting. It was a great effort but I did manage to get myself sober in ten minutes.

I put my head under the coldwater tap and then drank some hot tea, which luckily had been brought into us. I think the walk up to Hackman's must have helped me because by the time I arrived there with Blondie I felt fine.

We went in but to our disappointment we found there wasn't going to be a dance, so, after I had drunk an orange squash and Mrs Searle a gin and lime, we returned to the Hall.

On our way back, whom should I meet but my own Officer from Delhi. We saluted and passed the time of day but I was at a loss because two days before I left for Mussoorie he had been taken to B.M.H. However, my partner and I arrived back at the Hall and I found Taffy still out to the world but I sobered him with some cold water and after dinner we went down to the cinema again.

Sunday turned out to be a lovely sunny day and in the morning we went for another walk and then had a drink. After lunch we had a sleep because we felt rather tired but after dinner we saw another film, "Assignment in Britanny" then once more returning to enjoy the pleasures of dreamland.

The next afternoon I took Taffy to see the M.O. about his suspected Ringworm and the lady doctor said it had been caught in time.

She gave Taffy some ointment and bandages for it telling him there was nothing to worry about. We left there and walked up to the bazaar where we bought some more film for the camera we had borrowed. We arrived back in time for tea having taken our time on the way.

I had arranged to go to another dance with Blondie and was getting dressed for dinner when one of the lads in the Hall asked me if I would care to make up a party. Mrs Searle had agreed and so did I. When we set off there were five boys and two ladies. The other lady had just arrived at the Hall and she was on the tall side, single and rather attractive, having a marvellous figure and a beautiful pair of legs.

We arrived at the Standard Restaurant and made ourselves comfortable at a table then one of the boys bought the first round of drinks. After the first dance there was a cabaret turn and it was a couple dancing a Rhapsody in Swing, which was very good. The pair of them glided about the floor and to finish the act the gent bent the lady backwards over his knee and as she went over she put one leg into the air. Her black dress fell back revealing a very shapely leg and then a white thigh until it was possible to see she had on a very thin pair of stockings.

Syd, myself and Taffy at Mossy Falls Mussoorie, August, 1944

My eyes stood out just like the rest of the boys' eyes did and then I noticed that Nora was looking at me with a smile on her face. At this I took off my specs and it certainly caused a laugh but to make things worse one of the lads asked her if she could see and she replied,

"You had better ask him!" – nodding towards me. I'm sure it must have been onc of the few occasions when I really blushed. The act finished and I replaced my specs. The rest of the evening passed on with all of us dancing in turn with the ladies.

The last dance I thoroughly enjoyed because I danced with Nora, she followed beautifully and of course the band were playing dreamy slow foxtrot tempos and all the lights were dimmed. It ended with a superbly played Bolero.

We all prepared to leave and one of the lads had been drinking rum all night but although he wasn't drunk he was a little over the mark.

He said he could walk okay and Blondie bet him he would fall over. He said he wouldn't but at that moment he slipped on something wet and finished up under the table. We all had a good laugh and then proceeded on our way home having had a very enjoyable evening.

The next day was our last one so after packing we had a short walk then came back for lunch.

At 2.00 p.m. we caught the down bus on our return journey and it wasn't as bad as when coming up and for curiosity I counted the bends in the road and in total there were some 500 in the 21 miles we travelled. We had to wait 30 minutes at Dehra Dun for our train but the time soon passed. There was nothing eventful to see except for the odd little town or village through which we passed.

We arrived back in Delhi the next day at lunchtime feeling very rejuvenated after our ten days glorious leave.

Chapter Eight

GOODBYE YOU OLD INDIAN SUMMER

With my return from a very refreshing leave I was bent on knuckling down to work again. This I commenced on the 31st August and in doing so I received a great surprise. I found that I was transferred into another section, which had been newly formed before I went on leave and in which I was greatly interested. Therefore, when I realised that my wish to get into the new department had come true I jumped like a two-year old. The saying that a change is as good as a rest was certainly the case this time.

The new post was far different to the general clerical work I had been doing and though I was now going to be a statistical typist, I had hopes of combining some draughtsmanship in the line of cartographical work. There were five of us on the staff and they included Sgt. Bernard Perry, a Sheffield chap, Cpl. Chopping, 'Chopper' to us all and full of beans, Cpl. Skidmore and L.A.C. 'Ginger' White, a very likeable and intelligent youth with a tendency to 'Creep'. However, I settled down to work with my new mates and looked forward to the future.

Because I had transferred to this new section it meant that I had to type correctly and efficiently so I, along with other personnel from various sections, was sent on a typing course. This was held three times a week and four hours per session. We were taught by an Indian civilian in an office in New Delhi whose method was very good as he got us to type in rhythm to any tune we cared to sing or hum. It worked tremendously and we all finished the course as qualified touch typists.

Besides taking an interest in my new position the next six weeks saw me hard at it with the Irstads. Being on the Committee my time was pretty full and during this period I think I only went down town half a dozen times. Occasionally I swam on my day off and a couple of times to the cinema also an invitation to have dinner at the flat of my friend Ron Hulme whom, I might add, was the perfect host and afterwards took me to another film show.

At the last General Meeting of the Club someone suggested that a dinner dance be held and this being agreed it was left to the discretion of a sub-committee to arrange things.

On the weekly committee night we set to work to see what was to be done and we all agreed that a dinner dance would be held on the 4th September, but at a later date we changed it to have the dinner on the 4th and the dance on the 15th and call it the Battle of Britain Dance. Each of us took on a special job, myself doing part of the advertising, whilst Steve, Ernie and Pat booked the Hall etc. We booked for fifty people at Davico's Restaurant on the Circle in New Delhi. Everyone who attended enjoyed it to the full and many said that it couldn't have been better if it had been in Blighty. A very good three-course dinner was served, this being the maximum obtainable, drinks were included and the total cost was Rs. 50.00 each.

The dance on the 15th was another terrific success and a profit of Rs. 200.00 was made for the C.O's Benevolent Fund. Invitations had gone out to all the RAF, brasshats but Sir Richard Pierce was unable to attend. However, we did have the honour of Air Marshal R. G. Goddard the senior Personnel Officer for SE Asia.

I had a very interesting part to play, much to my delight, when I had to go to all the ladies' residences such as the W.A.A.C.(I)'s Hostel, W.E.C. and the Wrens Hostel collecting them for the dance and I'm certain there was no man who didn't have a partner. Advertising had been well carried out and around 2200 hours the Press came to take photos of dancers enjoying themselves wearing party hats and throwing streamers all over each other. I don't think the

Irstads ever had so much publicity.

Since returning from leave there was one occasion of which I shall always feel very proud. Ron Hulme asked me to play in the Band again but would I make sure that my best K.D. uniform was 'bulled' up and brasses sparkling because we were going to play at a dinner dance at the Viceregal Lodge for the Viceroy of India. What an honour! There was the Viceroy, General Wavell, General Aukinleck and Air Chief Marshal Sir Richard Pierce, all with their wives and many very well known Indian dignitaries. It was a night I shall always remember.

During the excitement of the past six weeks I received a great piece of news. I learned on the ninth of September that I had been promoted to Leading Aircraftsman having past the trade test, which I sat in June last.

With the results of my typing test being added on I obtained a pass mark of 98%, also my pay was increased to £10 per month.

On the 16th September, our section was ordered to pack, ready to move to Kandy in Ceylon. This had been in the offing for sometime and sections were ready to go but as usual there was much panic with everyone bumping into someone else and within 48 hours we were ready. However, at 1100 hours on the 17th, Air Vice Marshal Weedon C.B.E., dashed into our office and said, "Alright lads, put your charts back onto the walls." That was that and we didn't move although some other sections did.

After that little bit of panic all seemed to quieten down considerably and I was still busy almost every night of the week with the Club, running Tombola, whist drives, on duty in the Club Room besides attending meetings. During this quiet period we were moved out from under canvas and re-billeted in a brick barrack block where it was much more comfortable.

Thursday the 12th October I was invited to the W.A.A.C(I)'s dance at the Stadium and although the setting was beautiful I can't say that I enjoyed it. It was held in the quadrangle under a star spangled sky, the air was cool and it could have been a good show. There was plenty to eat and drink, good music but insufficient women for partners. I think the ratio was something like four men to one woman; it was really impossible to dance. Everything seemed to be going all right until about 2300 hours. I was standing about ten yards from the bar talking to Stan Porrett one of my room mates, when without the slightest warning all hell broke loose.

Someone at the bar yelled, "You bastard!" and the next minute the same fellow had cracked his glass on the edge of the bar and jabbed it into the jugular vein of the chap next to him. Blood spurted all over and both of them were covered but the attacker wasn't satisfied with that, he floored his opponent and then proceeded to kick his head in. It all happened so quickly and it must have been five minutes before anyone could get near them. We learned later that the wounded man an RAF, Warrant Officer, died from loss of blood.

After this Stan and I decided it would be a good idea if we returned to our billet and bed.

A few days later Stan felt ill and was itching all over so one of the N.C.O's told him to report sick and see the M.O. We guessed it to be Prickly Heat, which had turned septic, so off Stan went and within half an hour he was back at work. Wing Commander Lord saw him in the corridor, "What the blazes are you doing here Porrett?"

"The M.O. sent me back sir, implying that I was malingering."

"Did he, be-damned!?" said the Winco. "Come with me."

The Winco took Stan straight into the A.V.M. and explained to him. The A.V.M. immediately rang the Command Senior Medical Officer who happened to be an Air Commodore with his office just down our corridor. The result – Stan was on his way home within hours and the M.O. who was involved and of a low rank was posted to the forward areas or to put it another way – the jungle.

This incident was the last bit of excitement up to the 4th November when I was posted to

Kandy. The same old panic. "You're going", "You're not going", "Pack", "Unpack." I was all mixed up. However, on Saturday the 6th after the Group Captain had argued it out with the A.V.M., I was posted, definitely. Just by myself except of course for one officer. There was no need to pack because I had already done that in the panic in September.

As anyone in the Forces knows, that when one is posted to another Unit then that person has to be cleared from all the various sections and obtain a kind of credit clearance. This I had almost done, having been to equipment section, medical and orderly room, accounts and others until I came to the armoury.

The Warrant Officer wouldn't clear me because I hadn't a Sten Gun. He wouldn't listen when I told him that I had never brought one with me from Blighty.

"Everyone has a gun of some sort when posted overseas," he said.

"But sir..." I could get no further. Just then his phone rang and a voice asked, "Is L.A.C. Priestley with you?" It was W /C Lord.

"Yes, sir," replied the W.O., "but I can't clear him without a gun."

"Nonsense," said the Winco, "If he needs protection then I've got my own 45."

Within ten minutes I was back with the Wing Commander receiving my final instructions.

So, at 5.30 a.m. on the 8th November I boarded a Dakota aircraft with W/C Lord and Flt/Lt Brown at Palam Airfield. Within thirty minutes we had run down the flarepath and risen into the air bound for Ceylon. There was plenty of room on board so all three of us kipped down for same sleep but not before we had seen a marvellous sunrise.

There wasn't really much to see on the way south because the ground was flat and barren. We passed over Hyderabad and twenty minutes later we touched down at Hakimpet to refuel. We didn't stay long and we were soon taking off again. Over southern India we ran into a little bad weather and had to climb to 13,000ft. to get over it but everything was all right. We arrived at Ratmalana airfield about 1600 hours.

When we left the plane with our luggage the W/C and Flt. Lt. went into the Officers' Mess and I remained outside to take care of our belongings. Suddenly I heard, "Priestley, what are you doing?" It was W/C Lord.

"Looking after our kit, sir," I replied. "Nonsense, come here and have some tea." So it was that I had tea in the Officers' Mess and was treated as a person, not another rank. After this we were taken to the nearest station by lorry with all our kit. We boarded the 1830 hours train, which was the Mountbatten Special to Kandy. As we disembarked from the train Sqd/Ldr MacLachlan who had everything arranged for accommodation and the transport, which was to take us to the camp just the other side of Kandy, met us.

There wasn't enough room in the back of the bus so I had to ride up front with the driver and this suited me admirably. We pulled away from the station and soon we were passing through the town of Kandy and as we left it behind we came into what reminded me of an English country lane. The night was jet-black and the headlamps of the bus were like two huge searchlights piercing the inky blackness.

Twisting and twining along the greasy roads owing to the recent rain, a high speed could not be maintained, especially when taking the numerous sharp bends. It took some twenty minutes to reach camp, which was about 2,000 feet above sea level and situated amidst a forest of tall silent giants – a coconut plantation.

We were taken to the Officers' Mess and I vas told to wait in the P.M.C's office whilst my two officers went for a meal. I must have waited for fifteen minutes when a sergeant came in. Later I found he was from Bradford.

"I don't know what I'm supposed to do with you. Would you like something to eat?"

"I would very much, thank you," I replied.

"Come with me and I'll see what I can do," So he took me over to the Officers' kitchen where I found my two officers sitting.

"Can Priestley join you, sir?" he asked.

"Certainly Sergeant," then turning to me, "Come in Priestley, I'm sorry, I forgot about you," said W/C Lord.

After the meal of boiled ham, salad and coffee the officers and I had a smoke and a chat for a while then they left me in the Admin Office where eventually the sergeant returned and said he could fix me up with accommodation. He certainly did. That night I slept in a bed in the officers' quarters and thoroughly enjoyed the comfort.

The following day I reported to my new office and my new job. I was informed by Flt/Lt Brown that for the present I would have to help L.A.C. Alan Gordon, the other chap in the office, to get things organised for a while and then I should go onto my draughtsman's work.

I had met Alan Gordon in Delhi through the medium of the A.C.S.E.A. Players and when I enquired if he was doing anything of the kind here he informed me that they were almost ready for the production of J. B. Priestley's play, "They Came To A City."

"We are at the moment short of stage staff. How would you like to give a hand?" he asked.

"By all means, when do I start?" "Tomorrow night in the Camp Cinema," was the reply.

This short conversation led to my being occupied for the next week with the Priestley Play – no, not mine.

The play was a great success and after two showings outside the camp we went to the Chunking Restaurant in Kandy to have supper but the last of these outings was the best. It was a jolly party with several Wrens being there, also one WAAF. All the dishes were Chinese and though this was my first taste of it I enjoyed it but wasn't tempted to use the chopsticks. The main course was a delicious shark dish. After the last show the players closed down for a rest with the intention to start a new production in the New Year.

For the next few weeks I spent most of my nights in the NAAFI and soon palled up with another Taffy and Ken, a Birmingham lad. I was settling down quite well to the serenity of my new camp, which was certainly better than the model City of New Delhi. The atmosphere was better and the scenery marvellous with tall stately palms, a quiet but somewhat dirty river at the bottom of the camp all surrounded by green foliaged mountains.

Everything seemed to be going smoothly up to the 11th December when suddenly I was rushed into the 48th Indian General Hospital with Diphtheritic Otitis Externa (L). It was Diphtheria in my left ear.

However, before continuing the story of my illness, I wish to describe part of the surrounding area. Two thirds of Ceylon is covered by jungle where brilliant orchids, flowering trees and shrubs grow. Colombo is the modern capital but it used to be Kandy, which was also an independent kingdom until 1918. Kandy itself is a hill city and a very pleasant place with a beautiful lake opposite the Temple of the Tooth. However, the outstanding feature of the city is the Botanical Garden in nearby Peradeniya.

On the edge of the river, which runs through our camp we could watch the Dhobi Wallah, as the launderer was called. He did the washing and ironing of our clothes and no soap was used because the women beat the dirt out on boulders at the side of the river and the irons were big flat ones with charcoal inside them to give the heat.

It was said that the elephant urine in the river helped to bleach out tunics.

Chapter Nine

INDIAN GENERAL HOSPITAL

48 I.G.H., was about two miles from 'C' camp and situated on a small hill over-looking the little village of Katagastota. The hospital in peacetime used to be a boys school, a sort of monastery and through the courtesy of the Ceylonese Government had been turned into a hospital for British Troops. In front of the main entrance there was a large sports field where many hours were spent by 'up' patients watching inter-service and civilian matches taking place. These games included cricket, football and hockey.

On being admitted I was put into Ward 4, which is the Medical Ward and being a diphtheria case I was put into isolation on the veranda. There were several other servicemen with the same complaint and I recognised one of these as George Richardson, the corporal who slept on the next charpoy to me back in camp. He had been in three days and having become friendly with the sister he asked her if I could be put in the bed next to him. George hailed from Derbyshire and during a conversation I found out that he lived only some 15 miles from me just over the Yorkshire border back home, so really we were close neighbours.

The second day in hospital brought me an inspection from the M.O., and later my first treatment. What treatment! Sister Coleman, the army nurse, administered it. She belonged to the Queen Alexandras Royal Army Nursing services Q.A.R.A.N.S. She approached my bed with a surgical tray upon which rested a hypodermic needle loaded with anti-diph serum. George Richardson was chuckling to himself and I asked,

"What are you grinning at?" "You'll see – or rather feel in a minute!" he replied.

Well I did feel. Over I turned onto my stomach and down came the bedclothes, pyjama trousers and the hypo.

"Relax," was the only word I heard from the Sister. Then it came! Four inches of cold steel into my buttocks. That was that, I knew what George was laughing at.

Every four days we all had the same treatment, first one cheek and then the other. Soon it was like sitting on a hornet's nest.

After the first week Sister Coleman went onto night duty for a fortnight which left us with two other Sisters Q.A.R.A.N.S. Betsy Harper and Molly Morgan. Two nicer nurses I have never met, they were so full of fun and could give a joke as well as take one.

Betsy was one of those quiet, efficient girls and most of the boys used to call her 'rigor mortis' but George and I grew to like her very much. As for Molly, she was entirely different but still efficient, she liked an extra good time and we knew it. 'Attractive' was written all over her face and I think she knew how much we admired her figure because every time she came near to our beds she would stand with her back to the sunlight and give us a crafty wink. Her uniform was almost transparent; it was most unfortunate that we were patients.

I remember one day a new diph. patient arrived on the veranda and it wasn't long before Molly came around with the hypo. The new boy was sitting in his pyjamas with his legs outside the bed when she reached him.

"Come along," she addressed him, "this is for you so drop your trousers."

Unfortunately, not having had treatment before he didn't know the routine so he stood up outside the bed, turned his back on Molly, dropped his pyjamas and bent down. Then the tittering started and Molly, the tyke she was, pushed the chap face down onto the bed and hardly giving him time to get comfortable, she struck. From two feet away she almost threw the needle at him and he gave out a loud, "Ow-w-w-!"

There was uproar at the other end of the veranda and as she passed us on her way back she said,

"And all of you had better stop laughing or else you will get the same next time."

"Did you play darts for the local Pub at home Sister?" I asked, still chuckling. CRASH! A library book came whizzing through the air straight at my head.

"Just you wait," was her remark. I did wait. The next day was my turn for the needle and Molly threw. "Ow-w-w!"

So the days passed with medical inspections and treatment and in the evenings we spent most of the time playing Monopoly.

Each day brought us closer to Molly and Betsy, metaphorically speaking of course, and they certainly looked after us but unlike the ordinary patients we were allowed to have honey and malt extract, lime juice and sugared barley sweets, all provided by the Red Cross from Australia.

On the 23rd December I lost my bed mate because he was getting better and was taken out of isolation and put into the open ward. This partly broke up the Monopoly school and many are the times when the two nurses have chased me back onto the veranda.

I had an R.E. sergeant in the next bed to me instead of George and he was just the same. We also had a NAAFI sergeant in the ward and the same day that George left, the R.E. sergeant had a chat with the other sergeant from the NAAFI.

"How about getting some beer in for tomorrow night?" asked the R.E.

"I'd like to very much but I'm afraid it's impossible. The C.O. wouldn't allow it," was the reply.

"Now don't give me that line. Look! Either you get some beer in for the boys or else the R.E's don't do any repairs on your NAAFI for twelve months."

Well, Christmas Eve arrived and not only did we get two crates of beer but the R.E. sergeant acquired some bottles of sherry and whisky from their Mess. The next day the orderlies and the nurses were at us all day to return the medicine glasses.

Christmas Day 1944 and what a day! I was improving in health and was allowed to go into the other ward to chat to George. All the diph. cases along with one or two others were more than merry and Molly, Betsy and Capt. Mills the M.O., having been to a dance the night before, were worse than us.

I sat on the end of George's bed to have my Christmas dinner and then more fun came. All the patients had been served with turkey, chicken, veg and stuffing when Molly came across to George and I and asked,

"Do you want any more stuffing?"

"No thank you," I replied. "Well shout up the Ward and see if anyone else wants stuffing," said Molly.

At this I started laughing and bellowed up the Ward, "Say chaps, Molly wants to know if any of you want stuffing?"

Crack! Molly's hand hit me right at the back of my neck.

"You're at it again," she cried, but laughed as much as we did.

That same night we lay in our beds watching the Sisters on their way to a dance. After we had made sure there were no more to pass we started another bottle party. We finished the last bottle about 2230 hours but none of us could get to sleep so we chatted to each other until midnight and then we started 'booking' the Sisters in. All the bottles we had emptied were stood across the pathway and as the first Sister came past I recognised her as Betsy. "Serg.," I softly called to my bed mate. "Betsy's here and she's going behind the bushes so we can't see her." "Goodnight," bawled the sergeant.

"You devils," cried Betsy, "get to sleep."

All the time this was taking place she was getting nearer to the row of bottles. Crash! Over they went.

Betsy, boyfriend and all; It was the moment the boys had waited for and there was uproarious laughter.

The rest of the week passed quietly as did New Years' Eve because we were not allowed to celebrate that. On the 2nd of January, I was discharged as fit and returned to my Unit. I saw my Camp M.O. the following morning that said he would take another swab just to be on the safe side. This he did at 10.00 a.m. and at 1.30 p.m. I was on my way back to 48 I.G.H. The swab was positive.

For a further three weeks I was under observation and during this time Molly was transferred to the Military Hospital in Colombo. Finally convinced that I was clear of diphtheria! Capt. Mills decided to send me to 28 Indian Convalescent Depot (B.I.), which, was up in the hills of Ceylon at a small place, called Dyatalawa.

To get there we left by train from Peradeniya Station in Kandy. It was a very pleasant journey on a single track built by Canadian engineers. Slowly we climbed up on the twisting journey through coconut groves and tea plantations It was a beautiful sight to see Ceylonese women dressed in multi-coloured saris, tediously picking the leaves from the small bushes and putting them into the big baskets fastened to their backs.

I arrived at the Convalescent Camp on the 24th January and from the very first day I knew I wouldn't like it. The surrounding district had much in common with the Derbyshire Moors back home but the camp itself was situated in a wooded hollow. The first three weeks were really awful and strict daily routi'nes were adhered to. To give you an idea here were the Daily Routine Orders:

0645	Reveille
0700	Roll call on Parade ground
0715	Dismiss
0800	Breakfast
0900	Roll Call
0915	P.T., which include anything from Rugger Touch with a medicine ball to a 10-mile route march or a 4-mile cross-country run.
1015	NAAFI
1045	Roll Call
1100	Lecture
1200	Break
1300	Lunch or Tiffin
1400	Roll Call
1415	Organised Games
1600 } 2215 }	Your own time.

The routine never altered and if anyone went sick we had to hope for the best. The M.O. was crazy. Often he would greet you with a Nazi salute when you entered his office and one day he said to a patient, "You don't want to see me you want to see a doctor."

Then on another occasion he sat outside with the sick parade and the peculiar thing was that they were all new arrivals and didn't know him. After ten minutes he remarked, "When is this bloody M.O. coming?"

No wonder we nicknamed him Mad Carew.

On the fourth week of my stay at 28 I.C.D. I had a stroke of luck when Tosh Noyes the resident R.S.M. came and enquired if any of us could play a musical instrument and if so would we be willing to form a small dance band.

There were five of us who stepped forward and this was the line-up:

Jimmy Hayworth on Alto Sax and Clarinet, Johnny Birch on Hawaiian Guitar, Stan Cole on Piano, Eddie on Spanish Guitar, Cyril on Drums and myself on Double Bass.

We had a practice that same afternoon and played at our first dance in the Sergeants' Mess that same evening. The Q.M.S. helped us a great deal and rigged us out with black trousers and a red sash. We all had white shirts and although I say it myself we looked very smart.

That first dance set us off with a bang and the next evening we played at a dance for the other ranks. For four weeks we were in great demand and below was our weekly programme:

Monday	Officers' Mess or Wrens Mess
Tuesday	Tosh's Stag Party
Wednesday	Sgt's Mess
Thursday	B.O.R's
Friday	Naval Hospital
Saturday	Bandarawella Hotel.

All these dances earned us Rs.10 each night, which is about 15/- in old English money, but I would like to comment on two of our evenings, the first of which is Tosh's Stag Party. I have often seen impromptu concerts but never one like this. Admitted there were several good amateur turns on and the boys, the majority of whom were matelots, really enjoyed it. But the big fault with Tosh was he would come on and tell the filthiest jokes imaginable and not many of us liked him. Fortunately ladies were not permitted to attend.

One week Tosh was in hospital so we managed to put on a clean show. I might mention at this point that we had Max Newbould, the BBC theatre organist with us and he helped considerably. Max was on the permanent staff here and one day when I went to see him in his office he was having a right battle with a Black Mamba snake, which had crawled under the door. There was Max laying into it with a broom head and luckily he won.

The other evening I want to mention is a Saturday night at the Bandarawella Hotel. We all enjoyed this night because the acoustics were good and also the crowd of dancers. We were well paid because we arrived at 8.00 p.m., set up our instruments then went for a four course dinner and three double brandies each, all on the house. We commenced playing at 9.00 o'clock and at 11.00 o'clock I played waltzes on the piano whilst the rest of the band had a light supper and of course we had several drinks bought us by the guests and dancers.

The Army C.O. of the camp, who was a Colonel, tried his best to get all the band posted up there permanently but with us all being RAF tradesmen, Group Headquarters wouldn't entertain the idea. So, after seven glorious weeks we were split up and returned to our Units.

On returning to work I began to feel the after effects of my illness and I tried my best to work it off but it was of no use and at the end of the third week, following a mild heart attack whilst walking to work, I was readmitted to 48 I.G.H. with Chronic Bronchitis.

It was surprising how the place had changed in such a short space of time. Molly had been posted to Colombo and Betsy had left. The nursing orderly who helped to take care of me when I was in before was now a patient himself suffering with TB. There wasn't the same comradeship between patients as there had been before and the next three weeks I spent in there couldn't be described as good. But for one occasion there was no merriment as there was when George was in.

The one occasion was VE Day and we all received two bottles of beer each but the celebrating was far different to that at home. Several of the up patients, of which, I was one, were allowed to go into Kandy to witness the VE Parade. Many nations were represented along with our own Army, Navy and Air Force contingents, even the Kandy Boy Scouts turned out. General Browning who was Lord Louis deputy inspected all these. It really was worth seeing.

On the 14th May I was discharged from hospital and for a fortnight I really took things easy but on Saturday the 26th I went with Pat Ferryman, the WAAF Corporal in our section, into Kandy to see a religious procession called the Wesak.

It was a very impressive sight and everything was done by torchlight. The parade wasn't a huge one and only included what appeared to be small temple replicas mounted on bullock carts decoratively coloured, with children sat upon them in their religious regalia chanting native hymns. The town was packed with Singhalese and once or twice Pat and I were trapped in the swirling masses but quite safe.

The next few months I began to feel my old self again and once more indulged in sport. Corporal Cliff Kinch and I played many hours of tennis or went for long walks on our days off and sometimes found ourselves within a small native compound of which there were many quite near to camp the villagers were also friendly.

We were returning from the cinema one night with several other airmen, the moonlight was so bright one could have read a newspaper even though it was about 2300 hours. As we split up to go to our respective billets between the bashas (huts), one of the lads fell over what he thought was a small tree trunk left on the ground.

"Who left that bloody thing there?" he cried.

Then the 'log' moved. It was a Kobragoya, which was a sacred animal and had come up from the river and was like a small crocodile. We were doubled up with laughter.

A party of us arranged to take a 48-hour pass one weekend and go to a little village called Neuara Alyia. It was purposely built, another of the 'Bosses' ideas and about an hours ride by train and situated up in the hills above Kandy. It reminded me very much of the villages back home with the sloping roofs and smoke curling lazily up from the chimneys in the damp air. There was also a village pub and this gave the place its real atmosphere and it made a good change from the camp.

Ceylon is very beautiful when there is no monsoon, especially at night when the moon is riding along the treetops, casting fantastic but weird shadows from which come many strange jungle noises.

However, when we did get a monsoon there were times when it became frightening. For instance, on one occasion we had twelve inches of rain in 24 hours and the winds were so strong that a large palm tree was up-rooted and it crashed right across a Basha hut splitting it in two. Fortunately most of the lads were at the NAAFI so no one was hurt.

On another camp a coconut fell from a tree in the office area, hit an airman on the head and killed him. This resulted in a signal being sent from our HQ to all units in SE Asia to chop down any coconut trees situated immediately at the side of any wooden buildings.

Some nights Cliff and I would spend an evening playing solo with two other chaps or having a nice quiet chat over a pint of beer and smoking a pipe of tobacco. I may not have mentioned that Cliff was a Lancastrian and his father owned a pub somewhere near Preston. On Saturday nights we often went down to Kandy and passed our time away in the Pheonix Club, which was a club for other ranks only and was specially arranged for by Lord Louis himself.

It was a great place to relax in with easy chairs, settees and a marvellous bar, also a grand piano where quite a few musicians from the camp would gather for jazz sessions and sing-alongs.

Wednesday August 15th should have been a great night for us with it being VJ Night but no. Guards were put on the armoury; WAAF site and office area besides an extra fire piquet and the result was that only about 10% of the camp personnel was able to celebrate. In the canteen it looked as if the war had started, not finished. However, VJ + 2 was a little better and an all ranks dance was held in the NAAFI but still there wasn't that atmosphere that one would expect on such a night for rejoicing. There were only two pieces of excitement, one was when some fool threw a football onto the dance floor and everyone wanted to kick it out of the way. The other instance was where the officers in their Mess had given a baby elephant a bucket of beer to drink with the expected results. It may be called cruel but to see it wobbling all over the place trying to get back down the camp road was a very funny sight.

A view of the Phoenix Club and Tea Gardens where we had many happy moments

The following Wednesday Cliff and I went down into Kandy to see the Perehara, which is a yearly festival in peace time but during the war it had not taken place and this was the first time since 1940. We arrived in town early and made our way to the S.E.A.C. restaurant, which was another thoughtful arrangement made for the other ranks by the Supremo. There we had a four course dinner at a very reasonable price and were lucky enough to get a table near to the window overlooking the main street.

At 9.00 p.m. we heard the cracking of elephant hide whips and ten minutes later the whip men came into view. These whips were used to chase away the so-called evil spirits and each whip had a 20 to 30 feet lash on it which when cracked caused the crowd to hurriedly move back to avoid being hit. After these came one set of the world famous Kandyan Dancers dressed in all their jangling silver costumes which shone brightly in the light of the torches, which aligned the whole procession. Then came the first of the one hundred magnificently decorated elephants of which there are normally 400 during peacetime.

Temple of the Tooth, Kandy

In the centre of the procession came the bull elephant with its golden howdah in which was enshrined the Sacred Golden Tooth and this is supposedly one of Buddha's teeth which was placed here when he died and is classed as a relic of the Great Eastern God.

On either side of this was another large elephant upon which sat a Chieftain underneath a huge coloured umbrella and colours of every description could be seen both in the native Princes' dress and the ornamentation of the animals. Altogether this magnificent phenomenon took some one hour and forty minutes to pass below us. A few days later I went along to see the Temple of the Tooth where the relic is normally kept and once again the beauty of the structure was something never to be forgotten.

Monday 17th September, my other two buddies, Ron and Len, along with myself left for Colombo on a 14-day leave. Colombo is only eighty miles from Kandy and we travelled up in the Mountbatten Special, which took three and a half hours, strange as it may seem. From the station we took a taxi to Elscourt Manor the place where we were to stay. On arrival we found it to be a very large house in its own grounds, which was under the management of NAAFI/EFI. It was a marvellous building with two large lawns, highly polished dormitories and spacious bathrooms also spotless lounges, dining rooms and of course a bar.

On our second night there a dance had been arranged but it wasn't a great success because there were too many men and I think I had only two dances all evening. Half way through the dance all the lights fused and although some people ambled around in the dark the rest continued outside on the lawn. Luckily it was a glorious moonlight night and we were able to see what we were doing, so on the whole I think the majority enjoyed themselves.

The following day we decided to go swimming and around ten o'clock we went into town to the Governors' Pool on the shore where we swam for half an hour and then went and lay in the sun on the sand just up the beach. Len had an idea to go a little way down the beach near to the water and lie and wait for the waves to come in. It was marvellous lying there in the sun with big waves coming and sweeping over us but after a while it became rougher and some of the breakers were about four feet high so when they hit us they carried on right up the beach. We couldn't do much for laughing at times but later we were to regret it very much indeed. Sunburn can be classed as self-inflicted injuries.

Queen's Hotel in Kandy on the opposite corner to the Phoenix Club

Soon our thoughts turned to food, the sea air making us feel hungry so off we went and fed ourselves then after lunch we managed to locate one of Ron's pals whom he hadn't seen for two and a half years. Each of us was beginning to feel the sunburn especially on our legs and faces but we really had enjoyed it.

On several nights we had come from town along the Galle Face front and it had been magnificent with a full moon shining upon the white foam of the huge waves breaking on the shore and a strong breeze cooling us off from the heat of the day.

Saturday the 22nd, we went swimming at the biggest first class hotel the Galle Face Hotel which is a massive place for the up and ups but three days a week the pool is open for O.R's. In we walked, five of us like lords of the air and being in civvies people didn't know whether we were officers of O.R's and most of our leave we wore white shirts and shorts. We spent a couple of hours there and then returned to Elscourt for dinner and after this we wandered around to the open-air Fountains Café where we so often called for ice cream sodas in the evenings.

I think that for most of our leave we were down at Mount Lavinia, which was about seven miles along the coast, south of Colombo. It was a quiet and pleasant bay, which on Sundays was very crowded with men and women from all the services enjoying a little relaxation but we used to go down during the week and enjoy the piece and quiet. One day I had a little mishap. We climbed onto some rocks where we sat for a while letting the waves splash over us. I saw one wave coming and counteracted it, then turned to laugh at two of the lads playing silly devils and as I did so another wave came and swept me straight off the rocks onto the boys below. I was laughing so much I didn't realise that I had hurt myself. However, it wasn't too serious although I felt a little stiff for a few days and had to take things easy.

A view of the lake and bungalows overlooking Kandy

For the next couple of days we passed the time away by playing snooker and this caused a certain amount of fun because the cloth was ripped and whatever shot you played you scored something different. Wally, from the Parachute Regiment not able to reach the ball standing on the floor, slowly climbed onto the table on his hands and knees. His nose touching the cloth and his backside in the air was a very funny sight indeed.

Military General Hospital, Colombo

Whilst on leave I managed to contact Sisters Molly and Betsy who were now stationed at the Military General Hospital in Colombo. The latter was ill in bed with tonsillitis so I visited her once or twice and took her some flowers in appreciation for what she had done for others and myself when we were in hospital at Katagastota. She really was surprised and very pleased for the thought. For an hour we reminisced at what had happened down at 48 I.G.H. and the laughs we had when they were there.

The Clock Tower, Colombo

But going back to the leave itself there was another time when Wally and Len Croker tried surfing on some small pieces of wood about three feet long and eighteen inches wide down on the beach at Mount Lavinia. Some of the waves were around six feet high and Wally lay on one of these boards and in he came at some twenty miles per hour, straight through a girl's legs who was standing at the edge of the water with them open not realising what had happened so imagine the amount of laughter.

There was one day down at the Mount when I played a trick on Len. He had a very good physique as against my puny eight and a half stone, which he kept picking up and throwing me into the water. Anyhow, he did it once too often because when he threw me again I let myself sink to the bottom, turned over and swam underwater until I reached the sandy beach. I kept still and looked back where Len was and he and the others were panicking because they thought I had possibly drowned. Suddenly Len spotted me chuckling my head off, shouted some abusive language and then chased me along the beach. He didn't try it again but he saw the joke and laughed it off.

It was the best leave I have ever had and on the 29th September, and we all returned to camp.

However. I was destined for another short stay in 48 I.G.H. because on my return from leave I was asked the following day if I would care to make up a foursome at tennis. I agreed and at 6.00 p.m. after duty I went down to the tennis courts on the camp. At 6.10 p.m. I served the first ball of the match and was beginning to enjoy myself but after serving the third ball and jumping up to smash the return, I slipped. For a moment I was so interested in the game and so glad that I had won the point that I didn't give a thought as to what had happened.

When I picked myself up from the ground I realised that I had fractured my left wrist. The shock caused my suntan to go a dusky green and I felt sick but I managed to walk up to my billet and there Stuart Cohen pulled off my plimsolls and put on my chapleys for me. He then took me up to the M.I. Room and twenty minutes later I had seen the M.O. and was on my way back to hospital again. At 7.00 p.m. I was being taken up to Ward 2 with my wrist set and encased in Plaster of Paris.

Fountains Cafe, where we often called in the evenings

This is where we spent many a happy hour and here are the rocks I hurt myself on. Mount Lavinia Hotel is in the background

After having had something to eat I finally dozed off to sleep but about 2.00 a.m. I was awakened by the night Sister who asked, "How's your arm feel?"

"Fine thanks," was my reply, "I can't feel a thing."

"Just as I thought," she said, "Your plaster is on too tight and it's a good job I came round otherwise you may have lost your arm altogether."

She sent for the orderly who had put on the plaster and ordered him to cut it open. She then massaged it roughly for four hours to bring back the circulation. When the M.O. took off the plaster completely at 9.00 a.m. he found two lovely blisters nine inches long caused by the tightness of the cast. This mistake was the cause of my having to stay in hospital for another three weeks because I couldn't have another plaster on until I had got rid of the blisters.

Whilst I was in this time I was able to go down to the sports ground to watch a cricket match, which I thoroughly enjoyed but on my way back to the ward I had to climb a steep flight of steps and near the top I tripped and jarred my broken wrist. However, as I slipped I saw two feet just above my head and when I looked up it was Group Captain Wingfield who was one of my officers in the section. "Are you alright?" he asked.

The Farm Estate Tea Factory near Peradynia

"Yes Sir, thank you. What are you doing in here?"

"Oh! I got a touch of phlebitis but nothing to worry about, see you soon," and with that he let me pass.

So on the 22nd October I was discharged from 48 I.G.H. for the last time. Upon my return to work I didn't or couldn't do much in the office except run a few errands because of the pot on my arm.

There was only me on duty one Sunday along with Group Captain Kirby an Engineering Officer and I was just pottering about when he called me,

"Priestley, come and look at this."

So I went into his office and there he was looking out of the window and pointing upwards. There was a large aircraft flying above. "That's the bastard that's caused us so much trouble," he said.

It was a York aircraft, M.W.101 which was Lord Louis' personal plane and we had on paper been rushing around sending signals to the Air Ministry in London to get spare parts for it so that the Supremo could fly to China.

I was pleased after a fortnight to learn that I was being transferred to Command Statistics to work with the boys who I used to work with in Delhi. This section had been flown down here a few weeks earlier to build up the new HQ of Air Command, S.E.A. and when I found that they were coming Sqd/Ldr McLauchlan said I could go and meet them with the transport.

After moving to this section there appeared an order to the effect that certain personnel would be able to go to UK on Mid-Tour Leave. I was lucky enough to be one of these and four of us in the section sat and waited. Here was a chance for my arm to heal in the cold climate of home. Little did I realise that very shortly I would be saying goodbye to 48 I.G.H. and Ceylon. Apart from illness I enjoyed it here.

Chapter Ten

MID-TOUR LEAVE

On the 19th November 1945, I was notified to stand by ready to go on Mid-Tour Leave to the UK so the following morning I reported to the Orderly Room and was given a form stating that I was definitely one of the lucky ones who had qualified for the leave. First of all I went to the Air Movements Office and filled in an Air Priority Form in triplicate, which stated that I was to report to Cholovaram in Southern India by the 21st November and no later. I had a medical confirming that I was fit to travel by air even though I still had my arm in plaster and then proceeded to the Pay Accounts where I received Rs. 345 (£28). The most of this came because I hadn't drawn any pay whilst I was at the Convalescent Camp and had used my band money. Being the senior L.A.C., I was put in charge of a party of nine other personnel, one of which was Stuart Cohen but it was mainly to supervise Air Movement. The final instructions were that we had to leave Kandy at 1400 hours. Could we possibly be home for Christmas?

Perhaps not! However, we all climbed aboard the transport with the lads in turn giving me a hand because of my wrist. It was some twelve miles by gharry to Peradiniya Station where we made ourselves comfortable on the train bound for Colombo at 1515 hours, arriving there just as it was getting dark, 1830 hours to be exact. Everything had gone without a hitch so far and when we arrived at Colombo Fort Station there was a Flt/Lt. to meet us with a three ton lorry. We had hardly alighted from the train when he approached us and within minutes we were on our way to Ratmalana from where we were to leave by air at 0530 hours the next morning.

That same evening we went into the NAAFI/EFI for a drink and whilst standing at the bar I saw an airman looking at me and smiling, we shook hands. It was a lad called Dennis Holroyd who went to school with me and lived in the corner shop on our street. He was stationed here at Ratmalana so we had a good natter about home.

We thought Air Trooping started here but we were due for a disappointment. The lighting system had failed on the camp so we had to grope our way to the billets in which we were to be accommodated.

We didn't get a meal but somehow we managed until morning when we had breakfast for which we were very grateful.

At 0530 hours on the 21st we arose and prepared ourselves for the flight to Madras. We were weighed in at 32 S.P., 50lbs being the maximum weight allowed and embarked onto a Dakota Mk. IV. FL.652, which took off at 0615 hours and turned out to be quite a pleasant journey.

As we proceeded up the northwest coast of Ceylon we had a marvellous view of the terrain where in the distance we could see the mountains and immediately below us there was nothing else but dense jungle. After about an hours flying we ran into a cloudbank so the pilot took the Dak up to 8000 feet. One has to see to appreciate flying above the clouds and with it being early morning the sun was just coming up where the rays from it cast a fantasy of light and shadow upon what appeared to be folds and folds of cotton wool.

As we flew north and left the coast of Ceylon behind us we approached the southeast coast of India where the flat barren land, which I had left behind 12 months ago, came once more into view. There was no variation whatsoever in the landscape and within an hour we had touched down at St. Thomas Mount.

From the Airstrip we were taken by bus to Madras Central Station which was seven miles away and after waiting for more than an hour transport finally arrived to take us to Cholavaram, which happened to be a further fifteen miles on the other side of Madras.

On arrival there we found that the camp was full and fortunately for us we had to be billeted in the Officers quarters. It was very comfortable indeed with each room having two beds a dressing table and a wardrobe. Next day we did the usual thing of visiting the Orderly Room and the MI Room, afterwards returning to the aforementioned with our documents where we were told that there were thousands in front of us but we need not worry. Later we found this to be quite true because we stayed at this camp for fourteen days.

However, on the first night there, we decided to go into Madras and do a little shopping. I actually spent RS. 150 (£11), most of which was to buy a large suitcase.

After we had finished shopping we went and had dinner in a first class hotel which was managed and owned by the Bossotto Bros, the meal was excellent and to finish off the night four of us hired a taxi and had a pleasant trip back, each taking it easy and smoking a large cigar. For the next twelve days there was really nothing to do but go to the cinema on the camp and spend money in the canteen. The reason we spent money there was due to the fact that we had no 'irons' or plates with which to eat our meals, having been told at our unit that everything was 'laid on' so we were unable to use the Service Mess.

It is often said that many a true word is spoken in jest and this was proved on several occasions during our moves in transit. The first of these occasions was on the 31st November when we saw our names on the list to 'move off' and quite casually I remarked,

"Well, there's only an earthquake can stop us now!"

Believe it or not the following morning there was an earthquake on the west coast of India where the press reported that it was so violent a small island had appeared off the coast in the Indian Ocean. The result was that we were held up for five days but we finally left Cholavaram on the 5th December.

From the camp to the railway station at Avandi was not a great distance but notwithstanding the gharry broke down and this too followed a remark passed by Stuart as we climbed aboard that the lorry was sure to break down. A long wait at the station preceded a short journey in a 'fifth' class carriage and after 45 minutes jostling we arrived at Arkonham. A few moments after arriving our third remark came true because this time we had just boarded the gharry when another boy remarked, "Something is bound to happen now!" and it did.

We passed over a small bridge hardly wide enough for the lorry to get over and the Indian soldier driving it was convinced that it would pass over trees. We persuaded him that this was not the case but not before he had made an unsuccessful, attempt to climb a telegraph pole. However, no one was hurt and we carried on only to be horrified on arrival to find ourselves in the midst of the Army.

Apparently this camp catered for the Army and RAF personnel in transit.

At the reception bay two sheets were provided for each person but no blanket and we wondered if we were in prison because the bunks in the billets were so high that the man in the top one was invisible and one doubted how he lived up there. He descended daily by parachute for his meals after which he disappeared again into the clouds, so to speak. It was suggested that he ought to be issued with two extra sheets and an oxygen mask.

We had very high hopes of leaving here within a very short time but unfortunately 700 A.L.F.S.E.A. personnel arrived with priority air passages and held us up once more for a further ten days.

The food on the whole at this camp was horrid with the main complaint being that it was always cold no matter what time one went for a meal. This and other things came to a head on the morning of the 18th December when, led by a few hotheads, the RAF personnel agreed to air their views to someone in authority. This someone was none other than the Prime Minister Mr C. R. Attlee and this was the text of the message:

"URGENT. FOR YOUR ATTENTION. APPROXIMATELY 250 RAF REPATS AWAITING AIR TRANSIT TO UK. MAJORITY HAVING SERVED THREE MONTHS OVER STIPULATED TIME REFER YOU TO YOUR PROMISE RE GETTING US HOME FOR CHRISTMAS.

WE HAVE BEEN HELD IN TRANSIT IN INDIA OVER ONE MONTH AND ARE GETTING NO SATISFACTION FROM OUR SUPERIORS, HENCE THE CABLE. WE WANT ACTION, REPEAT ACTION FROM GOVERNMENT AT PRESENT SOCIALIST MAJORITY AND DEMAND OUR RIGHTS. EXPEDITE REPLY AT ONCE.

SPEED IS ESSENTIAL. ENDS WITH HOPE."

That night certain persons helped by a few beers set off fire extinguishers and tore down notice boards etc., but six of us on our manifest kept out of the way and we were having a drink in the canteen when a message came over the Tannoy.

"All personnel of Manifest 146 will report to the control room in the admin. block immediately."

What could this be we thought to ourselves? So we all went across there expecting anything but good news but we were told that twenty of us would be leaving in the morning but unfortunately four men had to stay behind to make room for Aircrew personnel. So the O.C. Party called out the names at random and I am sorry to say that Ray and Pete Grant, two of our pals, were two of the four unlucky ones. Both were on their way home having served on the Air Sea Rescue boats on the Irrawaddy River in Burma.

At 0630 hours the following morning we took off from Arkonham in very clear weather and the journey on the whole was very good then at 1000 hours we arrived at Poona but we didn't stay long. In fact just one hour and this was to have a meal and re-fuel so we didn't get the pleasure of looking around this pukka-pukka place of world renown. At 1130 we left Poona in an almost new Dakota, which was definitely more comfortable than the last one.

A few days after we arrived at Mauripur, Karachi, we found a small shop on the edge of the camp which sold mementos, trinkets etc., including military arm flashes and badges. Stuart pointed to one, which we recognised as our HQ Badge. This was a further thought, which Lord Louis put into practice. The badge was a circle with the blue head of a Pheonix super-imposed on a red and white background, in other words, the Pheonix Rising from the Ashes. We all bought a set and the local Indian tailor sewed press-studs on to the badges and left arm of our blue uniforms, which we were called upon to wear at this time of the year. Even in India it was wise to wear something warm, so, when we put on our uniforms with our Command flash A.C.S.E.A. (Air Command South East Asia) at the top of our sleeves on the shoulder and the Pheonix below that, we really looked smart.

The left sleeve of my uniform looked more like an Americans because it also had my brass Band Harp pinned just above my L.A.C. Props insignia and near the cuff was my inverted chevron for good behaviour, or should I say undetected crime after three years service.

It was after Christmas on about the 29th December, that we were all ordered into one of the two cinemas on camp. What for? We did not know but we soon found out.

We had just made ourselves comfortable when a Senior N.C.O. called us all to attention. We all stood and looked at the stage. Who should walk on but Air Marshal R. G. Goddard from our own Headquarters and as I remarked earlier he was the Personnel Officer for the whole of South East Asia Command.

"Sit down," he said. He then continued looking straight at our small party who were sat together near the front and remarked,

"You people who are from Headquarters can keep quiet because you know most of the answers." Then looking towards the rest of the audience he said,

"Anyone else who wishes to ask a question may do so."

The Air Marshal had recognised the arm flashes on our uniforms and also recognised some of our faces. He answered many vital questions and seemed to satisfy the majority of personnel but he did point out that the main reason for his visit was because of the disturbances at Arkonham. Being the officer we knew him to be, he was very sympathetic but warned us not to try anything like that again. MUTINY! you may ask? Very, very nearly.

Apart from that there wasn't much to mention about the sordid stay we had at Mauripur except perhaps that it gave us a chance to see parts of Karachi and also enabled us to spend our worst Christmas and New Years' eve in the services.

Whilst here I went sick so that I could have the pot removed from my arm but the medic who tried to cut it off with something like a pair of bolt cutters nearly broke it again with the effort he put into it.

Never mind, the relief was worth it when he threw the pot into a bin and there was no more itching.

Our stay lasted over a fortnight and our hopes of being home for Christmas were completely shattered, moreover because we had written to our families telling them that we would be home for this Christmas. What a disappointment to everyone.

At last, after much waiting, we finally left Mauripur at 0700 hours on the 4th January, 1946 although out of the original nine who left Kandy on the 20th November last, only four were on our plane. If we were disappointed only heaven knows what our parents and families were thinking. Mind you, we were more fortunate than some poor devils that had taken off a few days earlier because we had heard that two transport planes had crashed in the bad weather on their way home with much loss of life. It must have been fate when we were held back.

Most of the route was over the Arabian Sea and we had to wear Mae West jackets, which were fully appreciated because of the cold weather. For five hours we kept a steady course and at 1030 hours local time we touched down at a staging post called Shajah in Persia. Here we had a good welcome with a magnificent meal of eggs and chips and the way we attacked that meal would have given anyone the impression that we hadn't eaten for weeks.

We didn't stay long enough to see much of this post but a good description of it would be, 'an outpost in the desert' for that's all it appeared to be. So at 1200 hours after refuelling and giving the aircrew a rest we saw the runway of Shajah slip quickly below us as we started on another leg of our journey, setting a straight course up the length of the Persian Gulf. Officially we should have followed the west coast of the Gulf but our pilot decided to change direction and set a course up the middle of it.

As we reached Basra at the North East tip of the Gulf we changed course again and proceeded direct to Habbaniya by flying in between the rivers Tigris and Euphrates and at Habbaniya we touched down for the second time that day, which was about 5 o'clock local time. It was here, owing to bad weather that we had a further 17 hours delay but I think after nine hours flying we welcomed the chance to stretch our legs and get some fresh air.

At midday the following day we set off for Lydda in Palestine and whilst on this part of the journey we witnessed one of the most beautiful sights I have ever seen from the air. We were flying at 8,000 feet over Transjordania in between the Dead Sea and the Sea of Galilee, the passage was a little bumpy and huge rain clouds surrounded us on all sides when suddenly on the port side we came to a break in the clouds. About five miles away and some 2,000 feet below a very large black cloud was slowly rising and as it rose there appeared underneath it a beautiful sunlit valley in which lie the silver sprinkled Dead Sea. It was like a curtain going up on a new ballet but as quickly as it appeared so it vanished and once more our company was the rain cloud.

Soon after this we arrived at Lydda on the coast and I'm pleased to say everything was quiet and calm especially after hearing the news about the happenings and uprisings. Our stay at Lydda amounted to 48 hours for the purpose of getting acclimatised but in that short time we were very impressed with the Palestinian landscape with certain parts of it being likened unto some of our English countryside.

There were plenty of the 'Red Devils' Paratroopers patrolling the surrounding districts because of the local troubles but on the second morning of our stay two of the Paratroopers asked us if we would like to take some fruit home. Of course the answer was in the affirmative and we set off across the fields with the two guards in attendance. Half an hours' walk brought us to a Jewish orchard just inside a Kibbutz and our eyes and mouths opened with amazement at the sight of so much fruit on the trees. Then the pickings commenced and we all took part in gathering the harvest, each of us ladened with oranges, lemons, grapefruit etc., and as we made our way back to camp and being a little thirsty after our long walk we ate one or two of the oranges to quench our thirst and moisten our throats.

The grapefruits were the biggest I had ever seen but managed to get three of them into my suitcase. One fruit was large enough for breakfast for a family of four.

What a 'squeeze.'

It was a squeeze too because Stu Cohen had over-loaded himself with presents and had asked me to put some into my suitcase and then drop them off at his home in the West End of London if I arrived home first, so this I did.

So much for our rest at Lydda and at 11.30 a.m. on the 7th January we left the troubled 'State' behind and set a straight course for Bardia. From 5,000 feet we could see the bombed landing strips and wrecked vehicles below us, which had suffered in the battles of a few years ago but as we left Bardia behind us a further half hour brought us to our next port of call, El Adam in North Africa.

It was here that we had a little more bad luck because on reaching the reception building the Captain told us that one of the crew was ill and being unable to get relief from Cairo we would have to stay a few days. Realising our misfortune we decided to make the most of a bad job and having been accommodated in first class billets, the entire cleaning etc., being done by German POW's, we settled down.

The following day we received permission to visit Tobruk, the scene of so many famous battles, so ten of us climbed aboard a truck to go the seventeen miles and as we drove along we once again saw many wrecks of trucks and tanks. We were travelling on the back of an open lorry at about fifty miles per hour and the floor of same appeared to be covered in coal dust or something similar. As we took interest in the surroundings suddenly, to me, the whole landscape diminished. I wondered what had happened! Then one of the lads asked me to look at my specs, I took them off and found that the heat of the sun in the desert had softened the frames and the force of the wind had blown both the lens out. Guess where? Into the dust on the lorry bottom. We all grovelled about in the dirt and finally found them but with them being of the circular type it was fairly easy to re-set them. Having had a good laugh about it we were brought back to earth with a bump.

About four miles from Tobruk, lying at the foot of a small hill, we saw a British Military Cemetery with thousands of white crosses in their neat rows and in the centre of all these there was a stone memorial for those fallen in battle. It brought a lump to one's throat.

Ten minutes later we arrived at Tobruk and alighted from the transport at Windy Corner where we found the NAAFI/EFI, which stands on a hill over-looking the harbour in the path of all winds, hence the name, Windy Corner. Here we all enjoyed a wash and brush up, which we really needed after the journey because we were all covered in the horrible dust from the lorry.

Having to be back at El Adam by 5.00 p.m. we made the most of our five hour stay and proceeded to sight-see the town or what was left of it because to my memory there wasn't a building left intact. Our soldiers had made a good job of cleaning up and the streets were spotless, the battered houses and buildings had been patched up with empty petrol cans and whitewashed over so that from a distance nothing appeared to be amiss. We walked along the edge of the harbour and in the water we saw ships of every description which had been sunk at various times, there were twenty in all. One of these was a huge Italian liner called REX, which was said to still have bodies of Italian families on board.

So when we enquired as to why it couldn't be cleared we were told that divers were unable to get near because a giant squid was loose in the bay and it was dangerous for anyone to go near it. Several of us explored one or two shelled houses and collected at least one souvenir each, some German and some Italian. We returned to Windy Corner and after a small snack prepared by the three ladies of the staff we managed to get a lift back to El Adam, arriving at 4.30.p.m.

On the ninth we were greeted with the news that our sick aircrew chap was well again but when the aircraft was taken on air test it was found to be u/s. This caused another three days delay so finally it was the 12th January when we set off for the UK. However, as the aircraft gathered speed we braced ourselves for lift-off when suddenly we felt the brakes applied and a few minutes later we came to a halt. Apparently one of the propeller blades had 'Feathered' which luckily the pilot had seen and stopped for a safety check, so this cost us another day. It could have cost us our lives.

The next leg of our journey wasn't very interesting because we flew mainly over the Med., and the only important thing worth seeing was the island of Sicily which we flew over direct. At 2.30 p.m. we touched down at Elmas in southern Sardinia but only stopping to have a meal and refuel again we soon set off on the last stage of our journey home.

As we approached the south coast of France we could see the tiny lights of Marseilles far below us but that was the only thing we saw until passing over our own Portsmouth with its lights gleaming. Fifteen minutes later we alighted on Blighty soil at 11.10 p m. at Membury in Berkshire. I shall never forget that night because of the 12° of frost and the brilliant moonlight also because of a remark I made on getting out of the aircraft.

"Isn't it 'FLIPPING' cold?" I said, not realising that it was a WAAF standing at the bottom of the steps. I think my face went red, even in the cold. We stayed the night and the next morning we went to 9 P.D.C. Hunsdon in Hertfordshire and here we stayed another night before getting documented and paid etc. and then finally to catch the trains to our respective destinations.

As I walked onto St. Pancras Station with my kit I received several strange looks from the Military Police because I was wearing brown suede shoes with my blues. This was because as I climbed onto the aircraft at El Adam I caught my toe on the top step and ripped off the sole of my service shoe. The only other pair I had with me was the suede ones, hence the looks but nothing was said. They must have realised that I had arrived from overseas.

At last I was on a very well earned Mid-Tour leave eight weeks after leaving Ceylon. However before catching my train I found time to get a taxi and call on Mr and Mrs Cohen to drop off Stuart's presents but when I arrived at their flat Stuart had beaten me to it and was anxiously waiting for me. His parents made me very welcome and with a little time to spare he took me for a splendid meal in the West End. Two hours later I was on my way home to Sheffield and looking forward to seeing my parents again.

Chapter Eleven

RETURN TO S.E.A.C.

The leave was to last a month and it was full of activity being able to see my family and friends again. All my peacetime pals were in the forces somewhere but I was able to make new friends and it was amazing how the left arm of my uniform with the A.C.S.E.A. badges on it seemed to attract the opposite sex when I went to the local dances. Some even thought I was an American until they heard my Yorkshire accent.

However, the 28 days soon passed and on the 12th February I returned to 9 P.D.C. after having spent a reasonably good leave and awaited the draft being made up to return to S.E.A.C. The following day the Adjutant broadcast over the camp Tannoy asking for a bassist to play in the camp dance band. I applied for the vacancy and being accepted, played the following night at a dance in the NAAFI for other ranks. The outcome of this was that I wangled myself off the draft, which left Southampton in the Capetown Castle on the 23rd of February with Stuart and many other service pals from A.C.S.E.A on board.

I played at several dances in the next few weeks and this enabled me to scrounge two more 48-hour passes and travel home for the weekend. However, my stay was short lived because on the 4th March a signal arrived from HQ, A.C.S.E.A, saying that I had to report back to Singapore immediately because I was urgently required. On hearing the news and realising that I would have to return I approached Corporal Brockley in the Orderly Room who happened to have been in the same building as me in New Delhi and he managed to get a signal off to my unit asking for permission to fly me back with Air Passage Priority. Working out that there would be no reply for at least seven days I asked the Adjutant for that number of days leave and was very pleased with myself when it was sanctioned.

Returning from this leave on March 12th I had another five days at Hunsdon and played in the band once more before finally reporting to North Weald on the 18th where I was fixed up with my air passage.

For three days I stayed at North Weald and had two good evenings in Epping and Bishop Stortford with two young aircrew sergeants who were sleeping in beds either side of me. On one of these nights we missed the last bus from Epping which was going past the camp so we asked at the local Police Station if it was possible for us to sleep in one of the cells The duty sergeant agreed but we told him to call us at 6.00 a.m. to enable us to get back to camp in time for Reveille. We really appreciated this help because in one of the pubs we had called at, one of the sergeants introduced us to a drink called Russian Stout, which was very potent and so strong that it took it all its time to pour out of the bottle.

On Thursday the 21st I left for Bourne in Cambridgeshire where I expected to catch my plane, however, after sleeping at Bourne overnight a group of us went by transport next morning to Upwood, which was about 27 miles away. On arriving at Upwood we had a small snack and at 0750 hours we saw the English countryside quickly recede below us. Once in the air we climbed rapidly in our four engined 'bird' of the Liberator class and flying to the east of London we headed for the French coast on course for Le Havre.

As we passed over the town a new course was set and we headed for North Africa but it was another four and a half hours before we crossed the south coast of France. At 4.30 p.m. our wheels touched down at Castel Benito a few miles from Tripoli. It felt grand to step out of the plane after nine hours flying especially into the warm sunshine of Africa and it was such a contrast to the cold winter of England. It was so peaceful too and this made one think that this was another world.

There wasn't really anything of note at this staging post and after a meal and a shower; I went with Gerry, one of the aircrew chaps, to the camp cinema. Coming out at 10.00 p.m. we were quite in need of our beds and we slept; 0750 hours the following morning we once more climbed 'into the blue' and the skipper set the nose of the plane on a line for Cairo. This gave me a chance to see more of the Western Desert, which I had flown over a few months earlier but there was nothing but sand to see and 5½ hours flying, brought us into Egypt at Cairo West.

We disembarked and boarded the waiting transport, which was soon speeding along the main highway to Cairo. It was a 17 miles journey along an almost straight road and as far as I can remember there were only two bends in it. We shortly arrived at the transit camp and were quickly allotted our respective tents where we had a much-needed wash and then proceeded to the canteen to have dinner.

After the meal Gerry and I enquired if we could go into Cairo to have a look around and permission was given provided we were back at 11.30 p m. We had to take a chance and were very lucky to get a lift in a private car driven by an Englishman and as soon as I had closed the door his foot went down hard on the accelerator and we shot away with a roar. In the distance we were able to see the famous Pyramids at Gizeh and the scene was most fitting because the moon was just appearing between two of them. The scenery on either side of the road flashed by us as our driver very expertly handled the car and fifteen minutes later we arrived at Cairo. It was the first time the needle of the speedometer had fallen below 50 m.p.h.

We thanked our host and made our way across a beautiful bridge over the River Nile with stone lions some fifteen feet high guarding either end and having crossed the bridge we hit the night life of this Egyptian Capital.

This was the time when we both fancied a drink and we soon found a sort of beer "off shop" on a corner. We went in and asked for two beers and the Egyptian behind the counter reached up onto a shelf and took down a bottle from which he poured about an inch of liquid into each glass and just filled them up with cold water. Gerry and I looked at each other with puzzled expressions paid a nominal amount and took a sip. It was great; in fact it tasted as good as some bitter beers we could get at home.

We carried on sight-seeing and to me it was like a huge fairyland with all its different coloured neon lights, which advertised anything from matches to cinema shows. Gerry and I walked this way and that viewing different buildings one of which was the well-known Tedder Club named after the famous Air Chief Marshal but after an hour we thought it high time that we had a meal.

We were recommended by some soldiers to go to the Washington Night Club and after paying admission fees we were shown to a table on the balcony. Gerry ordered dinner for the both of us and whilst waiting we sampled a bottle of beer which was totally different to the one earlier. There was a cabaret on at the time and although we missed the first two acts through being late, the rest was marvellous. Whilst eating a very good three-course meal we thrilled at the acrobats of a first class Egyptian act of father, son and daughter. They would have done justice to any English stage. But I think the highlight of the night, for the benefit of the troops, was the very Eastern dance performed by a dusky yashmaked maiden in the proverbial veils. The band then finished off the cabaret and having enjoyed our meal we decided to make our way back to the transit camp and having a further piece of luck we cadged another lift and finally arrived back at 11.00 p.m. but not in default.

The following morning on the 24th March we left Cairo on our next hop, which turned out to be thrilling and amusing. Once more I flew over Transjordania but this time in an easterly direction. It was after a few hours flying and we had crossed the Persian border that the Flight Engineer called two of us up to the control cabin. There wasn't really room for two of us so I was told to go below the pilot into a small well, which was mainly used by the Bomb Aimer or Navigator on operational sorties. It was a marvellous view as I lie there on my stomach looking through the Perspex observation window.

"The Skipper wants you to watch this," he said.

The Skipper turned his head towards us and enquired, "Okay?" We replied, "Yes, thank you."

He then made himself comfortable and told us to hang on. We needed to because he slowly eased the control column forward and the nose of the huge bomber with all four engines racing faster and faster, hurtled to the desolate desert below. At first we were only interested in the dive but as we flew lower we could make out one or two tents of the nomad herdsmen tending their goats and a few stray camels.

Within a few minutes we were within feet of the ground and as we went no more than 100 feet above the sand, direct for one of the tents the nomad fled for dear life from his herd into his tent. I suppose his first thought was that his abode would give him protection but alas, as the skipper pulled back his control stick we shot into the air, the slipstream from the Liberators four engines caught the tent of the nomad whisking it away from over his head and along the ground for about 100 yards. Whilst this had been going on the goats and camels had scattered in all directions frightened by the noise. We couldn't stop laughing. Although it was a funny experience I felt sorry for the herdsman as he stood shaking his fist in the air in anger.

The navigator put us onto our correct course again and at 11.30 a.m. we landed at Shaibah in northern Persia. We should have had a meal there and then pushed on but the aircrew of another Liberator on the tarmac were pals of our crew so they decided to go into Basra on the binge while the passengers of both kites had another night's sleep.

The following morning we were up early and after breakfast were detailed to do an unusual job. The aircrews arrived a little 'under the weather' following their night in Basra and were having trouble getting the aircraft started. All the passengers formed a circle and as we walked round we each in turn had to push the four bladed propellers round and round in order to get compression. There we were walking around in circles getting nowhere. We eventually won and standing back, the skipper finally started up the engines.

The next part of the journey was somewhat monotonous except for one instance when our plane tried to play wing tip tiggy with the other plane and I think everyone was glad when we touched down at Mauripur at 7.00 p.m. in the evening.

From here I expected to change planes to fly all the way to Singapore but here my Priority Air passage finished and I was refused a B.O.A.C. passage because I possessed no 'rings pips or crowns' on my uniform, I was just another rank. Instead I left by Dakota the next day for Poona where I stayed for 48 hours.

I was still in the company of Gerry the aircrew sergeant and on the night of the 27th we went into Poona to a dance in a big marquee but only succeeded in getting drunk on just the right number – eight double rums. I climbed into my bunk, which was the top one of a three-tier type unit about 0030 hours, oh! I did feel rough and then I was called at 0230 hours to catch my flight to Madras.

"Come along Priestley – there's a plane waiting for you," called a voice from the floor below.

Ouch! What a feeling in my stomach every time we hit an air pocket, but I managed to keep everything down, thank goodness.

I stayed at Madras for three days waiting for a ship and finally I started on the last leg back to HQ embarking on H.M.S. SAINFOIN on Saturday 30th March, setting sail the following morning.

It wasn't an exciting trip by any means in fact it was very dull. The only thing of interest was seeing the Nicobar Islands and the coast of Sumatra. There was just one exception to the monotony and that was one day, away behind us, we could see a tropical storm with its terrific lightning flashes and claps of thunder. How glad we were not to be in the middle of it.

Whilst sailing down the Straits of Malacca there was a little excitement on our last night on board. We just missed a Chinese type junk by about five feet and that was about all, it had sailed right across our bows in the dark with only one little light showing and it was only by chance that thc lookout saw it.

On Friday the 5th April we nosed our way in between one or two small islands before coming into the world famous Singapore Harbour. We hung around for a couple of hours before finally manoeuvring into position and tying up at Collyer Quay. Within an hour we had disembarked and were taken straight to 60 P.T.C., for a meal and then dispersal to our respective units.

So this was Singapore and I had returned to S.E.A.C.

Chapter Twelve

SINGAPORE

By 1700 hours on the day of arrival at Singapore I was inside Tanglin Barracks, which used to be the main depot for the Royal Artillery but had been made available for RAF personnel. I was fixed up with a vacant charploy opposite one of my old buddies from Kandy and he was of course Corporal Kinch who happened to be having 14-days' leave on camp and being free he asked me to go with him for a view of the local surroundings.

A view of the Supreme Court steps where the surrender took place

A general view of the Supreme Court and Municipal Buildings

To slightly digress, whilst I had been away in England the whole of S.E.A.C. headquarters had been transferred from Kandy to Singapore, this being possible because the dropping of the Atom Bomb on Hiroshima had finally forced the Japanese to surrender and so end the war in the Far East. The Japanese in this area had unconditionally surrendered to Lord Louis Mountbatten on the steps of the Supreme Court, which is pictured above. I only wish that I had been there to witness the historic occasion, which must have really created an auspicious sight when the Japanese Generals handed over their swords to the 'Supremo' on the front of this magnificent building. The ceremony took place on the 12th September –1945.

Returning to the point in question, the invitation from Kinch was a good start and soon after dinner we set off from the camp when Cliff suggested that we walked and I'm glad we did because I was able to take a good look at the rest of the area surrounding the camp. It was like a huge park but on the other hand with all the bungalow type billets it resembled a hospital in its own grounds.

The billets were quite large and were capable of holding 154 men where in each one there were four rows of charpoys with 3ft space in between them. A billet in itself was divided into two sections with washbasins, showers and latrines in the centre. As we walked down the drive it was then that it appeared to be more like a park where on either side of us were small embankments of closely cut grass or near the curbstones there was a foot or so of beautiful flowerbeds and borders.

We had walked slowly down the driveway and it took us a good ten minutes to get into Tanglin Road, which was the main road past the camp leading into Singapore about five miles away. After a while we arrived at one of the 'Worlds', which are so famous out here and the one we came to was the Great World the other two being the Happy World and the Little World.

The 'Worlds' can be best described by saying that they have much in common with the Pleasure Beach at Blackpool except for one or two major differences such as the Big Dipper and the Fun House, there were neither here.

There was of course a boxing stadium also used for wrestling, a Chinese Theatre where the cast and dialogue were strictly Chinese, several shops where one might buy anything at a price and right in the centre of the entertainment enclosure cabaret dances were held where a person had to book a dance by giving a ticket to the girl that you danced with. It was three tickets for one Malayan dollar or else a girl to yourself for one hour for ten dollars which was £1.3.4d in our money. So you see if you had the money you could enjoy yourself – perhaps. We only stayed an hour but enjoyed every minute even if I didn't spend anything.

One of the Three Worlds

The following day I moved over to another billet where my other workmates were and to my surprise who should be there but Stuart Cohen and some of the chaps who had left me behind in England when they returned by sea from Southampton. It was good to see them all again. It took me the whole of the day to get organised, sorting things out etc., but that was really a sheer waste of time because my stay at Tanglin only lasted for three days, but before I left I had the opportunity of meeting some very charming people.

Within the three days Ron Worley, who was from Romford and his pal Derek asked me to go to a café where they always went to play records on the radiogramme.

The Badoeing Café as it was called, was situated in a street by the name of Dhoby Ghat about half way into Singapore. It was a pleasant little place and spotlessly clean being owned by the Lee family who were Malayan-Javanese. This family was a happy little gathering and had two small girls, Lily (11) and Nellie (8) who both made a fuss of Ron Worley.

For an hour we played records and enjoyed the company of this grand family and before leaving Ron took our photographs with the two girls and their baby brother but unfortunately they didn't come out properly and ironically we never saw the Lee family again.

On Monday the 8th April I started work in our new office block, which was in the Union Building and we were on the top floor of Winchester House overlooking Clifford Pier where at a later date the 'Supremo' met the new Governor of Malaya.

I was formerly introduced to my new officer-in-charge who was Squadron Officer Sheila MacKenzie and was most delightful, was exceptionally tall, 5ft 11 inches and very pretty with more of a sweet child's face. She was also slim, 24 years of age and had fair hair with blue eyes. In my short stay I grew to like her very much.

Union Building and Winchester House which were our temporary Headquarters before moving up to Changi

A view of Collyer Quay from the Union Building

On the Tuesday we moved from Tanglin Barracks to a much nicer camp at Changi and in doing so I had my first glimpse of the jail, which the Japanese made so famous or should I say infamous and now unoccupied. I think everyone had heard at one time or another of the Japanese atrocities which took place there and as we drove past the main entrance we could see the wooden stakes on the beach nearby where some of the tortures had been carried out.

Changi camp was very similar to Tanglin except that the billets were three storeys high and much better for amenities. At the far end of the camp we had a sports field and a club for other ranks only and beyond that we had the sea fenced off on the shore with kinds of railway sleepers driven in upright as a precaution against sharks. It was here that we spent many hours of free time. Not a hundred yards in front of our residence was the Changi Airfield with the largest runway in the Far East.

The Air Chief officially opened it shortly after our arrival but until we got used to it the noise was very frightening whenever any aircraft landed on the metal runway, which was just below our billets.

The move from town of staff and equipment wasn't completed until the following Saturday when we were very thankful that there were some Jap POW's to help us to do it and I must say that they worked very hard.

There was one instance however when my sympathetic feelings came to the fore. A large metal cupboard had to be moved down three flights of stairs in Winchester House onto a lorry being used in the move. Four Jap prisoners managed to lift it onto their shoulders and then moved to get it through the door but just then the front end of the cabinet caught the door jamb with the result that one of the Japs at the back took the pointed corner at his end right into his shoulder making a deep gouge, which oozed blood everywhere.

Just then Sqd. Off. MacKenzie came by and I asked her if the injured one could get some First Aid because he was human like everyone else. At first she hesitated but then she agreed, so the wounded prisoner was sent for treatment.

It was really amazing to see the POW's because now that the war was over and they didn't know which rank was which by our uniform markings they saluted everyone as though at any time they would be subjected to some sort of punishment similar to that which had been dealt out to our lads.

The Shackle Club, Singapore

During the transitional period of the move all our staff received privilege coupons to dine at the Shackle Club for lunch and I do thank the NAAFI/EFI for such marvellous service and organisation. The food was exceptional and what made it better was the fact that it was served by very smart Chinese and Malayan girls of around 15 and 16 years of age.

Singapore is strictly an island and is joined to the Malayan Peninsular by a causeway or small raised bank across the Johore Strait. Sir Stamford Raffles was the founder of Singapore hence the names Raffles Square and Raffles Hotel. Much is owed to him for the work he put into it to make it the place as it is known today.

After the move I only went into the town three times and two of those were to do a little shopping but I was greatly impressed by the cleanliness of the streets. It was rather amusing to see the popular trishaw, which was an ordinary cycle with a sidecar for two attached to it. There was just one other occasion when Cliff and I went to the Happy World with two of the WAAFS for a meal and a dance which went down very well and as we had our meal we could see below us a beautiful swimming pool, which reflected the decorative lights of the surrounding places of entertainment.

Such places as Raffles Square, Municipal Buildings, The Docks, Cavanagh and Anderson Bridges I shall never forget; also the streets where the local inhabitants hang out their laundry from poles extending from the windowsills. The Chinese and Malayans trotting about in wooden sandals with their rhythmic clip-clop! clip-clop; the solid wheel bumpity-bump of their out of date trackless trams; these too I shall always remember.

Although on the 20th May I had to report to 60 P.T.C. again, this time it was on my way home for good because my demob number had been called. Including myself there were six boys who were leaving our office, either on repatriation or demob and getting together we decided to hold a farewell party and invite the rest of the staff.

The night arranged for this social evening was Friday 17th and seeing that our office was a very large one we agreed to hold it there, with permission of course. Everything had been ordered with regard to drink, food and music, also the re-shuffling of the desks etc. to make, it similar to a night club-cum-cabaret. At 8.00 p.m. everything started with a good swing and for half an hour everyone began to get settled in. Unfortunately the electric supply failed and left us without lights and music, the outcome was that the party turned out to be a booze-up and when one or two of the younger end started getting rowdy we decided to pack up. However, several of us who were sober, including Sheila Mac who was always game for having fun, left the office and went up to the swimming pool to finish off the evening with a very pleasant hours' moonlight bathing. It was well-turned midnight when we finally returned to our quarters.

Below and overleaf are other well-known landmarks in Singapore but the Raffles Hotel was for officers and VIPs only although there were quite a few civilians staying there who had returned now the war was over.

The Raffles Hotel

Cavanagh Bridge under which many sampans pass daily whilst trading their wares

It is worth a point of mention to say that the reason Tanglin and Changi camps looked so fresh and tidy was because all the trimming of the hedges, roadside and trees was done by the Japanese POW's who seemed to relish in it.

Before completing my story I also ought to mention that on the camp at Changi we had a very good little theatre in which several concerts were given and these varied from recitals of straight music to big band arrangements by the Station Dance Band. The Theatre Group also put on plays by Rattigan and Priestley etc., but the highlight of my stay on the camp was the night when the Welfare Group put on a Benefit Revue in aid of St. Dunstan's Home for the Blind. It was a tremendous success and overleaf is the programme frontispiece:

By kind permission of the Allied Air Commander-in-Chief
SIR KEITH PARK, K.C.B., K.B.E., M.C., D.F.C.

AIR COMMAND SOUTH EAST ASIA WELFARE

Presents

AT THE

ASTRA THEATRE CHANGI

THE WELFARE PRODUCTION

"GO FLY A KITE"

A BENEFIT REVUE

IN AID OF

ST. DUNSTAN'S HOME FOR THE BLIND

Souvenir Programme *Price* **50** *cents.*

THE

STAGE CLUB

SINGAPORE

(under the distinguished patronage of Mr. John Gielgud)

Presents

"WHILE THE SUN SHINES"

A COMEDY

IN THREE ACTS

BY

TERENCE RATTIGAN

PRODUCED

BY

DONALD CASH

PROGRAMME

WHILE THE SUN SHINES

A COMEDY
IN THREE ACTS
By
TERENCE RATTIGAN

CHARACTERS
(IN ORDER OF APPEARANCE)

HORTON	*Mark Scammell*
THE EARL OF HARPENDEN	*Richard Vernon*
MULVANEY	*Donald Cash*
LADY ELISABETH	*Maureen Scholfield*
THE DUKE OF AYR AND STIRLING	*Arthur Baster*
LIEUTENANT COLBERT	*Robert Wilson*
MABEL CRUM	*Anne Orpen*

PRODUCED
By
DONALD CASH.

SETTINGS
By
REGINALD SIMMONS.

ALL MEMBERS OF THE CAST APPEAR BY KIND PERMISSION OF THEIR RESPECTIVE COMMANDING OFFICERS.

DUFFLEBAG

Opus 1	Ted Heath
Basie's Basement	Woody Herman
Softly as in the Morning Sunrise	Artie Shaw
Poor Butterfly	Benny Goodman
Lonesome Road	Tommy Dorsey
Save it, Pretty Mama	Lionel Hampton
Record Session	Harry James
Drop Me off at Harlem	Duke Ellington
A Pretty Girl is like a Melody	Red Nichols
Relaxin at Touro	Muggsy Spanier
Jump for Me	Count Basie
My Guy's Come Back	Ted Heath

Ron Worley was a Big Band fanatic and the above are some sort of his record collection of which there were hundreds he kept in a tin kit box.

Ron Worley (left), Stuart (centre) and Derek

Permission was given to Ron to use service transport for visiting military camps and to give his Swing Sessions to other personnel and his equipment and records was so heavy that Stuart, Derek and myself used to go with him to give assistance.

As I explained when in India that when a serviceman leaves a permanent camp then he has to get clearance from all sections. So on the 19th this is what I did and when I had almost finished the rounds there was only one item left. During Service life certain numbers have to be remembered, for instance 1250, which is ones identity card; a 252, which is a charge sheet and people try very hard not to appear on one. There is also a 295 which everyone does try for and that is a leave pass and people try to get as many as possible but some numbers like the last three of one's Service number are very important because they are always called out on pay parade for identity in drawing your fortnightly money. However at this stage I think that the most important number is 2520A and that's your Demob book, namely your Service and Release Book. This contains your service record, good or bad, rank achieved and any decorations that have been awarded. W/Cdr. W.B.E. Powell who also hailed from Sheffield, coincidentally, signed mine.

The rest of the day was taken up by saying farewell to all the lads and lasses in our section including Sqd/Off. MacKenzie.

"Keep taking the tablets," I said to her as I shook her hand.

She had to smile because her complexion had a yellow hue to it due to her taking Mepacrine Tablets to ward off Malaria. They were horrible to take and many of us dodged them although on some of us they had no effect.

After the last cheerio I returned to my billet to pack the rest of my kit and a new Khaki Drill uniform I had recently purchased I sold to the young lad in the next bed to me for 14 dollars.

So, on the 20th May 1946 I theoretically finished my duties in the service of the Royal Air Force and at 9.45 a.m. I left for 60 P.T.C, Tengah where I actually commenced my final days.

This particular area around the Cathedral brought back memories of some small towns in England with the trees and a beautiful park skirting the front of the building. This, along with the multi-coloured flowerbeds was an idyllic place to relax.

St. Andrews Cathedral, Singapore

A view of Anderson Bridge and Empress Place from Fullerton

Chapter Thirteen

SUB-CHEESE FINIS

The above title is an interpretation of Urdu meaning 'The End' and this chapter is dedicated to this purpose before returning to Civvy Street.

We arrived at Tengah to spend a grim ten days in this transit camp before catching the boat and for three days we chased about doing nothing but repeat what we had been doing at Changi, that is, getting cleared.

The accommodation was really appalling with each tent having eight charpoys instead of the standard six. If one wanted a meal he had to queue in a hot sun with 2000 other men and when the meal was finally received the food wasn't what one could call first class. The Dining Hall was a series of open sided marquees and flies came in onto the food by the thousands. Anti-malarial measures resulted in punishment of no less than 28 days detention for the most-minute offence whilst ten miles away precautions had been relaxed for weeks.

A special notice board was prominently displayed with the penalties detailed in full.

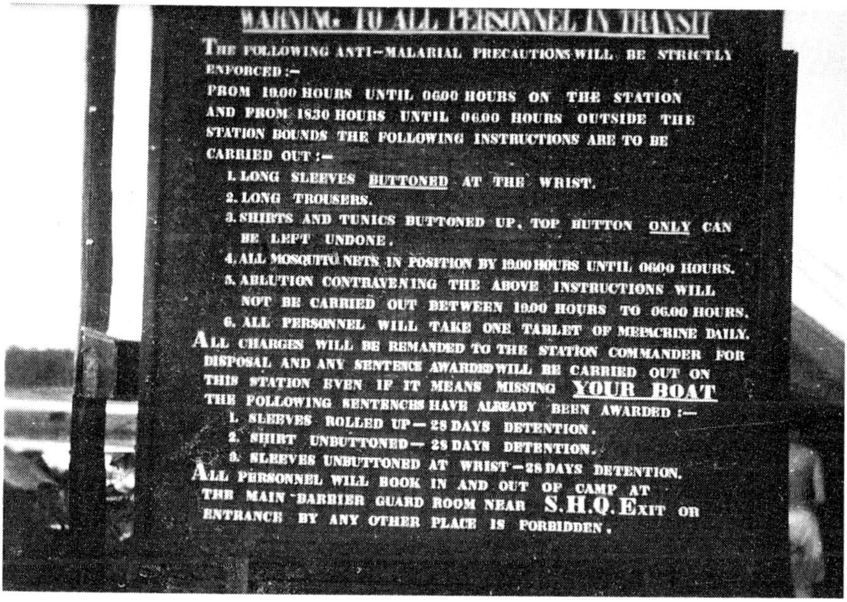

WARNING - TO ALL PERSONNEL IN TRANSIT

The following anti-malarial precautions will be strictly enforced:

From 1900 hours until 0600 hours on the Station and from 1830 hours until 0600 hours outside the Station Bounds the following instructions are to be carried out.

*1. Long sleeves to be **BUTTONED** AT THE WRIST.*

2. Long Trousers.

3. Shirts and Tunics buttoned up.

Top button only can be left undone.

4. All mosquito nets in position by 1900 hours until 0600 hours.

5. Ablution contravening the above instruction will not be carried out between 1900 hours and 0600 hours.

6. All personnel will take one tablet of Mepacrine daily.

All charges will be remanded to the Station Commander for disposal and any sentence awarded will be carried out on the Station even if it means missing YOUR BOAT. The following sentences have already been awarded:

1. Sleeves rolled up - 28 days detention.

2. Shirt unbuttoned - 28 days detention.

3. Sleeves unbuttoned at wrist - 28 days detention.

All personnel will book in and out of camp at the Main Barrier Guard Room near S.H.Q. Exit and Entrance by any other place is forbidden.

Tengah wasn't far from Changi and we reached it by crossing 'The Causeway', which is pictured below. A transit camp is totally different to the luxury of a camp like the one we had left behind. Here we were accommodated under canvas and the odd few in the 'splender' of a wooden hut.

The amenities were very poor and the ablutions were in the open air whilst the Mess was really non-existent.

Still here we were and if we wanted to get home then we had to put up with it, rules and the lot.

It was of course our final part of service and deep down everyone was willing to put up with any discomfort before setting off on our last journey.

The Causeway between Singapore and the Mainland

The queue for a meal outside the mess at Tengah

There was only one NAAFI on the camp and that was built to hold 400 whereas there were 2000 men available to use it. I ask you, is there any wonder that we were sick and fed up with this moth-eaten camp so you can imagine our relief when Friday the 31st came around.

Leaving Tengah at 11.00 a.m. we arrived at Collier Quay thirty minutes before we finally walked up that proverbial gangplank but we were due for an early disappointment because this ship, the SS 'Maloja', a P & O boat, was one of the old type with the mess decks instead of the new cafeteria type. However, this was to be our last trip by sea so we couldn't really grumble and when all is said and done, it was going the right way home.

Notwithstanding we did get one lovely surprise and that was instead of staying in port for 24 hours as expected, at 4.00 p.m. we cast off and the journey commenced. We edged our way carefully up the backwater, which led out of Singapore Harbour and I'm pleased to say a military band had been rushed down to the quayside to give us a 'Royal' send-off. As the music gradually faded away in the quiet of the evening we took our last glimpse of Singapore. Whether it was all part of the send-off I cannot say but as we nosed our way into the open sea, three Hellcats and three Corsairs of the Fleet Air Arm escorted us for some ten miles and in a final salute they shot over the bows and stern of the ship at mast high, each pilot in turn waving us goodbye. I know that each one of us on board appreciated this last act of gratitude.

Taking an all round view of the 'Maloja' one couldn't say that it was a good ship and four things stood out above anything else. It was slow and only being able to achieve 16 knots at full speed; the food on the whole was very poor, especially the bread. Most of us only ate the crust because the centre could be taken out and made into dough balls, which were always thrown out of the open portholes. Accommodation was as I said before, on mess decks with eighteen men to each table, half of who slept on the open decks upstairs and the other half almost sleeping on top of each other, on tables and under them. Last but not least of the grievances was against the amenities on board where one canteen supplied tea or minerals three times per day and if anyone wanted either of these drinks it meant queuing with the other 3500 troops. Cigarettes were of the poorest Indian quality and toilet requisites ran out before the journey ended and other items in the canteen were sold at prices far above the usual troopship ones.

To keep our minds occupied, the staff of the ship tried to appease us by running Tombola every afternoon and another interest, but not as frequent, was the horse racing. It cost a shilling per ticket for the Totalisator and the same for the Race Double, which was on the third and sixth races. We all had a race card with six horses in each race and these were obviously all-fictitious names such as:

'Married' by Batchelor out of 'Pity',
'Eno's' by Colonels out of 'Sorts',
'Blind Date' by Katie out of 'Hope'.
'Nautical Bellow' by R.S.M out of 'Tannoy',
'Gasping' by Old Soldier out of 'Fags'.
'Beauty' by Camouflage out of 'Jars',
'Helluva Time' by Bright Young Thing out of 'Mummy s Sight'.

There were many others too on the Race Card at the Equatorial Meeting of the Maloja Jockey Club. It was all good fun and helped to pass many an hour of enjoyment.

The game was controlled somewhere on the ship. Where? We did not know and never found out but a commentary on each race was given over the Tannoy. At the end of the voyage it was announced that £400 had been made from the troops indulgence of the various rackets and that 10% went to charity – but who knows which one?

On Monday the 3rd June a broadcast was made and this was to ask for artists who were willing to take part in a ship's concert. I saw this as a chance to pass some time away instead of lounging about the decks. For a fortnight a small party of us rehearsed every afternoon and our first show was given on the night that we reached Aden but I will give more details of the concert later on.

This last chapter may appear to be full of moans and groans but one can't get away from the plain and true facts of life. I say this because I have in mind another instance, which angered the troops. There were four hundred first and second-class passengers on board, 25% of who were Dutch and English civilians with their families. These people were allowed the use of the whole of the port side of the promenade deck whilst 3,500 troops used as best they could the starboard side and the general opinion of the servicemen was this. A troopship is a troopship not half and half and the main thing being civilians, some foreigners at that, they must have volunteered to go abroad in the first place. We didn't, so let them wait until they are able to get 100% passenger service on a passenger ship, not push out the troops who had for three or four years fought for the freedom of such people. I wonder how much the Shipping Lines really gained in profit after this trip?

As one can see, the journey home was very dull and except for the concerts the only thing of interest were the sights of the various coastlines of the many countries which we passed by.

Tuesday morning we sailed past the south coast of Ceylon with its barren shore and in the distance we could see the tall mountain range running north to Adam's Peak. This was so called because there is supposedly a huge footprint on the mountain and local inhabitants say it is the footprint of Adam in the Bible as he passed through the area.

When I was stationed in Ceylon I was able to go on several excursions to various places as I have said earlier but Adam's Peak was one place I was unable to get to see although some of my pals have had that pleasure.

Wednesday we reached the southeast coast of India and at twelve knots we crawled along the coast for two days until coming into the great Port of Bombay. I never thought I would see this place again but here I was and at 2.00 p.m. we docked at the Alexandria Dock and were told that we would be staying until Monday. What a setback but realising that there was a need for fresh supplies and water it wasn't too bad and to compensate for this the O.C. Troops very kindly allowed us shore leave. Naturally, like many other chaps, I took advantage of this for one reason only, I wanted a good meal and I knew exactly where I could get one. Bombay hadn't altered very much in three years but one thing was obvious and that was, there were very few military personnel about now and this was mainly due to the end of the war and the repatriation of time served servicemen.

Having taken a last look at this magnificent city and replenished myself with a good meal I returned to the ship along with all the others who had taken advantage of the short shore leave and settled down to a restful night.

At 5.00 a.m. on Whit Monday we pulled away from Alexandria Dock assisted by two tugs and after an hour and a half of manoeuvring we nosed our way into the Arabian Sea. There wasn't a great deal we could do except lounge about the decks and the only immediate enjoyment we had was by taking our final look at the Far East and after dark, our last glimpse of the constellation, the Southern Cross in the night sky.

During our sail across the Arabian Sea towards Aden one or two lads thought that they would try to launder their smalls by putting them on a piece of thick string and let them hang in the wash of the ship. If they were lucky they retrieved it in spotless and bleached condition but if they were unlucky the only thing they received in return was a bundle of shredded rags.

One other racket which the crew organised was a periodical mileage tote and this was done by a line which was dragging astern with a type of mile-o-meter attached to it and as this revolved it recorded the mileage and bets were taken as to how many miles we had travelled each twenty four hours. The jackpot was very rewarding.

For the next few days I was busy with rehearsals and the producer said, "At the rate of progress shown we should be able to put our first production in front of an audience by Friday night."

I'm pleased to say the opening night was a great success and the first batch of troops who saw it fully appreciated the effort, which had been put into it.

The concert party members were a good crowd, full of spirit and none of the snobbishness one might expect amongst first and third rate turns. The show itself consisted of a few sketches, P.T.I's doing acrobatics which were not very easy on a rolling ship; a conjuror, a couple of musicians and one chap by the name of 'Ricky,' was a professional female impersonator. He went down exceptionally well with the boys especially when he left the stage, sat on the O.C. Troops, lap and sang 'Daddy. I want a diamond ring.'

The majority of the concert party were RAF lads but we also had two nurses from the Field Army Nursing Yeomanry, F.A.N.Y's for short, two nurses from the Red Cross and three Army lads, in all there were about twenty of us. After each show we returned to the Officers' mess where we were provided with sandwiches and tea and we usually finished off with a little sing song. After the first show, as we came from the mess, we could see the lights of Aden on the starboard beam and from that we knew that we were entering the Red Sea through the Straits of Bab El Mandeb.

S.S. MALOJA

By kind permission of Commodore J. ALDER SMITH
and Lt.-Col. V. E. C. DASHWOOD, M.C. (O.C. Troops)

"D'YE HEAR THERE"

A SHOW AT SEA

PRODUCED BY

RALPH FIGUE

JUNE, 1946

Programme

Crossed Keys	Stan Topping
Song	Ben Milnes
"In Lighter Vein"	Reg Humphries
D'ye See Here	Eurwyn
Monologue	Doug Tetlow
It's Naughty But It's Nice	Ricky
Winter in Torquay	Elaine Mellor Sally Shaw Allen Young

Songs *Duet with*	M. F. Lawrence Ernest Barnes
Wings Over Maloja	Stan Topping Bill Dale Percy Hayselden Sally Shaw
The Other Side of the Picture	Nan Dickinson Sally Shaw Ricky
D'ye Hear There	Gerry Williams Leonard Good
Songs	Ernest Barnes

The King

Accompanist	Leonard Good
Stage Manager	Jack Skilbeck
Properties	Ron Priestley

*With **grateful acknowledgments** for the kind assistance of the Ship's Company*

The following day was very hot indeed and most of us walked about with only a pair of shorts on and even the deck seemed to burn one's feet if you wore no shoes. During the day we had a message from the Bridge saying that we were passing the Twelve Apostles, which were a small group of islands of volcanic rock where on some of them there were lighthouses with a keeper on them who was the only inhabitant. Their main use was for navigational purposes with there being so much movement of shipping in that area and more so now that the war was over.

It was on the evening of the 17th June that I had the opportunity of seeing a glorious sunset. This one was quite different to any other I had seen previously because for the first time I was able to see the sun go down inch by inch until it disappeared beyond the horizon. Some might say,

"Well! what's so unusual about that?"

It is this. Practically every sunset I have seen has always been partially obscured by clouds or mist but this one wasn't and as I gazed at it there appeared to be long tongues of flame shooting from its outline. I think that astrologically this is called the Corona and what a marvellous sight it was. I doubt if ever I shall see this sight again or the vivid array of colours cast off by this huge planet.

At 10.30 a.m. on the 18th we stopped in the bay just off Teufik having sailed slowly up the Red Sea past such well-known places as Port Sudan on our left and Jedda on our right in Suadi Arabia. We didn't stay very long because four convoys are allowed through the Canal each day, two up and two down, so at 14.30 hours we pushed into the Suez Canal entrance.

The Canal is approximately one hundred miles long and stretches from Port Said in the Mediterranean to Port Teufik in the Gulf of Suez so, after sailing up it for a further one and a half hours we entered one of the several lakes in the Canal. This one was The Great Bitter Lake and like the one at El Ballah it served to allow ships to pass each other en-route to their various destinations.

As we passed through the lake we saw two Italian warships anchored across the way and all was very quiet and peaceful as we reached the Suez Canal proper. It was just the same as I had seen it back in 1943 with vegetation on one side and the desert of Arabia on the other, however, we finally arrived at Port Said at about 0230 hour in the morning

There was now no need to keep a sharp lookout for enemy aircraft and submarines as we did on our way out to the Far East and as we 'cruised' through the Med, this time westward, it became more of a holiday as each day passed by.

At 11.30 p.m. on Friday the 21st June we saw Malta or rather the lights of Malta just before we 'turned in' for the night. The following morning at 10.00 a.m. we passed within three miles of Pantalleria where once again I was seeing many of the sights I saw a few years earlier and one vision in particular was the 'cardboard rock' which I described before on page ? of this book. Monday the 24th we at last saw Gibraltar where we really had a good view of the British Settlement as through the Straits we sailed but this time for home.

Leaving Gib. behind we turned north sailing up the coast of Spain and the next day we passed the mouth of the River Tagus where, on the northern bank stands Lisbon, the capital of Portugal. It was quite pleasant as we sailed through the Bay of Biscay, the sea was very calm and not the rough and heavy one to which we associate it, also we didn't have to worry about lurking 'U-boats' now that the war was over.

We were on our way home and I think that everyone on board the 'Maloja' had adopted a couldn't-care less attitude and was looking forward to reaching England to meet their families once again.

Wednesday the 26th June, after giving the concert for eleven consecutive shows, the party was to hold a farewell gathering in the Officers' Lounge where plenty of Gin etc. was provided along with various eats and at 9.00 p.m. we commenced our little do. For half an hour or more we had great fun by going right through the show but with everyone doing the other actors parts, it was a riot. Then we started a singsong of popular tunes and we were just beginning to enjoy it when at 10.45 p.m. the Purser sent down a message telling us to pack it in. Now this caused some discontentment amongst us because O.C. Troops had told us that we could go on until midnight. Even the officers in the Concert Party objected.

So after much argument and dissent we had to break up the celebrations. Many things were suggested as to what we should do with the Purser but nothing was accepted although Mrs Lawrence one of the F.A.N.Y's, said that she would report the incident and many others to her husband who was a Director on this same Shipping Line.

Thursday morning arrived and everyone was keyed up, having packed our gear and belongings the previous night because we were due to arrive at Southampton this day and in the early morning we saw Portland Bill off the Devon coast – this was our first glimpse of Blighty.

All day we sailed up the English Channel and after tea we passed the Isle of Wight entering Southampton Water at 6.30 p.m. As we moved towards our berth we passed those two magnificent ships, the Queen Mary and Queen Elizabeth where from one porthole of the Elizabeth some flighty young thing greeted us by waving her silk frilly knickers at us. I wouldn't have been at all surprised to learn that she was a G.I. bride.

We tied up at 7.30 p.m. in front of the Elizabeth and I'm sure the whole of Southampton must have heard the cheer. Several boys' relations had managed to get down to the docks and catcalls, cheers; laughter and tears were all mixed into a crowded hour of excitement.

The journey had seemed an eternity at times but now we had made it, everyone seemed so happy, we were home.

As everyone rushed to the rails a voice came booming over the Ship's Tannoy.

"Will all personnel break up and move from the starboard side because the ship is listing dangerously towards the quay!"

The tilt was to be expected when some 3000 troops stood on one side of the decks, however, we all dispersed and the ship righted itself.

An Air Commodore Howe came on board to greet us with words to this effect.

"I have come here today to thank one and all officers and other ranks for the splendid work which you have done in S.E.A.C. and if any of you think of rejoining the services..."

Nothing could be heard above the noise, which came from the lads on deck, it's a wonder the boat didn't sink. What a welcome and in RAF parlance, what a load of 'bull shit'. Maybe it would have been different had we returned from Europe where so many poor chaps had been 'roughing it' this past twelve months.

When it came to disembarking, everyone, including the army lads was given priority over the RAF personnel and this caused some ill feeling. However, we did have the last laugh because when our turn came we never went through the Customs and all those who disembarked earlier did get checked out. We didn't leave the ship until the following afternoon when the NAAFI provided us with free char and cakes. Many thanks to this wonderful organisation for the service they had given to all the Forces over the years. At 6.30 p.m. we pulled out of Southampton by train and headed for Kirkham in Lancashire where the demob centre was situated.

On the train the excitement had died down and chaps were looking through the windows at the green fields and trees, villages and towns of this their beloved Blighty and as darkness approached almost everyone got his head down for some well earned sleep in expectation of the morrow.

We arrived at Lytham St Annes station at 3.30 a.m. and before the train had come to a halt a corporal jumped into our compartment from the platform with the words,

"Come on lads you're getting demobbed on Sunday."

Transport whisked us away from the station and travelling sometimes at 60 miles per hour we finally reached Warton, which is next door to Kirkham so to speak. We weren't given the chance to go to bed because we were busy filling in forms etc., in preparation for our demob. and after a meal we started on the release scheme. Never have I seen anything so well organised in the RAF. The 645 of us were rushed here and there for medicals, cash and disposal of surplus kit but after a hectic Saturday we managed to get a good night's sleep.

On Sunday the 30th June we were up with the lark and the final 'do' was on. Transport took us to Kirkham to the main release centre and here we started,

"Sign this, sign that, keep that, and give us this."

It was all that we heard for two hours which also included our choosing of the famous 'demob suit' etc. and 36 hours from entering the centre we had been cleared, paid and above all, demobbed and month's paid leave.

At 12.30 p.m. we turned our backs on a Royal Air Force camp for the last time as the buses took us to Preston Station where we were to catch the trains for our various destinations, all of us kitted out in new suits and a trilby hat. My suit was dark brown and the overcoat was light brown herringbone tweed. I wonder what Mum and Dad would say when they saw me?

As the tears in my eyes swelled up the day I left home to join up over five years ago, so they did today, mainly this time with relief and thanksgiving.

In conclusion, for myself, I want to say, "THANK YOU," to my Commanders in South East Asia Command, especially the 'Supremo' Admiral Lord Louis Mountbatten and for those and my fellow servicemen for bringing us safely back home to the ones we love.

THANK YOU.

"TO MY MAKER, LORD GOD OUR FATHER AND ONLY SON, LORD JESUS CHRIST." - AMEN.

1st July 1946.
(Also my Dad's birthday)

All these facts are reliable and true and taken from many notes, which I made and kept during my service with the Royal Air Force in South East Asia during World War II. The story is also compiled on three 90-minute cassette tapes and the final recording was made on the 12th January 1982. The music on the tapes was by the Southern Band of the Royal Air Force and the narration by myself, 1044159, L.A.C. Ron Priestely – ex-RAF.